Summer Sunrise

By Daphne C. Murrell

All words written in
Bold Italicized TW Cen MT TYPE
represent the Padawin language.

Published in the United States of America

Mountain Paradise Publishers.

ISBN-13:978-0615958286
ISBN-10:0615958281

Dedication

This book is dedicated in loving memory to my brother,
William Carey Wall, Sr., "Bill",
who really believed I hung the moon.

One

Jonathan Wright ran his fingers through his thinning hair, sighing as he gazed out his office window to the lush valley below. Pulling his hand back, he discovered a few loose, gray strands. *If I don't stop this little habit, I'm gonna end up completely bald before my 60th birthday.* It was coming up quickly.

He leaned back in the squeaky chair—bought twelve years ago—and frowned at his stubbornness. Yes, the church could afford a new chair. Yes, his wife had told him it was despicably ugly. No, he wouldn't get a new chair when this one still worked fine. It was comfortable, it was familiar, and it was one of the few things at this church that hadn't changed in the past four years.

He wasn't complaining about the changes; these were changes pastors prayed for, dreamed about, and pleaded for God to bring. The church had tripled in size, and he and Kyle Sarkos, his youth and music minister, had managed to keep it in tact these four years on their own. But as he stared at the church records sitting before him, it was obvious he must do something to catch up with the changes.

Stop stressing over this, Jonathan; it's a good position to be in. You can still be the pastor and shepherd this flock, but you can't continue to do everything. Kyle's hands are full too. Somewhere something has to give, and if you don't hire a new staff member, this church will start to fall apart. Two people cannot keep seven hundred taught and spiritually fed. It's time to grow.

He hated the thought of bringing in someone new. He and Kyle worked together marvelously. Kyle had started as an interim music director, but within a few months, the church hired him full time. He was an extremely talented young man, but his heart for leading worship was what had impressed Jonathan most. Before Kyle, the church had grown at a slow, steady pace. But after he came on, and then also began handling the youth, people came out of everywhere to First Baptist of Dockrey, Alabama, and the church could barely contain them all. They needed to build, they needed to train workers, they needed someone who could organize this many people into a productive and growing group that would continue to reach the community for Christ. He hated to admit it, but he was too old to keep up this pace. It was more important to think of the needs of the church than to try and continue beyond what was possible for just two men.

He heard the door to the outer office open, and the squealing sounds that followed made him smile. Kyle and Cindy had brought the twins with them. With Kylla, their oldest, now in Kindergarten, the couple would often bring their two-year olds, Devin and Denay, to play on the pre-school playground which sat just outside of Cindy's desk window. They were adorable kids—active, but adorable. Denay had a scream that could pierce an eardrum, but a smile that could charm any heart. Devin was so full of mischief, it was a wonder Cindy could keep an eye on him while she worked. If not for the locked gate, it would be impossible.

It's a miracle Devin hasn't picked the lock yet, Jonathan chuckled to himself.

He stood from his chair, which once again squeaked and groaned at his every move, and stretched his arms above his head. He walked over to the door and began to make moaning sounds.

"What that?" he heard Devin whisper. Denay squealed.

"I don't know," Kyle replied to his son. "A monster?"

"A monkster?" Devin whispered again. "Let's go get him!"

"Nooooo!" Denay screamed out. "He eat us!"

Cindy's voice of frustration finally broke in. "There are no monsters in the church. Kyle, stop telling them that."

"Uh huh," Devin quickly informed. "Dere's one live under the baptizing tub!"

"Devin!" Cindy replied in horror at the thought.

"Daddy said!" Devin explained.

Kyle smiled sheepishly and shrugged his shoulders in helplessness. "It seemed like a good story at the time."

Cindy pulled Denay up into one arm and took Devin's hand with the other. "We're going out to the playground where there are *no* monsters whatsoever."

Denay's eyes grew wide as she looked at her mother and gave a huge nod. "Oh, yes there are."

Devin smiled in agreement and said, "He lives unduh da sandbox."

Cindy turned back to Kyle who immediately said, "They came up with that one on their own."

"Yeah," Devin continued, "and dis one is bwown."

"The one under the baptizing tub is blue," Denay explained.

Cindy took the children and headed toward the back door in a huff.

Jonathan emerged from his office and stared with Kyle out the window at the adorable trio. "God is good," he said to the younger man whose blond hair and perfect features beamed with pride.

"Very," he agreed as he watched his beautiful wife, long blond hair, handle her two blond-headed bundles. "However, I don't think Cindy is gonna be quite as *good* when she gets me alone again. She doesn't like my monsters."

"Devin obviously does."

"I know." Kyle raised his eyebrows mischievously. "I can't help it. He gets so animated whenever we start—and one thing leads to another, and before I know it … well … we've created another monster."

Jonathan sighed. He wished life could always stay as simple as this. "How 'bout I save you from an immediate reprimand? Come into my office with me. We need to discuss some business issues about the church."

"I'm there," Kyle said quickly as he pushed past Jonathan, noticing Cindy was on her way inside.

Jonathan followed him, closed the door, and then ran his hand through his hair again. More gray strands. He listlessly sat in the squeaky chair and then leaned back as far as he could.

"This is serious?" Kyle asked his pastor. "I thought you were just trying to bail me out."

Bringing his hands together in a pyramid, Jonathan admitted, "Fraid so. I've been avoiding the inevitable for a long time."

"What is it? Is there a problem?"

"Yes and no. Our church has grown." He paused to collect his thoughts then continued. "It's too big for the two of us anymore."

Kyle merely nodded. "I know. So, what are we gonna do?"

Jonathan exhaled slowly and glanced out the window to the beautiful beginnings of autumn in the northern Alabama valley. "We've gotta hire a third staff member … at *least* a third one. We probably need more than that."

Kyle acknowledged with another nod. "What position?"

"Not totally sure. How are you with continuing both youth and music?"

"Hey, I'm happy. I'm not overtaxed in any way—well, as far as those two ministries alone are concerned. It's all the other stuff I have to do that gets taxing."

"Most churches our size have already split up those ministries."

"Because most churches have music ministers who hate youth ministry."

"And you love it." Jonathan had recognized that shortly after Kyle came. "So we don't need to go there?"

"No sir."

"Allrighty, then …" Jonathan moved forward, squeaking the chair again. He glanced down at the sheets before him which had been compiled by the *Church Steering Committee.* "Education, maybe? Church administration? Someone who can come in here and take over all the organizing and such—leaving me to simply pastor the people … and you to work with youth and music."

Kyle considered it carefully. He knew that adding a new person would greatly change the dynamics of the church office and their working relationships. The three office staff, he, Jonathan, and his wife, Cindy, had practically become family. There was no stress, no confusion, and everyone knew how to handle everyone else. No matter how wonderful the new person might be, it would mean a major change to how things were right now.

"That's probably the right decision," Kyle finally settled. "I know it would do you a world of good to not have to worry with all that. You could just preach, teach, and then go visit with the people as you see fit … just like you used to."

"Yep," Jonathan said half-heartedly. "But it also means relinquishing control in a lot of areas where I've been in charge for thirty years." He glanced up at Kyle with one raised eyebrow. "Do you think that makes me a control freak? A bad pastor?"

"I think that makes you human."

"*That* I most definitely am."

☼☼☼

Annie Williams stood on the back of the pool's deck at her new log cabin and admired the colors that were beginning to show. The sourwoods were already a deep red, and the hickories were showing a hint of yellow. She and Stephen had finally *retired.* His contract was over, and for the first time since college, he had no obligations to anyone. After years of worldwide fame and fortune as a popular musician, he was now released to live a normal life with his family … if you could call it *normal.* The 15-foot fence that surrounded their property—which connected to Annie's parents—would always be a stark reminder that their version of *normal* would forever be drastically different from most others.

Four-year old Ellie came through the sliding glass door onto the deck to be with her mother. "I miss Stevie," she said nearly in tears.

Annie reached down and pulled her up into her arms. "Me too."

They had moved to Dockrey this past summer, and since Stevie had just turned five, he was eligible for Kindergarten. She and Stephen had labored over the decision. In New York, they had assumed they would hire tutors, but since they planned to take some time off and be in Dockrey for a few years, public school seemed the best option. Annie was beginning to wonder now. It was hard to send her little bundle of blond curls away every morning, but Stevie loved it. He had never been able to spend time with other children except when visiting the Wrights in Dockrey. Here he always had his cousins surrounding him. To him, Alabama was heaven.

"How are my girls?" Stephen asked sleepily as he joined them on the deck. After giving them a second look, he began to shake his head. "Are we all sad again this morning because Stevie is at school?"

Ellie nodded and buried her head into Annie's shoulder. The compassion in Stephen's blue eyes melted Annie's heart. How did she manage to end up with the man of her dreams? He held out his arms for Ellie, and she went to him readily. Soothing her soft blond curls which matched his own, he gently made promises of fun and frolic for them the rest of the day.

"You're going to spoil her," Annie said with only a hint of seriousness.

"And this is a problem?"

She shook her head and turned back to the valley—*her* valley. She was home again.

Two

Angie Collins stared at her youngest child, Carter, only two, and nearly broke into tears again. Something was definitely wrong. She had excused it for a long time, but as a doctor, she had to face facts.

Four-year-old Cassie came running up the back steps of their deck on the Pacific island of Padawin screaming in delight. Angie turned her attention to her daughter and quickly wiped the tear that had slid from the edge of one eye.

"What is it, sweetie?" she asked warmly as she held out her arms.

"A crab!" Cassie said bright-eyed as she proudly displayed the small creature. It was squirming all over trying to escape her grasp.

"He's a pretty one," Angie smiled as she pulled her onto her lap.

"Can't we keep *this* one?"

Angie shook her head as she reached up to put a long strand of Cassie's hair behind her ear. "We don't keep wild animals as pets. You know we always let them go at dark."

"But if we make him a little home, and he thinks we're nice, then he won't be wild anymore."

There was no end to this child's logic. *Is it possible that she's only four?*

"It's wild, sweetie. God made him wild—we're gonna let him stay wild."

Cassie turned back and looked at her mother with one green eye and the other brown. "But if we don't save him, someone else will just eat him."

She tried not to grin. She knew Cassie was working hard to play on every emotion she had.

"We don't keep wild animals as pets."

Cassie sighed in defeat and hopped down from her mother's lap. She walked over to Carter and held out the crab. "Isn't he pretty?"

As was typical, the two-year-old crawled over and touched the top of the crab's shell. He refused to walk. He was now twenty-five months old, and he had yet to even try. Whenever Angie attempted to stand him on his feet, he would scream in either terror or pain, and they weren't sure which. He was content to let his father, missionary Michael Collins, tote him around the village at Podakind, and anywhere else they might go. Angie kept thinking perhaps he was a slow learner, but his mind was sharp. At two he could already identify the letters of the alphabet and count to ten. Mentally, his development was excellent.

"Can we go swim at the beach?" Cassie asked.

"After I finish in the clinic today, we'll all go down."

"Even Daddy?" Cassie asked excitedly.

"You bet!"

Geechern—the young tribal lady who had worked with Angie the five years she had served as a medical missionary—came bounding onto the back deck. Angie smiled in delight at Geechern's condition. She was exceptionally brilliant, but had been born into a tribe where women were second-class and given very little credit. Because of the influence of Christianity, women were now more esteemed. Michael had taught the men, both by the Word of God and by example, that women were gifts from God, not to be used and abused, but to be treasured. Because of Geechern's intelligence and stubborn nature, it was believed she would never marry. But as she panted and sweated in her eighth month of pregnancy, Angie felt humbled at the changes she had seen God bring about in this village.

"Someone waiting in the clinic?" Angie asked her assistant in the native Padawin language.

"A man has been cut with a knife. He was chopping a new hunting path and the blade swung down onto his shin. It does not look good."

"Let me see what I can do for him," Angie said as she stood up. She smiled at the thought that Geechern had not used the word *stupid* to describe the man's negligent behavior. Before her marriage to Kateem, Geechern hadn't cared much for men or their macho attitudes.

"I will watch your angels," Geechern said warmly as she plopped down on the deck next to Cassie and Carter. ***"What kind of creature are you bringing home today?"***

Cassie held up the crab and began to explain to Geechern in fluent Padawin how she had stalked and captured her prize pet for the day. She glanced back up at her mother with pleading eyes again, but Angie merely shook her head. That was the rule: a wild animal was always let go at sunset.

She walked toward the clinic door, which was connected to the house, and geared her mind for the sight of the sliced up leg. The deeper she went into this third pregnancy, the more nauseous she became over things like this. Michael kept suggesting they try and leave Padawin for another furlough in the states before Christmas. She had delivered both Cassie and Carter a month early. This one was due in December. To stay in Padawin until after the holidays would almost be foolish, but Angie loved Christmas on the island. She desperately wanted Carter to experience the traditions they had created during their celebration of Christ's birth. Cassie, though only four, already looked forward to them.

When she opened the door, she immediately propped herself on the frame as she saw the wound. One of the men standing in the waiting area ran to her.

"Are you okay, Dr. Angie?" he asked as he took her arm. ***"Should I go get Brother Mike?"***

"I'll be fine. This cow makes it hard for me to handle blood sometimes."

Had anyone other than a local villager heard, they would have laughed in confusion. But there were several Padawin words with which she constantly struggled, and one was the word for *pregnancy*. It was very similar to *cow*, and no matter how hard she tried, she could not remember the change of inflection. She finally gave up and just accredited it to her southern drawl.

"Let us get him into the surgery room and see what we can do."

"Are you going to cut my leg off?" the hurt man asked in sudden alarm.

She grinned at him and shook her head gently. ***"Not even if you gave me all the shrimp in the sea."***

The man relaxed. Everyone knew that Dr. Angie loved her shrimp.

As she cleaned and sewed him up, she thought of her home in Dockrey. The leaves would be beginning to show color. The air would be crisp and cool in the mornings. Her father, pastor Jonathan Wright, would be pulling out his soft flannel shirts from storage, and her mother, Barbara, would be planting mums and pansies in the church flower beds. As another wave of nausea flowed through her, the thought of heading to Alabama seemed more appealing. Maybe Michael was right—maybe it was time to go.

☼☼☼

Andie Mason moaned as she glanced in the mirror before returning to the living room where four of her five children were supposed to be busy with their schoolwork. The youngest, Alaina, or *Lainey*, as everyone now called her, was standing just inside the door patiently waiting for her mother to finish using the restroom. Andie tried to remember the last time she went to the potty without a shadow.

"What's wrong, Mommy?" Lainey asked as Andie continued to look in the mirror.

"Mommy's hair keeps changing colors on me," she said as she turned off the light and motioned Lainey back toward the front of the house.

"Mimi says you need to get your hair out of a bottle like she does."

Andie grinned. "She did, did she?" She picked up a pair of dirty socks and a Batman costume on her way down the hall. She tossed them into the clothesbasket already overflowing with dirty clothes. "Did Mimi also say which color I should go with?"

"Huh?" Lainey had no idea what the *bottle* was all about.

Barbara Wright, Andie's mother, had actually been gray for many years. But one morning she woke up, looked in the mirror and told her husband, *I do not feel as old as I look. Today, I become a beautiful brunette again.* And that was that.

The commotion Andie heard before she reached the living room let her know that the hopes of her children doing their work had been merely hopes. She was tempted to walk in and begin yelling right away, but it had been a particularly stressful morning. Instead, she peeked around the corner to see exactly what was happening. Her first thought at what she saw was to begin reprimands immediately, but the children were having too much fun. They had pulled off all the cushions from the sectional couch and laid them in a row along the floor. Ashley, her eight-year old, took a long run on top of the now cushion-less couch, made a flying leap off the end from the arm, and soared through the air until she hit the row of cushions.

"Cool!" yelled Arly, the ten-year old. He jumped up on the couch and prepared for his own flight. "Move Ashley! It's my turn!"

Adam, the oldest, and a fairly reasonable twelve-year old, quickly gave directions for the way to get the most air when leaving the arm. Andie shook her head in unbelief. Arly took off, barely keeping his feet on the couch as he rounded the curvy part. When he hit the arm, he spread his limbs out wide and soared even farther than Ashley. The kids laughed in a chorus.

"I am *not* doing this," Aimee began to protest. "Something could be broken." The rather serious six-year old always tended to be reticent about anything questionable.

"You're such a *girl*," Arly began to taunt her.

Aimee wouldn't budge. "I know you're trying to be mean to me, but I actually *like* being a girl."

Adam cut in. "Well, if you're not going, I'm taking my next turn."

Andie watched as her oldest hopped onto the couch and started the procedure. By the time he flew off the end, the kids were screaming with laughter again. Jumping so far, he nearly went past the cushions.

Aimee, still the voice of reason, warned them all. "You know Mom's gonna have a cow when she sees this."

"You're the only cow Mom ever had," Arly said as he stuck his tongue out.

Andie finally entered the scene, hands on hips, and stern look on her face.

"Uh oh," Ashley whispered.

"Would someone mind explaining exactly *what* is going on here?" she asked soberly.

Aimee stood up immediately. "Adam and Arly decided to pull the cushions off the couch and do flying things."

Andie nodded as she walked over to the arrangement. She glanced up and down the couch, then over at the cushions that were now in disarray from being landed upon.

Lainey walked up beside her mother and pulled on her shirt. "Can *I* do it, Mama?"

She shook her head firmly. "No, you cannot." She looked at her other children. Their expressions were totally guilt-ridden. Andie glanced down at Lainey and added, "Because it's not *your* turn yet." At that, all the children, especially Aimee, changed their looks to complete surprise.

A little alarmed, Aimee asked, "Then whose turn is it, Mama?"

Andie pulled off her sandals, pushed up her sleeves, and hopped onto the couch. "Mine," she whispered. The eyes of each child grew wide.

"Go, Mom," Adam said with an astonished whisper.

Andie started the run, rounded the couch corner, hit the arm, and took off.

"Mom!" Ashley screamed as Andie flew through the air. "You're gonna miss the cushions!"

As soon as Andie landed, she knew it had been a big mistake. She had indeed missed the cushions—completely—and the pain in her right ankle was reminding her that she should always scope out things like this. This would not be her first, but her sixth broken bone. Was that acceptable considering she was thirty-seven?

✡✡✡

Ring, ring, ring! It was impossible for Cindy to get any work done at the office for the time she had to spend on the phone, but she believed it to be as much a ministry as anything else at First Baptist. She tried to give each person who called special attention, but with the budget needing to be balanced and bulletins needing to be printed, it was getting exasperating.

"Good morning. First Baptist Church," she said trying to muster up some cheer.

"Hey, Miss Cindy, it's Adam." She sighed with relief. It was Andie's oldest son, Jonathan's grandson. This wouldn't be a conversation for *her.*

"Whatcha need, buddy?"

"Is Gaga in?"

"Sure is. I'll get him on the line."

Cindy buzzed Jonathan and informed him that Adam needed to talk. *If only we had just one line,* Cindy thought. *Then only one person could talk at a time. That would free me up a little.*

"What's up, guy?" Jonathan said as he picked up the phone. He was thankful for the reprieve, and he adored his grandchildren, all ten of them.

"Mama's broken something, I think," Adam said with hesitation.

"Something? Something like a lamp or the dishwasher?"

"A body part."

He closed his eyes and rubbed his temples. Andie had to be the most accident-prone person on the planet, but she had managed to stay catastrophe free since having five children. "What do you think she's broken?"

"I'm guessing her ankle. It's all swollen and … well … it's just kind of hanging there on her leg."

"Hanging there?" He was now beginning to feel some alarm.

"Yeah. I tried to call Dad, but he's not answering his cell. He must be busy hammering or sawing or something."

"I'll be right there." He hung up and immediately called his wife. It took six rings before she answered.

"Hello?"

"Barb? You need to get to Andie's right away," he said a little too nervously.

"Oh no, why?"

"Adam thinks she's broken her ankle. I'll take her to the ER; you stay with the kids."

"What did she do *this* time?"

"Don't be too hard on her. She hasn't had an *accident* in over twelve years. Just keep that in mind, okay?"

He smiled as Barbara laughed and told him, "*You* keep that in mind too!"

Three

On Friday morning, Billy Marcum awoke to the annoying demand of the alarm buzzing intermittently. He tried to find it without opening his eyes, but after knocking over a glass left on his stand from last night, he realized it was hopeless. He finally sat up in the bed and glanced around until he found the clock. Oh yeah … he had put it across the room to force him out of bed. He rolled to the edge and managed to get up without stumbling. Is this how every morning would feel for the rest of his life?

Mornings had never been good for him. He didn't drink or party anymore, but he still found himself staying up until two or three each night watching television. He supposed the saying that old habits die hard must be true. He tried to keep his balance as he swaggered toward the refrigerator. What on earth had possessed him to sell everything he owned, buy a houseboat and a motorcycle, and go back to school? Where had his head been? Here he was at thirty-five preparing to student teach for the rest of the semester. Was he nuts?

He pulled open the fridge and frowned as he realized it was empty. Did he have enough cash to drive through McDonalds this morning? He swayed with the boat over to his dresser and picked up his wallet. Five dollars. He could eat on that. Was there enough gas in the bike? He couldn't remember. What time did he actually get in bed last night?

After dressing and trying to make his hair look presentable only to be flattened by the helmet, he walked outside into the cool dampness of the morning. It seldom rained until he had bought the motorcycle; now it seemed to rain almost every day. He locked the boat, pulled on his raingear, put on the helmet, and took off for McDonalds. Did he really want to teach school? Really?

After wolfing down a biscuit and coffee, he headed on to the school. He remembered high school well. That had been the apex of his life. He was a star athlete in the tiny town of Dockrey. He was good-looking, and with Angie Wright, the gorgeous preacher's daughter by his side, life had been perfect. But when graduation was over, Angie left for med-school to become a missionary, and he went to the University of North Alabama in hopes of becoming a science teacher. Angie eventually did finish school and became a medical missionary. But Billy? He dropped out of school, started working at a men's clothing store, and eventually married … twice. The first marriage was probably out of love;

he wasn't sure anymore. The second one was purely on the rebound from the first, along with a lot of alcohol, a gorgeous girl, and the convenience of being in Las Vegas.

He locked his helmet inside the luggage of his Kawasaki Concours and ran a brush through his hair. A couple of girl students walked by and gave him the twice-over. He smiled and locked up the brush. Sometimes it was a curse to look like he did. In his younger years he had taken great advantage of women. But as he grew older, he began to want more from a relationship. It appeared impossible. The smart, deep and methodical women never seemed to be in the places he hung out. And going back to school with a bunch of coeds three years ago had been a recipe for social disaster. He learned quickly that an eighteen year old who looked twenty-six was not a good idea for a man in his thirties. Finally he just gave up. Cindy, his twin sister who was married to a minister back in Dockrey, had told him otherwise. He was happy for her and her little family, but that kind of life was not meant for Billy Marcum. He was a loner … thus the boat … and the bike.

The principal greeted him enthusiastically and pointed him in the direction of the science department. He expressed how pleased he was to have such a *mature* man student teaching for a change. Billy replied appreciatively, but inside all he could think was, *Lock up your teenage girls; this may be the biggest mistake of my life.*

Walking through the hall, he received stares and glares from the students. He shook his head and wondered what he had gotten himself into. *God*, he half prayed—he still didn't know if he really believed in God—*You'd better work some kind of miracle with all of this. I know girls. I can reject just as easily as not, but pretty little girls with jilted feelings can become ugly little liars. This is all I've ever wanted to do. Please don't let me fail. Please give me … something … I don't know what … to keep my head on straight here.*

He found the science and math department, and walked through the double front doors. Next task: locate Mr. Culbertson's room. No names were posted on the doors. A tall, husky boy brushed past him.

"Excuse me," Billy called to him. "I'm trying to find Mr. Culbertson's room."

The boy looked back. "Mr. C.?"

"Science teacher," Billy clarified.

"That's Mr. C.'s—last room up there on the left."

"Thanks. Appreciate it."

"No problem."

The boy was wearing a jersey, obviously a football player with tonight's game on his mind. He had the world by the tail and science was the least of his concerns. Billy smiled and shook his head as he walked down the hallway. He remembered that feeling well—it had been wonderful. Too bad real life was as far from that as these kids could ever imagine.

He found the door and walked inside hesitantly. An older man was slumped over a podium writing down a few things before class began. He wore a dress shirt with dress pants and had thick glasses, the typical science teacher type. Billy would definitely be breaking that mold this semester.

"Mr. Culbertson?" he asked.

The man looked up quickly and gave him a warm smile. "You must be Billy Marcum." He placed the pencil behind his ear, shuffled over still humpbacked, and extended his hand. Billy shook it firmly; something his father had taught him to be important.

"Yes sir, I'm Billy. What do I need to do?"

"A lot," Mr. Culbertson laughed. "Are you sure you're up for high school science?"

"I'd better be. If not, I just wasted some good years and a whole lot of money."

"Well, you've got nine weeks to find out," the teacher said as he patted him on the back. "Let me get you the books and start explaining where we are. This weekend you can begin making lesson plans for next week, and you get to take the wheel starting Monday."

He sat at Mr. Culbertson's desk through first and second periods. The man was an awesome teacher. Billy felt inferior knowing he would have to teach in front of him for the rest of the semester. One positive thing: he would be graded and guided by the best. This man knew how to connect with teenagers, and he knew how to make science sound like the best thing in school.

After second period, Mr. Culbertson explained it was planning period and he was free to do whatever until fourth. He nodded but just continued to sit after Mr. C. left. He had no idea what to do. He decided to walk out into the hallway and observe. As soon as he stepped out the door, he heard a teacher sailing into two students, one being the football player who had given him directions to the classroom.

"You know the rules," she went on. "If you have a failing grade in a class, you don't play in the game Friday night. I'll turn you both in right now if you can't give me a better excuse."

The boys shrugged helplessly. Finally, the one Billy had talked with spoke up. "We only missed one assignment. How can that be failing a class?"

"Easy!" she exclaimed as she threw her hands into the air. "You've only had *two* assignments this term so far! Even if you had made 100's on your first assignment, which I know for a fact *neither* of you did, to not turn in today's work would give you a 50 average. You boys aren't the brightest bulbs in the box, but I'm sure you're familiar with the fact that a

50 is an *F*."

"But it's just *one* assignment," the boy tried to reason. "We can't be failing a class over one simple homework assignment."

Billy listened intently as he watched the teacher's blond ponytail bob back and forth. This was an interesting situation. Would the teacher cave? Would he cave if he were in charge?

"Okay, boys," she continued, ponytail going to town as she talked, "since this is math class, let's do a little math. There are two grades in my grade book at this point in time. One would be your first homework assignment earlier this week. The second would be the big, fat zero sitting in there from today. What that means is that both of you are failing Algebra Two. At what point did you think those two grades were equal to passing?"

Both boys stuffed their hands into their pockets and remained speechless.

"I'm *not* Coach Grey." There went the ponytail again, this time accompanied by a slender finger pointing in their faces. "I don't *pass* students simply because they wear a number on their shirts or because they can throw and catch a ball … any ball … any sport. You're in Algebra Two, I'm your teacher, and if you intend to play tonight, you'd better turn in those assignments before the end of the day."

"The end of the day?" the other boy began to complain. "How are we gonna get it done by then?"

"I don't know. You're the geniuses. You're the guys who thought you could swing in here today with no homework and walk out unscathed."

Billy laughed silently. They probably had no idea what *unscathed* meant.

"I could say *forget it* and go ahead and write you up for the week. I'm actually being nice about all this. Because I can promise you: if you ever do this again, there'll be no second chance or end of the day opportunity."

"If you were really being nice, you'd just let it go this time."

"Oh, no," she said shaking her finger fiercely. "Don't tempt me, Randy. To actually offer you until the end of the day is not my style. I'll give you this one opportunity. If it ever happens again, I won't be this *nice*."

"I think you're nice," the second guy grinned adoringly.

The teacher shook her head and said, "You can't charm me out of homework either, Kurt."

The boys realized it was set in stone. Their only chance to play tonight was to somehow get that homework completed by the end of the day.

"We'll have it," Randy grudgingly gave in.

"Good. Now, you should both say *thank you* to me for being so lenient and head out for third period."

"Thank you, Ms. Marcum," Kurt smiled weakly.

"Yeah, thanks," Randy said turning to go.

Billy's heart dropped. *Ms. Marcum*? No way. He waited to see if the teacher would turn, but she continued to stare and shake her head even after the boys left the building. He would have to find out eventually—he might as well go on and take the chance. She definitely had a strong southern drawl, but just about anyone in north Alabama would.

"Excuse me," he said softly as he approached her.

When she swung around, her ponytail flopped again, but the expression on her face when she saw Billy was almost frightening. She immediately pulled off the narrow, dark-rimmed glasses and rubbed her nose. "Billy?" she asked breathlessly. "Billy Marcum?"

He couldn't believe it. It was Samantha. How on earth did this happen? "You teach here?" he asked, then felt like kicking himself for such a stupid question.

"Yeah," she said slowly as she took a step back. "Nine years. What are *you* doing here?"

He blew up at his hair and then leaned back against the wall. "Would you believe I'm student teaching this semester with Mr. Culbertson?"

She laughed slightly and replaced her glasses as she shook her head in sheer disbelief. "No. I don't. You went back to school?"

He nodded. "Three years ago."

"What brought that on?"

"Well, Dad died from a heart attack about five years ago."

Sam immediately caught herself from the shock of the statement. "Oh no. I'm so sorry. He was a wonderful man."

"Yes, he was," he agreed trying to avoid her eyes. This was extremely awkward. "Then three years ago … Mom … well …" he still couldn't say it after all this time.

"No," she whispered as she stepped up to him for the first time. "What happened?"

He actually thought he might have to fight back tears. "I can't believe I still want to cry about this."

"It's okay. It's what people do when they have feelings."

He winced slightly. He knew she wasn't digging at him, but she might as well be. "She had cancer."

Sam reached up and touched his shoulder compassionately. "I'm so sorry. I can't imagine what you've been through. So all of that prompted you to go back to school and get your degree?"

He only nodded. His emotions were still threatening to overcome him. Talking about his parents with Samantha was almost unbearable.

"You want to go get some coffee?" she finally offered. "This is my break time too."

"Sure," he said as he tried to sigh himself out of the emotions.

"Science teacher, huh?" she said as they began to walk. "I never thought you had it in you."

"No one did. Not even me."

Samantha Marcum was silent for a while. She couldn't believe that being next to her ex-husband like this could bring back so many feelings. She had sworn to never speak with him again; he had hurt her badly, and she was determined that he would be the last person to ever worm his way inside her life. It had worked. She had closed herself off, finished her B.S. in math and then gone on for her Master's. In her nine years of teaching, she had managed to remain distant from her co-workers, and instead had poured her life and passion into her students. They had become her surrogate children, and she had dedicated herself to making sure they all understood that a good use of education could open doors that could lead them away from anything and take them to anywhere. She knew firsthand.

As she led Billy to the teacher's lounge, part of her still wanted to slap the dog out of him. He had been cruel and insensitive when their brief marriage ended. She could still feel bile rise in her throat as he made some snide remark about Angie Wright, the woman of his dreams, and that Samantha would simply never be her. But a whirlwind breezed through her head as she realized the man walking beside her had changed. He was broken, almost humbled somehow. He had lost both parents, the two people who had always believed he was better than he acted, and apparently that loss had triggered a transformation.

When Sam had met Billy, she had just started the University of North Alabama as a freshman. Her past had been so horrible and painful that she wanted to travel as far from Toombs County, Georgia, as she possibly could. She studied like crazy hoping to somehow get scholarship money to pay for school. UNA offered her the best deal. She left Toombs County vowing never to return, and so far, she had kept that vow. But Billy Marcum had shown up very early. He had dropped out of school and was a cocky twenty-one-year old with a good paying job and a sports car. He hung out with his buddies at the student center on campus. Why he ever struck up a conversation with her was beyond her comprehension; he'd always fancied the socialite, snazzy-dressing types that caked on make-up and hair spray. Sam had been studying in a pair of sweats with a ponytail.

She stopped suddenly as her face flushed realizing she still wore the same stupid ponytail. She couldn't help it; it was just too convenient … or something.

"Is anything wrong?" he asked stopping with her.

She shook her head and chuckled. "Not really. I was just thinking you're probably wondering if I ever do anything with my hair."

He grinned as they picked up the pace again. "I've always been rather partial to your ponytail."

Four

"So you call what I'm doing *whining*?" Jonathan asked his wife on Saturday evening as they climbed into bed. It had been a stressful day at Andie's as they had tried to manage the kids who were feeling horribly guilty that their mother was in surgery because of their flying stint in the living room. "Whining?" he asked again.

"Yes, dear," she sighed as she rubbed lotion into her arms. "You've whined all evening to Stephen and Kyle about having to hire a new staff member. You've moaned and complained and griped, and frankly, I've just about seen my limit with it."

He was shocked. His wife was never at her limit with anyone. After raising three very rambunctious and stubborn daughters, one reticent and uncommunicative son, and doling out love and discipline to ten generally overactive grandchildren, the concept of *seeing her limit* had never happened. Now suddenly with her adoring husband of forty years she was about to *see her limit*?

"Stop looking like a whipped puppy," she said sternly as she peered over at him.

"How do you expect me to look? I've just learned that I'm a whiner and that I've practically caused you to go gray again."

"For heaven's sake, Jonathan! I cannot see for the life of me why you're struggling with this decision! You come home everyday absolutely exhausted from work. Pastoring used to be a pleasure for you … it energized you … but now it's become a chore. The only time you're truly happy anymore is when you're delivering a sermon—which you complain about when you get home because you didn't have enough time to prepare." She now reached over and gently touched his arm. "Sweetie, this church has grown beyond just you. You're a shepherd, dear, not a CEO. You preach and reach the people. You touch their lives and meet their needs in a divine way. God's gifted you with a unique ability to connect with folks on a personal level. *That* is what has built this church more than anything … and *that* is what's going to keep this church going. If you don't relinquish control of the other areas to someone new, the church will suffer. They won't have *that* pastor any longer, but a …"

"… whining, sniffling …" he bemoaned still stewing in his pity party.

"They'll have," she interrupted him, "a burned out man of God who cannot adequately fulfill any position any longer because he's stretched to the seams." She leaned down and kissed his rapidly thinning head of hair. "You're too wonderful a man, Jonathan, to go out in a whimper."

Whimper? Whining? Am I really that bad?

✿✿✿

"Flying through the air, huh," Doug Mason said shaking his head as he sat beside his wife, Andie, on her hospital bed. "Just when I think I can leave you alone with the kids again, you go and pull something like this."

She smiled groggily still fairly sedated, as the surgery had been extremely invasive. "Will I walk again?"

"That's a big ten-four, but the doc says that you should avoid flying again for the next … oh, sixty years or so."

"I'll keep that in mind. How are the kids?"

"Looking like a group of cats that ate the pet canary. Well, except for Aimee. She's sort of been gloating about the whole thing. Arly's gonna pop her in the mouth if she doesn't stop."

"Are they at Mom's and Dad's?"

"Nope. Would you believe Stephen and Annie took them home tonight?"

She looked up alarmed. "Do you think that's good?"

He shrugged and sighed. "I don't really care. They offered; I accepted. Now that they're living here and want to be a part of this great, big, happy family, they might as well get broken in with our brood."

She actually managed a giggle through the medication. "Our *brood* will most definitely break them in."

✿✿✿

On Sunday morning, Stephen began to wonder if he'd ever been this exhausted in his entire life. Getting his own two ready for anything had always been a chore, but with Andie's added five, getting to church had become a three-ring circus. He was appreciative at how Adam had tried to help—but when the cinnamon rolls burned because Adam had forgotten he had put them in at too high a temperature hoping to cook them quicker because everyone had gotten up late, it set the pace for the rest of the morning. Aimee's hose had a run, and she refused to wear them to church. Ashley's bangs were growing out so someone needed to do something with her hair or she would never be able to see during Sunday School and would miss all the questions in Bible competition. Arly was insistent that he wear a tie like Uncle Stephen, but since he'd never learned to tie one, he had managed a knot that no one could get undone, thus it had to be cut from his neck. Lainey and Ellie thought the idea of spending the weekend together was grand. They were exactly the same age, even sharing the same birthday, and as four-year old cousins, mischief was on the menu. After being fully dressed and perfectly ready, they went outside and slid down the wet slide along with swinging on the wet swings. By the time Annie realized they were gone, they were covered in mud from head to toe. She had to change her own clothes after bathing them and getting them ready a second time.

As they finally climbed into the Mason van to head for church, Stephen looked over at Annie and said, "She didn't break her ankle on accident; the poor woman needed a sabbatical."

Annie nodded as sweat beaded up on her forehead. "I think two kids are plenty, don't you?"

He stared down the road and tried to imagine going through this on a daily basis. "Plenty." That was quite a confession for Stephen who had always wanted a house full.

☼☼☼

Before Jonathan left for the fateful deacons' meeting that Sunday afternoon, Barbara came over and put her arms around him. "Sweetie, you're not facing a firing squad. These men are your biggest supporters."

"That's not what worries me."

"Then what is it?"

"It's change, Barbara," he sighed in defeat. "For thirty years I've served this church and had a wonderful time doing so."

"No," she stopped him. "For twenty-nine years you've served this church and had a wonderful time. For the past year you've been miserable. It's too much. Even if you were thirty again, it would still be too much. Change can be good, honey. Ten grandchildren prove that. Who would've thought that anything could be more fulfilling than raising your own kids? But suddenly a whole new generation comes on the scene, and life takes on an even deeper meaning." She caressed his face and stared at him with deep compassion. "Our church family has grown, Jonathan. It's time for change."

☼☼☼

Charles Emerson, chairman of the deacons nodded in understanding as Jonathan laid out his decision. He actually felt empathy for Jonathan's reticence. The man had given his all to this church and had done more than anyone could ever imagine. To bring in someone new to take over the administrative and educational decisions had to be scary.

"If you believe this is what we need to do," Charles finally spoke in his drawn out, slow, southern speech, "we're behind you one hundred percent."

Ricky Tatum, one of the younger deacons on the board, nodded his agreement. "I think it's a good decision. But I'd like to make a suggestion."

All the deacons gave him their attention.

"I think any decisions this newguy makes need to be run by the pastor. He needs to still be in charge. He's led this church in the right direction all these years, and he still needs to be the bottom line. I'm uncomfortable with bringing in someone new and giving him all this power. He doesn't know us. He'll be making decisions based on programs and research, not based on the hearts of the people that make up our congregation."

"Listen men," David Deaton broke in. "I think we're all on the same page. Remember this: all decisions have to be approved by the deacon board. All committee reports and suggestions have to fly by us for approval. Shoot, even Jonathan's decisions have to come here before they go to the church. It'll be the same with the new staff member. Jonathan is the head of this board, this church. In a very real sense, his stamp of approval or veto will still be the ruling factor."

The deacons nodded in agreement. It seemed a safe assumption.

Jonathan placed the cap on the dry erase marker and leaned on his hands as he bent over the large table. "It's time," was all he could say. "It really is time."

Five

Billy awoke on Monday morning feeling as though he'd been dragged behind a semi. He'd obviously slept at some point that night because the sound of the irritating alarm had jarred him from a dream. He rolled from his bed and moaned as thunder boomed and lightning flashed. The boat swayed from the wind and the heavy rain, and he nearly tumbled over as he went to the other side of the room to turn off the clock. At least he had breakfast available on the boat this morning.

He poured a mug of coffee and stuck a frozen sausage-biscuit in the microwave. Who was he kidding? Billy Marcum a teacher? An educator? Today he began student teaching. He had his lesson plans down, but the thought of facing those teenagers suddenly made his stomach turn. He remembered how cocky and intolerant he had been in high school. Could this possibly be some kind of recompense for his bad behavior back then?

Get over it! he spoke to himself out loud. *You haven't even started teaching yet, and you've already convinced yourself that you're a failure. Where's that confidence that used to ooze from you years ago.*

But it was more than just the teaching—there was also Samantha. Seeing her again only reminded him of the jerk he used to be. He had hoped that by somehow going back to school and completing his degree, he could atone for and change the past. It might have worked, but with Sam next door … five days a week … for the entire term … there would always be this reminder that he had left a string of disappointed people. No matter what he accomplished at this point in time, he could never make up for the grief and pain he had caused his parents … or Sam.

The microwave beeped and he pulled out the biscuit, burning his hand in the process. He dropped it to the floor and ran to the sink to let cold water pour over the burn. When relief came, he picked up the biscuit, blew it off as though somehow his breath could magically remove the germs and dirt, and then he sat at the table to have his breakfast. The first bite presented its evidence that his breath hadn't removed much of anything—invisible grit was laced all through it.

Samantha. He remembered their first meeting that evening in the student center. He was there playing pool with some college buddies, acting as though he himself was still a student. While his friends were making the effort to do something productive with their lives, he was a loser, a dropout ... in a word, a disappointment. There was a beauty pageant rehearsal going on that evening, so the girls he usually flirted with were all gone. Sam was studying on one of the couches, books and papers spread out everywhere, as she twisted her long, blond ponytail. She had taken off her glasses for a moment to rub her tired eyes, and that's when she found him staring at her as he waited his turn by the billiard table. She immediately diverted her look and placed her glasses back on her nose to read again. He was struck. She wasn't flirting with him; in fact, it appeared she was avoiding him. Girls didn't do that to Billy Marcum.

He finished his game and then moseyed over to the couch where she was studying. "You certainly seem intent on what you're doing," he had started the conversation.

She looked up at him, obviously surprised that he'd spoken to her. "Chemistry," was all she said.

"Ooooo. What year are you?"

"Freshman," she replied not looking up.

He picked up the chemistry book and plopped down on the couch beside her. "Why is a freshman taking Chemistry?"

"Because I CLEP'ed the general sciences." She still wouldn't look at him.

"You're kidding?" he had laughed. "You don't look like a genius."

This caught her attention and she looked up at him. "What does that mean?"

His charm began to pour forth then. "Well, this really *cute* freshman girl is sitting over here studying an upper level science course … what is wrong with this picture?"

"I don't know. What else is a freshman girl supposed to be doing with her education?"

"I have this philosophy: never let college get in the way of your education."

She had looked completely confused. That statement definitely needed clearing up. "I have no idea what that means."

"See, college is more than just books and papers," Billy had said as he gently shut her book. "There is more than just science and English and math … blah, blah, blah. You do know that, don't you?"

He flashed his most charming smile, and that was when Sam began to blush. As a couple of minutes turned into an hour, and he continued to talk and tease with her, she began to have a good time for the first time since being at UNA. She had been so focused on studying—so she could break the bonds of her past—that developing a social life had never occurred to her.

"This place is about to close up," he had said as he handed her back the chemistry book. "It appears that I've wasted a lot of your precious study time."

"Actually, you did," she told him as she packed her things in her bag.

"Is there anything I can do to gain forgiveness?" His charm never stopped.

"No, not a thing. I hope you can live with the guilt of it."

With that said, she had stood and started for the door. He was floored again. He'd just spent over an hour flirting with a girl he would have never noticed on a normal night, and she was cutting him off as though he had been more of a nuisance rather than a pleasant distraction.

"Hey! Hang on!" He ran after her. "What's the hurry?"

"No hurry. The place is closing. It's time to leave."

Billy just stared at her in disbelief.

She asked him, "Is there something else you wanted to say?"

He was speechless. Billy Marcum was talking to a girl and he was completely speechless. "I guess not."

"Okay, then," Sam turned back toward the door. "I've got to finish my chemistry."

When she had left, one of his buddies came up behind him and slapped him on the back. "Slumming tonight, I see."

For some reason the statement took offense with Billy. He wasn't sure what it was about that girl, but something had captivated him that night that reminded him of his times with Angie Wright. This girl was not as stunning as Angie, but her conversation and demeanor forced him to think fast and laugh often. In fact, what had started out as flirting turned into genuine dialogue somewhere during the evening. That was rare.

A crack of lightning brought Billy back to the present. It was time to get moving. He had thirty minutes to get dressed and ride his Concours to school … in the rain.

☼☼☼

"A motorcycle?" Sam laughed as she came up beside him in the parking lot. "You ride a motorcycle now?"

He could feel the heat rising in his cheeks. Why did it bother him that she thought this was ridiculous?

"This is nothing," he mumbled as he joined her on the sidewalk. "You should see where I live."

"Oh my," she stopped laughing. "Really? You didn't get another ritzy little apartment?"

"I *did.* For several years." He paused as he started up the steps. "Then I went back to school. I downsized, you might say."

"I'll have to confess, you've got me really curious now. I may have to come over just to see where you live."

Billy laughed. *Remember that: girls can be curious about where I live. Great pickup line.* He then grimaced at the thought. He was through with that kind of life and *those* kinds of girls.

His morning was horrible. Mr. C. had been called from the room only five minutes after first period started and was informed that his wife had been rushed to the hospital with a stroke. Billy was on his own. When third period, planning period, began, Sam came to greet him at the door.

"How's it going?" she asked innocently. The look on his face caught her by surprise. "What on earth is wrong?" she asked as she walked in and joined him at the podium where he seemed frozen.

"I'm an idiot," he sighed as he shook his head. "Whatever made me think I could do this?"

"Been there, done that," she said confidently. "Mr. C. will help pull you through all of this. He has a wonderful command of the classroom."

"Mr. C. wasn't here." He explained the call about the stroke.

She looked at him with a compassion he couldn't imagine she could still have for him. His heart melted. He now remembered why he had fallen so easily for this girl who was drastically different from every other—she had a heart of gold.

"Okay, pretty boy, sit down and listen for a change," she said soberly as she grabbed his arm and led him toward the chair at the desk. He smiled; she used to call him *pretty boy* after they had married. She pulled off her glasses and began to lecture. "I know you. You came in here and thought you would charm stars into all of their eyes. You flashed your gorgeous smile and told a couple of cutesy jokes, then you assumed you would have everyone eating out of the palm of your hand." She looked him in the eye. "Am I right?"

He nodded, a little embarrassed. "I sort of hoped … maybe …"

"Listen, teenagers are wonderful people. They're full of potential and energy, and most of them are still not afraid to dream; they haven't had the life sucked out of them yet. But they're willing to test their limits … to push you so they can see just how much they can get away with. Most of them have no desire to work anymore than they have to. However, since you're responsibility is to give them an education, your first duty is to make sure they're learning. Because of that, you have to come off as an ogre in the beginning."

"An ogre?" he said weakly. "They didn't teach me this in college."

"You can be a *nice* ogre," she assured him, "but you have to be an ogre. You have to be relentless in making them understand that there are requirements they must fulfill in order to pass your course, and that you'll not put up with anything that interferes with that. You have to set the standard up front. Then as time passes, you can begin to build some relationships and have some influence on them. You can loosen up and joke a little. But until that point, you've got to let them know that you'll meet *your* objective of teaching them regardless of how much or little they like you or your class."

He laid his forehead down on the desk. What little confidence he might have had left was now dripping from his brain. "I'm an idiot. I don't think I can do this."

"Be the ogre, pretty boy," she said softly as she squatted down beside him at his chair. "You can be very persuasive, you know."

He turned his head to the side to look at her. "I can?"

"Very …" She grinned with a hint of suggestiveness. Popping her glasses back on, she pushed them up the bridge of her nose, and then gave a wave goodbye.

Six

Jonathan finally dialed the number that had been sitting before him nearly an hour. Why was this so hard? This was normal procedure for growing churches. It must be the idea of just picking someone out of the blue that bothered him most. He wanted someone *safe*, someone he knew, someone he could trust, but he had been out of circulation way too long to know any old buddies who might be in the education/administration arena. To trust a complete stranger with the structuring and ordering of the church was a daunting matter.

Dial, Jonathan, dial.

When Ronnie Friar was finally punched through, a hint of relief managed to sway through him. Ronnie was his friend, his pal from seminary, a man of integrity that he had talked with many times over the past thirty-five years of pastoring who always seemed to have wisdom for every situation. Having him work with the Alabama Baptist Convention at this point in time should be a plus.

"What kind of trouble are you in now?" Ronnie teased as he answered the phone.

"Up to my neck," he replied with a laugh. "I'm crossing my fingers that you've still got that magic wand of yours."

"From what I've read lately, you seem to be taking the world by storm—you don't need my magic wand. Your church is busting out on all sides. How many are you running now in Sunday School?"

"True numbers or *ministerially* speaking?" he laughed. That had been a joke between them for many years. Often there were actual numbers of attendance and such in a church, then there were numbers that ministers tended to add … *oh, these guys were counting money* … *we did a service at the nursing home today* … *the Arnold family with their eight kids came in late and didn't get counted.* And of course, you never gave the exact number. If a church ran two hundred sixty-seven in Sunday School on average, the pastor always rounded it *up*. *Yes, we have about three hundred on most Sundays.* After years in ministry, Jonathan automatically understood what most pastors were saying. This had been something he had tried to avoid. However, no one knew that, and he was probably accused of padding his numbers and his ego along with the rest of them.

"We're having about five hundred fifty in Sunday School, seven hundred or so in worship," he told him. "Two morning services … both smack dab full."

"Whew. You building yet?"

"Start in a month. It took a while to acquire the property beside us, but it's ours now."

"Way to go. I hate to see that beautiful sanctuary you've already got divided up into rooms."

"We're going to turn it into the youth and children's building. Split it in half, and divvy it up."

"You've done an awesome work there, Jonathan. You should be proud—or humbled—seeing that God used you mightily in all this."

"Well, the word *overwhelmed* seems to be more on the offering of late."

"Too much, huh?"

"Between myself, the music/youth man, who does an exceptional job, and our secretary, ditto, it's just too much for the three of us. We've got to add a staff member." He paused then added, "and I'm hoping like crazy you've got some suggestions."

"Education?"

"Education … administration—it's just too much for me to try and shepherd the people anymore with all the business and organizing that's needed to keep this many members on track."

"I can imagine. In fact, I'm sitting here wondering what took you so long? Why didn't you do this two hundred people ago?"

"Because I'm stubborn," he chuckled. "So, who can you recommend? Surely there's someone you know who can come into our church and fit right in and work miracles and get me off the hook."

"I wish I could. The only ones I would recommend are so close to retirement they can taste it, and they're not gonna budge to go to a first-time position to iron out the mess some stubborn pastor has gotten himself into."

Jonathan grinned. "No mess here, buddy … just need."

"That's what they all say. The best I can do for you is get a list of résumé's and mail them up. Look through them, make some calls, narrow them down, and hand the best of the best to your committee."

"That's not what I wanted to hear."

"I wish I could do more, Jonathan. You deserve someone who's sharp as a tack but personal and warm. I just don't know anyone to fit that bill that would be willing to leave at this point, but I'll keep my ears open."

"That shouldn't be too hard," Jonathan threw in causing both of them to laugh. Ronnie Friar was known for his large ears.

✿✿✿

Angie leaned against the sink at her island home, peeling potatoes, thankful that her morning had been uneventful. One child with a cold and one woman with an intestinal parasite had been simply handled. The machete incident last week had almost taken it out of her.

She glanced out the double glass doors to see her two children playing contentedly on the deck. Cassie was helping Carter build a road with blocks so his trucks could drive across. Poor Carter. His inability to walk never seemed to bother him. He was a happy and peaceful child, seldom complaining or demanding. Cassie, on the other hand, wanted answers for everything, and would push the limits of anyone who couldn't satisfy her inquisitive mind.

The baby gave Angie a sharp kick, and she giggled at the wonder of what this one might be like. She thought of Andie's five children and how different each one had been. Every child was a unique creation of God. Even her best friend, Cindy Sarkos, said that her twins were as opposite as any two kids could be. As she thought of Dockrey, it stung her heart for a moment. She knew it would be foolish to wait and leave for the States after Christmas. This baby would probably be early too, and she didn't need to have it here. The plan was to go home, Michael was pushing to go home, and it was time for her to make a decision.

She smiled as she noticed Michael slowly creeping up the back steps to startle his unsuspecting children. It had been four months since they had been to Taveren, the capital city, and his hair had grown out bushy again. It was bleached from the sun, and that, along with his tanned skin, gave him the appearance more like a surfer-dude than a missionary. As he made his way to the top of the stairs undetected, he suddenly pounced toward the children with a loud roar. Both kids squealed in delight and then immediately made their way into their father's arms—Cassie running, Carter crawling. *Will he ever walk*, she wondered?

As Michael stood to tote them inside, she opened the door for them.

"Look what I caught," he grinned. "Wild animals from the jungle were sitting on our back deck ready to eat us."

She leaned over to kiss him. "Hey, sweetie. How was your morning?"

"The crop is huge this year," he said as he let Cassie down. "I'll feel very comfortable leaving everyone here with this harvest when we go back to Alabama."

She tried to smile. She loved her home and her family and friends there, but Padawin was in her blood—it was her passion. She sighed and went back to the sink to finish the potatoes. Michael placed Carter on the floor and walked over to his wife, putting his arms round her from the back and burying his head into her long, sandy-brown hair.

"We'll be back, Angie," he said softly. "We always come back. We belong here."

"I know," she tried to sound confident. "But leaving is so hard. We do so much here that no one else can do. These people depend on us."

"And these people did just fine before either of us showed up." He turned her around to face him. "The men can handle the crops. Sojay and Joshua can lead the church, and even the other tribes have said they can come to their villages to hold services. Geechern can handle the clinic just fine."

"But Geechern's baby will be here soon, and …"

"… and so will ours." Michael looked at her soberly. "We can't wait much longer, Ang. We need to get you out of here; we need to go home."

He then looked down to Carter, and back up at Angie. "And we need to find out what's wrong with our little man. They can't do that here."

She agreed as tears began to form in her eyes. Carter was indeed the trump card. "I know," she barely uttered. "I just hope … well … that whatever it is …" she fought back the tears, "… that it won't hurt."

Michael leaned in and kissed her forehead. "We'll have to trust God. He gifted us with Carter, and we're doing the best we know how to do. He'll guide us, be with us, and with our boy as well."

She nodded slowly then reached up and put her free arm around her husband's neck to pull him close. "Let's go home. You're right; it's time."

Seven

After the tardy bell rang, three more students waltzed in as though this was normal procedure.

"You'll need to bring me a tardy pass," Billy said as he looked up from the podium. The students probably couldn't hear him for the noise of the class. Since the bell had rung, every single person had continued talking, with the exception of one girl who sat in the back corner reading a thick novel. The three late students didn't bother to acknowledge his comment—they walked on to their seats.

"I said," he repeated considerably louder this time, "that you need to bring me tardy passes."

The class got quiet suddenly.

"Yeah, right," one of the three snickered.

"Actually, I'm being serious," Billy said sternly. "You three will need to head up to the office and return with a tardy pass each."

"We weren't even ten seconds late," another one said snidely. "I'm not gonna get a pass for that."

"Last time I checked, I was in charge of this class." He remained firm. "My understanding of procedure at this school is that any student who walks into my class after a tardy bell is required to bring me a pass."

"Let me explain procedure to you," the first student smirked as he stood with an air of confidence. Billy actually found this humorous because it reminded him of himself at that age. "You're not really considered *tardy* unless class has actually started. So, technically speaking, I ain't late."

The class laughed at the boy who was now clearly proud of himself. He then turned toward Billy to see his response.

"That is not *my* procedure," he said without a blink. "Go get a pass."

The boy sat there and stared. This wasn't actually about all three boys. This boy was obviously the leader, and if Billy dealt with him, he would be dealing with them all. No one budged.

"Did I not make my point?" Billy asked him.

"You're not making the best first impression here, Mr. Teacher," the boy remarked sarcastically. "If you're gonna go and change the rules, you need to let us know first."

"I think what you meant to say is that if I intend to *enforce* the rules I need to let you know first."

"Yeah, whatever," the boy shrugged him off this time and turned around to talk to the person behind him.

"Let me make this *very* clear," Billy said loudly, startling the entire class this time. "I intend to enforce every rule this school has designed. I intend to begin class promptly after the bell. I intend to assign homework, give quizzes, and grade notes. I intend to teach you the subject of Biology in every way imaginable with the hope that it will somehow seep into your minds. I also intend to see three tardy passes from you gentlemen before I allow you into my classroom. Consider this a declaration of all my intentions." He stepped out from behind the podium to emphasize his final point. "And if anyone here is just a little unsure about any other school or classroom rules, let me suggest to you that the way to figure it out is not to break them first. Ask—I'll be glad to make my *procedures* and *intentions* clear prior to any foolish decisions based on false assumptions."

The class stared. He wondered if they'd even understood what he just said. The one boy was still testing him, with the other two glancing back and forth from Billy to their fearless leader.

"You need to get your passes," Billy said unmoved.

"And if I don't?" the leader asked.

"Let me put it this way," he remained calm, "if I have to ask you again for a pass, that'll immediately be detention this afternoon."

"You can't give us detention," the boy said smugly. "We have practice."

"I can … I will … and your best bet to be at practice today is to get out of your seat right now and bring me a pass."

The other two boys had had enough. If the big boy wanted detention, he could have it. They were getting a pass.

☼☼☼

Sam finished explaining factoring integers, for probably the sixth time, and then went to her desk to grade more homework papers. As the class worked quietly, she tried to concentrate on the job at hand, but Billy's helplessness kept creeping up in her mind. It was unlike him to be out of sorts. The one characteristic that had dominated his past was confidence, and even though some of that confidence she had loathed, some of it had been the main attraction. When she first saw him in the hall again last Friday, all she had wanted to do was slap him and yell *how dare* he be there. But when he told her of his parents' deaths, and then as tears welled up, her defenses melted. Then this morning, the complete loss of self-assurance had again taken her by surprise.

There was a knock on the door, and she looked up to see who it was. Paulo. She smiled warmly and motioned him to come on in. No other student in the entire school would have even considered knocking, but Paulo was different. He had secretly become her *special project.* The fourth son of Mexican immigrants, probably illegal, he had too many strikes against him already. But he had an eager heart, was a remarkable athlete, and had diligently given himself to learning. She knew that if Paulo would continue to apply himself, he could do anything he wanted in this world. She was determined to nudge him in the best direction, one that took him away from the Hispanic gangs that his brothers had fallen into.

"What is it, Paulo?" she asked as he approached her desk.

He placed his Algebra II book down and opened it to where his finger had marked the spot for tonight's homework. "I was working on this, trying to get a jump on it before I left school, and Ms. Marcum, I just keep struggling here. I cannot understand this."

"You're making it too hard, Paulo. Watch." She began to describe as clearly as possible how to work the problem. Paulo repeated each step verbally to make sure he understood.

"Right there," he stopped her. "Why do you do that?"

"You need to put the numbers in their simplest terms. It makes working the problem so much easier."

"But I can't figure it right. How do we get to the simplest terms?"

She continued to explain. As she did, a few students wrongly assumed her attention was far from the class, and a little murmur or two of discussion began to ensue. Sam nipped it immediately.

"I don't recall giving permission for conversation," she said strictly. "Did I not assign enough work to keep you occupied? Should I give you more?"

The class quieted automatically, and everything went back to normal.

When the final bell of the day rang, the class exited eagerly. Sam closed up her books, collected the papers she had not yet finished grading, and grabbed her keys to lock the door. Her curiosity, however, got the best of her. How had Billy fared? At lunchtime he looked horrible. He was still concerned that he had chosen the wrong profession, but several of the teachers in the lounge had assured him that classroom experience was a wonderful encourager—the more he did it, the better he would become. Sam had tried to ignore him, still overwhelmed that he had suddenly showed back up in her life, but it appeared he was avoiding her just as much.

After locking her door, she walked to Mr. C.'s room and glanced inside. He was sitting at the desk thumbing through the pages of his plan book.

"How'd the first day end?" she asked as she walked into the room.

"Better than it started," was all he said as he continued looking through his lesson plans.

"So, do the kids think you're an ogre?"

He smiled this time and slightly nodded as he wrote something down on a notepad. "I'm afraid so." He finished writing, dropped the pen, and gave her his attention. "One boy even has detention … a football player, no less. I think word got out quickly, and after that everyone pretty much stared at me like I had the plague."

"Very good. Give them a couple of weeks with Mr. Ogre, and then you can begin to let up some. Believe me, they'll have a much better appreciation for your charm when they realize they can't run all over you."

"I'm taking your word for it," he said as he stood up. "Is it still raining?"

"I think so. Do you need a ride?"

He chuckled and shook his head. "It's rained for the past three years … ever since I bought that stupid bike. I'm used to getting drenched by now."

"Stupid?" she said surprised. "I thought it looked rather cool. I don't believe I've ever seen anything quite like it."

He looked down at her as they walked from his desk toward the hallway. "You're impressed with my bike?"

"I didn't say I wanted to hop on, just that it looked really cool. What kind is it?"

"Kawasaki Concours. It's a sports-tourer."

"Well, that means absolutely nothing to me," she confessed as he locked the door. "But the maroonish-red color is awfully pretty."

He laughed. "I definitely was *not* going for *pretty* when I picked it out."

"Then you should have picked black." They continued down the hall and out the double doors. "So, tell me about your house. You've got me really curious."

He shook his head and insisted, "Don't even think about that. You wouldn't believe me if I told you."

She reached up and slugged him slightly in the arm. "Billy Marcum! Stop holding out on me! What's the deal with this house of yours?"

He simply continued to shake his head. "You're *not* seeing my house. Final answer."

"What if I follow you home?" she threatened.

He stopped walking and looked down at her. "What is this fascination you have?"

"You started it. It's your fault. You began it this morning, and it just won't leave my little, one-track mind. I won't let up until I see where you live."

He shook his head in defiance. "No."

"I'll bring dinner?" she suggested. "Something good that I know you like. Just give me directions and I'll be there at six o'clock."

"You're crazy. I'm not telling you where I live."

"Chinese?" she continued, running behind him as he headed toward his bike. "You obviously have no papers to grade tonight. It looks like the perfect opportunity."

"You have papers," he said pointing down to a full stack in her hand. "I wouldn't want to keep you from your work."

"Trust me, these will be done in forty-five minutes."

He stopped at his bike, unlocked his luggage, pulled out a helmet, and then his rain suit. Sam was smiling expectantly at him. He merely laughed and finally said, "Meet me at the pier at six o'clock."

"I didn't say I wanted to picnic. I want to see your mysterious house."

"Meet me at the docks and I promise you we'll eat in *my house* for supper."

☼☼☼

Sam pulled into the parking lot at the marina promptly at six o'clock. She immediately spotted Billy standing next to his red bike. She parked beside him, rolled down her window and asked, "Do I need to follow you somewhere?"

"Show me the food," he said soberly.

She lifted up two bags. "Do you have drinks?"

He nodded. "Get out, then."

"Here?"

"Yes … *here.*"

She handed the bags of food to him through the window, and then rolled it up. She got out, locked her car, and motioned for him to lead the way. As he started down the pier, she finally realized what was happening. "Don't tell me you live on a boat."

"Okay … I won't tell," he said as he stopped at one and jumped onto the side. "But at some point you're probably gonna figure it out." He placed the bags down and offered her a hand. She laughed as she took it, and he pulled her onto the boat.

"I can't believe this," she said looking over the houseboat.

"Disappointed?"

"Are you kidding? This is so cool! You actually live on a boat!"

"Well, come on in and let me show you my kitchen/living room/bedroom. We can eat in the kitchen or up on the fishing deck."

"No picnics, I said. We're dining inside tonight." She stopped him before going through the door. "You do have air-conditioning, don't you?"

"Yes, but it won't be long … just a few weeks … before it's cool enough to turn it off and open up the windows."

"I'll come back then and we can have our dinner al-fresco. But tonight, let's avoid the heat and humidity."

It turned into just plain fun. Sam was totally flabbergasted to discover that Cindy had married a minister, had three kids, and was a church secretary. Cindy was most definitely the twin of Billy; they were too much alike. During her marriage to Billy, Cindy had been the wildest girl Sam had ever known. In fact, she had often felt uncomfortable around her because of her escapades. To suddenly learn that she had changed her ways dramatically made Sam long to see her again.

"She's always begging me to come to church on Sundays and eat dinner with her family," Billy explained. "Why don't we do that some day? You can hop on the back of the Kawasaki, and …"

"We'll take my car," Sam interrupted quickly.

☼☼☼

As Sam climbed into her bed that night, for the first time in a long while she felt a twinge of loneliness. She and Billy had talked and laughed for nearly three hours. They had done no reminiscing, but had merely caught up. Relaxing in his boat had almost seemed like old times, and the longer the evening wore on, the more she realized that he wasn't the same man she had married almost fourteen years ago, and he was most definitely not the man she had divorced. He had been her only love … ever … but he had hurt her so deeply that she could never bring herself to open up to any one again, especially not a man. She wanted to kick herself for being curious about his house and volunteering to bring dinner, but now that the night was through, she felt almost fulfilled in some way. Now what?

Eight

Doug helped Andie into the bed and brought her three different pills. She wearily took them from his hand and popped all three into her mouth, following them with several large gulps of water.

"How can you do that?" he asked in amazement as she swallowed all three at the same time.

"Spite," she replied.

"Explain that one to me, babe. You can swallow three pills out of spite?"

She nodded as she took another swallow. "Annie always gagged when she took pills, and it drove me up the wall. I practiced swallowing M&M's whole until I could get five down at a time."

He looked at her in near disgust. "You swallowed candy just to eat at your little sister?"

"You'll never understand sibling rivalry, Mr. only-child. You'd be surprised at the things we used to do."

"Oh, I doubt that. After the things you do right now … flying off the end of couches, totally destroying your ankle … swallowing M&M's doesn't seem near as surprising."

She hunkered down in the bed, careful not to jar her wrapped ankle which was propped on a huge, fluffy pillow. "Don't get testy with me, Doug. My ankle might hurt, but there's nothing wrong with my slugging arm."

He stood up quickly and backed away. "Thanks for the warning, Ms. Ali. I'll be sure to keep my distance from the nest whenever making sarcastic remarks."

"My memory's long, pal. I might just wait until you're sound asleep … and then WHAM! I take my revenge."

"You know, sometimes it's really hard to believe you're a pastor's daughter."

✡✡✡

"I'm not whining," Jonathan insisted as he crawled in bed beside his wife. "I'm merely saying that I'm very disappointed Ronnie couldn't give me a recommendation. It means we have to start from scratch. I was hoping for a little better take-off."

Barbara fluffed her pillow, leaned over to kiss him, and then said flatly, "You *are* whining."

✡✡✡

Cindy Sarkos couldn't believe what she was reading: Angie Wright

Collins, her best friend since middle school, would be returning to Dockrey sometime next week. What a Friday it was turning out to be! Waiting at the post office had been a large envelope from the state convention which she knew contained the résumés Jonathan had requested. She would be glad when the new staff member arrived. As much as she loved the church and being married to one of its ministers, it was becoming increasingly harder to find time alone with Kyle and the children. If he wasn't busy with some kind of meeting, often out of either of his fields, then she was trying to play catch-up with all of the records and organizing that seemed to keep piling up. The only hope of reprieve was to get someone new … and fast.

When Jonathan finally walked in, he looked unusually haggard for a Friday. Fridays were their good days. Fridays were fun: lunches out, laughter and dreaming days. If Jonathan was starting Friday with a frown, that wasn't a good sign.

"For you," she said with a gentle smile as she handed him the large envelope.

"That was quick," he mumbled as he took it from her, still unpleasant. "I only called him Monday."

"You must carry a lot of pull with the head honchos down there in Montgomery."

"Not enough," he grumbled heading directly for his office. No bantering today.

Jonathan closed the door and dropped the package onto his desk. He walked to the window and stared down at the valley below. Within the next month the colors would begin to show significant change. It was a good change, a beautiful change, a welcomed change from the heat. Even when the leaves were finally gone, it was good. Winter was a time of resting. The cold and the shorter days weren't gloomy or dreary; they were opportunities to stay inside, snuggle with family, and do things out of the norm. Then spring always brought the promise and hope of new life, while summer brought fun and recreation. Change *could* be good, but everything within him told him that *this* change was trouble.

How can I think that? What else am I supposed to do? I can't keep going like I am. Should I retire? Is it time for a new pastor here who can do bigger and better things, one who can give more than twenty-four hours a day? Jonathan sighed and shook his head. He dropped into his chair and took comfort again in the old familiar squeak. *No. No man needs to do what I'm doing. Life is not about church and work alone; life is about relationships. I've always said that. If the ministry is causing my relationships to suffer, Cindy and Kyle's relationships to suffer, then it's time for change.*

He pulled open the envelope and began to read through the various résumés. It was easier tossing the *no's* than finding the *yes's*. He told himself he had to come up with at least five, but after two hours of thumbing through and dissecting thirty-five résumés, all he could consider in good conscience were four. He had told the committee five, but this was the best he could do. At first he considered reading through them all again, then quickly dismissed that idea. They would have to settle for four; these were the only ones that stuck out as suitable for the job at Dockrey.

☼☼☼

"Mrs. Mason," the doctor said soberly, "you might as well face the fact that you're going to be down for at least six weeks."

Andie groaned.

The doctor shook his head. "Listen … you try to fly like a ten year old, you're going to have consequences. I don't have a miracle cure for you. You snapped your ankle, we put it back together with nuts and bolts, and now you have to cooperate by staying off it until everything heals."

"Did I mention that I have five kids?" she asked sarcastically.

"Did I mention you're not ten years old?"

Doug chuckled. "That was good, doc. Yeah, I think you mentioned that."

She glared at him, and then he noticed that she had balled her fist. He was glad the doctor was present. He would look mighty silly trying to run from a crippled mother.

"I homeschool," she added.

"Congratulations," the doctor continued joining her sardonic mood. "I don't believe standing is mandatory for that."

"No … only cooking, cleaning, laundry, pets …"

He rubbed his scrubby, peppered beard and pulled off his round, wire-rimmed glasses. This time he grinned. "I think it's time those five flying children of yours learned the meaning of household chores."

"Three," Doug interrupted.

"I thought you just said you had five children."

"We do. But only three of the five were flying."

☼☼☼

"Cassie, sweetie, you don't need all of these in Alabama," Angie tried to explain as Cassie stuffed all her swimsuits into her luggage. "You might swim for just a couple of weeks at Aunt Annie's and Uncle Stephen's, but it's going to start getting cold. We won't swim there like we do here."

"Will it snow?" Cassie wondered as she continued shoving in all the swimsuits.

"It might, but that will be later," she said gently as she began removing one swimsuit at a time. "First we have autumn, remember? We saw pictures of Mommy and her sisters in the pretty leaves."

"Do the trees die?" Cassie asked this time. "Daddy says leaves make food for the trees. If the leaves aren't green, they're dying."

"Well, that's true." She was trying to answer all the incessant questions with patience. "But only the leaves die, not the trees. In spring, the leaves come back, beautiful and in so many different colors of green that it's awesome."

"But how do the trees *eat* if they have no *food*?"

"They don't … I suppose." Angie was a doctor of medicine, not agriculture. Michael had planted this knowledge in his daughter; he should be the one fielding the questions.

"Then they *have* to die," Cassie concluded.

"But they don't. They sort of … well … hibernate! Like bears!" Angie was proud. That should stop this particular line of questioning.

Her little head bobbed in contentment as she ran her hand over her favorite swimsuit.

"Is that the one you want to take?" Angie asked her.

She nodded. "It looks like Princess Leia in Star Wars. Can we fly in a spaceship to Alabama?"

"No, just an airplane."

"But how come Leia gets to ride in a spaceship and I don't? Daddy says I'm a princess too. Can't all princesses ride in spaceships?"

"Cinderella rode in a horse and buggy," Angie said as she got up to go into another room. This conversation could go on and on.

"Carriage, Mama," Cassie corrected as she got up to follow. "It was a carriage, remember? But only it was really a punkin'."

"Yes, and the horses were rats," Angie barely recalled.

"Mice, not rats. And the mice weren't horses. The mice were the people that drove the carriage."

Angie reached down and picked up Carter who was intently looking through a book of sea creatures. "I must be crazy," she said to him. "What on earth am I doing having a third child? I can't even handle the two I've already got."

"Cwab," Carter said as he pointed out a crab in the book. "He pinch."

"Where is everybody?" Michael yelled from the living room. "Has my family already left for Alabama without me?"

Cassie tore into the other room and raced into her father's arms. "Daddy! Can we fly a spaceship to Alabama?"

"You bet," he said matching her wide eyes.

Cassie turned around and gloated. "See, Mama. Daddy says we can."

"I know. Daddy would promise you the moon if you asked," Angie smiled as she came in and handed Carter to his daddy.

"Are we packed?" Michael asked her as he nuzzled his beard into Carter's face causing the little boy to cackle at the sensation.

"*We* are almost packed." She paused to take a deep breath. "I've had the world's most inquisitive child on my tail every minute of the morning. I have answered every question from how cats mate to why trees don't die when they lose their leaves."

Michael laughed. "Those cats *were* loud last night."

"I agree, but you always give out partial information to her. Then she thinks on it all night, and here I am in the morning having to explain the birds and the bees to a four year old … and how trees hibernate." She walked up to him and stepped within an inch of his face. "You need to be a little more thorough, Dr. Collins."

"I'll keep that in mind, Dr. Angie," he said as he put down the two wiggling children.

Cassie ran back to her room and Carter crawled over to a small pile of toys on the floor.

"So … uh … what did you tell her?" he wondered.

"About which thing?"

"Well … you know … the cats … mating."

She looked at him squarely and without a hint of a grin she said, "Everything."

☼☼☼

"This is an unbelievable swing, Dad," Arly said in awe as his father finished tying off a hickory stick for the handle. The rope hung high from the top of a large oak branch which jutted out over a steep incline. "Can I go first?"

"I don't think so," Doug said as he bit his lip while pulling the knot as tightly as possible. "I'm gonna give it a go to make sure it's safe."

Adam shook his head doubtfully. "Do you think that's a good idea? I mean … remember Mom? What if you take a tumble and then …well … our whole household could just fall apart."

Doug gave his eldest son a smirk as he pulled on the handle of the swing. "I am *not* your mother. I've never told you guys this, but your mom has a tendency to be a bit accident prone. She's put on a good front all these years since having kids, but apparently it was all show. The woman in there moaning and groaning on the couch? *That* is your real mother."

"Can you blame her for complaining, though?" Ashley said, practically the spitting image of her mother with long, dark wavy hair and big brown eyes. "Her ankle was hanging, Daddy. It looked really nasty. You should've seen it."

"That's okay, Ash," Doug said as he took a start, ran off the bank beside the tree, and twirled around over the steep hill. He landed with his feet firmly planted on the other side. "I saw three other breaks. They never look too good."

"Cool!" yelled Arly. "I'm next!"

"Patience, my young grasshopper," Doug said with an Asian accent. "Watch and learn from the master."

"Careful, Dad," Adam said soberly. "I'm serious about you not getting hurt."

"Me too," Doug grinned as he ran off the bank in the opposite direction this time. "Woo-hoo!" He twirled a couple of times before straightening up to land squarely on his feet again. "Nothing to it." He handed the rope to Arly. "Your turn."

"So cool," Arly said as he grabbed the handle.

"Now, you've gotta keep your bearings about you, or you'll end up like your mother," Doug warned. "For now, just run and swing around over the hill, then land. Come back around. No fancy stuff."

"But Dad," Ashley protested, "I want to twirl like a ballerina like you did."

Doug gave her a somber stare. "That was *not* like a ballerina. It was more like Spiderman, you know, flipping around on his web strings."

Arly ran as fast as he could holding tightly to the hickory handle. As he swung over the incline, it seemed like being thirty feet in the air. He screamed in delight. He nearly hit the tree trying to stop, but managed to turn around immediately and do it again.

"Mission accomplished," Doug whispered as he headed toward the glassed in back porch where Andie had been watching the whole scene. He opened the door and smiled sympathetically as he walked in.

"You get an A for ingenuity this time," she smiled at him.

"I promised you I'd get them out of the house for a while. I always keep my word." He eased himself down beside her on the couch, careful not to move her leg. "Tomorrow we'll take them over to Stephen and Annie's; they can swim 'til they drop."

"Always keep your word, huh?"

"Don't bring up the bathroom," he said as he put his hands up in innocence. "That'll take a little longer than just thirty minutes."

"I know. You could work on the bathroom tomorrow while the kids and I are at Annie's."

"But Stephen was going to grill Delmonico steaks," he protested.

"I'll promise to call when he puts yours on the grill."

Nine

Billy made the students clear their desks as he explained the different parts to the test. "First, there are ten true and false questions. After that, you'll find ten matching then ten fill in the blanks. It winds up with ten multiple choice followed by three essay questions."

"Little something for everyone, huh Mr. Marcum," asked one of the girls.

"Absolutely," he grinned, trying to act sure of himself. "You're bound to find something you like on here."

"I'd like an A on mine," a girl on the front row smiled.

"Me too. I hope you've got what it takes to pull one out," he said seriously again.

As the students worked, he tried to get past his nerves. What if the test was too hard, or even worse, too easy? But then, what if no one passed? What if he was a terrible teacher after all? He knew he probably shouldn't base his teaching career on the first examination he gave, but insecurity seemed to plague him lately. He needed a break after this first week. Perhaps he should pay Cindy a visit for the weekend.

When the final class of the day rolled around, he felt a little confidence at last. Several in each class had made perfect scores, while the rest pretty much went as expected. This was a good sign. He had obviously taught those who wanted to learn, and he would have to work on those who didn't care.

As soon as the bell rang, students quickly rushed out to get ready for the weekend. Several even bid him goodbye. Before locking up, he decided to call Cindy and see if she and Kyle felt like some company for the weekend.

"Hello?" she answered.

"Hey, Cin. How's the wife and mom gig going?"

She giggled at her twin brother's description. "The *gig* is going just fine. I'm driving Kylla home from Kindergarten as we speak."

"How's she doing in school? Probably impressing everyone right and left, I imagine."

"Spoken like a truly biased uncle. How was your first week of school, Mr. Marcum?"

"Interesting. It took a bit to get the kids to actually listen to me, but after all the tests today, it appears *somebody* is listening."

"Good for you. I'm proud to hear it."

"I was thinking about maybe making a visit this weekend."

"Come on down!" she said excitedly. "You know we have plenty of room."

"There's a home football game tonight. I thought I'd stay for that seeing how most of the players grace my classes each day. I might drive up there tomorrow; be there for lunch."

"We're having lunch at Stephen and Annie's, but I'm sure you could come on over. I'll ask them if you want."

He thought for a moment. He really didn't care to face any of the Wright family. After his past with Angie, and his obvious continual pining over her, he felt uncomfortable around them.

"I don't think so," he finally answered. "I'll go on to the house and let myself in. I'll see y'all when you get there. Take your time, okay? Don't rush back to entertain me."

"If you insist, but I know Annie would love to have you visit."

"Some other time. I promise."

He hung up and let a smile linger. He was happy at how she had managed to put her life together. In fact, it had been her change that had motivated him to make changes of his own. Going back to school had been the farthest thing on his mind, but after losing his father and then his mother's battle with cancer, money and women just didn't fulfill anything anymore. He kept thinking he would get over it, but when he discovered his mother was dying, he was empty. He had nothing left on which to fall back—it was then he decided to finish his education.

"Hey, pretty boy," came Sam's voice from the door. "How'd your day go?"

He looked over and was warmed by her smile. How she managed to get past his hurting her was beyond him, but he was genuinely thankful. Had he faced his first week of school with a still bitter ex-wife next door, he probably would have quit.

"My week ended pretty well, ponytail."

She blushed slightly. "I know, I know. You'd think by this time in life I could've figured out something different to do with this mess," she said flicking her hair.

"Aww, it's not a mess. It's actually cute as a button."

"Again, let's reiterate that I'm over thirty, and *cute as a button* is probably not the look I should be going for." She came into the room and picked up a stack of tests setting beside his arms. "Are you one of these *test always on Fridays* teachers?"

"Test every five days. At some point they'll stop falling on Fridays."

"Yuck … you'd give a test on Monday?"

"Yuck … yeah," he said as he took the tests from her. "I'm fresh out of college where they don't give a flip when you get a test. I need to season myself for several more years … like you … before my sympathetic side kicks in."

She grinned and shook her head. "I see the *ogre* aspect has kicked in however."

"Well, it works. Let me know when ogre time has run out and I can begin being *charming* again."

"No, no, no," she wagged a finger in his face. "Ogre time never fully runs out; it just becomes diminished."

He sighed in exasperation. "How come there's not an *ogre* class in college? I feel so cheated."

She glanced through the tests. "Fairly typical … a few A's … a few more B's … a lot of C's … and so on. It looks like you did just fine, Mr. Marcum."

"Thank-you, Ms. Marcum. I'll take that as a compliment from a veteran of war."

She laughed as she nudged her glasses up on her nose. "I'm not a veteran, not yet. But it would do you some good to go see one with me. Got any plans this afternoon?"

He placed the tests with the other exams and then eased himself up from the chair. "I was gonna go to the game tonight. Thought I'd see if these whipper-snappers have any talent."

"But what about right now?"

He shook his head.

"Come with me. I'm headed to the hospital to see Mr. C. and his wife. I'm sure he'd be thrilled to hear about your week."

He hesitated. "Eeee … I don't do hospitals."

"Who does? It's just life, sometimes."

"Uh … they sort of remind me of Mother being sick and having to be there so much …"

"Didn't Cindy have her babies in a hospital?"

"Well … yeah … but …"

"Did you visit her then?"

He nodded.

"Then keep that memory. Follow me to the house on your bike. I need to pick up a gift I bought for them yesterday. We can ride together to the hospital and then get something to eat before the game."

He only nodded again as he took out his keys. Had he just been railroaded? If so, he wasn't about to complain.

✪✪✪

"So, tell me about them," Barbara said as she placed a plate of cookies in front of Jonathan. "You narrowed it down from thirty-five to four. Describe the lucky four."

He nervously ran his hand through his hair as he took in the aroma of the chocolate chips. Familiarity—Barbara had made these many times through the years to comfort her family. How he hated the thought of change. He had been through plenty of changes the last few years, and though they were taxing, the results were eventually good. Annie had married and become a world-renown musician. Angie had left for the mission field and married also. Alex, his only son, had married and was now a much sought after musician in California. All had given him grandchildren. He had offered Kyle Sarkos a huge chance to start over in ministry at Dockrey, and it had been the smartest call Jonathan had ever made for the church.

"Stop wandering," she said with a frown as she joined him at the table. "Tell me about the four wonderful men you picked out today."

"I don't *know* if they're wonderful; I just know that they have impressive résumés."

"Then tell me about their résumés … and stop sulking."

He looked over at her and refused to smile. Was he the only one who understood the severity of what was about to occur?

"Speak, Jonathan," she said firmly as she took a bite of a cookie. "I'll help you see the positive side in all this. But give me some information to go on, please."

"Okay." He might as well hash it out with the one who loved him most. If anyone could see the positive side of a situation, it was Barbara. "One guy has been at a church in Florida for about ten years and is ready to get back to his home state in Alabama. He's well qualified and apparently well liked at the church. Another man has eight children and wants to find a church in a more rural setting."

"Eight children? And he's a minister? How can they afford to eat?"

"They probably live off of potatoes and ground beef; we've been there before. The third guy seems to be really good but has problems with seizures."

"Seizures? Really?"

"The last guy is a former Navy Seal."

Her jaw dropped. "You're kidding? What's he doing in the ministry? Not that there's anything wrong with that. It's just … well … odd."

"According to his testimony page, he saw two buddies blown to pieces on a mission, and he says it was God getting his attention."

She stared in horror. "Bless his heart. That'd work for me."

"Apparently he has done some exceptional things at the churches he has served. He actually has a doctorate."

"Does that mean he would outrank you?"

"No," he said soberly. "I will remain the senior pastor … a doctorless pastor no less … but still *the* pastor."

☼☼☼

Emotions poured over Billy as he followed Sam into the driveway of *her* house. It had been *their* house when they had married—it was a gift from his parents. They were so thrilled he was settling down that they wanted to give them a solid start. They bought this small place as a wedding gift, but when the divorce was settled, his parents had insisted Sam keep it. They were so humiliated at his behavior, irresponsibility, and inability to commit, that they had given the house to her in hopes that it might make up for his unforgiveable conduct.

He stepped off the bike and watched as she grabbed her things from the seat of the car. What he was sensing wasn't déjà vu, but instead what might have been. Had he never left her, this be their normal afternoon. He stood silently behind her as she unlocked the door and then slowly followed her inside. What a change.

"Wow," he said in awe. "You've done a lot of work in here."

"Do you like it?" She was preoccupied with getting what she came for.

"I'm highly impressed. When did you add the hardwood floors?"

"Nine years ago," she yelled out as she went down the short hallway. "When I actually started getting paid, it was my first goal for the house."

He gazed around the living room. It was inviting and cozy. The fireplace. He remembered how excited they had been when they saw it. In fact, it had been the deciding factor on choosing this particular house. Billy had never built a fire in his life, and the first few times he tried had been disastrous. But after a few lessons, he finally mastered the art. He recalled the first night they had managed to get it going. They had pulled blankets and pillows on the floor and …

Don't go there, Billy, he told himself. *Don't remember Sam that way.* But it was hard. This had been *their* place. For two years life had been ideal for them, and this house carried many wonderful memories. But he had been a jerk. He had been so full of himself he just couldn't imagine settling with one woman for the rest of his life—how could that be eternally fulfilling? He began to look more at what he did *not* have rather than what he *did* have. And the result was a fast decline in what had been a blissful relationship. He ran his hand along the glass fireplace door as more memories rushed through his mind.

"Are you ready?" she said coming back into the room.

He jerked his hand away as though she might have known what he was thinking. "Yeah. Whenever you are."

"Take these," she said as she handed him a vase from the table containing three orange roses. "I got these for her yesterday too. I knew I wouldn't have a whole lot of time to shop between school and the game tonight. Let's go."

He followed her out, turning back to get one final glimpse of the house. It was odd to see it again, and he wondered, not for the first time, if leaving Sam had been his biggest mistake … ever.

Ten

Billy hated hospitals. He hated the smells, the sounds, the sterile environment, and the even cutesy uniforms. In his mind he was seeing his mother hooked up to every kind of wire and tube imaginable. The last month of her life she had been moved back home to Cindy's, and he had forced himself to visit each week. When he finally came to the realization that she was indeed dying, he was afraid he would forget to tell her something important—something she needed to know. He hadn't had that privilege with his dad. James Marcum suddenly had a massive heart attack in the middle of the night with no warning. He died even before the ambulance could arrive.

"Think of Cindy," Sam said gently as she read his eyes in the elevator. "Hospitals aren't just places of death, Billy. They're places of hope and healing too."

He nodded as he leaned down to smell the roses he held. Sam smiled compassionately at him, and once again he felt that twinge of disappointment at what might have been. They stepped off the elevator and made their way down the hallway to Mrs. Culbertson's room.

"Knock, knock," she said gently as she cracked open the door.

"Sam?" Mr. C. stood up and came over to her. "Come on in, honey. How are you?"

Sam reached out to give the bent over man a tight hug. "I'm wonderful. How are you two?" She moved over to the bed and reached down to embrace the frail woman.

"Better," the lady struggled to say. "Slow."

Sam chuckled as she caressed the woman's face. "Then it looks like you and Mr. C. will make a great pair. He's not the fastest kid on the block, you know."

"Watch it, Samantha," he chided.

"Remember Billy? Your student teacher?" She pointed back at Billy who was trying to hide behind the roses as he remained outside the door.

"Come on in, Billy," Mr. C. said cordially as he motioned him inside. "I'm glad you came. I want to know about your week." He looked over at his wife as he pulled Billy by the arm. "Lora, this is the young man I told you is student teaching for me—Billy Marcum."

Lora gazed at him in confusion as she said, "Greetings." She then looked over at Sam. "Marcum? Relative?"

Sam laughed and nodded. "Actually he is, but it's distant."

And with that simple confession, she went on as though nothing unusual had happened. Billy was stunned. She hadn't hesitated with her answer. He had been waiting for students to ask if they were related somehow, and he had racked his brain to come up with something that wasn't a lie. He had finally decided the only thing he could do was say they were related in no way whatsoever. Apparently Sam was a little more creative in her thinking … and apparently she had indeed been thinking about it.

After several minutes of visiting, Sam excused herself to make a phone call. Billy stood uncomfortably in the room with the two elderly people he barely knew. He tried to relax but felt extremely ill at ease. Mrs. C. could barely get out one word at a time, and Mr. C., who had not left her side since Monday, could barely keep his eyes open.

"Are you a Christian, Billy?" Mr. C. asked out of the blue.

"Excuse me?" he replied, not exactly sure what the man was asking.

"Are you a Christian? Do you have a relationship with the Lord?"

"Uh … well …" how did he answer? "I was pretty much raised in church. My dad was a deacon, and my mom worked with preschoolers for years."

"They're active in church?"

"They were," Billy said lowly. "My father died around five years ago—my mother two."

"So…sorry," Mrs. Culbertson managed to say. Then she took a deep breath and added, "God … is … good."

"Yeah," Billy nodded, although he didn't know if he agreed. God hadn't been good to him. Why did God take both of his parents in such a short time? But then, what had Billy ever done to deserve anything good from God? If he let himself, he could easily believe he was the reason for his parents' death—that could have been God's payback for all the shenanigans he had pulled over the years.

"How are you and Sam related?" Mr. C. went with a different line of questioning.

Out of the frying pan and into the fire, Billy thought. *I should have elaborated on the church thing. I'm not quite as clever as Sam on this matter.*

"By marriage," Billy managed to say.

"How so?"

"Uh … someone in her family married someone in my family," he phrased almost as a question. *Sam, where are you? Get off the phone!*

"Were your fathers brothers … or something like that?"

He shook his head slowly. "Uh … not quite."

"Grandparents?" Mr. C. continued.

"Mmmm … no." Billy was getting antsy. How could Sam just roll things off like this? Suddenly she walked back into the room.

"Allrighty," she said with a big smile. "And what are we all so deeply discussing?" Their faces were serious. "Gas prices?"

"No," Mr. C. spoke up. "I had just asked Billy how you two were related.

Sam merely continued to smile. "And what did Mr. Marcum say?"

"He said *by marriage*, but doesn't seem to know who married whom."

She laughed this time. "Oh, he knows."

Mr. C. raised his eyebrows this time and Mrs. C. showed the first sign of life.

"Billy and I were married years ago," Sam threw out as no big deal. "Haven't seen each other since the divorce until Monday morning. Can you imagine our surprise?"

"*You* were married?" Mr. C. asked in unbelief. "You never mentioned before that you were married."

"Well, it was no big deal," she continued with the same nonchalant air. "We were kids—really young—thought we were madly in love, you know? It was one of those huge mistakes you make that you just can't take back. You move on."

"Hmmm, marriage is never something you throw off lightly," Mr. C. said with concern.

"Oh, it wasn't thrown off lightly," Sam assured him. "There was a lot of hurt, a lot of heartbreak, and a lot of loss. But like I said, you move on."

"I see."

☼☼☼

The football game turned out to be the most fun Billy had experienced in years, especially since entering school again. He and Sam had gone together, grabbing a couple of hot dogs at the game and then splitting a box of popcorn. She yelled at the players and the cheerleaders until she was so hoarse that she was barely audible by the end of the third quarter. As they drove back to the house, they pulled through Dairy Queen and got a milkshake hoping the cold on her throat might ease some of the trauma.

When they arrived, he unlocked her door and made sure all was fine before he turned to go.

"Oh … uh …" he stammered to ask her. "I'm going to Cindy's tomorrow. You mentioned wanting to see her again. You could come … if you wanted."

"Would she mind?" she asked with a raspy whisper.

"Are you kidding? She's into this whole domestic thing. Wife, mother, and gracious host—she'd be thrilled. I was gonna stay the night, go to church with them the next morning. Are you up for that, or do you want to come back tomorrow night?"

"Do they have room? Three kids, and then you?"

"It's my parents' house. When Cindy and Kyle moved in, they closed in that huge garage for Mother. They have more room than they know what to do with."

"Wow," she said softly. "Okay, I suppose." She thought a bit more. "Why not?"

"Great." He smiled at the idea of spending time with both Sam and Cindy. "You wanna drop by the boat and pick me up, or do you want to take the bike?"

She shook her head firmly. "I'll pick you up. I can't imagine stuffing a Sunday dress inside that luggage of yours. However, I would like a ride on that thing one of these days … when it's not raining."

"Consider it done."

☼☼☼

"Why is Alabama so far away?" Cassie complained for at least the tenth time.

"Because it's on the other side of the big earth ball," Michael explained patiently. Angie smiled; he seemed to have no trouble fielding all the questions his daughter's eager mind offered.

"The round globe?" Cassie remembered the model in their home her father used often to tell his children as well as members of the tribes about God's great creation. He nodded.

"Why can I not see the ocean anymore?" she asked as she climbed onto his lap. "Are we in space? Is that why it's dark?"

"We're in a part of space. We're up above the earth. See all the stars?"

"Are we going to a star? Is that what Alabama is?"

"No, Alabama is a big piece of land in the United States."

"Why can't we swim in the ocean in Alabama?"

"Because we won't be near enough. It takes hours to go to the ocean from Mimi and Gaga's house."

"We'll swim in the pool, right? A big bathtub." She shook her head. "That sounds too small."

"As long as it's warm enough, we'll swim," he tried to make her understand.

The questions and answers continued. Angie cuddled a sleeping Carter as baby number three kicked and turned inside of her, and she felt, for the first time, a sense of relief at heading home. She gently ran her hand over Carter's legs and tried to imagine why he wouldn't walk—why he *couldn't* walk. He could crawl, he could use his legs, and he had passed every motor test as a baby that indicated he was perfectly developed. Was he lazy? No. He could move all over the world if he had to or wanted to. Something had to have happened since his birth that was causing pain or pressure that made this normal feat impossible for him.

"You okay?" Michael asked as he reached over to touch her hand.

"Thinking about Carter. I hope we find some answers while we're here."

"We will," he assured her. "He's a special little guy, isn't he?" Michael reached up and gently ran his hand over Carter's smooth, browned face. "He loves his books."

"Takes after his Daddy," she grinned as she leaned her head on his shoulder.

"You'll have to admit I've done better about all the books."

"Apparently playing with your children is more fun than reading at this point."

"Indeed it is."

When she had first come to Padawin, she was floored at the amount books Michael had, as well as their complete disarray. She convinced him to build some shelves for the house, and then she organized them around the room. Until Cassie had been born, he kept a constant supply coming in. In the evenings, if they weren't playing their guitars on the back deck beneath the moonlit slopes of volcanic Mount Podakind, he was reading. But when Cassie came, he developed a new hobby. Every free moment was spent adoring his firstborn, and to this day, Angie had never once heard him raise his voice to either child in anger. He disciplined, but with such tenderness and understanding that she felt guilty every time she expressed frustration toward the kids for any reason. He was a gem, and she took comfort in knowing that her children were being raised by a man that would always place them above any other care in his life.

"Daddy?" came Cassie's voice again in question, but this time accompanied by a yawn.

"What is it, sweetheart?".

"I'm think I'm just tired of flying," she said as she laid her head on his chest.

"Me too. Close your eyes and imagine Han Solo is taking you to Coruscant."

"With Chewey?" she asked, eyes becoming bright again.

"Of course. And you're on the Millennium Falcon."

"At light speed?"

Angie mumbled, "I wish."

☼☼☼

"Okay," Stephen said sternly to all the children as they stood on the deck of the pool at the log cabin, "I am the lifeguard here today. What I say goes. Is that understood?"

Adam, Arly, Ashley, Aimee, Lainey, Stevie, Ellie, Kylla, Devin and Denay all looked at him with eager anticipation and gave the required military salute. Uncle Stephen had a way of making everything fun. Even as he explained all the taxing rules, pacing back and forth like a sergeant at boot camp, they knew he was only playing a game with them.

"When I blow this whistle," and he blew it loudly, "everyone is to get out of the pool and line up by age immediately. Is that understood?"

"But Daddy," Ellie reminded him, "Lainey and I are exactly the same age. Who goes first?"

"Aha!" Stephen spun around to the little cousins. "That is *not* entirely true. I believe Lainey came into this world a couple of hours before you, Private. That would give her precedence."

"I get to be president?" Lainey asked excitedly. "Shouldn't that mean that I get to be in the very front of the line?"

Stephen turned around to the adults standing beneath the shade of the deck. "When did four-year olds become such smart alecks?"

"Stephen," Annie rolled her eyes, "please let the children get in the pool. I think you've rattled on long enough."

Stephen looked at them all—eyeball to eyeball—and finally blew a long, loud whistle as he motioned them into the water. The kids screamed in delight and jumped in rambunctiously, splashing Stephen in the process. He walked back to the adults and gave his wife a long, sloppy kiss.

"Wow," Cindy said in awe. "It doesn't take much to get you energized."

"You have no idea how energizing all of this is to me," Stephen beamed. "Do you realize that for the first time in my life I have nothing to do, nothing to prove, no dates to keep, no interviews to hold, no songs to write, no meetings to arrange, no musicians to deal with, and no albums to record? I am free to just be a normal guy."

"Normal guys don't kiss their wives like that in public," Andie added from her seat under the shading where her foot was propped. "That was a private kiss."

"Oh, you're one to talk," Annie laughed. "You were always trying to make your private married life public to poor Angie and me all those years. You used to freak us out, you know?"

"It wasn't *private*; I was just sharing with my dear sisters."

"Oooo," Cindy grinned as she took a seat. "You can share with me, Andie."

Andie laughed loudly and shook her head. "I have five kids and a broken ankle; there's nothing to tell at the moment!"

Cindy leaned over to her. "Then perhaps you should let Annie tell you about her love life for a change."

"No way," Annie said as she held up her hand. "I never kiss and tell."

"No, you just kiss in plain sight of everybody to begin with," Andie grimaced.

Jonathan and Barbara joined the group through the French doors. "Good morning!" Barbara called out as she carried a bowl of potato salad. "Annie, do you want this in the kitchen?"

"Just put it on the counter, Moms."

Barbara went back into the house, and Jonathan walked over to the edge of the pool. "How is my spawn faring today?" he called to them all.

"Hey Gaga!" Lainey called out. "You need to come in and swim!"

"I don't think I'm allowed. My thinning hair might clog your filter."

"Awww, Gaga!" Arly griped as he climbed out of the pool and walked up to him. "Come on in and swim. Adam and I will clean the filter."

The adults behind them laughed because Jonathan's thinning hair had become a constant point of conversation. The children just assumed it probably *would* clog the filter. Jonathan turned around and gave them all a severe look. The laughter only grew.

Eleven

"This is like being in a time warp," Sam whispered to Billy as they drove up to Cindy's house. "It's almost as though nothing has changed."

"Tell me about it. That's how I felt yesterday when I went to our … *your* … house."

She looked at him with a compassion he still couldn't understand. "I'm sorry. I didn't even think about that when I took you there."

"It's okay," he said quickly. "I'm the product of my own creation."

"I've always felt guilty about taking the house, you know? But I was so desperate to get on with my life—and it was such an amazing offer—I figured why not. It's been an incredible asset to me too. As I went on in school, it was wonderful. I didn't have to live on campus. I could go back to my home and just study like crazy."

He used his key of many years and opened the front door. Smiling he took in the aroma of some kind of delicious goody that had been baked recently. It was still unbelievable that Cindy could cook … and cook well. Before meeting Kyle, she had probably never cooked anything more than a Pop-Tart. Now, she could whip up just about any order.

"What is that luscious smell?" Sam said breathlessly as she followed him inside.

"I have no idea." He dropped his bag and headed toward the kitchen. "But I'm definitely going to investigate." She let her things fall as well and followed him to the source of the delightful fragrance.

"Cherry cobbler," he said as he stood over it and breathed deeply. Cindy had left him a note. He picked it up and read it out loud.

> *Billy, I was supposed to take a dessert to Stephen and Annie's today, but since you were coming, I decided to make extra. There's fresh bread in the pantry, and lunchmeat and cheese in the fridge. If you'll put your plate of cobbler in the microwave for 30 seconds, then add a scoop of ice cream from the freezer, you may just die of delight! ☺ We should be back sometime later this afternoon. If, however, you change your mind, you're welcome to join us. They live on the property behind the Wrights.*
>
> *Love, Cindy*

"Who are Stephen and Annie?" Sam asked as she leaned down to smell the cobbler.

"Stephen and Annie Williams? You've never heard of them?"

"Should I have?"

"You don't know the song *Autumn Sunset*?"

"Of course I do." She stared at him in confusion, then suddenly the realization hit her. "Wait a minute. Are you talking about *the* Stephen and Annie Williams? The musicians? They live in Dockrey?"

He sort of hesitated as he explained, "Annie Williams is Angie's sister. Her brother Alex played in Stephen's band. Stephen came home for Alex's wedding, met Annie … and well … as they say … the rest is history."

Her jaw dropped and her eyes grew round. "You've got to be kidding me?" She leaned against the wall and thought about what she had just learned. "I can't believe this."

"You a fan?"

"Huge. I always loved Stephen's music, but when their first album together came out—that Christmas thing—I fell in love with her voice. I had no idea she was from Dockrey! This is unbelievable"

"We can go over there if you want. Cindy invited me yesterday, but I don't care much for hanging around the Wrights. I feel like I'm sort of the blight in their otherwise perfect lives."

"Why would you think that?"

He wouldn't look at her as he mumbled, "Angie."

"Oh," she said curtly.

They stood in silence for a bit, avoiding each other's eyes then decided to settle in their rooms.

"You take the garage apartment; I'll take the playroom."

"The playroom?"

"My parents' old bedroom. It's the *playroom* now. There's a nice pullout couch bed in there."

"Are you sure?"

"It's great. Here," he opened the door to the apartment. "Here's your room."

She walked inside as he turned on the light and was amazed. It had to be the biggest room she'd ever seen. It contained a kitchen, a dining area and a living room all in one.

"Over there," he pointed to a door, "is the bedroom. Just make yourself at home."

"Are you sure you don't want to stay in here? I feel like maybe I'm putting you out seeing that you spend most of your nights rocking back and forth on that boat."

He smiled one of his charming smiles and said, "I like the rocking—it drifts me right off to sleep." That was a lie. He never *drifted* off to sleep at all anymore.

☼☼☼

"A Navy Seal?" Kyle and Stephen were astonished as Jonathan described the last of the four candidates.

"Sir! Yes, sir!" Kyle saluted.

"And he has a doctorate," Jonathan added.

Stephen could tell Jonathan was tense. "What bothers you about all this? You keep saying that it's something the church needs to do … that *you* need to do."

"It is. And in all probability it's going to end up being one of these four guys."

"They seem qualified," Stephen observed. "But how do you start deciding which is the right one?"

"Ahhh … that's the key question. Lucky for me, that's not my job. I just get the résumés. It's up to the committee from here on out."

"Do you get to approve him?" Stephen wondered. "After all, you've led this church for thirty years."

"More or less. I'm sure if I give a thumbs down to their final choice, they'll move on, but I doubt I would do that. If the committee has done all the praying and all the interviewing, I'm not going to disapprove of their decision because I have some odd hunch … or constipation that day."

Kyle raised his eyebrows. "Constipation?"

"Yeah. Barbara thinks that's what all my uneasiness boils down to. She says I need to relax, eat more fiber, and enjoy the prospects of a new man coming in to relieve me."

Stephen laughed as he stood to check the steaks. "Maybe that's what's wrong with Annie when she gets in one of her foul moods."

Jonathan shook his head and smiled. "Nope. You just married one of the Wright sisters. They're stubborn-headed and opinionated. And then Annie, well, she's pretty moody by nature. I wouldn't suggest bringing up the *constipation* issue."

"Tell me about it," Stephen said gravely. "And don't ever credit anything to PMS."

"Daddy," Devin said as he pulled anxiously on Kyle's sleeve, water dripping everywhere. "Potty."

"Can't Mama take you?" Kyle said as he glanced over to Cindy.

"She said tell Daddy." Devin was starting to dance.

Cindy yelled from across the deck. "I do the pottying with Kylla and Denay! You get the privilege with your son!"

"Daddy, hurry," Devin said desperately.

"Let's go," Kyle whispered as he dipped down to pick up the anxious boy. He ran to the bathroom at the pool house, dripping the entire way.

✡✡✡

Harold "Hal" Bridges looked over his financial situation and frowned at the prospects. If he didn't get work soon, he was going to have to do something lowly. Surely some church somewhere in the entire United States needed an administrator! He punched the numbers in again on the calculator—they didn't lie. At least he had been wise enough to put out résumés before the church had actually fired him. But now the severance pay was just about gone, and he and his wife were down to only her meager salary. This wasn't how he wanted to live. He couldn't believe the people in that church had concocted such stories about him. All he was doing was what he had been hired to do. They told him to come in and shape it up—make it a place that was capable of growth—train the people to bring in other people. That's what he had done! Where was the problem?

"Hal!" his wife, Lisa, called from the other room. "I'm going to work! Do I need to bring home anything when I come?"

"Food!" he yelled back.

Twelve

Cindy was confused when they pulled into their driveway. She had expected to see Billy's odd, red motorcycle, but instead, a small white car was sitting there.

"Who's that?" Kyle asked. "Did Billy buy a car?"

"With what? He's barely scraping by right now."

"Do they pay him to student teach?"

"I don't think so. In fact, I think *he's* still paying tuition."

Kyle parked the van, and they began the process of herding three very tired children toward the house for baths and supper. Cindy opened the unlocked door and cautiously moved inside. Who's car was in the driveway? She listened for noises and heard subtle laughter coming from what had been her mother's apartment. She smiled slightly in relief knowing that Billy indeed must be here.

"Head upstairs, baby," she told Kylla. "Daddy will get your bath going."

"I thought I only had to deal with Devin," Kyle protested with a smile. "Aren't Kylla and Denay your responsibility?"

Cindy gently pinched his cheek and said, "I'm just gonna say *hey* to Billy. I'll be up to bathe them all in a minute. You get the water going."

He smiled, arms full of the twins who were ready to drop off to sleep any minute, and leaned over to kiss her lightly. "I'll do it. Visit with your brother."

She shook her head as she tousled Devin's hair. "You'll never do it on your own as sleepy as they are. They'll drown before you get through."

"Hey. I'm the dad; I can handle this."

He managed to get them up the stairs. That was a positive feat, so Cindy headed to the apartment.

"Billy boy," she called as she walked in. "Who's car?" When Cindy looked to the couch and saw Sam sitting there, she felt her knees buckle. "Samantha?"

Sam smiled sheepishly and gave a tiny wave. "Billy invited me. I hope it's okay."

Cindy put her hand to her mouth in shock and tried to fight away the tears building in her eyes. Sam. She loved Sam like a sister. When Billy had divorced her, Cindy thought she would die. But here she was, in her house, looking as adorable as ever—blond ponytail still in tow—pushing her glasses upon her nose.

"*You* are welcome here anytime," Cindy said as she moved to the couch with open arms. "Billy must always call first." She winked at her twin.

Sam stood and the girls melted into an embrace. She pulled off her glasses to dry her eyes.

"How in the world are you?" Cindy asked still overcome with shock and a flood of emotions.

"Very well. I'm teaching … have been for several years."

"I figured as much. You can't imagine how often I think about you." Cindy looked deeply at her. "I can't believe you're standing here in my home right now. Would someone mind explaining how this happened?"

"I'll let Sam tell you all about it," Billy said as he stood. "I want to go see the kids."

"Upstairs in the bath. Make sure they don't drown, okay? Kyle promised me he could handle it, but …"

"I'll give him a hand; you two catch up," he smiled with pleasure.

After he left, Cindy took Sam's hands and led her back to the couch. "Tell me you are *not* seeing him again," she said soberly. "He's changed, I'll admit that, but he didn't deserve you then, and he still doesn't."

Sam waved her off. "No, it's nothing like that, let me assure you. He's student teaching right next door to me."

"You're kidding?"

"Odd, isn't it?" Sam leaned back on the couch. "I could have killed him when I first saw him there in the hall, then I had to think: if Billy Marcum is student teaching, something big must have happened. He told me about your parents, and I couldn't help but feel sorry for him."

"Well, don't feel *too* sorry for him." Cindy looked at her and still shook her head in disbelief. "I can't believe you're here. How are you doing?"

"I'm still in the house. I teach high school math. I read a lot, and have found that I like fixing up my little home. That's pretty much my life, but I like it. It's what I've always wanted."

Cindy nodded. "What about your parents."

Sam shifted her gaze to the window as she replied, "I still don't talk to them. What would I say, especially after all this time?"

"I don't know, Sam. It's just so hard for me to imagine. My parents were my only grounding for so many years. When Daddy died, I thought I would too. I couldn't imagine how I could go on without him."

"He was a wonderful man. I didn't tell Billy this, but on that first day after he told me … when I got home, I just wept over both of their deaths. They were more like parents to me than my own."

"They felt that way about you too." Cindy paused then added, "They agonized over the divorce."

Sam only nodded. "But what about you?" She smiled changing the subject. "A church secretary? How on earth did that happen? When I last saw you, you were as far from anything religious imaginable. In fact, I still can't picture you doing this whole *homebody* thing."

"It was a miserable trip from where I was to where I am now. I was actually involved with a married man when Daddy died. Angie Wright talked some sense into me." Cindy felt horrible for mentioning Angie's name, but it was the truth. "Sam, I wish you could know Angie. She's not the person you think she is."

"It really doesn't matter, does it? She'll always be the woman Billy wanted, and I'll always be the woman who wasn't her."

"But that's just it; Billy didn't want Angie … not the real Angie. For crying out loud, she's a missionary with two kids and one on the way!"

"What? Angie? The seductress? The most sensual woman on the planet?"

Cindy shook her head. "She's not like that at all. She and Billy had this thing in high school. I think she was the only female he could never conquer and it ate at him. You know that old saying, the things you can't have you want the most?"

"But I thought …" Sam paused to remember. "I thought she was his first."

"His first love, maybe, but that was it. She was so fed up with him by the end of high school that she barely even spoke to him."

"And now she's a missionary? But wasn't she kind of … loose?"

"Listen, don't judge Angie by how Billy and I turned out. She was pretty much the voice of reason in the midst of our heady rebelliousness. And contrary to what Billy might have led you to believe, when she married, she was a virgin."

Sam was utterly confused. For all these years she had believed Angie Wright was this super sexual being that had so intoxicated Billy that no one would ever compare to her in his life. Now she was discovering that it was all in his mind?

"She's fun," Cindy went on. "She loves life, and she loves the Lord. She's a missionary doctor."

"A doctor!" Sam now exclaimed. "You cannot imagine how completely foolish this all sounds. She's a doctor?"

"A medical missionary on a Pacific island, only she's on her way back here right now. Her third baby is due in December. Anyway—after Angie set me straight about my life, Mother developed cancer the first time. It was Angie who convinced me to leave everything I had in Florence and move back here with Mother. Angie's dad, the pastor, managed to get me a temporary job as secretary so that my hours would be flexible during mother's treatments. Kyle came on as the music minister, and without going into a lot of gory details, here we are." Cindy put out her hands and smiled. "Happily ever after, so far …"

The children came to life for a short while when they realized Uncle Billy was visiting, and then when they met Sam, the twins took to her immediately. Kylla had a tendency to be standoffish until she was sure she was wanted. Sam took notice of this and began to make a special effort to reach out to her. But something Sam hadn't expected also happened—Billy adored the children. A gnawing sense of loss began to eat away as she watched him play and tease with all three of them throughout the evening. Devin delighted in the way Billy kept sneaking strings of spaghetti from his little plate, and Sam wondered if this had always been a part of his personality. Had they remained married, would they have had children by now? Would Billy be working and she at home? Would they have run into his arms each evening when he returned from the job? She still felt raw from her discovery that Angie Wright was really a sweet and gentle soul rather than the image of seduction she had been led to believe.

When everyone had said their goodnights and settled into bed, Samantha lay awake a long time trying to re-sort the images of her past. The one that kept cropping up was the night she had revealed her life to Billy. They had been to a bar, dancing, laughing and drinking—she still wondered how they managed to make it to his apartment safely. He opened another bottle of wine, and they sat around his living room talking. She had had way too much alcohol, and this time when He asked her about her family, she opened up readily—crying, talking, and confessing.

"My dad was a high school football star … small town and small time. He had no ambition for a future, got mother pregnant during his senior year, and then married her after graduation. He was a drunk—an A-number-one drunk. He'd come in totally doused and then proceed to blame her for his miserable life. He did things to her that a little girl should never see her parents doing."

Billy had flinched when she told him this. To him, at that point in time, she was still this cute, smart girl, outside of his normal realm of influence that he was taken with. The truth probably was that all he wanted was a different kind of conquest, but this conversation was about to change all that.

"I figured right then," Sam continued, "that I wouldn't ever get married. When school started, life was good. I got away from it all for seven hours a day. I dealt with the nights because I could shut out the noise and the screaming and the yelling and just sleep. Then third grade came."

She had shifted in her seat and realized she was telling more than she had wanted. She remembered shaking slightly at the thought of actually reliving all of it. "Mother had some kind of mental breakdown. She just went nuts. Suddenly she couldn't tell the difference between our life and the television. Anyone she didn't know personally was part of some horrible conspiracy designed to destroy our family. She would force me to stay home from school if a murder mystery had been on TV because she was convinced they were actually after us.

"Then Daddy went ballistic with her because she couldn't realize how he abused her. He could do whatever he wanted and she was thrilled to death. He wasn't the enemy in her mind; everyone else was. HRS started visiting because of my missed school, and they warned Daddy that if I didn't start making it to school, they'd take me away. Well, Mama went off the deep end then; she just knew HRS was part of the conspiracy. When they threatened to have him arrested, he finally caved in and made sure I made it to the bus every morning, which meant holding back my screaming mother every single day. As you can imagine, that pretty much kicked his drinking up another notch."

Billy stared at her in complete bewilderment. "Your mom screamed for you not to go to school?"

"It was horrible and embarrassing. The kids then started making fun of me because of my crazy mother. But this great thing happened … at least for Daddy. Because of mother's now obvious handicap, he started getting government money. And because mother had a kid, he got a little more money."

Billy nodded as the lights came on. "He quit work, didn't he?"

"Oh yeah," Sam confirmed. "And he pretty much hated me. I don't know why. I never even spoke to him. I stayed out of the way, watched a lot of television and read a lot of books. Sometimes Mother would insist that I sleep with her so she could protect me, but other than that, I was a nonentity in that house. Then I turned twelve."

At this point, Sam had stood up and staggered to a window. It seemed hot and suffocating in the room. She was shaking worse now as she came to the bad part of the story.

"The bad part?" Billy had responded in shock. "It gets worse?"

She tried not to cry, but the more she thought about her past, the more terrified she became. She couldn't believe she was telling Billy—wonderfully charming and amazingly handsome Billy—this part of her life. He would walk out on her for sure when she finished telling about the way her father had sold her to her two uncles as a way to make extra cash. She wasn't worthy of someone like Billy Marcum. He would realize now that she wasn't this wonderfully educated young lady with a bright future. Instead, he would see her for what she really was: white trash. A used and abused girl who had had two abortions before she reached her sixteenth birthday, and both pregnancies were from her uncles.

“Oh, Sam,” Billy had said in total compassion as he came up behind her and put his arms around her tightly. She kept waiting for him to leave or to tell her to go or to do something, but he only held her. When she managed to pull herself together, she tried to leave, but Billy insisted she stay. She thought he was just being polite because she was so tipsy, but instead, this became the first of many nights they shared. Two months later, Billy had proposed, and Sam believed that all her dreams were about to come true.

Thirteen

"These look really impressive," Floyd told Jonathan as the committee looked over the four résumés that had been copied for each member. "You know how to do your job well, pastor."

Jonathan smiled and nodded, but the compliment didn't erase the sinking feeling.

"This Florida gentleman looks appealing," said Tonya Rogers. "And he has some staying power. Ten years is a long time to be at a church."

Jonathan raised his eyebrows.

"Well," she said quickly, "that doesn't compare to your thirty, Pastor Jon, but it's a good start."

He rubbed his temple. He had read over these résumés more times than he should have. He knew every detail, every church, and every degree each man held, but the committee was seeing them for the first time. He waited for the last one, and sure enough, the anticipated response came.

"Navy Seal!" exclaimed Tom Richards. "You don't see that on a ministerial résumé too often."

"What's his name?" Stan Preston asked as he quickly found the paper. "Harold Bridges. Where's he from?"

"Arizona," Nancy Beth Tate read. "You never see that in Alabama. Why's he trying to come here?"

"Maybe he's got family here like the guy from Florida," Tonya surmised.

"Well, lookey here," Floyd pointed out. "The guy has a doctorate from the seminary in California. Do you think he'd even consider us?"

"Really?" Stan asked excitedly. "I wonder why he didn't put that up front in his name: Dr. Harold Bridges?"

"Probably just a humble guy," Nancy Beth assumed. "He knew we'd read it sooner or later." They all paused as they read down the résumé. "I don't know about ya'll, but I have a good feeling about this one."

"Me too," Stan agreed. "Navy Seal, the guy knows authority, doctorate, the guy's educated—I'm thinking we should maybe pursue this one first."

Tom Richards was the only one that suggested caution. "I don't know, y'all. We need to be careful about what we're doing here. The life of this church lies in our hands."

"We're not calling him, Tom," Nancy Beth scolded. "We just think we should start here."

"He may not even be interested in us," Floyd frowned. "Probably won't be, but we can start with him."

Tom looked through the papers and took in all the information. "But why from Arizona? And if he went to seminary in California, his family must be out west somewhere. Why does he want to come here?"

"Because he's heard of all that Southern hospitality," Nancy Beth grinned endearingly. "He wants to experience it for himself."

"No kids too," Floyd brought up.

Stan chuckled and added, "That sure beats eight kids."

An alarm suddenly went off in Jonathan's head. "What's wrong with a man having kids."

"Not kids, pastor—eight of 'em," Stan clarified.

"And eight is too many?" Jonathan asked him.

"It is in *my* opinion," Stan stated.

Jonathan sighed as he placed his papers on the table. *And we're off.*

☼☼☼

"Hello?" answered Hal Bridges on Sunday evening.

"Mr. Bridges, I mean *Dr.* Bridges?"

"Yes it is. May I ask who's calling?" Hal sat gingerly on the couch and crossed his fingers.

"My name is Floyd Benson, and I'm calling on behalf of First Baptist Church in Dockrey, Alabama."

"Alabama?" Hal grinned as he smiled. Alabama would be perfect. That should be far enough from Arizona.

☼☼☼

"Will Mimi and Gaga be waiting for us when we get off the plane?" Cassie wondered as she wiggled uncomfortably beneath the tight strap of the seat belt.

"At least." Angie smiled at the thought of seeing her parents again.

"What does that mean?"

"Many probably wanted to come and pick us up from the airport, but I can guarantee Mimi and Gaga will be there."

"Who else would come?"

"I don't know. You've got aunts and uncles and cousins all living there, so we won't find out until we arrive."

When the jet finally landed and the passengers were cleared to leave, Michael unbuckled Carter and handed him to Angie. He was thrilled to be released from the seat, and began hugging and kissing his mother as though she were the reason for his freedom. Michael then helped Cassie to the floor and gave her the bag she had carried on with her choice toys and books. He reached over for Carter so Angie could carry her massive purse. Once they were in the aisle, they slowly moved out the door of the jet and through the airport until they reached the waiting area.

"Angie!" Barbara screamed out. "Over here! We're over here!"

Angie followed the scream and saw her mother waving frantically. She immediately left her little family and took off, trusting that Michael would keep the kids in tow. When she reached Barbara, she embraced her with all her might and held tightly as they both cried.

"This is the crying-est bunch of women I've ever known," Jonathan said smugly as he stared down at Angie.

"Oh, Daddy," Angie grinned through her tears. "Your just jealous 'cause I got to Moms first." She held on to her mother a little longer, then broke the hug and went for her father.

Michael appeared holding Cassie's hand and carrying Carter in his other arm. When Barbara spotted the children, the crying started all over again. She reached for Carter, who had no idea who this woman was, and nuzzled him on her shoulder. Then she bent down to see Cassie.

"Hello, Mimi," Cassie said seriously. "I remember you pretty good. Did you know that I am Cassie?"

Barbara couldn't speak; she simply reached out and pulled Cassie to her. At this moment, Barbara tried to figure out which was worse: missing her daughter of thirty-five years, or missing the wonder of watching these grandchildren grow.

✪✪✪

Billy joined Sam at the table in the teacher's lounge during lunch. This was the first time they had actually sat together in this particular room. They had tried hard to keep their distance to a certain degree hoping no one would put their last names together. But after the wonderful weekend at Cindy's, they felt a camaraderie and kinship that pulled them together. Billy was concerned that since Mr. C. knew they had been married, it might be quickly spread about the campus, but Sam assured him Mr. C. wasn't that kind of man.

"Her children are adorable," Sam commented as she bit into a fried bologna sandwich. "I can't believe how much they look like them. Blond hair, blue eyes …"

"You do know that Kylla isn't Cindy's?" He assumed she had been told.

"No! You're kidding? Kyle had another child before meeting Cindy?"

"He had been married for ten years to, get this, Martin Sartin's daughter, you know, that actor guy."

Her face grew another degree of astonishment. "Are you for real?"

"His wife had left him while she was pregnant, convincing Kyle the baby wasn't his," Billy tried to explain the sordid story. "Then she was murdered."

"I remember reading about that!"

"He was delivered this child complete with his name on the birth certificate. When Kyle and Cindy married, she adopted Kylla immediately."

"I don't believe it. She got an instant family."

"I thought she was nuts. I couldn't imagine my sister getting married, much less willingly raising someone else's kid. But it didn't take long for me to realize that she and Kyle … and Kylla too … had something really special together—something I'd never find."

"What makes you think that? You're not impossible."

He leaned in to whisper so none of the other teachers would hear. "If I couldn't make it with you, ponytail, I couldn't make it with anyone."

She blushed. That probably was true. She was willing to put up with almost anything … anything except Angie Wright. His obsession with that woman had been Sam's only weakness. She could handle his going out with the guys, coming home drunk, even squandering money, but she couldn't compete with his visions of Angie. How odd to find out that she was closer to pristine than sultry.

"Well, people like you and me probably weren't meant for the whole marriage thing," Sam finally stated.

"You're the perfect marriage candidate," Billy exclaimed a little too loudly.

A teacher from across the table overheard him and commented, "If you two got married, Sam wouldn't even have to change her name."

Another teacher jumped in. "Great idea! Two single people, good-looking—you two ought to think of the benefits. You'd have two salaries, tax breaks …"

"Wo," Billy said as he held up his hands. "I am not the marrying type."

The first teacher noted, "Apparently Sam isn't either—perfect match!"

☼☼☼

Hal Bridges looked over the information he had jotted down from his phone conversation with Floyd Benson the previous evening. He smoothed his cropped hair and reached down to remove a piece of lint from his starched khakis. Lisa was heating up leftovers for lunch and anxious to hear the news before heading to bed. She hated night shifts at the hospital, but it paid time and a half, and it was less likely for her to run into someone from the church. This church had been particularly bitter and hateful, and she wondered how such a group could call themselves Christians. She brought in the plates of roast beef and yawned deeply as she sat across from Hal.

"First," he began, "it's in Alabama."

Lisa's eyes grew wide. "You put out résumés in Alabama?"

"I sent a résumé' to every state with a Baptist Convention. Maybe the southeast will be a little more welcoming."

"I hope so. You go through churches like people go through toothpicks."

He slapped the table in agitation. "It's not me! They hire me to do a job, and then they tie my hands when I try to do it. Am I supposed to just sit there and be the puppet of every pastor I work under?"

"Apparently nobody else sees it like that. Churches tend to think that the pastor is in charge."

"That's ridiculous. I am a church administrator. For the most part, that makes me the CEO. It's pitiful how pastors become so easily intimidated when you approach them with things *they* need to change. Oh, sure, let them criticize the church right and left, but don't ever suggest to them that they might possibly be part of the problem."

"I don't know that everyone agrees with your philosophy. In fact, I don't think anyone does."

"Listen, I will not be treated like a second class staff member at a church. I know what I'm doing, and I demand others respect that."

"If you say so," she sighed. "What's the salary?"

"A lot better than what the last church paid me."

"Really?" Lisa perked up at this. Her brown eyes were tired and sagging, and her short, bleached hair was slightly wild from heavy hairspray being doused in the rain. "How sure do you think this is?"

He leaned back in the chair and looked over the printed notes he had taken. "Ninety-nine point nine percent sure."

"That sure?"

"It doesn't take me long to size up a church and its needs. First, you listen to the committee, then the pastor, then you just look. Before I leave from there on our trial Sunday, they'll wonder how they ever lived without me."

"That's fine, Hal, but could you please ease up some on everyone? I'm really tired of moving around."

"You make it sound like it's my fault," he said with irritation. "I don't like moving any more than you do! But I won't sit around and twiddle my thumbs while these churches try to get their acts together."

"Okay, okay, simmer down. What else?"

"They're running around seven hundred now. The pastor and the music guy have been trying to handle it all on their own. It's bursting at the seams; they're starting a building program this next month."

"Sounds exciting … and promising."

"Indeed."

Fourteen

Angie breathed a warm sigh as she stared around the apartment located over her parents' garage. This was her home—the place where she had grown up. That sense of belonging gave her deep comfort. It was true that she loved Padawin and its people, and that she had carved out a wonderful life there for her and her family. Padawin was home now, but being back in Dockrey, in her old house, made her realize all she was missing in this compartment of her life. Her children would know very little of their cousins and their grandparents. They would grow up in a tribal atmosphere far away from American culture. That would be both bad and good. She smiled at the thought. *No one races crabs across their living room floor on a rainy day in the US.*

Michael walked in carrying another load of luggage, carefully balancing their two guitars amidst it all.

"Where's Carter?" Angie asked with only slight concern. Michael was ten times more cautious than she when it came to their kids.

"His Mimi's got him. We need to see about a doctor for him as soon as possible."

She winced. Sometimes she could almost forget about Carter's problem, and being home had allowed that for a few, precious moments. "I know. Let me get online and see if I recognize any names from school; I'll start there." She turned back to face him. "However, I need to get myself to a doctor too. I'd love to see how things are going down here," she grinned as she rubbed her tummy.

"We're not gonna find out what it is," he said firmly. "I like surprises."

"For Pete's sake! *I* want to know! Everybody else finds out the sex of their child; it's common practice now."

He smiled mischievously as he put his arms around her. "And when have you ever done anything common?"

She stared at him and eventually nodded. "Okay … you win again. But," and she placed her forehead to his, "if we have another one, the deal is this: we are going to find out. That's my only concession for this."

"Are you planning on a fourth?" he laughed. "Are we in competition with Andie and Doug?"

"I want a houseful!"

"We have a houseful!"

"Ahh," she exhaled loudly, "but I have a wonderfully creative builder husband who can just keep adding on to the house."

"If we keep at it like this we're gonna have to start building up rather than out."

"That would be interesting—a skyscraper at Podakind!"

Cassie came walking in with her own bags. "Am I staying in here?" she wondered at the large room.

"Not unless you want to," Angie told her. "You're welcome to stay in my old bedroom. It's just down the hall."

Cassie's eyes lit up. "Really? Are your old toys in there?"

"Some of them. Wanna go see?"

"Yeah," she responded in awe. "Right now."

Angie led Cassie to the room and was pleasantly surprised to see that someone had finally organized it. After medical school and then seminary, Angie had just thrown boxes in and stacked piles of books wherever there was an empty space. She wondered if her mother had gotten tired of closing the door when company came.

"This is so pretty," Cassie breathed as she walked into the room. "I love purple, Mama."

So had Angie. Purple curtains still hung on the gabled window, and the walls were a light lavender. The bedspread was covered with large purple flowers looking like something pulled out of the sixties. And sitting on top of the pillow sham was a purple bunny with a beautiful jeweled necklace. Angie had never seen the rabbit before. She noticed a card in the bunny's arms.

"Look at this," Angie said as she sat on the edge of the bed. She picked up the envelope and held it out for Cassie to see. "Do you know what that says?"

Cassie recognized her name immediately. "Mama," she whispered. "Is it from the tooth fairy?"

Angie tilted her head to the side in confusion. "I doubt that. What makes you think it's from the tooth fairy?"

"Because the tooth fairy lives in a purple room and has little purple wings. Maybe this is her house."

To be so practical, Cassie also had a great imagination.

"No, the tooth fairy doesn't live here. Why don't you read the card and see who it's from?"

Cassie carefully pulled open the top and then lifted it out. It was covered with balloons and confetti, with confetti falling out of the card. Cassie squealed in delight. Pretty things like this were rare in Padawin.

"Mama," she was still whispering, "who is it from?"

Cassie handed the card back to Angie who read:

> *Dear Cassie, I am so proud to have my beautiful little granddaughter living with me for a short while. I hope you enjoy staying in your mother's room, but I know that strange places can sometimes be scary. So, I found you a special friend to help keep you*

company in your new room. His name is Snuffy, he is very soft, and he needs to be cuddled a lot.

Angie smiled gently as her eyes began to water; she had had a stuffed rabbit named Snuffy while growing up too.

If you need anything at all, remember that your Mimi is here to get it for you. Have a good stay. Love Mimi.

"Oh, Mama, he is so pretty, and he is mine," Cassie now said with a little more excitement. "Can I hold him?"

"Mimi said he needed to be cuddled," Angie reminded her as she reached for the bunny and handed it to Cassie.

Cassie took it and carefully pulled it into a hug. "He is so, so soft. How did he get so soft?"

"Some bunnies are just born that way." Angie reached over and ran her hand across the purple fur; indeed it was soft. Cassie would have no trouble adjusting to a new room, or a new house.

The spoiling had already begun.

☼☼☼

"Does your ankle really hurt that bad still?" Lainey asked Andie as she sat beside the couch on the floor.

"Not as bad, but still quite a bit. That's why I keep taking this medicine that makes me so sleepy."

Lainey sat thoughtfully for a moment. "I miss the food you cook. Adam and Arly don't even make good peanut butter and jelly sandwiches. It's all gunky when they finish."

"Gunky?" She smiled at the appreciation. It was nice to know even the smallest of things meant something to her children. The older three dared not complain about anything; they still bore guilt from feeling responsible. But Aimee and Lainey made it perfectly clear they didn't care for the new arrangement.

"And Daddy can't cook at all," Lainey went on. "He can't even make my noodles right, Mommy. He put too much salt in them last night."

"Salt? He put salt in them?"

Lainey nodded as she made a face. "They were horrible, but Ashley said I should just go ahead and eat them and not complain. I ate what I could, but had to drink a lot of Kool-aid. I think tonight I might just eat cereal. Do you think he'll put salt in my cereal?"

"Guess what?" Andie asked her excitedly.

"What?"

"We don't have to eat here tonight!"

Lainey grinned big. "Where are we eating?"

"At Mimi and Gaga's."

"Yea!" Lainey jumped up and clapped her hands.

"But there's more," Andie told her. Lainey looked as though she were about to burst. The eating must be really bad. "Cassie and Aunt Angie will be there."

"Cassie! Yea for Cassie!"

"And Ellie too."

The excitement now tripled. Andie had to confess she was excited also at seeing Angie and her family again despite the drowsy effects of the medicine. It had been two years since the last visit, or more aptly, the last child. If Angie and Michael kept it up, they would be home every two years just to have babies. She grinned. If they could surpass her on the number of children, it would take a lot of pressure off. For some reason, when she told folks she had five kids, stares of utter amazement always followed.

Adam walked in with jelly on his left arm and down his pants. "Lainey, your sandwich is ready."

"What's with all the jelly?" Andie asked him.

"I dropped the knife, then when I bent down to pick it up, I accidentally knocked off the whole jar." He looked mortified. "Sorry. I cleaned it all good—well, except for me. I'm gonna change right now."

She smiled compassionately. No matter what she said, she couldn't lift the guilt from her children. In truth, she was the one responsible for the accident. Had she been a good mother, a responsible mother, a thinking mother, she would have reprimanded them all, made them put up the cushions, and then given them more work as punishment for such reckless behavior. But instead, well, she was immobile. She was going to have to do something about the food situation, however. Her kids couldn't live off of peanut butter and jelly for lunch and salted ramen noodles for supper. Between Annie, her mother, and now Angie, maybe something could be worked out until she could get back on her feet … in six weeks.

✲✲✲

Jonathan, Kyle and Cindy sat in the front office of the church laughing hysterically at the antics of the twins out on the playground. Whatever the argument was about, no one knew, but the level of hysteria and know-it-all-ness that was ensuing was purely comical. Cindy knew in a little while one would gain the upper hand and the other would come storming in to tell, so it was only a matter of time before the adults knew the scoop.

"I hear the committee has already contacted a guy about the staff position," Kyle noted. "The Navy Seal."

Jonathan nodded and sighed. "Yeah, they jumped on him right away … very impressed."

"Do you think we'll have to salute when he walks in a room?" Cindy joked.

Jonathan raised his eyebrows but wouldn't smile. "I hope not. I'm getting too old to throw my hands up during random times of the day."

"You're not old," Kyle punched his arm lightly. "You're merely a seasoned veteran in the faith. By the way, when is your sixtieth birthday?"

"November," he replied bleakly. "I hope the buzzards don't start circling before then."

"You know something?" Cindy asked thoughtfully. "Sixty isn't near as old now as I used to think it was. Shoot, neither is forty! I remember Angie and me talking about how we dreaded turning thirty. Our Sunday School teacher was thirty, and we thought she was ancient."

Jonathan scowled at her. "Thank you for expressing the views of the youth of our church. I feel so much more comforted now."

"That was junior high," Cindy said to clarify it was not her judgment now. "We thought everybody was old back then."

"You two were quite the pair. I hope you can behave while she's home on furlough," Jonathan said firmly.

"Don't count on it! It's all I can do not to run over there right now and visit. It's driving me crazy! Angie is home and I'm sitting here typing out the budget for Wednesday night's business meeting! Life is so unfair!"

"Trust me, Angie is collapsed somewhere from jet lag. Cassie, on the other hand, is probably running the house by now."

"Angie wrote that she was very stong-headed and extremely inquisitive."

"Very … on both accounts," Jonathan finally smiled. "And totally adorable. You won't believe them when you see them. They're so tanned and everyone has bleached out hair."

"How about the little boy?" Kyle wondered. "Can he walk yet?"

Jonathan shook his head. "They're gonna try to find a doctor as soon as possible and have some tests run."

"Shouldn't something have been noticed at birth?" Kyle asked again. "I mean, they do all sorts of odd things to them when they're babies to make sure everything is developing right. You'd think they would have picked something up."

"That's what concerns Angie. She feels like if it was something he was born with, the doctors would have known immediately—she would have known immediately. She thinks something's happened since birth—since he was about eight months or so. He was pulling up then, but sometime after that, he just stopped … and then he never even tried to walk."

Devin was running toward the door now. Apparently Denay had won the argument.

☼☼☼

Annie sat on the pool deck with Ellie as they swayed back and forth in the swing. She was reading to her out of a new Bible storybook. As was typical, the little blonde was down to her underwear. It was nearly impossible to keep clothes on the child. Annie was thankful her father was the pastor, because had any other pastor visited and experienced the antics of Ellie, rumors would have no doubt been started. Twice Ellie had greeted her grandfather at the door completely naked, and then once, as Jonathan and Barbara were eating dinner with them, Ellie had managed to sneak out the back, strip down to nothing, put on her swimmies and jump into the pool. When everyone went out to cut a watermelon, there was Ellie in all her glory.

"Mama?" Ellie asked as she looked at the pictures of Adam and Eve. "Why did they mess up like that?"

"You mean why did they sin?"

"Yeah. Things were very good. Why didn't they just obey God?"

"Why don't you always obey Daddy and me?"

Ellie thought on this one. "I'm just a kid."

"But they were like kids too. Even though they looked older because that's how God had created them, they probably weren't even as old as you." Annie actually wondered about that. It was a good point, but it wasn't fact. For all she knew, they could have been in the Garden thirty years before eating from the tree. "Just like you, they wondered if their heavenly Father's rules were really the best."

Ellie nodded as she took in the idea. "But you know what? They blew it for all of us. If they could have just left that tree alone, we would all be naked … but happy."

The thought took Annie by surprise. Here she thought she was conveying the concept of sin to her precious little girl, but Ellie's only fascination was the fact that the couple was allowed to walk around with no clothes.

"That's right, Ellie," she could only agree. "Naked, but happy."

Fifteen

"How'd things go today?" Sam asked Billy as she peeked inside his room after the last bell. "Better than your first week?"

"Mr. C. was here today. Things went a lot smoother. And you know what—the man is not an ogre. I'm beginning to think there are holes in your theory."

"Mr. C.'s been here for forty years; he doesn't have to be an ogre. He's taught some of these kids' grandparents. His legacy precedes him."

"They definitely respect him."

As they left the building and headed toward the parking lot, she asked him, "So tell me, all that stuff the preacher talked about on Sunday, do you believe it?"

He shrugged. "I guess so. I was brought up with that. My parents believed it, and Cindy believes it. I guess somewhere down there I believe it too."

"No," she said as she shook her head. "You might think it's the truth, but you don't believe it."

He looked puzzled. "You're gonna have to explain that one to me, ponytail. I think it's truth, yet I don't believe it?"

"Yeah, think about it. You've heard it all your life so you just assume it's the truth. But you don't live your life like it's truth. I mean, what about the whole sin thing? Do you really believe that sin sends people to hell? Do you believe God does that?"

He felt like he was in the hospital again being drilled by Mr. C. He hated discussing religion as much as he hated discussing politics. Nobody was ever totally right in his opinion.

"I suppose I believe that. Some people deserve to go to hell, you know?"

"Yeah," she nodded bitterly. "Like my father … and my two uncles."

"Most definitely." His face began to burn red with anger.

"But what about us?" she wondered. "We haven't done anything like that, but we're sure guilty of a whole bundle of other sins … if there are such things. Do we go to hell just for them?"

He hated to even think on that. If hell was real, he was bound to go. He had not only messed up his own life royally, he had done a good job of doing it to others also … starting with Sam. He believed God had given him the opportunity to sort of atone for all his stupid mistakes when he had married her. He had the chance to take someone whose life had been horrible and help to heal it, but he had been as selfish as ever and eventually walked out on her too.

"Look," he stopped walking and turned her toward him. "I'm not the person to discuss religion with. But I'll say this—if anyone ever deserved hell, it would be me. I don't even pretend to think God would want me in heaven, in a place where people like my parents go for doing the right things in life. I've made my choices, and unfortunately, all my choices led me away from God. You need to talk to somebody else."

He turned quickly and started for his motorcycle, but Sam ran after him, grabbing his arm.

"You're not that bad Billy," she said tenderly. "We've all made mistakes."

"But you're not talking about mistakes, you're talking about sin … deliberately turning your life away from God. That's me."

"But what about Cindy? She was right up there with you, and you know that. But look at her now. She's like this … I don't know … saint or something. She's even married to a minister … working in a church! If God could do that to her, couldn't he do that to you?"

He unlocked the luggage on his bike, pulled out the helmet, and then placed his pack of papers inside. "Like I said, I'm not the person to ask. Talk to Cindy, shoot, talk to Pastor Jon, or even Kyle. Come back with me this weekend if you want, but don't ask me about God; I'm a lost cause."

As Sam watched him drive away, she felt like slapping herself. Seeing him so despondent about life still ate at her. Last month, had someone told her Billy had lost his spark, she would have laughed and said he deserved it, but to actually see him like this was hard to handle. He had needed to be notched down a degree or two, but it almost seemed as though he had hit bottom. What was he living for? What hope was there in his life? He had said with total conviction that marriage was out of the picture, and he even appeared ready to give up teaching after a rough first few days. What had ripped all that confidence away? But what ate at her even more was why in heaven's name did she care.

✪✪✪

Mayhem was the only word to describe the Wright house that evening. With all three sisters and their families present, the entire place was filled with chaos. Nine grandchildren managed to move in and out of every room as they played games and chased each other. Even Carter was in on the excitement. Twice Angie had found him attempting to crawl up the stairs only to hear him scream at his failure. She pulled him up to her and tried not to think about his condition or all the possibilities of what might be wrong. It seemed so unfair. Cindy had dropped by briefly after work to say hello, and it nearly broke Angie's heart to watch Devin and

Denay join Carter on the floor because he was unable to run with them. They were barely a month apart in age. To see these two-year olds active and playful only magnified what might be wrong with her little boy. She whispered a prayer of health for the child growing inside her now. She wondered if she could bear another one with a physical issue.

After cleaning up the supper dishes, the adults found themselves on the screened-in back porch with several different discussions going on at once. Angie took another depth of comfort in her family. Having to go through the testing she knew Carter would need, all during the impending arrival of a third child, knowing that her parents and her sisters would be there with her through it all gave a sense of relief. Michael would be her compassion, her support, but her other family would be her laughter and her reminder that God works all things for the good.

"So what are we hoping for?" Annie asked Angie about the baby to be. "Do we want a boy or a girl?"

Angie chuckled and replied, "I honestly don't care; I'm just ready for it to get here."

"Surely, you're kidding," Andie exclaimed. "Right now life is easy. Nursing, middle of the night feedings, crazy hours … what were you thinking having a third child?" She winked.

"Well, I could always crack my ankle in half and then lie around and let everyone else do the work," Angie snapped back. She then said in a mocking tone, "Just bring me the baby, and I'll do my part."

"Very funny," Andie scowled. "Like I'm enjoying this? Is that what you think?"

"With five kids and suddenly you have a debilitating break?" Annie exclaimed. "Yeah! I'm thinking you're loving it!"

"You know what, though?" Andie said as she leaned into her sisters to speak discreetly. "You'd think the break would be nice, but it's not worth all the griping. Nobody can cook, nobody can get the laundry right, and the house is a wreck."

Angie laughed. "And the house being a wreck is a problem? You should see mine!"

Annie, the perfectionist, and Angie's worse critic concerning neatness, commented, "With five kids you can't let things get out of hand, Ang. Remember that as you keep spitting them out. Another kid, another mess."

"Do you know how I view mess?" Angie asked her. "A mess is merely evidence of something wonderful having been done. I invite the mess, and invite the messers!"

"You're hopeless." Annie rolled her eyes. "But seriously," she turned back to Andie, "why don't you let me come over and help with the laundry and lunch? Then, if it's convenient, you can all come over to my house for supper. It didn't occur to me that Doug was as helpless in the kitchen as Stephen. After all these years you'd think he could cook something."

Andie leaned in again. "He added salt to the ramen noodles."

Annie shook her head. "That's pretty bad. I don't even think Stephen would have done that."

"Let me help too," Angie offered. "I've got no responsibilities at the moment. I'd be glad to do some cooking and such, but I'm not cleaning any windows."

"Doug can clean windows," Andie admitted. "But it takes a whole lot of nagging to get him there."

✪✪✪

Billy lay back in his bed as the boat rocked gently on the water. He couldn't get Sam off his mind. When she had mentioned her father and her uncles today, it had stabbed his heart hideously. She deserved so much more in this life than she had been dealt, and he had once had the chance to offer it to her. But instead, he gave into his stupid selfishness, and not only had he lost Sam, but he had removed any hope she ever had of truly changing the course of her life.

The first two years of their marriage had been wonderful. They spent all their time together. They fished, they camped, and they saw every movie that came out. They played cards, backgammon, Othello, and even Scrabble. It didn't matter—as long as they were together, life was fun. Then his old buddies began to make subtle comments about how Billy Marcum had been tamed by the ball and chain. He didn't feel that way, but the talk was biting.

"Yeah, you can't do a thing anymore without the wife's permission."

"Poor Billy, he's not allowed to have any fun."

"When you went out of circulation, we only assumed it would be with the girls. We didn't realize the wife wouldn't let you do anything."

The truth was, he enjoyed life with Sam. He had no desire to get drunk and hang out playing pool with the guys anymore. He had Sam, and she was wonderful. They cooked together, played together, did everything together, and it was fulfilling in every way. But the more the guys hounded him, the more they made it sound like Sam had a noose around his neck and he was inches from being hanged. The thing that dug him the most was that when he started hanging out with them again, coming home late at times, Sam never complained. She smiled and said he was free to do whatever he wanted. She spent the time studying and expressed no grief over his changed behavior. A part of him had wanted her to gripe, to say she missed him and that he needed to shape up. That was when he began to push.

He would sometimes stay out all night. And then when he was with her, he began to pick at her, to do things to deliberately hurt her or cause her to react. But still, she endured. To her, each day was a chance for a new start, and she faced it as though things would be fine in the morning.

The clincher came one evening as they had finished supper and she had cleaned the kitchen by herself as he sat out on the patio with a beer. In times past, he would have helped her, but he was set on forcing her to give him his freedom, a freedom six months before he would have never dreamed of wanting. When she had finished, she went to the couch to study. He knew she had tests and papers coming up, but he wasn't going to pitch in to do anything. He made her carry the load herself. After all, she had married *him*. She was the one benefiting from this arrangement. She was the one with the shaky past that needed to find herself and needed someone to lean on. He had been just fine before her, and he would be just as fine when she was gone.

After two beers, he walked inside the house and began to gripe about something. She acknowledged his presence but went back to her studying. And that was when he let it slip.

"Angie Wright knew how to keep a man happy. She knew everything I ever wanted."

Sam didn't even look up. She stopped writing, pulled off her glasses, and merely stared at her paper. He had dealt the final and fatal blow. She could deal with the drinking, she could deal with his being out all weekend, she could even deal with his moping around the house, but she couldn't handle being compared to his ideal … and he knew that well.

All she had said was, "Pack and leave, and never come back, please."

He didn't have to be told twice. He couldn't have handled the guilt of walking out on her from his own volition—she was too vulnerable, too used, and too hurt from her past. He really did care for her, but he had been convinced that marriage was a prison, and he needed to be released. He had carefully manipulated the relationship to the point that eventually he knew Sam would initiate the divorce. As he walked out, he turned to tell her goodbye, but he didn't have the heart. He almost had second thoughts. Seeing her there in what had been their home where they had shared so much joy and she had found healing for a season, he felt like a heel. But then, isn't that what Billy Marcum had always been? Who was she to think she could change him? No one could.

But the deaths of his parents had done the trick. As he tried to force the thoughts from his mind so he could drift off to sleep, he kept seeing Sam's expression when he had told her about their deaths. It had been a fresh loss for her. They had loved her like a daughter and become the endearing parents she had never known. The divorce had not only cost her a marriage, but also a family. And right now, if he could find any more tears, he would weep—not for himself, but for Sam. She had found a small taste of fulfillment in teaching, but she had shut herself off from any other relationships, and he knew the dubious honor went fully to him. He could have healed the hurts of her past, but instead, he merely put the final nail in the coffin.

I am nothing more than a selfish imbecile.

Sixteen

"This is really kind of cool," Sam said on Saturday morning as she stood in the middle of the houseboat. "It's like the whole house is a waterbed."

He smiled as he threw the last of his things in his bag. Not a single person had made a positive comment about his living on a boat since he had bought it. "Wanna trade for awhile?" he asked jokingly.

She turned toward him. "I know you're only teasing, but the truth is, I'd love to. It's almost like camping, isn't it?"

"Almost." He picked up his bag and looked around to see if he had missed anything obvious. All seemed to be in order. "Ready, Rudolph?"

"Ready, Santa," she replied without missing a beat. It was funny how even though they had been apart for so many years, little habits still popped up as though it were yesterday. After watching *Rudolph the Red-nosed Reindeer* their first Christmas together, they had developed the practice of copying Rudolph and Santa whenever they went anywhere. It had slipped out of his mouth by accident this time, but when she responded promptly with her line, he couldn't help but smile.

He locked up the boat and they climbed into her car for a weekend at Cindy's. He hoped Sam could keep her questions about religion at bay until they got there. Cindy seemed sure of herself concerning Christianity, and he felt confident Cindy could be the one to help sort out Sam's confusion. Personally, he didn't want to think about God. He knew his life's history, and at thirty-five, he honestly believed it was too late for change.

✪✪✪

"Why again is the church waiting so long to see me?" Hal asked Floyd Benson during another call. "What's wrong with next weekend?"

"We just assumed that you needed time to work things out in your own church," Floyd replied. "They're probably not going to be real thrilled at the prospect of you pulling out and leaving them."

"If God wants me in Dockrey, Alabama, then this church will have to understand," Hal said firmly. "I don't like to dally around, Floyd." He could tell by the man's voice that he was aged, and that most would have felt the need to refer to him as *Mr. Benson*, but Hal had learned the sooner he put himself on the same ground as others, especially those older than he, the sooner he got the respect he needed to successfully carry out his duties. "If it's time to move on, then it's time to move now. I don't want to linger on this for weeks on end."

"I guess I could talk to the committee and see if we could speed it up a little," Floyd told him. "We weren't supposed to meet again until a week after next Sunday, though."

"Tell you what, Floyd, you call an emergency meeting on Sunday afternoon and try to get me there next weekend."

"Well, Nancy Beth won't be here. I'd like the whole committee's input before I make a decision. Plans and preparations will need to be made before you visit. We'll want a church-wide supper and a time for members at large to talk with you and ask you questions."

A red flag went up in Hal's mind immediately. "Hang on just a minute, Floyd. Are you saying that I'm gonna have to sit before a firing squad of unprofessionals and be questioned about my ability to do this job?"

Floyd was apparently taken aback as he answered right away. "No sir. We just wanted the church to get a chance to know you. Everyone's excited about the prospect of all you can do. It's not a drilling time; it's a get-to-know-you time."

Hal smiled at the no *sir* and shifted gears quickly. "Oh, great then!" he said cheerfully. "Look, don't go to a lot of trouble for me. We can save the whole *get-to-know-you* thing for when I actually move there." He still needed to push the time up. "Is there any way you can contact this *Nancy Beth* about the date over the phone?"

"Probably. I'll see what I can do."

When he hung up, he stood immediately and began to pace and think.

If I can get there next week and hook them, I would say I'm giving a two-week notice here. Augh! But two-week's notice would have to be from like a Sunday or something, so it'd really be three weeks. Wait … I could say I gave it on a Wednesday. That would give me less time. This is gonna work … it's gonna work. Now, to find out as much as I can about this pastor and music guy. I need to have my ducks in a row before I go in and start changing the lineup.

✪✪✪

"Where are we going, Mama?" Cassie asked as Angie buckled her into the car-seat of the Wright's minivan.

"We're going to see Devin and Denay," she replied happily. Angie loved Cindy like another sister. And as close as Angie and especially Annie were, there were things and situations in life that Angie had shared with Cindy that had given them a special bond. To spend an afternoon with their families together was just another one of those blessings she wouldn't forget to count while in Dockrey.

"And Kylla will play with me?" Cassie asked excitedly as she cradled the purple bunny.

"Yes indeedy, she will," Angie met the excitement.

Michael buckled Carter in on the other side and then removed the diaper bag from his shoulder tossing it to the floor. "Let's go."

☼☼☼

Sam and Billy pulled up to Cindy's shortly after lunch. They had gobbled down some fast food before leaving town and had laughed almost the entire time. He was in a good mood, and his old charm had begun to shine through for a few brief moments. Sam was especially interested in how taken he was with Cindy's children. True, they were completely adorable, but to hear him talk about them as he did was surreal. He had never cared for children before.

As she parked the car, they both wondered to whom the white van belonged.

"I have no idea," he told her. "It looks like Pastor Jon's to be honest with you. Maybe he's talking over church stuff with them or something."

As they got out, they could hear the squeals of delighted children coming from the back.

"I wonder what's going on out there," she more commented than asked.

"I can guarantee you I'm gonna find out," he said as he grabbed out his bag with a huge smile and started for the door.

Once inside, the laughter of adults was every bit as loud as the squeals they had heard from the children.

"Cindy?" Billy called out not seeing anyone in the living room.

"We're out in the sunroom!"

"Just drop your things here," he told Sam. "We can settle in later. I want to see what's so funny."

"That makes two of us."

As soon as they stepped through the door of the glass room, Billy froze. Sam looked up at him in confusion. There was another couple with Cindy and Kyle, and they were obviously having a great time. The man had bleached hair, and the woman was beautifully tanned, in fact, she was the most beautiful woman Sam believed she had ever seen. She was holding a toddler and kissing him over and over as he giggled incessantly.

"Hi guys," Cindy said as she tried to calm her laugh. "Come on in and have a seat."

Billy moved almost like a zombie, but Sam walked on in as though all were well and fine.

"What a beautiful little boy," Sam said as she waved at the toddler. "I don't believe I've ever seen a baby so tanned. Are you guys from Florida or something?"

"Way farther than that," Cindy said laughing again. "This is Angie and Michael Collins. They're missionaries in the South Pacific."

Sam reached out her hand to shake Angie's before the full meaning of who this woman was had registered. Just as Angie took her hand, she realized *this* was Angie Wright.

"This is Samantha … uh … do you still go by Marcum?" Cindy asked.

She only nodded as she shook hands. She had become a zombie now too.

"Are you guys related?" Angie wondered.

"This is Billy's ex-wife," Cindy explained so matter-of-factly that Sam almost believed there was no reason to be uncomfortable here. But that was not the case. Here before her very eyes was the one woman she had hated and blamed for the loss of her marriage for over ten years now. Even though Cindy had convinced her last week that Angie was nothing like Billy had described, she couldn't simply release years of bitterness. She glanced over at Billy, but he was staring at the ground. This was ten times worse for him.

As the afternoon wore on, something happened that Sam would have never believed: she found herself admiring Angie. Yes, her beauty was breathtaking, but so was her obvious love and adoration for her husband and children. By suppertime, she felt as though she had found a new friend, and as much as she kept telling herself that *this* was the woman who had ruined her life, she was finding it harder to believe.

As for Billy, he avoided the entire trio of women for the remainder of the day. Luckily for him the men ended up grilling outside on the back deck while they watched the children occupy themselves on the massive play set in the yard. He found himself staring at Cassie most of the time. She looked just like Angie with the exceptions of the sun-streaked hair and the one brown eye. Even some of her mannerisms reminded him of her. Occasionally he would glance inside and watch the ladies talk. He adored each of them for different reasons. In fact, the three people he had cared for most in the entire world, other than his parents, were sitting there together. He wondered how Sam was faring, but as he watched, she was just as animated as the others. But then, Angie had that effect on people. She was the kind of woman that made you feel like you had known her all your life. A friend like Angie could have changed Sam's life years back.

☼☼☼

"She's nothing like I thought she would be," Sam confessed to Cindy that night after Angie's family had left and all the kids were in bed. "She was really wonderful. No wonder Billy loved her so much."

At this statement, Cindy burst into laughter.

"What's so funny?" Sam asked perplexed by the outburst.

"Billy never *loved* Angie Wright!" Cindy insisted. "He just always had this thing about the fact that she wouldn't sleep with him … or much of anything else, come to think of it. She was like the mountain that he never conquered."

"I don't think so. I think he really cared for her."

Cindy reached over and put her hand on Sam's knee. "Trust me on this one—Billy was not in love with Angie."

"But … he always …" she stopped. She didn't need to discuss this with Cindy. Her reasons for divorcing Billy were all tied to Angie in her mind. They seemed almost silly now having met the woman.

"Listen to me," Cindy said with deep compassion. "The only woman Billy ever loved was you. You found his heart, Sam. I don't know how, but you found it. Angie occupied his mind a lot of the time, as well as other body parts we won't go into, but she never had his heart."

"But I thought …"

Cindy put up her hand. "Forget what you thought. It galled Billy that she wouldn't sleep with him. He tried everything under the sun, even offered to *pay* me to convince her." Cindy shook her head in disgust. "Can you believe that? She got sick of him by our senior year, but agreed to go with him to the prom if he promised to keep his hands off of her. We even double-dated to make sure he couldn't try anything sly while they were alone." Cindy looked at Sam with a sad expression. "That's why when you guys divorced, it killed me. I knew he had found the love of his life, but I couldn't understand why on earth he wasn't fighting for you."

Sam didn't know what to say. If Billy had loved her so much, why had he worked so hard to push her away? She had never done anything to cause him grief … anything except *not* be Angie Wright. She really believed that was her only shortcoming. Had she been Angie, all would have been fine. But she lost Billy, and he had pushed her to that point by waving the banner of Angie ever before her pitiful soul.

"Listen to me," Cindy said seriously. "I told you before, Billy didn't deserve you. Whatever his reasons were for being the jerk he was in your marriage, I can promise you they had nothing to do with Angie. And I can tell you this too—he doesn't deserve you now either. I'm thrilled to see you again, Sam, and I love you like a sister, but don't let Billy weave any kind of deceptive charm over you. He's changed some, but inside, he's still the self-centered little boy he always was. Until he's willing to give it all over to God and let God change him from the inside out, he'll continue to do whatever seems best for Billy … and not those he cares for."

Sam nodded in understanding. He would always be poison to her. It was partly because of his charm and looks, but the fact that he had cared for her like he did those first few years and brought healing to her bruised and battered life played a huge part. Because of his love and attention, she had come to believe that she wasn't just *white trash* destined to repeat her parents' mistakes. Because of him, she believed some dreams could come true, even if they didn't include him.

"You do understand me, don't you?" Cindy asked.

She nodded. "I understand. And believe me when I say this, I'm not ready to give myself to anyone again, least of all Billy." But as she thought about Cindy's words, she also felt confused. "What do you mean he needs to let God change him from the inside out? How does God change people?"

"God can make beauty from ashes, Sam. I ought to know."

"But how?" She knew nothing of what it meant to trust God. All she knew was how to protect herself from others, and if God was really out there, that included Him too. What kind of God would allow a child to be repeatedly raped by her uncles in exchange for money to her father? What kind of God would allow a girl to experience two abortions before the age of sixteen? How could He change anybody when He honestly didn't seem to care?

Seventeen

"Next week?" Jonathan asked Floyd in total shock. "He wants to come next week? What's the rush?"

"He says he doesn't like to dally around," Floyd explained to the whole committee with the exception of Nancy Beth. "He says if God wants him here, then here is where he needs to be … and as soon as possible."

Tonya was not so much concerned with his coming as she was with the preparations. "But that only gives us a week to try and put together a dinner and social."

"He wasn't real hyped up about the whole social thing," Floyd told them. "He says we should wait and do that after he gets here permanently."

The man's already got this call sealed up and stuck in his pocket, Jonathan thought to himself.

As though reading Jonathan's mind, Tom spoke up. "I don't like being rushed into this. In fact, all we had agreed to do was *talk* with Hal Bridges first … before the other men. He's acting as though we're already issuing him a call."

"Hang on, Tom," Stan interrupted. "That's not entirely true. We agreed to check him out first before dealing with any of the other men. That's all we're doing."

"No, it's not," Tom disagreed. "If we're having him come here next week for an interview, we're in essence saying that we're issuing him a call. I think you need to call him back and let him know he's not the only man under consideration."

"But he is the only man," Tonya wanted to clarify. "I thought we'd agreed to check him out first. Does that not include a weekend visitation?"

"No, it doesn't," Tom told them all. "Look, I know you guys haven't actually formed a committee in probably ten years to pick out a new staff member. I've been on several search committees in previous churches. There are certain things we need to do before Mr. Bridges steps one foot inside this church."

"Such as?" Stan asked.

"We need to call his references," Tom began. "We need to talk to other churches where he's served. We need to call his present pastor. We need to check into his financial background."

"Hold on there just a minute," Stan broke in this time with a little anger. "I'm sorry, but I don't like this idea of *checking up* on potential staff members. I think it shows a lack of respect for the minister. Are you suggesting that he's deceptive or something?"

"All I'm saying is that when you check into some of these things, you find problems. No man is perfect. No matter how many résumés we look at, not a single one represents a perfect person. Our best bet is to check into the man's background and determine that his flaws are things this church can live with."

Jonathan wanted to stand on the table, clap his hands and yell *hear, hear*, but instead he settled for a little cough.

"You okay, pastor?" Tonya asked.

"Fine," Jonathan assured her. "Just fine." Boy, was he glad he had Tom on this committee.

"I don't know, Tom," Floyd began. "I kind of think it would be insulting too. After all, he's a minister of the gospel. He deserves our trust. Do you make it a habit of checking into our pastor's financial statements?"

Jonathan once again wanted to yell, only this time to say, *No, Tom doesn't, but there have been plenty on and off over the years who have!*

"You guys need to trust me on this," Tom said adamantly. "We need to take our time. The reason all that information is on the résumé is for us to use. We need to use it and use it wisely. We need to be concerned about the needs of this church first."

"This church *needs* an administrator," Tonya stressed. "And the sooner, the better. Pastor John and Kyle are swamped up to their eyeballs with all that's going on. They need relief, and the church needs to move on."

"Look," Floyd brought up, "this is why we have a committee. Let's put it to the vote."

"But Nancy Beth's not here," Stan reminded him. "The whole committee has to vote before we can do anything."

"I talked with her this afternoon; she's all for it," Floyd revealed.

☼☼☼

Jonathan tried to concentrate on his adorable grandchildren, Cassie and Carter, as they played out imaginary scenarios in his backyard, but what was happening at the church continued to run through his mind like a siren of warning. Emergency meeting of the search committee for the purpose of initiating a call the coming weekend? No church-wide question-answer session? No checking into references or with former churches? This church had obviously forgotten all the trouble with their former pastor. And why not? That had been over thirty years ago. And for the past four years, there had been no opposition whatsoever. The only member of this church who had been against him resigned over the hiring of Cindy Marcum, and since then, it had been smooth sailing. They had forgotten that not everyone is always what they seem.

"And which dwarf are we today?" Barbara asked cheerfully as she joined him. "Still Grumpy?"

He looked at her with disdain. "That's not even cute any more, Barbara. Serious things are happening, and you keep acting as though this is just another simple step in the process of life."

"For starters," she said soberly, "I'm not trying to be cute. I'm merely trying to encourage you and put your focus back where it needs to be."

"And where is that?"

"On the fact that God is in control of all of this."

He gave a sigh of doubt this time. "Sometimes, I wonder. This committee doesn't seem to care about seeking the Lord. I know what can happen to a church when a move is made out of God's will. There's a high possibility that things could go horribly wrong."

"Actually, the odds are an even fifty/fifty," she suggested. "There's a good chance God will bring an incredible person in here who will fit right in and usher more showers of blessings. However," she paused to give Jonathan a warm smile, "there's also a good chance God wants to shake things up a bit."

This alarmed him. "For what earthly reason!"

"Ah," she shook her head slowly, "that is precisely the point, sweetie. Perhaps for no *earthly* reason, but for a heavenly one. It's been many years since we've been through the fire, Jonathan. God has blessed us and this church so richly that it might just be time to see if our faith comes out as sparkling gold."

"No, thank you," he mumbled as he leaned back in the bench swing beneath a huge hickory tree.

"Tsk, tsk," she shook a finger at him. "We can't accept the good things from God and reject the hard. I believe you may have possibly become a little too comfortable, Pastor Jon."

He leaned to the side and glared at her in disbelief.

"It's *possibly* true, Jonathan. I've seen you stand strong in the Lord through some very daunting circumstances, but lately, honey, everything's been so easy. Welcome the rod, Jonathan—welcome the rod."

Welcome the rod. This was one of his biggest points of advice when counseling others. He equated the discipline and testing of the Lord with a rod of correction. When God brings the rod into our lives, we are to welcome it as from His hand, as something good, as a means by which God would work out the negative and intertwine the positive. He had been there many times, but as much as he hated to admit it, Barbara was right. It had been at least four years since he had received any opposition in any way whatsoever. It had been four years since anyone had questioned his leadership or authority in the church, the community, even among his family. His three girls were happy and successful in their pursuits, all married to wonderful men of God. His only son had finally overcome the horrific demons in his own life, and was married to a wonderfully encouraging woman with whom he shared a precious little girl. The church had grown beyond anything he could have imagined possible in Dockrey, and any idea he put forth was readily embraced. Life indeed had become very good and extremely easy.

"I want to be beyond the rod," he confessed softly. "I want life to remain easy, comfortable, and stress free."

She gave him a warm smile and gently touched his hand as she said, "That would be heaven, dear, and that ain't gonna happen here."

☼☼☼

Angie's nerves were so on edge as she punched in the number that Michael almost wished he had gone ahead and done it himself. He rubbed her back in encouragement and gave her shoulder a tight squeeze as they sat together on the couch in the upstairs apartment. She sighed as she went through a series of explanations concerning what to press in order to be directed to the correct office. After several drawn out instructions followed by several different presses, the phone rang in the office of her old colleague from med school.

"Dr. Taylor's office," came the answer. "How may I help you?"

"Yes," Angie replied, somewhat caught off guard at receiving a live person after the series of automated responses. "Dr. Levi Taylor is an old friend of mine. I need him to give me a call when he gets a chance."

"May I have your name, please?"

"Dr. Angie Collins."

Michael tapped her shoulder and shook his head. "Wright," he reminded her. "He won't know your married name."

"I mean Dr. Angie Wright," she said quickly. "I wasn't married back then."

"Okay. Angie Wright," the secretary repeated slowly. "Is this in regard to anything specific or just a friendly call?"

"If you could just have him call me, that's all he needs to know." She didn't want to go into details. The story was too long.

"Could you hold just a second?" the secretary asked.

"Sure."

She sighed slightly at having taken the first step toward getting Carter's condition diagnosed. A smile drew across her face.

"What is it?" Michael asked softly concerning her smile.

"His hold music is James Taylor. Levi loved James Taylor. I wonder why she put me on hold?" She tapped impatiently as time passed. "The woman didn't even get my number. I would've hung up by now and just assumed she would eventually pass on the message, but without the number …"

Suddenly the music cut off and a merry voice spoke instead. "Angie the angel? Is it really you?"

She smiled again, bigger this time. "Levi Taylor, you haven't changed a bit, have you?"

"You bet I have!" he laughed. "Now they *pay* me to do all this gory stuff."

"Did you ever get that convertible?"

"Yes, ma'am. And it's even faster than Dr. McDoogle."

"Oh, please," she blushed. McDoogle had made a pass on her even before their first week of classes had finished.

"That could have been an easy *A* for you, you know?"

"You're starting to make me sick, Taylor," she griped. "Some doctor you turned out to be."

"Ah, but the kids love it."

"Thus, a pediatrician. I suppose they understand your mind better than the average adult."

"Absolutely. And what about you? Did you ever make it to the Philippines, or wherever it was you wanted to go?"

"Padawin," she corrected him. "And yes, I've been there for five years."

"Congratulations ... I think."

"You think?"

"Well, I don't know—you go through all this misery to become a doctor, and then you tail it off to some island where they pay you pennies. I guess ... congratulations."

"I'm very happy, in fact, I'm just plain tickled pink over it."

Levi laughed. "So what's up? Are you calling me from the island, or are you back here in the States for a little R and R?"

"Well, I'm in the States, but not for any rest. I'm soon to deliver baby number three."

"Wo, mama!" he exclaimed. "Number three? Please tell me you got married."

"What do you think?"

"Overly religious, very moral, completely whitewashed ... yep, you're married. So, I guess you're not calling me to rekindle some old flame you've nursed since school?"

"Flame? We never had a flame."

"Correction, *you* never had a flame," he explained. "Every guy within sight of you carried a flame ... except McDoogle. He had an all out blazing torch."

She was ready to change the subject. "Would you like to know the real reason I called, or are you gonna continue with the path of McDoogle?"

"I'm all ears," he told her, then quickly added, "no smart remarks about my ears, okay?"

"You deserve anything I might say after those comments concerning McDoogle."

"You're right … truce. So, what's up?"

Angie took a deep breath and then began. "It's my second child, Carter. He's just over two years, and he can't walk."

"Can't or won't?" Levi asked.

"Can't," she confirmed.

"Any other abnormalities concerning his development?"

"None at all that I've observed. He's very bright and expresses himself well. He's more like his dad, though, sort of reserved and quiet."

He chuckled faintly. "Definitely must be like Dad, then."

She ignored the suggestion that she could be on the loud side and went on. "It actually appears to be painful for him. He screams whenever you try to make him stand."

"Is he mobile?"

"Extremely. He can get anywhere he wants—anywhere but up."

"I see," was the only response this time.

After several seconds of silence, she asked, "What do you think?"

"What do *you* think?"

She closed her eyes and shook her head. "I don't want to think. I can't be objective about this. You know my heart is bigger than my head. I want to think that he's a lazy little boy and likes having his mama and daddy tote him around."

She could hear her old friend sigh. "How long has this been going on, Ang? Did he ever walk?"

"He pulled up. He was close to walking at about ten months or so—then he just stopped. He went back to crawling everywhere."

There was more silence.

"Are you in Alabama?"

"Dockrey."

"Where the heck is that?"

"Northwest," she smiled a little. "When I saw you were in Memphis, I figured it was an answer to prayer."

"I sure hope so," he said more soberly. "Make an appointment with Gail. I'll transfer you back. I'll tell her to give you top priority."

"Thanks, Levi. I really appreciate it."

"Angie?" he asked, still serious. "I hope you didn't wait too long with this."

"I know. I was limited with what I could actually find out in Padawin."

"Nobody forced you to stay there. You had to know that time was a factor in this?"

"I didn't know what to think. But as it moved on, I began to sense an urgency. So here I am."

"Can you come tomorrow?" he asked to her surprise.

"If you can fit me in, I can."

"Just come. When you get here, tell Gail at the receptionist's desk. We'll take it from there."

Angie could feel emotions begin to whirl around inside her. "Thanks … Levi. I appreciate it."

"I can't work miracles, Ang, but I'll do whatever I can."

Eighteen

Andie lay on the couch and tried to concentrate on Adam's math, but the numbers were starting to swirl around on the page. She rubbed her temples a few times and tried to focus, but the medicine was stronger than her will to teach pre-algebra.

"Adam, I can't concentrate," she finally admitted. "Tomorrow we'll do math first thing and see if I can actually make sense of all this."

"Sorry, Mom," he said softly. "I wish I could do it on my own. It's just that mixing numbers and letters throws me for a loop."

"Me too," she smiled as she touched his nose. "At least you can read music. There aren't many twelve year-olds around anymore who can boast that."

As he got up, he mumbled, "What's the point?"

"What's the point of what?" she asked him.

"Nothing." He tried to shrug it off as he moved toward the kitchen.

"Wait!" she called out to him.

He turned back, but wouldn't face her.

"What do you mean, '*what's the point*?'"

He just shook his head and tried to turn again.

"Adam Mason, explain yourself to me. I want to know why you said that. I thought you loved music."

He sighed, stared down at his feet and just stood there. She gave him time to collect his thoughts, but she realized he wasn't going to answer willfully.

"I want to know what the problem is. Adam, talk to me." She patted the couch for him to sit next to her again, but he remained where he was.

"I'm sorry, Mom," was all he said. "I'm just … just …" He threw up a hand in frustration.

"Adam, you can tell me anything. You know that. If there's something on your heart, which there obviously is, you need to let me hear it. Don't hold things in. You'd think your dad and I would have taught you that well by example."

He gave a small smile. Andie and Doug were famous for their open and animated *discussions*. He still hesitated, and Andie realized that whatever this was, it was big for him, and that it would obviously be something big for her as well or he wouldn't be holding out.

"Come on, Adam. Spit it out, son."

He looked up to the ceiling and finally said, "Now's not the time, Mom. Let's wait until you feel better. Okay?"

She gave a grave look and raised one eyebrow. He took a deep breath and sat on the table in front of her—not on the couch beside her.

"I guess … well …" he hesitated still. She listened patiently, allowing him the time he obviously needed. "Homeschooling has been really cool...and all. I mean, like, when I was younger, it was great working like crazy to get through so we could have the rest of the day to play."

He paused and looked away. She began to understand. Her heart dropped to her stomach. "And how is it now?" she asked him. "Be honest."

He looked back down at his pre-algebra book and sighed. "It's, I guess, just kind of tolerable. It's not that it's bad or anything, Mom. You do great. There are just things I … well … things that I miss, you know, that other kids are always talking about. And it's like all these years are going by, and I'm missing stuff. I know it's not important stuff, but it's … I guess it's the fun stuff … you know?"

She forced a smile. He was growing up and was no longer the silly, fun-loving little boy from her past. She had sensed his maturity often of late, and had seen the struggle within him. She hadn't known what it was, but it all made sense now. She knew her response was desperately important.

"It's okay, Adam," she smiled as she reached out her hand to him and made a fist. He responded in like and they gently hit them together. "Things change. I understand that."

He nodded slightly and looked back up toward the ceiling. "I want to go to pep rallies. I want to play in the band. I want to make fun of the science teacher, and I want to gripe about the bad cafeteria food."

Andie forced herself to grin, but inside she could feel herself falling apart. Was she losing her firstborn? Were they about to turn a corner that led to a point of no return? The medicine was really strong right now and was playing havoc with her emotions, but she needed her mind and heart to be strong.

"So, what would you like to play in the band?" she managed to get out. "I don't believe they have positions for guitar or piano."

He shrugged. "Who cares? Like you said, I read music real well. I don't know … maybe even the drums. That'd be sort of cool, and it'd be really different."

She scowled for a moment. "Drums? Well, that's just what this house needs: a little more chaos."

He chuckled and sighed as he finally made eye contact. "Mom, I love our house … and our family. I even think the chaos is fine. I just … just …" He struggled for the words.

"Adam," she interrupted him, "you don't have to explain anymore. It's okay. I'm not saying it's an automatic *yes*, but your dad and I will talk about it, and we'll weigh it all out like we adults tend to do, and we'll probably talk about it some more …" She smiled at him again. "And eventually we'll get back with you."

She laid her head back on the couch and closed her eyes as images swirled around inside her head from the medicine. She could almost talk herself out of taking it except for the merciless throbbing in her ankle. When the medication kicked in, the constant throbbing dulled to a steady ache.

"I'm drifting, buddy," she murmured. "Go practice your drums."

As he walked off, she stretched her eyes open for a glance at the lanky young man. This was a conversation that would stay imbedded in her mind for as long as she lived.

✡✡✡

Sam popped into the science room during third period break to check up on both teachers. Mr. C was sitting at his desk laughing as Billy demonstrated some unusual antic at the front of the room. She pulled off her glasses and finally asked out of complete bewilderment, "What are you doing?"

Both men were startled, but then burst out in hilarity.

"This Mr. Marcum is quite the story teller," Mr. C said. "However, Billy, I don't think you should share that particular experience with the students. It could put ideas into their heads, and liquid nitrogen is not something to be trifled with … well … except maybe in that case."

The men laughed again for a moment as she stared in ignorance. Mr. C finally stood, stretched, and ambled toward the door. "I needed a good laugh, Billy. Thanks."

"Where you going?" Billy asked as Mr. C. pulled the keys from his pocket.

"The hospital. They may let Lora go home in the next couple of days. The neurologist is supposed to be there in about 20 minutes."

"How's she doing?" Sam asked with concern. "I didn't get up to see her this past weekend."

"Don't really know," he replied unenthusiastically. "I'll find out in twenty minutes."

She nodded and waved as he left the room, then made her way to Billy who was now standing at the small lectern.

"Going to the game Friday?" she asked as she glanced at his plan book.

"Too cold," he said with a shiver, shaking his head. "The temperature's supposed to get down in the forties."

"What do you mean? That's perfect football weather! You get all bundled up and drink a ton of hot cocoa while screaming and jumping for your team."

"Yeah, that part's fine," he explained, "but when you're on a bike going and coming, it's downright miserable."

"Well, what if someone with an actual car and a heater was willing to let you ride along?"

"That would be a different situation altogether," he smiled at her. Why was it that his smile could so easily disarm her? "Do you know of someone who'd be willing to do such a thing?"

"I've heard of a generous, brave soul that might be willing," she teased. "Are you up for it?"

He breathed a deep sigh and leaned against the podium. "Sam, at this point in my life, I can use all the charity I can get. But I'll be honest," he glanced at her for just a second with a hint of humiliation, "it's very hard. For all my life I had everything I ever wanted. But when I decided to go back to school, get my degree, and start teaching, I gave it all up. It's almost like I'm up the proverbial creek …"

"However," she stopped his analogy with one of her own, "you are not without a paddle. Your degree, as well as this experience right here and now, will give you all the momentum you need when you're finally allowed to pull anchor and let go."

He smiled again and shook his head. "Leave it to you to not let me feel sorry for myself."

She spoke seriously this time. "I admire what you've done, Billy. Not many guys with a past like yours would ever dream of doing such a thing. I mean really, the last place I ever expected to find you after all these years was in a high school … next door to me."

He stood tall and reached up to run his hand through his smooth, blond hair, but his smile had faded. "You never really wanted to find me again, did you?"

"Honestly, no." She stuck her glasses back on and turned toward the chalkboard. "I confess that I did imagine it a few times. In my imagination I was always complete and happy, and you were desperately alone. You would tell me what a fool you'd been and how horrible your life had turned out since you left. I would tell you how sad that was, but that losing you was the best thing that ever happened to me. I explained how it helped me grow up, how it helped me realize the only person I could ever depend on was me, and how I would make sure I'd never let myself down again. I would sort of pat you on the back and then walk away proudly, believing that you were pining away for all that you lost."

She traced her name on the board in the dust of the chalk.

"Grow up?" he asked her softly. "You've always been grown. From the time you were a little kid you had to think like a grown-up, make decisions like a grown-up, defend yourself like a grown-up."

"Only on the outside. Inside was this little girl who was craving to be cared for. I thought I had hidden her well … until you came along. Being with you tore down all those walls I had built to protect myself from the users in this world. I guess that's why it took me so long to get the message that you didn't want me anymore."

He jerked toward her and looked in disbelief. "Sam, that wasn't it..."

She put her hand up to stop him immediately. "I don't want to go there again," she said curtly. "For whatever reason, here we are." She held out her hands. "At first, I couldn't imagine ever being civil to you, but life moves on. And here you are … in my school … the next door down. The hard memories cut me to the core, but the good times remind me that we had something—something that probably should have stopped at friendship. But I didn't know where to draw the lines. I thought I could be a normal person and have a normal life."

"It wasn't you, Sam," he cried in exasperation. "Everything that went wrong with us was my fault!"

"Stop it!" she practically screamed. "I don't want to hash this out … not again … not anymore." She turned to leave the room.

"But you need to understand that there's nothing wrong with you," he insisted as he followed her to the door. "The decisions I made had nothing to do with you. They were just selfish acts made out of selfish influences. I wasn't even considering you in the process. All I wanted was what I thought was best for me."

She twisted back briefly as she said, "Then the question really is, Billy, what was it about me that wasn't the best for you? Why wasn't I good enough for you?"

When she left, Billy chose not to follow. What could he say? He had no answers for her. He had always done only what was best for him. If he could turn back time, he would start with Sam and would do everything he should have done but had been too blind to see at the time.

☼☼☼

"It's a really small town," Lisa Bridges said as she squinted at the tiny dot on the map where her husband was pointing.

"It has its own hospital," Hal told her. "And if you don't want to work there, Florence is about fifty miles one way, and Tupelo, Mississippi, about the same the other."

"Dockery, Alabama?" she repeated with a hint of disgust. "Is this what you've come to?"

He gave her a sharp look. "Don't embarrass yourself." He stood from the table and harshly pushed his chair beneath it. "We go where God opens the doors."

"We go," she said sarcastically, "when you force another church to slam its doors behind you."

He spun around quickly and grabbed her by the arm. "I'm going to make this as clear to you as I can—don't you ever second guess my motives or my calling." His voice was controlled and low, but his eyes were full of fire.

"Or what?" she replied with the same tone. "Are you gonna snap me in half like you did the enemy when you were a Navy Seal?" A mocking smile played upon her face now.

His grip grew tighter. "Believe me, I know how to make people snap … and it's not always physically."

"Believe me, I know. I've seen you do it over and over and over again. My question is, why the church? Why can't you just move on and let go of …"

"Enough!" he yelled this time. She had finally pushed the right button. "Don't you have to go to work?"

"Gladly," she said as she pulled away from his grip and straightened the sleeve of her shirt. "Someone has to make an honest living in this house."

She slammed the door before he could make his statement, but the anger that filled him was desperate for release.

"I am in control," he said slowly as he took several deep breaths. "I am moving on. This time I will have to be smarter … move more slowly … and watch … my … back …"

Nineteen

"Hey, gorgeous," Doug piped as he removed his socks before joining Andie in bed. "I love that look you get just before the drugs take you away. Where is it that you go when those things kick in?"

"Very funny," she moaned. "But this look has nothing to do with the medicine."

"Great, babe." He turned out the light and practically jumped into the bed. "Man, it's starting to get cold. Can I snuggle up next to you if I promise not to jar your foot in any way?"

"Which sister am I, Doug?" she replied instead.

"Uh … well … I guess the oldest sister?" He assumed that was the wrong answer, but he offered it anyway.

"I suppose that's what I boil down to at this point in life." Her tone was definitely morose.

"Babe, you're making no sense. Did you overdose or something?"

"Angie's the beautiful sister," she began to elaborate. "She's always been this knockout. When people meet her, they walk away thinking how breathtaking she is. And Annie's the talented sister. She's unbelievably smart and overwhelmingly musical. Shoot, she knew more about music than I did even after I got my degree—it just drips off her like honey." She turned to him in the darkness and asked again, "So what sister am I? What is it that defines me?"

"That's easy," he quipped. "You're the saucy one … the hot one. You're the one with all the spunk and the overflow of opinion."

He felt her body tense. That wasn't what he was hoping for. He quickly wanted to switch gears but nothing came to mind.

"Great," she mourned. "I feel so much better now."

"Babe, what's going on? Why the doom and gloom all of a sudden? You're this incredible lady. I mean, I've stood in awe of you my whole life. In fact, I can't believe you actually agreed to marry me. What were you thinking? And now … you're this unbelievable mom, but who could ever guess that you carried and birthed five kids? What's that song? One hot mama? That's you, babe! You're what every woman wishes she could be."

She reached over and took his hand. "Thanks. That's not really what I wanted to hear, but it works a little."

"Thank heaven for medication," he whispered.

"I'm being serious, Doug. Even the mom thing isn't mine alone anymore. For a long time I was the only sister that was a mother. But now Angie and Annie have their own brood …"

"But they don't have five," he reminded her promptly.

"But they're well on their way."

Doug leaned up this time and scratched his head. "You want to have more kids?"

"Lands sakes … no! I just want to be … I don't know … me!"

"You're making no sense, Andie. Seriously, did you take like an extra pill or something?"

"Adam talked with me today," she finally confessed. "I thought everything in life was running smoothly. Then I flew off the couch and decimated my ankle, and now my oldest son wants to go back to public school."

"Oh," he said as it all began to make sense. "And so you're thinking that somehow you've failed because your son is developing an excess of hormones?"

"Hormones? How do you tie this to hormones?"

"From twelve until—I don't know—I think I still suffer from it, these hormones start coming into a guy's life and begin to make him want things he never knew he wanted before."

"So you boil all this down to the birds and the bees?"

"No, it's much more than that. He's ready to fit in somewhere."

"He fits in here perfectly!" she protested. "He belongs here just fine."

"Andie, when we first started talking about homeschooling, you remember what we did? We prayed and asked God to make it clear. When we finally made the decision, we asked God to make it clear when it was time to stop?"

"And our son's hormones are now dictating God's will?"

"No, but God is putting into him a desire to branch out—to do something different. Look, he's here twenty-four seven with a brother and three little sisters."

"He's only twelve, Doug. Why does he want to leave us?"

"It's not like he's heading off to college or the military. He just wants to go to school like most other American guys his age? Was it your plan to keep him here forever?"

"Until he was eighteen. Why does he want to … to go away?"

He settled down beside her again. "Do you remember back when we were dating? Your dad never let us go anywhere. Our *dates* were made up of me sitting with you in church and then hanging out at your house the rest of the time. You couldn't even walk me out to my bike without your father standing at the front door watching us the whole time with every outside floodlight turned on full blast."

She chuckled. "I remember."

"We thought he'd never let us actually go out on a date all by ourselves. When he finally did, we thought we had reached heaven. Do you remember that?"

"Oh yeah. If he knew how passionate that first kiss was, he probably would've never let us out of his sight."

"He knew … that's why he held on so long. But he realized also that at some point he had to let you make your own choices. We were persistent. And just because we wanted to be alone now and then didn't mean we hated your family and were trying to pull ourselves away. We simply needed to explore some things on our own."

"We explored all right."

"But not too much," he reminded her. "We had our limits, Andie, mainly because your dad had made them very clear. He had made them clear to you all your life and made them clear to me for as long as I had mooned over you. I wasn't about to lose face with that man. And see, this is where Adam is right now."

"We were sixteen—almost seventeen!" Then her voice got softer. "He's only twelve."

"And he's a good boy, a responsible boy. I'm not saying that we let him go, I'm just saying let's explore the possibilities. We agreed from the beginning this would be open-ended. We never said homeschooling was gonna be it, now and forever, world without end. Let's talk it over with him. It could be just a temporary leaning. Ultimately, babe, the choice is ours. But God may be moving here, and if so, we need to be listening."

She sighed. "I just grew to believe we would do this until they all graduated."

"And you may do that—just maybe not with Adam. You may never get rid of Lainey. She hangs on you like white on rice."

"True. Maybe I should just start her in public school."

He reached up and caressed her cheek. "See, if you could get them all out of the house again during the day, when I come home for lunch … oooo, one hot mama strikes again."

"That's really pitiful, Doug."

"I told you, babe, it's all about hormones. And you bring them out in me pretty much all the time."

"So, I'm the saucy sister, huh?" She took his arm and pulled him closer.

"If they bottled what you've got, we couldn't say the name in public." He leaned over and kissed her as he added, "Or in front of your dad."

☼☼☼

"How's Mr. Ogre today?" Sam asked as she popped her head inside Billy's science lab. "Doing a little experimental stuff with the kids?"

He looked disheveled. "I have two more experiments planned for the semester, but after today's fiasco, I'm considering rewriting the lessons. Out of two chemistry classes, fifty-eight students, only one lab group got it right. What did I do wrong?"

"Who cares?" she replied cheerfully. "It's Friday! Nobody does anything right on Fridays. All we want is to get through the day and go watch football."

He stared up at her from his desk in shock. "Did I just hear you say that? Did those words actually come out of your mouth?"

She was apparently in a good mood. "All work and no play make Billy a grumpy boy."

He locked the last of the beakers up in a cabinet and removed his safety glasses. "My grumpiness has nothing to do with work or play. The three experiments will make up thirty percent of the chemistry grade. Right now, the majority of my students have a failing average. What kind of evaluation will that bring for student-teaching?"

"Was it a *pop* experiment?"

"What? What's a *pop* experiment?"

"Like a *pop* quiz, only it's an experiment. Did they know it was coming?"

"Of course they did," he answered defensively. "They've known for an entire week. We've gone over the procedure in class, and they were supposed to read the instructions again last night and then come prepared today with any questions they might have before we got started."

"Were there any questions?"

He shook his head.

"And somehow you take this to be your fault?"

"If only one lab group out of sixteen passes an assignment, apparently I messed up somehow. Yeah, I'd say it's my fault."

"And I would say that your students learned another very important life lesson today."

"Well, it certainly had nothing to do with chemistry," he mumbled.

"No, but an important lesson about life—when you're told to be prepared, then be prepared. I think that's a pretty valuable point, don't you?"

He smiled slightly and shook his head. "You've got your certificate nice and sealed up; you can afford to teach life lessons. I'm not a certified teacher yet."

"I can guarantee you that whatever that next experiment is, those classes will be much better prepared."

When the door to the outside was opened, the chilling wind blew right through him.

"Brrr," he shivered. "What a miserable day."

Sam punched him in the arm. "Snap out of it! We've got a game to travel to tonight."

He looked down at her in surprise. After their last discussion, he had assumed he wouldn't be traveling with her to the game. Things had gotten pretty ugly.

"You still want me to go?" he asked her.

"Yeah. Why?"

"I thought you didn't like me anymore."

She laughed. "Of course I don't, but that doesn't mean I have to neglect you. I don't behave like you do."

He stopped and took her arm. "That was low, Sam." He shook his head and gave a slight smile. "I'm serious, though. You chewed me out the last time we spoke. I don't know if I'm coming or going with you sometimes."

"You're going. I'll pick you up about five-thirty. It's a long ride to the game. We'll grab something to eat on the way."

And with that she walked off with a wave. He watched as she opened her door, got in, and then drove off. Maybe there was still hope after all. Maybe she just had a lot unresolved feelings she needed to get off her chest first. Whatever the reason, he found himself smiling at the thought of spending the evening with her again.

"Mr. Marcum," came a younger voice beside him accompanied by a tap on his shoulder.

Billy looked down to see Paulo holding open his anatomy book.

"Paulo?" he asked the junior. "Shouldn't you be getting ready for the game?"

"I have a few minutes," he explained through a fading accent. "I don't understand something here." He pointed to a picture of the circulatory system in his book. "I can't get how the lungs get the oxygen to the blood. I keep reading it and looking at this diagram, but it isn't making sense to me."

He gladly showed him and explained the process, and then found delight as Paulo's eyes lit up in understanding. After thanking him profusely, the boy practically danced toward the field house. Billy smiled to himself and found a deep sense of satisfaction.

I'm doing the right thing here. This is why I want to teach … so the ones out there like Paulo can have a fighting chance in this world. Sam's right. I can't make them all love chemistry, but I can teach them about life in the process.

The day was finally looking up.

Twenty

When Angie began to giggle, Michael shook his head in confusion. The ride in the van to Memphis had been very serious so far, and the conversation had consisted of all the *what ifs* they could possibly imagine, most of them negative. She had brought along a book about the life of Lottie Moon, one of the most celebrated foreign missionaries of Southern Baptists. When she picked it up to read, he never imagined laughter would ensue.

"What's so funny about Lottie Moon?" he wondered as her giggling continued. "I didn't realize she was such a comedienne."

"You know what?" she grinned as she turned toward him.

He glanced at her and was again struck by her extreme beauty. How did he end up with such a jewel? "What?" he replied.

"I'm sure stuff like this wouldn't be so funny if I had been an only child," she said as she tried to suppress her smile.

"Stuff like what?"

She giggled again and started shaking her head. "It could be completely innocent, and all Annie or Andie had to do was look my way, and we'd all lose it."

"Tell me, please! What is so funny?"

She regained control and said, "Lottie Moon had a cousin named … Fannie Moon Butts." With that said, her laughter burst into full bloom.

Apparently it was a multiple sibling humor thing, because he was still waiting for a punch line as she continued to laugh hysterically. She looked over at him and tears were actually rolling down her cheeks.

"Michael!" she exclaimed. "Is that not funny?"

He was confused. "What part? That she had a cousin?"

"For crying out loud! Her name! Fannie … Moon … Butts!"

He still was in the dark. "Well, I'll admit I don't care to choose either of the three for our next child, but … what?"

"Do you not see the connection between all three names?" she asked in unbelief.

"Fanny!" Carter suddenly yelled from the middle seat. "Tan your fanny!" He began to giggle also.

Michael finally began to nod in understanding as a smile started to appear. "Okay … it's coming together now." He looked in his rear view mirror to catch Carter's eyes. "Daddy doesn't tan your fanny—only Mommy does. Daddy feeds you chocolate cake. Remember that."

Angie reached over and slapped his arm. "No one would ever

believe that you've made me the disciplinarian in this family. I was always the soft-hearted girl—the one who would give into anyone."

"Hey, we choose our roles carefully."

Angie turned around in her seat and reached her hand back to touch Carter's little foot. "Just remember that if Mommy didn't make the chocolate cake, Daddy would be feeding you fish jerky and dates."

Michael smiled at his blessings. Even if Carter's situation turned out to be the worst imaginable, he was still blessed beyond what he could have ever dreamed. God had given him all it took to survive this far; God would give them all that was needed to take the next step.

"So, is this Dr. James Taylor someone I need to worry about?" Michael asked.

"Levi Taylor," she corrected him. "For what reason should you be worried?"

"You tell me. My first meeting with one of your ex-boyfriends nearly blew me back to Padawin."

This time she lovingly rubbed his arm. "Billy Marcum had nothing over you."

"No … nothing at all," he mumbled sarcastically. "Just great looks and an oozing of charm. What am I gonna discover when we walk into this other guy's lair … I mean office?"

"The first thing you're gonna discover is that he has alarmingly large ears—and they choose to stick out rather than lay flat."

"Sounds good; keep going."

"And we never had a *thing*. Levi was a good friend, a good study partner, and the only guy that ever saw me throw up during a medical procedure. He helped me get things cleaned up and all before anyone knew. He sort of saved my skin that day."

"What was the situation?"

"A burn victim," she grimaced. "He had already died from the explosion … some kind of chemical thing. But the smell and the oozing from his body was just … well … it was too much for me."

"You trust him? I mean really trust him."

She looked back at her little boy. "I'd trust him with my own life, so I'd definitely trust him with Carter." She touched Michael's knee and added, "He'll do everything possible."

When they found the office building, it was more like a miniature skyscraper. Carter marveled at its size because nothing comparable to it existed in Padawin, not even in Taveren. He cooed at the elevator ride and loved the bright decorations and toys that filled the waiting room. As Michael held Carter, Angie went to the window and waited for the receptionist to slide the glass open.

"May I help you," the fresh-faced young blond asked her.

"My name is Angie Collins."

The lady's countenance fell slightly when Angie introduced herself, but she managed a smile and nod. "I'm Gail. I'm Dr. Taylor's … Levi's wife."

Angie responded with a warm expression as she realized this woman would be fully aware of her situation.

"We're in no hurry," she told Gail. "I know he's fitting us in. We brought plenty to keep ourselves occupied, and Carter's not a fussy child at all."

"Lucky you," Gail grinned from obvious experience with many fussy children.

"Not that lucky," Angie laughed as she patted her tummy. "Our oldest? Very fussy … very stubborn. And who knows about this one?"

"He doesn't plan to keep you waiting. I think he's dying to see you actually."

"That makes two of us."

Angie moved to where Michael was standing and she wrapped her arm in his. Carter was playing with a massive maze-like machine that held all kinds of balls that could be moved along twisted, metal rods. She softly repeated a phrase from their wedding vows.

"*Through the good that may lighten our ways and the bad that may darken our days* … I had no idea when I made that promise to you how good the good would be … or how bad the bad could be."

Michael leaned his head toward hers and gently kissed her cheek. "I never dreamed when you said those words they would ever be for real."

"That's because you didn't know me. I sincerely meant every word."

"I know you now," he smiled tenderly, "and I still can't believe you married me."

Carter made a small exclamation as he completed a cycle with the colorful beads. Angie knelt down beside him and gave him a warm hug for the accomplishment. She looked back up toward Michael and said, "We ought to see where we can get one of these. He doesn't have to move anywhere to play with it, yet it's loaded with activity."

Michael knelt down with them and added, "By the time we return to Padawin, maybe he won't be so stationary."

A pudgy nurse with a pleasant face and compassionate eyes opened the door to the back rooms. "Angie Collins?" she asked sweetly.

Angie turned to her immediately and raised a finger. "That would be me."

"You're a little old for a pediatric patient," the nurse teased.

Angie reached down and picked up Carter. "This is the patient. I'm just an old friend."

The nurse's smile grew large as she poked her finger at Carter's little nose. "Now *that's* more like it. What's your name, big boy?"

Carter grinned at the nurse but then shyly turned his head into

Angie's body.

"Tell her your name, buddy," Angie encouraged as she kissed the top of his head.

The nurse pulled on his sock this time as she said, "You are one tanned little boy." She then glanced up at Angie and over to Michael and added, "In fact, all of you are rather dark … but you don't look ethnic at all."

"We live on a Pacific Island," Angie explained. "We're here for the upcoming holidays … and …" she looked down to her belly, "… to see this one makes it here safely."

The nurse nodded and then gave her attention to Carter again. "I guess if you won't tell me your name, I'll just have to call you Koozi-Bob."

Angie jumbled Carter in her arms and whispered, "That's not your name! Do you want her to call you Koozi-Bob?"

Carter shook his head and looked back at the nurse. He was close to speaking, but his mouth just wouldn't open. As much as Cassie was like Angie, Carter was like Michael—shy and reticent.

"Okay, Koozi-Bob," the nurse motioned them back with her, "let's see how much you weigh."

They followed her to a brightly colored room.

"Have him stand right here," she nodded toward a cute contraption. "We'll check his weight first and then his height."

Angie smiled but inside emotion began to well. "He can't stand," she said softly, "thus, our visit here today."

"Well, then Koozi-Bob," the nurse moved right on as though nothing out of the ordinary had been mentioned. "You'd better plop yourself in the little boat here."

She pointed toward a boat that was obviously used for weighing the smaller patients. Carter smiled at the nurse as Angie sat him in the boat, and she knew it was just a matter of time before he would warm to the lady. She was working hard to win him over.

"All-righty," the nurse sighed as she recorded his weight. "You're a mighty big boy, Koozi-Bob. You nearly broke my boat. I bet you ride in a boat a lot, huh? Being on an island and all."

Carter nodded, but still wouldn't speak.

The nurse reached to a roll of stickers on a shelf and pulled off four for him. "But since you didn't break my boat, I'm gonna give you some of these stickers. What do you think about that?"

Carter took them hesitantly and smiled shyly again. She then led the family down a hallway to a room that was also brightly decorated. In fact, anything that would have made this place appear to be a doctor's office was well camouflaged. Carter had never been to a doctor, other than his mother, so he had no fears to begin with, and all the colors and decorum fascinated him.

"How old is he?" the nurse asked as she made a few notes on her paper.

"A little over two years," Angie replied.

"Has he ever walked?"

Angie only shook her head this time. The lady wrote down a few more lines.

"Does he crawl or pull up?"

"He crawls very well, but hasn't pulled up for at least a year. He did a little—close to his first birthday—then he stopped."

She nodded as she jotted down a few more things, then she looked up at Carter again and grinned. "Well, Koozi-Bob, Dr. Taylor will be here in a minute to give you a good once over. I'll see you then, okay?"

Carter nodded and smiled, but still refused to speak. He liked her though, and Angie found herself adoring her son as his little personality oozed through his facial expressions.

"He's a cutie," the nurse said as she turned to the door.

The three of them sat silently as they waited for the doctor. All the prayers, pleadings, worries and wonderings were about to be faced. There was nothing left to say at this point, and Michael was thankful that as vocal and expressive as Angie could be, there were moments like these when she could stay quiet and leave him to his thoughts. He watched as she cuddled Carter gently, but didn't smother him. His inquisitive eyes took in all the details of the room, and she seemed to follow his attention as she glanced to every area he did. It was almost as though she instinctively knew his thoughts. When her eyes finally met Michael's, she gave him a nervous look that let him know she was anxious over the possibilities.

"God has us all in His hands," he reminded her softly. "Even your Dr. Taylor."

She smiled slightly, and kissed the top of Carter's head. "I'm afraid we may have waited too long, Michael."

He shook his head. "There's no such thing—God directed us."

"But you kept trying to get me to leave earlier."

"A month or two wouldn't have made a difference."

"You never know," she said as she bit her bottom lip.

Suddenly the door burst open, and a tall, thin man glided in. "Angie the angel!" he exclaimed as he looked down to where she was seated. "I can't believe you're here!"

She stood immediately and handed Carter to Michael. As soon as Michael saw her eyes, he knew she would start crying. He took Carter quickly, and she reached out to Dr. Levi Taylor. Sure enough, the sobs began.

"Hey … hey," Dr. Taylor said calmly as he stroked her long hair. "This is gonna be all right."

She gained control fairly fast and then backed away to get a good look at her old friend. "You have changed," she said as she reached up to touch his ears. "What did you do?"

"Had my ears tacked," he said proudly. "Some of us get money for playing doctor."

Michael scowled slightly as the man was indeed more handsome than Angie had described. He had looked forward to seeing those large ears protruding.

"I thought you'd be paying off some of those student loans," she teased.

"I'm working on it," the tall doctor grinned, "but some issues take greater priority in life. I told the surgeon I wanted a set of lips like this girl I knew in med-school, but when I described you to him, he just shook his head and said no one was that perfect."

Michael raised his eyebrows in alarm.

Angie sighed and shook her head. "Funny how the things I hated most growing up turned out to be my most flattering features … or so I've been told."

Dr. Taylor now turned his attention toward Michael and Carter. He extended his hand to Michael and said, "So you're the dude that tamed the savage beast."

Michael felt that familiar self-consciousness that always overtook him when he met someone from Angie's past. He shook the doctor's hand as he juggled Carter to one knee.

"This is Michael," Angie introduced as she went to stand beside him and put her hand on his shoulder. "He's my rock and the holder of my heart."

Levi Taylor put a hand up to his chest and looked at Michael in admiration. Next, he glanced down at Carter and kneeled on one knee so he could be eye to eye with him.

"And who is this little fellow?" the doctor asked. "What's your name, guy?"

"I name is Koozi-Bob," Carter said promptly.

All three adults looked in surprise.

"I see nurse Nancy has already gotten a hold of you," Dr. Taylor said. "She's a mess."

"He liked her, but wouldn't say a word to her," Angie told him.

Levi gave Carter a good once-over, and Angie knew he was evaluating his outer appearance. Levi talked nonchalantly about his life since med-school as he poked, rubbed, pulled, pushed, and prodded around on an unsuspecting Carter. After a few minutes, Levi held out his hands toward the boy who immediately responded with a smile.

"You're good," Angie said with admiration. "I'll have to keep all that in mind when I'm examining little ones in the Pacific."

Levi took Carter in his arms and then walked over to an examination table. "Yeah, kids aren't near as scared of doctors as they used to be."

"No wonder," Angie agreed as she looked around the office. "This place looks more like a playground than a place of medical expertise."

"Uh huh," he grunted as he prodded around on Carter a little more. "That's the idea."

There was a small bit of silence as he continued until Carter suddenly screamed out in pain. Angie and Michael both jumped to their feet.

"Sorry, Koozi-Bob," Dr. Taylor said quickly as he pushed a green button on the wall and gently sat Carter up on the table. "I was trying to give a tickle test and obviously messed it up. How about this?" He poked Carter in the ribs and the fearful look turned into giggling almost immediately. "Ah … I found that tickle spot!" He then squeezed Carter's knee at which he let out a full-blown laugh. "And another! Man, I'm good."

The door opened and Nurse Nancy poked her head inside. "You rang?"

"Koozi-Bob here needs an elephant and a rabbit as soon as we can get to it," the doctor told her.

"This afternoon?"

"If it's possible. What do you think?"

"I'll make the call right away." The nurse then looked over to Carter and added, "How you doing, Koozi-Bob?"

"His tickler definitely works," the doctor replied.

"Ah, we did a tickle test, did we?" the nurse grinned.

After she left, Angie came up to Levi with a concerned look. "You did way more than a tickle test there. And what's with the elephant and rabbit thing you ordered? I assume that was code for something."

As the doctor lifted Carter and placed him back in his mother's arms, he explained, "Developmentally, muscularly—yada, yada, yada—he appears to be fine. There's no obvious abnormality. Reflexes are fine and doing what they ought to do."

Michael now stood and asked, "And the scream? Was that normal too?"

Levi shook his head this time. "No. As soon as I found that, I knew we needed to do a couple of scans … thus the bunny and elephant."

"Bunny wabbit?" Carter asked in delight.

"That's right, Koozi-Bob," Dr. Taylor said as he tousled Carter's hair. "I have some buddies who are gonna give you two new friends today. They want you to do a couple of tricks for them first, and then you can have two cute little animals to take back with you to Alabama. How does that sound?"

Carter only nodded this time as Angie gently ran her chin over the top of his little head. "What are you thinking?" she asked him.

"What are *you* thinking?" the doctor asked her again as he had on the phone. "I'm sure you've got some idea."

She shook her head. "I don't know. I wanted to believe it was developmental."

"Have a seat," Levi told them both, and they sat back down as he wheeled a stool from beside the table. "Right now I can only guess, but I feel like there must be something growing around his spine." He looked them both eye to eye as he continued. "At the moment, there doesn't seem to be any real pain associated with it unless it's pressed just the right way … like when he stands. It's probably wrapped around some kind of nerve and has imbedded itself there. The scans this afternoon should reveal something."

"What's the prognosis?" Angie asked right away. "What are we looking at if this is actually the case?"

He sighed and folded his arms. "You know I can't answer that at this point."

"You can give us at least some ideas," she countered, "possible scenarios."

"All I'd be doing would be giving you false fear … or false hope. I don't know, Angie."

Michael spoke up this time. "Will there be surgery involved."

"Well, that I can answer … definitely," Levi replied as Angie was already nodding her head. "I don't know how invasive or how successful the chances are because I don't know what we're dealing with or if this is even the problem. But I can almost guarantee that surgery will ensue."

"How soon?" Michael wanted to know.

This time Angie answered, "As soon as possible."

"Yeah," Levi agreed. "Like the beginning of next week."

"Will you do it?" Angie asked him.

"It depends. If it's going to be really involved we'll need to enlist a neuro-specialist. But I'll assist—either way you can know I'll be there."

Angie reached out her hand to him and he took it. "Thanks," she said tearfully. "I'll owe you."

"You already owe me," he grinned. "Throw-up up on the burn victim?"

She smiled through her tears and nodded. "How can I make it up to you?"

"Stay with my wife and me tonight and through this whole ordeal."

Michael broke in again. "We can get a hotel. Thanks though."

"I insist," Dr. Taylor said as he stood. "We could catch up, and it would give me a good opportunity to observe Koozi-Bob here in a more natural setting."

Carter grinned, but Michael sighed. He stood along with Levi Taylor and stuck out his hand in thanks. "I appreciate all you're doing, but there's no need to invade your home."

Angie could sense Michael's insecurity and knew it was time to intervene. "How about an alternate plan?" she suggested. "Could we do dinner or something instead? I'd really like to be alone with Michael and Carter tonight as we sort through it all. This will be the end of a lot of questions, and we'd like to think on it together—just us."

The doctor threw up his hands in surrender and said, "Okay, but my home's still open. It'll get taxing and stressful when the surgery happens."

"Oh, we won't be in a hotel then," Angie stated. "We'll be right beside him."

Levi nodded as he opened the door. "I'll be back with you in a minute with all the details. Hopefully we can get those tests scheduled this afternoon and get moving right away."

When he finally left, Michael kissed the top of Angie's head and then sat next to her and Carter.

"Thank you," he said with relief. "I wasn't comfortable staying with *Dr. Smoothie* at all."

"Dr. Smoothie?"

"Yeah. Apparently his newly pinned back ears have given him a … never mind." He looked at her squarely. "I have a hard time with your old boyfriends, Ang. I just do."

She leaned into him and said, "He's *not* an old boyfriend, Michael."

"Does he know that?"

Twenty-One

Angie was pleased with the sophistication of the testing equipment at the children's hospital. The technicians did a wonderful job convincing Carter to be very still while they took pictures inside his body. Afterwards, Levi had arranged a room for them at the Fed Ex House where they tried to relax as they began the next phase of waiting. Once he reviewed the results, he would call, set up a meeting with them and help to make some definite plans about what should come next. When the phone rang, Angie jumped from the bed and raced for her purse.

"Hello?" she answered.

"Angie, its Levi."

He was serious—no joking involved. She knew this meant it was probably one of the worse scenarios.

"What have you found?" she asked him.

"What don't you guys come on to my office? I have everything laid out here. I can show you what's going on, and we can decide the best course of action to take."

"Okay. Then we can all go out to eat afterward?"

"Maybe," was the reply. "If you're up for it."

She closed her phone and looked toward Michael as her lip began to quiver.

"What is it?" he asked with concern. "Bad news?"

She bit back the tears. "He wouldn't say, but I picked up that it must be."

He came over and placed his arms around her. "We'll get through this, Angie. God's in control. Carter belonged to Him before he belonged to us. He'll guide us … okay?"

She buried her face in his shoulder for a moment as she fought to keep herself from sobbing. She knew there could have been simple possibilities with Carter's condition, but after Levi's response, she realized none of those would apply. She knew it was cancer, and she knew the treatments ahead for her little boy would be invasive and gruesome.

"Let's pray before we go," she managed to whisper. "I need more than my strength alone to face this."

He took her hand and led her to her knees.

☼☼☼

"Right here," Levi said as he pointed his pen to a large mass at the base of Carter's spine. "I'll be honest with you both; the fact that it's contained in just this area alone is close to miraculous. I can't imagine why it hasn't spread throughout the whole abdomen."

"Is it benign or malignant?" Michael asked.

"At this point we can't know," Levi told him, "but it's got to be removed. We'll do a biopsy on the tissue once we've gone in." He pointed to a specific area and explained, "The tumor is pushing on these nerves. As long as Carter doesn't use them, he doesn't feel it. But as soon as he begins putting pressure this way," he pointed his pen up on the image, "it affects this whole area. This is why he can crawl just fine, but can't stand or walk. Frankly, it seems that he should be in a lot more pain than he is."

"Maybe he is," Michael suggested, "but just doesn't know any better."

"No," Levi disagreed. "He's too pleasant of a child. If he were suffering from the pain it seems he should be suffering from, you would have known it."

They all stared at the images silently. Angie was fighting her emotions once again. She had known this was one of the possibilities, but she didn't want to face the fact that her two-year old could have cancer. Yet here it was staring her in the face, and she knew it was time to put her emotions as a mother aside and begin to deal with it all realistically. She could cry when they got back to the room at the Fed Ex House, but for now she had to ask the right questions.

"What are we looking at treatment-wise?" she began.

"Surgery, first, of course. We'll try to get as much of the cancerous tissue as possible. Then the possibility of chemotherapy is strong."

"Why not radiation?" Michael wondered. "Wouldn't that be less … painful … or sickening?"

"He may have to have both," Levi said honestly. "Right now, and I hate to say it like this, we're not near as interested in your son's comfort as we are in saving his life."

She gulped at the reality, and Michael nodded in understanding.

"What if we had done this sooner?" Angie asked as the guilt inside her began to build even more.

"I honestly don't think it would have mattered much," Dr. Taylor answered. "I mean, it's a big old thing, but it hasn't affected any area other than his walking. If you had brought him in here paralyzed, I might have said you waited too long. But for now, I think it's all gonna be fine. Besides, if you didn't think it was cancerous, why did you come to me in the first place, a child oncologist? You had to have some inkling, Angie?"

She nodded as her emotions were running too deep again.

"You mentioned we may need to see a neurosurgeon or something," Michael got back to business. "Is this going to be the case?"

"Yeah, most definitely. But there's no need for a meeting. I'll assist him. In fact, I'll make the call right now so we can go ahead and set up a time for the surgery. The sooner, the better."

Michael put his arm around her waist as he nodded in agreement. Carter was still drowsy and slow from the medications they had given to calm him. As she gently rubbed the top of his little head with her lips, Michael could feel the tears begin to form in his own eyes. His son did indeed have cancer, and as easy and gentle as life had always been for the two-year old, it was now about to become extremely disturbed.

✪✪✪

"I had no idea she was *that* beautiful," Gail Taylor told her husband that night as he flipped channels while lying silently on the couch.

He made no remark.

"She appears to be in true love; they're on their third child," she added.

Levi still said nothing. Angie had always been his dream, his ideal, and when they had started dating last year, she had asked why he never married. He honestly told her it was because of Angie Wright. When Angie called the office yesterday, Levi could hardly contain himself. Gail then took last night to explain all her insecurities and frustrations with him since their ten-month marriage had begun, and that the sudden appearance of Angie Wright back into his life was not helping.

The thing that hit Levi the hardest, however, was the complete *unremarkableness* of her husband. He had anticipated meeting this extremely charismatic character who had managed to be the lucky man to sweep her off her feet, but instead he found Michael to be gentle, humble, and very unassuming. And it was obvious she adored him. Indeed, she was carrying his third child, and whatever it was about him that she found attractive, it seemed to hold them together tightly.

"I never thought I'd have to meet her," Gail continued. "I thought you said she was a missionary or something."

He looked at her with a scowl. "Her son has cancer. She left the islands to seek treatment for him. What would you have her do?"

"Why you?" she wondered in exasperation. "Of all the doctors in the world she could have called—why you?"

He was beginning to get disgusted. "Perhaps because I'm a specialist in just the area she suspected?"

"But she's not even from Tennessee!"

He stood up from the couch abruptly and tossed the remote on a cushion. "What would you have me do, Gail? Tell her to go away? Tell her to find someone else to take care of her sick little boy? I didn't ask her to call me!"

"No, but you sure didn't waste any time seeing her again. You have a waiting list of patients pleading to get into your office for an evaluation, and you schedule them a month or two down the road. Dr. Full-lips calls you up one day and you conveniently fit her in the next! Now you've got surgery scheduled for Monday! It would appear someone is getting special treatment!"

"Sue me!" he yelled as he headed toward the stairs. "Or leave me! Whatever! I didn't ask for her to walk back into my life. I never thought I'd see her again."

"So you married me … second best." She pouted as she folded her arms and sat back in her recliner.

"I told you from the beginning I'd always care for her. My money and future seemed strong enough for you at that time. I'm not the one wavering here. You knew where my heart stood concerning Angie. I'm not about to walk out on us just because she's showed up again. Besides, she's married and apparently very much in love."

"Very …" she repeated.

"Then either get over it or get out," he said without looking down from the top banister.

☼☼☼

The phone call from Angie had disturbed Jonathan almost to a breaking point. He was struggling enough with his unfounded, yet gut-feeling fears about Hal Bridges, but to hear his little grandson had cancer was unbearable.

"Are they staying on through Monday?" Barbara asked, very broken herself from the news.

"No. They're coming back in the morning … should be here by lunch." He sighed and inadvertently removed a few more hairs as he ran his hand nervously over his head. "She wants us to have a prayer gathering tomorrow night for Carter. It seems to be really serious."

Barbara wiped a tear in understanding and went to the kitchen for the church directory. "I was thinking about having a dinner for them, but at this point, maybe we should call for a fast instead."

"I think that's a good idea," he agreed. "Begin calling the prayer chain, and ask any … who are willing … to begin a fast tonight."

"I'm on it."

He walked through the house and onto the back porch where he spotted Cassie out in the yard playing. He was able to smile through his frustration as he was reminded that at any time in the world there would always be great sorrow … but always great hope too. Cassie's curiosity and inquisitiveness were non-stop. Even though she had spent very little time with her grandparents, she had no trouble communicating and opening up to them. Jonathan chuckled at some of the conversations he had had with her since their arrival. He whispered a prayer of thanksgiving for being able to get to know this child, and then added a prayer of hope to get the privilege of knowing her brother just as well some day.

Twenty-Two

Billy slouched down in the passenger's seat of Sam's car. She insisted on paying for his dinner as they pulled up to the drive-through.

"I can afford a burger and fries," he complained.

"I don't know how," she countered. "Come on, Billy, swallow that pride of yours. You're a student, and you have no source of income. I have a job and no debts."

"I don't need pity or handouts."

"Yes, you do," she laughed. "You need all the pity and handouts you can get right now! Stop griping and let me pay for your supper."

He stopped arguing as she pulled up to the window, paid for the food, and then handed him the bag.

"Sort it out, will you?" she asked as she pulled back onto the highway. "Hand me the fries first. I want to eat them before they get cold."

He handed her a pack of French fries and then worked on wrapping her chicken sandwich with a napkin. He gave it to her and then dug in the sack for his own food.

"Are you still in a bad mood about the chemistry experiment?" she asked him

"Probably," he half mumbled.

"Okay, that's obviously not it."

"What makes you say that?"

"If that's what's got you miffed, you'd know it. It must be something else."

He sighed. "I guess."

Sam chuckled as she shook her head. "It's so odd seeing this side of you … and very refreshing."

"Refreshing? You *like* seeing me in emotional torment?"

"I like seeing you be real. The Billy I remember seldom let his guard down. In fact, if everything wasn't right, you just pretended it was. No problems, no worries, no reality. Life was all about happily-ever-after, and even if it weren't, you just ignored it."

"So you actually *prefer* this miserable side of me."

She smiled and glanced over at him. "Yeah … I think I do."

Billy enjoyed watching his students play football, cheer, and play in the band, and they were all thrilled to see him there. Apparently their struggles with the chemistry experiment didn't affect their ability to appreciate a good, close game. He also took great pleasure watching Sam interact with the students. He knew, for the most part, they were her whole life. She didn't have much going on where other relationships were concerned. She kept to herself and gave her energies to teaching.

The chit-chat between the two of them was easy and shallow at the game. He was thankful she gave up trying to pull out his problem, for in truth, it was all about her. At times it seemed all was fine between them and there still stood a chance of hope somewhere. Then in the middle of something, she would reveal all the pent up hurt she still held, and it seemed even a friendship would be impossible. He had to be careful, because the reality was that the only woman he had ever really loved was Sam. Every other girl in his life was purely passing … even his marriage to Kirstie. He knew his second marriage was mainly off the rebound from Sam, and he was half-drunk in the process. And then Angie, well, Angie was merely a dream … nothing more.

Kirstie. Sam. How could he tell Sam he had been married a second time, just a few months after their divorce? It would probably sever any ties he was struggling to hang on to right now. It would almost be as big an insult and hurt to her as their divorce had been. His best bet was to keep it a secret and hope she never found out. But what if she did? What if Cindy let it slip … or anyone else in Dockrey? But then again, exactly what was he hoping to gain from this rekindled relationship with Sam? Did he actually believe that somewhere down the road they might end up together again? Could she forgive him so fully that she would trust her heart to him? He doubted that, so why the anguish? Why not just tell her the truth, get it out in the open, and be done with it?

He looked over at her as she gently sang with the radio while driving down the road, occasionally lifting a finger to nudge her glasses up on her nose. He couldn't tell her. If there was even a small chance that this woman would take him back, he had to protect it at all costs. If it looked like things were going to happen, then he would come clean. Until then, total confession was senseless.

"You're in deep thought tonight," she remarked as the song ended. "What's running through your head, pretty boy?"

"You know me," he tried to make light of it. "I'm incapable of having a deep thought inside this muddled brain."

"Oh, I don't believe that."

"Which? The deep thought or the muddled brain?"

"The deep thought," she giggled. "I'll definitely agree with the muddling."

"Do you think it's possible for a brain to explode from so much stuff being crammed into it at one time? It's like I don't have a chance to breathe anymore, much less think deep thoughts. The depth of my thinking has to do with chemical equations and body organs. I must have been crazy to think this thirty-five year-old brain could handle such an endeavor."

"But look how far you've come," she reminded him. "A few more weeks and you'll be ready to take on the heart of the education system."

He laughed slightly. "I hope I can take it on half as well as you have."

"Shoot, by then you'll have figured out the perfect combination between ogre and dazzler, and all the rest of us will just be standing in your dust wondering what overtook us."

"Right," he mumbled as he lowered himself in the seat again.

As she pulled into the parking lot of the marina, he grabbed his coat from the back seat and began to put it on. Turning up the collar around his neck he prepared to face the biting cold he knew awaited him on the boat. He refused to keep the heat on when he wasn't there in order to save on propane, and right now he almost wished he could just lie down in the back seat of the car.

"Thanks for the ride," he told her sincerely as he delayed getting out. "It was a fun night."

"I enjoyed it too," she nodded as she kept her head straight ahead. "Are you going to Dockrey this weekend?"

"I don't think so. I was gonna go over all the lab reports and see if anyone was even close to knowing what they were doing."

He could see her smiling as she continued to look forward.

"What are you smiling about?" he asked her.

Without turning toward him, she explained, "All this seems so weird … this moment, I mean. When I knew you before, from the very first moment we met, you were always flirting with me. You would use any excuse you could to try and coax me into a snuggle or a kiss … or more." She grinned even bigger. "I used to make myself anticipate your advances so I could be prepared to ward you off, or at least appear to not enjoy them."

"Appear?"

"Yeah, as though I were harder to get than I really wanted to be."

"You *were* hard to get!" he exclaimed. "I wondered if you would ever warm up to me."

He could tell she was uncomfortable. He wasn't sure why, and he wasn't sure what this conversation was really about. In truth, he was thrilled to still be in the warm car, whatever the reason.

She continued, "I just kept telling myself it wasn't real—that you were playing some kind of game with me. I figured as long as I could make myself believe that, I'd be safe."

"Safe from what?"

"Your adamant advances."

"I'd say you held me off pretty good."

Her smile faded, but her head never turned. "On the outside maybe, but inside I had already embraced you. I knew it was only a matter of time before you found the key to break through my defenses, and when you finally did, I was almost relieved."

He was touched. She had never told him that before. She had always led him to believe that her feelings for him were shallow until their first night together. He reached for her hand and softly intertwined his fingers with hers. She squeezed back but still wouldn't face him.

"It's so easy for me at times to feel transported back to then," she almost whispered. "Times like now, when we've had fun, when there are no pressures, I can almost believe that life can be perfect again. Even now it seems like we should go back to the house, light up a fire, and throw a few blankets and pillows on the floor."

Immediately he was transported to those scenes. He held her hand tighter and then squeezed his eyes shut. Did she know what those thoughts did to him? Was she asking him to go home with her, or was she just sharing her heart? He had to stay clear-headed where she was concerned. He had devastated her once—he wasn't going to let himself do that to her again.

"Well," he tried to lighten the mood, "a nice fire sounds wonderful seeing that I'm about to walk into a rocking iceberg. Think of me when you step into your warm house."

She finally turned to him. "Every time I step through that door I think about you … every single day since you left. I always wonder why you're not there, what I did that was so wrong to warrant losing you."

"Sam …"

"I know, I know …" she let go of his hand, "it wasn't me … it was you." She sighed. "You can tell me that all you want, Billy, but I'll never completely believe it."

"But that's the truth," he insisted. "You were wonderful … you were fine."

"Then why couldn't you stay with me?"

"Because *they* all talked me out of it! They kept insisting I was missing out on … on what I used to think was life. A few drinks and a stroll down memory lane were very convincing."

"And I obviously wasn't."

"You can't believe that. Until I met you, I was this self-centered, egotistical jerk. You found something in me no one else ever did. Then those guys waltzed back in and reminded me of who I used to be, and how uncomplicated life had been, and they got me thinking. And I was thinking all the wrong things, Sam. I hated what I was doing to you … to us … but the booze could anesthetize all that. And somehow the idea that I was this macho, smooth-talking, looking-out-for-number-one type guy again made me feel … man, I don't know what."

"Free?" she offered.

He sighed. "I guess. Only I didn't realize then that I was never bound by you. You gave me all the freedom I wanted. You never complained, never nagged. And somewhere inside I knew all that too, but I had sort of set my course and was determined to drive you away."

"Well," she said with a sad smile as she put the car in gear, "congratulations—you succeeded."

Billy now looked out the front of the car. There was really nothing left to say. Apologizing was worthless. Atonement was impossible. In truth, he didn't even deserve to be sitting here with her having any kind of civil conversation. When all was said and done, he had destroyed the best part of his life when he had destroyed their marriage.

"I have no excuses, Sam," he finally confessed in the silence. "And the thing you said about feeling transported back in time, I never feel that way when I'm with you. I always remember what I did and what I shattered. When I look at you, I just feel guilt."

He opened the door and got out quickly. He pulled the collar of his jacket tighter around his neck and then thrust his hands into the pockets. He wanted to wait for her to leave, but she just sat there. He couldn't believe he was hurting her all over again—he didn't want that at all. Finally, he made his way toward the boat, his head down against the biting wind. Once on the deck, he looked back. She was at last pulling out of the lot.

"If I could go back, Sam, I would do it all so differently," he spoke softly through the cold, his breath showing in the frigid night. "I would treasure you in every way. I would give you the world … I would give you *my* world."

Twenty-Three

All day Saturday the sanctuary at First Baptist of Dockrey was spotted with many members, in and out throughout the day, on their knees. Prayers were being offered up for Michael, Angie, and especially little Carter and all that would ensue during the coming weeks. Someone would stand and pray for the surgery, then another would feel led to pray for the treatments. Many stood to pray for Angie as she prepared to deliver another child in the midst of it all. Some prayed for Cassie and how all this would affect her as she was away from the only home she had known and wouldn't see her parents or brother for days at a time.

As the day of prayer and fasting drew to an end, Michael and Angie felt encouraged that all was under the watchful eye of a loving heavenly Father. No matter what happened, they would be given the strength to endure. No matter the results, life would indeed go on, and it would still be filled with purpose and meaning.

That night, as they lay in bed, Angie reached over and took his hand. "Thank you for being such a rock through all of this," she whispered to him. "Your faith that God will work it out for the best has been a huge comfort to me."

He put his arm around her and pulled her close. "I know you may find this hard to believe, but I'll always see my worst days as behind me. Nothing, not even this, compares with what life was like growing up. Carter knows love. He knows peace. He knows true serenity and acceptance and joy. I don't want to lose him, Angie, and I don't want him to know pain or suffering, but I would choose all of that for him … and for us … over what my life was like as a child."

She shivered at the thought. To her, this was the worst scenario imaginable, but he was right—things could indeed be more unbearable.

"Keep reminding me of that, okay?" she said sincerely. "And keep reminding me that we have more than one child to consider through all of this. I was touched by the prayers people prayed for Cassie and for this little one inside right now. Sometimes, Michael, I feel like if I lose Carter, I'll lose everything … like I won't be able to go on, but God has given us two others … two little gifts that need the same love and devotion."

"Don't worry about that. You're doing wonderfully with the others. You eat well …"

"Very well," she giggled slightly.

"Which is good. And you even rest well. This little one," he touched her tummy, "is being treated just fine. And as independent as Cassie is, it's almost like God made her that way just for this moment. She's really enjoyed spending time with your parents and has astounded them with her *essence.*"

She snickered. "Good word, sweetie. She's never been a clingy child, has she?"

"No. And right now she's surrounded by grandparents, aunts, uncles, and cousins who are more than thrilled to take up where we might have to leave off on occasion."

She breathed a sigh of genuine relief as she snuggled closer to his chest. When the baby gave a strong kick, he placed his hand down on her stomach again and rubbed it gently.

"How do you sleep with all that going on?" he asked her, having felt the kick against his side.

"You know me, once I'm asleep I'm out for the night, except the occasional trip to the potty. Also, these punches remind me that this little one is doing just fine. That's a good enough reason to drift off into peaceful sleep."

"This is a really big baby."

"Tell me about it—feels like an octopus sometimes."

Her voice was getting groggy. He kissed the top of her head and rubbed her shoulder. "Good night, Dr. Angie. Sweet dreams."

"Good night," she murmured lazily. "Sleep tight. Don't let the bed bugs bite."

✪✪✪

Jonathan lay in bed with a sense of peace for the first time in a long while. The strength and maturity the church had shown today in their support and care for his family had encouraged him. Even if the devil himself were to walk into the church, there would always be a remnant that would know and recognize real truth.

"You okay?" Barbara asked as she turned in the bed to face him. "You haven't slept all night."

"Was I keeping you awake?"

"No. I couldn't sleep either. I wish somehow I could take all this away from Angie and Michael. I wish I had the power to just put my hands on that little boy and make him whole again."

"Welcome the rod, honey," he said soberly. "Welcome the rod."

She leaned up on an elbow and asked with astonishment, "Have we had a change of heart suddenly?"

He smiled through the darkness, through *all* of the darkness, and replied, "I think we have."

"So you don't think the church is about to call a monster to work with you?"

"On the contrary, I think that's exactly what's about to happen. But

God has a plan; He's up to something. I don't know what He's gonna do through all this, but whatever it is, I'll accept it as from His hand, and pray that my integrity will hold together."

She reached over and gently touched his cheek. "You are indeed a man of character and integrity, Jonathan Wright. You'll make it through this."

He took her hand and gently kissed it. "Only because I have you beside me through it all. Who would've ever thought that life's journey would've taken us this far. I think back to those first years when we were married."

"That first church was horrible," she reminisced with him. "I was ready for you to quit the ministry."

"Really? You never told me that."

"Of course not! I knew God had called you to pastor. It wasn't *my* plan. I knew the Lord enough to know that I needed to support you, not pull you away from your destiny."

"Destiny," he chuckled. "That makes it all sound so noble."

"It is noble, sweetie. And even through all that, God still provided the support we needed."

"You're thinking of the Adams, aren't you?"

"Yes," she agreed with a fond memory. "They sent us away to their condo on the beach for a week to let us escape a bit … and gather our thoughts."

"We'd never been to anything so plush in all our lives."

"Nor have been since."

"Nope. And what a week it was. Eating incredible food, watching the sunrise on the balcony."

"I'll never forget something you said that last morning we were there."

"I know what you're thinking," he broke in. "We had gotten up early, while it was still dark, just so we could see the entire sunrise."

"We sat out there on that balcony, awed by the incredible beauty of something so common, and you said, 'Go God! Keep on making the common things look breathtaking.' And then you turned to me and told me that our life was just like that summer sunrise. Every day we got up, we could either choose to see the beauty in this world, or we could choose to see the common."

"And that's where we are now, Barb. Each morning, the sun *will* rise. Carter *will* have surgery. This church *will* call a new man to come in and take control. Life *will* go on … but in the midst of it all, each day *will* have a sunrise. And we can see the beauty and the glory of God in it, or we can see the struggles that are just a natural part of life on earth."

She gave a small laugh. "Stephen Williams has nothing over you. That was some of the most poetic talk I've ever heard! If only you could sing, sweetie."

☼☼☼

Jonathan still felt that peace as he stood in the pulpit the next morning and announced the plans for the following weekend.

"Our search committee has invited Dr. Hal Bridges to visit this coming weekend," he explained with a smile. "It seems they believe this man is the one to help lead our church in a new direction. He will arrive on Friday evening and be staying at the bed and breakfast with his wife, Lisa. On Saturday, I'll walk him around the church and show him all the facilities, the plans for the new building project, and discuss the programs going on here at present. On Saturday evening, we'll have a church-wide covered dish supper at six o'clock so everyone can get a chance to meet him. He'll preach next Sunday morning, and then we'll vote after the service on whether to extend him a call. I hope you all will attend and pray for God's direction concerning the calling of a new staff member. I know this is short notice, but when things start moving, sometimes we just need to take a big breath and catch up."

The congregation laughed gently. They loved their pastor. As was typical, his tie was already loosened, his hair was disheveled, but his pleasant expression and genuine heart made every person sitting in a pew feel at ease and at home. They had no way of knowing that in his spirit he was already offering deep intercession for this body that he knew would very soon come under attack from the enemy like never before. As Kyle began the worship time, Jonathan focused his mind on the Lord, and prayed for wisdom to speak words that would encourage this congregation to hang on to the Lord with all their might.

The whole morning worship seemed odd to Annie. First, there was at last the diminishing of the paparazzi down to only two obvious ones. When they had first come back to Dockrey this past summer, they couldn't dream of going to church or anywhere else, except for her parents' house which still had a twelve-foot fence surrounding it. The tabloids were insisting Stephen and Annie had left New York for Alabama because they were having *serious marital problems* and needed to work through some things. Many *sources close to the couple* had given exclusive interviews describing the deep conflicts going on inside their marriage away from the public eye. For about three months, photographers roosted and hovered in the town hoping for a photo to either prove or disprove the international claims being published. After awhile, however, when the only evidence was that the Williams' had indeed retired and were enjoying family life, with no intentions of putting out any new albums or doing any more tours, the interest began to wane. The past month had allowed Stephen and Annie to almost become *normal.* The one thing going for them was the small-town life of Dockrey.

There were no other celebrities within hundreds of miles, so for a tabloid to camp in the dinky place with no hope of any news for months on end, wasted time was becoming wasted money. She grinned to herself as one of the obvious photographers kept leaning around a pew for a glance at the famous couple. She simply scooted closer to Stephen, at which he put his arm around her shoulder and gave her a loving smile, unaware she was still trying to discourage the rumors.

The second odd thing in church was Billy Marcum. This had been the third time this month he had shown up for a service. She knew it couldn't be Angie because he had attended even before she returned. Why he was here wasn't obvious, because he remained preoccupied throughout the entire service. He never sang a song, never looked at a Bible, and never even glanced at Jonathan during the sermon. Annie knew he had returned to school and was almost finished—a miracle in itself—but to see him in church again was mind-boggling. It reminded her of high school when he and Angie were on-again off-again with their romance. During the off-again times, he would sit with his parents and look as though the world had come to an end, and that was exactly how he looked at this moment.

Then third, there was her father's sermon. He was a good preacher, but today there was a passion in his voice that almost begged the church to not be deceived but to always be on its guard. She watched in bewilderment as tears came to his eyes several times and emotion choked his voice. She chalked it up to the situation with Angie and Carter. This was difficult for everyone in the family, but what else could be expected? Angie had waited far too long to get medical attention for her son's condition, and now the prognosis was more bleak than any wanted to accept.

When Annie, Stephen, and their two little ones walked out of the church that morning, no strangers followed. She squeezed his hand and said, "I don't think we're famous anymore."

He winked down at her and nodded. "Feels weird, doesn't it?"

"I have an idea," she said with a wide grin. "Since no one's going to Moms' and Dad's today because Angie and Michael want some alone time with Cassie and Carter, why don't I call Andie and see if we can get some chicken and fixins and go over there for Sunday dinner?"

Andie was delighted, so Stephen drove through Jack's, picked up the food, and the blue Escalade headed toward the Mason residence.

After filling up on fried chicken and mashed potatoes with gravy, the adults sat around the back deck and watched the children attempt to out-do each other on the swing Doug had made.

"Thanks for lunch, guys," Andie said as she tried to arrange her thickly bandaged ankle into a more comfortable position. "The kids were really bummed when they found out Moms wasn't making dinner today."

Doug sighed, "Apparently my children don't like my cooking."

"Tell them it could be worse," Stephen suggested. "I could be the one having to cook for them."

Annie laughed. "That *would* be worse. Stephen can't cook a thing. I do think he's learned how to warm water in the microwave now."

"It's weird not being at Moms' and Dad's on Sunday," Andie bemoaned. "It's like I've done that forever. But I understand. I can't imagine what Michael and Angie are going through right now. All my kids are very healthy and always have been."

"Ours too," Stephen agreed. "It reminds me of all I have to be thankful for."

Annie sighed one of her moody sighs and shook her head. "I do feel sorry for them in one sense, but in another, they sort of brought all this on themselves."

With that statement, every adult eye turned toward her in question.

"Oh, come on," she said soberly, "you can't tell me that if one of those kids out there," she pointed toward the group at the swing, "couldn't walk by fifteen or sixteen months, we wouldn't have drug them to every doctor in this vicinity until an answer had be given."

Andie quickly defended, "But Angie doesn't live in this *vicinity*. She doesn't have access to all the specialists we do."

"But she could have had access," Annie spoke back immediately. "She could have brought Carter back to the States with a medical emergency or something. Nothing was holding her there except her own blind hope. And the fact that she's a doctor makes the whole thing more unbelievable. She even said that this tumor thing was pretty much what she had anticipated."

"But Padawin is different," Andie tried to explain how Angie's heart works. "There people deal with handicaps and illnesses in their own way. To them they're just a natural part of life. People aren't ostracized for their differences. No one was hounding her right and left about what might be *wrong* or *abnormal* about her child."

"Please," Annie was now becoming more sarcastic and defensive. "If I had lived on the moon, and my child couldn't walk, I'd have found a way to float back if I had to. It's like Angie chose to bury her head in the sand, and Michael obviously didn't have what it took to pull it out until now. She actually wanted to stay in Padawin until after Christmas! Can you imagine? What was she thinking?"

Andie was now getting a little sarcastic and defensive herself. "She was thinking that she was in Padawin because of God's calling, and that He would give and take away and deal with her as He saw fit."

"He also gave her a brain to know when her child needed extra help."

"And He gave her a heart that kept her where she was until now."

Stephen and Doug had long since stopped contributing to the conversation. When two Wright girls start going at each other, the best thing is to stay out of the middle. However, when they're going at each other over the case of the third sister, it's close to dangerous to even be in earshot.

"You've got to be kidding me," Annie groaned. "You're gonna take up for her over this?"

"What do you expect me to do? Condemn her? The fact is the decision has already been made. She's here now, Carter's been diagnosed, and treatment begins this week. I'm choosing to support her and be whatever she needs me to be at this present time."

"I'm not saying this to her face," Annie insisted. "And I wouldn't. But I'm not gonna pretend with the rest of you that I think her choices were wise. I think what she did was stupid and that if Carter … well … if he doesn't make it, she's ultimately to blame."

"Don't you think she feels that way already? She's not walking around with her head in the clouds oblivious to reality. She knows the cost of time. But what's the point of dwelling on what can't be changed? She needs our support and our love and our prayers, so that's what I'm giving her."

"I didn't say I wasn't giving her those things, I'm just saying that if God doesn't pull out a miracle here, we don't need to sit around and say *Oh, it was just Carter's time … he was just put here for a little bit.* I think she made a grave mistake, and I think the consequences could be severe."

"What if God does choose to pull out a miracle?" Stephen suddenly interjected. Everyone looked at him in shock, especially Doug. "He could, you know. When Lazarus was sick, Jesus deliberately delayed heading that way because He had something other than healing in mind. He was gonna let Lazarus die and then raise him from the dead. I believe God's will is gonna be done one way or the other where Carter is concerned. If God had wanted him here a year ago, he would've been here a year ago." Stephen paused as he saw Annie fuming inside, but then added, "Carter's here now. God will do exactly what He wants. And it doesn't matter what Angie did or didn't do—God is ultimately in control."

Annie stared in silence for only a moment then said, "Gee, maybe you should take up preaching now that you're out of the entertainment business."

She had very little to say the rest of the afternoon.

Twenty-Four

Billy lay back on the couch at Cindy's house with a glass of iced tea and a full stomach. The twins and Kylla were engrossed in some movie where a cucumber was singing opera in a bathroom. He wondered if the movie writer felt like all creativity had been spent on cute little animals to the point that we now had to resort to singing vegetables for entertainment. Complain as he might, he found himself caught up in the story and even laughed so loud once that Denay asked him to quiet down. As the movie ended and Kylla put in another of the same kind for round two, he decided to look for the adults and find some more mature conversation.

It didn't take long for him to hear serious tones of talking out in the sunroom. The door was open, so he walked on in to find a tearful Cindy and a forlorn Kyle.

"Am I interrupting?" he asked cautiously.

"No," she said softly. "Come on out and take my mind somewhere else."

"If you want your mind elsewhere, go in there with the kids. They're watching vegetables sing and dance around a bathroom," Billy suggested.

Cindy smiled and shook her head. "I know those movies by heart. Give me a new distraction. What's the latest in your life?"

He sat down and placed his empty tea glass on a side table. "Not much. I'm still doing the student-teaching, I still live on a houseboat, and I've been totally broke—financially-speaking—for a good three years now. What's the latest with you guys?" He grinned big.

"I wish Mom's estate could give you more money a month," Cindy told him.

"Hey, I'm not complaining. That estate has paid for my schooling … schooling that Mom had no idea of knowing if I would complete or not. The extra five hundred dollars pays for docking fees, electricity, propane, and motorcycle gas. It feeds me for the most part … not well … but enough to live with. Why do you think I drive down here whenever I can? I know you probably think it's my fascination with the fact that you can cook a roast now, but the truth is I just need a good meal now and then."

"Why don't you take the leftovers back with you?" she suggested. "We're always throwing most of them out. The kids aren't big roast fans."

"Gladly!"

"So what's the latest with Sam? Why didn't she come this weekend?"

He groaned softly as he placed his hands behind his head. "I didn't ask her to come. We went to the game together Friday night and sort of had a … I don't know what it was … an uncomfortable discussion, I suppose."

"About what?"

"Us," he said vaguely.

She sat up a little straighter. "Us? I didn't realize you guys were an *Us* again."

"Technically, we're not. It just seems like we end up together a lot because of our working situation. Inevitably we wind up talking about the past, and it usually ends up with me being a jerk again and Sam being a victim."

"Well, that's pretty much what happened."

He glared over at her. "Believe me, I know that. I don't need you or her reminding me about it whenever the opportunity arises."

"I don't want to see her hurt again."

"And you think I do?"

"I don't know, but I hope not."

"I have no intentions of ever hurting her again. I know what I did was deplorable."

"Well then, what are you doing with her now? Please don't tell me that you have some kind of hope for reconciliation."

"Have I ever said that?"

She looked out through the glassed-in room and shook her head. "It's just been a hard day—a hard weekend—for me. Angie's little boy has a massive tumor on his spine. He goes in for surgery this week. Until they get inside and get a real look at it, they don't know what kind of prognosis to offer."

"Wow," he said sympathetically. "I had no idea. When Pastor Jon said to remember them in prayer, I just thought he was talking about the new baby. They seemed so happy when we were here the other day."

"They are," she confirmed. "Their faith is strong. I don't know if I could face something like that with the same kind of strength. I guess that's why the whole thing with Sam and you scares me. I don't want to see another person unnecessarily hurt."

"I'm not gonna hurt her, Cindy."

"Not on purpose," she said doubtfully.

He blew out the tension in a deep breath and shook his head. "What do you think I'm gonna do to her?"

"For starters, dating her is a bad idea … a bad idea from the get-go."

"I'm not *dating* her," he asserted this time. "It's far from that, believe me."

"Promise me you won't then."

He gave a frustrated look. "I can't promise that exclusively. Right now I'm in no position to date anyone, and that includes Sam. But I can't say what might happen down the road."

"Get your degree, graduate, and get a job. Get settled down and stable. When you're totally out of transition, then maybe …" She closed her eyes and then shook her head again. "Goodness, Billy, maybe not even then." She got up and started to leave the room. "This is just as depressing as Angie's situation."

"No one's dying here," Billy interjected.

"If you start seeing Sam again, she might as well be dead." And with that she left.

Billy looked over at Kyle. "She absolutely doesn't trust me. Doesn't she think I'm capable of change?"

Kyle smiled slightly and gave a sideways nod. "I believe she thinks you're capable—she just wants to see it all happen first."

Billy stood and went to a long pane of glass. "What else can I do? I quit everything I was to go back to school and become a *responsible* adult. I'm on the last leg of getting my Master's. What do I have to do to prove to her that I'm worthy of at least a little respect."

Kyle sat back thoughtfully before he answered. "She's proud of you—she really is. And she's seen the changes. But with Sam, she's worried. It's hard for her to think that when it comes to women … well … that you're actually capable of change. She's afraid if anything really bad were to happen to Sam again, it might push her over the edge … or something."

Billy made no comment but continued to stare out the window. He agreed with Cindy. But what if Sam wanted to try again? Sometimes it seemed like she really wanted to start over and forget the past. Then at other times it seemed like the past loomed between them larger than ever.

Kyle stood up and went over to him. "It's sort of like you and Sam are in the fourth quarter of the game and you're two points behind. Your team has the ball, fourth down, ten to go, with fifty yards to the goal. You're the quarterback, Billy. You hold the options and you call the play."

Billy chuckled and nodded. "True."

"The easiest thing here would be to go for a field goal. If you make it, you win."

"Fifty yards is a long try for a field goal."

"Exactly! Or, you could send your only receiver, Sam, down the field for a mega pass. There's a fifty-fifty chance it could work."

Billy nodded, then asked, "And if it doesn't?"

"Sam blames herself … again … even though it was your pass …

and your call. See, you left her, but in her mind, it was because of her. And look, women are just like that. They internalize everything. You can tell her until you're blue in the face that your divorce was all about you … but the truth is, Billy, you handed her the ball, and when the game was over, she felt like it was her fault."

This made sense to Billy. For the first time he began to understand what she must have felt through the divorce. "So, coach, what do you suggest I do?"

"Keep the ball," Kyle said simply. "Don't give Sam the chance to fail this time. Finish student teaching and there's a first down. Get a job, and you have another first down. Get rid of the boat and get a real life and move on down the field. Then when you're close to the goal, and it's not impossible, give the ball to Sam and let her have the chance to score again. Only this time, you let her win the game."

He turned to Kyle and offered his hand. Kyle took it and shook it.

"Thanks," Billy said sincerely. "And all this time I thought you were just a sissy musician."

"Hey, if vegetables can sing, I can surely draw parallels from football to be used in the game of life."

Twenty-Five

Annie marveled again at the unusual conviction with which her father preached during the evening worship. For most of the service she still reeled over Stephen's contradiction with her that afternoon. She knew she probably had stepped over the line a bit, but she was talking with Andie, with family, and it was never meant for Angie's ears. She was just speaking her mind, something she had always done. True, it had gotten her into much trouble over the years, but family accepts you for who you are. This was one thing she had looked forward to with being back in Dockrey. In New York she had to constantly be on her toes in the public eye. At every turn there was a photographer or a reporter flashing a camera or screaming questions. One wrong look or biting word could turn a bad mood into a full-blown, press-created, mega situation. This was home, and she should have the freedom to make mistakes, or to simply be herself again.

Near the end of the service, she reached over and took Stephen's hand, her first gesture of communication with him since the incident. He looked at her in surprise. She smiled warmly and just held his hand. She didn't want to be at odds with him. He was her life, her love, and her dream.

Things seemed fine as they all said their good-byes while leaving from church. Stevie and Ellie took up most of the conversation and busyness as they drove home and then prepared for bed. When Ellie was down, she looked around the house for Stephen and finally found him outside on the pool's deck.

"Mind if I join you?" she asked innocently.

"Only if you promise to be nice," he replied in the darkness.

She ignored the hint of sarcasm and sat with him on the gliding loveseat. "I don't want this to be hanging over us, Stephen. I want to clear the air."

He stared out over the moonlit valley behind the pool. "Annie, I know you relish the right to speak your mind," he began, "but you don't need to always exercise that right without restraint."

"I thought you liked the fact that I'm opinionated and stubborn. You said when you married me it would keep life from being boring."

He didn't reply right away. "When we married, I used to leave my towels on the floor, drop my clothes wherever I was finished with them, leave my shoes wherever they came off, and I never carried a finished coffee cup to the kitchen. I didn't need to. I had a hired staff all around me who was paid to clean up my messes."

He got up from the seat and walked over to the edge of the pool where the moon was reflecting on the still, clear water.

"What's your point?" she asked as she remained seated.

He turned back to face her in the darkness. "I hang up my used towels now, and I throw my clothes in the clothes hamper. I put my shoes in the closet, and not only do I take my cups to the kitchen, but I rinse them out and place them in the dishwasher."

She gave no response.

"You told me I should do those things because it made me a better man. Leaving my messes for other people—when all it took was less than a minute of my time—was evidence of a lack of character." He looked back to the valley. "I took your words to heart and allowed myself to change."

She saw now where he was heading. Part of her was hurt because of the criticism, but a larger part was growing angrier each moment. Adrenaline was rushing through her body, and she knew if she didn't get control, she would lash out at him.

"Your words can cause some pretty horrible messes, Annie," he finally put out. "And I feel it shows a lack of character, just as much as me leaving wet towels in the middle of the floor for you to step over or for Mabel to pick up and wash. I made the effort to change my thinking and my actions."

She bit her lip with emotion. She was being scolded, and she didn't like it at all. He had no right to treat her as though she were a mindless child. "What I said today wasn't meant as some declaration in stone," she said slowly through her anger. "I was with family, and I was just sharing some thoughts I had about my family."

"No," he said with a bit more firmness and conviction. "It wasn't just about family; it was about Angie. Next to me, she's the closest person to you in the world. Do you know how that scares me? What kind of things do you feel about me? What kind of innocent mistakes have I made that you've judged and criticized in your head?"

"I was just making an observation," she said with frustration as she at last stood and walked over to him beside the pool. "They were feelings I had that I wanted to verbalize and get out."

"They were feelings you should have kept to yourself and removed from your mind."

"So I have to weigh my words from now on?" she asked bitterly. "I don't have the freedom to speak my mind or express my opinion? Suddenly everything I say and do is on trial?"

"Yes," he said plainly. "I learned to pick up my towels because it was a right thing to do. You can learn that sometimes laying your opinions out in the open is *not* a right thing to do. Sometimes you need to think before you speak, and you need to make sure no one is gonna be left cleaning up the emotional mess you leave when you *speak your mind* or *share your opinion*."

She held back the anger that was longing to be unleashed. She had given him a piece of her mind a few times before they had fallen in love and married, but for six years, she had only adored him. At this moment she was wondering if she had made a big mistake. Had he felt this way all along but never said anything? Was this just the tip of the iceberg?

Rather than speak, she turned to leave.

"So, that's it?" he asked. "Nothing to say?"

She turned back and spat out, "I'm weighing my words. You'd rather not hear what I have to say at the moment."

"On the contrary, I'd love to hear what you have to say. I'd like to know if any of this is sinking in, or if you're gonna let it all simmer and fester until it explodes anyway."

She looked at him in astonishment. "What are you saying to me? In the years I've known you, you've never treated me like this. Suddenly I feel like an outcast, like I don't deserve you or your forgiveness."

"So far, I've heard no apology or request for forgiveness."

"Why should I say I did something wrong when I did what I've always done? There was no personal attack in my comments!" she yelled in her frustration.

"Everything about it was personal!" he matched her tone. "Here is your sister, Angie, with the biggest heart in the world, giving her life and her family for the sake of the gospel, and because she didn't jump in a manner that was consistent with your liking, you say she deserves any retribution that's heaped upon her!"

"Well, then maybe you married the wrong sister!" Her anger had finally reached its breaking point. "Obviously my heart is pitifully small and unable to muster up whatever is necessary to make me loving enough to please you. I had no idea we had all these issues lurking beneath the surface."

"Don't make this argument about us." He wouldn't let her out so easily. "This is about your insensitivity to someone very close to you who needs your support at this moment more than any other time in her life."

"And I am supportive of her!"

"Baloney!" He stepped over to where she was standing near the French doors to the house. "Every time she says something in the future, you'll look at Andie or me and roll your eyes like we all have this little private knowledge about how incapable Angie is. I don't want to be a part of that game, and Andie didn't either. And when you put your arms around Angie and tell her everything will be all right, I don't want to be sickened by some two-faced put-on that you're doing!"

"Stop it!" she screamed out this time. She breathed deeply to gain control of her senses. "Enough." She was slow and deliberate. "I don't know what kind of fiend you think I am, but I'm not the person you're describing."

"Sometimes," he slouched, "you can be." He walked back toward the pool. "You can tear me apart if you want, and you can tear down my musicians, but don't do this to Angie … not right now."

She stared in silence as her body literally pumped from rage. She knew at this point it would be better to leave his presence than continue to try and reason with him. She opened one of the doors and walked through into the house. She was startled to find Stevie standing there, wide-eyed and fearful.

"Mommy?" he asked cautiously. "Are you and Daddy mad?"

She knelt down beside him and pulled him into a gentle embrace. He had heard. They had never fought like this before, and even she was fearful about what had just transpired. She pulled him back and looked him in the eye. "It's okay," she assured him. "We're just tired and need to go to bed."

She took his hand and led him back to his own room where she tucked him in again and kissed his forehead.

"Don't worry, Stevie," she tried to sound confident. "Everything's all right. Sleep tight, okay?"

"Okay." He seemed to believe her.

She left the room and stood in the hallway. What did she do now? The adrenaline had eased, and all she felt was exhaustion from the day and extreme panic about where she stood with Stephen. He wasn't backing down or showing any sense of contrition, yet her stubbornness was insisting he had made more of this than was there. To admit she was wrong would be … well … admitting she was wrong. And Annie Wright Williams was never wrong.

She turned toward the bedroom, but she knew she would never sleep in this kind of condition. She also knew it was highly unlikely that Stephen would join her in their bed that night. They had never spent a night apart and had never gone to bed angry. Was she so stubborn that she was willing to sacrifice all that was wonderful in her marriage to simply protect her pride?

God, why is this so hard?, she whispered in aggravation. *Am I really that bad? Is that really what I've become? I was just … sharing … just passing on my thoughts … just talking sister to sister. I wasn't condemning. Stephen misunderstood. Why should I apologize for something that didn't really happen?*

Praying was the wrong action for trying to justify her situation, because as she finished pleading her case to God, the conviction finally came. She could see the selfishness, the thoughtlessness, and then the stubbornness that had followed. Now she had to decide which was more important—to save face with herself, or to go to Stephen and admit she was wrong. The thought of sleeping alone for the first time in six years was sobering. She headed for the outside deck.

He still stood by the water in the moonlight. Not only had she dishonored her sister through all of this, she had lashed out at him too. Eating humble pie was literally something Annie had never done before in her life. She wasn't even sure how to start. When he didn't look back to see who had opened the door, she knew this would be harder than she hoped.

"I don't exactly know how to make all of this right, Stephen," she confessed delicately. "All I know is that I've hurt the people I care about most."

He continued staring out toward the valley as he said, "You do know how to make it right, Annie. You just don't want to do it."

She walked up beside him. "True. This is very hard for me."

He wouldn't respond.

"You're not gonna make it easy for me at all, are you?" she asked as she began to feel remorse sweep over her.

"I've watched you do this over and over again, but today … this was too far. It was really, really wrong."

She closed her eyes, sighed deeply, and finally acknowledged, "I *was* wrong." Tears began to sting her eyes as she longed for him to reach out to her, and anguish began to pierce her heart as he remained silent and unmoved in the night. "I admit that what I said today was from a heart that is judgmental and critical. I know that I have my own … standards … and ideals. And when people fall short of them in my estimation, I'm quick to announce it. I also know that just because I feel a certain way about something, it doesn't mean it's the only way … or even the right way to feel."

He slowly turned toward her. "Do you realize how many times I lie down at night and wonder what you're judging me about? What standards have I failed to meet in your eyes?"

She shook her head and insisted, "Stephen, I love you more than anything. I don't judge you."

"You love Angie. You love your parents. But you're quick to cut them down to size when you talk to me about them some times."

"That's just passing talk," she tried to justify again.

"And who do you pass talk around with concerning me?"

She could sense his fear now. She wanted to take his hand and guarantee him she would lay down her life for him if it was necessary, yet here she was refusing to fully humble herself before him. If she couldn't be honest with Stephen, what hope was there? If her pride was so strong that she was willing to sacrifice him, what could life possibly hold for her?

"I'm sorry," she said in total embarrassment. "I guess I've always been like this … and everyone has always just accepted this about me … probably because they were afraid to counter me. I never want you to fear what I think about you or ever doubt my love for you. Sometimes, Stephen, my heart gets so black when I don't understand other people. I guess there was this part of me that was angry with Angie for not doing something sooner." A tear escaped. "I don't want her to go through this pain. I don't want her to lose Carter. I suppose being judgmental toward her helped to take away some of my pain … maybe. Maybe blaming her was a way to ease … I don't know … all she would feel if something horrible happened."

She stepped back a bit and wiped her eyes. "It doesn't really make sense. It's just this mechanism I've developed over the years to somehow harden me to the hurts of others. I guess … I don't know." She sniffed a few times and then added, "But I don't like it."

He turned toward her and gradually reached out his hand. As much as she wanted to take it, for the first time in her life she felt she didn't deserve it. She didn't deserve him. She didn't deserve two wonderful, healthy, adorable children. She didn't deserve the closeness of two sisters or the support of her parents. She had been blessed beyond most, but she had been too blind to really see what she had.

"I don't like it either, Annie," he said gently. "There's so much I love and adore about you, but this part of you has always scared me."

He stepped closer to her and took her hand this time.

"Can you forgive me?" she asked as she looked up into his face barely visible in the moonlight. "Can you help me move past this? Can you show me how to open my heart instead of protecting it with all these tactics I've used over the course of my life?"

"I was alone for so long, Annie, that when I found you, I was afraid to open my heart too. And you blew me off royally, you know."

"I was just as scared as you were," she admitted.

"No you weren't—because if I walked out on you, you had a family to fall back on. I had nothing … no one. And over the years, every time you've started in on someone, my gut would go into knots wondering how you really felt about me."

"I love you, Stephen. I really do," she wanted him to believe the depth of her commitment. "I could never hurt you."

"But you hurt others so easily, others whom you love too."

"I know that now," she said as another tear fell from her eye. "And I've been so wrong."

He put his arms all the way around her and pulled her close to his body. "You're so complex. I sometimes feel like I'm drowning around you. I love our life, Annie. I love living here, and living together. I love our kids. I love our family. I love playing cards and watching old movies with you. But I get so scared that one day you're gonna wake up and find out that I'm not really this major entertainer … all of that was just an act … I didn't know what else to do. The truth is I'm just a simple guy who likes simple things like sunsets and laughter. I don't want to have to second guess my every move. I just want to be able to sit back and do nothing if that's how I feel, or get out and do it all if that's how I feel … and not be judged about my timing or my motives."

She pulled her head back and gently kissed him with trembling lips. "You can do anything you want, and I'll be right by your side, adoring you the whole way."

"That's all I want. I just want to trust you, Annie. I want to trust that what I hear you say and see you do is for real. Don't hide from me."

"I won't," she promised. "I'm yours, heart and soul. If you can learn to pick up towels, it's time I learned to weigh my words."

"Heart and soul?" he asked hesitantly. "What about body?"

She gave a small smile. "I thought you'd never ask."

This time her kiss was far from gentle. When he scooped her in his arms, she let out a burst of laughter at the thought.

"What's so funny?" he asked as he nudged the door closed behind them.

"Are you actually carrying me up to the bedroom?"

"Unless you'd rather stop at the couch?"

She glanced over to it. "Stevie's been up once already. I'd hate for him to walk in on us. He'd never see the couch the same again."

"The bedroom it is then."

As he carried her down the hall, she kissed him again and again. Humble pie was much better than she had ever imagined.

Twenty-Six

"Moms, tell me you're kidding," Annie bellowed over the phone early Monday morning after taking Stevie to Kindergarten. "Exactly what did the headline say?"

"I'm holding it in my hand, sweetie. It says *The Real Reason the Williams Left for Alabama*, and then it has a picture of you and Angie embracing. Beneath that it says, *Annie Comforts Sister over Dying Son.*"

"For crying out loud," she moaned as she poured another cup of coffee. "So much for no more paparazzi. I wondered why people suddenly appeared outside the fence again this morning. How many were at your house?"

"At least fifty or so were at the front gate."

"Also, so much for Stephen and I going to Memphis tomorrow for the surgery."

"I'm so sorry, Annie. I know you wanted to be there for Angie," her mother tried to comfort.

"Does she know yet?"

"They're all still asleep as far as I know."

"When do they leave today?"

"They have to check in at four-thirty. I think they're planning on leaving around one o'clock."

Annie hated this part of her life. Somehow the press had gotten wind of Carter's situation, and now that would be the story for Stephen and Annie the next few weeks. They would be followed again everywhere they went, limiting their travels to only the Wrights' house. No church for at least another month. The news seekers would also inundate Angie and Michael with questions and photographs. She had better alert the Memphis police and get them planning on security control at the hospital right away.

"Why don't you let me bring something over for lunch so we can spend a little time with them before they go?" Annie suggested.

"Way ahead of you. I'm making a big pot of potato soup for everyone who wants to come. Just come on over whenever you all get going."

"Thanks, Moms, and I really am sorry about all this."

"Would you stop fretting about it? We all accept this is just a part of your life now. In fact, the lack of people camping outside the fence at my house has almost seemed strange of late. We're back to normal now." Barbara gave a little laugh.

Stephen walked in as she hung up the phone. He snuggled her from the back and gave a growl.

"Morning, my beast," she said, setting down her cup and turning to face him. "You're up early."

"I'm working toward actually seeing the sunrise again one of these days," he told her. "Coffee ready?"

"If I'm up, there's coffee." She pointed him toward the pot. "You're never gonna believe what happened today."

"Today? It's barely started. How could something already have happened that's actually newsworthy?" he said hunting for his favorite mug.

"Moms went to the grocery store this morning and found a major tabloid posting the story of Carter's cancer."

He jerked his head toward her and his face grew white. "No way! How?"

"Who knows? But it literally makes me sick to my stomach."

He stopped dealing with his coffee and stared into space. "Maybe it was a bad idea coming back here after all. If they can't dig anything up on us, they start on your family. How low can these people go?"

"Pretty low. Moms says there's a picture of me hugging Angie and they're claiming this is the real reason we came back to Alabama." She frowned at him and added, "At least they think our marriage is back on track."

He shook his head as he finished stirring his coffee and grabbed a piece of cheese toast from the tray on the stove. "Is it warm enough to have breakfast outside?"

"It's a little too chilly for my tastes. You Yankees would probably have no problem with it." She grinned at him and winked.

"How long do I have to live down here before I stop being a Yankee?"

"Hmmm, we'll see," she said as she motioned him toward the den.

✪✪✪

When Stephen and Annie left later that morning, the gate at their own house was packed with strangers again.

"These people need to get a life," Annie grumbled as the guards cleared a path for the Escalade to pass.

"This is their life," Stephen responded.

"I still wonder how they all found out."

"All it takes is one to dig up some dirt, and within hours the whole world knows."

"Sometimes I wish we kept a machine gun in here and I could just open a window and go to town on them all—watching them fall and start running for their lives … one by one."

He sniggered. "Yeah, that would stop the whole paparazzi thing—

Annie Williams on trial for killing thirty-two running innocents with cameras."

"Well, at least it'd be the *truth* instead of all the baloney they make up most of the time."

The Wright house was just as bad. People were snapping pictures right and left and screaming out questions to Annie. She refused to look anywhere but straight ahead.

"Nasty mens," Ellie muttered from the back seat.

Stephen laughed and looked over to Annie. "She picks up fast, doesn't she?"

"That's right, baby," Annie said as she turned back to her girl. "They are nasty. They stick their noses into other people's business, and if they can come up with enough garbage, they get paid well. In fact, I think that pretty much sums up their job—garbage men."

"You shouldn't insult garbage guys like that. *They* actually perform a much appreciated task," Stephen added.

"True," she agreed as they passed through the gate. "Do you ever wonder if the whole fame thing is worth this? It's utterly ridiculous! We won't even be able to go to church again for awhile. And I was really hoping the two of us could get away and go out to eat sometime soon … all by ourselves … no children, no photographers."

"Yeah, to that little Italian place we went to when we went out the first time."

"Ricatoni's," she smiled in remembrance. "That would've been nice."

"This will cool down eventually. We're gonna outlast them, you know? Someday we'll be so boring that the only people who can stand us will be each other."

"I look forward to it."

Once inside, Cassie and Ellie immediately took up together as the adults sat around the fireplace. The talk was light, and everyone was discussing the crowd outside the fence. Right now, the most important thing was to feel the love and closeness of family. Within a few minutes, Andie and Doug arrived with their kids.

"Are you cutting out on work today?" Angie asked him as he helped Andie hobble through the door.

"Today and tomorrow," he told her. "We'll be up at Memphis with the rest of you while Mr. Carter's doing his thing."

Annie screamed in frustration because *she* would not be going to Memphis. Doug looked over at her in shock. "Or I could stay here, if you'd rather?"

Angie laughed as she took Andie's hand and helped guide her to the recliner. "She's not yelling at you, Doug, at least not yet. Moms saw a tabloid at the supermarket today saying the real reason Annie's here is to help me through Carter's cancer."

Andie's jaw dropped. "You're kidding? No wonder the crowd was so big outside. I knew it had to be something, but never figured this. How'd they find out?"

"Who knows?" Annie moaned. "But it's not fair. There's no way Stephen and I can go tomorrow with all of this going on."

"Really?" Andie asked as she gently eased herself into the chair. "They'd follow you into the hospital?"

"They'd go anywhere and do anything," Annie explained. "I've already notified the hospital and the police about it. It'll be bad enough having them follow Angie around for the next while, but if we show up too, chaos will ensue."

"You're not gonna be there?" Andie nearly cried. "That will be awful! How can you not be there?"

"It's all Stephen's fault," Annie said as she pointed over at him. "He just had to be a celebrity."

"Hang on, there," Doug cut in. "You could have fallen in love with anyone in the world, but no, you had to pick one of the *most* famous. Annie, you never do anything half way. I'm sorry, but I think Stephen's off the hook here. Everything is your fault, and I think we should all just agree to that right now."

"Everything?" Annie grinned as she joined the teasing mood deciding to try and keep the morning light. "Andie's ankle isn't my fault. She did that all on her own."

"Well," Doug shook his head, "I'm sure if we really thought about this, it would eventually fall back to you."

The morning remained pleasant, and at noon everyone gathered around the table for potato soup and grilled cheese sandwiches. The noise was typically loud with the adults involved in animated conversation, throwing opinions around the table. But the added excitement of Andie's five, Angie's two, and Annie's little Ellie, seemed to raise the whole scene up another notch or two. It was at that point that Stephen had a revelation. He stood from his seat and gently clanged his spoon against his glass until everyone, including the youngest girls, looked up at him in eager anticipation.

"I have realized something," Stephen began. "Wasn't it just last week that Dad preached about how nothing happens without a reason?" Everyone halfway nodded. "This whole tabloid thing has gotten Annie and myself especially in a tizzy. I even thought to myself, *Why couldn't it have happened after the surgery? At least we could have been there for the surgery*, you know?" He paused and looked around the room. "I now know why."

"Spit it out, Sherlock," Andie said in desperation, "'cause I'm still pretty ticked about the whole thing."

"We keep the kids," he responded flatly. "There's no way that a bit of *this*"—he made some wild hand motions to describe the pandemonium—"won't follow to the waiting room in Memphis."

He smiled as Annie frowned. "Your heart is bigger than your brain," she mumbled.

"Probably," he sighed, "but if we kept all the kids at our place, you all would be free to relax and not have to deal with any … uh …"

"Problems that might arise," Annie interjected.

"Exactly," he confirmed.

Everyone around the room, including the children, sort of looked at him in amazement.

Finally Andie asked, "Are you sure you're that noble? Do you know what you're really volunteering to do?"

"Actually, I have no idea how we're gonna manage, but it's the least we can do," he said with a hopeful grin. "We did keep the Mason gang for a whole night and somehow survived. This can't be much worse."

Lainey looked up at Stephen and asked, "Can we swim in your pool?"

Adam jumped in to reply, "Too cold, Lainey."

"Actually," Stephen put a finger in the air, "it's heated."

Arly raised an eyebrow. "Cool." He thought a moment more and then added, "We could even swim when it snows."

"It's gonna snow?" Ashley asked.

Annie answered quickly, "Not tomorrow. But it will be rather chilly. We'll have to have some important rules about getting in and out of the water." Annie looked next to her at Angie. "What about Cassie? Do you want her to go with you … be there with you through all of this … or can she stay also?"

Angie looked to Michael for direction. She seemed to struggle with making even the smallest decisions lately. "What do you think?"

Michael smiled and took her hand. He knew everything had become emotional for her. "I think Cassie would much rather stay at Aunt Annie's log cabin and swim in the pool with her cousins than sit around in a hospital for endless hours listening to boring grown-ups talk." He then motioned for Cassie to come near. "What about it, Cassie? Do you want to stay and swim tomorrow or go with us to the hospital?"

Cassie gave a serious look and responded with a definitive, "Stay."

"Stay it is, then," Michael smiled at her. He looked to Angie for her reaction. She was comfortable with the decision.

Andie soberly turned to her older two, Adam and Arly, and said, "And you two had better be a help and *not* a hindrance. You know what I'm saying?"

"Yes, Ma'am," Adam said quickly, obviously relieved that he wouldn't have to make the long trip to Memphis, plus be cooped up inside a hospital all day.

"Me too, Mom," Arly agreed.

"I can help too," came Aimee's ever-present voice of reason. "I'll make sure Lainey, Ellie and Cassie don't break the rules."

Andie looked at Aimee and sternly commented, "Just make sure *you* don't break the rules."

Twenty-Seven

The drive to Memphis was tense and quiet. Michael spent much of his time concerned about Angie. This pregnancy had been uneventful. With both Cassie and Carter she had struggled with high blood pressure, not to mention each one coming a month early. This one had brought no problems ... so far. With a late December due date, there was a good possibility it could arrive within the next month. Carter would still be recovering from tomorrow's surgery, and Angie would naturally want to meet his every need. But with a new baby, the amount of time and energy she could spend with him would be limited. And she was huge already. He wondered if it was possible that she had miscalculated the date.

Thank you, Lord, for so much family around right now. And give me extra insight to see when she's pushing too hard and too far. He thought for a moment, and then added, *And if at all possible, could You please let this one wait until the due date? I know You've already got the plan down, but it would be so much easier on all of us ... Angie, me, Cassie, and the new baby ... if it could come on time ... instead of early ... just this once.*

Angie's thoughts were far from the new baby. She was only thinking of Carter. Even if the surgery were successful in removing the cancer, there could still be permanent damage that might prevent him from ever walking. What if she had come last year when she first began to realize his development was off? This scenario would be totally different. If Carter's prognosis ended up negative, she would always blame herself. Could she live with that kind of guilt for the rest of her life? And what about Cassie? As a mother, she owed her so much more than she had given lately. Michael took up plenty of time with their firstborn, but Cassie needed her mother's attention. When she wasn't in the clinic or fretting over Carter, she was exhausted and resting on the couch.

God, you gave me more than one child, but only one child seems to occupy my mind and heart at the moment. I adore Cassie, but her questions and constant curiosity wear me out. And this little one I'm carrying seems unimportant at the moment. It was so different with the first two. I thought of them every minute and imagined what life would be like when they came. Right now, I'm just pleading with You not to let this one come before I'm ready to handle a new baby.

She sighed as she tried to exhale the stress and tension. She glanced back at Carter who was sleeping soundly in his seat. He was so pleasant and easygoing. How would he handle the invasiveness of all that was about to happen to him? Would it change him?

Michael reached over and took her hand. "It's all gonna be okay," he assured her. "We're in the palm of God's hand."

She tried to smile. "I know that in my head, but my heart is struggling to catch up."

When they arrived at the hospital, Carter again was fascinated by the tall buildings. He and Michael carried on quite a conversation as they made their way up to his room, and Michael acted as though all this was normal procedure. Angie was close to falling apart inside and was thankful for his strength and calm as they sat in the room awaiting a nurse and orders.

"I don't wike this place," Carter suddenly announced.

Michael looked down at him with a silly expression. "And why not? I think it's rather neat. Look at all the animals on the wall."

Carter looked around at the animals, but his expression didn't change. "Don't wike it."

"I like it," Michael continued with the positive comments.

"I don't wike the cage," Carter explained as he looked toward the bed with the high bars surrounding it.

Michael laughed slightly. "That's because they think you're a tiger. Grrrrrr...." He reached down and tickled Carter. "You'd better not bite them or they may just send you on to the zoo."

"I don't wike the smell," Carter went on.

"Really?" Michael asked him with surprise. "I thought it sort of smelled like Mommy."

This got Angie's attention. "Me?"

"Yeah, that whole alcohol - Betadine kind of smell—I never go into the clinic unless it's to see you, and it always smells like that."

"That's called being *sterile*."

"I didn't say it was *bad*, just that it reminds me of you."

She gave him a reprimanding look and shook her head. She gazed back at Carter who was still taking in all the details of the room. Michael lifted him and twirled him for a moment, then took him over to the bed and placed him inside.

"What do you think, Tiger?" he asked as Carter sat still.

Carter looked around the *cage* briefly and then he began to smile. "Grrrr," he said with a mischievous grin. "I a mean tiger and I bites people."

Angie chuckled and quickly added, "You're a nice tiger, and you only bite ... like ... rats and things that are nasty like that."

"Antwope," Carter added.

"What?" she wondered.

"He meant *antelope*," Michael told her.

"How does a two-year old know what an *antelope* is?"

"We were watching lions on the Discovery Channel the other

night."

"I a lion!" Carter suddenly announced.

Just then, the door opened and in walked a very tall nurse. Carter looked at her and gave a long growl.

"Goodness," the nurse said with a start. "What have we gotten ourselves into?"

Angie pointed toward Michael and stated, "Any troubles you might have are strictly from his father."

Michael leaned over to pick Carter up and then whispered as he pulled him close, "No biting, tiger. Okay? Your mom would have a fit with that."

Carter whispered back, "I not a tiger; I a lion. I bites antwopes."

☼☼☼

Sam strolled down to Billy's classroom when their planning period began. As she peeked inside the door, she saw a morose expression on his face as he stared out into space. Her first thought was to leave him with his gloom and head back to her own room, but curiosity got the best of her. What could have Billy Marcum so down again this morning?

"What's bugging you?" she asked as she walked on in.

He turned to her with a start and gave a sigh. "Just trying to figure out the whole God thing."

"Okay," she frowned. "That's deep for morning thoughts. Why are you thinking about God this morning? I thought you'd sort of written off religion."

"I guess … maybe … I don't know. I get so turned around with all of it. I mean, I know my sister made some incredible changes. Her life is like one hundred eighty degrees different, and she says it's all because of God. I'd like to think that my parents are … well … reaping the benefits of all those years they gave to serving God. I hope they're in a heaven, somewhere—doing whatever it is you do there. Then there's Angie and her missionary husband … giving their lives to tell people about God … but … I mean … is it even fair that they have to suffer like this when they've given everything up to serve Him?"

"How are they suffering?"

"You don't know?"

She shook her head.

"Their little boy … he's having surgery this morning."

"You're kidding?" She was shocked at the news. "Why? He was awful cute … looked really healthy to me."

"He can't walk. He's never walked. They found out last week he has this massive tumor on his spine that's been causing all the problems."

"Wow," she said in understanding. "He seemed so happy. I never noticed he couldn't walk."

He banged his fist on the podium. "Why!" he practically yelled.

"Why does God do senseless stuff like this to innocent people? Why you? Why them? Why not the horrible people in this world that deliberately harm others? Why not your father or your uncles? Why not … why not …" his voice got lower, "why not … me … instead of Angie?"

She shrugged. She was as clueless as he. In fact, when it came to God, she had no idea whatsoever about anything. Did He exist? If so, then how did she fit in? Would her past keep her out of heaven, or would God consider her a victim? Could He have prevented all the abuse, or did He engineer it? Thoughts about God blew her mind too much to consider them.

She put her hand on his shoulder and tried to give an encouraging smile. "Well, maybe He's planning on a miracle or something. I can't help you in this area. Is someone gonna inform you of the outcome?"

He shook his head. "I try not to let them know I care. They all probably think I still carry a torch for Angie, and to show a little interest might raise some eyebrows."

"Will Cindy know anything tonight?"

"She's there now … at the hospital.

"Then give her a call tonight. Think of a good reason to talk, and then casually ask about the little boy."

He thought for a moment. "Want to come to Cindy's for Thanksgiving?"

Her eyes grew wide. "Where did that come from? What a random thought—Angie's boy … to me coming for Thanksgiving?"

"It'd be a good reason to call Cindy."

She smiled in acknowledgment. "Sounds like a plan. I suppose I could sacrifice my Thanksgiving traditions for you to find some info on Angie."

✡✡✡

The waiting room was crowded and tense, but not near as crowded or tense as it would have been had all the children come along. The surgery had been going on nearly five hours with no real updates, except to say Carter's vitals were fine. Michael was extremely thankful for all the family and friends there to help keep Angie's mind in a better place. He was more impressed with Andie than he had ever been. When they had first met, she had been cold and non-accepting of him. He began to think that her personality was the same. Once the ice was broken, however, he realized that beneath the cool surface was a woman with deep compassion and great loyalty to family. Even though she spent most of her time on a recliner with her foot propped up, she constantly kept conversation going for Angie's sake, never letting silence linger for long. Then, interspersed between the conversations, she would ask if Angie needed anything. Was she hungry, thirsty, did she need to get some fresh air, was the baby kicking, was everything all right?

"Dr. Collins?" the receptionist called out from the desk.

Immediately Michael and Angie rushed toward the lady.

"Is there news?" Angie asked first.

"Yes," the lady smiled. "They've finished, and the doctors will be here in a moment to let you know how everything went."

Angie sighed as this first milestone was past, but immediately tears began to form in her eyes. Michael noticed her going pale and put his arms around her quickly, pulling her close.

"It's okay," he whispered softly. "God's in control."

The family immediately rallied around her speaking words of encouragement and hope.

It seemed like an eternity before Dr. Taylor and the neurosurgeon appeared. When they did, they asked to speak with Angie and Michael alone in the hallway outside the room. The couple quickly made their way through the door and looked tersely into the faces of the doctors.

"First," Levi Taylor started, "it all went just fine."

Angie gave a small cry of relief.

He continued. "It was a mess in there, to say the least. It was enormous and was wrapped around the spine like nothing I've ever seen before."

The other surgeon added, "But it was all contained. It's like the thing just grew bigger, but never spread."

"It was deeply imbedded into everything, however," Levi explained. "That's why it took so long."

"We'd think we had it all in one area, and something would tell me to pull back a flap of tissue, and there would be more traces."

Levi shook his head. "I've never seen anything like it. And I can't believe Carter had no pain with all that in there, except for pressure from trying to walk."

Angie began to go into doctor mode for the first time. "Do you feel like you got it all?"

"We got it," the second surgeon told her confidently. "Like I said, I'd start to move on, and then I'd think we'd better check under here or over there again before moving, and there would be tendrils of the tumor still clinging. It was definitely clean before we closed up."

Angie nodded as she thought. "What about damage? Do you think he'll be able to walk? Do you think it'll return? What kind of prognosis are we looking at here?"

Levi smiled. "I think the prognosis is very positive."

Tears began to form again as Angie closed her eyes in relief.

"So, he'll walk?" Michael asked for the first time.

"I don't see why not," the other doctor told him. "We'll run some tests on the mass and see if it gives us any more information, but as far as any structural or permanent damage, there appears to be none. The biggest problem was the pressure it was putting on that area of his spine. Now that it's been released, he should be back to normal … well, as soon as he recovers."

"Yes," Angie pulled herself together again, "and what are we looking at as far as recovery is concerned?"

"A lot of pain," Levi said honestly. "We'll keep him heavily sedated for several days. He'll whine and moan a lot, but he won't remember anything that's happening."

She nodded in understanding.

"We'll slowly begin to bring him out of it around Friday afternoon," Levi clarified. "Then we'll need to get him eating and begin to do some physical therapy to prepare him for standing … and hopefully, walking."

Angie was a mother again now, and the emotions caught up with her fully. As she began to sob in relief, Michael pulled her to him with one hand and reached the other out to thank the doctors.

"Thank you," he said sincerely and humbly.

"I'll be checking in with you on and off during the afternoon," Levi let him know. "If I might suggest, why don't you two and your entourage go out for something to eat? We won't let Carter rouse today at all. When you get back, he should be resting soundly in his room."

Angie shook her head. "We'll stay. Just let us know when you're moving him so we can be with him as soon as possible."

Levi reiterated, "He won't know you're here, Angie. You might as well get out for just a little bit."

"His head may not know," she said soberly, "but his heart most assuredly will."

As Angie and Michael thanked them again and returned to the waiting area to tell friends and family, Levi shook his head. How did this missionary manage to snag the most beautiful woman in the world? Michael Collins was so unassuming, completely humble, almost boring. Yet Angie looked to him for so much; he could see it in her eyes.

"Beautiful gal," his surgeon friend said as they moved down the hallway.

"Tell me about it," Levi bemoaned. "She's the one that got away."

☼☼☼

Billy put aside the papers he had finished grading and went to the fridge for a Coke. Only one left. He reached into his pocket for his wallet to see if he had enough to buy another pack. Fifteen dollars. He'd better not. Instead of Coke, he filled a glass with ice and then water. He sat down on the couch and pulled out his phone. He really wanted to know how Carter's surgery had turned out, but he didn't want to seem too eager. The truth was that he was happy for Angie and her marriage and her family. And when it came right down to it, it was Sam that he actually loved and wanted to be with. But in his own inevitable way, selfishness had cost him everything he really cared about. At least Sam was willing to spend Thanksgiving with them. That one morsel gave him something to smile about.

He punched in Cindy's number and waited for an answer.

"Hey—what's up?"

"Thanksgiving," he began. "You mentioned having a big to-do at your place for all of us. Is that still on?"

"Actually, the Wrights have asked if we would spend it with them again this year."

He hesitated. He didn't want to invite himself, nor Sam.

"You know you're welcome," she told him. "They even said as much."

"Well," did he bring Sam into it? "I suppose, but I was really calling to see about bringing Sam with me. She's all alone on holidays, and I thought the least we could do was ask her for Thanksgiving. Actually, I've already asked her because I thought it was gonna be at your house."

"No problem!" Cindy piped in immediately. "You know how they are: the more the merrier."

"Could you ask before I give Sam a definite answer?"

"I don't have to ask, Billy," she assured him. "Trust me—they'll be thrilled."

"Well, I'll tell her it's a *yes* then, but I'd be more comfortable if you'd ask."

"Wow, is there actually a little sense of propriety going on with you?"

He smirked at her question. "By the way," he tried to sneak in quickly, "didn't Angie's kid have surgery today?"

"Yes!" she said with excitement. "We were all there … just got in, in fact."

"How'd it go?"

"It was great. They got all of the tumor and believe he should be a normal little boy after the recovery."

He looked up to heaven and mouthed a *thank you.* "That's good to hear. Angie and Michael should be very relieved."

"Very. I probably won't see them for a month, though. They'll be staying in Memphis until he's ready to come home. That's my luck—my best friend comes home from a tropical island and has to spend most of her time *away* from me."

"I'll see if I can bring Sam home this weekend to cheer you up."

"That would be wonderful."

Twenty-Eight

The recovery for Carter was going to be miserable. Even though he was not fully awake, the next few days he cried often. Angie and Michael hadn't left the room since his return, and they were worn out from the ordeal. They had a room reserved at the Fed Ex House, but neither was willing to leave. Michael had pleaded with Angie to at least go for one night. She could shower, rest, and take care of baby number three, but she wouldn't consider it. She spent much of her time singing and talking to Carter, and then trying to comfort him whenever he would begin to whimper.

After one of Levi's visits, Michael followed him discreetly out into the hall.

"Dr. Taylor," Michael called out as he jogged after him to catch up.

"Michael," Levi said turning back to him.

"Thanks for … well … for everything. I wish I could get Angie to leave for just a little while, but she won't budge."

"Carter's oblivious to all that's happening right now."

"I know, but it doesn't change the fact that she's gonna be right there with him through it all."

"She needs to think about more than just Carter right now," Levi said soberly.

"I know that too. She was early with both Cassie and Carter. I'm afraid if she doesn't get some real rest, this one's gonna come early also. She's so big; I can't imagine her hanging on much longer."

Levi nodded and chuckled. "Is there any way you can force her? You managed to persuade her heart to marry you—perhaps you can convince her of the importance of some genuine rest."

He shook his head. "I doubt it. But I do thank you for trying. Maybe when he wakes up she'll be willing to let us take turns being here … and being at the Fed Ex House."

Levi thought for a moment about how to encourage Angie to leave. "I may have an idea."

"Really?" He looked hopeful.

"Maybe I can work something out to actually get Carter to *my* house … get him out of here … thus get Angie out of here."

Michael sighed deeply and smiled. "That would be … wow … asking too much. But I thank you anyway."

"Nothing's too much for Angie," Levi affirmed. "I'll see what I can do."

☼☼☼

Jonathan, Kyle and Cindy sat around the church office as they made plans for the impending arrival of Hal and Lisa Bridges. Hal had insisted they stay in a hotel rather than with any of the church members, even the family that owned a bed and breakfast. He had also insisted that no *social* event or special supper be held for them.

"This is really inconvenient," Cindy complained as she hung up the phone from booking reservations at a hotel in Russellville, 28 miles away. "Every time they come to the church during the visit they'll have to travel that miserable two-lane road."

"Everything about this whole ordeal is inconvenient," Jonathan agreed. "With all that's going on with Angie right now, I'd really rather have had my focus there than try to deal with this whole process."

Kyle agreed, "That's where you should be. Why couldn't he come next weekend instead?"

"Good question," Jonathan mulled. "I've asked myself that more than once this week."

Cindy laughed quietly and asked, "Is it possible to dislike someone before you've ever met them?"

Kyle and Jonathan both looked at her soberly.

"Very," Jonathan replied.

Cindy rolled her eyes and pulled out the page from the printer. She handed the piece to Jonathan and explained, "Here's the schedule for the weekend. They arrive at the airport in Birmingham at three o'clock and get a rental car, then they have supper with the committee at seven o'clock at Fourth Street Grill …"

"Fourth Street Grill?" Jonathan asked in surprise. "I thought they were eating at Tom Richards' house?"

"That's been nixed too," Cindy told him.

"Tom changed his mind?"

"No, *Dr. Bridges*. And would you believe he told me that was how I needed to address him?"

Jonathan's eyebrows flew up. "Are you serious?"

"That's what I said when he told me," Cindy giggled. "I hope I can handle him all right, Pastor Jon. We're so informal and relaxed around here. Shoot, we don't even call the family doctor by *doctor*. At this rate, I'll be fired before the man even starts working!"

"Nobody's firing anybody," Jonathan said firmly. He looked back down to the schedule. "On Saturday we tour the church that morning. Lunch at noon. What?" He glanced down at Cindy. "We look for housing Saturday afternoon?"

"That's what *Dr. Bridges* said."

"He hasn't even stepped foot in this church, and he's already planning to find a house?" Jonathan ran his hand through his hair and shook his head in unbelief.

Kyle just smiled as he said, "I guess he's pretty sure of himself."

☼☼☼

Lisa Bridges stared at her husband in utter shock. "You gave up the lease! Why on earth did you give up the lease?"

"Because we didn't have the money to pay for another month."

"We can get the money! Getting another house is almost …"

"We won't be here another month!" Hal insisted sternly.

"You hope," she muttered under her breath as she removed her jacket and dropped her purse onto the table.

"Don't leave your purse there," he said automatically.

"Excuse me?"

"Don't junk up the house," he rephrased. "Take your purse to the bedroom and put it on the shelf where it belongs."

"Let me get this straight," she whipped her head around to face him. "I work all weekend long and then nights throughout the week to make up for the fact that you can't seem to keep a job and you're telling me I can't drop my purse on the table?"

Hal glared at her and bit the sides of his cheeks.

"Save your obsessions for the churches," she said through gritted teeth. "I'm going to shower and then go to bed."

"Are you packed?" he asked as he followed her to the bedroom.

She mumbled beneath her breath and turned back to face him. "Would you lay off me? I will pack *after* I have slept and can think clearly!"

"I told you to pack last night before you left."

"It doesn't take hours to pack for a brief weekend. I'll pack when I wake up."

"Remember: this is the South. They'll be very conservative. None of that ultra-fancy stuff, and try to lessen the make-up a bit, will you?"

"Would you like me to dye my hair brown instead of blond too?" she asked sarcastically.

"Whatever. Just try to fit in."

"Me?" she laughed. "That's some advice you could certainly take to heart."

☼☼☼

Billy lay back on the couch and flipped through the channels on his tiny television. There was no high school game tonight and nothing good was on Friday night programming. He was totally bored. He should have gone on to Cindy's, but he had to wait until Saturday afternoon because Sam had a meeting that morning. Sam. Now there was a thought to brighten his evening. He should have suggested they do something tonight, but he was down to three dollars and didn't get his allowance until Monday. He assumed she would take her car tomorrow and he wouldn't have to pay for gas.

A knock outside the boat caught him by surprise. He turned off the television and made his way to the door. When he opened it, Sam greeted him with a huge smile and a paper sack.

"Sam? What are you doing here?"

"I had absolutely nothing to do, which is rare, and thought I'd come by and celebrate with you," she grinned.

"Come on in," he said as he offered his hand to get her on board. "What are we celebrating?"

"The success of Angie's baby boy!"

"Well … okay," he said hesitantly as he helped her through the door.

"I figured it was as good a reason as any," she laughed. "Let's go up top."

"It's a little chilly, don't you think?"

She held up the bag and said, "This will warm us up. Grab a couple glasses and let's go."

He was suddenly alarmed. "What have you got in there?"

She slowly pulled out a bottle of wine. "Just like old times."

He winced slightly and then slowly shook his head. "I can't, Sam. I … uh … don't drink anymore."

Her eyes grew wide. "What? Wait, let me get this straight. Billy Marcum doesn't consume alcohol?"

He shook his head.

"You're kidding me?" She was laughing now. "When on earth did that happen?"

He started to tell her, but she put her hand up to stop him.

"Wait," she said quickly. "Let's go up top first. I'll just imbibe directly from the bottle, and you can give me all the gory details."

He shrugged and motioned for her to lead the way. She climbed the ladder stairs, opened the hatch-like door, and then stepped onto the top deck of the boat. She looked up at the stars, gave a big grin, and then reached into the bag for the bottle. She sat down as she removed the top, and then looked over at him.

"Now," she said, "tell me about your lack of liquor. What prompted such an idea?"

He sat down on one of the padded benches and watched as she turned the bottle up. The temptation to join was strong. "My mom," he started.

She finished a large gulp, held the bottle in her lap, and then nodded her head. "How did she manage that? You were quite the drinker."

"It was near the end," he explained. "She told me how proud she was that I'd gone back to school. She pleaded with me to stick with it. She was so scared that after she died I would just give up on everything and become … I don't know … a bum or something. She was really worried about my drinking. While she was … dying … I got wasted in Dockrey a couple of times. You know, just trying to deal with it all … trying to handle the inevitability of what was happening. It bothered her. A couple of days before she died, she had this real heart-to-heart with me. She pleaded with me to stop the drinking. I tried to explain it wasn't something I did all the time, just something on occasion to numb the pain."

"Yeah, right," she mumbled cynically.

"Well, that's kind of what it had boiled down to. I wasn't into it like when you knew me. I was in school. I had to think clearly."

"So you told her you'd stop drinking?"

"At first, I just said I'd slow down, but she wouldn't accept that. She wanted a promise that I'd stop. Those times she saw me drunk scared the daylights out of her. She said she couldn't die in peace if she thought I'd go out and get drunk to stop the pain."

She stared at him in astonishment. "Wow. I had no idea. And you've kept that promise all this time?"

He nodded. "I promised my mom on her death bed. I don't think even *I* could be that heartless … go back on something I promised her just before she died."

Sam turned the bottle up again. "I feel a little guilty," she confessed as she wiped her lips. "But it was your promise, not mine. I'm proud that you can do that. It's just one more piece of evidence to prove that you're not the same man you once were."

He looked at her and wondered if he had changed enough to ever have a chance of getting her back. "How changed do you think I am?"

She took another drink and stared at him for a while. "A lot," she finally replied.

"Like how."

"Like, oh, I don't know, Billy, a lot of ways. You're just different in a lot of ways."

As the evening went on, she got significantly drunk. She had intended on sharing the bottle, but since Billy wasn't drinking any, she had ended up with way more than what should have been her part. She talked freely into the night, not really revealing anything, just going over hurts from her life growing up, and then sharing certain things that had happened over the years they were apart.

"Did you ever date anyone after me?" he asked at one point.

She laughed and nodded. "One guy," she managed to slur out. "Keith Wiggington."

He recognized the name and was stunned. "The professor? The chemistry guy?"

She nodded. "Mr. C set us up. He goes to his church or something like that. We went out a few times, and he was a really nice guy, but I couldn't be what he wanted."

"What did he want?"

"A good *Christian* girl," she said despondently. "I went to church with him a couple of times, but I just couldn't get past the fact that here I was, this prostitute for hire, walking down the aisles next to all these good people."

His face turned red. "You were *not* a prostitute! Don't ever say that. You were forced to do what you did."

"We can butter it up all we want, but it still boils down to the fact that I had sex with men for money."

"But you didn't get the money! Your father forced you to …"

"My *pimp* got all the loot," she laughed out this time. "I didn't see a cent of it."

"Sam." Billy came over next to her. "I don't want to hear you talk like this. What happened to you had nothing to do with you. It was the result of a perverted man who …"

"What do you mean it had nothing to do with me?" she countered. "It had everything to do with me! I was there for every stinking moment of it. I can remember their breath, and how their hands felt as they …"

"Stop it!" he yelled as he took the bottle from her. "You've had enough of this."

She laughed again. "You think taking that away will make me forget it all? You've got to be kidding! Every moment of every day I remember what happened to me. I always think to myself how funny it is that I tried so hard to run away from it, but it'll never leave. It's always here," she pointed to her heart, "and it'll always tell me what I really am."

He closed his eyes and shook his head. "Sam," he said gently, "that's not true. You're wonderful."

Again the hideous laugh resounded. "This from the man who divorced me … from the man who so hated what I was that he couldn't bear the thought of sleeping with me anymore."

"That's not why I left! I've told you that over and over again."

"Please, Billy," she pleaded, "just admit the truth. For once, admit the truth."

He took her hands in his and tried to find reason in her eyes. "The truth is that I loved you, Sam, but I was a complete and total jerk. My friends tried to make me think that marriage had tied me down and turned me into something I didn't want to be. When I was wasted and empty, it was easy to believe that. If only I had known what I really had with you, I would have never walked out … I would have never pushed you like I did."

She patted his hand and smiled. "It's okay, Billy. I knew it was too good to be true anyway. I didn't deserve you."

"Sam, please. Don't believe that. I was the one who didn't deserve you. You should've had so much more than what I gave you."

Her expression became serious as she told him, "No. All I ever wanted was what you gave me. That's all I ever wanted, Billy. Just us."

As the evening had gone on, clouds had slowly moved in. And as she continued to look him in the eyes, rain began to drizzle.

"We need to go inside," he told her. "You'll get wet and sick."

She smiled a drunken smile. "Who cares?"

"I care."

He pulled her up to her feet. She was extremely wobbly.

"I like the rain," she giggled as she tried to sit back down.

"I bet you do right now. You probably like everything at the moment." He put her arm around his neck and moved them both toward the hatch. "Let me go down first. Try to stay right behind me so you don't fall."

They maneuvered through the door and onto the ladder. He went down slowly so he could catch her if she should happen to trip. She was trying to be careful, and the look of intensity on her face almost made him smile. She had a little bobble and he managed to catch her in his arms.

"Now, this is nice," she smiled up at him.

He grinned back. "I have a question for you."

"Anything."

"Why the ponytail?" he wondered. "And why the glasses still?"

She looked up at him as she slowly regained her balance and moved away slightly. "You don't like my ponytail?"

"I think your ponytail's adorable," he assured her. "It's just that when you wear your hair down, you look really … well … attractive."

"Sexy?" she beamed.

"Actually, yes."

"And I suppose without the glasses you think I'm even sexier, huh?"

"You really are. Why don't you get contacts or something? I've just been curious."

She continued to smile as she reached back to the band holding her ponytail. She slowly pulled it from her hair and then shook out her long, blond locks.

"Better?" she asked.

"I wasn't asking you to take down your hair," he said seriously. "I was just curious. That's all."

She then reached up and removed the glasses. Without thinking, she tossed them across the room. She put her arms around his neck, still standing on the stairs, and smiled as she looked at him.

"Even better?" she asked this time.

There they were … those gorgeous, deep green eyes. Billy put his hands on her waist, not in an embrace, but to steady her. He tried not to think about what she was doing to him at the moment, but to think about the fact that she was really drunk and completely unaware of her actions.

"If I didn't know better," he said as he pulled her on down the stairs to the floor, "I would think you were trying to seduce me."

At this she laughed again. "Good thing you know better, then!" She released her arms from his neck and wobbled over toward the couch. "I wouldn't dream of seducing you, Billy Marcum. I'm still trying to figure out how on earth to be friends with you. I mean, how do you turn off everything we once had and just decide to forget it and be *friends*?"

He helped her down to the couch. "Well, you've done a pretty good job of it. I didn't realize it was such a struggle."

"It's always a struggle, you know?"

"It is?"

"Sure! For me, at least. I mean, I hated you … until you walked back into my life … into my school … into my dreams. Now I just think about you and wonder how I keep my head together where you're concerned. I know you would never have me as a lover again, so how do I be the best friend you could ever want so that you won't walk out on me again?"

His heart dropped. She was still afraid he would hurt her. "I don't want to hurt you again, Sam. Really, I don't."

"You won't leave me anymore?" she asked as her eyes began to grow heavy.

He reached over and lightly smoothed her hair. "I wouldn't dream of it."

She smiled sleepily as she leaned over to lay her head on his shoulder. Then she wearily said, "You don't have to love me, Billy. If you'll just like me, I can almost be happy again."

His heart could have stopped. He pulled her close and held her tightly as he thought of her words. Had she taken a dagger and plunged it into his chest he couldn't have hurt worse.

"I do love you, Sam," he whispered. "I always have, and I always will."

Twenty-Nine

They began to wean Carter off the sedative late Friday evening, but it wasn't until early Saturday morning that he finally awakened. Around four-thirty Angie began to hear him whimper again. She immediately jumped up and went over to him, a habit that had pretty much ensued for the past four days. She had not gotten more than two hours of sleep at a time since Tuesday morning.

"Hey, sweetie," she said softly as she gently touched his arm. "It's Mommy. How are you?"

He rolled his head back and forth but wouldn't open his eyes. She saw his lips pucker a few times as though he were about to cry, but then they would stop. She continued to rub his arm and speak to him.

"Can you wake up for Mommy? You've been asleep a long time."

He rolled his head a few more times, and this time a small little cry escaped. She immediately put both hands down inside the caged bed in an effort to try and cradle him.

"Mommy?" he finally managed with his eyes still closed.

"That's right, sweetie. Mommy's here. Are you still very sleepy?"

He rolled his head again. "Ow, Mommy."

"I know, baby," she told him as she tried to caress him as much as possible from the awkward position. She would have picked him up in a moment, but the clumsiness of the new baby in front pushing her against the crib would have been catastrophic had she tried. Of course, the IV in his arm as well as the wound in his back would have presented their own problems, but at the moment all she could think of was holding and comforting him.

"Owwww," he moaned a little louder this time.

"Can you open your eyes and look at Mommy?"

He rolled his head back and forth. She actually smiled. He was such a pleasant being that to see him slightly cantankerous, like his sister often could be, was a little humorous.

"Your back hurts, doesn't it?" she asked as she continued to gently touch him.

He nodded this time as his lips pouted.

"Dr. Taylor did some work on your back," she tried to explain although she knew he probably couldn't understand. "It may help you walk, Carter. Wouldn't that be fun?"

"No!" he yelled out this time.

The yell finally woke Michael. He rubbed his eyes for a moment until he realized Angie was at Carter's bed talking to him. He immediately went to the crib.

"Is he awake?" he asked with excitement. This had been the longest time he had not communicated with one of his children since they had been born.

"He's getting there," she explained. "He's having some pain."

Michael was alarmed. "Should he be?"

She frowned. "Oh, yeah. He'll been in pain for quite a while."

He reached down to touch his son. "Hey, tiger. How ya' doin'?"

Carter moaned a few more times and then said, "I not a tiger. I a lion."

Michael sighed with relief as he put his other arm on Angie's neck. "I think he's back."

☼☼☼

Jonathan sat in his office on Saturday morning with mixed feelings. He was thrilled to know Carter had awakened and demanded food. Angie had promised to get some sleep today, so that in itself gave him a reason to breathe a little easier. But as he sat, he awaited the entrance of Hal Bridges. Once again, the norm would have been for Jonathan to have met with him and the committee last night, but he was learning that Hal had a knack for getting things done his way. Jonathan didn't want to be here right now. He wanted to be on the way to Memphis with Barbara, Cassie and Andie to see his little grandson, but here he sat on pins and needles as though a tornado was about to storm through and he was helpless to do anything to stop it.

When he heard voices at the front door, he whispered another prayer, stood from his creaky chair, smoothed his thinning hair, and left his office to greet the group. As committee members poured into the office, Hal Bridges and his wife, Lisa, entered last. The man was impressive to say the least. He was easily over six feet, just like Jonathan, and was impeccably dressed. He wore tailored slacks and a starched maroon shirt with an expensive looking silk tie. Jonathan tried not to slouch as he felt very self-conscious in his wrinkled khakis and long sleeve polo.

"Pastor Jon," Floyd Benson began, "this is Dr. Hal Bridges."

Jonathan stuck out his hand in greeting and Hal took it firmly.

"Pastor," Hal said.

"Hal," Jonathan replied.

Nancy Beth spoke quickly to correct Jonathan, "It's *Dr. Bridges*."

"Oh, I think *Hal* will be plenty acceptable," Jonathan said sternly.

"Whatever you think, *pastor*," Hal said with sense of controlled humility.

"So, where do we start?" Jonathan asked right away hoping to move from the awkwardness of the moment.

"Right here should do fine," Hal told them as he began to survey the office area. "How many secretaries do you have?"

"Just one," Jonathan replied.

"That's it? One secretary for a church this size?"

"She's very efficient," Jonathan gave by way of explanation. "She's done the job adequately, and we've never seen the need to hire anyone extra. And she certainly hasn't done any complaining."

"I see," was Hal's only remark.

He continued inspecting various aspects of the room until he came to what was obviously Jonathan's door as it was noted by a small sign. "May I?" he asked as he reached for the handle.

"Sure. Why not?"

Hal opened the door and walked inside. He looked around the office and read a couple of titles from the various books that covered all the shelves as well as were stacked on the floor and the desk.

"Looks like you could use some more shelving in here," Hal commented.

"Perhaps," Jonathan nodded. "But there are more pressing needs at the moment. I feel like a few misplaced books here and there are a small price to pay for a new building in a growing church."

"Absolutely," Hal said as he glanced around at the slight chaos.

He left the room and then walked over to Kyle's office. This time he didn't ask. He opened the door and walked on in. The size of the office shocked him.

"Wow," he said as he looked back. "This room bigger than yours, pastor."

"Yes, Kyle works hard and deserves his space. Plus, he has all this music equipment and such, tables for discipleship meetings … and you can call me Jon if you like."

"Surely he doesn't work harder than you," Hal doubted.

"I don't know. Some weeks I know he puts in more hours. He totes kids off to youth camp; he does Christmas and Easter musicals. I've seen lights on up here at ten o'clock at night and found him nailing sets together at times. He also brings youth in here for discipleship and does a lot of family counseling. He's an asset."

Hal nodded again and then closed the door. "May I see the rest of the facilities?"

"Gladly."

Jonathan, followed by the committee, showed Hal the sanctuary area, the education building, the gymnasium, and where ground had just been broken for the new building. Hal made few comments, but jotted down notes here and there as various areas were seen. Once the tour was finished, Hal looked over his notes and began.

"How many Sunday morning services do you have?" he asked first.

"Two," Jonathan replied.

"How long have you had two services?"

"Two years."

"Why did you wait so long to begin building?"

"This was as quick as we could get to it," Jonathan tried to say without sounding defensive.

Hal gave him a sharp look. "It's my understanding that you actually have some Sunday School classes meeting in homes. Is that correct?"

"A few. We had to divide some classes because of size, and there was nowhere left to put them. People gladly volunteered their homes, and it's been a big blessing."

"Hmmm. So you've outgrown the church for two years, but this was the earliest you could get around to solving the problem? That sounds a little irresponsible, pastor."

Jonathan saw a slight wince on the face of Lisa, the first indication that she even existed in Hal's world.

"That's why *you're* here today, Hal," Jonathan put forth. "To take up some of the responsibility so we can manage to stay on our feet as we continue to transition."

"And not a moment too soon at that," Hal murmured.

He glanced down over his notes, and then asked, "Where were you planning my office to be?"

Jonathan deferred to Tom Richards. Tom cleared his throat and began to explain, "Well, we really don't have a legitimate office for you. We thought you could move into the Sunday School office until the building project was finished. At that time you'll have your own space."

Hal raised an eyebrow. "You're kidding me, right?"

Tom didn't miss a beat. "No, sir, I'm very serious. We told you we were in a period of transition and that everyone had to make sacrifices for a while until the new building is complete."

"No offense, but I believe we could make some other sacrifices. Like, say, we move the minister of music into the choir room. Throw him a desk and a few chairs in there in the corner, and it'll probably even make it easier for him … not having to run back and forth when he needs something from the choir room."

Jonathan marveled at the way the committee cowered at his suggestion. He, however, would not bow to this intimidation.

"Not gonna happen," Jonathan said forcefully.

Everyone turned to look at him, and Hal's expression was extremely severe.

"No offense, *Hal*," Jonathan continued, "but Kyle has been here for almost five years and has contributed to the success of this church in more ways than I could mention. I'm not saying you have to prove yourself, but I'm not bumping Kyle out of his office in order for you to move in. If you don't want the Sunday School office, then go pick a bigger room somewhere and we'll clear it out for you. But Kyle stays."

Nancy Beth reminded him, "But there are no more rooms available. It would mean moving out another Sunday School class."

"We'll do whatever we have to do, but Kyle stays in his office." Jonathan folded his arms in resolve. "If Hal is dissatisfied with the office you chose, then he can decide on another option … displacing a class, or learning right off the bat how the rest of us have sacrificed to see this church grow and change."

Hal looked down at his list and made another note. "I can sacrifice, pastor. But I hope that in the future this church will learn how to be more responsible in its decisions so as not to *displace* anyone at any time. Good leadership can do a whole lot for that."

Jonathan knew it was a backhanded jab, but he merely smiled because he had won the first victory: keeping Kyle in his office.

Thirty

Billy began to panic when he awoke so late. It was nine-thirty and Sam was sound asleep on the bed. He rolled over and tried to gently nudge her.

"Sam, when is your meeting?"

She didn't budge.

"Sam!" he tried to be a little more forceful. "You need to get up and get … well … I don't know … cleaned up or something."

She only moaned as she slowly rolled over.

"It's nine-thirty," he continued. "You've got a meeting with some parents today. You need to get up Sam."

She slowly tried to open her eyes. She put up her hand to shade the sun that was beaming through the slats in the blinds. "Turn off the lights and speak softly. My head's killing me."

"Great," he mumbled. "You've got a hangover. Sam, you've got to get up—you've got a meeting this morning with the Johnson parents."

Slowly reality began to dawn. "Oh, man. I'm in no shape to deal with Mrs. Johnson today."

"Tell me about it," he agreed as he tried to help her up.

"Stop!" she yelled out quickly. She dropped back down onto the bed. "I don't even want to try and get vertical at the moment."

"When is your meeting?" he asked again. "You've got to get up and get ready."

She rolled her head around and tried to make sense of the morning. "Why am I here?"

"You came over last night and nearly emptied a bottle of wine."

She only nodded as she put her hand up to her head. "And I ended up in your bed, I suppose?"

"Barely," he explained as he tried to get her to sit up again. "You zonked out on the couch. I managed to get you into a dining chair long enough to pull the bed out."

She opened her eyes again and looked around her. "I appear to be fully clothed, so I assume nothing happened."

"Well," he decided to tease her a bit, "when you took down your ponytail and threw your glasses across the room, I began to wonder. But you assured me you were not trying to seduce me, so I stopped worrying."

She shook her head. "I did not. You're making that up."

"I am." If she didn't remember, there was no reason to let her know otherwise. "Why don't you head to the shower, and I'll make a pot of coffee? We'll see if we can get you on level enough ground to handle Mrs. Johnson today."

"I don't think that's possible on even a good day," she moaned as he helped her up from the bed.

Once inside the tiny shower, she let the warm water run down her body. She didn't even have what it took to soap or scrub. Her head was pounding, and she was definitely getting more nauseous with each passing minute. The thought of coffee wasn't very appealing, but if it could help her out of this condition, it was worth a try.

As she managed to open her eyes again, she noticed Billy's shampoo. She reached over, pulled up the cap, and sniffed the familiar fragrance. A smile actually came to her face as old memories flooded her muddled mind. For a few brief times in her miserable life, she really did have a taste of *happily ever after*. Billy had been beyond Prince Charming, and their life together had seemed even better than a fairytale. But her smile faded as she was again reminded that all that was over. It was then that she realized she had no idea where her glasses were.

"Did I actually throw them across the room?" she wondered. "Nawww."

☼☼☼

Cassie, unlike her little brother, was not the least bit impressed with the buildings in Memphis. In fact, she found them ugly and intrusive. She couldn't understand why people would cut down beautiful trees to put up such big and hideous structures. In some ways, she even found Dockrey offensive. She loved her grandparents' back yard, but she hated the front where hundreds of people hung out at the gate of late. In the back she could hear the birds sing and watch the trees sway and it could almost seem like she was back on her island in Padawin, only without the mountain, without the river, and without the ocean.

As they walked into the hospital, she immediately expressed alarm. "What happens if the building falls? We won't be able to get out fast enough."

Barbara gently tightened the grip on her hand and assured her, "It won't fall, honey. It's been made to be very strong and hold a lot of people safely."

Cassie accepted the answer because she knew she had no other choice if she wanted to see her family again. She had never been without them, but she understood why Carter couldn't walk, and she understood how important it was for them all to be here with him right now. They had given her the choice to stay in Dockrey or stay with them, and as her father explained all the ramifications of her decision, she decided playing at her grandparents in loneliness would beat the boredom of living in this massive structure for many days.

She really didn't like the elevator. She thought the building was caving in and gave a small cry of panic. Andie managed a soft laugh and explained that they were going up, not down, and that the elevator would bring them even closer to her parents and little brother. She tried to be a big girl, but she knew now that when she did see her mommy and daddy, she would most definitely cry.

When they walked down the long hallway and finally turned a corner to where Carter's room was, Cassie held her breath. Would they really be there? Would she really get to feel her mommy's arms around her again and be able to touch her daddy's rough face? As the door opened, she saw all three of them sitting happily on the bed.

"Mommy!" she breathed in excitement.

"Sweetie!" Angie called back.

Cassie ran to her mother and threw her arms around her neck, holding tightly as if she would never allow herself to let go again. Then the tears began to fall.

"Are you okay, baby?" Angie asked tenderly.

Cassie pulled back a little and nodded. "Is Carter okay?"

"Ask him yourself?" Angie replied.

Cassie looked next to where she and her mother were sitting, and there sat her smiling father and pale-faced little brother.

"Carter, you okay?" she asked him.

"I got ouch on my back," he answered seriously. "Them doctors were digging in there."

Andie laughed at his description as she stuck her crutches together and plopped onto a chair. "I know that feeling! Been there several times these past few weeks."

Michael reached over and touched Cassie's cheek. "How's my big girl?"

She reached back and ran her hand across his three-day beard. He leaned over and gave her a kiss and then helped Carter to give a little kiss.

"Okay, everyone," Barbara said cheerfully as she tried to get through the emotional moment. "It's lunch time. Andie and I will be glad to go down to the cafeteria and get everyone something to eat. Can I take some orders?"

"Andie can stay with us, Moms," Angie spoke quickly. She knew her mother was trying to give the family some time alone. "She doesn't need to be up on that ankle."

Andie contradicted her. "Actually, I do need to be up on the ankle. The doctor has said it's time to start *rehabilitating* the thing. So, I'll hobble down to the food place with Moms."

☼☼☼

Lisa threw her purse on the floor of the rental car as she and Hal left for the hotel in Russellville after a long day of meetings with the committee and house shopping.

"What were you trying to pull?" she yelled as they drove away from the church. "Challenging the pastor before you even get called? We *need* this, Hal! We need *you* to get a job …"

"… to pay off *your* massive debts …" he interjected.

"Yeah, well, that's kind of what we agreed to, was it not? Nevertheless, we're not in the man's presence even an hour, and you already begin hinting at his irresponsibility!"

Very calmly he gave details of the previous night's meeting. "I told them last night that most times a pastor is very reluctant to admit his failings in the church."

"He seems like a nice guy, Hal, a man with genuine concern."

"And I'm sure he is, but if I'm to come in and do *my* job, it means there are things the pastor has always done that he'll no longer do. For heaven's sake, the man has been here for thirty years! He needs help, this church needs a fresh change, and I'm the one to do it."

"But you countered him. You made him …"

"I told the committee to expect that," he clarified. "I baited them, and then I baited him. As it turns out, *Pastor Jon* did everything according to plan—my plan. And if all goes well, that's how it'll be from now on."

"Why?" she asked in exasperation. "Why can't you just go into a church and be *normal?* Why can't you just *fit in?*"

"Fit in? They're not hiring me to fit in! They're hiring me to come in and turn this place around! And there's no way to do that if they remain under the leadership of this guy! I'm their answer. The sooner they all realize that, the sooner this church takes off."

"This whole persona you've created, the *take-charge-minister* guy, why has it never worked before? Why are we yet planning another move?"

"Trust me: this will be different."

"Because …?"

"We're in the South now, honey," he said with a slightly exaggerated accent. "People here are trusting and believing."

"I think the real word you're looking for is *gullible.*"

Hal gave her a sharp look with anger burning in his eyes. "If I didn't know better, I'd think you don't believe I'm adequate at what I do."

"All I know is that for the past four years I've managed to bring in most of the money. That was *not* the deal."

Hal's chuckle was slightly vicious as he said, "It'll be different here … very different."

"I certainly hope so."

✪✪✪

Barbara looked with concern at Angie. Her eyes were tired and her demeanor seemed broken. She had barely slept since the surgery, and that had to be bad for the new baby on the way. Barbara would have gladly taken her place, but she knew Angie would never leave Carter's side. At least Cassie had been compliant enough to stay in Dockrey, thus taking a little stress off of Angie and Michael. When Michael left the room once, Barbara made some excuse to follow him out.

"Is she as tired and worn out as she looks," she asked as they walked down the hallway.

"*I'm* so exhausted that I've just about reached *my* limit," he told her, "and I've slept more than she has and I'm not carrying a baby. I don't see how she can keep holding up." He paused and turned toward Barbara. "I'm worried—really worried. There's no way anybody can make her stop doing what she's doing. She's just Angie. Her heart is always concerned about those she loves … never about herself."

"But what about the baby?"

He shook his head. "Until it gets here and she holds it in her arms, it won't concern her. The flesh and blood of Carter is ever before her. So, he will be the priority … no matter what."

"And you couldn't pry Cassie from her now if you tried."

"I don't know if she'll go back with you or not," he sighed. "This is hard on her … being separated from us."

She smiled with great understanding in her eyes as she patted his back. "I packed her a bag just in case. I assumed as much. They won't let her stay in the hospital, will they?"

"No. But we have a room reserved at the Fed Ex House. I could try to talk Angie into staying with Cassie for a night, and then maybe we could switch off some."

She shook her head. She doubted it would work.

"It's worth a try," he offered weakly.

☼☼☼

Levi couldn't believe Gail was being so unreasonable.

"Can you not put yourself in her place?" he asked this time. "She's thousands of miles from home, her son has just had major surgery, and now he faces weeks of chemotherapy and pretty heavy physical therapy. She's eight months pregnant and is totally exhausted, not to mention the fact of feeling incredibly guilty over having to abandon her four-year-old."

"And so you just want me to invite this woman into our home for a month. This is *the woman* that I always feared, the one I always knew you would love more, but the one I never thought I would have to face because she was somewhere in the middle of the Pacific Ocean!"

"She's only a friend," he tried to reason with her. "She was never anything more than that! She never even considered a relationship with me!"

"It's not *her* I'm worried about! For crying out loud, Levi, this is my competition! This is the woman who captured your heart."

He hung his head and dropped down into one of the empty office chairs. Everyone else had gone to lunch, and he thought this would be the best time to present his idea to Gail.

"She's happily married," he said feebly. "She has two kids and one on the way. What could possibly happen?"

"In reality, nothing," she admitted. "I've seen her, and I've seen her with her family. You don't stand a chance of tearing that apart."

"Then what are you afraid of?"

"She *owns* your heart," she now responded with tears welling up in her eyes. "How do I treat this woman with hospitality in my own home knowing all the time that you're walking around regretting she's not your wife—that she's not the one who lives there with you?"

He looked down and tried to come up with a way to explain it all to her. "Because it's the *right* thing to do."

"The *right* thing? Since when has that mattered to you … the man who takes exorbitant amounts of money from the parents of children who are dying?"

"Since … since … *that* surgery," he said as he gave her a strange look. "You know I don't believe in God."

She nodded. He didn't even want to be married in a church.

"But Carter's surgery was bizarre." He stood and began to wring his hands. "It was almost as if we weren't in there doing it. There's no way we could have guessed where that tumor had ended up … all those little nooks and crannies … but there we were, hour after hour, pulling back pieces here and there and cleaning even more spots."

She looked at him completely dumbfounded. "You think *God* did that?"

"I don't know! But something did." He sat back down. "I know the one thing that Angie was always committed to was her thing with God. All those years of medical training were simply so she could pack up and take off to some underprivileged nation and bring medicine … for pennies a day … just so she could tell people about how great her God was. When they came in with Carter, I wanted to blurt out to her, *Where is your loving God now?*" He shook the thoughts from his head. "I didn't say it, but when we were doing the surgery, every fiber of my being was screaming to me, *Here's Angie's loving God. He's working through you to bring life back to her little boy.*"

She couldn't believe what she was hearing. She had been raised in church but had wandered far away during college. She assumed one day she would get back, but when she married Levi, that seemed impossible. Was it even probable that he was telling her he might believe that God is for real?

"What are you saying, Levi?"

He turned his chair so that he faced her. "I'm not sure, but all I know is that for the first time in my life I feel like I need to do something *bigger* than just me … than just what I can get out of it. I know Angie will never be mine, but to offer her our house seems … well … *right.* That's all I can say. And I know Angie. If I tell her to let her family come and stay with us this next month or two, she'd never do it. But if *you* assured her that you wanted to do this too, she might." He sighed and looked down at his big feet. "It's the right thing to do, Gail. That's all I know to tell you—it's the right thing to do."

☼☼☼

By the time Sam and Billy made it to Cindy's, she had hoped the hangover would have eased. But as they sat in the sunroom watching the twins and Kylla play outside on the unusually warm day, her aching head and bitter nausea managed to thrive. She shouldn't have come, but she missed Cindy so much. Just being with her was almost like having a family again.

"You're not quite right today," Cindy said as they prepared a simple dinner in the kitchen late that afternoon.

Sam chuckled. "You noticed?"

"Well … yeah. What's the problem?"

She gave a deep sigh and looked over at Cindy who was stirring the spaghetti sauce. "I got pretty drunk last night. I took a bottle of wine over to Billy's and …" She stopped immediately when she saw the expression on Cindy's face. "Billy didn't drink a drop of it," she said insistently.

Cindy stared at her in unbelief. "You're telling me that you brought alcohol to his place, got drunk, and he never touched it?"

"I swear he didn't. In fact, he told me about the promise he made to your mother. I felt like a real heel. But I was most definitely in the mood to escape … at least a little bit … so I went ahead and partook. The result—today."

Cindy put down her spoon and turned toward Sam. "He didn't even take a swallow?"

She shook her head. "And he woke me up this morning …"

Cindy's eyebrows flew up as she asked, "You slept with him?"

"… he woke me up … fully clothed … nothing happened." Sam began to realize that Cindy must doubt a lot of the changes in Billy's life. "He was a perfect gentleman, Cindy. I got wasted on his upper deck, and somehow he managed to get me inside, get me into bed, and get me awake and sober enough this morning to be at a parent's meeting at the school."

Cindy crossed her arms and looked at Sam in frustration. "You can't trust him, Sam. No matter what happens in Billy's life, it always comes back to Billy getting what Billy wants."

She wasn't sure if she agreed. "How do you know? I mean, what has he done to prove that it all eventually just revolves around him in the end?"

"Look at his life, Sam. Every decision he's ever made was to somehow benefit his own self. And he's never cared who he hurt or destroyed in the process."

"What about his decision to stop drinking?"

"Don't be fooled. I don't think it's ever been really tested. I think he's avoided places where liquor tempts him, and he's avoided people who tempt him. He's concentrated on school … and … well, let's face it: he's pretty much broke. He can barely afford to eat as it is. He doesn't have what it takes financially to go out and party every weekend."

"His friends would have been glad to set him up."

"But he's avoided them. He's given himself to school."

She was confused. "And you don't think that's noble enough?"

Cindy came over and put her hand on Sam's arm. "You can't change a man from the outside in. I ought to know. You have to change who you are on the inside before you can really change. Billy wants to do good, but his life hasn't changed. Some of his habits have been put on hold … it's amazing what guilt can do for you, especially when looking into the eyes of your dying mother. But for Billy to really make a change, something else has got to happen … something that won't let him mask what's inside, but rather will reveal what's inside for what it really is."

"And what is that?" Sam wondered. She was completely bewildered.

"Sin," Cindy said flatly.

She nodded this time. "Oh … the whole *God* thing. That's what you're talking about, isn't it?"

Cindy had prayed and pleaded with God to give her an opportunity to share what He had done in her life with Sam, and it appeared as though that time had come. She silently prayed again for God to give her the words to share about His transforming love and power without turning Sam off to the Truth.

"Sam, you remember what my life was like before."

Sam only nodded.

"And what I am now is totally different."

"Totally," she agreed.

"That's what I want for Billy … and for you."

Thirty-One

"Where's Cassie?" Jonathan asked Barbara as she came in that evening.

"She stayed," Barbara yawned as she handed one of her grocery bags to him. "It was just too much for her to leave them again."

He figured. "And how was Carter?"

"He's a real trooper. What else can you say about him? He had major surgery on Tuesday, and today he was just happy to be alive. He talked about how bad his back hurt, but it didn't seem to have any effect on his personality."

"What about Angie?"

She put down her bags and turned to him in near grief as she shook her head. "I don't know how she can hold up through all of this. She looks horrible. She hasn't slept soundly since the day they checked him into the hospital. And poor Michael is about to come undone. He's more worried about Angie than he is Carter."

He wasn't surprised. "Why don't they stay at the Fed Ex House?"

"Michael plans to tonight. He was going to insist that Angie go and take Cassie with her, but if she refuses, he says he plans to take Cassie anyway. Someone's got to give her some attention in the middle of all this."

"And then when the new baby comes, more mayhem will be added to the ruckus."

"I'm trying not to be distraught over all of this," but she couldn't finish the statement. She fell into tears and into Jonathan's arms as she let the stress and distress of the day wash through her.

"I understand, hon," he said gently. "We knew there'd be days like this. We've gotten through them before, and God will see us through these too."

She took comfort in his words, because they had been through much over the years. "It'll be interesting to so what God has up his sleeve for this one."

"He's always had a purpose, hasn't He?" He continued to rub her back.

"Always."

She tried to gain control as she pulled back and looked up at him. "How was the new minister? You did get to meet him, didn't you?"

"Oh, yes," he went immediately into a frown. "The illustrious *Dr. Bridges* most definitely made an appearance."

"And …?"

"And he was everything I hoped for and more."

She furled her eyebrows and grimaced. "Really? That bad?"

"Let's just say, in *Dr. Bridges'* mind he has already analyzed, diagnosed and set a course of action for First Baptist of Dockrey."

"Which is?"

"To put the irresponsible pastor in his proper place."

Her mouth opened wide. "And what place would that be?"

"Somewhere behind *Dr. Bridges.*"

☼☼☼

Gail and Levi walked into Carter's room, with Levi holding tightly to her hand. He knew there was no way he could ever explain to her that he loved her more at this moment than any other time in their life together. He knew what she was sacrificing to carry out this wish, and he hoped there would be some way he could let her know.

"How's my favorite family?" he said jovially as he closed the door behind them. "And who is this pretty little girl?" He had never seen Cassie.

Michael answered, knowing Angie was about to drop. "This is our Cassie. She's a very *big* girl."

"You certainly are," Levi said as he knelt down to her. "You stayed with Grandma and Grandpa all week so Mom and Dad could help out your little brother. There aren't a lot of sisters in the world who would do that."

"Are you the doctor?" Cassie asked.

"I am." Levi marveled at the spitting image of Angie.

"I don't like your hospital," Cassie said frankly.

"Cassie!" Angie exclaimed.

"It's okay," Levi calmed her immediately. "Not everybody does. What do you think is wrong with it, Cassie?"

She gave a look as if to say *where do I start.* "It's way too big and way too tall. And you made all the trees die to build it. Why do you have to kill the trees to save people?"

Wo. She definitely had the free spirit of her mother living inside her.

"Well," Levi tried to state his position simply, "there are a lot of people all over the place that need our help really, really bad. A small building could never help all the people. We would have to tell many people every day to just go back home and stay very sick because we couldn't help them. And as for the trees, if we cut one down here, we can plant a brand new one somewhere else." Well, that was a stretch. He had never personally planted a tree in his life, but in the eyes of a four-year-old, that seemed like good reasoning.

"Where?" She was persistent.

"Cassie, enough!" Angie said with exasperation.

"Bright child," Levi laughed.

"Can you tell her father has a Doctorate of Agriculture?" Angie raised an eyebrow.

"No offense," Levi said with a big smile, "but I definitely saw more of her mother in that little exchange. Hard-headed, stubborn, opinionated."

"But her Daddy is the one who fills her head with all these ideas."

Levi was amazed at the resemblance between Cassie and Angie. He shook his head at the vision. "Anyway," he continued, "Gail and I are here with an offer."

"So, this isn't your official *doctor's visit*?" Angie teased, probably the first time she had showed any energy all day.

"Well, it is … but more than that too. We want you and your family to come stay with us while Carter goes through his treatment."

Angie's jaw dropped.

"Listen," Gail jumped into the conversation, "I know you may feel awkward about this, but we have so much room. You really need to be resting in your condition, and any friend of Levi's … is a friend of mine."

Angie shook her head. "There's no way I could impose on you like this."

For the first time in his life, Michael actually said something aggressive and decisive. "We'd be delighted."

Angie turned and looked at him in utter amazement. "Are you serious?"

"Listen," Michael looked at her with deep compassion, "I can't bear to watch you go on and on like this. At some point, Ang, you're gonna come apart. And not only you, but baby number three is in there fighting for its chance to be a part of our life together. I'll do anything I have to."

Levi tried to lighten the mood. "A man with conviction … how do you fight against that?"

"But all the equipment and stuff that he needs in order to be monitored …" Angie tried to be the voice of reason.

"… will be provided for at the house," Levi guaranteed her. "Between me and you and Gail, we should be able to monitor all of it adequately."

Angie now looked over to Gail. "Are you sure? This will be a major disruption in your nice, quiet life. I don't think you really know what you're asking."

"On the contrary," Gail replied, "I know exactly what I'm asking. I would be honored to have your family spend some time with us."

"This isn't *some* time," Angie laughed. "It's practically moving in!"

"Then our house will at last seem like a home!" Gail said cheerfully. "It's about time."

☼☼☼

Stephen sat quietly out by the pool as he thumbed through all the important numbers on his cell phone. Record producers, personal numbers for celebrities, television and movie directors, writers, people with whom he had worked and come to know well for the fourteen years he had been involved with the music business. He had looked forward to retirement and being able to spend unlimited amounts of time with his family, having absolutely no projects hanging over his head. But now … it didn't seem near as inviting. It had been five months since he and Annie had given their farewell concert in New York at Carnegie Hall. The concert had been recorded and televised on a major network, and a massive ball had followed with one of the biggest who's who of celebrities ever created.

He sighed as he continued looking through his numbers. Each name brought out another memory. Some were good and represented successful accomplishments. Others were stressful as he had worked with odd and overly creative temperaments and obsessive perfectionists. The fact was that he didn't miss the people—he simply missed the work. He couldn't remember a time in his life when he hadn't been busy with music in some form or another. And all he missed right now was a reason to be doing something.

"Meditating?" Annie asked as she joined him outside.

"Hmmm," was all he replied.

"We won't have many more warmish nights like this. Pretty soon it'll be downright cold."

"You do know that *your* cold is very relative as compared to *my* cold?"

She laughed as she reached for his hand. "It'll even be cold enough for you Yankees to consider it cold."

He closed up his phone and stuck it inside his pocket.

"Making a call to someone?" she asked.

"Not really," he began as he started a small confession, "just contemplating the possibility."

"To whom?" she wondered.

"I'm not sure. I was just thinking that with all of this time on my hands, I could possibly do some work here at home for somebody."

She was shocked. "I thought you were in retirement?"

"Yeah, at thirty-five I'm retired. The reprieve has been nice, but I'm starting to get antsy just sitting here doing nothing."

"Doing nothing? I could fix that, you know?"

"In what way?"

"I could teach you to cook, do laundry, clean the pool …"

He laughed. "No thanks. The reason I worked so hard in the first place was so I didn't have to do those things; I can pay someone else to do them."

"Or marry someone who will."

"You're catching on."

She sat thoughtfully. She had no idea he was surfing on the edge of boredom here in Dockrey. She had just assumed he loved slowing down as much as she.

"The stars are gorgeous out here, aren't they?" she asked him.

"Definitely. In fact, everything about here is gorgeous."

"Except the lack of work."

He leaned back and took a deep breath. "I do love it here, Annie. I don't want to leave. I like the lack of people, the lack of busyness, the lack of stress. I like the fact that my time is my own, that I can have all the freedom in the world to be with you and the kids, and that the paparazzi … well … never mind about them. They've managed to follow us even down here. But it won't always be like that."

"I know. I just had no idea that you were unfulfilled."

"Happy … but not fulfilled."

She glanced over at him. "Wait. Didn't we have this conversation before?"

He smiled sheepishly. "About six years ago, I believe."

"That first week that we met."

"And you got so mad at me I didn't think you'd ever speak to me again."

"I almost didn't. You kept telling me that happiness equaled fulfillment, and I kept insisting that it was possible to be happy and yet not completely fulfilled."

He nodded as he recalled the major quarrel.

She grinned and squeezed his hand. "Are you saying now that you're indeed happy but no longer fulfilled?"

"I'm afraid to admit it. You might not speak to me again."

"Oh, I'll still speak to you, but I do believe some sort of apology is in order."

"Apology offered."

"And apology accepted."

They sat in silence for a little while as they looked out at the stars and enjoyed the gentle breeze that would occasionally blow in with sudden wisps.

"Maybe we should have another kid?" she suggested out of the blue.

He looked at her in total shock. "You're kidding, right? When Ellie was born you said you would never be dragged through that ordeal again. In fact, I think I remember you saying something about me whacking you on the head with a hammer if you ever suggested it."

She laughed again. "I wasn't talking about *me* having it. With you being so bored, I figured you could carry it, birth it, and do the middle of the night nursings this time."

He grinned at her and shook his head. "I would almost take you up on that, except for Ellie's birth was a little more … uh … intense than Stevie's. I don't think I have the constitution for it."

"Well, that fact, and also that it's completely impossible."

He smoothed his thumb over the back of her hand. "Not that another child wouldn't thrill me. You know I've always wanted a houseful. Plus, there's this competition going on in your family: Andie has five, Angie has a third one on the way, and we're just sitting here with two, nice and happy in our brand new log cabin with a heated pool in the middle of the Alabama wilderness."

"Yeah, but Alex only has one. He blows the competition idea."

"But he's a guy. That totally knocks him out of the *three-sister-ring*."

She gave him a serious look and clarified, "I really was kidding about having another baby. It's nice to be out of diapers for a while."

"Its official then," he said forlornly. "I'm really bored, and I need to find some kind of work to do."

The conversation was starting to bother Annie more. They had discussed throughout their entire marriage the wonderful life they would have when he was finally finished with his contract. Had something happened to change all those dreams?

"What exactly do you want to do?" she wondered. "Do you want to go back to writing and recording and touring again?"

He answered quickly, "No, nothing like that at all. I don't want to have to leave here. I like it here. I just want to be able to do something with my time other than watch the grass grow."

"Like what?"

"Oh, I'm not sure." He thought for a moment and then said, "Maybe something like Benjamin Brenner."

Her eyebrows flew up in alarm. "Benjamin Brenner? What made you think of him? Of all the people in the business, what brought his work to the forefront?"

"I like him," he answered plainly. "He's this neat guy who's incredibly talented and has the ability to literally make a movie come to life. When you sit through something he scored, the music itself is almost like a mini-movie. How cool would that be to take a story, come up with a melodic theme, and then write a score that flows throughout the entire script. *That* would be awesome."

She wanted to say no more. There was now a huge hollow hole in the pit of her stomach. She knew something about Ben Brenner that Stephen was clueless about: he was Stephen's biological father. Even before they had married, Edrew Williams, the man who had married Stephen's mother and raised him, had told her that the reason he had hated and mistreated Stephen all those years was because he wasn't really his son. Ben had gotten Ellen, Stephen's mother, pregnant and offered to pay for an abortion. After being rejected by her family and having her hands mutilated by her father, Edrew came to the rescue, marrying her and promising to raise Stephen as his own son. Ellen never wanted Stephen to know, and she had made Edrew promise not to tell him. Annie wondered often if she should come clean with him and just tell him the truth, but something inside her felt as though she would be dishonoring Ellen's wishes. She had never met the woman, but she had great respect for how she had raised Stephen and made sure that he succeeded where she couldn't.

Finally Annie tried to redirect his thoughts. "I don't know … that's a huge undertaking for a first try. What about something else for a starter? Something simpler."

"Such as?"

"Well … maybe doing a theme song for a movie or something … or a television show. Something that's sort of … you just sit down and do it and then it's over."

"Annie, I could write a theme song in one day. Besides, I've done that many times. I want something new and challenging. I want something *big*."

As she leaned back and closed her eyes, she began to wonder if perhaps having another baby might not be a good idea. It would be a great distraction from Benjamin Brenner, and would most definitely give Stephen something new to do. She wondered if it would be considered selfish by God if she actually prayed for twins … no, triplets. That would be a major distraction … times three.

☼☼☼

Billy was beginning to panic again. He had not seen Sam in over an hour, and it was getting late. She had remained under the effects of the hangover most of the day, so he had tried not to bother her. But as the big clock in the living room chimed midnight, and she was nowhere to be found in the house, he decided it was time to *bother*.

After one more search, he at last saw her blond hair shining in the moonlight through the doors of the sunroom. He literally heaved a sigh of relief and made his way outside to see if everything was all right.

"Hey ponytail," he said gently. "You okay?"

She looked over at him and smiled a tired smiled. "Yeah." No glasses … her eyes melted him again. She then turned her gaze back to the stars. "It's so nice and peaceful here. I needed a little down time I suppose. I haven't felt the best today, and I thought maybe coming out here for a while would clear my head." She smiled again. "I was right."

He sat down beside her on the top stair and glanced up at the stars.

"This almost feels like home," she confessed softly. "I have so many memories of sitting out here like this. You and Cindy would always come out to smoke, and since your parents hated it so much, they never dreamed of joining you. So you guys would talk about all the things you didn't want your parents to hear or know." She gave him a devilish grin. "You two were quite the characters back then."

He shook his head. "I'm not exactly proud of all that anymore. Just another of my bad vices to be reminded of."

"And when did you stop smoking? Was that another promise you made to your mother on her deathbed?"

"Actually, no." He stretched out his legs and rubbed his arms as the lateness of the night was beginning to turn cool. "I was sort of forced out of smoking. When Mother died and I had to go on the monthly allowance, I stood in the grocery store one afternoon with a carton of cigarettes in one hand and a pile of frozen dinners in the other. I actually weighed them in my head … which could I do without the easiest? After a rather stupid argument with myself, I decided I would really need to eat if I planned on finishing school. So, I put the cigarettes back and went and got several more dinners."

"Just cold turkey like that?" She was amazed. "You just upped and said no more?"

He laughed slightly. "Well, it's not like I had much of a choice. Every time I craved one I'd remember that I could eat supper that night when I got home."

She looked over at him with a genuinely sympathetic expression. "So you only eat supper? That's your only meal?"

"I got a meal ticket at the cafeteria during the week. That was included in Mother's will."

She smiled and shook her head. "Your mother was a smart lady."

"That, she was," he agreed. "She was so proud of what I'd already done, but she knew me too well. She knew I'd use her death as the perfect excuse to quit school, get drunk a lot, and probably end up dead on the side of the road somewhere. She figured holding my feet to the fire, even after she was gone, would be my only hope."

She took a deep breath as her teeth began to chatter from the chill. She looked over at him sadly and said, "I'm really sorry about bringing the wine over last night and then going ahead and getting wasted even after you told me you didn't drink anymore. That was incredibly insensitive of me."

He shrugged it off. "No problem. It's always better to get drunk with someone than alone."

"Yeah, but … *that* was wrong. I should have sucked it up and said, *Let's play Scrabble or something.*"

"Scrabble?" he laughed. "Yeah … that's sounds way better," he added sarcastically.

"It's just that I went there with my mind set to … I guess the best way to say it is that I wanted to empty my soul, so to speak. I wanted everything off my mind and out of my brain for a while. I just didn't want to have to deliberately think."

"That's why I let you stay the night. I knew you were most definitely *out of your brain* and in no condition whatsoever to drive home."

Sam slowly stood and stretched her arms to the sky. "Thanks," was all she replied. It had always been hard for her to let go of any form of guilt. "I guess it's getting late."

"Past midnight."

She looked over at him and grinned as she asked, "And you haven't turned back into a mouse yet?"

"Nope. But I have this great glass slipper I found back on the stairs at the palace. I was thinking about trying to find the chick who left it."

She grabbed his hand and dragged him toward the door to the sunroom. "When Billy Marcum starts playing *Cinderella*, it's definitely time to call it a night."

Thirty-Two

Jonathan looked out over the congregation on Sunday morning and was awed by the number of people present. It had been two years since the whole church had met together in the sanctuary. This morning one hundred fifty chairs had been placed in every spot available so the church could meet as one to hear Hal and then vote at the end of the service. For just a brief moment, his heart was warmed by the sounds of fellowship and joy as he looked out at the flock he had shepherded for thirty years. Then Hal Bridges appeared.

When Hal came to the platform, Jonathan was dismayed. The man had suddenly developed a humble demeanor. He was still impeccably dressed, this time with a crisp white shirt, a solid black suit, and again, a stylish, yet conservative tie. His hair was in perfect place, not a strand sticking out from anywhere, and as he went to a seat on the platform, he walked with what seemed to be a measured calculation.

Jonathan almost ran his hand through his hair from sheer nervousness, but figured it was probably already in bad shape from just making it through the morning Sunday School time. Hal had put him through the third degree as they had walked around the church and peered into various classes. He had made many comments under his breath about the condition of the rooms, the shabbiness of the carpet, the staining on the walls. He talked about the way appearances could make or break a church when people were visiting and dangling on the edge of decision. He hoped there would be enough funds available to give the existing building a good facelift. Of course, Jonathan didn't mention the fact that most people thought this was the most beautiful sanctuary within a hundred miles. Its exposed wood and giant beams brought a homey feel to the worship while so many other churches seemed sterile and cold.

He wanted to tell Hal, *Dr. Bridges*, that the chair on the platform he had taken was Kyle's, but at this point it seemed a worthless effort. The man, no matter how humble his appearance, was definitely in the mindset to promote himself at all costs. Kyle would figure it out quickly enough when he walked in with the choir. He could simply join them in the loft if need be. Hal had wanted to meet Kyle, but of all mornings, Kylla had a stomach virus, and the result was Kyle rushing in way later than normal. Of course, Hal had his comments about that.

"Does the man not have a wife?" he had asked.

"Yes …" Jonathan had patiently replied, "… a very lovely and responsible one. However, she teaches the senior high girls' class, and they decided it was more important that *she* been here on time rather than Kyle."

Hmmm was becoming Hal's classic response to everything he seemed to disagree with yet didn't care to argue about at the moment.

The church had a special presentation for Kyle and Cindy this morning, and Jonathan now was wishing he had put it off until the evening service when Hal would be gone. This was a wonderful surprise for the couple who had given so much to this church over the past five years, and the excitement of *Dr. Bridges* would somewhat overshadow the whole gift.

As the choir made their way into the loft, Kyle looked slightly disheveled himself, something that rarely happened. Luckily, Billy was here for the weekend, and he and Samantha had volunteered to keep Kylla at home during Sunday morning. Kyle automatically headed for his seat, but stopped short when he realized it was occupied. He glanced over at Jonathan who could only give him a weak smile. Kyle shrugged his shoulders, looked back toward the choir, and managed to find an empty chair at the front of the loft.

Andie was doing an exceptional job at the morning prelude, but Jonathan still felt amiss because Angie was in Memphis with her son, and Annie had to stay home again because of the onslaught of the paparazzi. Just when he thought life was beginning to feel normal for the first time in many years, it appeared his world was being turned upside down. He glanced toward heaven, whispered a quick prayer, and moved to the pulpit.

As usual, he was light and fun with his announcements. There was a bit of give and take with the congregation, and before he knew what was happening, he had loosened his tie and forgotten completely about the judging eyes sitting on the platform right behind him. As he ended his part, he called Doug to come and make a special presentation. Doug's antics always brought humor to anything he did. His simple walk from the choir loft to the pulpit in his robe brought laughter right away. As he fumbled for an envelope, it fell across the pulpit and down off the platform onto the floor in front. More laughter. Tom Richards, who was sitting on the front row with the search committee, graciously retrieved it and handed it back, at which Doug gave a deep bow. Laughter ensued yet again.

"If I can hang on to this thing now, I have a special presentation to make here," Doug began. He looked back at the choir loft and continued, "Could Kyle and Cindy Sarkos please come to the office … I mean, the pulpit." The laughter returned as a shocked Kyle and Cindy maneuvered their way to the platform.

"Kyle and Cindy," he said more seriously now, "this church owes you both a great debt of gratitude. You guys have served us faithfully above and beyond the call of duty in so many ways, that when I started to try and list them, I soon realized it would take up most of the pastor's sermon, and I wanted to stay in good standing with the preacher … if you know what I mean." It was impossible for him to be the straight man, and the people laughed again. "But anyone who's been in this church for the past few years is bound to have been touched by your ministries in one way or another, so there probably isn't a need to go on about them anyway."

Kyle and Cindy were clueless.

"Because you guys got married in such a whirlwind, and were just beginning here, you never really got a proper honeymoon. So the choir decided that we ought to do something totally frivolous and send you two off somewhere so you could *honey* and *moon* over each other for a few days. We were thinking the mountains or something," then he motioned his hand out toward the congregation. "But as others in the church got wind of it, they all decided to chip in too and just blow this thing out of the water."

Cindy began to shake slightly with emotion as she realized what was happening. Kyle put his arm around her waist and smiled.

"This is a little token … well, that's not true … it's a pretty big token when you come right down to it … a big token for the huge assets you both have been to our church." He handed the envelope to Kyle. "These are tickets for a mega cruise down through various Mexican ports and the Caribbean."

Cindy's hand came up to her mouth now and tears began to form in her eyes.

"You leave this Friday," and Doug put his hand up to stop any complaints they might have. "We've already arranged for people to take your children … well, I mean take *care* of them … not swipe them or anything, so all you have to concentrate on is packing."

Kyle now had tears building up in his eyes as he opened the envelope which held airline tickets, ship tickets, and a check for an amount he couldn't yet see.

Doug went on, "I know you probably feel a little overwhelmed by all this and think you should say something eloquent and sweet, but we've all agreed that you should forget it for now and just give us a great slide show when you return."

Very gently Kyle shoved Doug to the side and took the pulpit. "You bet I'm gonna say something." Kyle gathered his composure for just a moment. "First, let me say that this church is like no other I've ever been a part of in my entire life. When I came to Dockrey … I came home. You embraced me, you embraced my family, and you made us a part of you. And knowing that this trip is from you … and is done out of love

… will make it far sweeter than had we planned it ourselves. I'm sure Cindy would say something nice and sweet too, but she would have to squeeze it in between sobs, which would probably cut into Pastor Jon's sermon also … and I would hate to ruin such a great working relationship." The congregation laughed again, then broke into applause, and finally came to their feet as Kyle and Cindy made their way back to their seats.

"Well," Jonathan began as he returned to the pulpit, "this is quite a start to what promises to be a very big morning. As most of you know, Hal Bridges is here today in view of a call as Minister of Education to our church."

Jonathan knew he would have to pray and confess this afternoon because the refusal to use the title of *doctor* was done with a hint of malice in his heart.

"The search committee will be recommending him, and after the service today we'll have a vote as to whether this is the desire of the church as a whole. So, I'll call on Floyd Benson, the chairman of this committee, to introduce Hal to you, and then we'll let Hal tell you whatever is on his heart. Floyd?"

Floyd walked up to the platform and smiled proudly as he grasped the pulpit with both hands. He looked like a man who had indeed carried out a great accomplishment.

"First, let me say that we're honored this morning to present *Dr.* Hal Bridges to you. Our church is so blessed to have found a man as qualified, educated, and experienced as Dr. Bridges. He served ten years in the military as a specialist in the Navy Seals, received his BA in Education Administration from Pepperdine University in Malibu, California, and then went on to Golden Gate Baptist Theological Seminary in Mill Valley, California to get his MA and ThD in Church Administration and Education. He pastored while attending college and seminary, until his final year in seminary when he became Minister of Education and Administration at First Baptist Church of Newton, California. He stayed there for two years until called to serve at Community Friendship Baptist in Phoenix, Arizona five years ago. He comes with great recommendations from professors and pastors alike, as well as a four-star Navy Captain who had the pleasure of working with him for several years. A man of impeccable character and great vision, Dr. Bridges desires to unite with us, not only as a staff member, but as a member of this fellowship to work beside us as we seek to grow First Baptist for the glory of God. Please welcome Dr. Bridges as he shares with you his conviction that God has indeed called him to now serve us at this time."

Floyd confidently held out his hand toward Hal as the congregation broke out in applause. Jonathan watched as Hal stood swiftly, adjusted his suit button, and then moved with dignified steps toward the pulpit. Whatever Hal Bridges was, Jonathan thought, he was *not* like Dockrey. He was not a man who belonged here. He could only hope that Hal would indeed desire to be a *member of this fellowship* who would *work beside us as we seek to grow for the glory of God.*

Hal took his time before beginning his address. He appeared to look into the eye of every church member seated out front. He held an air of self-assurance as he nodded his head in an approving manner toward the people who were staring back at him. It was almost as if they were the ones under scrutiny.

"Good morning," he finally spoke. The church responded in like reply. "As I stand here before you, please do not think that this is a decision made impetuously or without greatly weighing both the benefits and detriments that accompany it. My only desire is to follow the call of God to wherever He leads me so that I may fulfill my eternal purpose—the purpose for which I was created and sent to this planet."

As Hal went on with his flowery speech, Jonathan found his eyes wandering to the wife, Lisa Bridges. There was something totally odd and misplaced about her. She was as impeccable in her appearance as Hal. Her shortly cropped blond hair was perfectly styled, her make-up flawless, and her light pink suit fit as though it had been meticulously tailored to her slender figure. But there was something in her eyes that seemed out of place. It wasn't as if this was a couple united in the call, but more like Hal was the golden prize and she was the certificate that accompanied it. As he spoke, there was no look of admiration or even anticipation in her gaze. She was like a robot he remembered seeing in some odd science fiction movie he had watched with Arly and Adam recently—programmed to be the perfect complement to the man who had chosen her … and nothing more.

Hal's speech went on and on. Jonathan had actually offered to let him preach, but Hal insisted he wasn't a preacher, but an administrator. Besides, Hal commented on the fact that he wanted to hear Jonathan preach before making *his* ultimate decision concerning coming to Dockrey. *No pressure there*, Jonathan smiled to himself. *Perhaps I could settle all this today and just preach a really botched up sermon.* He glanced down at his watch. Hal had been talking for fifteen minutes now. Jonathan looked back toward Kyle.

Kyle mouthed the words, "Do I need to shorten the worship?"

He smiled and shook his head. If Hal didn't want to preach, he should have just shut up and sat down. But his speech went on and on. After twenty-five minutes, he finally began to wind it up.

"As far as the cut in pay and the lower benefits, I can deal with those if this is indeed where God is calling me. So, in closing, I would just like to say, I hope this is a partnership between you and me, a partnership between myself and *Pastor* Wright, a partnership between me and Kyle. If we are to take this church out of the struggling situation it has been led into, it will require the cooperation of us all. As Paul said, we must *press on toward the prize*. That is all I desire to do … press on for what is the absolute best for this church, this community, this nation, and this world … for the glory of God." He stood tall for a moment, and then leaned back down to finish. "Thank you."

The applause began slowly, but it eventually caught on and finally the whole church joined. Hal stayed at the pulpit a few moments longer. It sounded more like the speech of a political candidate than it did a minister coming to serve the Lord at a new church. Jonathan went up and shook his hand, smiling graciously the entire time. When Hal finally went back to Kyle's seat on the platform, Jonathan asked the congregation to bow with him in prayer.

Kyle went on with the music part of the service as planned, although he was extremely nervous about time. Since they were televised on the local cable station, it was imperative they keep their services to one hour only or they would have to edit out either the beginning or the end. But every time Kyle would give Jonathan a questioning look, he would give him a reassuring smile and nod to just continue on.

When at last the offering was finished, Jonathan came to the pulpit for what was anticipated to be a sermon. He smiled warmly at the faces of those whom he had shepherded for many, many years

"Well," he finally said, "it appears we didn't have to worry about Doug or Cindy taking up my preaching time, but old Hal here did a pretty good job." There were a few chuckles at this statement. "But you know what? That's fine. This morning, in just a few minutes, we'll be deciding on the possibility of a new direction for our church. I think having Hal speak to us about his ideas and concerns, and then our moving into a time of praise and worship with Kyle where we focus only on adoring our Lord and Creator, that this is an appropriate place to bring our service to a close. Normally, we would offer an invitation for salvation or rededication, or for whatever decision the Lord might have laid on your heart. But this morning I'd like to offer this altar to you as an invitation to pray. Your vote will be a deciding factor in the future of this church."

The faces of the people were trying hard to read Jonathan Wright. Was he for or against Hal Bridges? This wasn't exactly what anyone had expected. As Jonathan called the instrumentalists up to play and Kyle up to sing the invitation hymn alone, he then invited church members to come to the altar and pray.

The first ones to the front were Hal and Lisa Bridges. Slowly people began to flood the aisles and go down on their knees in prayer as Kyle appropriately sang "Have Thine Own Way, Lord." Jonathan didn't kneel.

He sat in his chair and merely bowed his head. *Father, You have this church, and you have this moment in Your hands. Do whatever it is that You wish to do: not my will, but Yours be done.*

When Jonathan had come to this church in view of a call thirty years ago, the vote had to be ninety percent. But because of the huge division caused by the previous pastor, so many business meetings had failed to accomplish anything with a ninety percent vote. Once Jonathan had been voted in, a revision of the Constitution and By-Laws changed the vote to only sixty percent. Jonathan had never believed that was a good number. If something passed by a sixty percent vote only, that meant over a third of the church disagreed. How would the church respond to *Dr.* Hal Bridges?

Thirty-Three

As the committee and the church staff waited in the lobby for the vote to be counted, Tom Richards came over to Jonathan and motioned him off to the side.

"I have to tell you this," Tom said softly so that no one else could hear him. "You presented the motion wrong this morning."

Jonathan chuckled. "Parliamentary Procedure has never been my strong point."

Tom shook his head. "It had nothing to do with your procedure." He leaned toward Jonathan's ear and spoke even softer. "You said the committee was unanimously presenting Hal to the church."

Jonathan pulled back to look him squarely in the eye. "It wasn't unanimous?"

"Not at all," he said discreetly. "I didn't like him from the moment he began insisting on pushing up the schedule. And there were a lot of vague things on his résumé'." He paused and sighed. "I've done this before, Jonathan, in other churches. Now-a-days, you have to check people out. A man can pad a résumé' in ways that would blow your mind. We've got a good thing going on here in this church, and I would hate to see it destroyed by someone who could have been *found out* had we *checked him out* more thoroughly."

"The vote's still got to come in, Tom. Who knows?"

"I *do* know," Tom said firmly. "That stupid sixty percent rule will pass anything. Most churches I've been in require an eighty-five percent vote; that sure is a lot more practical."

"I don't like the sixty percent thing myself, but there it is ... in black and white ... and after what this church went through before me, I doubt it'll ever change."

"Before this guy is through with us, it might change ... it just might."

Tom and Jonathan nonchalantly moved back toward the rest of the group.

"So, how many years were you in the Navy?" Kyle asked Hal as he loosened his tie.

What had been a series of jovial and light exchanges suddenly became sober as the look on Hal's face became intense.

"Ten years," he said grimly. "I don't really like to talk about it much." Hal opened up his hands and stared down at them in silence for a moment. "These hands," he declared through nearly gritted teeth, "have killed men … these bare hands. It was out of duty and obedience to my commanding officers, but still …"

Everyone just gawked in silence.

"I don't like to talk about those days if I can at all help it," he continued, "but people seem to have a gory curiosity about it, so I oblige the questions."

Of course, this made Kyle look like a heel for asking what was meant to be basic conversation. Jonathan immediately jumped to Kyle's defense.

"Well, let's face it Hal," he said as he slapped his back, "you don't meet an ex Navy Seal every day. I suppose it's one of those things you learn to live with and deal with over the course of the years."

"I try," Hal replied as he slowly wiped his hands together. "But there are some stains in life that even time can't erase—some wounds that time can never heal."

The mood definitely became dark after this. The only salvation was Devin and Denay and all their toddler energy. The focus quickly, and *gratefully*, shifted to the adorable little blonds.

A few more minutes passed before the counting committee finally returned with the results. John Cramer gave Jonathan a rather severe look as he handed the envelope to Floyd Benson. Jonathan tried to interpret John's expression, but John could say nothing. Whatever the results, he knew John wasn't pleased.

Floyd carefully opened the envelope and only stared at the paper he had pulled out. "This is the actual vote?"

"Counted five times," said Ricky Tatum.

"Well … okay. Not what I expected, but it's still okay."

Everyone looked intently at Floyd, anticipating in their own minds what the result actually was.

Nancy Beth had had enough of the suspense. "For crying out loud, Floyd!" she nearly yelled. "What was the vote?"

Floyd raised a bushy red eyebrow and said, "Sixty percent for Hal: forty percent against."

Everyone began to look at each other in alarm. This was not what they had wanted. Ever since the sixty percent rule had been enacted, no vote had actually been that close. And as far as staff members were concerned, Jonathan's vote thirty years ago had been ninety-eight percent, and Kyle's had even been one hundred.

"This isn't a problem, is it?" Hal finally asked. "You did say a sixty percent vote would get me in?"

"Well, yeah," Stan told him, "but to actually be voted in with *only* a sixty percent vote … that's not very reassuring."

"Sure it is," Hal nearly chimed. "You've got a big church here. The bigger the church, the more reasons you have to find differing opinions on things."

"But sixty percent?" Tonya questioned. "How could forty percent of the church not see you as this great addition, this awesome asset?"

"Easily," Hal continued on with the confidence. "You've got to understand what you brought before them this morning. It was so much more than just saying *hire Hal.* This church was voting on whether they really want to go through with expansion, with growth—in other words, they were voting on big change. Sixty percent said *absolutely! Count us on board with this.* Forty percent said *you've got to prove this to us.*"

"Well, you're wrong there," Tom spoke up this time. Everyone turned to Tom. "This church voted one hundred percent to make all the changes we've called you to make. There were no doubts and no hesitations."

"In fact," Kyle interrupted, "Jonathan wouldn't even consider doing it if the whole church wasn't behind the decision. Churches split over things like this."

"Of course they do," Hal agreed. "And your one hundred percent moving to sixty percent merely shows that this is a normal church. That one hundred percent vote for change is easy to come by when you don't put any specifics on the table. But when you suddenly offer up a name, a plan, and a budget, things look a little different."

All Jonathan could think of at the moment was that Hal Bridges was one smooth talker. He was also shocked that a forty percent negative vote didn't seem to bother him in the least.

"Here's the bottom line," Jonathan finally said as he tried to draw the shocker to a close. "Hal, you've been called to this church as Minister of Education. Do you accept this call, or do you reject it?"

Hal smiled and stuck out his hand to Jonathan. "I gladly accept it and look forward to doing great things with you in the very near future."

Jonathan shook his hand, worked up a smile, and then said, "And I can't wait to see all that God has in store for this church as a result of calling you here."

No one was quite sure whether Jonathan's statement was a declaration of gladness or of doom, but Hal Bridges seemed utterly delighted over the whole thing. As the committee took him out to the church van to leave for dinner at the local steak house, Kyle, Cindy, Barbara, Jonathan, Ricky Tatum and John Cramer lingered in the lobby watching them pat each other's backs getting into the van.

"What just happened here, Pastor Jon?" Ricky asked as he turned to Jonathan, obviously reeling from the shock of the vote. "One more person here today could have literally made that vote fifty-nine percent."

Jonathan shook his head and gave another smile more of resolution and confidence rather than warmth and gladness. "I believe we'll have to just chalk this one up to the sovereignty of God, folks. Can't explain it, but it happened, and somehow through it all, God is in control."

Barbara came up beside Jonathan and put her arm through his. "Welcome the rod, sweetie. Welcome the rod."

☼☼☼

Annie was purely sick over the result of the vote. "Our being there could have changed the whole outcome!" she shouted as she rampaged through the log cabin that Sunday afternoon. Everyone had been over to her place for Sunday dinner, and when she had heard the whole scenario, she began going ballistic. Now that everyone had left, she returned to her expressions of complete disgust.

"This is absolutely unbelievable! The stupid paparazzi! Those ridiculous, lying magazines! How could this have happened? How could the church be so stupid and so blind to have just voted him in like that?"

Stephen tried to calm her. "We have to just believe like your dad said: God's in control here."

"In control of what? What on earth was accomplished this morning?"

"I don't know, honey, but I'm not gonna sit here and question God through all of this. And we don't even know if this is good or bad. The man hasn't even started working yet."

"Don't insult my parents like that … or my sister for that matter!" she said bitingly.

"I'm not saying their impressions of this guy were wrong," he defended. "I'm just saying there may be more going on here than what we're seeing on the surface. What was that your dad used to say all the time? *God is up to something*? Remember, anytime something started happening that we knew would shake up our world, he would always say *God was up to something*. That's all this is."

"Like what? What could He possibly be up to!" she snarled.

"I don't know," he threw his hands up in desperation. "I'm *not* God. I just trust Him … that's all."

She gave a controlled growl of rage and turned to leave the room. When the door slammed upstairs in the studio, he knew some unusual music would soon be played on the piano as she let out her frustration. Sure enough, a Nocturne by Chopin began to be pounded out unmercifully.

He shook his head. *I should record these sessions of anger and make an album out of them. Never has such emotion been put into music. Even Chopin himself would applaud that version of his work.*

☼☼☼

As Sam dropped Billy off at his boat, she found herself smiling at him unaware. It had been unusually *normal* with him this weekend. He had paid a little extra attention to her on Saturday because of her miserable condition. And today, as they cared for Kylla together, she had seen a tender side of him that reminded her why she had fallen in love with him in the first place. The more time she spent around him, the more his faults and failures, and yes, even the wounds he had caused her, began to fade.

"What are you smiling at, ponytail?" he asked as he closed the trunk of her car and caught her in the middle of a silly grin.

She blushed slightly and shook her head. "Nothing really … just stuff."

He took a step toward her. "That is not an acceptable answer. What's running through that pretty little head of yours?"

She just shook her head as she continued smiling. "My thoughts are still my own."

He looked down at her and gave a deep sigh. "Well, I'll gladly share my happy thoughts with you." He leaned on the back of her car and dropped his bag to the ground. "I'm happy you came to Cindy's with me this weekend. I'm happy you were there with me to help take care of Kylla. I've enjoyed riding with you today and just shooting the breeze about anything at all that came to our minds." He reached out his hand to hers and waited for her to slowly take it. "And now, I'm *really* happy that you're holding my hand."

She blushed again. "Is that what I'm doing? Holding your hand? We're not just shaking hands to say goodbye?"

He reached out his other hand to hers, and when she took it, he pulled her to him. "We're definitely *not* shaking hands now."

"What are we doing now?" she barely managed to get out as he scooted farther down the back of the car so he could be even with her eyes.

"I know what I'd like to do," he said as a smile began to form. "I'd like to pretend that …" He stopped. *Don't do this now, Billy* he told himself. *Don't give her the ball yet. Wait until you're ready. Finish school, get a job, be a man she can really trust with her life.*

But he knew she was already falling. She whispered to him, "We don't have to pretend anything, Billy. We're adults, remember? We can do whatever we want to do."

The temptation for him was so strong that he had to make himself close his eyes. The only woman he wanted in the entire world was offering herself to him, but if he took her now, he could still make a huge mistake again. To hurt her and to lose her trust would be as fatal as putting a bullet through her heart.

"*You're* an adult," he finally said. "I'm this overgrown adolescent who is so close to being an adult I can almost taste it."

She leaned her head against his and closed her eyes.

"Ponytail," he said fondly, "having you this close to me is almost too much to resist. Every memory of every good time we ever had together is rushing through my whole body at this very moment. But part of being an adult is learning to make wise choices. It's learning to put other's needs before my own wants."

Sam, still keeping her eyes closed, nearly pleaded, "But what if our wants are the same?"

He finally pulled back, put his hands up to her face, and said, "If our wants are the same at this exact instant, then that means I have to do everything I possibly can to never lose your trust … or your *love* again."

Sam tried to look in his eyes, but the intensity of what she was feeling was overwhelming. He couldn't know how deeply she had fallen for him again. Although he had just confessed his love for her, it was still too soon for her to actually *say* it. Maybe he was right—they needed to wait. They needed to wait until all the barriers and walls and wounds from the past were completely torn down and healed. She had to be able to look at him with no regrets and tell him her heart before they could go any further.

"You're very right," she finally admitted. "But you must know something."

He turned her face up so she would look at him. When she did, he smiled reassuringly. "What must I know?"

She reached her hand over her chest and said, "You've always had my heart, Billy Marcum. You always will. And if you were to walk out on me at this point, you would kill me all over again. I don't think I could bear it."

"I will never, never, never walk out on you again, Sam. Never. I promise you that."

She didn't want the tears to spill. She could feel them starting, but she didn't want him to see the depth of it all right now. So she pulled away and shook it off, smiling as though all was fine in the world.

He seemed to know what she was doing, so he obliged by grabbing his bag and turning toward the pier.

"I'll see you in school tomorrow," he said lightly as he swung his bag to the other hand.

"If you're lucky," she grinned, twisting toward her car. "I might play hooky. You never know."

"You'll break my heart if you're not there."

She opened the door but turned back to say, "Well, then I guess I'd better show up."

Thirty-Four

The flight back to Phoenix was pure bliss for Hal, but Lisa's stomach was in knots and she kept telling him so. She couldn't believe he had pulled this off once again.

"You need to chill," he told her. "Things are going to be just fine this time. You'll see."

"It must be nice to have such a high opinion of yourself."

"It is," he replied arrogantly. "I've told you time and time again—I could do church work in my sleep. Shoot, I could write a book on the subject."

"There's an idea," she said sarcastically. "Why don't you give that a try? Then we could stop hopping around to churches every few months when you fail to prove your *supposed* expertise again."

His laugh was almost evil. "Not even your pessimistic mentality can bring me down today. I've got this situation completely under my control."

"And this is different because ...?"

"Because this is a *loving* church. This church has no problems, no divisions. The pastor is this easy-going guy who's been there since Moses, and the music minister is a good natured fellow with an incredibly gorgeous wife who will serve as a great side track."

"While you do what? Tear them all apart? It doesn't make sense, Hal. I don't get the point."

"The *point*," he said more severely now, "is that these people sit in their cushy jobs making great salaries that are funded by well-meaning people who think they are next to God and know everything. You think I'm a phony? I grew up in this stuff! I know the phonies. My job is to expose these people for who they really are—vultures that live off of the sacrifices of others."

"Oh, please," she moaned as she rolled her eyes. "You have yet to reveal anything except your own incompetence, *Dr.* Bridges."

"I'll let you get by with as many insults as you want today," he merely smiled. "This time will be different. I can feel it. That scraggly pastor and his little flunky of a music man will be putty in a few weeks."

"That *scraggly* pastor has already seen right through you. He was pretty quick to shoot back at your little digs all weekend."

"And the committee was *devastated* at his defensive sensitivity. That Nancy Beth lady told me so. I explained to you before that I laid the foundation, and then I baited the man. And remember, this is a big church in a dinky little town. Rumors spread quickly there. There's no such thing as suburbs in that area. In fact, I wouldn't even doubt that before I'm finished, these people will actually call *me* as their pastor."

"You don't pastor, remember?"

"Their ignorance could be my bliss. Farmers, hillbillies, red necks … what do they know about anything? Dr. Hal Bridges from California could be their salvation from southern ignorance."

"Good heavens, Hal!" she cried. "You're a complete idiot! Those people aren't ignorant. Just because they have a southern drawl and take life a little slower than you're used to doesn't make them some sort of uneducated, ill-bred brood."

He just smiled. By the time he returned in two weeks, he would have a plan that would blow that church apart and then eventually hail him as a leader of unmatchable insight. He had at last found what he had been looking for all these years, and it was invigorating to finally feel the breath of victory on his neck.

☼☼☼

Stephen sat at the baby grand in the upstairs studio and plunked out a few melancholy chords. Annie wasn't fit to be with at the moment, and as she talked to Angie over the phone, venting her frustrations from Sunday's events, he was glad she was going at it with someone other than him. He loved her with all his heart and could in no way imagine life without her, but the more intense sides of her personality could be hard to swallow at times. And when they emerged, he was never sure the best way to handle them. Sometimes she needed to talk and talk and talk until it was all out of her mind, and then she would go on as if nothing had ever happened. Then at other times she would need to be left alone with her thoughts for a few hours, and on occasion, a few days, and then all would return to normal. If he could figure out the clues as to which was needed each time, life would be so much simpler. He had always heard women were complicated, but he had no idea how true that was until he had married this particular version.

He looked around his studio and noted that he needed to work on the acoustic insulation. Of course, at this point, there was no good reason to do it. To soundproof the room wasn't a necessity seeing that he was doing nothing professional with his music. He had realized quickly this wasn't a subject to discuss with Annie. She took it personally that he wasn't enjoying his life with her and the kids, but that wasn't it at all. Creating music was what he did … it was as much a part of him as his family had become. Heaven knows they didn't need the money. If he never sold another song in his life they would have no worries. It was simply that he needed *something* to do. He needed a few hours a day where he could escape into his own world of work and produce something that was needed somewhere by someone.

He pulled out his cell phone again and clicked through all the numbers. What possibilities were lying out there just waiting for his call to produce them? Bill Turn of CBS had always wanted him to do some work. The movie producer, Stephen Cleinberg, had asked him several times to consider scoring a movie for him. Then there were several ad executives who had pleaded with him to come on board and do some commercials. Now *that* would be a funny turnaround. Annie had left advertising to join him on the stage. He could now leave the stage and move into advertising.

"Yuck," he chuckled to himself. "I could be writing songs about dog food. Life actually could be worse than this."

As he got near the end of his list, something caught his eye—XYZ Music.

"Wo," he whispered. "I had no idea I had that."

He punched in the details, and sure enough, it was a California number.

"When did I get this?" he wondered out loud. "How long has that been in here?"

Benjamin Brenner's music company, XYZ Music, was the place through which all of Brenner's work was done. Stephen would love to try his hand at scoring a movie, but his private dream was to one day learn from the best, Ben Brenner himself. In fact, Brenner had even suggested as much to him several years back. The thought had always kicked around in the corners of his mind, but there had been no way he could have given that kind of time to any projects other than his own recording and touring. But now, maybe it could actually happen. He wouldn't even have to leave home to work.

He almost punched in to dial the number when he heard Annie coming up the stairs. Now was not the time to be involved in something she questioned. He could do this later. He quickly shut the phone and replaced it inside his front pocket.

"So, what are you doing to occupy your mind this evening?" she asked listlessly.

"Not much," he confessed as he closed the piano lid and got up.

She dropped down on the plush couch in the studio and leaned her head back against the soft cushion.

"How's Angie?" he asked as he joined her.

"Tired is the best word I can come up with. But there's a positive note on her end. The doctor friend who's done all this has asked them to move into his house for the next month and let Carter be cared for there. He can go to the hospital for his treatments, but the physical therapist and the nurses will come to the house to do their thing."

"That is a positive note," he said with slight relief. "Maybe it'll help them all relax more … even Angie. Do you think she'll carry this baby to term?"

She shrugged. "Who knows? She hasn't yet."

"If it does come early, she's gonna need you and Barbara really bad. There's no way she can handle a newborn on top of what's happening with Carter."

She looked over at him with a tired smile. "That's very sweet of you." She reached out for his hand. He took it and slid over next to her. "Can you handle our two if I need to go up there for a while?"

"Our two?" He grinned and nodded. "But please do not add Andie's crew. I don't think I can do the Mason clan again for a while."

"I know what you mean." She pulled his hand up to her lips and gave the back of it a gentle kiss. "I love them all to death, but five kids can be a little … oh …"

"Overwhelming?"

"That's the word."

They sat quietly as Annie softly rubbed his hand. The one negative about being back around family was that you not only had to deal with your own stresses, you had to deal with theirs also because they were always before you. When you're a thousand miles away, all you can do is pray when you think of them and move on. But when you're in the midst of it all, you feel obligated to somehow help fix it. Right now she wished she could heal Andie's ankle, kick Hal Bridge's rear, as well as the search committee, excluding Tom Richards, and then head up to Memphis to take over all of Angie's responsibilities so she could rest and unwind. But as it stood, she was no better off than if she were still a thousand miles away.

"Would it be possible for us to pay a visit to Angie in Memphis when she moves into the doctor's house?" Stephen questioned.

"I don't know. If he has some kind of security or gate or something, I guess. But chances are he has nothing at all that would protect any of us from the camera SWAT teams."

He chuckled. "You're probably right. In fact, to even get you up there unnoticed to help out would take some major sidestepping."

Annie grinned. "It's been done before."

"I know. I'll never forget you hiding in the back of your dad's pickup when you were pregnant just so you and Andie and Angie could go to the mall."

"I'll never forget it either. I almost threw up during and after." She sighed. "I was seriously thinking about getting away somewhere before the talk with Angie," she told him as she picked a piece of lint off one of the cushions.

"Really?" He was surprised. "Like where?"

She smiled impishly and just shook her head. "You wouldn't believe me if I told you."

"Come on, you've got me really curious now. Where? Where do you want to go?"

She shook her head again and leaned back against the couch. He wouldn't accept *no* for an answer. He slowly moved up to her neck and began to gently kiss the side. She wiggled at the sensation.

"Are you trying to force it out of me?" she asked as she squirmed again.

"Not *force*, more like *coerce*."

"Is there a difference?"

"Yes. One sounds much more civilized."

She tried to move slightly away, but Stephen pulled her back. As she looked into his eyes he could see she was beginning to thaw from the emotionally icy day. She leaned in and gave him an unexpected kiss to which he was delighted. In fact, he had now forgotten all about the mysterious trip.

"Greece," she whispered as she stopped to breathe for a moment.

He pulled back and looked at her. "When you said *get away*, you were serious."

"I'm always serious," she teased. "Didn't you know that?"

"I'm learning. But Greece, wow, I didn't expect that. You really want to take a trip to Greece?"

"Well, not now, but sometime I'd like to go back there again. It was one of those places we always went to on tour that I felt I could never get enough of. Everything about it was so enchanting … the history, the white villas, the beaches, the people. I think I fell in love with it, but never really got the chance to know it."

He was again totally stunned by this woman. "You will never cease to amaze me."

"Why do you say that?"

"We've been married for almost six years, and that's the first time you've ever told me about your fascination with Greece. What other secrets are you hiding in that muddled mind of yours?"

"Muddled?"

Stephen pushed her back on the couch and gave her a look of warning. "Don't even try to argue that point with me. Your mind has been muddled, befuddled, and downright out of sorts all afternoon."

She smirked up at him as she asked, "And is this your suggested form of psychotherapy? You're gonna pin me to the couch?"

"Absolutely," he whispered as he leaned down to kiss her again. "What are the kids doing right now?"

"Watching TV," she whispered back. "But if you're about to do what I think you're about to do, I would suggest locking the studio door.

They could come barging in at any moment."

"Boy, would that be a shock." He kissed her again and grinned. "I'm locking the door. We might as well initiate this room too."

Thirty-Five

Sunday night church at First Baptist was odd. Everyone seemed stunned concerning the vote, yet not surprised that Hal had been called to fill the position. The worship was forced and stale, Jonathan's sermon seemed to carry no conviction or power, and after the service, most people just left rather than stand around and visit for the usual long time.

Cindy had stayed home with Kylla, so when Kyle walked in, she immediately asked about the church's reaction. As he explained the atmosphere that evening, she sort of nodded in understanding and went back to moving the twins toward bed. They had stayed home with her and were already bathed and fed. Kylla was zonked out, part from exhaustion and part from the Phenergan. He peeked in on her to see that all was well and then joined Cindy in saying goodnight to the twins. He was thankful that even though they may be fireballs in the daytime, when it came time for bed, they dropped in an instant. He listened to their sweet prayers, and then took Cindy's hand as she called out her final goodnight.

Once in their room, Kyle slowly began to undo his tie. He rolled his neck around a few moments to try and loosen the tension that had been building since before dawn with Kylla's throwing up, then the Hal Bridges speech and Navy Seal discussion, all the way through the strain in the church that evening. When Cindy turned around and recognized his condition, she immediately went to him and began to finish his tie.

"You need a good night's rest," she said as she pulled the end of the tie through the knot.

"As do you," he responded.

"Not as much as you. I got a reprieve this evening. I got to spend my time with three of my favorite people. You had to face the awkwardness of this whole day again."

He closed his eyes and rubbed the back of his neck.

"Come here," she said as she led him toward the bed. "Let's work some of this out of you."

He didn't resist as she unbuttoned his shirt and made him lay on his stomach so she could massage his back. She climbed up on the bed, straddled his torso and began to knead the tense muscles all through his body. He wanted to thank her, to praise her, and to tell her how wonderful she was, but he was so exhausted, and her hands felt so good, that all he could do was just lie there and soak it up.

"Can you believe the church gave us a cruise?" she began.

He knew he didn't have to answer. This was all part of helping him wind down and let go of the day. It didn't happen often, but the few times that it had were just as needed as this moment now.

"I'll miss the kids, but being alone with you for a whole week will be almost like a taste of heaven," she continued.

He understood exactly. They had never really been alone since the day they married. Kylla was there from the beginning, his daughter from a previous marriage, and she had always been included in anything they did. Then there were the years spent caring for Cindy's mother as she battled cancer. To be alone with her anywhere would be wonderful. Any time they even had an opportunity to leave town to eat out was a huge blessing.

"Can you imagine going to those exotic, romantic places … just the two of us?" she asked.

That was it. He was unwound. He rolled over and pulled her down in the bed beside him.

"I guess you can," she giggled.

He said nothing. All he could do was stare at the most beautiful woman he had ever known. Sometimes it was still hard to believe that this was his wife. But not only his wife, she was his confidant', his best friend, and his partner for life. He could never grasp the life she had lived before he had met her. She had been as wild and worldly as one could get, but to him she had never been anything other than wonderful, Godly, supportive, and a huge right arm in his ministry.

"I'll have to confess," he finally spoke, "that I still can't believe it." He ran her silky blond hair through his fingers. "No kids, no church, no responsibilities."

"No house to clean or meals to cook."

"Just the two of us." He smiled as he leaned over to kiss her. "We may never want to come back."

She dreamed with him, but then reminded him of reality. "You know that won't happen. We'll be missing the kids the first day. We'll want to call and make sure everything is okay. We'll have to force ourselves to think about each other."

"Speak for yourself," he mumbled as he kissed her again. "I'm forgetting about the kids right now, and they're just down the hall."

"Do we have kids?" she teased as she enjoyed the moment alone.

"I think so."

Later that night as they sank into bed, Kyle held her close and drifted into a peaceful sleep. He didn't want to imagine what life without Cindy would ever be like. At the moment, life was harder than either of them had ever known before. They had been raised as fairly wealthy and privileged kids. Their parents had seen them through whatever pursuits they had wanted. Life had come easily for them. Then both of their worlds had crumbled. Kyle's wife had left him, and Cindy's father had died from a heart attack, only to be followed with the devastation of her mother developing cancer. Yet through those dark times, they found each other and found hope and life again.

But now things were hard. The huge house they had inherited from Cindy's mother was becoming a financial burden. The power bills were high. There were many things in need of repair, the first being a new roof. The air-conditioning unit had finally blown at the last of September. They didn't have the money to replace it, but since fall was beginning, they could at least open the windows and enjoy the breeze. The church was growing but didn't want to raise salaries because of the need to bring in a new staff member.

Kyle had hinted that they might think about selling the house, and Cindy tried to pretend she agreed, but he knew her heart. This had been her mother's gift to her; this house was literally her inheritance. It was more than just a structure—it was the foundation of her life. He knew she would give it up if he asked, but he didn't want to do that. He had thought about trying to begin music lessons. He could do them after school during the week. It would cut in on some wonderful family time, and he would have to leave earlier for work in the mornings in order to be out by three o'clock, but it would bring in some much needed extra money.

However, at this moment, with Cindy lying in his arms and her love for him stronger than ever, he honestly didn't care. God had worked some incredible miracles before. Whatever He had planned for them at this point in time, Kyle would gladly face it. And with the church offering them this unbelievable get-away, it would allow them some time to think and pray about their future as they relaxed and enjoyed each other for the first time in their life together.

She sighed as she rolled over, and he let her slip from his arm. But the moon on her face took his breath away again.

"I'll find some way to keep this house for you, Cindy," he whispered as he watched her sleep. "I promise I will."

☼☼☼

When Angie first awoke on Monday morning she nearly believed she was back in Padawin. Had it not been for the darkness of the room and the unfamiliar sound of the air conditioner, she could have almost been transported for a few brief minutes. It felt unusual to be rested and refreshed. She glanced over at little Cassie who was curled up in a ball next to her. As much as she had protested when Michael insisted she take her to the Fed Ex House and spend the night, she was now glad. In fact, she felt a little guilty for the way she had treated Michael before leaving.

"I will not abandon my child," she had told him through gritted teeth and exhausted anger. "If you want to go to a strange room for a night and pretend there's nothing wrong with your son, go ahead, but I'm not budging."

Rather than respond in like attitude, he had simply lifted a sleepy Cassie into his arms and said, "You *have* abandoned a child … two in fact. Cassie can't stay the night here again; they've made that policy clear. I know how much you want to stay with Carter, but Angie, if you don't get some rest, that little one you're carrying now isn't gonna arrive with the best start. And this one," he kissed Cassie's cheek, "needs some alone time with her mother."

In truth, Angie had very little fight left in her. As tears grew heavy in her eyes, Michael simply came to her, put his arm around her, and then pulled her to the shoulder that Cassie was not occupying.

"You are my rock," was all she could say as she sobbed into his shirt for a few moments.

And he was. She knew Carter had been well tended by his father that night, and she also knew Cassie desperately needed to be back in touch with her family, her foundation, her identity. She and Angie had talked close to eleven o'clock Sunday night. Cassie had many questions about why they were still here, why Carter was in such pain, why Angie couldn't doctor him, and why they had to be in this big city instead of back home with Mimi and Gaga. She missed Geechern, she missed fishing, she missed the ocean and the river, and she missed the easy way of life that Padawin offered. Angie could only smile and agree with her on that point.

She reached over and gently pulled a strand of Cassie's bleached hair from across her still tanned face. The four-year-old stirred slightly and then opened her eyes. She smiled as the first thing she saw was her mother.

"Are we home?" she asked sleepily.

Angie shook her head and gave a warm smile. "Not even close," she replied.

The smile faded, but Cassie scooted over to her and took comfort as Angie held her in a tender embrace.

"I really want to go home," she pleaded softly. "I don't like Alabama and America very much."

Angie was thankful to be relaxed, because had she not been, she could have burst into tears again. She kissed the top of Cassie's head and said, "It isn't always like this. Carter has been very sick."

"He never acted sick."

"He couldn't walk, sweetie. That's a kind of sickness."

"But when he didn't act sick, you say he is sick. And now that he is supposed to be better, he is acting sick. How can he be better and not *feel* better?"

"Because the thing that was making him sick had to be taken out of him. That's why we're here. They had to cut into his body and pull out all this yucky stuff."

Cassie rolled back to look up at her mother with searching eyes. "Couldn't they have just left it in there? He didn't hurt when it was in there."

"Actually, it did hurt him. Whenever he would try to stand up and be a big boy … like me and you and Daddy … it would hurt so badly that he just stopped trying. And sweetie, eventually that stuff would have spread throughout his whole body and …" She couldn't finish the sentence.

"And what?" Cassie was always curious.

Angie tried not to dwell on her statement. "He could have died."

Cassie rolled back onto Angie's pillow and stared up at the ceiling. It was hard to believe this child was only four. Lainey and Ellie seemed so care-free and unconcerned about the things of life, but Cassie always pondered and questioned and studied her world.

"Is it better to hurt than to die?" Cassie finally asked.

Angie sighed and plopped down onto the pillow beside her. Sometimes reasoning with Cassie was impossible. "I think God made us want to fight to live as much in this life as we can. That's why He shows doctors and scientists ways to help heal all the hurting people in the world. And then when we've done all the living we can do, that's when it's time to die."

Cassie bit her lip as she considered that idea. "So Carter still gets to fight then?"

"Absolutely."

Suddenly Angie gave a yelp as the baby kicked sharply against her ribs. Cassie stared up at her in surprise.

"What was that about?" Cassie asked wide-eyed.

"It was *this* one," Angie grinned as she took Cassie's hand and placed it on her abdomen. It kicked again.

"Wo, baby!" Cassie exclaimed. "Mama, how can it do that in there?"

Angie shook her head. "I think it's getting really tired of hanging around inside. It's kicking me and saying, *Let me out*!"

Cassie giggled. "Then take it out. Why do you keep waiting? I want to see it. I want to know if it's a girl or a boy."

"It's not ready yet," Angie found herself trying to explain yet another point. "It wouldn't be able to breathe well yet."

"Well, how in the world is it breathing in there right now?"

Angie rolled her eyes. "It's not. I breathe for it."

It kicked again, and Cassie laughed at the sensation this time. Angie reached up and pushed Cassie's hair behind her ears. Cassie put her arms around her mother and squeezed her tightly for a while. After a long silence, Cassie gave a mischievous look and whispered, "I hope it's a boy again."

This took Angie by surprise. "Really? I would think you wanted a sister, someone you could play with and all."

Cassie looked at Angie as though she didn't have a brain in her head. "I play with Carter all the time. And besides, girls are afraid of bugs and stuff. Lainey told me if I ever put a cricket on her again she would drown me in the pool. A cricket? A cricket? It's so tiny. I was wishing I had a crab to throw on her!"

Angie laughed as the baby kicked again. "Your cousins didn't grow up in Padawin."

"So, Padawin girls are different than Alabama girls?"

Angie nodded and affirmed, "Quite different."

☼☼☼

Billy checked his wallet to make sure he still had the two dollars for gas. Still there. He sighed with relief as he poured the last of the milk into a bowl of Frosted Flakes. Thankfully, today was payday. He almost wished his mother had set up the allowance so he would be paid once a week rather than once a month. He had learned quickly not to squander his money, but it seemed that by the end of each month, he was always down to the wire like this. After this morning's cereal, there wouldn't be an ounce of food left in the boat, his bike was almost dry, and he had two dollars in his wallet. When he walked into Kennedy Nelson's office today for the five hundred dollar check, he hoped the look of desperation wouldn't show. One good thing about Kennedy, though—he was always encouraging. Although he and Billy were close in age, Kennedy had been a young man with vision and direction. As the lawyer who handled Billy's mother's estate, he was efficient, knowledgeable, but also very compassionate where Billy was concerned. Several times he had wanted to give up, and when he walked into Kennedy's office to get the monthly check, he would spout off a bit. But somehow Kennedy always managed to urge him on in his pursuits.

"Pay your dues now, Billy," he always said as Billy would gripe. "This won't last forever. And when it's over, you've got a real life out there waiting for you."

He nodded to himself at the thought. Perhaps Kennedy was right. And if there was a possibility that Sam could be in the picture again, it made the goal even more enticing. Last night with her had almost been impossible to refuse, but he always kept his discussion with Kyle in the back of his mind. He had to make sure he was ready to take care of her for real before handing her the ball in their relationship. Had she stayed last night, it would have been too immature, and the pressure for the relationship to be rekindled would have been too intense.

He grabbed the remote and zapped on the television to check the weather. The only thing worse than riding the Kawasaki in the cold, was riding it in the cold and the rain. The weatherman stood before the large map and predicted both cold and rain for the week. He sighed, turned off the TV, and tossed the remote to the bed which he had yet to roll back into a couch. Suddenly the phone rang.

"Great," he mumbled. "I suppose a call this early would have to be more bad news."

He went to the kitchen area where his phone was charging and glanced at the display. "Kennedy?" He clicked it on. "Hello?"

"Billy, great!" he replied in his typical upbeat manner. How was it possible for anyone to be so perky at this time of the morning, especially when it was freezing outside and a forecast of rain loomed in the distance?

"Yeah, it's me. What's up?"

"Can you set aside a little more time to meet with me today when you come by? There are some issues we need to discuss."

Issues? Great. That's exactly what I need in my life right now: more issues.

"I suppose," Billy moaned reluctantly. "What are these *issues* all about?"

"Your finances," he said flatly.

He closed his eyes and rolled his head back. Could it possibly get any worse? "I'll be there about three-thirty."

"Alright, see you then. Bye."

"Yeah, bye."

He glanced down at the time on the phone. He would have to hurry if he was going to get gas before school. He went to the closet and pulled out his cold weather riding suit to put on over his clothes. Thank goodness he had purchased it before he had become *poor*. It had been a lifesaver these past few years.

He went over and turned off the heat completely, and then made sure everything possible that could be turned off was. He didn't want to have to pay extra money for any convenience. He even reached back and unplugged the refrigerator for the day. No sense running the electricity when nothing was inside. And if it was going to be as cool as the weatherman had said, he could actually keep his groceries outside on the deck of the boat a few days.

He grabbed his wallet, his helmet, and his book satchel and headed out the door to begin his last month of classes. With the first of November starting, he should probably go ahead and begin preparing the kids for their semester exams. As slow as some of these students were, he wondered if they would ever get it.

One month to go ... just one more month.

Thirty-Six

Gail Taylor struggled to get her mascara on without making a mess. Today, Angie Wright, the woman she feared most in the world, would be moving into her house indefinitely. When Levi had finally told her last year the reason for his hold up in pursuing anything deeper in their relationship, she had almost laughed. Levi, a man who had nothing to do with God, had fallen in love with a missionary who wanted nothing to do with him. Could she handle moving on in a relationship with him even though his heart would forever belong to someone else? Considering that the woman lived on a Pacific island somewhere on the other side of the world and that her life was totally devoted to the Lord, of course she could! In her mind this had been a win-win situation. Levi was charming, funny, a great conversationalist, not half bad-looking, and then rich—all in all a nice package. Could she live with the fact that her competition was a woman she would never have to meet? No problem. The woman could look like Miss America and it wouldn't matter. For all practical purposes, she didn't exist, at least not in *their* world of high society parties and materialism.

She finished her mascara and then looked up toward heaven. "Is this my punishment?" she griped to God. "I suppose this is what I get for trying to think I could run away from You."

She shook her head and moved into the expansive bedroom to get her colorful scrubs on for the day. Levi, as was typical, had already showered, shaved, dressed, and was in the midst of who knows what number cup of coffee. She wasn't really sure if it was just her insane jealousy or not, but he seemed to be a little lighter in step and attitude this morning. As she pulled on her clothes, he passed by with a whistle and went into the bathroom to brush his teeth.

"Not eating breakfast again?" he asked on the way.

"Not if I have to compete with Miss Gorgeous Missionary … who happens to be very pregnant yet still looks like she weighs a hundred pounds."

He glanced around the doorway. "Are you still in a tizzy about her? I thought we talked through this last night."

"No, you talked through it. You convinced yourself that Angie is happily married with a growing family, and that the only place you fit into her life is to be the savior of her son."

"Don't tell *her* that," he retorted with a grin. "She might begin to think I have a god complex."

He went back to his teeth, and she slid into her shoes. How was she supposed to act when Angie was right here, constantly around, caring for her children, doting on her husband, and desperately needing Levi's expertise for the very life of her son? Perhaps she should stop by the bookstore on the way home and buy a large novel. She could try to divert her misery somewhere else until the woman was finally gone. And then at that point she could try to put her marriage back together again. There was no way Levi could live under the same roof with the *only woman who would ever have his heart* and not realize that Gail was just an accessory in his life. She was merely a distraction from what his heart truly desired. But she had tried her best to be a big distraction. She had been the perfect wife for him in their brief marriage. In fact, he had told her several times that marrying her had been one of the smartest moves he had ever made.

"Ready, my striking wife?" he asked as he turned off the bathroom light and walked back into the bedroom.

She glared up at him. "Why are you doing this?"

"Doing what?" he asked innocently. "We do this same dance every morning."

"But the music has obviously changed."

He shook his head as he grabbed his coat. "I'm not gonna keep on with this, Gail."

"But you told me …"

"I told you long ago, before I knew what kind of life we could have together, that Angie was the only woman I could ever love."

"And when she waltzed back in, it sure did throw you for a loop. You moped and groaned and …"

"… and acted like a man whose life was being turned upside down." He took her hand. "I had to think through it all, baby. You know how I am. I like being in control. I like getting my own way. I like to call the shots. Here I was standing face to face with the one thing I wanted and could never manage to get."

"And how do you think that makes me feel? I'm second best, Levi. I'm second choice. I'm a hand-me-down rather than a Tiffany gown."

He shook his head, pulled her into his arms, and kissed her warmly. "*You* are most definitely a Tiffany gown."

☼☼☼

Sam removed her glasses and rubbed her eyes. How could this morning have turned out so miserable after such a great weekend? It was only third period, but each class had gotten worse. If she hadn't managed to get control, she would have given the entire group detention. It must be the anticipation of the upcoming holidays although they were still three weeks away from Thanksgiving.

Thanksgiving. For the first time in ten years she would spend a holiday with someone again. Immediately her thoughts went to Billy. She had practically thrown herself at him last night, but he had graciously sent her on. The changes in him still baffled her at times. It was hard for her to believe she had gotten wasted on Friday night, ended up in his bed, yet awoke fully clothed and uncompromised. That was nothing like the old Billy. Then there was last night. Rather than take her up on her offer to spend another night, he chose to be a gentlemen. She had been relieved as she drove away, because as much as she hated to admit it, she was falling for him again.

Not *falling again*; she had never gotten up from the first time. In the ten years they had been apart, she had thought about him every day. She often wondered where he was, what he was doing, and who he was with now. She had sworn to herself she wouldn't get into a situation like that again. From now on, she would guard her heart with a fierceness she had never known before. And she had done a great job. She dated a few men on and off, but never had she come close to even considering falling in love. But here it was happening all over again.

It could have been easier for her to have hated him … had he not moved into the classroom next door, had his parents not died, had he still been cocky and on top of the world. She could even resist his incredible good looks and unending charm, but his broken heart was what drew her to him this time around. He had been humbled, and so much so that he was willing to change his whole life just to find meaning and a purpose again. If she could somehow be a part of his new life, she knew it would be different this time. Maybe she wouldn't be alone after all. And days like today, when everything that gave her life meaning was falling apart, it would be okay, because there would be more than *this*. He would go home with her and they would share their hurts together, their triumphs, their failures, their joys … their lives.

She longed to go next door and peek in to see him. If she could just lay eyes on him she knew it would settle her heart … then again, it could set it all aflutter. As the students began to pour into classrooms sensing the time for the bell was near, she grabbed her glasses and headed out the door. She just needed to see him.

As she walked into the hallway, she saw him leaning against the wall just outside his door. His head was propped back, and he had one leg up with his foot on the wall behind him. If it was at all possible, he seemed to look even more handsome than ever. Her heart pounded at the sight. She moved slowly toward his room. Whatever he was thinking must be weighing on him heavily.

"Hey, pretty boy," she said loud enough for him to hear above the bustle of the hallway.

He immediately opened his eyes and looked toward her. His smile melted her.

"How's your morning gone?" she asked nonchalantly.

"Horrible."

"Yours too," she laughed. "I'm glad to hear it's not just me."

"What did these kids do this weekend to get them so riled up?"

"I assume it's the approaching holiday."

"Veteran's Day?" he remarked. "They're this rambunctious over Veteran's Day?"

"No. Thanksgiving."

"Thanksgiving? That's three weeks away!"

"I suppose it's gonna be a long November, then."

He blew out a long breath and stood up straight. "Maybe it was the Halloween weekend. Whatever. All I know is that this day is only beginning."

"Well, perhaps tomorrow will be better. We can hope, can't we?"

His expression didn't change. "I don't know. With my luck lately, tomorrow could be ten times worse."

"Or not …" she suggested.

Billy looked down at her and appreciated how she was trying to encourage him, but she didn't realize it was way more than just the students eating at him. This meeting with the lawyer was looming over him like a thunderhead about to burst. Something was wrong, and he had no idea what. Had his mother's estate run out of money? Would this be his last check? Would he even get a check? Would he have to take out a loan just to live this last month of his schooling?

"Where are you?" she asked.

"Apparently, up that same creek again."

Just then the bell rang and students began to dash through the doorways into their classrooms.

"Why?" she wondered. "What's happened?"

"Mom's lawyer called me this morning. There seems to be some kind of financial problem. He needs to meet with me this afternoon."

"What kind of financial problem?"

"He didn't say, but it must be pretty serious. We need to meet longer than usual to discuss it at length. He wouldn't go into it over the phone."

Since the hallway had cleared because of the bell, Sam reached over and took his hand. "Oh, Billy, I'm so sorry."

"It's gonna be hard to make it through this last month."

"Will you get your check at least—your five hundred for this month?"

"I don't know … hopefully. If not, I don't exactly know what I'll do."

She pulled herself closer to him, still holding his hand. "I know what you'll do—you'll move in with me."

His eyes grew large. "I couldn't do that."

"Why not?" she whispered. "It would solve your problem and get you through the last month."

"Because," he hesitated, "it would be hard … you know … to be with you … after all this … and not really be *with* you." He squeezed her hand as he looked past the glasses into her hopeful green eyes.

"I'll be strong enough for both of us," she half-teased. "Separate rooms and all. We'll just share the food."

He smiled and shook his head. "Let's wait and see what the verdict is. Maybe there's enough for me to get through this last month and a half, and then I can move in with Cindy until I get a job."

"Tell you what," she proposed as she finally released his hand, "you go to your meeting this afternoon, and then come on over to my place. I'll make supper, and we'll talk about any plans or changes that need to be made. Until then, remember that you're not totally up that creek yet. Okay?"

It was all he could do not to pull her to him and hold her tightly in thankfulness. Just to know she was on his side and willing to do whatever was necessary to see him through this was mind boggling. He didn't deserve what was happening between them again—and what was happening was a second chance.

☼☼☼

When Angie and Cassie walked into Carter's hospital room, the sight awaiting them warmed Angie to the bone. Michael was laid out on the twin bed and Carter was lying on top of him. Both were sound asleep. She put her finger to her lips to make sure Cassie would stay quiet so they could sleep on, but just as they both settled quietly onto the couch, a nurse came barging in to announce it was time for a blood pressure and temperature check.

Cassie looked up angrily at the nurse and bellowed, "Are you crazy, lady? They're asleep. We respect people when they sleep!"

If the nurse hadn't wakened Michael, Cassie's pronouncement most certainly did.

"Cassie!" Angie quickly jumped in to explain. "At our house, we consider naptime to be important. We try to *respect* each other's need to sleep."

"And that's a very good rule," the nurse said softly this time. "I should remember that and be more quiet when I walk into a room. I didn't think they would still be sleeping at eleven o'clock in the morning." The nurse then looked at Angie to clarify her entrance. "Shift change … I just came on. Really, I had no idea they were still asleep."

"It's no problem," Angie assured her. "And you're right—they should be up by now."

Michael groggily shifted Carter as he tried to sit up. "We had a rough night."

"How so?" Now Angie was worried.

"He missed his mommy," Michael told her. "But we finally made it through. He woke up a few times, and about five this morning he was determined to get out of bed." Michael gave a tired smile and said, "So, I just joined him. Thank goodness we weren't still in the room with the caged bed."

Angie went over and sat beside them. She gave Michael a gentle kiss and then softly rubbed the top of Carter's back. "Well, Cassie and I slept wonderfully. I have a slight twinge of guilt over how good I actually feel."

"You shouldn't," Michael spoke up immediately. "You're carrying another child, Angie. Try to remember that in the midst of all this."

She glanced down to her belly and then gave him an incredulous look. "Do you think I've forgotten?"

He raised an eyebrow and said, "At times, yes. I feel much better knowing you got a good night's sleep."

"Mama's fun to sleep with," Cassie piped up as she joined the conversation. "She hugs on you all night long."

"Yes," he grinned. "I know. I've missed my night long hugs lately."

Angie touched his cheek and reminded him, "Tonight. We'll be at Levi's tonight. I'm sure we'll get our own bed."

His brows furled. "Don't be so sure. Dr. Taylor might even place us in separate rooms … wouldn't put it past him."

Angie smirked and guaranteed him, "If he does, one of us is moving … quickly."

When Carter finally managed to awaken, he was thrilled to see his mother. He actually cried out of desperation when she took him in her arms.

"Sweetie, it's okay," she reassured him. "Mommy had to get some sleep."

"Mommy went bye bye," he complained through a whimper.

"I know, but only for a little while." She made him look her in the eye. "I'm here again. See? Everything's alright."

Carter kept his arms around her neck. "You won't go bye bye?"

"No," she said firmly. And with that pronouncement, he seemed content.

No matter how uncomfortable the arrangement at Levi's might be for Michael at the moment, it would do wonders for all their morale. They could be together in an almost normal setting, and they could live comfortably as Carter went through his treatments.

Thirty-Seven

Billy parked the bike, removed his helmet, and began to take off the riding suit. The temperature had barely risen above forty today, and it would freeze tonight. Just the thought of facing that boat again in the winter, plus the very real possibility that he might have no money today sent a shiver through him.

Just another month and a half. If worse comes to worse, I can move in with Sam. It will be hard, but I'll do whatever it takes to make sure I finish this degree. He then looked up. *Mother, I'm gonna do this … I'm gonna complete this part of my life … no matter what. And when I do, I hope you'll somehow know it was because I promised you I would … and that I didn't break this promise … finally.*

He stuffed the riding suit into a piece of the side luggage and walked up to the office. Every time he came here it reminded him how much of life he had wasted. He would have already been as successful in teaching as Kennedy was in legal matters had he only stuck with his schooling years ago. He felt as though he was a mere child in Kennedy's eyes, although the man had always been more than respectful and positive toward him. To think they were only months apart in age was always humbling for Billy.

"Hey, Billy!" Kennedy greeted as he entered the receptionist's area. "I was just coming to check if you had called. I thought you might have forgotten about our meeting."

"Are you kidding? I get paid today. I *can't* miss a meeting on the first Monday of the month."

"So that's why you come by here every month?" Kennedy teased. "I thought it was my intensely charismatic personality!"

"Well, that too."

Kennedy didn't comment about the check, so Billy assumed that meant all was still fine where it was concerned. When Kennedy motioned him into the office, he could swear Miss James, the receptionist, had winked at him. She had made it known many times she was ready and willing to do whatever his heart desired. If things worked out between him and Sam, eventually he would wear a ring again, and that ring was a wonderful deterrent for forward ladies.

"Have a seat, Billy," Kennedy said as he sat behind his big desk and opened up a thick folder. "How are things going for you?"

Billy really didn't care for the chit chat. He wanted the man to just spill it all out so he could begin figuring how to get on with his life. "At the moment things are pretty tense."

Kennedy looked up at him in surprise. "For real?"

He nodded.

"Why?"

"Why?" Billy repeated the question. "You called me this morning to tell me we had to discuss some important financial issues. How do you think I should be? Loosey-goosey?"

Kennedy laughed and shook his head. "I am so sorry. Have you thought all day there was some kind of problem with your finances?"

"What was I supposed to think?"

Kennedy stopped laughing and looked at him man to man. "You were supposed to think I would always be up front with you … as much as I possibly could. You were also supposed to think that if something were about to happen that would be negative for you, I wouldn't beat around the bush to let you know. I thought you knew me better than that."

He hung his head. This was more like a father chastising a son. Would he ever grow up?

"I apologize," Billy managed to mumble. "It's been really hard lately. I had two dollars in my wallet when you called me this morning that I had to spend on gas in order to just make it to school. And with gas prices going up and down all the time, I don't know how I'm gonna continue to make it on my allowance. So, when you call to say we have *financial issues* to discuss, can you understand how I might be a little pessimistic about it all?"

Kennedy only nodded. He pulled out an envelope from the folder and handed it to Billy. "It's finally time for you to read this," he said with a smile. "And please, put your worries aside for the moment."

He reached for the letter and immediately recognized the handwriting. "It's from … Mother?"

Kennedy nodded again. "If you'd like, I can leave the room while you read it. Then when you're ready to discuss it, you can call me back in."

"No. Stay. You know what's in here?"

"I know the main gist of it. I haven't read it, nor do I have a copy. But I do know what she's going to tell you."

Billy's hands shook as he stared at his name on the front. This was almost too emotional for him to handle—a letter from his mother. Obviously she had written it prior to her death, and this day seemed to have some significance about it. He carefully opened the envelope, treating it as though it were a priceless treasure. As he pulled out the familiar stationary, he was thankful she had never cared for the computer. Because this was written in her own handwriting, that made it more special.

Dearest Billy,

If you're reading this letter, then it means this would have been one of the proudest moments in my life. As I lie here in this bed, still struggling with the sickness that has invaded my body, I'm so thankful that it hasn't poisoned my mind. It's a difficult thing to try and decide how to take care of your children after you're gone. I know that your father and I spoiled you and Cindy more than we should have, but when you both finally came into our lives, after years of struggling and praying and hoping and aching and crying for children, it was hard not to give you everything you wanted.

Even as I write this, I can only hope that you kept your promise and stayed on course with your schooling. You're too bright and gifted to lay your life at the feet of materialism. Much like Cindy, you sold yourself to a lie that happiness could be found only in worldly pleasures and fleshly appetites. As I watched Cindy's life transform into something beautiful and worthy, all I could do was hope and pray that you would someday do the same.

Now, as you are a month away from graduating, you need to know that the $500 a month I set aside as your allowance was very hard to do. Part of me wanted to do so much more, but I know you, Billy. If you ever got a taste of your old life again, you'd forget the sacrifice and run back to it with open arms. Kennedy and I spent hours trying to decide exactly how much would be needed for you to survive until school was finished. If you're reading this, you need to know that I understand how hard this has been for you, but you also need to know that I could never, ever be prouder of you.

Up until now, you and Cindy have been led to believe that your inheritance was: the house for Cindy, and tuition and a monthly allowance for you. What you didn't know was that this was only part of it. Everything else, however, has depended on what you did with your schooling. If you finished, then the rest of the inheritance was to be split between you both. If you quit at any time, then everything else was to go to Cindy. I know she will be fair and will do whatever is just and right with the money, but I hope that it doesn't all fall into her hands. I hope, I pray, with everything inside me that you'll one day read this letter and know how important it is to make sacrifices in life in order to improve the quality of the gift God has given you.

I have instructed Kennedy to make the final transfer the month before your graduation. He is to cash in all our financial investments and disperse them to you and Cindy fifty-fifty. I know that if you've endeavored to be faithful to your promise to me, then you'll endeavor to responsibly handle what you're about to receive.

I would say to you, "Good luck," but at this point, you no longer need luck. With a degree and a genuine accomplishment almost behind you, you can finally be your own man. Use this inheritance wisely, Billy. Now that you've come to understand the real meaning of "having" and "not having," the way you handle this gift will be drastically different than if you had received it immediately after my death.

I love you, my son, and I'll go to my grave believing that you completed your degree and are reading this letter.

All My Love,
Mother

Billy was stunned. His first thoughts were simply that he was reading a letter from his mother. It was almost as if she was speaking to him from the grave. But slowly, as he moved through the body, he realized he was about to receive some type of monetary compensation. When he looked up at Kennedy, there was a huge smile spread across the lawyer's face.

"What do you think?" Kennedy asked him.

"I don't know what to think. There's more than just Cindy getting the house and me getting tuition?"

"Oh yeah—quite a bit."

Billy looked confused. He shook his head and asked, "How much are we talking about?"

Kennedy put up a finger. "First, there is a point that your mother insisted I make very clear to you."

"Sure … what is it?"

"She only gave you five hundred a month because she was afraid you would give up if she made it too easy. She wanted to make you fight for this."

He sighed as he glanced back down at the letter. "Why the month *before* graduation? Why not afterward?"

"She was a good lady, Billy—a gracious lady. She wanted you to be able to celebrate, and she somehow wanted to be a part of that. She figured your inheritance would help take the load off your back, plus it would give you the chance to do whatever you needed to do to get going in the real world again. You could buy a house … one that doesn't rock back and forth with the waves. Shoot!" Kennedy laughed, "you could actually buy a car!"

That thought was sobering as his hands were still freezing from the cold ride here. "So, how much are we talking about? I had no idea there was more money out there somewhere."

"Well, you're mother had invested it all. Your father's social security and retirement were more than enough to take care of her after his death. But they both had some incredible insurance policies and your dad had some unbelievable investments." He reached back into the folder and pulled out another envelope. "Instead of your typical $500 check, this is exactly half of all your mother's investments." He handed the envelope to Billy.

He stood to take it, and then just held it in his hands a minute. It must be several thousand if he could get a car. The smartest thing would be not to spend it, but to immediately put it into savings. This was it; after this payment there would be nothing more from his mother. School would be over, and he would again be on his own.

He looked back at Kennedy who just continued to smile a silly smile. Finally, he began to undo the back flap. As he pulled out the check, he was almost afraid to look. He imagined that whatever had been there had been significantly depleted from his last three years at college. But when he turned the check over to see the amount, he literally felt his knees buckle beneath him. Kennedy immediately ran to his rescue.

"You alright?" he asked as he helped him back down to the chair.

"Where did this come from?" Billy could barely ask.

"Your dad had made some good investments over the years. Plus, like I said, your mother never used his insurance policy. She just cashed it in and then immediately began to pop some into CD's and some into the market. Your tuition was paid from the interest on all of this. When she died, I was given power of attorney to get her policy and do the same thing until … well, until you graduated … or didn't … at which point everything would have gone to Cindy."

All Billy could do was stare at the check. In his hand he was holding a voucher worth $4,368,000. Just a few minutes ago he was wondering how he was going to manage another month and a half, and now he was holding a check for more money than he could even imagine.

"So, you're saying my parents were millionaires?" He still couldn't believe this was happening.

"More important than that, *you* are now a millionaire. In fact, you were all along, you just didn't know it."

He leaned back in the chair and continued to look at his check. "So, what do I do now?"

"If I were you, I'd go make a deposit," Kennedy grinned. "And then, perhaps, I'd buy a car."

He sighed as he stood. "I guess so. I guess … I think … I don't know what I think." He laughed at last. "Does Cindy know?"

"Not yet. Your mother wrote her a letter too. I was instructed to do the same thing with her—give her the letter and then give her the check.

Cindy said she's busy up to her ears at the moment getting ready for a cruise this weekend. She asked if we could make the appointment after she got back."

Billy laughed again. "She needs this as much as I do! That house of theirs is starting to fall apart … well, not that bad, but it needs some help … and quick."

"Then I look forward to that meeting also." Kennedy reached out his hand to Billy. "And I want you to know, I'll miss all these get-togethers and updates with you each month."

"Really? I can't imagine why."

"Because rarely do I get to see a story unfold like this one. I have to tell you, Billy, there were a few times I wondered if you were gonna make it. You would get so discouraged and start talking about quitting until you could get your feet on the ground."

Billy interrupted to say, "And you would always talk me out of it." Things began to make sense now. "You knew if I could just pull through this, I'd be more than just a graduate on the other side … I'd be a millionaire."

"But more importantly, you'd be everything your mother ever dreamed you would be."

He nodded. Was this really happening?

He managed to make it by Miss James without anything suggestive coming out of her mouth. Once outside, the cold hit him squarely in the face. As he pulled his riding suit out of the luggage, he indeed wondered if he ought to get a car right away. He was going to graduate and then die from pneumonia if he didn't get off this bike during the winter months.

When he pulled up his riding bibs, his phone began to sing. He dug into his pocket, retrieved it, and tried to answer quickly so they wouldn't hang up. It was Sam.

"Sam?" he answered.

"Billy, hey. How is everything? I was starting to get worried."

He actually smiled. "You won't believe how everything is."

"Did you get paid?"

"Tell you what; forget supper at your place. We're going out tonight."

"No," she answered immediately and firmly.

"Yeah, come on. Let me take you somewhere for supper. That'll be a first."

"Billy, you can barely afford peanut butter and jelly on a daily basis. I'm not letting you spend money on me right after you get your check."

"Trust me on this: it isn't the regular check. I got a little more this time."

"Either way, you're not gonna spend any money on me."

"Samantha," he only called her that when he had an important point to make, "please let me do this. I *can* do this. It won't hurt me a bit this month."

She wavered. "Billy, I don't feel right about it. Just come over here and eat."

"Absolutely not!" he insisted. "Tonight, I'm taking you out, and that's final. Why don't you come pick me up so I don't have to ride my bike in the freezing rain?"

She thought a little longer. "Under one condition."

"Name it."

"If you get in a bind this month financially, you'll let me know and let me help out."

"Agreed!" he said amused. "Indeed, if I suffer financially this month, I will let you know."

"Okay, that sounds fair. So what do I wear?"

He thought for a moment. He wanted it to be nice, but not dressy. "How 'bout Blue Bayou? Ever eaten there?"

"Oh, I know where that is, but I've never been there. I've always wanted to though."

"It's very casual. Jeans or whatever is fine."

"Sounds like a date. When do I pick you up?"

"I've got a few things to do before I can get home, so how about we say around six o'clock."

"I'll be there."

When Sam hung up and Billy closed his phone, he finally let it all out with a loud whoop. He could be with her now! He didn't have to wait! He would graduate in the middle of December, and then he could begin making applications for teaching positions for the next school year. In the mean time, he could substitute teach and begin living happily ever after with the girl of his dreams.

Talk about your drastic changes! Life is about to become so much sweeter than I ever imagined.

Thirty-Eight

Most of Gail's day was spent on the phone directing various pieces of medical equipment to her house. The housekeeper was there to greet the suppliers and show them where to place all the boxes. She knew it would be somewhat chaotic when they arrived, but she had come to the point where she was simply ready for it all to begin so it could eventually end. How many hours would she spend watching Levi ogle over his true love, and how many days of it could she take before threatening to leave? He had sworn to her this was only a friendly gesture, that somehow it was his destiny, but that little lift that had been in his walk this morning had managed to stay there all day long.

When time to close the office finally came, they all cleaned up, locked up, and drove away. Everyone else went to their predictable homes with their predictable families, but Gail and Levi headed to the hospital to begin, what she was convinced would be the final days of her satisfying marriage. It had never been perfect, but it had always been enough. How was she supposed to compete with a woman who had captured his imagination years ago? And who knew, his whole vision of her could be more fantasy than reality. She most definitely couldn't compete with that.

As they greeted Angie and her family at Carter's room to lead them back to the Taylor house, Gail marveled again at how humble and grateful the couple was. She wanted to hate them for intruding into her wonderful life, but there was nothing pretentious about them. They were tired, they were displaced, and their innocent little boy was in a lot of pain. Not only that, he was about to undergo some severe treatments that would most probably make him sicker before they made him better.

As Michael followed the Mercedes up the impressive driveway, he began to feel even more intimidated at the thought of staying with Dr. Levi Taylor and his surgically tacked ears. Angie seemed to know exactly what his thoughts were.

She reached over and took his hand as she again reassured him. "If I had wanted to be with Levi Taylor, I would have been with him years ago."

"It's not just the man," he admitted. "It's the whole package. Look at this house—these grounds. Shoot, look at the car we've been following the past few miles."

"If I had wanted a house and grounds and a Mercedes, I wouldn't have become a missionary. Besides, *you* built our house. I think that's way more impressive than all this."

He laughed nervously. "No you don't, but I'll try and be happy with your sentiment."

As they entered the large, modern foyer, it was so perfect it didn't seem real. Obviously Levi Taylor did well in the cancer business. They chatted briefly about various characteristics of the house, but Michael and Angie were anxious to see their arrangements. In truth, they were exhausted from another strained day at the hospital, and if they could do so without being rude, they would just as soon drop into bed and be finished for the night.

☼☼☼

When Sam pulled into the port, it was just starting to drizzle. She had tried to call Billy to tell him she was on her way and to meet her outside, but his phone must have been turned off because all she kept getting was voicemail. She wrapped her coat around tightly and then jumped quickly from the car and ran down the dock to his boat. She climbed up on the edge and rapped loudly on the door.

"Sam!" he called out when he opened the door. "Get out of the rain! Why didn't you call?"

She gave him an exasperated look. "I did! Many times! Your phone must be off."

He pulled it out of his pocket. Sure enough, the battery was dead.

"Sorry," he said sheepishly. "I think the battery is on the blink."

She pulled off her glasses and went into the bathroom to wipe off the droplets of rain. "So, tell me what happened today at the lawyer's office. You left school a whipped puppy, and then called me in victorious triumph."

He only smiled as she emerged from the bathroom. "Later," he said to her.

"Later?" she smiled back. "Okay … so this is really good then?"

He came over to her and took both of her hands in his. "It changes everything, Sam … everything."

She liked the feeling of her hands in his. "So, I take it this means you won't be moving in with me … relieving us both of great temptation?"

"I don't have to move in with you to be tempted," he said as his old charm reappeared.

"Oh, my," she uttered softly as he pulled her closer. "Am I tempting you now?"

"Listen," he said as his lips nearly touched her face, "after today, nothing can stop us. Tonight, we can talk about everything … about us, our future, our plans … I've got something solid to build on now, Sam.

But I need to come clean with you too. We can't really start over until we lay everything out on the table."

He wanted to kiss her so badly he could barely breathe. He also wanted to pull off those stupid glasses so he could see clearly into her green eyes. As if she had read his mind, she released one hand and reached up to remove her glasses.

"I'm nearsighted," she whispered as she tossed the glasses onto the couch and reached back down for his hand.

He stared into her eyes for the longest time. He wanted to drink her in. He knew that after tonight they would be on track again, and he wanted to linger in this moment as long as he could. He wanted to remember what it was like to be on the brink of having every dream in his life come true.

"You do know that I love you," he whispered as he brought his lips to her ears. "No matter what happened in the past, I have always loved you."

Her hair in his face was intoxicating. He could smell her, hear her breathing, and was so close to tasting her again that he was struggling to keep his senses.

"Billy," she said softly as she pulled back so she could see his face. "The past has got to be over. I don't want to talk about it or think about it anymore. Okay? Can we just move on from here?"

It was finally too much for him. As her eyes pleaded for understanding, he leaned into her and kissed her for the first time in ten years. It was as though nothing in his life had ever mattered before this moment. Her response was eager and passionate, and as they both melted deeper into the kiss, he moved his hands up to her hair. He wanted to take out that blasted ponytail and run his fingers through that soft mane, but he remembered they still had a dinner date.

"We need to go eat," he tried to breathe out as he pulled away slightly.

"I'm not hungry anymore," she told him as she pulled him back into another kiss. He was losing himself to the passion fast.

"Neither am I, if we're being honest, but before this goes any further, there are things I need to say to you, Samantha. Important things."

He could feel his hands almost gain a mind of their own. They were heading down, and if he didn't stop it now, this would go too far. He had to tell her about his life after their divorce, his whirlwind marriage to Kirstie, his drinking, and a few more miserable adventures he had pursued before deciding to turn things around. She had to know everything this time. He couldn't afford to lose her trust ever again.

"Samantha," he whispered, "we can't … not right now. You have to trust me on this."

She put her head down on his chest and breathed heavily. "I do trust you, Billy," she admitted. "It took a while, but it's all okay now. It really is."

He gently kissed her forehead and said, "Then let's go eat some Cajun food. We can pick right back up when the night's over. Believe me; I'll have no problem with that."

His smile made her laugh, and she softly kissed him again before she released her hands and went to the couch for her glasses.

"Come on, pretty boy," she said as she took his hand and led him toward the door. "Wine and dine me tonight. I have a feeling you're gonna get really lucky when it's over."

Billy knew his heart was gone for sure this time.

☼☼☼

Once they were seated at Blue Bayou and began looking over their menus, Sam reached beneath the table to take his hand.

"You are one slick dude," she said subtly as she laced her fingers between his.

"What have I done this time? Whatever it is, it wasn't intentional."

She gazed around the room as she explained, "Great atmosphere, casual dress, pricey menu … the perfect place for us to do this. A little loud from the bar and the band, but intimate enough that we can sit over here in the corner and have our own personal discussion. I only hope the food is worth the price you insist on paying."

"It is," he said as he pulled their hands into his lap. "And don't look at the prices first. Look at the menu, find something you like, and then order it freely. Money is not a problem tonight."

She shook her head as she went back to the menu. "If you say so."

She decided on a shrimp po-boy sandwich with spicy fries, and he ordered the crawfish etoufee with Cajun chips and a salad. They sat back and enjoyed their sodas and laughed about how miserably the day had started and how things were finally beginning to look up.

As she explained a particularly embarrassing moment that had happened with one of the cheerleaders in her Algebra II class, Billy noticed a group of ladies sauntering toward the door from the outside. They were obviously out on the town for the night with nothing more in mind than having a good time. If Blue Bayou had not had its own bar, he would have sworn they had already visited one somewhere prior.

He turned back to Sam as she continued her story and wished he could reach up and take off her dark-rimmed glasses. Her green eyes were glowing tonight, and all he could think about was the boat before they had left … and now the boat when they would leave here. Suddenly life was good again.

As the ladies entered the restaurant, their exuberance continued. They were loud, almost to the point of being distracting, but he kept his attention on Sam. She was animated tonight and on top of the world. He understood—he felt exactly the same. Nothing could spoil this moment … nothing except a familiar laugh that now sounded above all others. It was unmistakable as it bellowed out past the bar and throughout the restaurant. He wanted to ignore it, but he had to know if it was she. Just as he glanced over, their eyes met.

God, no … please, he silently prayed. *Not tonight. Please don't do this to me tonight.*

It was too late. She had definitely seen him.

"Oh, my gosh!" she screamed across the room. "Billy Marcum!"

Sam immediately stopped telling her story and looked toward the woman. She didn't have a chance to ask who it was, because the tall brunette literally came running over to Billy. She leaned down and hugged him tightly and then pulled back to ogle over him.

"My gosh! You are as gorgeous as ever!" she continued. She glanced over at Sam. "I should have known you'd take up with another cute blond. That was my downfall, wasn't it? I wasn't a blond like your first wife."

Billy's head was spinning as all this was happening so fast. He had brought Sam to the restaurant to come clean with her, to tell her about his ridiculous marriage to Kirstie, but never in a million years did he expect his ex-wife to show up.

"What on earth have you been up to?" Kirstie continued in her typical flamboyant style. By now her companions had gathered around the table, and Billy knew his face had to be turning various shades of green.

"I'm in school … just about to finish," he said weakly.

Kirstie started roaring again with laughter. Yes, she was extremely beautiful, but poise and tact were not a part of her package. "No wonder I never see you around!" she spouted as she looked back to Sam. "And who might you be?"

Sam looked up at her, still in a daze as to who this was and what exactly was going on, and replied, "Samantha."

For the first time since walking through the door, Kirstie hushed. Her eyes grew big and her jaw dropped open. But the silence didn't last long.

"*The* Samantha, as in the *first wife* Samantha?" Kirstie wondered.

Billy now started to sink down in his seat. This couldn't be happening.

"I suppose that's it," Sam responded, obviously confused. "We were married."

"Nice to meet you, Samantha," Kirstie said with a big smile as she stuck out her hand. "I'm Kirstie Hester, the second wife."

Sam obliged the handshake, but suddenly her world fell apart … again … because of Billy Marcum. She could literally feel the doors, the walls, the fences and the barricades going up around her heart. She didn't hear another word the woman said beyond *the second wife.*

After what seemed like an eternity, Kirstie's friends insisted they move on to their table. She said her goodbyes to Billy and Sam as though nothing at all had happened. But the reality was that two worlds had just fallen apart.

Billy knew he should say something, but what? The very reason he had brought her here was to tell her the truth and to confess about his second marriage, but the hurt in her eyes had now replaced the glow, and he was afraid speak.

As soon as Sam could collect her thoughts and emotions, she stood and pushed her chair beneath the table.

"Please, don't go, Sam," he pleaded. "If you'll let me explain, it'll make a lot more sense than it does right now."

She shook her head. "I don't want to hear any of your explanations. The bottom line is that for … oh, man," her emotions were beginning to surface again, "… for the past few weeks, I thought things were … different. I thought we were open and honest." She looked down at him and her expression was extremely pained. "I thought you had changed and that I could really trust you. I thought the deception was over."

As soon as Billy stood, Sam turned to leave.

"Sam!" he called after her. "Wait!"

The waitress appeared with their food. "Sir," she said as she followed behind Billy who was now following Sam out the door. "Your food is here!"

He said nothing, but ran out the door after her.

"Sam! Please listen to me!" he yelled. "It was this spur of the moment thing! I didn't even love her!"

She was now opening the door to her car, but he ran up and stepped beside the door so she couldn't close it.

"We were barely divorced, and I was absolutely miserable," he continued.

"I don't want to hear about it," she echoed her point. "Please, let me leave."

"A big group of us went out to Vegas one weekend," he explained. "We both got dead drunk, and somewhere in the midst of all the cavorting we thought it would be funny to get married."

Sam looked up at him with disgust in her eyes. "And this is supposed to make me feel better?"

"We weren't even married a year … shoot … we didn't even live together six months! I still loved *you*, Sam. You can ask her."

"Yeah, yeah, yeah," she turned the key and cranked the car. "And you loved Angie Wright while you were married to me. If only you could learn to love the one you're with, you might have a decent shot at marriage the next time around."

She attempted to close the door, but he wouldn't move.

"We've already made a big enough scene here," she said tearfully. "Please, don't make me have to pull this car out with you hanging on to the door somehow."

He tried to make her understand. "The whole reason I brought you here was to tell you about Kirstie and the marriage … as well as a few other things I would really hate for you to be surprised by one day."

"Tonight?" she screamed in astonishment. "You waited until *tonight* to tell me about this?"

"I didn't think it would matter before. I didn't know we had a chance … a real chance … until today. That's why I insisted we go out … so I could just come clean with you, Sam." He paused hoping for some kind of response. There was none. "I love you, and I want to spend the rest of my life with you. Please find a way to forgive me and to chalk it all up to just one more of the stupid decisions I've made in my life."

Sam was obviously trying to keep tears from falling. "I'm tired of being on the wrong end of your stupid decisions," she managed to say as she put the car into gear and began to back out.

He realized it was hopeless and stepped out of the way. His least concern at the moment was that she was leaving him stranded with no ride at the restaurant. All he could think about was that his life was again in limbo, and he had no one to blame but himself. She was right; he should have told her long ago.

He watched as she sped away down the slippery street. The drizzle was now turning to rain, and Billy had no idea what to do or where to go. He had a bank account full of money, but the four million without Sam now seemed like nothing. Would he trade it all to have her back in his life? In a moment. But he knew Sam well. The chances were very high that she would never even speak to him again. So, he went back inside, paid the waitress for their drinks and all the food they wouldn't eat, and then headed down the street in the cold rain toward his boat. He could actually run the heat tonight with no worries, but his heart had become so numbed to anything other than its own pain, even the cold didn't trouble him. As the rain drenched his body, heavy tears, for the first time since his mother's death, began to drench his soul.

Thirty-Nine

After a wonderful dinner prepared by the cook, and an evening of meaningless chit chat that mostly consisted of Angie and Levi reminiscing about med school, the children conked out, Cassie in Michael's lap and Carter in Angie's. Michael carried a sleeping Cassie up the stairs to her room and gently placed her in bed. She never moved or moaned; she was out. He quickly bopped back down because he knew Angie would attempt the climb with Carter in tow if he didn't get there soon enough. He managed to transfer him to his shoulder and then pulled Angie up from the couch without too much fuss.

"There's no way we can adequately thank you for doing this," Angie said wearily before leaving with Michael to go upstairs. "I know you know that. I also know you wouldn't have offered if it didn't come from your hearts. Thank you so much. Right now that's all I have to give you."

Angie couldn't believe how relieved she was with the whole setup at Levi's. He had turned his upstairs game room into their own private little apartment. It came complete with a shower and a small wet bar. Connected to the room was what was meant to be a miniature home office, but it had yet to be furnished with anything. He had put a twin sized hospital bed in it for Carter, along with all the monitoring equipment, and then another twin bed for Cassie. In the game room, he added a queen sized bed for Michael and Angie, and had pushed aside the pool and ping pong tables.

"Our own room," Angie whispered to Michael as she looked around their home for the next month. "We'll actually have a little privacy again." She turned to him and gave a very suggestive smile. "We won't have to sneak away to be alone."

He blushed slightly. "That'll be nice." He pointed toward the pool table. "And if we get insomnia, we can always play a few games in the middle of the night."

"I don't believe I even know what insomnia feels like. I've never had trouble falling asleep … or staying asleep."

"That's because when you're awake you're always giving one hundred percent to someone or something."

"And look," she said as she walked out to a balcony. "We can overlook the gardens and the pond below. It'll almost be like our honeymoon again in Hawaii."

He laughed. "It won't even be close to that."

"Sure it will," she asserted as she took his hand and pulled him out with her. "We can walk out on this balcony for a breath of fresh air any time we wish. The only difference will be that there's no ocean in the horizon to take our breath away."

He leaned in to kiss her. "I don't need an ocean to take my breath away. Besides, I was such a nervous wreck in Hawaii. I never dreamed you would grow to love me like this."

"Ah, but I most certainly do." She wrapped her arms around his waist and pulled him in for another kiss. "You are my white knight, my prince, my rock."

"I'm also your plumber, your farmer, your …"

She stopped him with another kiss. "Yes, you're my everything. And right now, all I can think of is that we have a bed and a room all to ourselves again. The kids are asleep, the moon is … well … somewhere, I guess. It's definitely not Padawin or Hawaii, but I promise I can be just as romantic here as there, with or without seeing the moon."

He kissed her again as the thought of being with her alone began to swim around in his mind. Things had been so stressful and tense this last while that they had no time to be alone and unwind. As her hands moved down to his waist, he let himself get lost in her touch. Then suddenly he pulled back.

"What is it?" she asked as she only pulled him closer.

"The baby. Isn't it a little late in the pregnancy to … you know … do *this*?"

She laughed. Even after five years of marriage, he was still too shy to use certain phrases with her. "I don't care if this baby comes tomorrow. Tonight … it's me and you doing … you know … *this*."

He blushed. "I just don't want to do anything that would harm the baby."

"If you don't stop worrying about this baby, who is very well protected in there for the record, and start taking care of *my* immediate needs, you may end up doing *me* harm."

"You're sure it's okay?"

"Shut up, Michael, and let's … you know … do *this*," she grinned as she led him from the balcony back toward the bed.

They had no idea that Levi Taylor had been standing out on his patio beneath the balcony. It was an exchange that was meant to be personally intimate and playful, not overheard. But as he leaned against a post and quietly replayed the conversation, something struck him about the couple—they were deeply in love and committed to each other. As hard as their life had been recently, the playful banter between them indicated a deep need to reconnect in spite of it all. He and Gail had this tendency to pull away when things got tough. Somewhere down the road when life eased up and things got smoother, they would eventually find a way back into each others' arms. But Angie and Michael weren't just roommates. They weren't with each other out of a convenience to avoid loneliness. There was something deeper between them that he had observed, but couldn't label. He wondered if it were even possible for him and Gail to even relate on that level.

☼☼☼

Stephen was sound asleep when he felt Annie gently sit beside him on the bed. He slowly rolled over, opened his eyes, and was delighted as he saw his favorite mug being waved before his eyes full of steaming coffee.

"Wow," he said leisurely, "coffee in bed? To what do I owe this great surprise?"

She smiled with tired eyes as she waited for him to sit up so he could take the cup. "I didn't imagine you would just hop out of bed this morning, so I thought I'd give you something enticing."

He raised an eyebrow at her. "There are more enticing things than coffee, you know?"

Her laugh was weary. "But coffee is the best offer you're gonna get this morning."

Then he remembered. "How's Stevie?"

"Still dry heaving." She crawled in bed beside him. "I guess he's got this stomach virus in full force."

He took a sip of his hot coffee and sighed. "Bless his heart. He was having a hard time of it last night. Is there anything we can do, or do we just let it run its course?"

"I called the doctor a few minutes ago. They're gonna give him a prescription. Moms is going to pick it up for us and bring it over."

"Does that stop it?"

"No, but it does ease up the symptoms and helps him to sleep through some of it."

He nodded and took another sip.

"Thanks," she said as she snuggled up closer to him, "for cleaning it all up last night when he started. I was so exhausted. I think I had actually just fallen asleep."

"No problem. It's been a tense week for you."

She gave a slight chuckle. "Isn't it always?"

"Tense? No. Why would you say that?"

She sat up and stuck her hair behind her ears. "Living with me has got to be stressful for you. I mean, you had this simple life before I came along, and now you have to deal with my emotions, my complaints, and my upsets on a regular basis."

"I had this *boring* life before you came along," he clarified. "I wouldn't trade what we have for anything. Besides, this coffee in bed is really nice. You've never done that before. See, I never got little surprises like this before you came along."

"I'm really sorry for all the tension lately."

"Hey," he sat up straighter and looked in her eyes. "What's going on? Why are you so … uh … contrite this morning?"

"When I was taking my turn with Stevie last night, it made me think of Angie … and Carter. I found myself counting my blessings for only being up because my son had a stomach bug. Then I started thinking of all my other blessings." She took her finger and traced the side of his bare arm with it. "Everything good and wonderful in my life, Stephen, is because of you. Our family, our home, even the fact that my name is known around the world and plastered across the pages of magazines all over the country is good. My music would've never been heard by anyone had it not been for you. My happiness and joy right now are because of you. And yet I know that I don't always show that."

"Wow, you're really getting deep for the morning," he laughed slightly. "You usually save these discussions for the dark of night."

"I'm serious, Stephen. I know it seems like I take you and what we've got together for granted. And when you got up with Stevie last night … when I was so exhausted I could barely think straight … it reminded me even more of what a jewel you are."

He took another drink from his coffee and then set the mug down on the table beside the bed. "Honey," he said sweetly as he put his arm around her and pulled her close, "everything's okay. I don't hold any kind of malice toward you."

"But sometimes you doubt me. You told me that the other night out by the pool."

"Sometimes I do," he admitted, "but only when you go off on one of your tirades."

"And I shouldn't do that."

"But you do," he was quick to stop her. "And I understand. That's how you express yourself. In fact, that's sort of how all you sisters express yourselves."

"Not anymore. Angie isn't like that anymore. It's like she's made peace with her life somehow, and that no matter what happens, it's all okay. She's got Michael, she's got her kids, and she's got her work in Padawin. And for her, that's enough. Yet in my mind, I have so much more than she does. I married Stephen Williams! I dreamed about you for so many years. Who would've ever thought one day I would be sitting here next to you in our bed bringing you coffee?"

"A very noble act on your part, I must say," he winked as he reached over for his coffee again.

"And even Andie has settled down more. As long as you don't bring up politics, she's fairly sedate."

"I hate your family's political discussions. Not because I disagree, but because you all agree about the same things, but take an eternity and several arguments to finally get there."

She snickered as she laid her head back. "I know. That's sort of how we've always been. And see, I've loved that about us! But it's changing … at least, everyone else seems to be. But not me. I just keep burrowing my head down and going right along with whatever emotion or idea seems to crop up."

"You know what? You don't need to compare yourself to your sisters. You are three separate entities. You live your life on a totally different level than they do."

"And what level is that?" she wondered with a bit of self-pity.

"You are a creator," he tried to explain. "You will never be one that takes life as it comes. When stuff happens, you have to spill it out somehow. Sometimes, you do that through music or through writing. Sometimes, you do it through talking or hashing it all to pieces. You can't just let things happen to you and not respond—not process it." He smiled at her and gently kissed her nose. "And believe it or not, that's one of the things I love about you, yet it drives me crazy at the same time."

"You don't love it—you're just being nice to me right now."

"Oh, I do love it," he assured her. "I have laughed and been amused by it more than you know. But, yes, it has sent me in a tailspin just as often."

"It makes me wonder, though, how I can have everything in the world I ever dreamed of and yet still somehow be so displeased with life that I can fly off the handle like I do."

"You feel deeply. You think deeply. You react deeply. Besides, you're not all bad, you know?"

She looked up at him with a doubtful stare.

"Seriously," he grinned as he slid her down in the bed. "You have these gorgeous brown eyes that see right into my soul." He gently kissed each eye. "And you have these lips that are so inviting and lush that sometimes, when you're railing on and on about something, I just watch them and think, *I get to kiss them when she's finished.*"

"You do not think that," she giggled.

"Oh, yes I do. That's why I can smile when you go on a rampage. It's sort of like a secret delight of mine."

"I think you're making this up as you go along."

"And then," he moved his hand down her body, "there's the rest of you … very nice. Plus, you're an awesome musician, so you keep me on my toes where it counts the most. All in all, I'd say I got a pretty good package." He leaned into kiss her.

Suddenly a loud cry was heard from down the hall.

"Stevie's at it again," she said as she immediately began to get up. "Poor guy."

He fell back into the bed as she pushed him away.

"Sorry," she grinned as she leaned down to give him a final kiss. "Duty calls."

She started for the door, but then turned around for a final comment. "Thanks," she said sincerely. "I do know how blessed I am, whether I ever admit it or not."

☼☼☼

"Is this happening?" Cindy whispered to Kyle as the jet engines roared in preparation for take-off.

He squeezed her hand and leaned over to say, "Indeed. We are on our way to Miami, and then off for a one week cruise."

"And are our kids in good hands?"

"Great hands."

"And we're gonna be all alone?"

"Whenever we desire."

She closed her eyes as the plane began to race down the runway. "This is a dream, Kyle. This isn't really happening."

As the jet lifted off the ground, he squeezed her hand again. "If it's a dream, then don't wake me up. I can't believe I'm saying this, but I'm actually looking forward to being away from the children for a while."

"I'm afraid to say it," she confessed. "It would sound so … selfish … so un-motherly."

"You've been a mother since the day we got married. You deserve this more than anyone."

"*We* deserve this. Our marriage has been no easier for you than for me."

"Actually," he pulled her hand up and kissed it gently, "this marriage has been a picnic compared to my first one."

She chuckled and leaned into him to say, "Let's hear you say that after you've spent an entire week alone with me. This will be a first, you know."

"Oh yeah, and I'm planning on savoring every minute of it."

When the plane leveled off, she tried to relax. Flying was not her favorite mode of travel. In fact, she had expressed a lot of apprehension before leaving, but Kyle had assured her all would be fine. The trip to Miami would be brief, and then they would find their ship, their cabin, and they would sail off into the sunset.

"This is almost perfect," he said as he thumbed through a brochure of the cruise they would be taking.

"Almost? What are we missing?"

"A peace about going back. When we return to Dockrey, Dr. Hal Bridges will be there just a few days later. There's something really wrong about him, Cindy."

"And what's so odd about it is that a lot of the church obviously thinks that too. A sixty percent vote … how bizarre is that?"

"I wouldn't have come. No way … not if forty percent of the church had voted against me."

"And I can still see that odd look in his eyes when you asked him about being a Navy Seal. If it bothers him so much, he shouldn't put it in his résumé'. He has to know people are gonna ask him about it. And the truth is it's pointless as far as the ministry is concerned. There's no need for him to even bring it up."

Kyle shook his head again. "Things are gonna be very different when he comes."

"Maybe, maybe not. Not if we don't let them."

"No, it'll be different. You haven't worked in other churches. It can get bad among the staff. When you have someone with a really strong personality who refuses to blend in, it can cause major havoc."

"Yeah, but you've only talked about pastors being the problems. This guy won't be in charge. Pastor Jon will still be running the show, and even *Dr. Bridges* will have to answer to him."

He gave a breathy laugh and said, "I can't believe he tried to get my office."

"And Pastor Jon put a stop to it immediately."

"He hadn't even been called to the church yet! What is this guy thinking? That's what I'm telling you, Cindy—he's not a normal person."

"Okay," she put up her hands, "enough! I'm not spending my second chance for a honeymoon discussing some lunatic minister who's about to come in and rattle the church around. Let's talk about us … the trip. What do you want to do first when we get there?"

His forlorn expression immediately grew into a grin. "Lock the door and unpack."

"Why do we have to lock the door to unpack?"

He didn't answer. He just leaned over and kissed her.

"Oh," she whispered. "Silly me."

Forty

Billy was miserable. Even as he sat in Cracker Barrel eating a huge breakfast consisting of both pancakes and eggs, he couldn't manage to forget that money in his pocket and food in his stomach would never replace Sam. He had come so close to having it all, just like years before, only this time when he lost it, he knew exactly what he was losing. He wondered if she would make it to school today, Friday. She hadn't come the last three days, not since the fiasco at Blue Bayou. It was quite a shock for the school because Ms. Marcum never missed. She could be stuffed up with the worst cold of the year or running back and forth to the bathroom with a horrible stomach bug, but no matter what, she was always there. This was different though … this was a matter of the heart.

He paid his bill and smiled at the sweatshirt he passed on his way out. It had the large letters GRITS with the phrase *Girls Raised in the South* written beneath. Sam would have loved that. Her Southern accent was strong, and of all the things in her past she had tried to lose, that wasn't one of them. He had always gotten a kick out of watching movies with her and listening to her rail on about the fake accents of the actors. *For Pete's sake, they paid her $5 million to do this movie; the least she could have done was actually get a real Southerner to tell her how to pronounce the word y'all!*

But that was the past. It was clearer today than even Monday night that she never wanted to speak to him again. He had called, gone by her house countless times, done everything imaginable to see her, but she wouldn't respond. He had gotten so concerned that he asked Mr. C to check on her, which he did. She was fine, she needed time, and the last thing she ever wanted to do in the world was to face Billy Marcum again. Of course, that loaded Mr. C with a million questions that she refused to answer, thus leaving Billy with him for seven hours a day having to face the same questions.

The morning was definitely still cold, but at least the rain had gone. He pulled on his riding suit and determined that this weekend he would buy a car. He had hoped to do that earlier, but with all the problems with Sam, plus the fact that school was incessantly busy at the moment, he hadn't had the time to go to a dealership. One thing he had done, however—there was now a *For Sale* sign up on the boat and an ad in the paper. Hopefully that would be one mistake out of his life very soon.

As he stuffed his suit into the bike's luggage at the school, he noticed Sam's car was there. His heart skipped just for a moment, but then he knew it was pointless. She wasn't here for him. In fact, chances were high if he even so much as looked at her she would fall apart … or he might.

He passed through the door which led into the math and science building and saw that her room was open, but she wasn't standing outside as was typical for the start of school. He eased by and glanced in briefly; she was sitting at her desk looking through a stack of papers. He dared not pause lest she look up and see him. When he walked into his own class, there sat Mr. C at the desk giving him a really strong glare.

"She's back," Mr. C told him.

Billy nodded. "I know. I saw her car … well … and her too."

"And she's still not talking … about anything."

"And she probably won't." He placed his satchel on the podium and reached in for today's notes. He began writing the assignment for first period on the board as Mr. C. continued to stare at him.

"I'd really like to know what's going on here, Billy. I care about Sam deeply, I'd say almost like a daughter, but she won't let me in close enough to really reach her like that. I know you two were married, and obviously whatever this is about … it includes you."

He stopped writing for a moment and closed his eyes. Yes, it was all about him, but what could Mr. C. do? If Sam had no desire to open up to him, why should he? If she didn't want Mr. C. to know, it would be one more mistake for Billy to spill the truth.

"I … I can't … don't ask me to talk about it. If Sam wants you to know, she'll …"

"Hogwash!" Mr. C. suddenly exploded.

He stopped and turned abruptly towards the bent over man who had stood and was now walking toward him shaking a finger.

"Sam will never open up about anything! You must know that!" Mr. C. was more intense than Billy thought possible for the man. "I have taught beside this woman for nine years, and I know nothing about her life! When I found out you two were married, that was the most information I've ever managed to get. I have prayed for her, encouraged her, invited her to my house, my church, done everything I could possibly imagine just to try and break through that impermeable wall she has around her, but all to no avail." Mr. C was nearly in his face now. "Suddenly you waltz into our world, a person from her past, a husband no less, and she transforms into Susie Sunshine. Now, she's gone from school for three days, she won't answer her phone, and it all revolves around you." He backed down and sighed. "I care about her, Billy. And though I hardly know you, I care about you too. And whatever has transpired between the two of you has gotten you both torn into pieces, and I just sit here clueless and helpless."

Billy took a deep breath and put down the chalk. "Even if you knew it all, you'd still be helpless."

"Perhaps," he said with a nod, "but not clueless."

He brushed the chalk dust from his hands and then rubbed his groggy eyes. "Third period … at break," he said in defeat. "I'll talk to you about it then. I need to get ready for the bell right now."

Mr. C put his arm up on Billy's shoulder. "Son, I only want to help. There are things in life we can and cannot control. My wife's stroke? Uncontrollable. It's a *necessary* pain. It's something we have to deal with. It's a physical impossibility that was handed to us, and we must learn to live with it." He rubbed his shoulder now. "Your divorce, this mess you're handling now, it's controllable. It's an *unnecessary* pain. There'll be enough hard times in life ahead to face without adding all this to it."

"Tell that to Sam," was all he could say as he turned back to the board to finish his writing.

☼☼☼

Angie found herself smiling as she awoke in Michael's arms. There was no confusion as to where she was, but there was a sense of normalcy in sleeping next to him again. She slowly turned so she could face him. He was already awake.

"Good morning, Dr. Angie," he said with a tired smile. "Sleep well?"

"How could I not?" she answered as she reached her hand up to his chest. "You know how to put me at peace."

"I would love to take that as a compliment concerning my expertise in the bedroom," he grinned, "but the truth is, once you're asleep, you're out like a light."

"You don't give yourself enough credit. Perhaps the reason I'm always out like a light is because of you."

He laughed softly and ran the back of his hand down the side of her face. He would never know what he did in his life to deserve such a gift. And it was so much more than just her unmatchable beauty. Angie had to be the most vibrant, amazing, life-breathing creature on earth. And as she looked at him with adoring eyes, he couldn't imagine life being better. Even the loss of his son couldn't compare to losing her. She was his whole life. The children, as much of a blessing as they were, were more like the salt and pepper in his life. They were wonderful, but Angie was life itself. She had become the reason he even breathed. In fact, he had never lived before she came along—he had only existed.

"What are you thinking?" she asked with her playful smile as she studied the expression on his face.

"Can you not tell?" He now ran his hand down her body. "You, of course."

"Pleasant thoughts, I hope."

"Always."

She finally stretched and sat up in bed. "I suppose we should check on the tiger. I wonder how he did last night. I never heard him stir or complain."

"He stirred and complained quite a bit. I got up several times."

She was astonished. "You're kidding? Did you give him any pain medicine?"

"Twice."

She shook her head. "I slept through that? He cried, and I didn't hear him?"

"Well," he confessed, "it wasn't like he was loud or anything. I was just up a lot and was able to look in on him. I knew at what times he should take his medicine, so I gave it to him like they did at the hospital."

She furled her brow. "Why were you up? Apparently I don't work the same magic on you."

He shook his head and sat up with her. "It has nothing to do with you. It's your Dr. Taylor that bothers me."

"Levi? Why?"

He sat back against the wall and sighed. "Every time I get around someone from your past, I start feeling so inadequate again. In Padawin, life is simple and easy. It's almost like we're Adam and Eve there … like we belong together. But here everyone that knew you knows how incredible you are. I know they all look at me and think, *How did she end up with such a loser*?"

"Michael," she said sympathetically as she took his hand. "People do not think that."

"Yes they do."

"My family thinks you're perfect."

"They didn't at first. It took them quite a while to warm up to me. Over here, I'm still this pitiful, misunderstood little boy. It's almost like I'll never belong here."

She maneuvered her clumsy body until she could look at him face to face. "Anywhere that I am is where you belong. You are the other half of me. Until you came along, there was always a huge piece missing. Now, when I lie down at night or wake up in the morning, there's no more emptiness … and it's all because you're here."

"I have no doubts about you," he admitted, "even though I can't believe I can actually say that. You're so clear and affirming to me. But it's everyone else. They look at me with this great wonder in their eyes, and they act as though I'm the white elephant in the room."

"Sweetie, you have to reconcile all of this with your past. I can't change that … neither can you. You're the most incredible man I've ever known." She took his hand. "No, you're nothing at all like these shallow-minded, temporary-focused men that have always pursued me. In all the years before I met you, no one ever looked beyond what I was on the outside. That's why it was always so easy for me to refuse any advances. But you," she gave him the warmest smile she had, "you saw *me* … the real me. And whenever you look at these men and feel intimidated because you think they somehow feel superior to you, remember this—you won me fair and square. Every man in my life before you had their chance, but none of them had the qualities that I longed for, pleaded for … that I desperately needed. You, however," and she leaned up closer to him, "had everything. And my only regret about my past is that I ever doubted someone like you could really be out there."

His cheeks flushed as he pulled her to him. "For the record, I really like your *outside* too."

"Even with this growing basketball ever coming between us?" she moaned as she rubbed her tummy.

"More so." He held her quietly for a moment, and then added, "Thanks. I wish I could move beyond all these old insecurities, but they just seem to pop up now and again."

"It's okay," she said as she moved his hand to her tummy to feel the baby squirm. "Just so long as you never doubt *me*."

"You've never given me a reason to." The baby gave a strong kick. "That has to hurt."

"Nope. Only when it gets the ribs."

It kicked a few more times, and they both began to giggle.

"Are we crazy?" she asked Michael. "Having a zillion kids like this?"

"Definitely," he replied as he pulled her closer. "I guess we'll always have some kind of adventure going on in our lives."

"With three kids? You can count on it."

A gentle cry began to sound from the other room. Carter was waking. Michael immediately began to get up, but Angie pulled him back to the bed.

"I'll get him this time," she said firmly. "Why don't you try to get some more sleep?"

He shook his head. "I can't sleep if you're not beside me. It would be a worthless effort."

She leaned down to kiss his forehead and said, "Thank you. And you wonder how I could adore you so much."

Forty-One

As Billy unloaded the story to Mr. C. during their third period break, he never meant to tell him everything. But the compassion and care he showed toward both Sam and Billy seemed to urge him to spill it all. As he finally got to Monday night at Blue Bayou, Mr. C. just shook his head in near grief. He now knew everything. He knew Sam's past, he knew Billy's past, he knew all about their first marriage, and he knew that had things worked out Monday, Billy fully intended to bring Sam back to his boat for the night.

"So, that's it," Billy said with emotional exhaustion. "It's like we're doomed to live these separate, unfulfilled lives." He looked over to Mr. C. and said, "I'll never love anyone else. She's it for me—she's my soulmate. But she doesn't see that, or even if she does, she doesn't trust me. So … I just move on … I guess."

Mr. C. closed his eyes and nodded as he thought through all the information. So much about Sam must make sense to him now. "Wow," he said very softly. "I had no idea." The older gentleman looked at him with a deep compassion. In his eyes were reflected the years of wisdom born through both pain and joy. "How do I even start with you?" he said from a tender heart. "You both so desperately long for love, and long to give it … to each other … but you're lost in your pasts, and you have no idea how to move beyond your mistakes."

"It's all my fault," he began to say, but Mr. C. stopped him immediately.

"No, it's not, Billy. You're just as lost and hurting as she is."

"But I left her!" he protested. "I could've been everything to her … I could've saved her. But I chose my old path of selfishness and just left her there. I walked out on her and didn't bother to even look back to see how she survived."

"Son, you had no idea what love was," Mr. C. tried to explain. "Your parents weren't nearly as inept in raising you as Sam's were, but they also didn't do a good job of showing true love. The first time you were ever really shown love from your mother was in that letter you read on Monday afternoon."

"What? I knew my mother loved me!"

"I didn't say that," Mr. C. replied calmly. "I said the first time she really *showed* you true love was in that letter. Every other time in your life, she gave you exactly what you wanted. She didn't approve of all that you did, and she made that clear, but she never gave you an ultimatum. But as she lay dying, she realized that." Mr. C. shook his head again. "I feel for her too. Had she done that when you were twenty, or fifteen, or ten, your life would have been very different … and she knew that."

"My life wasn't her fault."

"On the contrary, your life and your failed marriage fall right back to your parents."

"You're wrong."

Mr. C. stood up and began to pace the front of the room. "Your struggles in your marriage were due to the fact that you needed Sam to love you in a way that your parents didn't."

"My failed marriage was due to my selfishness."

"I don't deny that. But just as your parents always gave into your selfishness, Sam did too." Mr. C. stopped and looked at him. "You tested her love for you, just like you always tested your parents. And she failed just as they always did by letting you get away with anything you wanted."

"That's not true!" Billy could feel his face turning hot. "Sam was an angel! I'm the one who messed up!"

"What you wanted was for Sam to love you enough to tell you to get your sorry butt out of her house and out of her life until you straightened up. You were pleading for her to say that she loved you too much to watch you continue to destroy what was good and right in your life. What you longed for was for her to fight for your marriage—to fight to keep you in her life. But just like your parents, she let you drown in your selfish defeat. And once again, you self-destructed."

"You can't pin this on Sam! I won't let you!"

"Billy," Mr. C. walked over to him and placed a hand on his shoulder again. "You and Sam were so young, so immature, and so clueless about real love, that your marriage was doomed before it started. It's easy in hindsight to say you made all those mistakes and you wish you could take them back, but it doesn't change the fact that what you needed from Sam, she didn't give you. And what she needed from you, unconditional love and acceptance, you didn't give her. And so here you are, years later, carrying the same emotional baggage and pain, and you somehow think you'll avoid the same mistakes this time?"

"I could've loved her … better," He looked up at him with real tears in his eyes. "This time … I could've done it right."

"You lied to her, Billy. You deceived her all these weeks you've been with her here at the school. You didn't tell her about the second marriage. Why? As you told me your story, you stressed you knew it would be important to Sam. You labored over when and how to tell her. And in typical Billy Marcum fashion, you waited until it was most convenient for *you* to unload the truth. Only this time, the truth beat you to it."

Billy slammed his hand on the desk. "Why didn't I tell her sooner?

Why did I wait? I blew it! Man, did I ever blow it this time!"

"Son, all you want in life … really … all you want is to be loved. And you don't have a clue as to how to go about it. Your sister found it, but she found it through sacrifice and suffering. That's where you find love, Billy. And that's where Sam will find it too."

"But she did sacrifice and suffer. She sacrificed and suffered because of me … because of what I was doing to her."

"No. She was just as selfish as you were. She was scared to death that if she really loved you—really made you face your destructive behavior, she would lose you. She was willing to watch you ruin your life with the hopes of somehow hanging on to you more than she was willing to pull you out of the pit." Mr. C. clapped his hands together one time and then pointed his finger directly in Billy's face. "And until the two of you realize that, and realize that rebuilding your marriage means rethinking your concepts of love, you're doomed to repeat the same mistakes again and again."

Billy sighed and wiped his eyes. "Fat chance of any of that happening now. She'll never speak to me again. She'll never trust me again."

"So you thought before. But there you were on Monday night ready to propose marriage once you got that inconvenient little deception out of the way."

Billy looked up at him. "You think she'll take me back?"

"Not completely. Something like this will always come up. You'll both pedal your frail little lives to the edge of love again and again, but until you realize that it's gonna take more than either of you have, you'll always fall short of having what you're desperately searching for."

His heart was breaking. "So how? How do I get there? How do I become what Sam needs me to be? How do I learn to love her like she needs to be loved?"

Mr. C. smiled tenderly and pointed his finger toward heaven. "I think you know. You have to surrender your life to the One who made you, and you have to let Him fulfill and complete you before you can ever be what she needs."

Billy shook his head. "God doesn't want me. I'm pretty sure of that."

"How do you know? Have you asked Him? Has He told you that somehow? Spelled it out in the clouds, perhaps?"

"I just know. I'm worthless when it comes to God. I've deliberately turned my back on Him so many times that He'd be a fool to even give me a second look."

"Then consider Him a fool if you must. Because right now, He longs for you to turn to Him and let Him clean up all the messes you've made all these years."

Billy spent the entire day at school longing to talk with Sam, but avoiding her vehemently. He knew any kind of encounter with her would probably bring an unnecessary confrontation, and it would be unprofessional of him to try and force something out of her in this controlled environment. He waited until he had gotten home, collected his thoughts, and was ready to go car shopping. He pulled on his riding bibs before leaving the boat, and then added the jacket as he approached the Kawasaki.

"Our days are numbered, baby," he said as he stuck the key in the bike and unlocked the handlebars.

He drove leisurely in the biting cold to Sam's. He needed to remain calm and just say what he had to say. He didn't need to let it blow up into any kind of real conversation. He had realized for the first time today while talking with Mr. C that he really wasn't ready for any kind of relationship with her. He had always wondered why Cindy so adamantly insisted he not see her again; perhaps this is what she saw too. His only concept of love had been to get what he wanted, and even though it was hard for him to swallow at the moment, the idea that he had been pushing Sam away in hopes that she would demand he change might be right after all. Over the years he had wondered many times why he did what he had done to her. He knew that he loved her, that he adored her, and when he saw her again in school those few weeks ago, it was as if nothing had changed in his heart. So why had he deliberately pushed her away?

He pulled into Sam's drive and parked behind her car. He removed his helmet and unzipped his jacket, but he left all the gear on. His intention was not to stay or to go inside. He was simply going to let her go, and then he would leave. He rang the doorbell twice and then took a step back. He didn't want to seem eager or intrusive. He knew she would probably want to slam the door, but that was her prerogative.

He waited patiently and wouldn't look up. He assumed she would look through the little hole and know it was him before opening the door. He wanted to seem as non-threatening as possible. To his surprise, he heard her unlock the door and turn the knob.

"What do you want?" she asked through a small crack.

"I just wanted to tell you something. Can I have a minute or two, just say what I need to say, and I'll be gone?"

She hesitated. He tried to see her through the crack. At last, she opened it wider and stepped into the threshold.

"Okay," she said with no emotion. "Speak, and then leave."

"That's my intention." He cleared his throat and began his well rehearsed speech. "First, I want you to know that I understand how wrong it was for me to never tell you about Kirstie. I kept trying to figure out if we actually had a chance or not." He paused, shook his head, and started again. "That's an excuse. It doesn't matter why. The fact is I didn't tell you, but I went on acting as though all was fine and clear between us. And I had no business letting things get … well … steamy between us again. I should've listened to Cindy and just kept everything simple and friendly."

She continued to stare at him with no emotion whatsoever.

"And everything I did at the end of our marriage," he continued, "was so wrong and misplaced. There is no excuse for it … period. I want to believe that what I feel for you right now is really love … and that I'd sacrifice my life to have you back with me again. But if my past and present are indicators of my future, then chances are, I'd hurt you all over again."

She took a deep breath and crossed her arms, but still remained silent.

"So, I'm just here to tell you I'll give you what you want … what you've obviously wanted all week … I'll leave you alone. I won't try to talk to you; I won't call you or approach you or anything. We'll just be civil if we happen to meet at school, and we'll leave it at that. And when the semester is up, I'll leave the Shoals area for good. I'll go back to Dockrey until I can find a job somewhere far away from here, and you'll never have to worry about running into me again … ever."

She continued to stare.

"That's it," he told her. "The end."

She sighed, nodded, and looked up toward the darkening sky. "I suppose Thanksgiving is out, then."

He looked at her in disbelief. "You still want to come with me for Thanksgiving?"

She shook her head. "No. I'm just being mean … sort of … I guess. I don't know what to say to you, Billy. Somewhere in the back of my mind I knew it wouldn't work out anyway." She put her hands in her pockets and looked away from him as she spoke. "I'm not meant to be with anyone. I'm messed up."

"Sam," he instinctively spoke her name and took a step toward her. She immediately backed away.

"Don't," she commanded. "I don't want your pity."

He pulled back.

She reached up and removed her glasses and rubbed the bridge of her nose. When she looked back at him, and he could see the green of her eyes so clearly, he almost changed his mind. He wanted to grab her and hold her and never let her go again.

"I still love you, Sam," he whispered to her. "I always will."

He forced himself to turn around and leave. He zipped his jacket as he approached his bike and refused to look back at her. He fastened his helmet and climbed on. He couldn't help but take one more glance. She hadn't moved. Her glasses in hand, and her arms wrapped around her in the chilly air—she looked helpless and alone. She *was* helpless and alone.

He backed the bike out of the drive, and quickly made his way down the road.

Sam watched until he was out of sight. So that was the end? She rubbed her arms in the frigid air and then went back inside. Like an emotionless zombie she closed and locked the door and then went to her kitchen. Even now, after all these years, it seemed like he should be standing there. He should be cutting up the salad or putting the pasta on to boil. She glanced at the empty fireplace and felt as though it would be completely normal to yell, *Billy, could you build a fire*? And after these last few days with him, she had allowed herself to dream again just a little bit. She bit her lip as she remembered inviting him to even move in with her if his money got cut off.

"What an idiot," she groaned. "Who did I think I was? Why would Billy Marcum ever want to be with someone like me?" She thought of Kirstie and her bigger-than-life boisterousness. Is that the kind of woman Billy really wanted?

She could feel herself beginning to lose control, and she tried to immediately redirect her thoughts to something productive, but the emotions were too strong. She put her hand to her mouth as though somehow she could stifle the sobs that were pushing up inside her throat, but it was pointless. They began to flow, and as they did, all she could do was drop to the floor and slowly fall to pieces … again.

Forty-Two

As Angie strolled through the back gardens at Levi's house, she found her heart longing again for Padawin. The pond was quaint, but it was nothing compared to the mighty rushing Grentawoo River or the sparkle and foam of the Pacific. And even though the garden was spotted with bits and pieces of beauty, deliberately placed in manicured beds, and designed to bring contrast to the concrete surrounding it, the continuous noise of cars and semis, sirens and planes, always shattered the possibility of true tranquility. And had she known that Levi Taylor was watching her from the patio doors, she would have been even more uneasy.

After a while, he snuck out of the house through a side door, and walked up to her unannounced.

"For crying out loud," she nearly screamed. "You scared the daylights out of me!"

He put his hand up to her shoulder to calm her. "Sorry. That wasn't my intention."

She was uncomfortable with his touch, so she moved away toward the pond, hoping it appeared natural.

"Where's the family?" he asked as he walked up next to her.

"Carter's sleeping, and Michael is trying to show Cassie how to shoot pool."

He squatted down to remove a leaf from the pond. "He's a really devoted father. I don't think I've ever seen a man quite as attentive to his kids as he is … and I've seen a lot of fathers over the years."

"That's probably because there isn't one as devoted—he's the best."

"He seems awfully devoted to you too."

She was still uncomfortable. "He is … very much."

He motioned her toward the sidewalk and they began to stroll through the various paths. "So, is that what it took to snag your heart? Complete devotion?"

"No, actually," she replied as she maintained a safe distance.

"Really? So, if anyone in your past had shown that kind of devotion, it wouldn't have captured your affections in the least."

She rolled her eyes. "I was shown more attention than I cared for in my past. That wasn't it."

"Then what? I'm extremely curious as to what it is about this man that so captivates you. Frankly, I find him rather … well … unremarkable."

Inside she began to seethe, but on the outside she smiled. "That's because you have no idea who he is … what he is."

"Tell me. I'd love to know how this man managed to win you when no one else could get even close. I mean, we used to call you the *snow queen* back in school."

She stopped walking and looked at him in astonishment. "Seriously? Y'all called me the *snow queen*?"

"Sure. You gave no men the time of day."

"That's a lie! I was very close to all of you. We were really good friends."

"I'm not talking about friendship," he said as he took her elbow and moved her along on the path. "Yeah, you were great friends with absolutely everybody. That's why no one could ever understand why you didn't date. You were the hottest girl alive, but no one could get near you."

"I really resent that. That's not fair. You make it sound like I should have just given myself to any and everybody that offered."

"Well, had you done that, you would have taken on the entire hospital staff … probably a few ladies included in the group too."

"You're being downright disgusting now. I'd rather not continue this discussion."

"I'm sorry. I guess I just can't figure out why you ended up with *him* when you could've had anybody in the world you wanted."

"Because he's the only one I ever wanted. Why is that so hard to understand?"

"But why? Why him? What was it … is it … about him that has you under his spell."

"I love him. He's my life. What's so hard to understand about that?"

"But why? Why are you so wrapped up in him? Why did you even marry him? I can't imagine him having the gall to propose."

Angie smiled, but only to herself. Had Levi known the true events surrounding her marriage, he would have found the whole thing even more unbelievable. But that was her story, and he had no right to hear it.

"I married him first of all because he was an incredible man of God."

"Ah, yes. The ever unmovable bastion of God. The one thing most of us never had."

"And I married him second of all because he had totally given and sacrificed his life for the sake of telling the world about God and His love … the very same call I was pursuing."

He shook his head and chuckled. "Gee, that sounds so romantic and breath-taking. I bet your love life just oozes with passion."

She stopped. "How dare you? My intimate life is none of your business. But for the record, I can't imagine any man with half the passion of Michael. And it's so much more than just some physical act that occurs between us when the mood is right. This is the man I have given my life to, the man who knows me better than anyone in the world, the man who shares my dream, shares my children, shares my mission, and most definitely shares my bed. If there's a happier woman, more satisfied, or more desperately in love than I am, I defy you to show her to me."

He laughed this time. "So that's all it takes to get you turned on? A guy who's into God?"

"No. It could never be just any *guy*—it took Michael. Everything about who he is and what he is … that's what it took. And when he holds me in his arms, or even touches me as he passes, it ignites me in a way that most people will never know because they settled for something less than their perfect one. And the thing that ties us even more—when I look at Cassie and Carter and see him in their eyes, I know they are the products of *us*. They are the results of a love I never thought I could find. And when this little one inside turns and tumbles," she reached down to touch her stomach, "I feel that same fire again." She glared at him to make her final point. "Anyone, including you, should be so lucky."

Angie then determined to leave. She turned and walked back quickly toward the house, but Levi ran behind her.

"Hey, don't get upset. I was just curious. It's not a problem."

"You always had this attitude about you … you and Dean and Jason. You would talk yourselves through the hard times by reminding each other that one day you'd have the big house and the Mercedes and any woman you wanted. And then you'd turn around and laugh at McDoogle, calling him a mid-life loser, when the only difference between you and him was about twenty years. And here you are … you've got the house, you've got the Mercedes, and I assume you've got the woman, but you're still grilling me about why I didn't fall all over you."

"I'm not *grilling* you."

"Oh, please!" she said throwing her hands up in frustration. "You're out here begging me to tell you that I somehow made a huge mistake with Michael, that all along I should've given you a chance—that somehow you're a superior person to him because he doesn't seem to be *remarkable* enough to you." Angie moved close to him this time. "Let me tell you about the man I married. I didn't even know he had a doctorate in Agriculture until weeks after our wedding."

"Bull," Levi said with playful eyes.

"No bull. I was putting away a bunch of books, and his diploma was lying at the bottom of the pile. When he came home for lunch, I wanted to know why he never told me. All he said was that I never asked." She smiled at the memory. "So, keep throwing around your doctorate, your house, your car, and your gardens back here, but always remember—it was never what Michael had that drew me into this love. It was always who he was. Nothing more, nothing less." She was about to leave for the house when she turned back to face him again. "And who he is will always be the man who won my heart, my love, and my passion."

She finally made it into the house and up the stairs to check on her family. Cassie was drawing pictures, and Michael was standing at the entrance to the balcony. When she opened the door to the room, he turned toward her and raised his eyebrows. "What were you two talking so intently about?

"Take a guess," she mumbled as she walked over to Cassie and leaned down to see the pictures.

"Me?"

"Bingo." She pointed down to one of the drawings and commented. "That's very good, sweetie. I love your sunshine."

"That's Geechern," Cassie told her as she pointed out one of the figures. "She is playing ball with me on the beach."

"I can see that," Angie smiled. "You're an excellent drawer."

"Uh," Michael walked over to the table, "so what were you saying about me?"

"To whom?" Angie asked nonchalantly as she glanced up at him with a teasing look.

He pinched her arm. "You know who I'm talking about. What did he say?"

She stood up all the way and rubbed the small of her back. "Over here," she motioned him with her head.

They walked over to the wet bar and she retrieved a glass from the cabinet for some water.

"Well?" he asked again.

She filled the glass, looked around his body at Cassie to make sure she wasn't listening, and then said, "He wanted to know what it was about you that so totally captivated me." She took a long drink.

"And you said?"

She was enjoying playing with him. She knew he was self conscious about it all, but she also knew he was convinced of her love for him. She leaned over to him and whispered in his ear, "I told him you were unbelievable in bed."

He blushed and laughed as he shook his head. "You did not, but thanks for the sentiment."

"Actually," she took another drink, "I did … more or less. I made it clear that I was an extremely satisfied woman."

He rubbed his face as if to try and erase the redness. "For someone so wonderful, you can be awfully wicked at times."

Forty-Three

Billy sat in front of the bar nearly 20 minutes before even getting off the bike. He had meant to buy a car. This was ridiculous. He was freezing, it was going to rain, and instead of getting something he could drive and stay dry in, he was sitting in front of a bar contemplating getting wasted for the first time in three years. He had watched several people come and go, and he knew this place was one of the more classy joints as far as clubs were concerned. Before, the thrill of going inside would have pushed him right on in, but at the moment, all he could feel was repulsion and bile. If he did this, he would go back on his promise to his mother. He would disappoint Cindy. He would disappoint himself. He didn't need alcohol to escape anymore—but that was before Sam.

He had now lost her a second time. On Monday he had been on top of the world. Every dream he could ever imagine was coming true, and then in a matter of minutes, it all fell apart.

He stepped off the bike, pulled off his riding suit, and stuffed it inside one compartment of the luggage. He then placed his helmet in the other and started for the door. He could hear music pulsating and already smell the smoke from the many cigarettes inside. He still wasn't sure if he hoped to see anyone he knew or not. He really just wanted to get so drunk that he couldn't remember anything and then pass out at a booth somewhere until he was sober enough to leave the next day. If Avery still worked here that would be no problem. If not, who knew where he would end up when the night was over? At this point, he didn't care. He just wanted to drink until he forgot.

He walked into the building and coughed immediately from the haze, but it didn't slow him down. He went directly to the bar, found a stool off to itself, and placed a $100 bill next to an empty glass.

"Yes, sir," the young bartender said immediately as he looked at Billy, removed the empty glass, and wiped the area with a dry cloth. "What can I get for you?"

"We'll start with some tequila, and just keep it coming for a while."

"As you wish," he said eagerly moving toward the other end of the bar.

Billy looked around impatiently to see if perhaps someone he knew might be there. It didn't take long to spot an old drinking buddy. Chase Moody, complete with cowboy hat, was standing at one of the billiard tables obviously trying to impress a *gorgeous babe* with his finesse and charm. Billy grinned. Chase was anything but charming. The girl didn't seem to mind, however. She was obviously enjoying the attention. When Chase looked his way, Billy raised up a hand. Chase had to look twice to believe it. He said something to the girl, and then they both came over to the bar.

His first tequila had arrived, so he quickly turned it up and guzzled it down. "Wooo!" Billy yelled as he slammed the glass on the bar. "Man! That burned like crazy!"

"It'll do that to you," Chase laughed as he came up and slapped Billy on the back. "Where on earth have you been, man?" Chase pulled him into a hug.

"What are you doing?" Billy asked trying to gain his composure after the drink and the manly hug. "I didn't think this was one of those kind of places."

Chase bellowed another laugh and yelled above the music, "If I were gonna be gay, you'd be my first choice, dude."

He wondered if he could even speak as his throat burned so badly. "Give me a minute. I haven't done this in a while."

"I'll say," Chase agreed. "What have you been doing?"

"Going to school. I went back to college to finish my degree."

"Tell me you're kidding, man. What are you gonna do?"

"Teach high school science. I'm student teaching right now."

The lady with him bobbled her eyebrows and commented, "Wow. If I had had a science teacher like you, I might have paid more attention in class."

"I'm being rude," Chase said suddenly. "Loretta, this is Billy Marcum. Billy, this is Loretta Aiken."

"Atkins," she corrected him quickly, never taking her eyes off of Billy.

"Sorry … Loretta Atkins," Chase corrected.

"So, you're the famous Billy Marcum," Loretta said with a grin that told Billy plenty. "I never thought I'd have the pleasure."

She reached out her hand toward Billy. He took it to be polite, but what this woman was obviously offering was nothing he wanted at this point in the night. He would have to be a lot drunker to put Sam out of his mind and settle for Loretta Atkins.

"You're a bit of a legend in these parts," she continued. "I was beginning to think you were all made up in their minds."

Billy looked over at Chase. "What kind of lies have you been telling about me?"

"Only the truth, dude," he said as he pushed his hat back. "You could walk into this bar at any time, pick out any girl in the place, and end up taking her home by the end of the evening … even if she came in with a date. That's the stuff dreams are made of, buddy."

"My, my," Loretta said as she shook her head and batted her eyes at him. "I'd like to know what kind of promises you make to get that kind of action."

Billy turned back and got another shot of tequila. Before he turned it up, he asked Chase, "Does this get any easier with time?"

Chase practically hooted as he said, "Sure! You drink enough of 'em and you get so drunk you don't feel anything—not even the burn."

"That's what I'm going for," Billy winced as he swallowed the next round.

After several shots, Billy asked for a beer, and the three of them moved to a table on the far side of the room. A few more of his old buddies showed up and welcomed him back to the scene, but the whole time Loretta kept inching closer and closer to him. He wanted to drink tonight; he didn't want a woman.

"If you move any closer," he told her at one point, "you'll be in my lap."

She only smiled and said, "Exactly."

Well, that made it clear. Her intentions were to leave with him and not Chase tonight. But the last thing he wanted was anyone other than Sam. Even as he felt the room beginning to spin and his head take on that old familiar buzz, his heart was still aching for her—and visions of her continued to swirl around his head.

"Look, Loretta," he finally said after several hours, "I don't want to be rude or anything to you, but you need to understand something about tonight."

"Tell Loretta everything, honey," she said as she ran her hand down the side of his face.

"Well … I'm here tonight because of … well … because of a girl I really, really love."

"And what did this *girl* do to you?" she asked with syrupy sympathy.

"We had a little …" he was trying to put it in a way that would make sense, get rid of Loretta, yet not hurt her in the process. "We sort of had a fight. I'm not here looking for any … uh … distractions … you know? I just wanted to kind of … well … drown myself for a little bit … and then head home."

"You can drown yourself in me all night."

"See … that's just it. I'm not wanting *that* kind of drowning," he tried a different approach. "I just want to … well … get lost in my own mind for the night … and then try to put it all back together tomorrow."

She wouldn't let up. "I know very well how to help you lose those thoughts of that silly girl. Besides, you don't need some *girl* pulling you down. What you need is a *woman*."

Suddenly, that thought stung Billy hard. Sam wasn't a *girl*; she was a full-grown, full-fledged, mature woman. Yet every time he thought about her or talked about her, she was always a *girl* in his mind. When he thought of Angie or Cindy or any number of other females, they were women. But somehow Sam was always this little *girl*—helpless, abused, and fragile.

"Where did you go, baby?" Loretta asked him as she turned his face around to hers. "I lost you there for a moment."

"You never had me," he said as he pushed her away and began to move himself toward the edge of the booth.

"Excuse me?" she said loudly. "Are you brushing me off?"

Chase heard the commotion from the pool table near their booth and looked over to see what was happening.

"This isn't what I came here for," Billy tried to explain as he made his way out of the booth. His head was spinning and his legs were wobbly. He was definitely drunk, but his mind was now more full of Sam than before. All he could wonder was why he couldn't see her as a woman.

"What's the problem here?" Chase asked as he walked up to the table.

"He's blowing me off," Loretta said flabbergasted. "You told me this would be a night I'd never forget, but this legend of yours doesn't think I'm good enough for him."

"Are you insulting Loretta here?" Chase asked Billy as he got right up in his face.

"I'm not insulting anyone," he said as his head continued to spin out of control. "I just don't need a woman tonight. Why can't anyone understand that?"

"I don't know where you've been or what you've been up to lately, but in here we're appreciative of people when they make good offers. I believe you're on the borderline of being impolite, my friend."

"I thought she was your woman anyway," Billy slurred. "Why are you pushing her off on me to begin with? You take her home tonight!"

Chase grabbed Billy by the collar and pulled him up to his face. "I know you're being rude now. If I didn't know you better, I'd punch that pretty face of yours."

"Do it, Chase," Loretta urged. "He thinks he's too good for me."

Billy put up his hands in surrender. "I don't think anything like that. Look, I'm in the middle of a relationship mess right now. I don't want to complicate it by trying to explain why I spent the night with another woman."

Chase shoved him down into the seat again. "I think you'd better leave. You ain't the same man. The Billy Marcum I knew would never turn down a woman and hurt her like you've done with Loretta here."

"Don't you see that I'd hurt her worse if I took her home?" Billy tried to reason with them. "My heart is somewhere else. It would be wrong."

At this statement Chase burst into laughter again. "You definitely ain't Billy Marcum! *Wrong* ain't even a part of his vocabulary."

"Problem here, gentlemen," a large man asked as he stood cautiously next to the table.

"Yeah!" Chase said immediately. "This jerk is messing with my lady! He's insulted her to high heaven."

The man looked at Loretta. "This true, ma'am?"

"Sure is," she agreed. "He's drunk as a skunk and needs to be removed before he starts in on someone else." She looped her arm into Chase's and gave a look of complete devastation.

"Okay, buddy," the man said as he lifted Billy from the booth by the arm. "Let's go. We don't want any trouble here tonight."

"Believe me," Billy said as he tried to straighten up, "neither do I."

The bouncer helped him to the door and then gave him a little shove on the way out. Billy was too wobbly to even stay upright. He fell against the door and then rolled onto the ground. It was raining again. The man pushed him away with his foot, and then closed the door behind him. Billy lay there a moment in the downpour.

He finally managed to pull himself up, and then had to remember where he was parked. After about five minutes of searching, he located the Kawasaki and then fumbled through his pockets for the key. He was miserable.

"Why!" he screamed from desperation into the rain. "Why can I forget where I parked, but I can't forget you, Sam!"

He reached into the wrong side of the luggage for his helmet, and angrily threw the riding suit to the ground. He went to the other side and got his helmet, put it on, but didn't bother to tighten the strap. It took him three tries to get onto the bike, but once he had it straddled, he felt he was in control again. He cranked the engine, put the machine into first gear, and then took off for the road. Luckily for him, he never even made it to the highway. He saw a car backing out just as he was approaching and he hit his brakes. The bike slid beneath him, pinning his leg. His shoulder hit the ground and immense pain shot throughout his upper body. When his head hit, it literally bounced several times from the impact. The strap was secure enough to keep the helmet on, but the pain from the hard bounce began to sear his temple. Once the crashing and bouncing had stopped, he lifted his head to try and get up, but everything went black.

Forty-Four

As Billy began to gain consciousness, he had no idea where he was or what was going on around him. He heard strange noises and voices and could make no sense of all the sounds running together.

"Hey, Crandall," he heard one man say who seemed to be standing right over him. "What do you call an ER motorcycle accident victim?"

"I don't think now's the time for that."

"An organ donor."

"Very funny. Let's get to his shoulder now."

Billy tried to open his eyes, but when any sliver of light reached them, the pain in his head became searing. He began to realize that the left side of his body, especially his shoulder, was throbbing intensely. He tried to shift for a moment, but hands immediately stilled him.

"Hold on there, buddy," came a strange voice again. "You don't need to move." Then the same voice yelled out, "Tell Dr. Potter he's starting to come to!"

"Are you crazy?" said another. "Not until we get this shoulder back in place."

"I know. If he's coming to, we'd better do it fast."

He felt several hands on his left shoulder and upper arm.

"Candy!" one of the voices called out. "Give us a hand here quick."

A female voice joined the group now. "What are we doing?"

"We need to get his shoulder in place."

"You haven't done that yet?" the lady asked annoyed. "What have you guys been doing?"

"Just help us, okay? Hold his legs."

As another set of hands went for his legs, Billy screamed out in pain again.

"Not the left one!"

"Sorry … I didn't realize there was a problem there."

He wanted to tell them he was fully aware of everything going on, but he couldn't manage to either open his eyes or utter a word.

"Ready? On three."

"Wait a minute … do you mean actually when you say three, or like the next breath after three?"

"On three, moron. Let's do this quick. This guy's gaining his senses."

"Go ahead, Crandall," said the female voice again.

"One, two, three."

As they placed the shoulder firmly in the socket, he yelled again. This time he managed to open his eyes.

"What … are … you …" he yelled out as he reached up to grab his shoulder.

"Settle down, buddy," said one of two younger men. "That'll be the worst of it tonight."

"What am I doing?" Billy wondered, still completely confused as to where he was and why he was there. "Where's Sam? I heard her just a minute ago?"

"Who?" one of the men asked.

"Sam? She was in here."

The other man shook his head and smiled. "You're pretty wasted, dude. You don't know what's going on, do you? No Sam has been in here all night. Did she call the ambulance for you?"

"What?" Billy asked as his shoulder continued throbbing in unbearable pain.

"I'm Dr. Crandall," the youngest looking man standing over him said. "Do you know what happened to you? Do you know where you are?"

Billy looked around for a moment and tried to ascertain his situation. "Uh … is this … a … a … hospital?"

"Very good," Dr. Crandall told him as he lifted a pen light to his eyes. "Do you know what day it is?"

Billy thought for a moment. "No idea."

The other young doctor snickered. "Who knows if that's from the concussion or from being dead drunk."

"I know," Crandall admitted. "Do you know why you're here?"

His mind was a jumbled mess. His head was killing him, the pain in his shoulder was growing more unbearable, and his leg was right behind with intensity. He couldn't remember what had happened.

"You were at a bar, dude," said the other doctor. "You decided to ride your bike home in the rain while you were totally wasted. What were you thinking?"

"I don't drink," Billy defended.

At this statement both of the doctors laughed.

"Well, you did tonight, man," the other one told him. "Big time."

He tried to remember what had happened that day. There was school, there was his mother's letter … no … that wasn't today. Mr. C. … he had talked with Mr. C. It was about Sam … yeah … it was bad with Sam.

"Sam's not here?" Billy asked them again.

"Sorry, guy," Dr. Crandall said with a sad smile. "We don't even know who Sam is. Do you remember what happened to you? Try to remember."

He closed his eyes again and thought. He had told Mr. C. everything on Friday.

"Is it Friday?" Billy asked Dr. Crandall.

"Not anymore," the doctor replied. "But it was when you got here. Keep going."

He tried hard to remember what had happened that day, but Monday night came back instead.

"Blue Bayou," he mumbled out.

"Nope," the doctor told him. "You weren't at the Blue Bayou, at least that's not where you ended up. Try again."

"Sam got mad … Kirstie came in … she blew everything. She just messed it up royally."

Dr. Crandall looked down at Billy with a tinge of sympathy. "So this has to do with a woman, huh? This Sam of yours."

"She won't even talk to me about it. I went there after school … apologized … just let her go."

"On Friday?"

He tried to nod, but the pain shot through his head again. "She still wanted to have Thanksgiving with me."

Dr. Crandall took his pulse. "And that was on Friday?"

"I really needed a car … but … I was so … oh man … what did I do?"

"You tell me," the doctor encouraged. "You needed a car and then what?"

"I did it, didn't I?"

"Did what?"

Tears begin to fall down the sides of his face. "Went to Blaze's."

"You're getting it now. What else?"

"Sorry, Mother … so sorry. It was Sam … I just couldn't bear … man. Mother … I am so sorry."

"What about your mother?"

Billy slowly shook his head from side to side as he looked up at Dr. Crandall. "I promised her I'd stop drinking. I stopped for three years."

"You tied a good one on tonight."

"Yeah. Sam and I are through. I just wanted to forget."

"Do you remember getting on your motorcycle to leave Blaze's?"

He closed his eyes and thought back. "Not really. I think I sort of got thrown out." He thought back again and again. He vaguely recalled getting on the bike, but that was all. "I can't remember it … just bits and pieces."

"Here we go," said another doctor, an older woman this time. "It's not near as bad as it could have been." She put three x-rays up on the screen. The two younger doctors walked over to view them with her. "It's a clean break right here. This guy came out lucky. It's a miracle for him that he never made it out of the parking lot. Had he hit the highway, he would have been dead for sure. Has he come to yet?"

"Just has," Dr. Crandall told her.

"What does he remember?" she asked as she turned her attention to Billy, pointing her pen light directly into his eyes again.

"Bits and pieces … it's slowly coming back."

"Mr. Marcum," she said sternly. "Do you know where you are?"

Billy nodded slightly. "The hospital."

"Do you know why you're here?"

"They said I wrecked the bike," he recalled, "but I don't remember it."

"I guess not," she mused as she checked his vital signs. "You took a big tumble, bashed your head pretty good. Thank God you had enough sense to at least put your helmet on. You've only got a slight concussion, but your left shoulder was out of socket and you've broken your lower left leg." The doctor continued looking over him. "We need to set your leg, Mr. Marcum, and then you're gonna need to go home. Who can you call?"

"Go home?" Billy asked in shock. "I can't move."

"You're drunk, Mr. Marcum," the doctor said flatly. "Too bad you didn't realize that *before* you got on the bike. Who can you call to come get you? When you're leg's set, you'll need to move on."

He had no idea who to call. There was only Cindy.

"My sister lives in Dockrey. That's it."

"Good looking guy like you and the only person you can call is your sister in Dockrey?" the doctor smiled. "No friends or relatives here in the Shoals?"

"None," Billy said sadly. "Not anymore."

"Alright, let's get your leg set … maybe you'll sober up a little more by then … then we'll let you call your sister." The doctor motioned for Dr. Crandall. "Why don't you do it, Crandall? Get Candy in here to assist. When you finish, call me back. And see what you can do about getting *hot rod* there a phone to call his sister."

"Yes, ma'am," Crandall agreed as he immediately began to move.

☼☼☼

Billy was still in a lot of pain, and his head wasn't any clearer than before, but Dr. Crandall was forcing a phone into his hand and telling him he had to call someone to come get him.

"You guys can't let me stay for just a little while?" Billy questioned.

"Look," Dr. Crandall said to him under his breath so no one else could hear, "you're pushing your luck in here. Every person in this ER would gladly hang you before they'd let you stay in one of these beds. You're like a double idiot in their eyes. You were incredibly drunk, and then you attempted to ride a motorcycle. Meanwhile, there are people out in the waiting area with heart failure, strokes, life-threatening situations, and you're in here taking up desperately needed space."

He nodded in understanding.

"I'm sorry," the doctor continued. "I feel for you. I don't know you, but from what I've put together, you seem to be a nice guy. You promised your mom you'd stop drinking—apparently you kept that promise for three years. But now your girl has totally jilted you, and you're lost and hurt and upset. So you tried to numb it with alcohol … just this once … and it turned into a fiasco."

"That's about the size of it."

"Nobody here cares. They want you out. Call your sister, and let's get things moving."

He looked down at the phone and tried to focus on the numbers, but then he looked back up at Dr. Crandall. "Do you care? You seem awful nice about all this."

Crandall smiled a sad smile. "Let's just say that I can relate."

"Girl problems?"

"Yeah. My fiancé' of two years called earlier this week to say she's *unsure* of our relationship lately. I know the real translation for that—I'm too busy, too far away, and she's found someone else to help fill in her time."

"Sorry. If she could be a little more patient, she'd have a great guy at the end of it all."

"Yeah, well … women, huh? Who can understand them?"

"I know that's right."

Dr. Crandall pointed at the phone. "You'd better make that call. They're not gonna be much more patient with you around here."

He punched in the numbers as Crandall left and waited for someone to answer. Cindy would probably be fighting mad when she heard his story. He glanced up at the clock. It was almost four o'clock in the morning. She would be really mad. It took six rings before someone answered.

"Hi, you've reached Cindy and Kyle's house," came the perky response.

He was about to speak when he realized it was the answering machine.

"We're on a cruise right now," her voice continued, "and will not be able to do anything for you until we get back. Listen for the beep and leave your name and number if it's that important. God bless you. Bye."

He pressed the off button and sat there helpless. He had forgotten about the cruise. He cursed under his breath as he tried to think of who else he could call. There were only two other numbers in the whole world he could actually remember. One was Jonathan Wright's; he still knew it from the years of calling when his mother had been sick. It was easier to get info from them than to call Cindy and get info plus a load of guilt. The other number was Sam's. No way.

"You still here?" the older woman doctor asked with disdain as she passed by him.

"Trying to get someone to pick me up," he said weakly as he held up the phone.

"Try harder," she said unsympathetically as she walked on.

To call Jonathan Wright would be the most humiliating thing in the world he could do. Absolutely not. That left Sam. He hated to do it, but he had no options left. There was literally no one left in his life to call for help. He turned on the phone, took a deep breath, and punched in Sam's number.

"Hello?" came the weak answer.

"Sam? It's me … Billy."

He heard her sigh. "It's four o'clock in the morning. What are you doing to me?"

"I'm in the ER, Sam," he said quickly knowing she would probably hang up any moment if he didn't get it out. "I had a bike wreck. I need help."

"What?" she asked immediately. "Are you alright?"

"I'm not really sure. I'm sort of groggy about it all."

"Where are you? What hospital?"

"Helen Keller. They need me to leave as soon as I can. Somebody's got to come get me."

She didn't reply.

"I called Cindy," he explained, "but I forgot she's on a cruise." He paused. "I didn't have any other choice." More silence. "I'm sorry, Sam, but I didn't know what else to do … who else to call. They're pushing me out of here, and I'm helpless." He closed his eyes and winced. "Can you please come get me?"

She waited for what seem like an eternity to him. "Give me a minute to get dressed, and I'll be right there."

He sighed with relief. "Thank you," was all he could say before she hung up.

Forty-Five

As Sam tried to gather her wits about her, she moved from the bed to the bathroom. She had slept miserably all week, and tonight had been no exception. When the phone rang, she was still in and out. She grabbed her jeans from the hook on the wall and began to dress as quickly as her body would respond.

Did I even ask if he was okay? she muttered to herself. *So what? He doesn't deserve my pity or empathy.*

She stopped for a second to catch her breath. *Why did he have to call me for help? I can't do this again. I can't be with him, can't be near him anymore. School was going to be hard enough … but now this.*

She looked through her closet and found her thick raincoat. *I'll just take him to the boat, see that he's settled, and that will be it. He'll have to get someone else to check on him if he needs anymore after that.*

She grabbed her keys from the hanger in the kitchen and made for the door. It was pouring outside. *No wonder he wrecked. No one should be driving in this mess … least of all a motorcycle.* She glanced at the clock on her dash as she cranked the engine. It was now four thirteen. *I wonder when it happened. Surely he wasn't driving around in the middle of the night. I bet he's been there a long time.*

It took her longer than she anticipated to make it to the hospital because of the rain. She pulled into the ER section of the building and parked beneath the cover at the door. Immediately a security guard knocked on her window. She rolled it down.

"You can't park here, ma'am," he told her.

"I'm picking up an ER patient," she clarified. "Can't I do this?"

He nodded. "Sorry … I didn't know. People have been trying to park here all night because of the weather. Try not to be too long. It's been really busy tonight. There's bound to be someone right behind you."

"I understand."

She turned off the car and got out. The biting wind struck her face and watered her eyes as she walked quickly toward the door. She wasn't sure where to find Billy, so she moved toward the information desk. As she was about to ask the lady for help, she spotted him sitting in a wheelchair in the corner of the waiting area. He looked horrible. His arm was in a sling and his leg in a cast and elevated. His head was leaned back against the wall, and his face was nearly green. She pulled herself together before going to him. She didn't want him to see the concern that was flooding through her.

She walked slowly through the crowded area to his corner and then gently said, "Billy?"

He gradually opened his eyes and looked around as in a daze.

"Billy, right here," she said as she squatted down next to him.

He turned toward her voice and tried to focus on her face. "Sam?"

"Yeah." She reached out and gently touched the hand in the sling. "You're in worse shape than I imagined."

He barely shook his head. "I'll be okay," he slurred slightly. "Just get me outta here … please."

It was then than Sam smelled the alcohol. She was floored. Had he actually gotten drunk? Had she driven him to go back on his promise to his mother? Guilt began to weigh on her like never before.

"Are you drunk, Billy?"

His head fell back against the wall, and she saw tears begin to slide down the sides of his face. In all the years before she had never seen him cry. She got on her knees and took his hand again, but this time she accidentally bumped against his sore shoulder.

"Augh!" he cried out sharply.

Every person in the area immediately looked over at him.

"I'm so sorry," she said instantly. "I didn't mean to hurt you."

"It's okay," he whispered. "You've gotta get me outta here."

A young doctor now approached them.

"Are you here to pick up Mr. Marcum?" he asked.

"Yes. I'm Sam," she said as she stood to her feet.

The doctor gave her a slight smile as he nodded, then he began to explain. "He's gonna be in a lot of pain the next several days. He's got a slight concussion … that shouldn't be a big problem, but I do have some directions you need to follow for the next twenty-four hours."

"Twenty-four hours?" she asked alarmed. "I was just gonna take him to his home; I wasn't planning on staying with him."

"Somebody has got to be with him," the doctor said adamantly. "There's no way he can be alone … not for a long while."

"You're kidding?"

She looked back down at Billy. She couldn't tell if he was asleep or awake. She knew Cindy was gone for the week, so that left nobody to care for him. She couldn't help but feel sorry for him, and the truth be known, this was all probably her fault.

"Okay," she conceded. "Tell me what I need to do."

"Here's a sheet," he said as he handed her the paper. "You've got to wake him every couple of hours." He went through all the head injury instructions with her first. "His shoulder was severely dislocated. It's gonna be fine, but it's gonna hurt like crazy for a while. His leg is broken right beneath the knee. The main thing to do there is keep it elevated for several days." He gave her another sheet and explained in more detail how to care for the shoulder and the leg.

He then gave an awkward hesitation. "He won't be getting up for a couple of days. You'll need to get him a urinal, probably even a bedpan."

"What?" she nearly shrieked. "I can't do that!"

The doctor only shrugged. "If you're the caregiver, even temporarily, I'd strongly suggest it for your sake."

She closed her eyes and nodded in understanding.

"Here are his prescriptions." He handed her several more papers. "Get them filled in the morning right away. He's gonna want that pain medicine as soon as the alcohol starts to wear off."

"Just how drunk was he?"

"Extremely."

She shook her head in astonishment and guilt.

The doctor wondered, "Does he do this often?"

"No," she said honestly. "At least not in three years."

"Yeah … that's what he said too." Crandall shook his head. "You also need to make an appointment with his regular doctor as soon as he's able to get up and around … like near the end of next week. He'll need to be checked fairly regularly through all of this."

She nodded. "I'll do what I can."

The doctor knelt down beside Billy and looked him over. "Mr. Marcum, Sam's here to take you home for a while. She's going to take good care of you. Listen to what she says and do what she tells you to do. Can you open your eyes and tell me you understand?"

He turned his head slightly, but wouldn't open his eyes as he said, "I'll listen to Sam."

"Alright, that's good enough," the doctor said almost sadly.

"Dr. Crandall," Billy slurred again.

"Yeah."

"Thank you for … uh … not being so tough on me … like all the others," he said sincerely. "It was a really bad week for me. Really bad."

"I understand."

Dr. Crandall stood back up and handed Sam his card. "Listen, if something were to happen, you know, just something bad, why don't you give me a call personally. Use the cell number. I might not be available right away, but leave a voicemail and I'll get back to you as soon as possible."

She looked at him with surprise. "Really? Personal cell?"

"Yeah. Just in case there's an emergency."

The doctor then took the brake off of the wheelchair and began to move Billy to the doors. When he pushed through to the outside, the cold brought Billy to life right away.

"Wo," he said as his head bobbled to and fro. "It's freezing out here."

"At least you're dry now," Dr. Crandall told him.

"My car's over here," Sam said as she moved ahead to open the door.

It was almost impossible to get Billy in without any pain. Dr. Crandall and Sam both had to lift him inside and then place his leg in a position that wouldn't hurt too much. They reclined his seat so his head could lay back.

"Do you have anything in here you could rest his arm on?" the doctor asked.

Sam looked around and thought. "Nothing."

Billy moaned.

"Wait," she said as she took off her thick raincoat. "Wad this up and stick it under there."

"Good thinking."

He took the coat and gently placed it beneath Billy's arm.

"I have a question," Sam said to Dr. Crandall as she began to shiver in the damp cold. "How am I gonna get him inside my house? I have no wheelchair, and I certainly don't have the strength to lift him like we just did."

He shrugged. "I have no idea. Once he comes out of the stupor, he can probably be a little more helpful."

"So what do I do? Just leave him in the car with the heater on until he sleeps off the drunkenness?"

"If you have to … I guess." Dr. Crandall looked nervously back at the building. "I need to go. They're expecting me in there."

"I understand." She looked at him and smiled. "Thank you. This isn't like him at all, you know. I appreciate your being understanding with him."

The doctor nodded and gave her a sad look again. "He loves you, you know? That's what all this is about. He nearly died over you tonight."

She felt her throat catch at the words. "It's not as simple as all that. I wish it were, but it's not."

"Yeah, that's pretty much the way it always is."

When Sam pulled into her drive at the house, she sat there for a while trying to decide how to get Billy out of the car. The rain was pouring, and he was obviously in a lot of pain. She could leave him in the car until the rain stopped, but the sooner she got him into the house, the sooner they could both rest.

"Billy," she said softly as she reached over to nudge his right arm, very careful not to touch or move his left.

"What?" he asked groggily. "What's wrong?"

"We need to get you out of the car and into the house."

He opened his eyes and tried to focus on her. "Where are we?"

"At my house. I know you're in a lot of pain, but you're gonna have to somehow walk inside. I'll come around and help you out the best I can, but I don't have the strength to do it alone." She looked at him sternly. "Do you understand?"

He shook his head and said, "Just take me to the boat. I can't be here."

"You can't be *there* right now. I've got to watch out for you for a few days. Let's get you inside the house and then we'll worry about all that later."

He looked at her and embarrassment showed all over his face. "This is so wrong, Sam. I can't do this to you."

"That's not an issue right now. All of this is awkward, and frankly, the timing stinks. But I'm all you've got at the moment, pretty boy. So, tell me we can cooperate enough to get you inside my house and into a bed."

"I can make it to the house," he assured her. "Just help me get up."

She reached over him and undid the seat belt release as she slowly eased the back of the seat into an upright position. Her hair brushed across his face.

"How can you do that to me?" he inadvertently asked out loud.

"Did I hurt you?" she asked alarmed. "I'm sorry."

He only shook his head. "Never, Sam. Never. Your hair smells so good. I love your hair … and your eyes."

She looked at him, puzzled about his comment, and wondered how clear his mind was at the moment. His blue eyes just stared back at her with intense longing. Again, all she wanted was to hold him close and assure him all would be fine. He was almost like a lost little boy, and for the first time in her life, she was actually going to take care of him.

"It's gonna be okay, Billy," she told him as she gently touched his cheek. "I'm gonna get you through this."

His right arm reached up and touched her face. "I'm sorry," was all he could say, and tears began to slide down his cheeks again.

She softly wiped a tear and then pulled herself back. "Showtime," she said with a weary smile. "Be ready for me. I'm getting out and then coming around."

The result was a complete debacle. The only thing that didn't happen while getting him to the house was a fall. Had he fallen, Sam doubted she would have ever gotten him up by herself. By the time they reached the house, they were both drenched from the rain, and Billy was literally crying from pain. She was tempted to let him stop at the couch, but her bedroom was only down the hall, and that's where he needed to be deposited. She could barely stand beneath the weight of his body as he leaned heavily on her, his right arm firmly around her shoulders. She kept moving him toward the door, as much with words as with steps. When they reached the room, she propped him against the wall as she pulled back the covers on the bed. Then she discovered their next dilemma.

"Billy, you're gonna have to get those wet clothes off. It's pointless for you to get in bed like that."

He nodded as he leaned against the wall, eyes closed, tears streaming down his face, grimacing in pain.

"Can you cut them off?" he asked faintly. "I can't do this, Sam." He sobbed for just a moment, and then added, "I'm so sorry."

"It's okay," she assured him again. "Can you stand there until I find some scissors?"

He only nodded slightly as he let out another weak cry.

She went to the kitchen and found her scissors right away. She was scared to death he would fall or slide to the floor before she returned. When she got back, he was still leaning against the wall, and he was still half-crying.

"I'm here," she told him confidently. "I'll get these wet clothes off of you, and then you can really relax."

"I'm so sorry."

"Billy, stop apologizing," she said as she tried to decide where to start. "I'll cut the shirt off first." She surveyed the problem. "Your sling is sopping wet too. We might as well take it off and let me throw it in the dryer for a bit."

She put the handle of the scissors in her mouth as she gently removed the sling. She had him rest his arm against her body as she carefully cut up the sleeve of his damaged shoulder all the way up through the collar. Once that was off, he managed to let the rest of the shirt slide to the floor. She removed his belt and cut through his pants next which had already been hacked up in the ER. This could have been unforgivably awkward had he not cried out in pain every few moments. She was able to ignore his body as she focused on trying to get him into the bed with the least amount of movement. Once in the bed, she propped his left leg up on two pillows, and then his arm on another. By now he was shivering from the wet, the cold, and the exposure. She pulled the covers up to his neck and went to her closet for another blanket.

When he finally seemed settled, she took his wet clothes and threw them into the garbage then put his sling in the dryer. She decided to turn up the heat in the house, hoping he hadn't gotten too chilled through the ordeal. When it seemed there was nothing else to do, she remembered all the papers and instructions the doctor had given her. She grabbed a spare umbrella and ran out to the car to retrieve the information. Looking through them, she decided her best plan of action at the moment was to just try and let him sleep until the sling was dry.

As she waited for the dryer to finish, she changed from her own wet clothes into a pair of warm flannel pajamas. She was shivering herself simply from being wet and cold for so long. She turned on her small bathroom heater and tried to warm her feet. She then pulled on a pair of wool socks and went to check the dryer. The sling was dry.

"Billy?" she said softly as she sat down carefully on the side of the bed. "I need to get your sling on again. It's dry and warm now."

He didn't move. She reached over the bed to his right arm and cautiously shook him. He awoke with a jolt.

"Mother?" he asked bewildered.

"No, it's Sam," she whispered.

"Sam?" He looked up at her and smiled. "Hey. Are we okay?"

She had no idea what he was talking about. "I need to get your sling back on. It's dry now."

"Sure … that'll be fine," he mumbled.

But as she tried to slip it over his head and around his arm, the pain became unbearable again, and he started to sob this time. It was mandatory that she get it on, so she merely continued to maneuver it until it was in the correct position. She felt horrible, and she was so tired at this point that she found herself beginning to cry too. When she finally got him settled, she felt exhaustion begin to creep over her. She looked at his face, and again tears were flowing down the sides even though he was still and probably asleep. She reached up and carefully wiped one side and then the other.

"So sorry," he managed to barely utter.

Her lip began to quiver. "It's okay," she assured him yet again. "Just sleep for awhile."

Forty-Six

When daylight began to shine through the cracks in the blinds, Sam opened her eyes and immediately glanced at her watch. It was nearly ten o'clock. She realized she had stayed next to Billy rather than go to the couch. She was supposed to wake him every two hours, but once she had drifted, she had been so tired that she never moved until now.

"Billy!" she said in a slight panic as she jostled his arm. "Billy, wake up! Wake up for just a moment!"

He slowly moved his head to the side and opened his eyes. When he saw her next to him, his eyes grew wide.

"What are you doing here?" he asked in surprise.

"Do you even know what's going on?" she asked as she sat up beside him in the bed.

He closed his eyes again and tried to move his neck around a bit to loosen up the pain. "It's slowly coming back to me."

"How do you feel? Do you need anything?"

He looked over at her again and she could tell he was embarrassed. "I need to go to the bathroom … really, really bad."

She turned away from him and got up off the bed. It was then that she remembered the doctor had told her to get a small urinal.

"I don't suppose you can get up?" she asked him.

"Well, as unclear as my head seems at the moment, there are a few things I do recognize." He closed his eyes in humiliation again. "First, I'm totally naked … not sure how that happened, but I know it's a fact. Second, I'm guessing there's no way I can get up from this bed without your help." He then glanced up at her again. "And third, even if I got up, if I remember correctly about last night, there's no way I'm gonna make it to the toilet without leaning on you significantly." He paused. "Does that sum up our situation pretty much?"

She smiled and nodded. "Pretty much." She started for the door. "Let me see what I kind find for you to help solve the problem. Then I'll get dressed and head for the drugstore. The first thing on the list will be a urinal."

Billy clinched his fists in complete and total disgrace. The events of the previous night were coming back to him quickly, and as much pain as his body was feeling at the moment, the mental anguish was ten times worse. He had sworn to Sam yesterday evening that he would be out of her life for good, and now here he was, literally depending on her mercy to even survive. The pain in his head, shoulder, and leg were almost to the point of being unbearable, but he wasn't about to complain. If he could just relieve himself, that would be a start, and then he could begin to think of a way to get out of her house and out her life again.

"Try this," she said as she came back into the room with a two liter soda container. "I cut the top off a little so … well … here. Give it a try. If you miss, you miss."

She handed him the container and left the room, shutting the door behind her.

☼☼☼

After collecting supplies from the drugstore, Sam went to the grocery and picked up some food to get them through the weekend. For the first time she thought about the days to come. Would he be able to finish his student-teaching? That would be horrible if he lost this semester because of the stupid accident. And it was all her fault. Why couldn't she just have accepted the whole second marriage thing and forgiven him and moved on? Because she was miserably sensitive. She was a messed up girl with no hope of ever getting her life together. And when the opportunity arose for her to have hope for something positive, she blew it again.

All the way home she thought about how to make sure he finished school so he could graduate in December. Her best bet was to call his advisor and see what could be worked out. There would be no way he go to school Monday, in fact, the whole week was doubtful. She would have to see what was absolutely necessary to get him through.

When she walked inside the house, she placed the bags on the kitchen counter and went back to check on him. He was sleeping soundly. She hated to wake him again, but she had to do this for twenty-four hours.

"Billy," she began the whole routine again. "How are you doing?"

He winced in pain as he began to come to.

"I have some pain medicine for you now," she said softly as she sat beside him on the bed. "Can you wake up and talk to me for a minute?"

He slowly opened his eyes and looked up at her. "I'm so sorry, Sam. You shouldn't be …"

"Shhh," she said immediately as she put her finger to his lips. "Stop apologizing to me. Just let me get you through this, and we'll deal with all the muddled feelings later."

He shook his head in mortification again. "Cindy will be home next weekend some time. As soon as I can, I'll …"

"But Cindy can't get you to school this next month. You might as well face the fact that I'm your best bet for the time being."

"You're kidding, right? There's no way I can make it to school like this."

"You'll lose this whole semester if you don't. You have to go!"

"How?" he asked her in disgust. "I can't even get up to go to the bathroom."

"I rented you a wheelchair for starters. I'm gonna call your advisor today and find out how many days you can miss without losing the whole term."

"You can't be serious."

"I know you're in unbelievable pain, but you're too close to being finished with all this. I'm gonna see you through this last month, and through your graduation. Whatever it takes, that's what we're gonna do."

He looked at her with a mixture of shock and devastation. "I can't ask you to do that."

"You didn't ask; I offered." She smiled at him warmly. "Right now, let's get the pain medicine going. I'll get you something to eat and then you can try and rest again."

"I can't eat, Sam. I'm really nauseous. Thanks, though."

"A little soup, maybe? How about some broth?"

"I really can't. Maybe later."

She returned in a few minutes with the medicine, a drink, and the newly purchased urinal. His face turned red.

"Take these and then tell me who your advisor is," she said as she handed him the pills and the drink. "And this," she held up the urinal, "I think you know what it's for."

Billy closed his eyes again. He took the pills, drank as little as possible of the Coke, and then rested his head again against the pillow.

"Your advisor?" Sam reminded him.

"Yeah … uh … Dr. Lockhart."

"Dr. Lockhart? She was mine too! She's a sweetheart. You get some rest, and I'll see what I can find out for you."

She tried Dr. Lockhart's home number, but there was no answer at the moment. She finally decided to take a nap and see if she could get a little sleep to make up for all she had lost last night. She lay down on the couch, and in no time she was out.

When she awoke, it was dark outside and was raining again. She glanced to the clock over the fireplace but couldn't make out the numbers. She reached for her glasses, put them on, and checked again.

"It's nine-fifteen!" she cried out. "Some caretaker I turned out to be. So much for waking him every two hours."

She scrambled off the couch and stumbled sleepily to the bedroom.

"Billy," she called out in a panic. "Wake up! Are you alright? Can you hear me?"

She was barely awake herself as she turned the light on and plopped down onto the bed beside him.

"Augh!" he cried out as his arm bobbled from her movement.

"I'm sorry," she said immediately as she reached down to soothe his arm. "I fell asleep and forgot to wake you. Are you doing okay? Is everything fine?"

He nodded as he tried to slowly open his eyes in the sudden light. "I'm okay. Look, I need to call Cindy."

"Can't. She's on a cruise."

He uttered a profanity and sighed in frustration.

"Would you just try and relax?"

"How? I promised you yesterday I'd be out of your life for good, and here I am, smack dab in the middle and totally dependent on you for … well … who knows how long? This is horribly humiliating! I just wanna get up and go home … only I can't move!"

"Billy, simmer down. For the moment there's not much you can do about it."

"There's not *anything* I can do about it! Sam, this is mortifying!" He closed his eyes and shook his head. "I want to get out of here. I want to go home."

She felt for him in so many ways. She had to do something to get him to face the inevitable fact that he was going to have to be here for at least a week. His face was still pale, and she could tell by his expression he was in a lot of pain. Then she remembered his medicine.

"Hey, you can have some more pain medicine," she said cheerfully. "Let me get that for you, and maybe we can try something to eat."

He shook his head again. "I can't eat, Sam. I'll throw it up all over the place. I'm really, really nauseous."

"I understand. I'll get your medicine, though."

Dr. Crandall had mentioned he might struggle with nausea for awhile, but she would continue to offer food until he took some. She got another pill for him and filled a smaller glass with ice and Coke. Just in case, she took a small plate of Goldfish crackers, a favorite of his, hoping he might take a bite or two.

"Ready?" she asked as she walked back into the room.

They both were embarrassed this time—he was relieving himself.

She quickly turned away and walked back into the hallway. "I'm sorry. I should have knocked."

He only sighed as he finished the job and set the urinal back on the bed stand. Could this possibly get any more humiliating? Yes, when he considered the fact that she would be the one emptying it.

"I'm finished," he said weakly, covering himself fully with the covers. "I'm sorry about that."

"No, I'm sorry," she said right away. "I should have thought about … well … I should have respected your privacy."

He gave a faint laugh. "Right," he said shaking his head. "I'm in your bed in your house, by force for the most part, and you should be respecting my privacy?"

"I wish you'd stop with all that." She came in and handed him the pill. "Let's forget about any circumstance right now except getting you better."

He popped the pill in his mouth and then took the Coke she offered. "Love to," he swallowed the drink and the pill, "but it's a little hard." He handed the glass back to her. "This hasn't been my best week, and it doesn't seem to be getting any better."

He tried to maneuver himself into a slightly different position, but he hit his shoulder in the process. He cried out again and fell back onto his pillow. He immediately put his hand up to his head to try and shield the pain that was now soaring from the concussion.

"Billy!" Sam cried out as she put the Coke on the table beside the urinal. She quickly went to the other side of the bed and sat down beside him. "What can I do? Please tell me something I can do to make it better? I can't handle seeing you in so much pain."

He only shook his head. There was nothing more she could possibly do.

"I feel so sorry about all of this," she said as she pulled the extra pillow up beside him and laid her head down.

"You? Why should you feel sorry? I'm the one who did it. I'm the one forcing myself into your home … into your life yet again … after I promised it wouldn't happen."

She took his hand and gently laced her fingers between his. "Why did you go back on your promise? Why did you get drunk? How could you have let me do that to you?"

He squeezed her hand slightly and sighed deeply. "Because I made such a mess of everything. I should've been straight with you right from the beginning. What's the point of staying sober and doing right when you still end up hurting the ones … the one … you love?"

"You can't let someone as insignificant as me ever rule the decisions in your life."

"Insignificant?" He turned his head toward her. "Sam, how can you call yourself insignificant?"

"Because that's what I should be to you, Billy. You deserve someone who's got it all together … someone who can roll with the punches. I'm this bundle of unresolved issues who will never be what you need in your life."

He looked at her intensely. "I need you right now."

She nodded. "But only for a little while. You'll be better, and you'll …"

"Sam," he stopped her. "Thanks … for being here … for getting me … for doing all this. I can't think straight enough to carry on a real conversation and make sense."

She leaned up and kissed his cheek, but when she moved back, he was staring longingly again.

"What are you thinking?" she whispered.

He tried to smile, but it was too hard. All he could do was think of what he had lost for the second time, and what he would be willing to do to get it back again. He finally just closed his eyes and rolled his head back on the pillow. Perhaps the pain medicine would kick in soon and help him forget the real condition of his life at the moment.

Forty-Seven

Saturday night was rough, but Sam managed a few hours of good sleep. As she stood in her kitchen late Sunday afternoon trying to find something that would be appetizing for Billy and entice him to at least attempt to eat, she thought of Dr. Crandall. He had said to call if there was any kind of problem—not eating would appear to be a problem. She jotted Crandall's name at the bottom of her list of things to do, then she began crossing off all that had been done.

Billy had no idea where his keys were to get into the boat for clothes and lesson plans, so Sam had gone to the police station to track down his belongings. Of course, they wouldn't release anything to her, so a cop had to go back with her to the house for Billy to sign papers allowing her to collect his stuff. Then she went to his boat and picked up some things he would need the next couple of weeks. After that, she dropped by the store and picked him up some pajamas, something he hadn't worn since elementary school, but she knew they would be warm and comfortable and loose enough for him to wear until he was back on his feet again.

Next on the list was to make three important phone calls. She grabbed her phone and headed for the couch. She could feel the lack of sleep catching up with her again.

"Hello?" came the answer for the first call.

"I need to speak with Dr. Lockhart, please."

"Speaking."

"Dr. Lockhart, I don't know if you remember me from years ago or not. This is Samantha Marcum."

"Sam! How could I forget you? One of my prize education students! How are you?"

"Doing well … for the most part."

"Still teaching?"

"Same place … high school math."

"How wonderful!"

"I'm calling about one of your students, Billy Marcum."

"Sure … wait … Marcum. I never connected the names before. Are you two related?"

"In a roundabout way," Sam rolled her eyes. She didn't want to get into this now. "He's been in a pretty severe motorcycle accident."

"Oh, no! Is he alright?"

"That's debatable at the moment. I mean he's fine as far as his mind and all … no permanent damage, but his body took quite a beating. He's got a concussion, his shoulder was dislocated, and his leg is broken."

"My, my, when did this happen?"

"Friday night. What we're wondering is how many days of student teaching he can miss and still pass the class."

"I don't think Billy's missed any days this term yet. But is he gonna be up to teaching in that kind of shape?"

"If I have anything to do about it, he will. I just need to know how many days he can miss this week without blowing his chances of graduating in December."

"He has three skips," Dr. Lockhart told her, "just like a regular class. But I'm sure we could manage something else if we needed to. Mr. C. is very easy to work with."

"I appreciate that. But let's start with what's regulation and see if he can handle it. If he's not able to get up by Wednesday, I'll give you a call and we'll move on from there."

Phone call number one was over and wonderfully successful. There was hope for Billy to finish the semester. Next, she dialed the principal. He needed to know that both she and Billy would be out the next three days. She would bring his lesson plans up to the school on Monday morning for Mr. C. and all should be fine on that end.

She crossed off all but the last line of her list—call Dr. Crandall. She went to her purse and pulled out the card he had given her. He had been so nice and understanding toward Billy in the ER. She felt guilty calling his personal cell, but that's what he had told her to do. All she wanted to know was if it was okay for him to still not be eating. It worried her, because if he didn't regain some strength soon, he would never make it back to school on Thursday, and for now, that's what she was shooting for. She punched in the number.

"Crandall," he answered after the first ring.

"Dr. Crandall? Wow, that was fast. Sorry … I was anticipating your voicemail."

"It's your lucky day," he replied cheerfully. "Actually, I'm off duty right now, so my phone was on."

"This is Samantha Marcum. I picked up Billy Marcum the other night from the ER … the motorcycle accident guy."

"Oh, yeah. How's he doing? Is there a problem?"

"Honestly, I think he's doing pretty well, except I can't get him to eat. He still complains about being too nauseous to eat anything."

"Really? Has he eaten anything at all?"

"Nothing … and he barely drinks too. He'll take a sip to get down his medicine, but that's all."

"Hmmm, I wouldn't say it's that serious, but he should be having something by now. Your best bet would be to call his regular doctor in the morning and see what he thinks."

"Yeah … uh … that would be a problem. He has no regular doctor … hasn't been to a doctor in years. In fact, the last time he went was back in Dockrey."

"Okay, that *could* be a problem," Dr. Crandall laughed slightly. "Uh … tell you what; my shift is nine to nine tonight. What don't you give me your address, and I could come by and see him in just a couple of minutes."

"Really? Are you kidding? An actual house call?"

Crandall laughed again. "Well, not actual, because you won't be charged for it. But I could look him over and talk to him a bit, and we could see if maybe something could be done or if there's actually another problem developing."

"Sure … that'd be wonderful," she smiled with relief. "It would take a huge load off my mind."

She gave him the address and then hung up the phone.

Wow, a house call. She looked around the room. It was a bit disheveled from all of the chaos surrounding Billy. She immediately began to pick things up and straighten the room. She got a glance of herself in the mirror and realized she'd probably better straighten herself up a little too. She finished with the house, then rushed to the bathroom, washed her face and began to put on make-up.

What am I doing? she wondered. *Since when did it matter if I wore make-up or looked nice for anyone?* She took down her ponytail and was brushing out her hair when the doorbell rang. She hesitated. There was no time to put her hair up. As she ran for the door she also realized she had forgotten her glasses at the sink. *Oh well.*

When the door opened, Jeremy Crandall looked floored. "Are you the same woman who picked up Mr. Marcum early Saturday morning?"

"Yeah," she smiled as she took a deep breath to release tension. "That was fast."

"I … uh … actually live fairly close to here."

"Really?" For some reason, this gave Sam a sense of comfort. "That's nice to know."

There was something about his eyes that seemed warm and gentle. He had a boyish face and she figured he looked much younger than he probably was, but there was also a calming maturity about him that put her at ease right away.

"Come on in," she told him. "I'm a little out of sorts. I haven't slept the best the past couple of nights."

"I bet," he laughed gently again. "What about Mr. Marcum?"

"He sleeps on and off pretty good. But as the medicine starts to wear off, he gets … well … moany."

"I don't blame him. I'd get *moany* too."

They stood in her living room slightly awkward for a moment.

"Would you like something to drink?" she asked suddenly. "Umm … Coke … or tea … coffee?"

"Actually, a cup of coffee would be wonderful."

She smiled, almost appreciative that he had taken her up on the offer. "It does sound wonderful. I'll get a pot brewing right now."

"Oh, that's okay. I didn't realize you had to make it."

"No, I'd love some myself … unless you're in a hurry or something."

"No … I … uh … don't have to be anywhere until nine tonight."

"Okay then, I'll put on a pot and you can check the patient back there. He's in the room off to the left."

"Sounds good."

Sam watched as Dr. Crandall moved slowly toward her bedroom. What a nice guy he seemed to be as he had such a kind demeanor. She wondered how old he really was. Even as he approached Billy's door, he did it softly and carefully, as though not to disturb the patient. How did he end up in the ER where everything was such hustle and bustle?

After looking over Billy and rousing him just enough to answer some questions, Dr. Crandall returned to the living room where Sam was arranging pillows on the couch. She had her glasses on now and her hair was pulled back in a ponytail. He nodded in recognition as he walked in. This was the girl he remembered picking up Mr. Marcum, not the beautiful green-eyed, long-haired beauty that had greeted him just a few minutes ago.

"Coffee's ready," she said cheerfully as she motioned him toward the kitchen. "Everything's there, whatever it is you might take in it: creamer, sugar, fake sugar."

He laughed gently. "I just take it black."

"Ooo, really? Do you actually enjoy it like that?"

"Hmmm, never thought about it," he confessed as he went to the pot and began to pour himself a cup. "I started drinking it in med school when I would be desperate to stay awake. I wasn't concerned with how it tasted; I just wanted something quick to pull me back to consciousness." He glanced back at her. "Would you like me to pour you one?"

"Already got it," she smiled as she reached down to the table and lifted her mug. "So, what do you think about Billy? Is the eating thing a problem?"

He brought his cup into the living room and joined her on the couch. "Actually, I think at this point it might be the medicine. At first, it was most likely the concussion. A lot of people react to that prescription with nausea, and sometimes all out vomiting. I'll give you a different one before I leave."

"Good. I hate to see him suffer any more than he already is."

They sat quietly for a few awkward moments, but he had some

serious curiosities running around in his head. He grabbed his nerve and finally said, "I didn't realize you and Mr. Marcum were married."

Sam almost choked on her coffee. "Excuse me," she gave a small laugh through a cough. "We're not … anymore."

"Oh," he nodded. "So, how long have you been … unmarried."

Sam smiled at his question. He was trying to be very polite. "We've been *divorced* for over ten years."

He nodded again as he took another swallow of his coffee. "But you're still close … friends and all."

Sam shrugged her shoulders and cocked her head to the side. "Sort of. The truth is … we hadn't spoken since the divorce until a few weeks ago. He's student-teaching in the classroom right next to mine."

"Really? So you're both teachers?"

"I've been teaching for nine years—high school math."

Dr. Crandall winced. "You wouldn't be impressed with my math skills."

"Oh, yeah? What was your best subject in school? Science? Anatomy?"

"You'd think," he smiled self-consciously as he leaned back on the couch. "Actually, I preferred the Language Arts. I loved reading and writing, stuff like that."

"So why a doctor? Why not an author or journalist or something?"

"Parental pressure, you might say. Both of my parents are doctors."

She raised her eyebrows in surprise. "You don't hear that often."

"Nope. And I was an only child. The demand was strong for me to go into medicine."

"I can imagine. So why an ER doctor? You like the fast pace?"

He shook his head this time. "Not really. I'm in residency right now … my last year. The ER seems to be the place they enjoy sticking us the most … especially when nights like Friday come along."

"Well, you were wonderful to Billy. I really appreciate the time you took with him. He told me how everyone was ticked with him for even being there. He said they aren't too sympathetic to motorcycle victims."

"It's tough," he explained. "So many of them come in beyond hope. It's hard to see why anyone would even ride one knowing how vulnerable and dangerous that can be."

"I don't know that he actually rides it by choice as much as necessity."

"How so?"

"He went back to school after he was thirty to finish his degree. Both parents had died, and he had no direction. He has no income except a $500 monthly allowance left him by his mother, and then she arranged to have his tuition paid. At the time, I suppose a motorcycle seemed like the best option."

"Yeah … well … that's something I never had to worry about."

"He didn't either until his parents died. He had a good job, a great apartment, plenty of money flowing in, but decided to trade it all for a degree."

Time passed quickly as they sat and talked for the next two hours. Dr. Crandall talked about his many adventures in med-school, and Sam shared some of the more wacky experiences she had gone through while teaching. As tired as she had been, she now felt a little energized. This was the first laughter she had had since the Monday night bomb, and it was a great release to think about something other than Billy for a change.

"I suppose I had better head on out," Dr. Crandall said despondently as he stretched on the couch.

"I thought your shift wasn't until nine?"

"Yeah, but I need to eat some supper first and get changed into my lovely doctor attire—scrubs."

Sam took their mugs to the kitchen. "It was fun having coffee with you. You actually drank three cups … all of them black. I'd say you must be a true coffee lover."

"Well, that's my typical evening habit," he explained as he waited by the couch for her to return from the kitchen. "I drink several cups before heading to work to sort of get me hyped up, and then once I'm there, the adrenaline takes over."

"Is that healthy?"

"Not at all, but then no one's worried about a doctor's health."

He opened the door and lingered a bit, apparently not wanting to leave.

"I really appreciate your dropping by, Dr. Crandall," she said trying to bring some finality to the conversation.

"Uh … look … you can just call me Jeremy if you don't mind. Even though I was supposed to be here on official medical business, I think our afternoon together warrants a first name basis, at least as far as I'm concerned."

She giggled and explained, "I've never in my life called any doctor by a first name. This might be quite an adjustment for me."

"Well, we'll have to work on it," he smiled again in that now familiar warm fashion. "Just try it out now … you can say *bye, Jeremy*, and we'll see how it comes out."

Sam nodded self-consciously and said, "Bye … Jeremy."

"Very good. See … with just a little practice, you could become a pro at that. Before you know it, you'll be saying *Jeremy this*, and *Jeremy that*."

"I don't know," she laughed. "It still seems … inappropriate."

"Hmmm, we'll have to change that somehow."

Forty-Eight

"Do you think there's no way we can all be together?" Andie asked with great irritation as she sat propped up in the recliner at Annie's home. "It's Daddy's sixtieth birthday! Surely Angie can come home for just a day or two."

"I don't think they can," Annie shook her head as she stirred another cup of coffee. "Carter is in physical therapy every day, as well as having to be monitored for all the … well … all the stuff they're doing to him."

"But she's a doctor. Surely she can therapize him and monitorize him herself for just a couple of days!"

Annie was getting more exasperated with Andie than the situation itself. "I'm not the one to discuss this with, okay? All I'm trying to do is plan the celebration … with or without Angie and her crew. *You* call Angie again and see if you can nudge her this way. I had no such luck."

"This is ridiculous!" Andie apparently wasn't listening to her arguments. "Everyone's home again for the first time in forever, and we can't even get together for a simple birthday party."

Annie was thankful for the phone ringing. She jumped up from the couch and moved quickly toward the kitchen before Andie threw in another comment.

"Hello?" she answered.

"Hey, sweetie. How's the morning going?" her mother asked cheerfully.

"Fair to partly cloudy. We're trying to plan Daddy's party, but the Angie issue seems to be an ever-present gloom hanging over the whole thing."

"Oh, my, then you won't want to hear this at all."

"What is it, Moms? What's happened?"

"The Monday morning tabloids have hit again."

"What is it now? The only time Stephen or I have even been out of the house is to take Stevie to school and pick him up. For crying out loud! What could they possibly have fabricated from that?"

"It's not you … not exactly. They've started in on Angie again."

"Angie? You're kidding!"

"They have this picture of her and that doctor walking outside, and he's got his hand on her arm."

"Dr. Taylor? The one they're staying with?"

"That's the one."

"And what does the headline say?"

"Trouble Brewing in Missionary's Paradise."

"Oh … my … gosh," Annie was fuming now. "How dare they!"

"We'd better alert Angie before it hits her in the face."

"I'll call her. Seeing that all this boils down to being my fault, the least I can do is be the one who breaks the news."

"Sweetie, listen," she said with motherly comfort, "this is just one of those silly facts of life we have to deal with. If it wasn't the paparazzi, it'd be some other ridiculous thing. And when you think about, it's downright absurd. These people are so desperate for outrageous news that they'd actually go after your sister, a missionary, to create a story."

"I know. I'll try to keep my head about it, but if it weren't for me, this wouldn't be happening."

"And if it weren't for me," Barbara laughed, "it wouldn't be happening either."

"You? How are you to blame for all of this?"

"I birthed you both! Had I not followed my heart and had two more girls after Andie, everyone would be just fine and happy in life, wouldn't they?"

She rolled her eyes. "Okay … point taken."

"Good. So, you'll call Angie?"

"Right away." She smiled and shook her head as she thought of her mother's comment. "And Moms, thanks for trying to take the burden off my shoulder."

"Ha! That'll be the day!"

☼☼☼

Angie explained the tabloid paper to Michael and expected an extremely negative reaction. "I'm sorry," she said as she finished, "you were watching—you know nothing they're claiming actually happened."

"You did disappear behind those big bushes for a little bit," he said doubtfully as he raised an eyebrow.

Her eyes grew wide in defense until she noticed the twinkle in his. "Are you playing with me?"

He shrugged and grinned. "Who really cares? This isn't our home. It doesn't matter what people here think. Let 'em say whatever they want. One day, we'll be sitting back on our deck in Padawin. Cassie and Carter will be running down the beach, and I'll be gently swinging baby number three to sleep while we watch the sun set on Mt. Podakind. That's our reality … not this crazy life over here."

She stared in confusion. "So, it doesn't bother you that my picture is all over the U.S. with *Dr. Smoothie* gently leading me by the elbow?"

"Are you in love with *Dr. Smoothie*?" he asked her as he came over and put his arms around her. "Are you carrying his third child? Are you about to leave the beauty of our life in Padawin for the comforts he could offer you?"

She put her arms around him too and replied, "Not on your life."

"Then, I'm good."

☼☼☼

Cindy stood on the deck of the ship and took in the gorgeous scenery as they approached the port. The warmth of the sun on her face almost made her feel reborn. It had been so chilly and rainy and dreary the past few days in Alabama, and just the weather itself here brought a good measure of cheer into her heart.

"You look pleasant," Kyle said as he came up and put his arm around her waist.

She looked over at him and gave a laugh.

"What?" he asked.

"You look like a tourist."

"That's because I am. I don't want there to be any confusion about the fact that I'm here purely for recreation and inane worthless living."

She nodded as she looked back to the port. "It's beautiful here, isn't it?"

"It could almost make you forget that we have a real life back in … where is it that we live again?"

She laughed. "I'm not *that* relaxed. I still wonder if the world will fall apart while we're away, and if it'll somehow be our fault."

"I guarantee you, the world won't fall apart. Our children are happily in the hands of caring people, and are probably being spoiled to death."

"To death? That's not comforting!"

"Bad choice of words," he said quickly. "How about … being spoiled beyond their wildest dreams?"

She nodded in acceptance. "I'll try to imagine that picture in my mind when I think about them. Then there's Billy. I wonder if he's managed to stay out of trouble since we've been gone. I didn't hear from him before we left. I somehow expected he would call and wish us a happy bon voyage or something."

"His thermostat could have been on *miserable* that day … or week."

"Who knows?" she sighed as she closed her eyes up to the sun.

"I'm wondering," he said playfully, "do you think they need any mission work done down here in the Caribbean?"

"Are you desiring to volunteer?"

"I don't know. I'm thinking … it's warm and gorgeous here year 'round … and no Hal Bridges."

She slapped his arm and shook her head. "If you don't leave Hal Bridges out of our vacation, you're sleeping alone tonight."

He looked at her in alarm. "Hal … who? Who are you talking about?"

"Better … much better."

☼☼☼

"You're kidding, right?" Hal practically yelled into the telephone. "You really expect me to pay that kind of money to rent that shabby shack?"

"Look, mister, I don't know who you are or where you're from, but at this point I have no desire to rent anything to you. I don't want the rude likes of you living in Dockrey anyway!"

Slam!

He crossed another house off the list. "You'd think they'd be grateful to have anyone renting from them."

He wasn't trying to be rude—he had just learned long ago that you *never* pay the asking price. People were always willing to negotiate, especially if you had a forceful personality. Apparently, the people in Dockrey didn't bend to *force* as easily as other places. Maybe Lisa had been right … people in the South weren't as ignorant as he supposed.

"That's stupid!" he muttered. "These people are just a little too proud for their own good." He jotted down the man's name he had spoken with. "I may have to teach him a lesson or two when I get settled well in Dockrey."

He looked down his list. There were only two houses left, and they had been at the bottom because they were the least favored. He didn't care. He wasn't about to bend to the ridiculous rental prices these people were asking. Hopefully, in just a few months, he could build his own house just like Jonathan Wright, or buy something comparable to what Kyle and Cindy Sarkos had. It wouldn't take this church long to see that they needed Hal Bridges just as much as those other two sentimental clowns.

Hal dialed the number and waited patiently for the answer.

"Hello?"

"Yes, I'm interested in the rental house you have on South Fourth Street."

"Okay, watcha wanna know?"

"First of all, how many bedrooms and bathrooms?"

"Two bedrooms, one full bath, and then another with a shower."

"I see," Hal jotted down on his notes. "And what are you asking for rental?"

"Five hundred security deposit and five hundred a month."

"You're kidding me, right?" He began the negotiating. "For a two bedroom house you're asking Five hundred dollars?"

"Sure am. It's a fairly new house, it's in superior shape, and I'd like to keep it that way. I ain't renting it for next to nothing to have some trashy people move in and tear it to shreds."

"Well, I can assure you that I am not *trashy people*, but I'm not about to pay five hundred a month, plus a deposit, for a dinky little two bedroom house."

"Then don't," the guy said flatly. "I got other houses for plenty less, but they're not near as nice as that one on Fourth Street. If you want to pay a trashier quality price, then I'll give you a trashier quality house."

"I most certainly do not want a poor quality house, but I don't want to pay extortionist prices for a decent one."

"Like I said before, mister, you don't have to pay anything to me. My price is firm."

"What about four hundred fifty? That seems a little more fair, don't you think?"

"You gotta be kiddin' me! I said five hundred dollars, and I meant five hundred dollars firm. You don't want to pay my askin' price, then look somewhere else."

"Nobody wants to pay that kind of price for a house that small. Apparently you don't need the money."

"Apparently," was the man's only response.

"What about four hundred sixty?" Hal offered this time. "That's still a ridiculous offer, but I'd be willing to go up that much."

The man now laughed. "You're one crazy person. I ain't renting it for less than five hundred dollars. Take it or leave it, mister."

"I guess I'll leave it then," Hal said with a disgusted sigh. "You obviously aren't in a rush to get this house off your hands."

"No problem. Have a nice day."

Click.

This was going nowhere fast. He had only one house left, and it was one he had hoped he wouldn't get to. It was definitely in the more shabby category than any of the others, but it did belong to a church member who would most probably *treat him right* if he were to take it, at least according to Floyd Benson. He dialed again.

"Hello?" a lady answered.

Hal smiled. Ladies tended to be way easier to handle than men. "Good morning. I was interested in your rental house out off of highway nineteen."

"Sure. It's in good shape—had a new roof put on it about three years ago. The kitchen appliances are furnished and in good working order, but no washer or dryer."

"How much are you asking?"

"Depends."

"Depends? Depends on what?" He had never heard of such a thing.

"How much work you're willing to put into it."

"Work?" He didn't like the sound of this. "I already have a job. I don't need to work."

"Where will you be working?"

"I'm the new staff member at First Baptist."

"Oh, yes! Hal Bridges! Floyd Benson said you might be calling me. My name is Alice Vordeman; I've been a member there all my life."

"Dr. Bridges," Hal said firmly.

"Excuse me?"

"I prefer being called *Dr. Bridges.*"

Alice laughed endearingly. "If we're gonna be neighbors, we might as well keep it neighborly from the beginning or you may end up getting your feelings hurt. Folks here prefer *friendly* over *protocol.*"

"But back to the work," he changed direction. He would have to deal with Alice Vordeman's addressing of him later. Right now he had to focus on getting a house. "I'm not sure what you mean by work."

"It's not that big a deal," she began to explain. "The house sits on an eight acre field … not very wooded. I like to keep it mowed. It's not hard to handle with the tractor … just a few hours a week. And then any repairs that might arise in the house you would need to take care of yourself."

"First of all, Alice, I'm not a farmer type fellow. In fact," he gave a little chuckle, "I've never been on a tractor in my life."

"Oh, there's nothing to it. I'm a five-foot-two skinny old grandmaw and I climb up there once a week to do the job. A big man like you could handle it with no problem."

"I'm not sure I really want to *handle* it," he tried to sound stern.

"But you could stay in the house for free. Well, you'd have to pay your own utilities, but keeping up repairs, which, naturally, I would pay for, and then keeping the field mowed, would be all you'd need to do for rent."

"Are you serious?" Hal was shocked. With the salary they were willing to pay him, some serious debts could be removed not having to pay rent. But mowing on a tractor? How demeaning.

"This almost sounds too good to be true, Alice. But I have to confess, I'm not all that thrilled with the idea of using a tractor. How much would you rent the house for without the mowing and repairs and all?"

"Five hundred a month."

"Five hundred?" What was it with people in this area? "That's a bit steep for an old house wouldn't you think?"

"But it's a big house and a very nice house. You couldn't come close to touching that anywhere else in Dockrey."

"But if I mow your field on the tractor and keep up repairs, I can stay there for free?"

"Sure! Seems like a wonderful trade-off in my opinion!"

He needed to think on that a moment. He had no intention of ever stepping foot on the tractor, but perhaps something else could be worked out.

"Tell you what, Alice," he said as he switched back into negotiator mode. “Let me talk to my wife, and I'll get back to you as soon as I can.”

“No problem. I'll hold it until I hear from you again.”

Free. That would be a wonderful situation. Certainly Alice Vordeman wouldn’t expect him to actually get atop a tractor and mow a field once she got to know the quality and class that he represented. Maybe something else could be worked out … eventually.

Forty-Nine

Stephen felt guilty for pulling up the number of XYZ Music again, but as Annie was occupied with Andie and the planning of Jonathan's party, and the kids were all swimming blissfully in the warm pool, he was all alone in the upstairs studio. He glanced out the large window next to the baby grand piano and literally felt his finger twitch to push the button. He knew Annie had an uneasy feeling concerning Ben Brenner—it had showed every single time he brought up the man's name over the years. But why? He was an incredibly talented guy and had done classic work that would go down in history as exceptional. What could possibly be so wrong with him that Annie would object to Stephen working with him? Yes, he had been married five times, but he wasn't seeking moral counsel, just an opportunity to create again.

He looked down at the name and number. All he wanted was to know if there was anything he could do for fun as he sat in Alabama with all the time in the world. A little writing here and there wouldn't take away from his retirement or from his time with the family. It would simply give him a pet project, something to do that would help satisfy the need to work.

Without another delay, he pressed the button and put the phone up to his ear. His hand actually shook as he waited for the rings to begin. When the first one sounded, he almost stopped the call, wondering what he was doing, and why he felt he should keep this from Annie. But as he labored the point, a receptionist answered the phone.

"XYZ Music. How may I direct your call?"

"Uh …" he felt foolish now. "Yes, this is Stephen Williams." Now he really felt foolish. "Wow, you probably think I'm an idiot. Right…Stephen Williams."

"Stephen Williams of *Autumn Sunset* fame?" she asked.

"Yes … and seriously, I really am Stephen Williams."

"I believe you, Mr. Williams," she replied calmly. "You wouldn't have this number unless you were someone Ben didn't mind having contact him. This is his personal office."

"Okay, I feel a little better now." He took a deep breath. "I was wondering … um … if Mr. Brenner was in."

"Not at the moment," she informed him. "He's on a trip to Chicago and won't be back for another week. I could have him call you as soon as he gets in if you like."

Now he was nervous. What if Ben called and Annie answered? That would be bad. But this was his personal cell; she never answered this.

"Well, I suppose I could just call him back … maybe. There's no real need or rush about any of it." Good plan.

"If that's what you prefer, Mr. Williams. But I would be more than glad to tell him you called."

"Yeah … you can tell him that, and that I'll try and get in touch with him sometime next week."

"No problem. Can I do anything else for you?"

"Uh … no. That'll be it."

"Very well, then. Nice talking with you, Mr. Williams."

"Good bye."

"Bye, bye, now."

Sweat was actually forming on his forehead as he quickly tucked the phone away in his pocket. Nothing happened, so there was nothing to hide. All was well. Ben wouldn't call back, and Stephen would only call again if he really felt urged to. No problem.

✿✿✿

Billy faintly heard Sam's voice as she tried to rouse him from a deep, drug-motivated sleep. He slowly opened his eyes and turned his head to where the sound was coming from. He finally managed to focus and found a smiling Sam waving a bowl in front of him.

"Think you can eat today?" she asked hopefully. "Dr. Crandall felt like it was maybe the medicine that was making you nauseous yesterday."

"Crandall? When did you speak to him?"

"Are you serious?" she asked with a laugh. "He spoke with you too."

"On the phone?" he wondered as he slowly tried to maneuver himself up in the bed.

"No, he was here yesterday afternoon. He talked with you about … well, I guess about how you were feeling. I don't really know because I didn't go in the room."

He held his breath as he moved to sit up against the wall.

"Wow!" Sam exclaimed in delight. "That's quite a feat … sitting up in bed all by yourself."

"It was no picnic. What's wrong with my arm again? Did I break it?"

"Nope," she said as she joined him on the side of the bed. "You dislocated your shoulder. It's your leg that's broken."

He nodded trying to remember all that had happened. "What day is it?"

"Monday. Are you gonna eat something?"

"Hmmm, I don't remember Saturday or Sunday … or Dr. Crandall."

"Eat? Are you gonna eat?"

"If it's that important, I'll most definitely eat. What have you got there?"

She handed him the bowl and said, "Chicken and rice soup. I'll get you some crackers or Goldfish if you want."

"That'd be nice. How 'bout the Goldfish?"

"Coming right up." She hopped up and left for the kitchen.

What are you doing in here? he asked himself as he took a spoonful of soup. *You've got to get out as soon as you possibly can. If you don't, it'll seem like Monday night never happened, and you'll doom Sam to repeat another heartache yet again. Don't pretend with her that everything is alright. She's gonna be nice … she's gonna act like nothing ever happened. Don't let her forget.*

"Here you go," she bounded in with a smile. Placing a small bowl of Goldfish crackers beside him on the bed, she sat down next to him.

"Look," he tried to talk without looking at her, "I need to get some clothes and see if I can get up and start thinking about getting home."

"Well, I'm certainly glad to hear that you feel like moving around, but you won't be out of here for at least another ten days. And I went by the boat and got you some clothes."

"Ten days? I can't stay here for ten days."

"Because?"

"Because I don't need to be here, Sam," he said a bit too angrily.

She looked at him with hurt and shock.

"No offense," he tried to say more calmly this time. "But you should be the last person having to look after me. Right now, the best thing for you is for me to be as far away from you as possible."

"Maybe—but the best thing for *you* is to be right here until we can get you mobile again."

"I think I would be alright if I could just …"

"Billy, stop!" she yelled. "Look, I understand all your feelings and pointless ideas right now. But the fact remains that you can't be on your own for a while. So, let's agree to call a truce and make the best of this until it's more feasible for you to leave. Besides, I've got to get you to school on Thursday if you plan to finish this term and graduate next month."

He rolled his eyes and leaned his head back against the headboard of the bed. "I don't care at this point if I graduate or not, especially if it means you have to take care of me."

"For crying out loud, Billy! Stop being such a baby!"

"What?" he looked over at her.

"I understand, okay? You don't want to be here in my house; you don't want to be near me. But it's absolutely ludicrous for you to storm out of here with your humiliated feelings and throw away an entire semester simply because you don't want to swallow your pride and let me see you through this. This doesn't change anything, other than the fact that I'm speaking to you. You're still a lying jerk, and I have no intentions of rekindling a relationship with you. However, I owe it to your parents, at least, to make sure you pull through this semester. Forget about you;

do this for your mother … okay? Can you look at it like that?"

He was silent. He didn't want her to help him. Just being near her practically broke his heart. How could he stay with her all this time and not fall even deeper for her?

"There are no valid arguments you can offer," she said flatly. "Either you stay here and do the right thing, or you leave and act like a total fool."

"Gee, you make it all so simple and logical, don't you?"

"That's because it is simple and logical."

They stared at each other for the longest time as he tried to put his thoughts together. The pain medicine was still causing his head to swirl, and it seemed impossible to think clearly. Yes, it would be a huge waste of money to throw off the entire term because of his pride. Also, he would have to have someone bring him groceries and supplies until Cindy got back. She was right: the simple and logical thing was just to stay put and let her tend to him until he could make it on his own.

"Okay," he reluctantly agreed. "But we get a few things straight."

"Right," she said as she shifted in the bed. "And these are the few things." She looked at him intensely. "You do what I tell you to do. You stop talking about leaving until I'm convinced you can handle things on your own. You don't even *think* about leaving here if it means you can't finish the term." She pointed a finger directly in his face. "Are these things clear?"

He bit his lip to control his mouth. "Those were not the *things* I was referring to."

"I don't really care," she sighed as she stood. "Those are my terms. You're so dazed and out of it that you really don't have enough sense to even make a decision." She looked back at him as she prepared to leave the room. "Can you just trust me on this one? Can you let me be in charge just this one time? You'll benefit greatly if you'll just go along with it."

He tried to smile, but it was purely by force.

She grinned at him. "You don't have to be happy about it. Just be willing to comply."

He nodded and slowly said, "Consider me reluctantly compliant, then."

She shook her head as she turned to leave. "That I'll do."

✿✿✿

"Why don't we do this?" Annie finally suggested. "We could have like a church-wide surprise party for his actual birthday, and then we could wait and celebrate with the family when Angie and Michael can make it."

"We'd be pushing Christmas if we wait for them," Andie gave the negative slant with a slight whine in her voice.

"You can't have it both ways!" Annie finally exploded from

exasperation at her sister. "If we plan around Angie, we're gonna have to wait—no options there, okay? If we want to celebrate his sixtieth on his sixtieth, then we're gonna have to make some plans that don't include her."

"You don't have to get testy about it."

"Testy? We've been sitting here for two hours trying to just come up with a date! We haven't even started planning the party itself! Get a grip on reality, sister, and let's at least set a day!"

Andie frowned and gave a deep sigh. "I just thought he deserved something more than an afterthought."

"I swear," she said trying to keep controlled, "I'll tell him how hard it was trying to do this, how much time it took to get it all together, and he'll be tickled pink that we did anything at all. Okay?"

"I still don't like it, but since you've gotten all rattled about this, I suppose I'd better go along with you."

"Augh!" Annie screamed out as she stood from the couch. "I am *rattled* because there's no other option, and yet you refuse to accept that!"

"I want Daddy's birthday to be special!"

"And you think I want something just thrown together?"

"Well, it would appear so. You're not even trying to see how we can get Angie here."

Annie twirled a strand of her long hair. "I must've been crazy to think life would settle down if we moved back to Dockrey. I forgot how hard-headed my sisters could be."

"I'm not the one being hard-headed about this."

Annie swung around to sail into her again, but found Andie smiling mischievously. She shook her head and closed her eyes in desperation. "Are you just baiting me?"

"Yeah … and it's so much fun."

"Two hours?" she replied in disbelief. "You did this to me for two hours?"

"Not really. It started out for real, but then watching you get riled up became just plain fun." She grinned. "I couldn't help it."

Annie fell back on the couch totally annoyed. "So, you actually agree with me on this so we can move beyond this pithy date-setting argument."

"Actually, I have an alternative suggestion."

"Anything … I'll agree to anything as long as it's realistic."

"We end up with three celebrations. We do the church-wide thing—I think that's a great idea. But we also do a small, intimate, family and close friends thing too … maybe even here at your place. Then, like you said, when Angie gets back, we celebrate one more time with just the family."

Annie's jaw dropped in amazement. "Seriously?"

"Absolutely! I'm very easy to get along with. Just ask Doug."

Annie shook her head and prepared to move on. "You'd better not be as ornery when we actually start planning the darned party. Remember that movie *Misery*? It's possible to have two broken ankles, if you know what I mean."

Fifty

The afternoon at Levi Taylor's house became increasingly stressful. Carter's physical therapy had been painful, and tabloid reporters were crawling along the property hoping to catch a shot of Angie and Levi in some passionate embrace. Eventually the police had to be called in to prevent trespassing and invasion of privacy. After supper, they all sat in the large living area with the massive vaulted ceiling. Angie cradled a very distressed Carter in her lap while Cassie played contentedly with a collection of small plastic animals on the floor.

"I probably should hire some security," Levi suggested as they discussed the situation. "It would at least hinder some of the reporters."

"Don't even dignify them by calling them *reporters*," Angie complained. "And don't worry about the security. The worse that could happen would be if they actually broke into your house. And if they did, it wouldn't be to steal. Then we could have them arrested and be minus one weasel—or just shoot them in self-defense."

Gail wondered, "Do you have to deal with this all the time … being Annie Williams' sister?"

Angie shook her head. "In Dockrey, it's sort of on and off. But we've been in Padawin a long time—nobody bothers us there."

"Is it hard living there?" Gail asked. "I could never imagine being in some remote area on an island surrounded only by tribal people. I'm sure that sounds shallow, but I think I'd probably die."

Angie smiled. "It doesn't mean you're shallow. There aren't a lot of people who'd find it appealing. It's a matter of calling really. See, to me, the States seem so hurried and stressed. Even when we come here to visit, I find myself longing for the simplicity of the islands again. And the reason has nothing to do with being deep or shallow or having a heart of sacrifice. It all amounts to the fact that I know that's where I belong. In Psalms it says God gives us the desires of our hearts if we'll take delight in Him. I've learned what that really means is that if we'll follow Him and take pleasure in Him, He begins to place within us His desires. He put a major longing for missions … and Padawin … in my heart … that's my desire. So, I guess you could boil it all down to a God thing if you wanted."

"A God thing," Levi repeated as if meditating on the idea. "Your whole commitment to God has always blown me away. How do you just … I don't know … just stay convinced that He's real … that He's really out there … somewhere. I mean, Angie, I've never seen any evidence that God exists."

"That's not true," Gail countered him.

"What?" he asked her. "Yes, it is. I've always told you that."

"Until you did Carter's surgery," she reminded him.

He quickly remembered, and his countenance changed immediately.

"What about it?" Angie asked him.

"It was all so … odd … the fact that we weren't comfortable with having found everything," he explained. "We'd pull back another flap of tissue, sometimes just randomly, and there would be more of the cancer."

Angie suggested, "Perhaps God was guiding you. Is that what you think?"

He shook his head. "I have no idea, but it was an unusual feeling. And why with Carter only? I've done many surgeries. Why don't I have that same feeling with all the others?"

Suddenly Michael interjected a comment. "Because maybe there weren't near the prayers being offered as in Carter's case. This little guy was literally bathed in petition to God."

Gail then asked, "So do you think Levi's surgery was an answer to prayer? I grew up in church, and I don't ever really remember God answering any prayers. I guess that's why it was so easy to turn away, you might say. I'm sort of like Levi; I just don't see any evidence that He's really around."

Angie gently kissed the top of Carter's head before she answered. "The problem isn't the evidence. The problem is that you refuse to see God."

"I'd love to see him!" Levi insisted. "But … well … in my eyes He's just not there."

"That's exactly my point," Angie told him. "When you have a child come into your office with a severe problem, you know nothing about that child. You're detached, you see him as a person who needs your services, and you begin the process of diagnosis and treatment. But how do his parents act toward him? Are they detached?"

He shook his head. "Of course not."

"Right—and by the time you've finished treating one of these children, spending long hours with them, are you still detached? Is he or she just another patient? When one dies, do you almost lose heart from the loss?"

He nodded this time.

"There you go, then," Angie smiled. "That's how it is with God. When you see a sunset, you just see an everyday occurrence that is mandated by the laws of nature. Me? I see God showing off His majesty. When you see how intricately the human body is designed, and how each individual system works with the others to promote life, you see an organism produced by an impersonal evolution. I see the hand of a loving God who thought of everything. When you see the green of the trees accented by the colors of the flowers and the sky, you see photosynthesis, seed-bearing, and atmosphere. I see the creative hand of God that even made the processes of nature have a form of beauty and delight. So, it's not that evidence of God doesn't exist—it's that you're so disconnected you're not capable of seeing Him."

Suddenly, in the middle of this deep conversation, Cassie came up to the adults and proclaimed, "It's because you are like all the America people."

"What do you mean, Cassie?" Levi asked her.

"You don't really know what is beautiful," she said as matter of fact.

"Cassie!" Angie exclaimed with embarrassment.

"No," Levi stopped Angie immediately. "Let her speak. For a four-year-old, she seems to have a good eye for observation. What do you mean, Cassie? How have I missed it when it comes to true beauty?"

Cassie plopped onto her father's lap and explained, "You have nice hair, and Miss Gail has lots of pretty clothes. You have a very big house and pretend water and plants outside. They make you happy. You like things that you make, not what God makes."

Levi nodded and gave a lopsided grin. "I never thought of that. What do you think is beautiful?"

Cassie smiled at the question. "The mountain, the river, the ocean, the berries, the trees, my friends. I don't like all your big buildings here. They kill the trees, you know? There had to be trees here one time. But they're dead. And all those trees back there," she pointed to the backyard where the gardens and the pond were, "you put them there. And you think they're pretty."

Angie quickly answered, "They are pretty, Cassie."

"It's okay, Angie," Levi assured her. "There's a lot of wisdom in those words." He looked back at Cassie. "And what about our house? What do you think about it?"

She looked cautiously at her mother. "It's not real."

"Cassie!" Angie exclaimed again.

"Angie," Levi said warmly, "would you let her talk? I think I'm getting more from her simple explanations than all your doctrinal arguments with me over the years. Cassie, why is my house not real?"

Cassie sighed and held out her arms, "Because it's not happy. You have nice floors and chairs, but there's no love on them."

Michael grinned. "At our home," he broke in, "whenever one of the kids makes a mess or stains something, we always say it's because we have children that we love. It kind of became a habit to call the stains *love spots*, because they were evidence that we cared more about the people than the property."

Levi nodded, obviously marveled by Cassie's depth of understanding.

"And you have a lot of bad air in here too," Cassie went on.

Everyone looked at her in surprise this time.

"What does that mean?" Angie asked her, almost afraid to hear her response.

"You don't use real air … ever. You just keep that old air coming in, and it's just the same over and over, going all around in that machine." She pointed at one of the air-conditioning ducts in the ceiling. "You never open up your windows." She pointed to the large windows up in the vaulted ceiling. "You can't even open those up. And Daddy and Mama open up those doors in our room for just a little bit, and we all take very big breaths, then they close them so we don't let your air out. But we should be letting it out so you could get some real air in here too."

Everyone sort of stared at her in silence then she almost whispered, "You can't see God because you don't like any of *His* stuff. You only like *your* stuff, and it's just not real."

☼☼☼

"Hey," Jeremy Crandall said sheepishly as Sam opened the door early that evening.

"Dr. Crandall," she called out in surprise, but then quickly corrected her address. "Jeremy."

"I was heading toward work and thought I'd stop by to see Mr. Marcum."

"Sure, come on in."

He walked graciously through the door and nodded at the warm and familiar living area. "How's the patient today?"

"Much better, actually. I didn't anticipate him being as alert today as he was."

"Good. I take it the change in medicine helped his appetite."

"Definitely. He ate some lunch and supper. I'm really hoping he'll make it to school on Thursday."

He shook his head slightly to the side. "I wouldn't bank on that."

"I'm not … just hoping."

"Is he up for a visit?"

"Check and see," she pointed toward the bedroom. "Would you like some coffee before you go?"

"I wouldn't want to put you out."

"I wouldn't have offered if I didn't want to."

He shrugged his shoulders and finally nodded. "Some coffee would be nice." He turned toward the bedroom, but stopped to say, "Make my cup like yours … all the cream and sugary stuff. I'd like to try it once."

"Sure."

He walked into Billy's room and woke him. "Mr. Marcum? Are you up for a doctor call?"

Billy slowly opened his eyes and looked up. "Crandall?"

"Yeah, you remember me. How are you feeling tonight?"

"Better than last night."

"I know that's right," Jeremy sympathized. "How's the shoulder?"

"Hurts like … well … worse than any of the rest."

"And your head?"

"It's okay today. I was surprised. I assumed with a concussion I'd be spinning around for days with a headache."

"Slight concussion. Be thankful you had enough sense to put on that helmet."

"You know what's funny about all this?" Billy said as he maneuvered himself up in the bed. "I don't even remember the accident. I remember being kicked out of the bar, trying to get my helmet on, and then everything else is a total blank."

"According to the accident report when they brought you in, you were high-tailing it out of the parking lot when a car started backing out. They say you tried to stop, but slid forever, fell over, and then smashed into the car anyway."

"Hmmm, did my bike make it?"

"I have no idea. But you did. I'd be very thankful for that."

Billy nodded in acknowledgment.

"So," Crandall wondered, "are you going back to a *murdercycle* or are you thinking about a car this time."

Billy smiled. "The funny thing is I was actually heading out to buy a car that evening. But I came by here, had a few words with Sam, and decided to just … well … ruin my life instead, I suppose."

"We all have days like that," Jeremy agreed. "Wasn't my best week either."

"Mine seems more like a decade now. And to top it off, I ended up hurting Sam again. I never meant to do that. And here I am stuck in her house at her mercy. Talk about your bad turn of events."

Jeremy smiled and commented, "I could think of a lot worse things than being stuck in a house alone with Sam."

Billy raised an eyebrow in surprise. "Well, yeah … but I was thinking more on her part … not necessarily mine."

Dr. Crandall immediately cleared his throat in embarrassment. "Yeah … well … that's none of my business. I'm just, well, Sam has been really … you're lucky … that's the bottom line … I think."

Billy immediately felt a twinge of jealousy, but as he gained control of his senses, he thought of Sam. This could be the perfect situation for her. If Dr. Crandall had some interest, this could be the best thing to ever happen to her. He was nice, professional, well-mannered, and easy to talk with. This could most definitely work.

Sam popped her head around the corner of the doorway and asked, "Billy, do you want some coffee. Dr. Crandall and I are gonna have a cup. Want to join us?"

He held back his deepest feelings and forced himself to say, "I don't think so. You guys go ahead. Thanks, but no thanks."

"What's the prognosis, doctor?" Sam asked. "Is he gonna live?"

"I'm afraid so. You won't be collecting any insurance money off of this guy."

"Ha!" she burst out. "Like that would happen!"

Billy tried to sleep as Dr. Crandall and Sam shared their coffee and conversation, but it was impossible. It was obvious the doctor had a slight infatuation developing. As to whether she returned the feelings, he couldn't tell. But if he really cared about Sam, really wanted what was best for her, the greatest thing he could do is encourage another relationship with someone who could take care of her, someone who could adore her and treat her like she needed to be treated. After his few encounters with Dr. Crandall, he believed this could possibly be the man to do that. Dr. Crandall had been very sympathetic with him during his ER experience when everyone else there had treated him like gangrene. Crandall had made sure he got to the car and was on his way to somewhere where he would be cared for. This was not a typical, self-centered man, like Billy—this was a man with a big heart. This needed to be Sam's destiny.

Look at it this way, he told himself. *As long as you're here at Sam's, it'll give Crandall a good reason to keep stopping by. So, swallow that pride, my man, and do something for someone else for a change. Give Sam a chance for a real life … a really good life … with someone who can love her and support like she needs.*

When Jeremy left, Sam stared out the front window as she watched him leave. What was happening here? The only man she had ever loved in her entire life was lying in her bed just a few feet away, but suddenly this new person had crept inside. What was he really doing stopping by to check on Billy? This was absolutely out of the norm for a doctor. She knew there had to be more to it than that. And the way he always lingered with her to have coffee after he had seen Billy was definitely out of the ordinary. How did this make her feel? She wasn't sure, but one thing she was sure of—Billy had to be at school on Thursday morning to finish out the semester. As far as she was concerned, that was the only thing that mattered right now, and that was what she would focus on for the time being.

Fifty-One

November was passing quickly. Billy had returned to school the following Thursday, and Jeremy Crandall had managed to show up every single afternoon to check on his progress and have a cup of coffee with Sam. The planning for Jonathan's three birthday celebrations was complete, and the church had been secretly notified of the party to take place on the special Sunday evening after worship. Carter was definitely making progress with his therapy, beginning to put some weight on his legs, but the chemo was making him terribly sick. Cindy and Kyle had made it back from their cruise with a new lease on life, and they were plunging themselves back into church work with a renewed vigor and zeal. And Hal Bridges was finalizing the plans for the move to Alabama.

"What do you mean *Friday morning*?" Hal yelled at the moving company. "I leave here on Monday morning, and plan to drive two days to Dockrey."

"We won't be finished packing your truck until Monday afternoon," the man tried to explain. "Are you sure you want to leave before we finish packing? That'll cost you extra insurance … you do realize that … to not have you here while we do the work."

"I don't care about the insurance," Hal bellowed. "The church is paying for the move. All I want is to have my belongings in Alabama by Wednesday."

"It ain't gonna happen, sir," the man said patiently. "We'll be going as fast as we can to get it there on Friday."

"You've got to be kidding me! I drive down the highway all the time and get barreled over by all these moving trucks passing me at light speed!"

"Well, that wouldn't be our company, then, sir. If you're not happy with our delivery date, then I suggest you try one of those companies that zoom by you on the highway. Friday is our date … and that's final."

Hal was getting really tired of people not cooperating with him. One positive thing through all of this was a rent-free house awaiting him in Alabama. Some of his debts would at last be taken care of.

"I'll go along with this," he said sternly, "simply because I gave you my word. But be advised that I am not at all pleased with the slow delivery."

Lisa came in as he hung up the phone. "Problems?" she asked innocently.

"Incompetent idiots," he blustered back. "Why is it that I have to bow to everybody else's schedule? Why, for once, can't the world do what I want?"

She ventured up behind him and actually wrapped her arms around his waist. "As I see it, this church in Dockrey pretty much *did* bow to your schedule. We leave next Monday for a new place with a new start, and that was all your doing."

He released a long breath and pulled her around to face him. "It was, wasn't it?" he smiled at her.

"Yep," she said as she leaned up toward his face. "And … you managed to get us a place for no rent. I'd say that was pretty good."

He nodded as she moved even closer.

"So if we analyze this carefully," she grinned seductively, "it would appear that you are in charge, my man."

He could feel his face growing warmer and his body rushing with desire. "If I didn't know better," he said slowly, "I'd swear you were about to kiss me."

"Very good," she said as she leaned into him.

☼☼☼

Angie was thankful for the Saturday reprieve. Carter had no therapy and no treatments. In fact, he was at a point where he didn't have to be monitored daily anymore. Between her and Gail and Levi, they were able to check all his vitals and make sure all was as it should be. She felt terribly sorry for him though. He had once been such a happy and pleasant child, but after all he had been through with this situation, he was now cranky and distrustful of everyone. He never knew anymore if even Angie or Michael were taking him to some chamber of pain and sickness when they approached him. It broke her heart to see her son so dismayed, but she knew this was ultimately the best thing for him.

Two photographers had been arrested for getting too close to the house, and Angie made sure she never ventured outside at all so there would be no more pictures to be had of any of them. She thought for sure the crowds would have thinned by now, but it actually seemed as though they were growing larger. Levi had to call the police each morning and afternoon when he left for work or arrived back home so they could get his car through peacefully. She tried desperately to find a bright spot in all of this, but her hope was sinking with each passing day. It seemed as though this period in time would never end.

On Sunday evening after everyone had watched a church service on television, including Levi and Gail, they lingered in the living room and talked about the sermon. Angie was surprised at how much Gail knew about some things with Scripture, and then how clueless she was about others. It was almost as if she had been raised in a church that went through the motions of being religious, but never focused on the excitement and joy of being a Christian.

"Mr. Doctor of Agriculture," Levi addressed Michael as Angie scooped Carter up in her arms for bed, "I think I've got a plant problem out back in the gardens. Could you walk out with me for a moment and take a look. You might have some suggestions."

Michael nodded and asked, "Those ferns around the pond?"

"Yep. Got any ideas?"

"I noticed those the other morning," Michael admitted as he arose with a stretch. "Let's go check it out."

Angie offered Michael a sympathetic smile as she motioned Cassie toward the stairs. She knew Michael wouldn't enjoy being alone with Levi, and she wouldn't enjoy putting the kids to bed alone as Cassie had donned a very stubborn attitude about life in general lately. She watched as he shuffled out the door behind Levi and prayed a silent prayer that God would boost his confidence a little as they discussed plants—a safe subject for Michael.

When Cassie started whimpering about having to sleep in the strange bed in the strange house with the strange people who didn't love God's *stuff*, Carter began to whine also. She gently shuffled Carter to one side of her body and then motioned for Cassie to climb up the stairs. They were both so tired and out of sorts that any type of reasoning would have been useless. They needed something familiar, something soothing. She rolled her eyes as she decided to do something she hadn't done in a long time—sing them to sleep. But rather than attempt an old, forgotten lullaby, she softly began to sing hymns in the Padawin language. She closed her eyes and imagined her and Michael sitting at the front of the big pavilion in Podakind leading music with their guitars. She could see the smiling faces of the people as they sang along, lifting their hands, closing their eyes, even a few dancing on occasion as they felt moved. She felt her own smile begin to grow as Cassie started to hum softly with her.

Within a few minutes, Carter dropped off to sleep, and Cassie's head had slumped on top of the growing baby in Angie's tummy. She did her best to get Carter down gently, and then managed to get Cassie to wobble over to her own bed. She tucked her in and kissed the top of her head as she brushed the long strands of hair out of her face.

"Mommy?" Cassie asked faintly.

"What is it, sweetie?"

"When can we go home?"

She sighed before answering. She really didn't know. "When the time is right, I suppose."

Cassie opened her eyes for a moment and gave her a brief glare as she whispered, "That means you don't know, doesn't it?"

"That's exactly what it means," she confessed as she ran her finger down the side of the sleepy face.

"Thought so," Cassie resigned as she rolled over and tucked her fists beneath her chin.

As Angie left the little bedroom and moved toward the French doors and the balcony in the game room, the baby gave a strong kick.

"Well, hello," she said with a start as she put her hand on her stomach. "You've been rather quiet lately. Didn't think you were getting enough attention? I suppose it's getting really crowded in there now. If you could just hold off for a couple of more weeks, it would be most appreciated."

The baby responded with another hard zing, and she nearly laughed out loud. She opened the large doors and breathed in the cool, fresh air as she ran her fingers through her long, presently stringy, hair. She heard voices in the garden and realized Michael and Levi must still be discussing the plants. She had left the lights off in the big room, so the men probably had no idea she was out on the balcony. She moved toward the railing and leaned slightly upon it as she strained her ears to hear how the conversation was going.

"It might work," she heard Michael say with a doubtful tone. "If it were me, I'd pull them up and start over … use something different this time. Analyze your soil too."

"Well … as a last resort. I'll try the treatments first. I'm not inundated with a whole lot of time at the moment. Landscaping won't fit into my agenda too easily." Levi knelt down and fumbled with the leaves of the ferns.

"Do you really like living like that?" Michael asked him much to Angie's shock. He was never forward or direct.

"Like what?"

"No time … no freedom to … well, I don't know … to plant flowers … to live."

"I suppose. This is what I've always wanted—a nice house in a nice neighborhood, a wife … gardens … a stable practice. What else is there?"

Michael stuck his hands in his pockets and gave a slight shrug like Angie had seen him do many times before. "I live in a concrete block house connected to a little clinic. It's nothing like any of this," he motioned to all of Levi's property. "And I don't even own it." He shuffled his feet slightly. "But I can come and go as I please. And when I walk in, there's these two adorable kids scrambling to my arms and this incredible woman … all literally infecting me with life." He paused a moment, and then added, "I wouldn't trade places with you for anything in the whole world."

Levi nodded as he used his shoe to move a few pebbles from the sidewalk. "Different strokes for different folks, I suppose."

"I suppose." There was a bit more silence. "Why do you think that is? How can one man strive so hard for certain things he believes will bring him fulfillment, while another has no desire for them at all?"

"Beats me, 'cause I'll be frank with you, man, I don't know how you do it. Living out there with just the basic necessities … no luxuries."

"Ah," Michael said as he held up a finger. "Therein may be the difference."

"Luxuries?"

"My kids … Angie … my freedom? *Those* are my luxuries. If I had to live without them, I could—I've done it before, but I wouldn't want to even dream of trying."

They moved slowly back toward the house, both silent and thoughtful for a short while. Then Levi commented, "I guess that's why Angie was so attracted to you. She always kind of had that mentality too. The rest of us would talk about our future practices and all the dreams and plans we had when we finally finished training, but Angie was unbending in her ideals." He gave a snide laugh. "If only I had known."

Michael stopped. "Known what?"

"Known that it was *that* kind of man she was looking for."

"Would you have changed … even for her? Would that have made *you* happy? To have had Angie, but," and again Michael motioned to all the surroundings, "but … none of *this*?"

Levi looked around as though he were seriously considering Michael's question. Angie leaned further on the railing to make sure she caught his answer. She still couldn't believe Michael was being so frank and forward with him.

"Good question," he finally responded. "I don't honestly know. Back then, I thought Angie was the most incredible woman I'd ever met. The first thing that strikes a person about her is her unbelievable beauty. I mean … it's matchless. But then you get to know her. Behind those lips and those eyes there's this vivacious, overflowing being that just … well … takes your breath away. And the more you're around her, the more you want to stay with her."

Levi looked back toward the moon again. "I don't know, Michael. I don't know if I could've traded all this to have had Angie. This was all I ever wanted … until I met her. But she didn't supersede all this—I just wanted *this* and *her* … both together."

Michael nodded in understanding. "You should see her in Padawin. She literally breathes life into that place. The people there think she's an angel … someone literally sent to them by God to heal not only their hurts, but their hearts as well. And as for me … she gave me life as much as she did our own children. But over there … it's like *she's* fulfilled and whole. She just floats through life unhurried, happy, full of laughter and love."

"She belongs there."

"Yes, she does."

"And," Angie could tell Levi was hesitating, "she belongs with you."

Michael pulled his head back in surprise.

"I hate to admit it," Levi continued, "but she does. I only knew Angie as a student, a learner. She was very idealistic and headstrong in her training. But to see her as a mother … man, what a transformation. And as a wife? I never imagined seeing her look at anyone the way she looks at you. It's almost as if you and that island brought out the true woman she was meant to be." He paused and looked over at Michael. "I wouldn't have done that for her." He shook his head. "I would've made her trade all that … for all *this*. And *this* would've never made her happy."

"So what about Gail? She seems to fit your mold perfectly. She likes the busyness, the money, the luxuries … all the same as you. Does that provide the glue you both need for a strong marriage?"

Levi laughed a little bit at this question. "There's not a whole lot of glue anywhere right now."

"Why not?"

"Jealousy. She's having a hard time feeling *secure* with Angie in the house."

"That would be your fault, wouldn't it?" Michael said bluntly. Angie couldn't believe this conversation.

"I suppose … but she knew all about Angie before we married. How was I to know that the missionary woman of my dreams would show up at my office with a son needing exactly my field of expertise?"

"That's not the point—you married *her*; maybe it's time you changed your dreams."

Levi laughed sarcastically. "That's easy for you to say. You're sleeping with *my* dream every night … in *my* house."

"Like I said, you need to change your dreams."

Angie took a deep breath. Michael was for the most part declaring Angie off limits to Levi, but at the same time encouraging him to consider a second look at Gail. Where did this daring confidence come from?

"Just like that, huh?" Levi asked him. "Just decide that one woman was wrong and the other is right and move on from there."

Michael reached up and rubbed his scraggly hair. "I had an incredibly miserable life. You probably didn't know that."

Levi shook his head.

"And like you, I had dreams. But I learned early on that people can't make or break my dreams. If my dreams depended on others, then I would have to live my life in great disappointment. Instead, I gave my life to meet the needs of others—that was my dream. And then one day, when I had no idea what was happening, this woman … this unbelievable woman … suddenly stepped up beside me and began to do the same thing."

"Angie … meeting the needs of others … pretty good description."

"And that's what happened between us," Michael tried to make him understand. "I had no idea there could be anyone out there like that … anyone who could just step into my life and work right along with me as if our goals were all one … united somehow. And what I'm trying to say here is … I guess … that in a lot of ways, you and Gail are there … just like Angie and I were. When it comes right down to it, you two really want the same things. The problem, however, is that you won't let go of something that was never possible in the first place."

Levi pursed his lips and folded his arms.

"Let me ask you something," Michael persisted. "What if something had … *developed* … between you and Angie back then? What if this is where you had brought her? What if this was the life you gave her? Wasn't that your dream? Isn't that how you imagined it? Even now … isn't that how you imagine it … even with Angie?"

Levi looked around at his gardens, at his house, at his life. "I suppose … yeah … I suppose I do."

Michael put his hands back in his pockets and shuffled his feet again. "And you think this would've made her happy?"

He made no comments. He just continued to stare at his belongings.

Michael went further. "When you come right down to it, happiness with somebody else isn't ownership; it's sharing. Wouldn't you agree?"

He gave a deep sigh, but still wouldn't respond.

"And it's not just sharing *stuff*, like you and Gail—it's sharing life, plans, hopes, fears. I don't know exactly why you two married, but whatever the reasons, even if they're weak, you can change. You can build something together … build your own dreams."

Levi rolled his tired head back and forth and gave a big yawn. "Why are we having this discussion? Are you telling me that I've overstepped some boundaries or something with your wife? Is this some type of ultimatum?"

Michael shook his head. "I know you don't believe in the bigger picture … that God did all of this for a reason."

Levi, slightly exasperated now, said, "Are you trying to tell me you believe God gave your kid cancer just so we could all be a part of this little reunion?"

"I'm saying that God has a way of engineering things to get our attention. Maybe God thought it was time to remind you that having it all may not be the answer to your biggest needs."

"And what about you? What about Angie? What about little Carter? You think this all-loving God just decided out of the blue to put you through this so I could somehow *see the light*?"

Michael walked up to Levi and put a hand on his shoulder, a very rare thing for him to do—make physical contact. "If through all of this you somehow begin to question your past thoughts about God, then I think my all-loving God just demonstrated the depths to which He's willing to go to prove His love for *you*."

"But why Angie?" Levi wanted to know. "Why not some other person's kid … some heathen … or whatever?"

Michael removed his hand and simply said, "Because nobody else really mattered enough to you, did they?"

Levi turned his back on Michael and looked back up to the sky. Michael would have stayed longer, but he felt it was time to leave and let the man think through some things on his own. Besides, with all the lights from the city and the gardens, there was very little to see in the night sky. His heart longed for the clear view of the stars in Padawin, the uncluttered and natural landscapes, and the freedom of life that awaited them there. But right now, he simply longed for Angie more than anything.

When he walked into the game room upstairs, his wish was immediately granted. She greeted him in the dark with a warm embrace and a passionate kiss.

"Hello, my knight in shining armor," she whispered in his ear.

"Hello … and wow. I would have come up sooner if I had known this was waiting for me."

"It wouldn't have been waiting had you come up sooner. I overheard your conversation with Levi."

He put his head down in embarrassment.

"Don't be shy about it," she said quickly. "It was wonderful to hear you talk to him like that. He's always been so cocky and self-assured. And what you said about Gail … all that's true too. He always treated girls like they were the lucky ones … not the special ones … all of them except me … and I was never one of *his* girls."

"He seems so bent on insisting he has everything he wants," Michael tried to sort out, "but at the same time that somehow life is empty without you. He doesn't get it that no *thing* or *person* will ever make him truly happy."

"Well," she kissed him again, "he certainly will never have me. You've already stepped into that position, and done a fine job with it, I might add."

He pulled her closer. "I don't deserve you. I don't know how I …"

She wouldn't let him finish. She kissed him again and put an end to any more conversation for a while.

Fifty-Two

On Monday morning Billy struggled with the crutches more than anything he could ever remember in his life. He had been in the wheelchair until yesterday when Dr. Crandall had presented him with his new mode of getting around. At first he was thrilled because this meant more independence from Sam. But after a few turns around the inside of the house, he quickly realized this was going to be no picnic. His left shoulder was still extremely sore, and having his left leg in a brace from his ankle to his hip made getting around almost impossible.

"It's gonna be hard," Crandall had told him. "It'll probably be worse before it gets better, but you need to start using that left arm again. For awhile, even though it'll be really awkward, try to put as much of your weight on the right arm. Eventually, you'll get your strength back in the left."

Thanks, Billy mumbled to himself as he tried to open the door to his classroom. *And when I get my strength back, I'll give you a nice one-two punch for moving in so fast on Sam … while I'm right there in the house with her.* He closed his eyes and sighed. *Don't do this, Billy. You want Sam with him. It's time for her to move on with someone who can really care for her.*

"Need some help?"

He didn't have to turn around. He knew it was Sam's familiar, sweet voice, always helpful, always thinking of ways to assist him.

"Unfortunately … yes," he breathed out in exasperation. "I'm beginning to wonder if I'll ever be able to be on my own again."

She patted his back as he shoved open the door to the science class. "If you need me, send a student down. Don't try to be Superman … okay?"

"Batman," he replied without smiling.

"What?"

"Superman was always sort of clueless," he explained with no emotion or facial expression. "He wasn't from our world. Batman was truly ingenious and tough … he was driven to it."

"Okay, Batman," he could tell she was trying not to laugh, "since we've left the bat-chair at home and you are forced to rely on the bat-crutches, if a need should arise before we return to the bat-cave, send one of your batty students down to fetch me." She started to leave, but turned back to ask, "What does that make me? Am I Alfred or Robin?"

He shook his head and finally smiled. Why did she always have to be so darned cute? "Neither," he told her. "You're Catwoman."

"Oooo," she slurred seductively. "I'll work on my purr today." As she left the room, she peeked back in and gave a low, "Meow."

By lunchtime he was miserable. He knew Sam would have some Tylenol, so he headed down to her room before dragging his aching leg and throbbing arm to the teacher's lounge. Her door was open, and he heard her voice before ever reaching the room. He peered inside prior to walking in not wanting to interrupt whatever was taking place. She and Paulo were bent over a book as she tried to explain some major concept of Algebra II. This was no problem, so Billy walked on in.

"Mr. Marcum," Paulo noticed him first. "I wish this Algebra made as much sense as Biology. This is gonna be the death of my high school career if I can't learn to make sense of it."

Billy smiled at his accent. Paulo had learned to speak English in the South, and though his native accent had faded somewhat, he used Southern diphthongs and pronunciations with many of his words.

"That's why I teach Science. But if anyone can possibly get math into your head, it would be Ms. Marcum."

Paulo shook his head doubtfully. "She is good, but I don't know if anyone is *that* good. I don't even know *why* anyone has to learn Algebra. Is there actually a real job out there, other than a math teacher, that would require you knowing how to do this stuff?"

He thought for a moment. "I think astronauts have to know Algebra."

Paulo shook his head, took out an imaginary notebook, and then pretended to mark something off. "I will take *astronaut* off of my wish list for things to be."

Sam laughed and patted his arm. "Don't write it off yet, Paulo. I'm telling you—all this makes perfect sense. You're just baffled for the moment. Go through the steps with me again and then we'll see if we can't work through a few more problems."

Billy leaned on his right crutch as he motioned for Sam's attention. "Before you get too deep in the Algebraic world again, I was wondering if you had a Tylenol."

"Sure," she smiled. "In my purse."

☼☼☼

As Hal and Lisa pulled into Dockrey on Wednesday afternoon, he gave a confident smile. "Welcome home."

"I certainly hope so," she mumbled. "I'm really tired of moving around."

"I have a good feeling about this place. The people are fairly gullible …"

"Nice," she interrupted him sternly. "Please call the people nice … not gullible. It scares me. It makes me think you're here to manipulate, not to fit in."

He shook his head as he followed the scrawled directions from Mrs. Alice Vordeman and turned left onto a country highway. "I do not *fit* in nor do I manipulate. I do what needs to be done." He glanced back down at the directions. "This sheet says Highway Nineteen, but this looks like a desolate country road. Why would anybody call this a highway?"

"It's not *desolate*—it's *quaint*. You'd better relearn some of your adjectives, Hal, or you're gonna offend people right and left."

He wasn't listening. "Would you call this a highway? A highway has four lanes, speaking of which, I haven't seen in 30 miles."

"This is Dockrey," she blustered. "It's not Birmingham! This is what a highway looks like in the Deep South in a small town in the middle of nowhere. Did you not pay attention when we were here before?"

"I just assumed … oh, never mind!" He was getting perturbed about it all. "Let's hope we can find Alice Vordeman's house easily. I can barely read the woman's handwriting. My dad used to call penmanship like that *chicken-scratch*. I now understand exactly what he meant. No wonder she's looking for someone to mow her field … she probably can't do it in an orderly fashion."

Lisa let out a small laugh. "I can't wait to see you on a tractor! That ought to be …"

He shushed her immediately. "I told you, I have no intention of getting on a tractor or mowing her field."

"And how do you plan to get out of that? We're getting a house rent free because you agreed to mow her field."

He shook his head at her ignorance. "Do you really think a good church lady is gonna put the new *Dr. Bridges* out on his tail? Eventually you'll begin to learn how people are, Lisa. Until then, just keep your mouth shut and follow me."

Mrs. Alice Vordeman was one lively, spunky lady. As they drove up into the yard of the newly built house where she now lived, she practically ran out the door and waved them down. She was probably in her late seventies, a widow, and very active in the church. Her kids and grandkids all lived in nice houses built around her property also, and Hal was about to inherit the *really* old home place. He grimaced for a moment as he thought about the fact that with all these relatives and nice houses, why was he about to move into the run-downed one, and why was he expected to mow the field. Couldn't one of her mooching relatives do that?

"Alice," he said smoothly as he stepped out of the car and reached out his hand.

Of course, Alice threw her arms around his neck and gave him a strangling hug. He wanted to push her away, but reminded himself quickly that he was in the South and this was how they did things down here. He managed one hand behind her back with a pitiful pat.

"I've got the key right here," she said enthusiastically as she dangled it from a small chain that also held some kind of reptilian paw. "Let me jump on the golf cart and you can follow me down there."

After saying that, she ran over to Lisa and strangled her also in a hug. Then she trotted down the cart painted exactly like the General Lee from the *Dukes of Hazard*, complete with the rebel flag, and she motioned big for them to follow. Hal and Lisa got back into their car and followed the General Lee down the gravel road about a half mile. When they turned into the drive and made it past the large hickories and oaks lining the way, the house practically loomed before them. It was very, very large, and very, very old.

"I didn't remember it being quite so … ancient," Hal mumbled as he stared at the looming edifice.

Alice hopped off the cart and motioned them on up the driveway and into the carport. "Welcome home!" she said cheerfully as she dangled the key and the claw again. "I hope this place will hold as many fond memories for you as it does for me."

"Me too," Hal said under his breath as he reached for the key, trying desperately to avoid the reptile appendage in the process. But just as he touched the key, Miss Alice let out a fierce growl. He drew back his hand.

"Just kidding," she grinned. "I want the keychain back. I got it on a trip to Florida several years back before my husband died. It's a 'gator claw." She held it up again and made it do clawing motions. "Cute, isn't it? I actually bought it for one of my grandsons who happened to be a Florida Gator fan at the time. But when we got back, he apparently had seen the error of his ways and turned his affections toward Auburn. Thank goodness! If he'd have said he was an Alabama fan … well … in this family that's just about as bad as being a Gator fan." Alice gave a hearty laugh and started clawing with the alligator paw again. "But I liked the claw after all, and I've always kept it on this spare key chain."

Hal nodded awkwardly as he waited for her to remove the key, and then took it graciously when she had finished.

Lisa stepped up and said, "We really want to thank you for doing this for us. We were concerned that …"

But Hal cut in, "We were concerned we might have a hard time getting a decent place to live with the salary cut I'm taking by coming here."

Alice waved off the notion. "Oh, don't worry about that. People here in Dockrey will take real good care of you. We love our preachers, and we treat them like royalty."

Obviously Mrs. Alice Vordeman didn't get the point of his statement. "Treating us like royalty won't pay the bills, however. We're gonna have to make some adjustments with this kind of pay cut."

"Then it's a good thing you're so sure the Lord called you here," she said as she motioned him to unlock the door from the carport. "You seemed awful intent on it. I was worried you might think the sixty-forty vote was an insult, but it just rolled right off your back the committee said."

Lisa looked over at Hal with a sarcastic smile as if to say, *I'd like to see you get out of that one.*

"Everything's in good working order," Alice told them as they walked in through the laundry room and into the kitchen. "The plugs and vents for the washer and dryer are all ready to be hooked up. The fridge is practically brand new. My old one gave out about six months before I moved into the new house. I bought this one thinking I'd take it over, but it didn't go with my new kitchen. Everything over there is stainless steel, so I thought I'd just leave it here."

Thank goodness, Hal thought, *because everything else in here is obviously as old as Moses.*

"And this stove is top of the line," Alice said proudly. "It might be a little old, but it cooks way better than that new-fangled thing I bought for my house. And if the electricity goes out, just use a lighter or a match and it lights up right away."

"Lights up?" Lisa asked in confusion.

"Gas," Alice explained. "It's a gas stove."

"Oh," Lisa said a bit unsure. "I don't recall ever using a gas stove."

"Goodness, honey," Alice exclaimed. "Once you do, you'll never want to go back to electricity again!"

Alice showed them how to automatically light the stove, but Lisa was still a little fearful of having an open flame driven by gas in her residence.

By the end of the tour, Lisa was highly impressed with the house. As old as it looked on the outside, it was obvious that it had been kept clean, painted, and in good repair on the inside.

"I thought about putting up some vinyl siding on the outside," Alice told them. "That stuff is so pretty, and it looks just like wood, you know? But I figured a military man like yourself could probably do it with no trouble at all. If you ever feel like doing any improvements, just let me know. I'll buy all the supplies and you can provide all the labor." She looked at them both and smiled big again. "This ought to be great fun! Just pretend you're one of the kids and treat us all like family."

She went on about a few more things, talking and pointing non-stop. And as she prepared to finally leave, she looked back at Hal and said, "Whenever you're ready to learn how to use the tractor, just drop by. It won't take any time for you to figure it out."

"As soon as I can," Hal lied. "It'll probably take all my time for a little bit to get settled in at the church and here at the house. But when I can get to the tractor and the field, I'll be sure to run by."

"Just remember," she smiled again, "it's your rent. Not a bad deal for such a comfortable house!"

And with that, Mrs. Alice Vordeman left like a whirlwind on the General Lee.

Hal walked slowly around the house, generally shaking his head and squinting at certain areas. "This place is a dump."

"Actually," Lisa countered him, "it's really rather nice. It's been well kept. And I love the hardwood floors."

He stomped a foot on the floor. "I wonder how old they are. We've never lived in anything this old before."

"We've never lived in anything this *big* before. It'll be fun decorating it. We can go with a country motif. I could make these cute little country bunnies to put all around the house. I have a pattern for them."

He looked at her with slight disgust and merely said, "Yee haw."

☼☼☼

Wednesday night dinner at the church was its typical hustle and bustle. As the years went by, it got bigger and bigger. And the more they expanded their children's and youth ministries, the bigger the number on Wednesdays. Jonathan smiled in pure delight at the sound of chaos with so many voices. This was *fellowship*. This was why they did this. Many were coming straight from work, and this gave them a great opportunity to wind down before going into Bible Study or into a department of children or teenagers where they would work and minister. It gave sustenance to the body, but at the same time provided a great sense of sustenance for the soul.

When Hal Bridges and his wife—Jonathan couldn't remember her name for the life of him—walked into the room, a sort of hush began to fall. It was definitely an awkward moment. Jonathan quickly moved over to Hal and reached out his hand.

"Welcome, Hal, to First Baptist of Dockrey," he said loudly so that all could hear and feel as though they were a part of the welcome.

Nancy Beth Tate immediately stood to her feet and began to clap. Slowly the clapping caught on, and after about ten seconds, most were applauding. Hal nodded humbly and waved to the crowd. In Jonathan's mind the man still appeared more like a politician than a minister.

"Let's go grab a plate and have a seat," he told the couple as he directed them to the serving line.

Jonathan and Barbara were both thankful that many people came up and greeted Hal during the dinner, because conversation had been very strained and unnatural. Barbara had never had trouble talking to anyone before. In fact, they had often joked that her spiritual gift was *gab*. But Hal and Lisa Bridges were two guarded individuals, and almost every response they gave was monosyllabic. When the bell buzzed for supper to break and for everyone to head to their places for the night, Barbara actually found herself perspiring.

"I see what you mean," she said to Jonathan as he grabbed his Bible before heading to the new members' class he taught. "They're hard to talk to."

He looked at her and shook his head in dismay. "Those are words I never thought I would hear coming from your mouth."

"Me either," she replied mournfully.

Fifty-Three

"You should have gone to the play-off game," Billy told Sam on Friday evening as they sat in her living room after Jeremy had left for the hospital. "This may be the last game of the season, and you'll have missed it."

She yawned as she flipped through a few more channels. "I'm just too tired. Besides, you'll be out of here in a couple of weeks, and I'll be all alone again. I might as well take advantage of a warm room with some warm company."

He glanced at the fire in the hearth and found himself mesmerized by the leaping flames. "You won't be completely alone. Dr. Crandall manages to make daily visits now. I've never seen a doctor so dedicated to his work before."

She blushed as she pulled off her glasses to rub the top of her nose.

"So," he wondered hesitantly, "… um … do you like him?"

She glanced over at him and put her glasses back on. "Maybe."

"Maybe? I don't think he's thinking *maybe*. I think the man is smitten with you."

"Yeah, well, it's sort of bad timing, you know?"

"Bad timing? Why? Because it's November … or something?"

She gave him a repugnant look. "No … because my ex-husband happens to be living with me at the moment. It doesn't make for the best situation to begin a new … relationship … or whatever it is."

"I think *relationship* is definitely where he's heading."

"Well, I'm not there … yet."

She pointed the remote back toward the television, but he wasn't satisfied with the answer. "Why? Is it me that's holding you back? I don't want to be the cause of something like that. You need to move forward with your life, Sam. I'll be out of here in two weeks."

"Yeah," she sighed as she turned off the TV. "I know."

"Like I said, I don't need to hold you back."

She looked at him again, but this time sadness prevailed. "You're not holding me back. I'm holding me back. You're just the good excuse I can use for the moment."

"But why? Crandall's a good guy. I mean, he's a doctor! What more could you want?"

She shook her head. "It's hard for you to understand. You don't have this … this monster of a past lurking inside you all the time. Billy, you're it … you're the only one I've ever actually told all that happened to me.

Even Ms. Allen didn't know it all, and what she knew she had to guess … and I just nodded … never actually said, *Yep, they all raped me repeatedly for the past few years.*"

"Ms. Allen … the math teacher who took you in back in high school?" He tried to ignore the description of her treatment. It literally felt like his blood could boil whenever she mentioned it.

Sam nodded. "I told you because … well … because I loved you … and somehow I trusted you."

His face grew hot with guilt and he put his head down. She immediately got up and went over to him.

"Don't feel like that," she insisted as she put an arm around his shoulder. "No matter how things ended up, it was sort of a healing for me. And even now, just having you back in my life, even though it's temporary, it's given me a security. It's like you're the only person in the world that I can let my walls down with because you're the only person who really knows everything there is to know about me." She reached up and gently caressed his hair. "I don't think I can ever do this again … let it all out." She bit her lip. "You're it for me where all that's concerned."

He stared at her and nearly trembled at her touch, but he couldn't speak. This isn't where he had wanted the conversation to go.

She smiled at him, removed her hand, and went on to explain, "But somehow this is enough. And when I realize how close we came to getting back together, it also lets me know that I can't just give my heart away to every nice guy who shows up at my doorstep to check on my ex-husband's physical condition."

"Jeremy Crandall is a *really* nice guy, though."

Sam furled her brows together. "If I didn't know better, I'd think you were trying to push something between the two of us."

"I just want to see you happy … really happy … settled down … and having all your dreams come true."

She smiled slightly and shook her head. "I don't really have any dreams, Billy. People like me can't afford to dream."

"Then maybe what I really want for you is to be able to dream for a change … dream, plan, and move toward something that leads to *happily ever after.* You deserve that, Sam."

She sighed and leaned back against the couch. "Even after all we've been through, it's still so easy to be with you. Even when I think about that woman you married after me … it still doesn't seem to change what we … have … or are … together. And I know the reason I feel that way is because, regardless of whether I *love* you or could ever *trust* you again, you're still the only one who really knows me."

All he wanted to do at that moment was pull her to him and swear that he would take care of her and always be there for her, but he knew his track record. And he also knew that even when he had tried to do right, Kirstie came sailing in at Blue Bayou and totally messed up everything. If he really loved Sam, and if he really wanted the best for her, he needed to push her toward someone else who was caring, gentle, and understanding. And as far as he knew, he had never met anyone that fit that bill more than Dr. Jeremy Crandall.

✿✿✿

"You better cover up with the blanket one more time," Andie yelled down toward Annie who was lying on the floor of the big Mason conversion van. "Here comes that high pick-up again. If that guy leans out the window one more time to try and see in, I may just swerve over and knock him to the road."

"Andie!" Barbara yelled in terror. "You would not!"

"Here he comes," Andie called out. "Are you covered?"

Annie didn't answer because she couldn't have been heard anyway, but Cindy Sarkos replied, "She's covered—not a spot of her showing anywhere."

This had to be the most ridiculous thing they had ever done. They all desperately wanted to see Angie in Memphis, but with all the crowds at the Wright house and outside Annie's property, it was impossible to ever leave without being followed. When Barbara and Cindy rode with Andie through the guarded gate at the Williams' place, the paparazzi went wild. They knew something was afoot. The plan was to get Annie under a blanket on the floor of Andie's van while still in the garage, and then when the photographers had given up, she would simply sit in a seat. These guys weren't buying the decoy this time. They all knew the van had to be headed to Memphis, and with a stop at Annie's, they also knew that she had to be in the vehicle somewhere. They were almost to Memphis, and the only thing Annie could possibly hope for was a few minutes now and then when she could remove the blanket from her face and breathe fresh air.

As the truck pulled up next to them on the highway, sure enough, a guy with a camera actually hung out the window as they both sped down the highway doing seventy miles per hour. Barbara nearly panicked as she watched Andie grip the wheel tighter.

"Don't you dare!" Barbara warned. "Get a hold of that temper, and pretend that everything is just fine."

"Just fine?" Andie bellowed back at her. "There's a moron hanging out the window trying to look inside my van!"

"And once we get to Dr. Taylor's house, that moron will be forced to stay outside the walls, and we can all visit peacefully with Angie … if we make it there in one piece." Barbara took a deep breath after the last statement.

Andie tried to regain her composure and pretend all was well, but she did feel sorry for Annie. It was bad enough that the photographers couldn't actually see Annie—had she sat in a seat visible to them all, a crash would have been likely. Was it really worth it for her to see Angie under these conditions? If it had been she, it was doubtful. But then, Annie and Angie had always been extremely close.

When they finally arrived at Levi's house, they couldn't believe the people outside the walls. It was just as bad as the Wright and William homes. Security had been alerted that they were coming, and a detailed description of the van, along with a license plate number had been given. After a brief few moments, they motioned the van through. There was no gate, so people immediately began to try and follow the van inside. A few stuns with tasers eventually got the crowd under control. Andie knew the garage was waiting for them, so she pulled inside, and the door began to close immediately.

"You can get up now," Andie said with sheer frustration. "I think we're actually safe."

Annie threw off the blanket and climbed up into a seat. "That has to be one of the worst experiences I've ever had."

"It could have been worse," Cindy commented. "You could have been car sick … or pregnant."

"Thanks," she grumbled back.

"Well, I can tell you one thing," Andie said shaking her head. "I'm NEVER doing that again—period."

Suddenly Angie sprang through the door, and everyone forgot about the misery of the trip. She threw her hands up in delight and squealed for joy, but the four ladies in the van just stared in shock.

"Oh … my … gosh," Andie drew out. "There's no way that baby's not coming soon."

"It's huge!" Cindy cried. "It doesn't even look normal … is it possible to be that big and not … not..."

"Explode?" Annie finished the question.

"Exactly," Cindy agreed.

Barbara quickly slid out from the van and ran to embrace her daughter. "How are you doing, sweetie?"

Angie held her tightly and cried for just a minute. "I'm okay … I really am. It's just a little emotional having you all here."

Barbara broke the hug and looked down at the massive baby. "When exactly are you due?"

"December 20th," Angie said doubtfully. "I hope it waits."

Andie snickered from behind her. "Fat chance. You'll probably go into labor today with all the excitement we'll bring."

As Annie appeared from the side door of the van, Angie began to giggle. Annie's face was red from the heat, and her hair was completely disheveled.

"Don't laugh," Annie said sternly. "I guarantee this will be the last trip

I make to Memphis to see you. You're gonna have to come home before this happens again."

"Rough trip?" Angie asked.

"Don't even get us started," Andie warned her.

"What is the deal with this?" Annie asked Angie as she reached down to touch her swollen tummy.

"Big, isn't it?" Angie grinned.

"What does the doctor say?" Annie wanted to know. "Are you raising a 20-pounder in there?"

Angie sort of blushed and put her head down as she told them, "I haven't seen a doctor yet."

"What?" they all yelled in unison.

"You've got to be kidding?" Annie was dumbfounded. "Why? What are you waiting for?"

Angie sighed and shook her head. "I just haven't gotten around to it. Levi knows someone who's willing to see me, but it's been so hard with Carter. He's struggling through these treatments, still not actually walking, although he's standing from time to time as he leans against something, and he's just plain … whiney. I figure that until this one," she rubbed her belly, "actually makes its appearance, I'd rather not worry about it."

All the other women exchanged tense glances, but Angie hurried them on into the house. As they went inside, they were immediately greeted by Cassie, Michael and Carter. The ladies were surprised at how sickly Carter looked.

"Wow," Cindy said stunned. "He's so … pale. Mother looked terrible too while she was taking her treatments."

"He has his good days and bad days," Angie explained. "Today he knows he has no physical therapy and no IV's. He's feeling good."

Levi and Gail had left early that morning for a weekend getaway. It had been months since they had done anything on their own, and with the family coming to visit Angie, they thought this would be a good time to leave the Collins alone. As soon as the ladies sat down in the posh living area, the catching up began. Michael wondered how it was possible for all those women to talk at the same time and understand what was being said. He didn't try to enter the conversation. Instead, he tried to pick out which one would be of most interest to him and tune in. It wasn't working. He ended up watching Carter most of the time who was also fascinated by all the chit chat.

"So," Angie continued, "is the new minister there yet?"

At this question, all yakking ceased.

"What?" Angie wondered.

"He came in Wednesday," Barbara began. "He had on his tie and coat looking like some advertisement in a business magazine."

Angie smiled. "I bet he felt out of place."

"Not Hal Bridges," Andie told her. "He has this way of making everyone else feel out of place."

Cindy laughed and slapped her leg. "That's exactly what I thought! When he stared at us like he did, I thought he was looking at us in disdain for such casual attire at church."

"He'd better get used to it," Andie sighed. "Daddy isn't going back to the Dark Ages for Wednesdays. In fact, if he didn't think it would offend half the church, he'd opt out of the suit and tie on Sundays too."

Annie chuckled, "As if he puts a lot of effort into his Sunday appearance. Moms, why don't you at least pull his tie all the way up before he leaves?"

"I do! When he walks out of that house, his tie is straight, his collar is buttoned, and believe it or not, his hair is combed."

Annie added, "What little there is of it."

Everyone laughed except Barbara. "You'd better not let him hear you say that. He's so self-conscious about it anyway."

"Daddy?" Angie exclaimed. "I never thought he was self-conscious about anything!"

"Fading hair is at the top of the list," Barbara warned. "And I'm serious; you girls had better not say a word about it to him."

Lunch was wonderful, and when it was time to leave, everyone was wishing they had a few more hours together. Angie walked them out the door while Michael notified security they were about to leave.

"So," Annie asked Angie mournfully, "are you sure there's no way you can make it for Thanksgiving on Thursday?"

Angie shook her head. "I'm just hoping we can be there for Christmas. Carter has another scan week after next. That should let us know if everything is working as it should."

Barbara reached over and gave Angie another big hug. "I'm so proud to see him standing a little. By Christmas, he'll be walking on his own."

Angie was getting teary again. "I hope so." She looked at all three ladies one at a time. "Thank you for coming. I needed this boost really bad."

"And you're gonna need another one when the baby comes," Barbara reminded her. "And I mean what I said—when you go into labor, give me a call. I'll be here as soon as I can, and I'll stay until you leave. You have enough pressure on you right now as it is. I'll be nanny, grandmaw, housemaid, and nurse all rolled into one."

Angie hugged her again and then stood back as the ladies entered the van and left. This had to be the hardest time in her life, but this visit was a huge boost for her morale. It was exactly what she needed—to reconnect with what was most important in life, the people she loved.

Fifty-Four

Jonathan wondered if there was any point in continuing the sermon Sunday morning. All eyes were on Hal Bridges—and why not? He had remained on the platform throughout the entire service with a pen in one hand and a bright green highlighter in the other. All morning he made huge marks in his bulletin with the highlighter and then followed by scribbling notes. It wasn't the highlighting or the scribbling that bothered Jonathan so much as it was the complete distraction it caused the congregation. If it had been anyone else sitting on the platform other than the new minister on his very first Sunday, he would have told the man to go sit in a pew and settle down … in front of the whole church. But he had enough propriety to pretend as if all was fine and well. That was *this* Sunday. This would not happen again next week. But Hal did it during the second morning service too, and the distraction was just as bad.

During discipleship time on Sunday afternoon before the evening worship, Jonathan suggested to Hal that he might want to sit in the congregation because the evening services were more *loose.*

"Really?" Hal replied with a knowing smile. "Having trouble sharing the platform, pastor?"

Jonathan was taken aback by the comment. "Not at all. But even during preaching Kyle has never sat on the platform. In fact, I can't think of any former staff member who has ever done that."

"Well, let me explain this as clearly as I can," Hal began in a patronizing manner. "You preach, and Kyle flaps his arms during the song part. All my work is done behind the scenes, so to speak. These people are paying me to do a job. They need to see me up front … just like you and Kyle … only I'm not preaching or singing. So, I think it best if you bend a little on this point and let me stay up there during the entire service. It will make people feel better about having me on board."

"Perhaps," Jonathan responded dubiously. "But all I think it'll do is make you look silly."

Hal's eyebrows flew up.

"We won't have half the people here tonight you saw this morning," he clarified. "There will be tons of empty pews out there, and you'll be sitting up there all alone—no choir or anything behind you."

Hal gave his condescending smile again. "Oh, I think I'll be just fine … silly or not. Don't worry, pastor, I'm not out to steal your thunder. I just want people to know I'm here."

☼☼☼

On Monday morning, the church office cranked up slowly as usual. Cindy and Kyle came in first at eight o'clock with Devin and Denay in tow. It was too cold for them to be outside, so Kyle let them play quietly with a few special toys in his office. There was also a television with a DVD player to occupy them later on if they began to get restless. Then a few minutes before nine, Hal came in. He was again in a suit and tie and he carried a polished briefcase.

"Good morning, Mrs. Sarkos," he said politely. "I assume the phone is connected to my office?"

"Yes … sir," she said uncomfortably. This all seemed so formal. "They did it Friday afternoon after you left."

"Hmm, I wish I could have been here to test it out," he said disturbed. "If it doesn't work properly, it could be disastrous seeing as I'm so far away and disconnected from the rest of you in here. Clear and immediate communication is vital if we're to keep things running smoothly."

"Things always run smoothly here," she said as she forced an enthusiastic smile.

"So it would appear. Where do we have staff meeting? Is it the pastor's office? Or I suppose it's Kyle's massive office. I imagine you could have a church business meeting in there if you had to."

Forcing another smile she asked, "Staff meeting?"

"Yes, where all the staff get together to discuss changes and needs for the church. I assume you have a weekly staff meeting."

Forget the smile. "Well, we usually sit around in here and have a cup of coffee and talk about how great Sunday was. Is that what you mean?"

He only stared at her.

"I guess not," she sighed.

"Would you buzz the pastor and tell him I'm ready to get started?" He said glancing at his watch. "This first one will probably run quite long."

"Pastor Jon's not here yet."

The expression on Hal's face was almost one of anger. "You're kidding? It's nine o'clock! Don't his office hours begin at nine?"

"Well, yeah, but …" Cindy was cut off by a big growl and huge screams suddenly bursting from Kyle's office.

Hal turned his head toward the door and whispered, "What the …?"

She now felt heat rising in her cheeks. "It's just Kyle … and the twins."

Hal looked back at her austerely. "Twins? Do they come here with you until time for daycare?"

Oh, boy. "They … uh … don't go to daycare."

"Then where do they go?"

She tried to smile again, but she had the sinking feeling he would not like her answer. "They just stay here … with us. Normally they play on the playground." She pointed out the big window which had a perfect view of the area. "But it's starting to get cold now, so we just bring them inside here."

His expression was downright scary. He didn't try to hide his disdain for the arrangement. "This isn't good," he said sternly. "This is a place of business, not a babysitting service."

He had succeeded in making her angry. "And we conduct business just fine here … always have … for five years."

Just then Jonathan burst through the door with his typical Monday morning excitement. "Greetings one and all! How do you like that weather out there?"

Hal looked down at his watch and then back up at Jonathan as he said, "Are you typically late for work, or has the weather got you off schedule for the moment?"

Jonathan's expression never changed as he smiled and replied, "Well, if you call nine-o-two *typically late*, then I guess I am. I always leave in time to get here at nine, but after talking with the security guys at the gate, and then applauding God for the incredible beauty of His creation, there are many days when it's nine-o-two, or even later, before I come bursting in."

Hal was not amused. "Where do we have staff meeting?"

"Right here," Jonathan said with a bounce. "Is the coffee ready, Cindy? I only had one cup at home this morning, and this chilly weather has got me hankering for another."

Hal stepped forward. "I don't think this is the appropriate place for a staff meeting. We have much to discuss, and just *hanging out* here casually will be a deterrent to getting things done."

"It's always worked before," Jonathan responded lightly. "Cindy? The coffee?"

She only nodded and pointed toward the small kitchen area.

"Pastor," Hal continued as he followed Jonathan toward the coffee maker, "I'm serious. I'd rather not have a staff meeting in here. Besides, the things we discuss are not meant for the secretary's ears. These are ministerial matters."

Cindy almost exploded, but this was the point where Jonathan stopped trying to play the nice game.

"Hal," Jonathan said with a bit of a bite, "we're all staff here. Cindy is as much a part of the ministry of this church as Kyle and myself. She goes above and beyond the call of duty in more areas than I could say, and it's all for the sake of ministry. If there are *ministerial* issues that need to be discussed, we most assuredly can talk of them in her presence … and even welcome her advice."

She wanted to stand and applaud, but instead she watched the different colors of red and pale that Hal turned. As he gritted his jaw, he moved away from Jonathan and picked up his briefcase.

"No wonder this church needs an administrator," he said with obvious forced control. "It's a miracle you've managed to maintain what you have. No staff planning, bringing kids to work, the pastor coming in whenever he feels like it." He paused, reached up to straighten his tie, and then practically commanded, "Staff meeting will be at nine-thirty in *my* office." He started for the door, and then turned back to add, "… *without* children or secretaries."

When he left, Jonathan looked over at Cindy. "Nice guy, wouldn't you say?"

"I can't believe what just happened. What's going on here, Pastor Jon?"

He took a long swallow of his coffee and smiled gently as he said, "Welcome the rod, Cindy. Welcome the rod."

At nine thirty-three, Jonathan and Kyle entered Hal's office. Hal glanced down at his watch and then back up at the two men.

"Is this the habit around here?" he asked them both. "Do we never get anywhere on time?"

"Uh … sorry," Kyle said meekly. "I was on the phone with one of my choir members. Her little girl is having a tonsillectomy today, and I wanted to let her know that I'd be praying for her and would try to make it over to the house tonight. She was a little distraught and wondered if we could pray right then, so I …"

"Mr. Sarkos," Hal said firmly, "I don't need a minute-by-minute rundown of your morning. Do what you have to do, but if a meeting is scheduled, do what you must to get here on time."

Jonathan jumped on that. "Even if it means disrupting ministry—the very reason we're here? We're to stop ministering in order to be at your meetings right on the dot?"

Hal narrowed his eyes and stared scathingly at Jonathan. "You can twist it however you want, pastor. But the bottom line is this—if we're going to run this church in a way that effectively ministers to all in this community, it will need to be done with order and punctuality. A nine-thirty meeting means nine-thirty, not nine-thirty-three." No one said anything, so Hal assumed his point was made. "Now, if you gentlemen will take your seats."

Jonathan and Kyle looked at each other sideways and then sat. Hal shuffled through several papers as though there were many things that needed to be addressed, and he was struggling with where to start.

Finally, he spoke up and asked, "Do either of you have anything you want to discuss before I get started."

Kyle looked at Jonathan and shrugged. Jonathan looked at Hal, took another long drink of his coffee and said, "I guess not. Shoot."

Hal raised an eyebrow. "I shall." He placed the paper in front of him on the desk, folded his hands on top and began. "I don't know where to start, gentlemen. When I saw all the statistics on this church, I assumed I was walking into a wonderful situation."

"And most would agree with you there," Jonathan remarked.

Hal cleared his throat. "However, what I've seen leads me to believe that you guys are just running on blind luck."

"What?" Kyle nearly laughed. "What on earth is so wrong with this church? Why do you think it's grown so much these past few years? You think that's blind luck? What about the work of the Holy Spirit?"

Hal stared him down as if to say *how dare you interrupt my speech?* "Is that what you call yourselves? The Holy Spirit? No wonder there's so much trouble brewing at the door."

"Hold on right there," Jonathan stopped him.

"No," Hal said firmly as he raised his voice. "I gave you the opportunity to speak before we started. You'll listen to what I have to say, and then you can make your inane excuses when I've finished."

Jonathan was absolutely stunned. If he could have imagined the worst scenario possible with the coming of a new staff member, it wouldn't have come close to what was happening right now.

"First, let me say," Hal continued with a commanding tone, "I was utterly embarrassed yesterday morning. I had noticed it the Sunday I visited in view of a call, but I just assumed it was a bad day."

Hal stood and ran his hand along one of the shelves, pulling back his finger to see a thick buildup of dust. He shook his head. "I would think a pastor who has been here for so long would have a little more respect for his congregation than to show up like you did and stand before them."

Jonathan had no idea what he was talking about, so he merely took another sip of his coffee and waited for the bomb.

"You obviously know how to comb you hair," Hal said sarcastically, "because it appears to be neatly in place at the moment. When you stand before a congregation, you're to look like a professional, not the absent-minded professor."

Kyle shook his head and mumbled, "You've gotta be kidding."

"You find that hard to swallow, *darling* Mr. Sarkos?" Hal bit back.

"What?" Kyle snapped. "Darling?"

"Oh, yes," Hal smiled almost wickedly. "Good looking guy, beautiful wife, perfect children, oozing with talent … you're just coasting through this place without a care in the world. A bigger church would have tossed you out before you could blink."

That hit Kyle like a two-by-four because a bigger church had asked him to leave. Of course, it had nothing to do with his talent, but was because his first wife had left him. But the very idea sent chills through him.

"Hang on a minute," Jonathan said with amusement. "I thought I was the one under fire at the moment. Why don't you finish crucifying me first, then you can get your nails for Kyle."

Hal shook his head. "There you go with that God-complex again. I'm beginning to see the picture more clearly now."

"So I have bad hair on Sunday mornings," Jonathan reminded him. "What else?"

"Your tie was halfway down your chest and your top button was open. And as if that wasn't bad enough, you had these silly cartoon characters dancing all over your tie. I kept waiting for you to push a button and watch the whole thing start flashing."

Jonathan smiled. "That would be my Fourth of July tie. It lights up with red, white and blue sparkles that look like fireworks."

It was obvious Kyle was suppressing a laugh.

"It's immature, idiotic, and unprofessional," Hal insisted.

"It was a gift from my grandchildren for Father's Day. The congregation knows that. When I wear it, it honors them and expresses the love and respect I have for them. The only person bothered by that tie yesterday morning was *you*."

Hal shook his head and replied, "I doubt that. I think the better statement would be that the only person bothered by that tie with the nerve to say anything about it was me."

"Okay, so you don't like my taste in ties … what's next?"

"It's your whole appearance, pastor. You look as far from anything professional as I've ever seen enter a pulpit."

"Maybe that's because I don't consider myself a *professional.* I consider myself a sinner like the rest of them, no better, no worse, completely redeemed by the incredible mercy and grace of God."

Hal shook his head as he gave a slight chuckle. "You really know how to turn everything back to your twisted idea of religion, don't you?"

"I only know that this church has had no problem with my hair, my tie, or my top button for thirty years," Jonathan said firmly. "What else do you have in your bag of tricks there?"

Hal now pulled out the bulletin on which he had highlighted many things and scribbled down notes. "Mr. Sarkos, are you the second pastor here or the music director?"

"Minister of Youth and Worship," Kyle replied cautiously.

"Yes … and do you find it necessary to preach your own little sermons before each song?"

"What?" Kyle was confused.

"In a *real* church … excuse me … a *professional* church … the song leader announces the song, and then leads the congregation in singing. Do you think we're all idiots and can't understand the words of the song enough to be able to sing and comprehend what we're singing at the same time?"

Kyle was noticeably blown away. He couldn't answer.

"Before you start in on the church's *darling*," Jonathan said smugly, "you'd better think twice. This church loves Kyle, and it's because of his worship-leading style."

"Once again," Hal shook his head, "so *people* have said. *People* who are irked tend to keep quiet."

"Baloney," Jonathan laughed. "Not in this church … in fact … not in any church I've ever served. My experience is that when people are dissatisfied, they make it downright clear in as many ways possible. It's the ones who think all is going well that never say anything."

"And so, once again, we play *the pastor with his head in the sand* game." Hal now removed his jacket. "You guys have got to understand something here—I'm not against you."

"Wow," Jonathan grinned. "Thanks for clearing that up. I think I might have been getting the wrong idea."

Hal looked back at him with contempt. "You're going to have to learn that this church hired me to make it run smoothly. That means when I see a problem, I fully intend to address it and see it eliminated. That's what I'm paid to do. This is no longer a little country church in the back woods of the typical Alabama small town. This is a growing, up and coming church, that needs some direction to help it take the next step. If you guys don't get in shape, this church is going to run off and leave you."

Jonathan stood this time and looked at Hal without a hint of amusement. "And follow who? You? Is that your plan, Hal?"

"I'm not suggesting anything other than some minor changes that need to be made in order for this church to continue moving forward."

"In that case, thank you for your concern, but no thanks," Jonathan said as he turned to leave the office.

"I'm not finished here!" Hal demanded. "There are other things we need to discuss."

"I'm finished," Jonathan told him. "And as far as staff meetings go, this isn't one. And when you have complaints about another staff member, you're to bring them to me … not humiliate them or demean them in front of someone."

"Then I suppose saying that the secretary running her own little personal daycare center in the church office would be inappropriate to discuss in front of the Youth Minister."

Kyle stood this time. "What?"

Jonathan turned back to Hal and said, "You're overstepping your boundaries here. Those kids have never once caused any disruption in the office. If they had, or if I had seen a problem, we would have dealt with it."

"Yes, I see how well you deal with obvious problems."

Jonathan motioned Kyle to the door. "Let's go, Kyle. This meeting is over."

Fifty-Five

Thanksgiving at Stephen and Annie's house should have been cancelled. With Kyle and Cindy there along with Jonathan and Barbara, the main discussion was Hal Bridges. Monday was only the tip of the iceberg. When Hal found out that Wednesday services had been cancelled because of the holidays, he blew up. How could a pastor cancel church so frivolously when there were people desperately in need of ministry at that time? Holidays didn't stop the need to minister the Gospel. It didn't matter to Hal that this was something that was done every year, not only at Thanksgiving, but during Christmas and Independence Day holidays too. Jonathan sighed as he imagined how he was going to handle those when they arrived.

Billy and Sam had come for the holidays. At first Billy denied the invitation, but when he realized Angie would still be in Memphis, he figured it would be good for Sam to get out and be around other happy people for a change. He didn't realize the doom and gloom that would be prevalent that Thursday. None of it seemed to faze Sam though. She was in the presence of Stephen and Annie Williams. She tried not to be star struck, but she was in the house of two of the world's greatest entertainers ever. And for some reason, little Ellie seemed to be taken with her. She would sit in her lap, hold her hand and walk around the pool, show her the bedroom and the playroom, and then wore Sam's glasses for most of the day. Sam stumbled a bit here and there, to which Annie would always insist that Ellie return the glasses, but Sam would try and say it was no big deal.

"Yeah, until you bust open your pretty head on the edge of one of our cabinets," Annie reasoned. "Then we have to take you to the ER … and that means trying to keep the paparazzi off your tail and out of the measly little hospital we have here because they just know that Stephen or I am hiding in the car somewhere."

When they got back to Kyle and Cindy's, Sam helped get Kylla in bed and even told her a bedtime story. When she came back down stairs, Billy was sprawled out on the couch in the living room watching a football game. She knew he had to be in pain after such a long day.

"Need anything?" she asked before sitting down.

"Naw, I'm fine. But thanks."

She knew Kyle and Cindy would be down in a moment and would probably want to stretch out and relax after getting the twins in bed, so rather than sit in the love seat or recliner, she gently lifted Billy's legs and propped them up in her lap.

"Is that okay?" she asked. "I know your leg is still sore."

"No problem. If you want, you can even give me a foot rub."

"That won't hurt?"

"Are you kidding?"

She smiled and shrugged, gently beginning to knead his feet.

"So, how was your day playing super-nanny?" he inquired teasingly.

She smiled.

"You and Ellie had a little thing going, then Kylla joined in after awhile. Cindy said you were telling her an unusual version of the Three Bears upstairs." He gave her a mischievous look. "Are we sensing the old biological clock beginning to tick there?"

She shook her head. "I'm not out to be a mommy by any means."

"Why not? You're a great teacher—a mom would just be another step forward … more of the same, only a little more intense."

"There are several obstacles to that path—a husband, for one. I'd rather not do it alone."

"I bet Dr. Crandall wouldn't mind playing daddy at all."

She glanced down at him, and he raised his eyebrows up and down.

"Would you lay off Dr. Crandall? I'm gonna have to think through all that … later … when my life settles back down again."

"You mean when I'm gone," he clarified.

"Partly that. There's a lot to consider with all of it, and you just made one of the points. If things … develop … between me and Jeremy, then somewhere down the road we'd probably have to make it permanent."

"You'd get married." He wanted to put it into plain wording to help her face it more realistically.

"Something like that. And then there would be other things to work through. Would I have to move? Sell my house? Give up my job?"

"Live in the lap of luxury with a great doctor."

"Give him kids …"

"Give him kids?" Billy laughed. "You make it sound like some miserable compulsion. Wouldn't you want to have kids?"

"I don't know," she confessed with some exasperated hesitancy. "Right now I just can't picture myself being a mom with Jeremy! It doesn't seem … *natural* … or something."

He gave her a puzzled look. "Could you picture yourself having kids with someone else?"

"I don't know. That's what I keep trying to tell you about him. He's definitely a great guy, an incredible catch, but I'm not fishing at the moment. Because of that, nothing sounds appealing."

"Are you still hung up on Dr. Wiggington?"

"Keith … the chemistry professor?"

"All the girls mooned over him big time."

"All the girls can have him," she rolled her eyes. "He was way too pristine for me. Conversation with him was downright uncomfortable. I would rather be tortured than sit through another dinner alone with him."

"Okay, so that means you don't want to have kids with Dr. Wiggington."

"I don't want to have kids with anybody, okay? End of discussion?"

"If you say so," he mused suspiciously. "But after watching you today, I think you have this huge maternal thing going on, and you're just afraid to admit it."

She dropped his left leg slightly, just enough to make him wince and cry out as she got up from the couch. "Thank you, Dr. Freud."

"Where are you going?" he asked as she started to leave the room.

"Outside for a breath of fresh air."

When Cindy and Kyle finally came down, she asked where Sam had gone. When Billy told her, she grabbed a light jacket and headed for the deck. She hadn't had a chance to be alone with her all day. Maybe she could get the opportunity to talk with her about some serious issues.

"Hey," she said gently as she joined her on the steps of the deck.

"It's nice out here, isn't it?" Sam said almost dreamily. "You can't see this many stars in Florence because of all the lights."

Cindy chuckled. "It's funny, because years ago I couldn't wait to leave this place and get to somewhere where the lights shone all night. And now, back here again almost seems like heaven."

"I can imagine. No bustling traffic, the sounds of nature … it's almost awesome in its simplicity."

Cindy agreed silently. "Didn't you grow up in a small town too?"

She grunted. "I wouldn't even call it a town. It was more like a community. In fact, we never even said its name. When people would ask where we were from, we'd just say *Toombs County*. It was a spot in the road, and I lived in a hole in the wall."

Cindy nodded as she pulled the jacket around her tightly. "I feel like I might need to apologize for the day."

"Why? For what?"

"We were all … well …" how did Cindy explain? "This new guy has really stirred the waters. I don't want you to think this is what church and Christianity are like. There's something wrong here right now, and we aren't sure how to handle it. We're having to talk through all of this and try to see God's perspective. It's hard."

Sam reached over and took her hand. "There are only two things I really know about Christianity—you and Mr. C. That's it. Mr. C. has always been this kind and caring soul. From the first day I stepped into that school until Tuesday afternoon when I left for the holidays, he's been this haven for me. He cares for me in ways I've never known before … almost like he is a surrogate father. And then there's you."

"Me?"

"I knew you well before. And to see the change in you … it's a miracle. And not only that, but you're so happy. How could anyone have gone from being this shallow, self-centered, materialistic girl to the incredible woman you are now? It took something bigger than anything I've ever known."

Cindy could almost cry if she would let herself. She squeezed Sam's hand. "Believe me, it was something big. Only God could've done this. And even when He started, I didn't want to give in. I tried so hard to hang on to all the things I thought gave my life meaning. I would never have believed that getting married, having kids, and settling down would be the greatest things I could do. But here I am." She leaned her head onto Sam's shoulder. "And I somehow want everyone I care about to know God in the same way."

Sam leaned her head onto Cindy's. "Then just keep on being who you are. Your life says way more than some minister who can't seem to get past himself."

Cindy gave a small chuckle. That pretty much summed up Hal Bridges in a nutshell. "So, back to the lighter side of life, why on earth are you putting up with my brother? I can't believe you're letting him live with you through all of this."

"What was I supposed to do? Make him go another whole semester after he's come so far. You know Billy as well as I do. It would be just like him to give up on the whole thing if he lost this semester."

"I know … but don't you think you've gone above and beyond the call of duty here?"

"I know what you're thinking," Sam assured her. "There's nothing going on between us. In fact, I'm sort of *seeing* the ER doctor that patched him up."

Cindy pulled back and looked at her in pure delight. "Sam, that's great! I didn't know that!"

"Well, it's not a big deal, and it's kind of awkward having Billy there all the time."

"Then kick him out!"

"No. I'm gonna get him through next week … his last week. When he's finished, all he has to do is write his final paper, take his orals, and he can move in with you for awhile."

Cindy shook her head. "You're an angel for all of this."

"No. I feel like it's a small way that I can honor your mom. She and your dad did so much for me. When I heard they were gone, it floored me. But when Billy explained how he promised her he would finish his degree … and then his accident … I felt like it was one final thing I could do … for her."

"Some promise," Cindy groaned. "If he would have kept his promise to never drink again, he wouldn't have had that wreck and you wouldn't have been forced to take him in and save his tail."

"Don't be so hard on him. He's trying to change too. But he doesn't have a Kyle there to move him on … or a mother."

Cindy put her arm around her and squeezed her shoulder. "But he's got you … only for the moment, I hope?"

"Only for the moment

☼☼☼

Jonathan stood in front of the mirror staring at himself on Sunday morning trying to decide exactly what to wear. There was really no middle ground. Either he wore what he always wore, a loud tie with an eventual unbuttoned shirt—or he went with Hal's *suggestion* and spiffed it up a bit. The real problem he was having, however, was what was the Christian thing to do? He knew Hal's intentions had nothing to do with the Lord, yet to ignore what had been said would be in direct defiance. Which was right?

He looked back down at the bed where he had laid out two different ties. This had never been a problem before with pastoring. In fact, this was one of the easier decisions. You wear a suit, you pick out a favorite tie you didn't wear last Sunday, and you go to church. When you get hot, sweaty, or just plain claustrophobic, you unbutton the top button and then go for it. But what did he do now?

"Jonathan Wright!" Barbara exclaimed as she walked into the room to put on her shoes. "What on earth are you doing? You're not even dressed yet!"

"I'm not sure what I should do." He pointed at the two ties. "I don't want to be outright rebellious about this whole thing, but I don't want to give in either. This is really pressuring me."

She smiled reassuringly as she looked at the ties. "Let's see, we have a plain blue tie, no design, almost identical to the one that *Dr.* Bridges wore last Sunday, and we have a tie that's red, white and blue with sparkling fireworks all over it." She looked back up at him with confidence. "I think the choice is obvious."

He raised an eyebrow. "Please share this information with me."

She picked up a tie and handed it to him as she said, "Try to keep your collar buttoned this morning, but make sure everyone knows that this patriotic attire is in honor of Pearl Harbor Day on the seventh … especially when you press the little thing in the back that makes the fireworks light up."

He took the tie and smiled. He liked the way she thought.

☼☼☼

Sam enjoyed hearing Jonathan Wright preach. She had only been to a few church services in her life. Ms. Allen had made her go when she had moved in with her during her senior year in high school, but Sam had been so self-conscious with all of the uppity girls there that all she did was try to survive until church was finished. The preacher back in Georgia had also talked over her head. She never understood any point he made. But this man was really different. He made the Bible seem alive and relevant for right now, and he always used personal illustrations to explain what he was saying. He was also funny. She had never seen a pastor with a flashing tie before. When he told the congregation he was honoring the memory of Pearl Harbor, the congregation literally applauded and came to their feet as he brought his tie to life. Of course, he turned it off when everyone settled back down in their pews, but she found herself smiling throughout the service as she would glance back at it.

The big distraction of the service, however, was the new minister on the platform. Every few minutes he would almost angrily take a green highlighter and mark through something on the bulletin and then add a few notes on the side. He became almost as amusing as the pastor. She wondered what he could possibly be doing and why he was so intent on it. She figured Pastor Jon would make him stop next week. It was hard to concentrate on the service at times with the man sitting there in an obvious stew.

☼☼☼

"Staff meeting, my office, nine-thirty sharp," Hal said as he peeked inside the door of the main office at nine-fifteen.

"Not today," Jonathan called back to him. "I'm heading to Tupelo. Three members in the hospital there … one having surgery this afternoon."

Hal looked highly offended. "Can it not wait until after staff meeting?"

"Pee wee football," Jonathan offered in explanation.

"What?"

"Arly has a pee wee football game at five-thirty. This is big stuff to him. I wouldn't miss it for the world."

"Who is Arly?"

"My grandson," Jonathan smiled proudly.

Hal was obviously perturbed. "Do you not feel that taking care of church issues should be a priority over football?"

"Arly's a church member. I guess that makes pee wee football an official church issue."

Hal grunted something undecipherable and then looked over at Kyle. "I guess it'll just be me and you this morning, then."

Jonathan immediately stepped up. "No," he said sternly.

"Excuse me?" Hal replied this time, clearly miffed.

"A staff meeting means *all* the staff," Jonathan clarified. "There will be no meetings where you share your little highlighted notes if we all can't be there."

Hal straightened himself, looking taller than usual, and said, "I don't believe that's your call, pastor. As church administrator, it's my duty to speak with …"

"Okay, Hal," Jonathan cut him off. "I'm not sure where the whole *church administrator* thing came in. You've talked about that from the beginning. You're the *Educational Director*," Jonathan enunciated the words deliberately. "Your job is to analyze the classes and structure of the programs in the church, and then arrange them in such a way where we are able to efficiently minister to the spiritual and emotional needs of the congregation. I would call you the *Minister of Education*, but you have yet to produce a license or certificate of ordination."

"What?" Hal questioned angrily as he face began to turn red. "Are you doubting my credentials?"

"All I know is that you've got all those diplomas gracing the wall in your office," Jonathan began, "looking very impressive and professional. But I see nothing indicating that you're actually a *minister*. In fact, I never remember reading in your resume' anything about when all that occurred. Perhaps in our next staff meeting we should hear about your *call* to the ministry and ordination. I would very much like to understand how that came about."

"Me too," Kyle piped in.

Hal looked at both of them as though he could shoot daggers through their hearts. In fact, Jonathan thought for a moment the man might lose control. Instead, he took a deep breath, straightened his plain-looking tie, and picked up his briefcase.

"I take it staff meeting will be postponed until tomorrow then?" he finally replied.

"Why not?" Jonathan grinned at the victorious feeling of finally having one upped Dr. Bridges.

Fifty-Six

Angie couldn't believe she was actually sweating as snow began to fall. Cassie stood on the balcony and squealed in delight at the first thing she had found in America that was wonderful. Michael held Carter, listless and pale, in his arms and showed the children how to catch snowflakes on their tongues. Cassie was going to town, but Carter didn't seem interested.

"Yowl!" Angie cried out as the baby gave a hard kick.

Cassie, Carter and Michael all looked inside immediately. She smiled back.

"It's okay," she assured. "Eat your snow. I think this one wants to join in the fun."

She lay down on the bed and tried to find a comfortable position. It probably wouldn't matter. As active as this baby had been lately, and as big as it was getting, it was unlikely she could fall asleep. She laid her head on one pillow, placed another between her knees, and then propped her back up with still another. Her back had been killing her lately. She knew she weighed a lot more than with either Carter or Cassie, but then she hadn't carried either of them full term. It couldn't be just regular weight gain because her appetite had been off significantly the past couple of weeks. This was going to be one huge baby.

Michael brought the kids back inside and coaxed Cassie into watching a movie for a little bit until he could get Carter down for a nap.

"Lay him next to me," Angie offered. "He can sleep here, and you and Cassie can go outside and …"

"No." Michael was firm in his denial. "You need some real rest. I'll take Carter to his bed, and Cassie can wait until I'm free for the snow."

Cassie gave a small pout, but she didn't argue the point. Carter looked so ill it was hard for his sister to not be sympathetic. Angie didn't argue either. She was so tired and miserable that the idea of merely closing her eyes seemed blissful.

Without putting Carter down, Michael managed to get Cassie settled on the couch with a DVD. Angie opened her eyes off and on during the process, but within no time she fell asleep.

Michael gave Cassie a gentle kiss on the forehead, and then he smiled as he heard Angie's breathing become deep. He walked softly to the bedroom where he placed Carter on his bed and lied down beside him.

"How you doing, buddy?" he asked as he cradled him in his arm.

Carter said nothing. He just snuggled deeper into his daddy's side. The treatments were taking their toll on him. He had refused to stand at all today when the physical therapist had tried to work with him, and there was no reward they could promise to make him try otherwise.

"Daddy, you wike heaven?" Carter asked out of the blue.

"What?" The question took Michael by surprise.

"It nice," Carter stated more than asked.

"Why do you want to know about heaven?" They had talked about heaven on and off, but had never really dwelt on it. One of the tribesmen had died several months back, and Michael had tried to explain to the children about heaven and how wonderful it is to leave our planet to go.

"I seen it," Carter whispered in near awe, his eyes big, his face smiling for the first time in days.

"What?" Michael asked again. What was his little son talking about? "When did you see heaven, Carter?"

"While I sleeping," he said as the smile began to fade. "I walk there." He relaxed on Michael's arm and closed his eyes. "I don't hurt there."

Suddenly Michael began to feel alarmed. "When was this, buddy? When did you see heaven?"

Carter opened his hollow eyes and looked up at Michael. "While I sleeping," he repeated.

"Last night?" Michael continued questioning him, but realized Carter had no concept of *last night*. "Was it after you went to bed … uh … last night." He knew he didn't understand. "After we had pizza?"

Carter smiled slightly. "I was sleeping, and then I walk. And he so nice. He hold me … and I don't hurt." Carter looked up at Michael. His eyes seemed so lifeless. "I stay, Daddy. I don't wike hurt."

"Stay?" Michael could feel tears begin to draw forth inside his whole body. "Stay here?"

Carter just shook his head and closed his eyes as he nestled again on Michael's arm. "Heaven."

Michael gently pulled him closer as a knot began to form in his stomach.

✡✡✡

Stephen reached into his pocket to pull out the vibrating phone. He flipped it open and glanced at the number. It wasn't one he recognized. It was almost impossible for anyone to get this number without having some major close contact to him, so he went ahead and answered the call.

"May I help you?" he answered in a very business-like manner just in case it was a call he didn't want.

"Yes, I'm trying to reach Stephen Williams. He had called me a little while back using this number. I thought I might reach him here."

Stephen was curious, but still didn't want to give out too much information. The paparazzi were going wild at the moment over the goldmine they had found with Angie in Memphis.

"May I ask who's calling?" Stephen decided to say.

"Sure. Ben Brenner."

Stephen's heart skipped a beat at the name. "Ben Brenner?"

"Yes, Stephen had called me, and I have to admit being really curious as to what it was about."

He gave a nervous laugh and finally confessed, "Well, this is Stephen. Sorry about the run-a-round, but I didn't recognize your number."

"Stephen! Great! I was beginning to think maybe my receptionist had given me a wrong number."

"I really apologize for that." He was humiliated now.

"Don't worry about it. I understand completely. I was thrilled to hear you called. I've actually been thinking about you quite a bit lately."

"Really?" That surprised Stephen. "About what?"

"I've been offered quite a daunting responsibility … so daunting, in fact, that I've seriously considered having someone work with me. Your name keeps popping up in my mind."

"You're kidding?" He was honored beyond words. "I had no idea you would consider working with me as a partner."

"And why not? You're one of the most talented young men in the world today. Who better to help me out with a three-movie saga that'll be the biggest fantasy production the world has ever seen?"

"Wo," He was taken back. "What is it? What's the movie?"

"No, no, no, dear Stephen," Ben teased him. "This is so much more than a movie. This will be a world-wide, magnanimous event, my boy. And I'm offering you the opportunity to be a part of it."

"Wow," he replied in pure awe. "I don't know what to say." He was being totally honest. Annie had made it clear she didn't want him working with Ben Brenner. And hadn't he left show business to be a family man … to live a normal life? If he stepped into this project, the *retirement* thing would be off in a big way.

"You say *yes*," Ben told him. "You say that you realize the two of us together would be an unbeatable force in the music field. You say this has *Oscar* written all over it, and that it's a deal you just can't refuse."

"I wish it were as simple as that. I've got a family now. I've got everything I ever wanted, and I retired from the business so I could enjoy all this. I'm not sure how stepping back into it right away, only after a few months, would wash with all my plans."

There was a moment of silence, and then Ben asked him, "Are these actually your plans … or are they Annie's?"

He was slightly insulted. "They're *ours*," he confirmed. "I've done the music thing a long time. I've been ready for a break, but never had a good reason. I've got three now."

A little more silence ensued.

"You haven't done this all *that* long," Ben countered. "I've been at it a few more years than you, and I can tell you, you never want to lose your edge—you never want to disappear. People will forget you just as quickly as they embraced you."

"Tell that to Annie. Her sister's in Memphis with a seriously sick kid and the people are flocking around her like vultures because they can't get to Annie here." He sighed. "The business can be good, but it's got some harrowing side effects."

"I won't disagree with you there. However, you have to make some compromising choices in life. You have a gift, Stephen, and I don't think it's quite right for you to just hole it up in the wall because you're ready to run from photographers. I'm not asking you to go on tour and put your face in music stores and magazines around the country. In fact, a lot of what you would do could be done in your own home."

"Really?" This was starting to sound promising.

"Sure. Scoring a movie is considerably different than promoting an album. The movie *is* the promotion."

"But if we're to collaborate, we'd have to be together. I don't envision you sliding over to Alabama to work here in my log cabin with me."

"You have a log cabin?" Ben laughed. "You really did go rural, didn't you?"

"It's a *nice* log cabin." He felt he needed to defend himself. "Even you would be impressed with it."

"Well, you could just sit there in your nice log cabin, pull up an old log next to the piano if you like, and put some notes on paper that describe the scenes. Then, yes, I could fly down and sit on another old log, and we could work up some of the major themes together. Or … if you ever felt adventurous … you could fly out to LA, and we could do a little of our writing in a more civilized environment—and there's always Skype."

He thought for a moment. "I'm not sure. I hope you don't expect an immediate answer. I'll need to think through this and talk it over with Annie. This isn't exactly what we had in mind when we retired."

"Just remember: you are who you are … and who you are is one of the greatest musicians and composers on the planet. Don't throw it all away on love."

What did Ben Brenner know about love? He'd been married and divorced five times.

"Well, I can tell you this," Stephen spoke firmly, "I'd rather have love and nothing musically, than to be number one and not have Annie."

"Ah, but that's only because you've managed to have both. Had you only found love, but no fame, you'd be singing a different song, my boy."

☼☼☼

Billy sat on the couch at Sam's and graded his chemistry experiments while Sam worked on Trigonometry tests. He was a little proud of himself for how well the experiments had turned out this time. Apparently the students had finally understood that when he scheduled a lab, a lab would indeed take place. He glanced over at Sam for a moment. Her glasses had slid down her nose, and her ponytail was bobbing back and forth as she looked from one page to the other. If he could have one wish come true, it would be that this could go on forever. The truth was that all of this could have happened, *would* have happened, had he not walked out of their marriage years ago. Life would have been so much sweeter had he let her stay inside it.

"I can't believe this is my last week of school," he said as he laid the last of the experiment papers on the pile.

"You mean your last week on *this* side of school," Sam corrected him as she looked up. "The teaching end requires quite a bit of work itself."

"Not for me. I'm not gonna sit down like you and make up a brand new test each year for the material. I plan on using the same test year after year."

She grinned knowingly. "And it'll only take one year for your students to realize that. They'll start saving them, making copies of them, and then selling to the following year's students."

"You're kidding? A high-schooler would be that resourceful?"

"In a heartbeat. If you actually want them to learn, you have to be one step ahead of them and ready to stick to your guns."

"So the ogre thing never really stops?"

"In some ways. But it always has to be lurking down there somewhere … and the kids have to believe that."

Billy threw his hands up in mock exasperation. "Now you tell me!"

She giggled and went back to her Trig tests. He watched in admiration. She would always serve as an inspiration to him. If he ever got to a point where he wondered if it was all worth it, he would remember Sam and what she had to fight for and get through in order to be where she is today. His little tragedies were nothing compared to hers.

The typical rhythmic knock let them know Jeremy Crandall had arrived for his daily visit. He was later than usual. Normally they would have only been home ten to fifteen minutes when he showed up, but today it was five-thirty.

"Wonder boy is late," Billy smirked as she got up from the couch to answer the door.

"Don't let him hear you call him that," she scolded with a finger over her lips as she reached for the knob.

"Why? Isn't he Mr. Perfect? I was just calling it as I see it."

"No, you weren't."

She opened the door, and a beaming Dr. Crandall stood there with two bags in his hands.

"Are we all up for Chinese tonight?" he asked with a big grin as he held them up.

"What?" Billy yelled from the couch. "Sam's not cooking? I don't want it if she didn't slave over it."

"Sorry, Bill," Jeremy said as he came inside. "I guess you're not eating then. But if it makes you feel any better, the lady who sold it to me was sweating … so somebody slaved over it." He handed the bags to Sam and continued. "Did you guys know it's flurrying outside?"

"Snow?" she asked excitedly.

"Yep. And if it keeps it up, we might actually see some ground cover later this evening," Jeremy told her as he removed his coat and gloves.

"Maybe the roads will ice up and you won't be able to make it to the hospital," Sam suggested.

"Not like this, they won't," he mourned. "With my luck, they'll ice up overnight and the other guys won't be able to make it in tomorrow morning … so I'll end up filling their shifts instead."

Billy shook his head. "Don't be so pessimistic, Doc. There's always hope, isn't there?"

Jeremy followed Sam into the kitchen. In his mind there was no hope of anything until Billy Marcum moved out of her house. No matter how much he and Sam talked and shared, Billy was always somewhere near. It was about to drive him crazy. Sam swore things were over between them, Billy swore things were over between them, but to be around them together, you would have to believe something was still going on. There were too many sideways glances, too many winks, and too many knowing looks to just be tolerating each other's company.

"Isn't this your last week, Bill?" he asked as he began to put on a pot of coffee.

"Sure is," Billy said as he maneuvered himself up onto the crutches to join them in the kitchen. "Friday is my last day."

"I bet you're excited," Jeremy tried to sound hopeful.

"Kind of, but it's a bad time to be graduating with a teaching degree," he complained hobbling toward the counter. "No positions will be open until the school year is over. I get to be a substitute for the next five months."

"That should be a great learning experience," Jeremy laughed. "I remember substitutes really well. There was this one lady who used to sub back in high school. Her name was actually Mrs. Battly. You can imagine the fun we had with her."

Billy raised an eyebrow. "You're not being very encouraging here, Doc. I was hoping for something a little more positive."

Jeremy shook his head as he pressed the button on the coffeemaker. The only positive thing he could think of for the moment was that Billy Marcum would be out of here in four days.

☼☼☼

Angie made her second middle-of-the-night trip to the bathroom. Her back was killing her, and her bladder was about to explode. As much as she wanted this baby to wait until the due date, she was beginning to wonder if she could physically hold off that long. After relieving herself, she stopped by the kids' room to peek in on the present babies in her life. Cassie was sleeping peacefully, probably dreaming about all the snow playing she and her Daddy had done. Her purple bunny was snuggled up next to her cheek, and her hair fell softly across the pillow behind her. Angie glanced back to Carter and noticed that all his cover was off, so she tip-toed to his bed to replace the sheet and blanket. Her kids had never known cold before.

As she covered him up, she reached her hand to caress his forehead. She nearly screamed in panic. He was burning up and sweating profusely.

"Michael!" she yelled from the little room. "Michael! Get in here quickly! Something's wrong with Carter!"

Michael immediately jumped up from the bed and ran toward Angie's voice. He had been in a deep sleep.

"Angie!" he called out. "Are you all right? Is the baby coming?"

"It's Carter!" she yelled back as Michael made his way into the room. "He has a really high fever! Go get Levi! We've got to get him to the ER now!"

She leaned over to pick him up, but Michael stopped her immediately.

"No!" he screamed. This woke Cassie. "Let me get him!" he pleaded. "You don't need to pick him up, Angie." He could see the tears in her eyes. "I know you want to, honey, but you just can't right now. Go get some clothes on. I'll get Levi, and then I'll carry Carter."

She nodded as she wiped her eyes and left Carter so she could get dressed.

"Daddy?" Cassie asked sleepily. "Is Carter okay?"

He knew he should answer her, but the lump in his throat wouldn't let him. He touched her cheek and just shrugged his shoulders. He quickly turned and left the room, running down the stairs two and three at a time to get Levi. He knew it was going to be a hard night, starting with getting through all the photographers camped outside the gate.

Fifty-Seven

Angie and Michael tried to be patient as Levi and another doctor on call checked Carter. Cassie had fallen back asleep in the waiting area as she used her bunny for a pillow and a blanket Michael had grabbed when they had rushed from the house. He put his arm around Angie and pulled her close. He knew she was beyond miserable. Her back was hurting terribly, but she couldn't sit and relax. And then all the adrenaline pumping through her body was having a wild effect on the baby. It was kicking and squirming constantly. She was physically exhausted from too little sleep already. As she leaned her head into his shoulder, she began to sob again. He wished he could do something, but he was just as helpless as she.

"Just cry, honey," he whispered to her. "I'd rather you let it all out than not."

She drew her arms around him and held him tightly. He felt the baby kick against his stomach as she gave a brief cry from the movement.

"This one's a booger, isn't it?" he chuckled.

She nodded slightly. "This feeling of dread keeps washing over me again and again. Something serious is wrong, and all the worse case scenarios keep playing themselves over and over in my mind."

"I wish they'd tell us something," Michael confessed as he rubbed her back. "They've got to know this is killing us."

Just then Gail returned from the snack area with a carrier of drinks.

"Here you guys go," she said weakly as she placed the holder on the table. "Coffee for you, Michael, and juice for you, Angie."

"I would almost kill for a cup of coffee right now," Angie said as she wiped her tears with the back of her hand.

He chuckled. "Yeah, that's just what that baby needs at this moment—a hefty dose of caffeine."

"Have you heard anything?" Gail wondered as she picked up her own cup.

"Nothing," he replied. "I guess, like they say, no news is good news."

Gail nodded, but Angie didn't look convinced. The baby gave another strong kick, and she jerked again, spilling a little of her juice.

"Are you okay?" Gail asked quickly as she went for a napkin. "Do you think the baby's coming?"

"I should be so lucky," Angie moaned taking the napkin and wiping down the front of her shirt. "I'm not even having Braxton-Hicks yet with this one. All that praying we did that God wouldn't let it come too soon—it apparently worked."

"I'll say," Gail smiled. "I could swear you've grown beyond what's normal since you've been with us. You must have a line backer in there!"

"Feels like an elephant," Angie admitted as she tried to take a deep breath. "It keeps punching me in the ribs. And when it hits one side, all of sudden the other side starts in too. It's like a one-two attack."

"I change my vote," Gail said with a silly grin. "It's a boxer." She blew on her coffee, grinned bigger, and added, "I sure hope it's a boy if it's going into boxing."

The doors to the room finally opened, and Levi walked through with a major discouraging look.

"Bad news," Angie said as soon as she saw his face.

He tried to speak, but all he could do was shake his head back and forth. Michael bit his lip trying not to explode with emotion.

"What is it?" Angie insisted, suddenly in control of her emotions. "Just be plain about it, Levi."

He rubbed his eyes, and tears were actually beginning to form. "It looks like it might be Staph." Angie closed her eyes. "But I think it's even worse than that."

"Worse?" Gail was shocked.

He nodded. "I really think some kind of infection has gotten into the bone around where the surgery was conducted. If so, it's probably been brewing in there for some time."

"So what do we do?" Michael asked, totally confused about the prognosis. "I assume he has to stay here … in the hospital."

Angie nodded as she put her hand up to her mouth.

"We're giving him some major antibiotics right now," Levi explained. "This is … uh … it's a total shock."

"It's the worst thing that could have happened other than the cancer reappearing," Angie told him. "This could become very touch and go."

Levi cleared his throat. "I'm afraid it already is touch and go."

Angie looked up at him. "What?"

"I don't know how we missed it," Levi said weakly. "Carter just doesn't complain like other children. Had he not had the fever, we might have never known."

Angie finally collapsed into a chair and put her face in her hands. "*I* should have known," she groaned as she shook her head. "He was so pale and weak. He wouldn't do anything today with the therapist, and when they administered the treatment, he just sat there … no whimpering … no complaining. I called him my *big boy* and told him how proud I was of him."

Michael was still confused. "What are you all saying here?" he wanted to know. "How serious is this?"

Levi looked over at Gail and then down at Angie before answering. "It's dead serious—that's as blunt as I can be."

"You're saying he could die over this?" Michael now asked with great alarm. "He's just fine, he's making progress, he's standing, and now he could die? How did it happen?"

Levi shrugged and held out his arms as a tear began to roll down his face. Gail went to take his hand, but Levi jerked away from her and left the room to return to Carter. She just stood there in humiliation.

☼☼☼

"Is the pastor late again?" Hal asked annoyed as he walked into the main church office on Tuesday morning. Cindy just glared at him. "What?" he exclaimed defensively. "He's been late every single morning since I've been here!"

Kyle stepped in to respond. "He's in Memphis."

"Memphis!" Hal bellowed. "I made it clear we were to have staff meeting this morning."

Cindy spoke this time. "It's his grandson."

"Really? What … is there another pee-wee football game?" Hal slung his briefcase to the counter.

"Different grandson," Kyle said not masking his rage. "Angie, the missionary, her son had surgery for a tumor on his spine last month. They discovered last night he's developed a Staph infection and a bone infection at the site. It's very serious."

"And no one felt the need to call me and let me know I'd be in charge?"

"Not at four o'clock in the morning," Kyle spat back. "And seeing as you didn't even know Angie was home with a child recovering from surgery, I can't imagine why anyone would call you anyway."

Hal ran his finger down his mustache as if to smooth it. "Seeing as no one has ever filled me in on the pastor's family, missionaries or not, how was I to know?" He reached for his briefcase. "Then I guess it's you and me."

Kyle shook his head in disbelief. "You gotta be kidding?"

Hal stared at him severely. "Not in the least. In my office … nine-thirty."

"I won't be there," Kyle said firmly. "Jonathan said there were to be no staff meetings without him present."

"I'm in charge at the moment," Hal blasted back. "Because of that, we do as I say."

Kyle laughed. "I don't know exactly where you get your pecking order, but no one has ever laid out this *in charge* business you keep insisting upon." Kyle turned to his office and said clearly as he walked, "When Jonathan returns, we'll meet … until then, I don't plan to step foot into your den."

Cindy watched as Hal nearly exploded, grabbed his briefcase, and shot out of the office. She couldn't help but smile. She jumped up from her chair and made her way into Kyle's office. The twins were sitting on the floor watching a DVD, and Kyle was standing behind them shaking his head, all red-faced.

"Bravo," she whispered as she raised her hands to him and clapped softly.

He rolled his eyes and held out his arms in frustration as he walked over to her. "What is the deal with that man? It's getting to the point that I can't even be civil around him. It's like I've got to be on the defensive all the time."

"Believe me, I can relate. Come out to my desk with me. The only meeting that needs to take place this morning is prayer. We need to pray for Carter. People will start calling soon, and I need to be free to answer their questions." Just then the phone rang. "See? It's already starting."

She jogged back into the office and picked up the receiver on the antiquated machine.

"Good morning, First Baptist," she said cheerfully.

"Cindy … it's Jonathan."

"Pastor Jon! How's Carter."

Kyle, who had followed her out, now moved quickly beside her to hear Jonathan's answer.

"It's even worse than they thought." They could hear the deep emotion in his voice. "Not only does he have the Staph and the bone thing, they've now discovered he has two types of blood infections?"

"What?" Cindy replied in horror. "How did this happen?"

"No one's sure."

"How's Angie holding up?" she wanted to know.

"As good as can be expected, I suppose. She's very tired, and she's enormous with this pregnancy. As a doctor, I think she understands the reality of this better than any of us, but at least she's being allowed to be a part of the planning with his treatment. It's killing her, though, to have to wear a mask and gloves around him. She wants to touch him, feel him, and she wants him to be able to see her face."

"I can imagine." Cindy bit her lip in turmoil. She was about to break out in tears. "Is there anything we can do here to help?"

"Actually," Jonathan said hesitantly, "it would be nice if someone could be with Annie at this time. She can't be here, and it's killing her."

"No problem," she said quickly. "I'll leave as soon as we hang up."

"Thanks. Just have Kyle answer the phone today."

☼☼☼

Annie sat on the couch and wept profusely after Jonathan's call. Her entire family was in Memphis right now, all rallying around Angie and praying and hoping together.

"It's not fair!" she screamed in despair. "I should be there! But I can't move from this place because of the stupid photographers super-glued to the fence! Why on earth did I ever think that this kind of life is what I wanted?"

The statement stung Stephen. He knew she was hurting, but *this kind of life* is what she bargained for when she married him. How would she feel when he told her he was considering going back to work with Benjamin Brenner in a contract that would keep him not only occupied for several years, but would also keep him in the public eye.

She stood and took her mug to the kitchen for another cup of coffee. "Is there any cheese toast left?" she asked as she glanced over at the empty cookie sheet.

He felt like a heel. "No … uh … I ate that extra piece. Sorry … you never eat more than two."

She waved it off. "It's okay. It's not that I'm all that hungry. I just feel hollow inside. I guess I thought another piece would fill up this emptiness." Her lip began to quiver again.

He walked over to her and put his arms around her. She dropped her head on his shoulder and began to cry again.

"I'm scared, Stephen," she confessed through her sobs. "I'm afraid for Angie. How do you deal with the death of a child?"

He shook his head and brushed the back of her hair with his fingers. "I hope we never have to find out."

☼☼☼

Michael sat on the edge of Carter's bed wearing gloves and a mask. He continued to hold his little hand and talk with him as though he were wide awake and hanging on his every word. Occasionally Carter would moan, but mostly he remained still. Michael tried to remind his little boy of all the wonderful things in life, and that this was only a small part of the big picture. One way or another, this would all be over some day.

"And remember the beach?" he said softly. "We would race our crabs and have picnics. And sometimes Daddy would take you riding on his back. Mommy read you lots of books." He paused as Carter slowly opened his eyes. "How you doin', buddy? Do you need anything?"

Carter almost smiled. "I seen it again," he said weakly. "I run, Daddy. I run fast, and I don't hurt."

The agony stabbed Michael like a swift sword. "What did you see, Carter?"

He did smile this time. "I seen heaven."

Michael closed his eyes and felt his emotions almost give way. "What's it like, buddy? Is it beautiful?"

"He is …" Carter mumbled softly as he began to drift back to sleep. "He … hold … me … too …"

Michael reached his hand over and ran it across Carter's smooth head, completely bare from the cancer treatments. He almost wished now he had not forced Angie to go to the Fed Ex House. She needed to be with Carter as much as he did, but with the new baby so close to coming, it was vital that she rest and take care of her own body as much as possible. Barbara and Andie were with her, and they would see to it she got what she needed.

Jonathan slipped quietly into the room and brought a cup of coffee to him. He took it eagerly and began to drink it immediately.

"Thanks," he said wearily. "Have you heard from the girls?"

Jonathan nodded as he sipped his own cup. "Angie's actually asleep. Hard to believe, isn't it?"

Michael shook his head. "I don't know how she's managing right now. She keeps switching into doctor mode whenever we start talking about it, but eventually that's gonna break."

Jonathan looked down at Carter. "I don't know how *you* are handling this, Michael. And you've been so strong for Angie. All she can say is that you are her rock."

Michael smiled. "I would give my life for her … for these kids." Tears were welling in his eyes as he looked up at Jonathan. "But that's not meant to be." He looked back down at Carter. "When God gave me Angie, he literally gave me my life back. And he gave me children … and a family. There has been a richness I can't explain." He looked back up at Jonathan and said, "Thank you for welcoming me into her life … into your life."

Jonathan nodded and patted his shoulder.

"He keeps telling me about heaven," Michael shared for the first time.

"Carter?"

"Yeah." He gently moved Carter's hand onto the pillow next to his head as he stood to stretch. "He says he can walk and run there—that he has no pain."

Jonathan raised his eyebrows. "He told you this?"

"Several times now. And he keeps mentioning a man … someone who holds him."

"Wow," Jonathan was stunned. "Do you think …?" he couldn't finish the thought in words.

"I don't know what to think. I know this—he hasn't complained or whined since we put him to bed last night. Levi says he has to be in a lot of pain, but somehow … in this *heaven* place he keeps dreaming about … he doesn't feel the pain."

Jonathan stepped closer and knelt down beside the bed. "What if it's not a dream?" he suggested, glancing briefly up at Michael.

"I've thought of that." He knelt beside Jonathan. "But it almost seems fatalistic. It's almost like admitting that Carter's sort of … already *there* … you know? And then you start to think that all this we're doing to him here," he pointed to the needles and machines, "is pointless. We're just prolonging the inevitable."

Jonathan put his arm around Michael's back. "Have you told, Angie?"

He shook his head. "I can't … not yet."

Jonathan nodded. The hope that an outcome where Carter lived here happily ever was fading quickly. As ministers, they had seen death many times, but it was mostly older people. Many had seen heaven and angels, and it wasn't long after that until they passed.

"Has he seen angels?" Jonathan wondered.

"I don't really know. Maybe that's who the *he* is that holds him. Maybe it's an angel."

Jonathan rubbed Michael's back again. "Oh … I don't think so. I think *He* is much greater than an angel."

Fifty-Eight

Hal Bridges stood before the entire church on Wednesday evening and gave an update on Carter. He tried to sound compassionate and broken, but the reality was he was still seething over all of it. It was Jonathan's business to stand before the church and bring up these issues. It wasn't his wife that was sick; it was his grandson. And not only that … but one he seldom even sees. His first responsibility was to this church.

It also galled Hal how centered everyone was on this kid. He had several proposals he intended to bring up seeing that the entire church was together, but all anyone could think about was the kid. He had suggested they call an impromptu business meeting, but one of the deacons, Ricky Tatum, acted as though that was the most irrelevant suggestion possible when this kid was lying sick in a hospital. They had already prayed—what else could be done? Where was the faith of these people? You lay it in the hands of God, and then you move on.

A lady in the back raised her hand. Hal had no idea who she was, so he recognized her by pointing.

"What kind of prognosis are they giving?" she asked.

"I have no idea," he sighed, getting very tired of the issue of this kid.

That's when Kyle jumped up. He came to the platform and practically shoved Hal to the side.

"Here's what we know as of five-ten this afternoon. I talked to Pastor Jon to let him know we'd be praying tonight, and he said there are many different issues to consider."

Hal folded his arms. They had already prayed, already discussed the kid, why did they have to hash it through one more time? And Kyle wasn't in charge. Hal had the meeting completely under control and was doing his best to steer it away from the emotional crisis that was clearly breaking out among the people.

"First," Kyle began, "it's way more than they thought." The congregation gave a few collective gasps. "Hal told you about the bone infection and the Staph complications, but they've also found today he has two types of blood infections."

Someone called out from the front, "How did he get them?"

Kyle shrugged his shoulders. "No one knows for sure. They say this is not uncommon to happen, but the severity of his particular case is unusual."

Hal was beginning to stew. This would most assuredly be an issue to be covered in the next staff meeting.

Another person raised his hand, but Kyle motioned for everyone to just listen.

"We need to pray for Angie in all of this," he continued. "She is major pregnant—and having to deal with all of this is taking its toll on her. Remember little Cassie too. She's in a daze. She has no idea what's happening. All she knows is that her brother went into the hospital last month happy, but unable to walk, and now he's as sick as a dog."

Hal raised an eyebrow. There was another child, and the lady was pregnant again?

"Remember Annie too," Kyle suggested. "This is really hard on her. You all know how close she and Angie are, but she can't leave home for the paparazzi."

Paparazzi? Hal was going to have to talk to someone about Jonathan's family. Apparently he was in the dark big time.

Now hands began to fly up, and Kyle answered the questions one by one. Hal realized quickly he had lost total control of the meeting. He glanced back to where Nancy Beth Tate was sitting, and he gave her a glare of discontent with what was happening. She merely shook her head and slightly shrugged her shoulders. He would let the committee know this was not how things were going to be conducted if he were to be the administrator of this church.

☼☼☼

Angie sat quietly on the couch as she stared out the large window on the lower level of the Fed Ex House. The baby inside was unusually still at the moment. She was thankful. The pounding her ribs had taken the past few days had become unbearable at times. She reached down and gently rubbed her tummy. "Just wait a little longer," she pleaded. "You've done well to stay in there this far."

"Who are you talking to?" Andie asked as she brought her a Sprite and a small bag of pretzels.

"This guy," Angie grinned sadly. "I don't see how I can hold out much longer. I've never come this close to the due date before."

Andie leaned down to the baby and said, "You'd better behave in there. We have enough problems to deal with out here as it is. Just listen to your Aunt Andie, and don't come out until we're good and ready."

Angie's smile warmed, and she reached out her hand to her sister who squeezed it tightly.

"Did anything happen while I slept?" Angie asked as she opened the pretzels and popped one into her mouth.

"Nothing … no calls at all," Andie said as she reached into the bag for a pretzel also. "Moms took Cassie to MacDonald's for a Happy Meal. Knowing Moms, she'll probably end up buying her a go-cart or something."

"I doubt that, unless they suddenly inherited a huge estate from some distant relative we never knew about."

"You'd be surprised how well they do now. Imagine, for all those years they raised four kids, put us through high school, put us through college … it's a wonder we had as much as we did. Now that they have no bills to pay where we're concerned, they do pretty good financially."

"Yeah … and no more of your broken bones."

Andie shook her head and reached down to rub her ankle. "This thing has reminded me of how clumsy I used to be."

"Awww, you weren't clumsy. You were just accident prone. There are people in Padawin just like you. I think some of you are just blessed with that gift."

"Well, it is a *blessing* I'd gladly give up in a moment."

The baby gave another swift kick; Angie gasped.

"Are you okay?" Andie asked quickly.

She smiled as she tried to shove the foot or the arm, whatever it was, back down and away from her ribs. "Okay is extremely relative right now. My son is dying, and I'm not okay with that. My baby is beating me up inside, but I'm okay with that, because that means one less child to worry about at the moment. My husband is standing solid and being strong through all of this … very okay. My son's doctor, an old friend, is so spiritually lost he couldn't see truth if it knocked him in the head … not okay at all. My younger sister can't be here with me because nosey journalists won't give her a moment's peace … not okay." Then she gave an easy smile again. "But my older sister and my mom have forced me to come back to this room and take a little nap … okay again."

"Well, do you want to head back to the hospital?" Andie asked as she stood and put pressure on the boot that now donned her ankle.

"Yes … as soon as we can. Have you been on your ankle too much?"

"Naw … it just aches and throbs still. But I'm thankful to be through with those crutches." Andie helped pull Angie up from the couch, and then remembered something. "Did you know Billy Marcum had a motorcycle wreck?"

Her eyes grew wide. "You're kidding! Is he okay?"

Andie gave a wicked grin as she replied, "Okay is very relative right now. He's on crutches and hobbles around everywhere … not okay. But he's living with that ex-wife of his until he finishes student-teaching … very okay … I think?"

"The cute blond?"

"The cute blond," Andie affirmed.

"Are they back together?" Angie wondered as she grabbed her purse and keys to head for the door.

"Not if Cindy has anything to do with it."

"Why not? I thought she liked the girl."

Andie grabbed her own purse and followed Angie. "She does … loves her to death, but she doesn't think Billy deserves her, or at least doesn't deserve a second chance with her."

"Hmmm," Angie mulled as she opened the door. "Cindy needs to mind her own business."

"I thought that too."

☼☼☼

Annie complied with Stephen's leading her up the stairs and into their bedroom blindfolded.

"What have you got up your sleeve?" she asked tiredly. "Is this some new and exciting passionate procedure you've devised? Being married to a creative temperament can have its limits, you know?"

"This is not about me," he assured her. "Just a little farther now."

When they had reached his planned destination, she heard soft music and smelled a wonderful, soothing scent.

"What have you done?" she asked him again, this time with a smile.

He slowly removed the blindfold to reveal the bathroom lit up by many candles as well as a full garden tub with bubbles and steaming water. She took in the view, the smell, and the sounds, and turned back around to face him.

"All about me, huh?" she asked doubtfully.

He gave her a sympathetic look and nodded his head. "Seriously … all about you." He reached his hand to her cheek and gently caressed her face. "This has been a tough month for you, and as if it couldn't be possible, it just got worse with Carter." He turned her around and pointed her toward the huge tub. "So, I want you to get into this hot bath, relax to the sounds of some wonderful music, enjoy the dim lights of the candles, and relax until you think you're about to drop. Then get out, dry off, and go to bed."

"And what about the kids?" she asked hopefully.

He whispered his reply, "All taken care of." He lifted up her long hair with one hand and softly kissed the back of her neck. Annie squirmed.

"And what do you get out of this?" she asked, still skeptical.

"Nothing more than a relaxed wife … I hope."

"Have I been that unbearable?"

"When you consider the circumstances, Annie, I think you've done very well. You've just been a little more emotional than usual. Between being holed up here in the house and not being able to be with Angie because of that, I wish I could just pay somebody to clean it up and make it all go away."

She turned back to him and placed her arms around his neck. "I wish I could make it all go away too … for Angie's sake."

"But you can't." He gently kissed her forehead and turned her back to the tub. "If you want to do anything for her right now, relax in your tub and spend some time in prayer. Outside of that, you're helpless—we all are."

When he left the bathroom, she took a moment to behold the sight again. He had to be the most wonderful husband on the face of the earth … maybe the whole universe. She slipped off her clothes and slowly placed a foot into the tub. Perfect. It was almost unbearably hot, but not to the point that she couldn't ease her way down. As she got used to the water, she sat all the way in and finally leaned against the bath pillow at the back. She let the bubbles seep in around her and smother her with their scent. The music flowed softly around the room, and as she leaned her head back and closed her eyes, she could almost forget what was happening in Memphis right now. Almost.

With a tear sliding down her face, she wondered how it could be possible to have anything left within her to cry again. Stephen was right—she had been extremely emotional this week, almost as if she had lost control. More than once the kids wanted to know why Mommy was crying, and she often found herself in tears even while eating a meal with the family. Maybe Stephen was right. If she could just relax enough tonight and let all the tension drain out, she could start tomorrow with a new lease on life.

✡✡✡

Jonathan was torn. He knew he should probably head back to Dockrey to give Kyle and Cindy a break on Friday, but what if Carter got worse while he was away. Barbara would be staying for certain, but he was ripped up inside about what to do. He knew he was an encourager for Michael who was trying to be strong about it all. Twice, when the two men had left the hospital for something to eat and to allow Michael to get cleaned up at the Fed Ex House, he had broken down before Jonathan. One time, he literally cried on his shoulder for nearly fifteen minutes. Jonathan understood the feeling … trying so hard to be strong for Angie and Cassie, but also mourning the condition of his son. It was a tough position to be in. Then there was the fact that Angie was so pregnant it seemed impossible she could go another day. He had told Jonathan he wouldn't know what to do if Angie went into labor. How do you choose between bringing a child into the world and holding the hand of another about to leave? Jonathan had no answer, not even a principle or a Scripture to pull out in support.

He decided to dial Kyle and see what his perspective was. One thing he could be certain of with Kyle—he was a man who walked with the Lord. Many times he had gone to him for comfort and advice, even though Kyle was close to thirty years younger. But he had been God's gift to Jonathan. For thirty years he had served at Dockrey, and even though he had friends in the church, there was no one who could really understand the struggles and blessings of the ministry … until Kyle came along. The two of them had found a kindred spirit between them, and it only made the job sweeter as the years went by.

But now there was Hal. Who was this man, and why in heaven's name had God brought him to Dockrey? As far as Jonathan had seen, there wasn't an ounce of compassion stored up within him, and at no time had he ever hinted of a walk with the Lord. Jonathan had prayed long and hard about how to deal with him, but he had gotten no answers. All he knew to do was to keep his faith strong and to continue leading the church in the direction he believed God had led him.

"Hello?" Kyle answered.

"Kyle, it's Jonathan. How are things going on the home front?"

"Who cares about the home front? How are things going up there? Is Carter better? Are they more hopeful now than they were this morning?"

He sighed as all the happenings of the day replayed in his mind. "Frankly, it's been another bad day. His fever spiked again this morning, and they tried maniacally to get it back down. It dropped a little … but …"

"Is he worse?" Kyle asked hesitantly. "I mean … isn't there something they can … it's not hopeless, is it … Jonathan?"

He could feel his own emotions begin to surface as he tried to find the words to tell Kyle that no one was hopeful about anything anymore. "I don't think they're giving him much … well … he's just not responding to the treatments. Maybe it could change, but for the moment, it doesn't look good."

"Wow," Kyle breathed out. "I don't know what to say."

"There's nothing to say. I know your heart. You feel for us, wish you could do something, but you're as helpless as we are. Just pray. That's all anyone can do now … just pray."

"You know it. And the prayer chain is standing on alert at all times. I'll call again and let them know the latest."

He nodded to himself as he thought of many in that church who were praying for his grandson right now. "Should I come on back home tonight … be there at the office tomorrow? I know this has put a strain on you and Cindy having to field all this by yourselves. I don't imagine *Dr. Bridges* has been much help."

"I'm ready to kick *Dr. Bridges* in the pants and send him on back to Arizona."

Jonathan gave a heartless chuckle. "Somehow, Kyle, I get the feeling that if we knew the real story, we'd learn that Arizona probably doesn't want him back."

"Really? What are you talking about?"

"I'm not sure, but I just have this hunch that our illustrious *Dr.*

Bridges isn't all he's cracked himself up to be."

"Do you think he's lying?"

Jonathan didn't want to put any more ideas into Kyle's head, especially based on speculation. "I'm not saying that. I just don't think that a man with the credentials he's supposed to have could have served at any church more than a few months with his kind of attitude. There's not a pastor in the world who would let a man like that come in and take over his church … shoot … not even take over anything … no pastor would even let him stay."

"I agree," Kyle said quickly. "He has relentlessly tried to pin me down this week since you left. He's called me … and you … every name under the sun to try and intimidate me into … something … I don't even know what. And I'm sorry, Pastor Jon, but I just keep putting the monkey on your back. I tell him we'll talk about all this when the pastor returns."

"Good boy, Kyle. You keep doing that."

"And look," Kyle wanted to assure him, "don't even think about coming back here. Stay on through Sunday if you need to. I'm sure Hal or I could preach if …"

"No," Jonathan said quickly. "No matter what happens here, I'll be in the pulpit Sunday morning. I may have to leave that afternoon, but I do *not* want our *Dr. Bridges* to be in control of that morning crowd. He managed to sway the committee with all his high-faluting-mumbo-jumbo. He could do the same with others in the church if we're not careful. I'm glad you managed to grab the reins from him on Wednesday night."

"I'm telling you, Jonathan—I could have bashed his teeth in."

Jonathan felt guilty for actually enjoying the mental vision that statement gave him. "Well, I could have bashed him a few times myself." It was time to switch gears. "Anyway, forgetting Hal and moving back to the more pressing problem at the moment—if you guys can handle the office one more day, I'll just stay here until Saturday afternoon."

"We've got it, boss," Kyle said in a chipper manner.

Jonathan couldn't resist. "Boss? You'd better not let Hal hear you say that."

Fifty-Nine

On Friday morning Billy was actually sad to finish his student teaching. He had come to know these kids pretty well, and they had finally come to a mutual understanding of how things were to be run under him. He realized this is how it would be when he started teaching for real. Each year he would have to train students about what to expect, and then make sure he always delivered what was promised. He remembered in high school, not so much in college, that some teachers were pushovers. He had decided, however, that Sam was to be his standard. He would never forget her philosophy about being an ogre. Even now as he looked out over the class, they were quietly working with the understanding that if they didn't choose to do it quietly, they would end up with more work to take home rather than one simple page of questions for the moment.

Sam. He owed her a lot. How could he repay her for all she had done these past weeks? The reality was he couldn't. But one thing he could do—he could leave her alone and let her move on with Dr. Crandall. He was the epitome of a nice guy. He was easygoing, had a dry sense of humor, was very courteous and thoughtful, and was about to have a great job somewhere as a likeable family physician. He was stable, motivated, and committed, would make a good husband, perhaps not the most passionate, and would definitely make a great father. This is what Sam needed most in her life. At the moment all she had was teaching, and that simply wasn't enough. She needed to be cared for and to have the opportunity to care deeply for someone else … someone other than good old wishy-washy Billy Marcum.

At least he had one more night with her. Cindy was scheduled to pick him up tomorrow morning, and then he would head back to Dockrey to live with them until he could get out on his own again. He had a prospective buyer for the boat, and would meet with him when he returned next Friday for his final interview and oral exam with Dr. Lockhart. But tonight he had Sam. He had made her promise he could take her out to eat, although she protested militantly that he didn't need to spend his money on her. He still hadn't told her about the inheritance money from his mother. In order to do that, it would mean bringing up that horrible Monday when he took her to Blue Bayou with the intention of coming clean and then proposing—only to have Kirstie walk in and totally blow his life. The best he could hope for now was to call her up on occasion when he was in Florence and perhaps have dinner with her and Jeremy Crandall.

☼☼☼

"Don't tell me," Hal said with a biting sarcastic tone, "the pastor will not be in *again* this morning."

Cindy was really struggling with being cordial to him. "Carter is worse," she said without looking up from her computer. "We told him to stay."

"And you would be the authority in this church?" Hal asked snidely.

She still wouldn't look up as she said, "No, but we would be the *seniority* and represent the heart of this church."

Hal was about to make another comment, but Kyle walked into the office. "Hey, hon," he said to Cindy as he walked up to her desk. "Can you pull up the order of services for December from last year? I wanted to do another candlelight service, but didn't want to duplicate anything."

Hal cleared his throat. "I don't suppose you're up for a staff meeting this morning?"

Kyle wouldn't acknowledge him. He kept talking to Cindy. "And do you remember the name of that song we found in my madrigal book from college? I think an a-cappella ensemble could do that somewhere in the middle."

"That was a gorgeous song," she agreed as she scrolled through the files on the computer.

"I said," Hal came out this time with a more forceful tone, "could we have a staff meeting?"

Kyle closed his eyes, controlled his anger, and turned toward Hal. "I made my interests in your staff meetings clear. When Jonathan gets back, we'll meet. Until then, forget it."

"Hmph," Hal muttered as he shook his head. "I'll tell you something, I don't know this pastor all that well, but from what I've seen, he's a slouch of a dressser, he shows up late every single day for work, and some days he doesn't show up at all."

Kyle looked back at him and said, "Well, I think for the first time we agree on something, Hal." Both Cindy and Hal looked at him in surprise. "You don't know Pastor Jon well at all … not at all."

☼☼☼

When Michael walked into Carter's room after lunch, he nearly went into a panic.

"Angie!" he whispered as loudly as he could. "Put on your mask and gloves!"

She looked up at him, her eyes swollen and pained, and shook her head. "Not anymore," she said weakly. "My son is gonna feel my touch and see my face before he dies. I don't want his last memories of me to be the smell of latex and the look of brooding, bloodshot eyes."

He understood, but there was more at stake. "The baby, Angie.

You've got to think about the baby."

"Michael, don't think me calloused here … or ignorant. I know exactly what I'm dealing with. But I have this gut-feeling that Carter isn't gonna make it … and this baby is. My faith right now is that God is gonna do what He's gonna do … and a mask and gloves won't change His plan—period."

Michael pulled up a chair beside her and stared down at his lifeless son. He didn't think it possible for Carter to look paler, but it was almost as if he was literally watching the life being sucked out. Each time he saw him, his breathing was more labored and his skin more pallid.

"How much longer can this go on?" he whispered in pure emotional agony.

She shrugged. "Who knows? If the medication doesn't start to have an effect, he could pass on within a day or two … or go into a coma."

He put his hand on her shoulder. She was in doctor mode right now which was good. It could allow him to share with her the things Carter had said. He had wanted to tell her, but she had been too torn up most of the time for him to even consider it.

"Carter says he's seen heaven." There. He said it.

She turned back and met his eyes. The look on her face told him it may not have been the right time.

"What?" she barely breathed out.

He reached up and removed his own mask this time. He had to agree with her. If God was really in charge here, no protection or lack of it would change His plans. He then pulled off his gloves and tossed them into the garbage.

"He says he can run there," Michael began. "He doesn't have any pain either." He took her hands in his and gently rubbed them.

She nodded as she acknowledged, "Then he really is going home. He's already placed his heart there, hasn't he?"

He couldn't speak; he only nodded. He watched tearfully as Angie carefully ran her finger down the side of Carter's cheek and then drew her hand across his hairless head. He didn't even look like the same little boy they had brought here a month ago.

"Did we do the right thing?" she asked, now moving out of doctor mode and back into mother mode. "Should we have just left him alone … let him not walk?"

"I doubt it," Michael sighed, completely understanding her train of thought. "The tumor would have eventually caused greater problems … and greater pain. I have to believe this was the plan all along."

She nodded with tears beginning to stream down both cheeks. "I used to be afraid of death … hated it." She moved a tube that was caught inside Carter's arm. "One reason I became a doctor was to stop it."

Michael rubbed her back as he tried to hold in his own tears.

She went on. "But Padawin changed that part of me. Somehow, over there everything has its time and place. Here in America we want to control stuff. We're such a selfish breed of humanity. We want to play God and build our communities bigger and better and stronger and more impenetrable, and while we do, we cut ourselves off from all that is simple and free. We wear our masks and gloves on every level. We protect ourselves from the things that really make us feel alive … from everything that makes us vulnerable."

She leaned back in her chair but kept a hand on Carter. "And we grow to fear and hate the things that are just a part of the process of living." She looked over at Michael, tears still streaming down her face. "A part of me wants to hate God right now, but it's the old part. There's this other part that keeps reminding me that I'll never again doubt how important a single second is with those I love. It reminds me that this earth isn't all there is to life … that there's an existence far greater and more magnificent than my mind can imagine. And my goal in this life is not to build things here on earth that I value or hold to, but rather to build things that have eternal value in the kingdom to come."

She looked back at Carter as he struggled to breathe in his sleep. "I have to confess something to you, Michael."

He leaned up to look at her. "What? What is it?"

"I never felt like he was ours for very long." And with that a small sob escaped.

"What do you mean?" He had never heard this before.

She took a deep breath and let it out slowly. "One reason I was so slow about trying to get him treatment was that I somehow knew he would be too weak to stand it. I kept thinking if we could just wait a little longer, let him grow a little bigger, let him become a little stronger, he would stand a better chance." She leaned her head back against Michael's shoulder. "But at some point I had to let him go. I guess this is that time."

Michael put his arm around her shoulder and pulled her tightly to him. She began to cry at full speed now. He couldn't help it and found himself doing the same. This was the first time they had done this together, and he figured they desperately needed it. He was thankful that Barbara, Jonathan and Andie had taken Cassie out and given the three of them time alone. They needed to get this part of the goodbye over so they could be strong for Cassie when it was finally ended.

Suddenly Carter began to stir. Michael motioned for Angie to look. She turned her head back to him and immediately knelt down beside him, awkward as it was with the baby inside.

"Sweetie," she said gently. "How are you doing today?"

When he opened his eyes, he smiled. "Mama," he whispered very softly.

"Yeah … it's Mama." She was thankful she had taken off the mask. "What have you been doing in your sleep?"

"I run again," he said with another smile.

She caressed his face with her bare hands and tried to keep her lip from quivering. "Can you run fast, baby?"

He smiled again, though weakly. "Fast. And I love dem boys, Mama."

She looked up at Michael. He shrugged.

"What boys, sweetie?" she asked him.

"Dem our boys," he tried to explain.

"I don't know those boys," she told him.

"Oh, mama," he said as though he thought she was teasing him. "Silly Mama."

Angie furled her brows and glanced back at Michael again. He still shook his head in confusion.

Suddenly, Carter opened his eyes wider than he had in days, and the smile on his face grew brighter.

Michael asked immediately, "What is it, buddy?"

Carter looked all around the room in wonder as he turned on his back slowly and painfully.

"I see dem," he whispered in awe. "Dey beautiful, Mama. See dem, Daddy?"

Michael got down on his knees beside Angie and put his bare hand on Carter's arm. "I don't see them, tiger. What do you see?"

Carter's eyes followed an unseen movement around the room, and his smile was larger than ever.

"Dey so bright and nice," he whispered as he turned to look at his parents this time. He stared deep into Angie's eyes and reached up his hand toward her face. She leaned down and kissed it as she took it in her own.

"I love you, Mama," he said weakly. "You nice wike angels."

Angie bit her lip to keep from crying.

Then he looked at Michael. Angie released his hand so he could touch his Daddy.

"You wike him, Daddy," Carter said this time. "You love me and you strong."

"Like who, buddy?" Michael wondered.

"Daddy," he said again with that teasing tone as though Michael should know what he was saying. Carter rubbed Michael's unshaved face and almost giggled like he had a hundred times before, but this time he acted as though he were relishing the touch.

"I love Cassie," Carter said as his eyes began to fade again. "and I love dem boys."

Angie and Michael just looked at each other in confusion.

"It … hurts … so … much … here," Carter now said as a tear rolled down the side of his face. "It always hurt."

"Always, sweetie?" Angie asked astonished at his confession. "Even in Padawin … even at home?"

He nodded slowly and closed his eyes as he relaxed his head against the pillow. "I go now?" he pleaded as he scrunched his face in pain. "I not hurt there." He opened his eyes and looked around the room again in awe. Then he looked back at his parents. "I go play? I run?"

How Angie kept from collapsing she didn't know. Everything within her was screaming to grab hold of him and make him swear he wouldn't leave. She felt Michael's body begin to shake next to hers and knew he was losing control fast.

"Carter … sweetie … I love you very, very much," she said through tears so thick she could no longer see his face clearly. "I'm so glad you lived with me for a little while." She then bit her lip and took one final breath before saying, "You can go now. It's okay, baby. You can go."

Michael grabbed Angie's shoulder and began to weep as she had never seen him weep before, but Carter was oblivious. His smile only grew bigger. Angie grabbed Michael and forced him to look back at their little boy.

"Dear God," Michael cried out, "what is he looking at? What does he see?"

Carter's face almost seemed to glow as his breathing became increasingly shallow with each breath.

Suddenly the door burst open and two nurses came barreling into the room with Levi.

"His vitals are dropping!" one of the nurses declared. "We heard them at the station."

Levi looked to Angie and asked desperately, "Angie, what's happening?"

"Look at him, Levi," she said through tears half of joy and half of distraught sorrow. "You look at him and tell me what's happening."

Levi stepped up beside the bed and saw the expression in Carter's eyes. The breathing was now minimal, but the look on the little boy's face was one of pure joy and bliss.

"What's he looking at?" Levi asked as he began to look around the room himself to see if he had missed something on the walls or ceiling.

"We're not sure," Angie replied, "but he says they're beautiful. And whatever he sees, he's ready to go with them."

Levi rubbed his eyes, half out of astonishment, and half out of utter irritation. "This can't be happening! He was doing so well! He was responding to treatment and to therapy! He's not supposed to do this!"

Michael touched his shoulder. "You did all you could do," he assured him. "It's out of your hands … out of our hands."

Levi threw off Michael's hand and stepped back. "But it shouldn't be!" he nearly screamed. "I should be able to heal him! I should be able to make him whole again … to make him walk! It wasn't supposed to happen like this!"

Michael and Angie only stared at Levi briefly. He stormed out of the room, and the parents turned back to their child. Carter was still smiling, though his breathing was almost nonexistent now. The only evidence that he was still alive was the continued slow blipping of the machine. They both reached down their hands and touched his little body again.

"Give him peace, Jesus," Angie whispered in prayer. "Take away the pain for good. Let him run … forever."

Within a few minutes the bleeping became a solid, single sound. Without even thinking, Angie reached up and turned off the machine. Carter's face, pale and truly lifeless now, still held a faint smile. She leaned down and kissed his forehead, then looked to Michael. He just shook his head in unbelief. He pulled Angie to him, and they both began to cry again. This couldn't be happening.

Sixty

On Saturday morning Cindy somehow managed to drive through her tears to Florence to pick up Billy. She had done more than just cry; she had sobbed, bawled, and almost pulled over twice to try and gain control. She couldn't process the fact that Angie's little boy was dead. Carter, who was born just a couple of weeks before her own twins, was now a lifeless shell lying in some room at the funeral home in Dockrey. Angie was picking out his burial clothes and his casket, and Cindy couldn't imagine how she was able to stand it. Yet when she had talked to her earlier that morning, she seemed resigned to her task and undaunted about what lay ahead.

Cindy prayed. *God, I don't think I could handle that … not at all. Losing my father and mother is nothing compared to losing a child. I know I should somehow minister to Angie right now, but all I have is fear and grief … and I just don't know what I could do or say that could make any difference in her life.*

She sighed at the unsettled feeling that had overcome her since hearing the news last night. The last thing she wanted at the moment was to spend an hour in the car with her self-centered brother as they made the drive back to Dockrey. He would probably talk about Angie in the past tense, and again bemoan the fact that she was married at all … much less to a missionary. Meanwhile, it was obvious that he was still trying to somehow romance Sam whom he had hurt severely years ago. She wondered how one person could be so egocentric and obsessed with his own agenda. He had changed some after their mother had battled cancer, but it wasn't complete. In so many ways he was still the self-centered brat he had always been.

As she pulled the minivan onto Sam's street, the unsettling took a deeper dive. It would be hard to say goodbye to Sam again. She literally loved her like a sister. She was one of the dearest people Cindy had ever known. It had been miserably hard to let her go when Billy divorced the first time. The whole family knew it was only because of Billy's jerked personality. It was impossible not to adore her. Yet here Cindy was … going through it all again. She knew when Billy left this time, the casual contact with Sam they had enjoyed the past few weeks would again be cut. It would be too awkward to try and keep up a relationship that no longer had any ties.

She pulled into the driveway, turned off the car, and then stared in the mirror as she tried to wipe away the smeared mascara and streaked blush. It was pointless. They would most certainly ask what the problem was, and Cindy would have to bring up Angie in the last conversation they would all have together. The pain became even bitterer.

✿✿✿

Sam tried to stay chipper throughout the morning as she helped Billy gather all his belongings. She knew this day was coming, the day when he would walk out of her life … again. Even though this time was much more civil, it didn't hurt any less. As they passed each other in the small hallway, they would smile, but not speak. There was so much she wanted to say to him, but they were only feelings and confusion, not things she could put into words. She kept thinking at some point they would sit and speak as they waited for Cindy, but time was passing quickly, and it seemed Billy had ended up with everything he owned being brought into Sam's house—their house.

"There she is," Billy said as he peeked out the blinds of the bedroom window. "I hope all this will fit into her van. I'm beginning to doubt it as the pile grows bigger."

"Well, you can always come back to get the rest."

"I suppose," he sighed as he took a deep breath and turned back toward Sam who was standing at the door of the bedroom. "You okay? You seem a little out of sorts this morning." he asked as he hobbled on his crutches toward the hall.

She nodded. She had hardly said three words all morning.

When Cindy knocked on the door, they both just stared at each other for a few moments. Neither could read the other's mind, but inside both of them turmoil was bubbling. How did they say goodbye … again?

"Hello?" Cindy called from the door. "I know you guys are here because the car is in the driveway."

Sam broke into a small smile as she headed for the door. "I'd better get that before she starts wondering what we're up to."

"Yeah," he agreed. "And she has a vivid imagination. Don't let it go on too long or she might shoot me for what she thinks I might do to you."

She turned back toward him in surprise. "What does she think you might to do me?"

Billy raised his eyebrows several times and suggested, "Everything I'd like to do to you."

She looked astonished. "And what might that be? What *would* you like to do to me?"

His grin nearly unnerved her. Why did he wait until the last day to suggest maybe the spark wasn't over?

Sam opened the door after another knock from Cindy and was shocked again, but this time it was over the condition of Cindy's face and eyes. "Are you all right?" she asked immediately with deep concern. "What's wrong?"

Cindy walked on into the house and was immediately greeted by Billy with a warm hug. She must look awful if Billy was actually offering to hug her.

"I'm afraid I got some bad news last night," she began, "and I haven't been able to shake the intense hurt from it all."

"What happened?" Sam asked right away. "Is everyone okay?"

Cindy shook her head. "Angie's little boy, Carter, died yesterday afternoon at LeBonheur Hospital in Memphis."

Both Sam and Billy were stunned.

"What?" he asked immediately. "I thought he was doing good. You said he was actually standing and such when you went to visit."

"He was," Cindy tried to explain as the tears began to choke her again. "But he got some kind of infection, and it just got out of control really fast."

"Good lands!" Sam exclaimed in a whisper. "I had no idea … I mean … how awful."

Cindy nodded, but the look of devastating concern on Billy's face was obvious. He was speechless. He merely went to the couch and sat down.

"How is Angie?" Sam wondered, although she felt a tinge of jealousy at Billy's response. She couldn't help it. Even though she knew Angie was in fact a wonderful person and not the seductive goddess she had been led to believe, she would always be Billy's ideal … and somehow, in the back of Sam's mind, she would always be the reason behind their divorce.

"Angie is surprisingly well at the moment," Cindy told them. "She's managing to do all that needs to be done in order to get ready for the funeral."

"Funeral?" Billy said as he turned toward them from the couch. "When is the funeral?"

"They're gonna have it on Monday morning."

Billy nodded and Sam tried to ignore the lump in her throat over his reaction. The moment was indeed awkward … again. *Great,* she thought. *The last thing on our minds when he left the first time was Angie … and it looks like that's gonna be the case this time too. Will I ever be able to live out from under her shadow?*

A vision of Jeremy Crandall came into her mind. Jeremy could be her ticket away from Billy if she would only let him. He did his best to make her feel like a princess, and she appreciated it all, but something was missing from their friendship that she just couldn't name. He wasn't the last thing on her mind before she went to bed or the first thing on her mind when she awoke. She didn't spend her spare time imagining all they could do together. She didn't wonder what it would be like to officially be his *girlfriend*, although that whole term sounded ridiculous as a thirty year old woman. She didn't imagine what kissing him would be like, or holding hands while Christmas shopping, or most of all, being married to him for the next fifty years. The only thing she wondered about now where Jeremy was concerned was whether or not he had what it took to get her mind off of her ex … once and for all.

As they slowly loaded the van, carefully stacking everything where Billy told them as he leaned on his crutches, she could feel the knot growing tighter in her stomach. A part of her wanted to scream for him not to go, and to just move back in and stay with her forever. But he had made it clear that things were indeed over this time. In fact, he had been so pushing her toward Jeremy that it almost seemed as if he was eager to get her affections in another direction. She hoped when he was finally gone she would be able to do just that. She couldn't spend another ten years mooning over a man who obviously didn't love her deeply enough to fight for her anymore.

As Billy prepared to leave, Cindy hugged Sam and thanked her again for all she had done toward helping him finish school. She insisted they keep in touch, but they both knew that wouldn't happen—it hadn't happened before. There were too many loose ends and raw emotions to continue opening the wounds over and over again.

Billy came up to Sam, leaned his crutches against the van, and pulled her into a warm embrace.

"Cindy will kill me for this," he whispered into her ear. "But I can't leave without trying to express how thankful I am for everything … absolutely everything you've done for me."

"You'd better be thankful," she teased him. "Not every girl in Alabama would be willing to put up with you like that."

He gently kissed her forehead and then let her go. He grabbed his crutches, poked himself to the seat, and then slowly maneuvered his way inside. They stared at each other as Cindy backed out of the driveway, and then he gave a final wave as the vehicle rounded the corner and drove out of sight.

I wonder who was on his mind, Sam thought as she turned toward her door to go inside. *Was it me … or was it Angie?*

☼☼☼

The funeral was becoming a pure circus. Stephen had anticipated the deluge of paparazzi, so he hired extra security for the sole purpose of keeping the event more like a funeral, and less like a movie premiere. The end result was that people had to show ID in order to get into the building. Many photographers and reporters had been thwarted, but many who had no credible identification had to be identified by someone already in the building.

"Pastor?" said one of the security men as he motioned Jonathan over toward the foyer. "There's a lady here with a Memphis ID. She says she's a friend of the family … that her husband was the doctor." He pointed toward one of the doors.

Jonathan recognized Gail Taylor and without delay walked over to her.

"Gail," he welcomed her warmly, "sorry about all this. It was gonna be crazy if we didn't have some kind of system."

"Believe me, I understand," she assured him. "After having them camped around my home the last few weeks, I don't blame you. I'm sure the church will be packed as it is just from friends and family."

He looked outside the door behind her. "Is Levi with you?"

She shook her head, and her face fell.

"What is it?" he asked as he took her elbow and led her to the side of the entrance area.

She was trying to get a deep breath and avoid crying. "I haven't seen him since Carter died. He took off … I don't know where … and he hasn't contacted me in any way."

"Do you have any ideas where he might be?"

She shook her head as tears began to pool in her eyes.

He reached down and wrapped his arms around her. "It'll be okay. Everyone who is touched by this death is having to work through a lot of emotion, a lot of disappointment, and a lot of questions. Give him some time. I'm sure he somehow feels responsible."

"I hate to interrupt," said the same security guard as he tapped Jonathan on the shoulder. "But there's another lady claiming to be a friend of the family. I recognize her from television, I think maybe a reporter, and she says she is, but insists that she's supposed to be here. She's also from out-of-state … really far out-of-state."

Jonathan followed the man's pointing finger to a beautiful blond standing anxiously in the doorway. Kelly McCall. He smiled and nodded. "She is a friend of the family. Let her in."

Jonathan looked back down at Gail. "Are you gonna be all right? Do you need some water or something?"

"I'm fine, but thank you," she said sincerely. "I'm gonna go find a seat in the back somewhere so I can slip out when it's over. I just felt like I should be here for Angie and Michael and Cassie."

"I'll be sure to tell them you're here."

He then went over to Kelly McCall.

"Pastor Jon," she exclaimed as he walked up beside her. She threw her arms around him and squeezed him tight. "I'm in complete shock about all of this. I came home early so I could be here."

"Thank you," he said with a tired smile. "Follow me and I'll take you to Annie. I'm sure she'd love to see you."

"Oh no, not now. I don't need to interrupt the family. I'll see her sometime this week."

"Nonsense," Jonathan maintained. "Trust me when I say any interruption or distraction is greatly appreciated."

He took her hand and led her toward the front of the church and out of the sanctuary to a room where the family was gathered. He opened the door, found Annie, and motioned her to come outside. When she walked out and saw Kelly, the two immediately embraced and began to cry.

"I can't believe you're here," Annie said in shock as she pulled away. "How sweet of you."

"We were coming anyway," Kelly told her as she pulled her toward a wall and away from anybody's hearing. "Johnny's team didn't make the playoffs … again. So, we're free for the holidays. He's got the girls still at his parents, but when Mother told me about Angie's baby, I told him I really wanted to go. He insisted I come on down."

"Wonderful," Annie said with a sense of ease. "It'll be nice to have something different on my agenda. Let's get together and catch up."

"Absolutely," Kelly hugged her again. "And when Johnny and the girls get here, we can do a whole big family *thing* together."

"That'll be great." Annie looked her in the eye and smiled warmly. "Thanks for being here. It means a lot to me."

Kelly shook her head. "I feel so helpless. But I also feel like I know Angie and her family because of our discussions the past few years. I couldn't believe it when Mother told me. How she found out so fast I'll never know."

Annie gave her a confused glare. "She's Vivian McCall," Annie reminded her. "She makes it her business to know everything."

"You're right," Kelly laughed. "She shouldn't be selling cars; she should be the editor of the newspaper!"

Sixty-One

Jonathan gave a moving and emotional service, and as hard as it was for him to speak, he was the only one who could truly do justice. Kyle sang a special song, and then Stephen sang. Angie had asked Annie to sing, but she said there would be no way she could possibly make it through. However, as the service neared the end, Angie suddenly came to her feet. Everyone carried a look of worry as they watched her make her way up the platform stairs and to the pulpit. Jonathan wasn't sure what was happening, but he relinquished his position and moved back as she went up and gripped her hands on either side of the podium.

"I know a lot of you here are asking some seriously hard questions right now," she began. "And believe me, I've asked them too. But I feel the need to let you know that all my questions have been answered." She looked out at the massive crowd that had come. "The answers aren't necessarily in line with what I hoped or wished, but nevertheless, they're answers … and they represent a truth that's bigger than my greatest fears or concerns.

"Some of you are asking why Carter? Why such a little boy? What had he done to deserve this? And what about Angie and Michael? What kind of God snatches life from those who serve Him and give their lives for Him?" The congregation was absolutely still. "I can't give you an exact answer, one that details all the ramifications Carter's death will have, but I know that God has us in the palm of His hand. And I know that Carter was one of His most precious creations. I also know that Carter is in a place now where he is whole … healthy … walking … and happy. Would I have liked for him to have been whole and healthy and happy around here at this very moment?" Angie looked deeply into the eyes of as many people as she could. "In a heartbeat," she whispered.

"But here we all are," she continued. "Grieving a great loss, but at the same time understanding that we're helpless to change it in any way. So where are the answers to all my questions? Where's the hope that I can wake up in the morning and anticipate the birth of yet another child? Where is the faith that I can go through all this again? What promise is there that if God took one child from me, He won't take another?" She smiled comfortingly at the grieving faces. "The problem doesn't lie in the answers, dear friends—because Jesus is the answer. The problem lies in our questions.

"Job suffered the loss of all his children at one time, and He asked God these same questions. God's reply was simple: *Job, where were you when*

I laid out the foundations of the earth? Do you understand how the dimensions were decided, and how it was just hung in the middle of the universe? Surely you know, because you keep talking as though you know exactly what the eternal outcome of every decision should be! Who told the oceans to come this far and then just stop? And as God goes on and on, He finally asks Job, *And what about death? Have you been there? Have you walked that valley of the shadow?*"

Angie's face glowed with a calm peace as she tried to explain. "Carter told Michael and me that he had seen heaven." Many in the congregation gasped. "He said it was wonderful, that he could run, and that he had no pain. He looked at us with pleading eyes and begged us to let him go *play there*." Angie's eyes were becoming tearful. "We told him to go." She paused and took a deep breath as the baby inside pushed against her lungs. "God has a plan. God has a perfect timing. This wasn't some arbitrary accident that Satan managed to pull off over God's head. My heavenly Father's eyes weren't diverted by some terrorist act in the Middle East as my son lay dying in a Memphis hospital." Angie shook her head. "He was right there with us. While holding Carter in His arms, He whispered to him it was time to go, and Carter was ready and willing.

"What about each of you? If the Father suddenly came calling you, would you be ready? What if it were your child? Would you think He'd made a mistake? Would you be like Job and try to assume that because He did things that moved you out of your comfort zone that He was suddenly unfair or out of control?

"I can't answer you all the *why's* that surround this, by I can answer the *Who*. A loving God, who holds not only the entire world in His hand, but now also holds my son—He had a plan. And that plan, from Carter's birth until Friday afternoon, was for that little boy to bring a few years of incredible joy and blessing into the lives of a few people."

She looked around the room, leaned into the pulpit microphone, and in a hushed voice said, "And here *you* are." She paused, and then added, "Why? Did the death of my boy provide a way of life for someone in this room? Is there someone in here who really doubts the love and the goodness of God? When our time in Alabama is finished, Michael and myself, along with Cassie and this new baby, will return to Padawin. We'll continue to share the love and power of Christ, and we'll not question God's motives or plans concerning Carter. But what about *you*? We know where Carter is, and we know he's thrilled with his new arrangement. We'll move on and continue to grow and minister and love and trust. But will you use this as an excuse to deny God's love? Rather than choose to believe that God is big enough to heal our lives after such a great loss, will you choose to run even farther?"

Gail Taylor's heart nearly pounded out of her chest. How did these people come to such wonderful conclusions about God? All she knew about God was that His demands and commands only limited her life and what she could enjoy. How did that equal with love and joy? How could Angie Collins stand up and declare all of this was part of some divine plan ordained before the foundations of the earth? The longer Angie talked, the clearer those answers became. *Because He loves me*, Gail thought.

Billy Marcum had wanted to curse God … again. He had cursed God at his father's death, cursed God at his mother's death, and wanted to curse God right now. He wanted to stand up and ask everyone why they were so willing to honor a God who ripped people from the lives of others. But after Angie's words, all he wanted to do was climb beneath a pew and plead for forgiveness. How dare he question God when Angie and Michael, missionaries who sacrificed everything for the cause of Christ, were so willing to accept suffering from the hand of God as well as blessing?

He stared at Angie, still so beautiful, and nearly glowing from her pregnancy. He had always carried a torch for her, but for the first time he saw something in her that touched him even deeper. And for some reason, it wasn't Angie that came to his mind as he thought about the need to stop his running and rebellion from God. It was Sam. How could he have so royally messed up his life, and then dragged her right down with him? At this moment, Angie's beauty didn't come close to the emotion that thoughts of Sam pulled up within him.

Angie now lifted her eyes toward heaven and began to sing softly in the Padawin language:

When the horn of the Lord will blow and time comes to an end
And the sunrise comes upon us bright and bright
When the ones who know the Lord go on to Heaven's special beach
And our names are called in Heaven I'll be there.

When our names are called in Heaven
When our names are called in Heaven
When our names are called in Heaven
When our names are called in Heaven I'll be there.

✪✪✪

Annie managed to survive the funeral and the food fellowship at her parents' home that Monday afternoon with a good sense of control. She and Andie took up most of the responsibility of greeting and arranging so her mother and Angie could be free. But it had caught up with her. She deeply resented the fact that the paparazzi had been the cause of keeping her and Angie apart during this last month. Angie had desperately needed the support and love of family, but it was too much trouble for anyone to make the trip unnoticed. And there was no way Annie could have stayed in Memphis. Photographers would have broken windows to get inside. She really, really hated this life. She had to be careful or she could almost find herself resenting Stephen because he was the initial cause.

But Thursday afternoon was her reprieve! She was going to spend the afternoon with Kelly McCall at Vivian's house, and they could escape to places long forgotten for a few brief hours behind the walled expanse. Unfortunately, the security that had to follow always reminded her that her life may never be normal again. But at least they would be out of sight once she was inside the McCall compound.

They were able to giggle and laugh for a long time, at least until Vivian showed up. Her presence managed to put a wet blanket on the freedom that had been blowing around. It was at that point the conversation began to turn serious. Kelly shared some of the struggles she was having in her marriage, and Annie in turn shared a few of hers. Kelly talked about her move to a news network as a reporter, and wondered if it was the right thing—to give up control of her work. Annie shared the frustrations of all that had happened since Angie's return, culminating in Carter's death and the bizarre need for security at the funeral.

As the afternoon wore on, the sharing got even deeper. Annie eventually shared about Hal Bridges and how his presence was causing unbelievable stress and tension at a church that had been wonderfully united for so many years. Kelly had been so sympathetic that Annie found herself sharing even more personal issues, family issues, things that had never been shared with anyone outside of family. It had been more cathartic than had she gone to a counselor and paid big bucks to get some emotional and mental release.

When the time came to leave, Annie felt refreshed, revived, and released of so much tension that she was practically walking on air. They made plans for Kelly and her family to come to the log cabin the following week where they would have a big party and give the husbands and children a chance to get to know each other too. It was amazing that someone who had been such a bitter enemy for so many years had turned out to be her closest friend outside of her sisters.

As Annie shut the door to leave, Vivian McCall listened carefully for what Kelly might do next. As presumed, she pulled out her phone and dialed up her no-good second-string husband as she headed for the back of the house to her old bedroom. Vivian knew she would be occupied for a long while as she talked to Johnny. There would probably not be a better time to move on the idea that had been brewing in her mind since overhearing the conversations that had just taken place between the two women.

Vivian picked up the phone, dialed information, and then said, "Yes, I would like the number of Hal Bridges in Dockrey, Alabama. Yes, I'll be glad to hold." There couldn't have been a more evil smile to have ever crossed a person's face.

☼☼☼

On Friday morning Kyle agreed to take Billy to the University for his final meeting with Dr. Lockhart. They had to bring the twins along with them or Hal would have pitched a fit having them at the office again with only one parent. Kyle hoped Jonathan would be in today so Cindy wouldn't have to face a day alone with just Hal.

"So," Kyle asked as he helped Billy out of the van, "you think you'll be through by noon?"

"Should be," he replied as he hooked the backpack behind an arm and leaned down on his crutches. "If I think it's gonna be later, I'll call your cell."

"Well, break a leg … er, never mind … you've obviously already done that. We're heading to my parents', and after lunch we'll meet with that guy who wants to buy your boat."

"Thanks," Billy nodded. "I owe you."

Kyle shook his head and waved him off as he pulled away in the van.

Billy turned toward the building and began his ascent up the steps. Once outside of Dr. Lockhart's office, he dropped into the small bench and tried to remember any last minute things he might have forgotten to look over. His palms were sweaty, and his leg was hurting more than usual because of the tension pulsing through his body. This was literally a do or die moment for him. A lot of time and money were invested in this meeting, and not only his own. He reached for his wallet and removed the letter his mother had written him and left with Kennedy. He ran his fingers over the writing and wished she could have been here to encourage him this one last time—but in a way, through this letter, she almost was.

Even as I write this, I can only hope that you kept your promise and stayed on course with your schooling. You are too bright and gifted to lay your life at the feet of materialism. Much like Cindy, you sold yourself to a lie that happiness could be found only in worldly pleasures and fleshly appetites. As I watched Cindy's life transform into something beautiful and worthy, all I could do was hope and pray that you would someday do the same.

He folded the letter and placed it back into his billfold as he tried to muster up the confidence he knew Dr. Lockhart would want to see. *Never look vulnerable*, she had told them in the beginning. *An air of confidence automatically makes people think you know what you're doing … even if you are totally clueless.* He chuckled as he plugged the wallet back into his pants and dried his palms on his khakis. He knew how to be cocky; that came easily. But would Dr. Lockhart know the difference between cocky and confident? He hoped not, because at this moment his confidence was at an all time low. Who did he think he was trying to waltz in here and pretend he could teach for a living? What idiotic school would be willing to hire him permanently? How long would it take everyone to realize he wasn't a teacher? He was a clothes salesman. He was a flunky, a dropout, a loser. He was a twice-divorced thirty-something who couldn't hold a relationship together if his life depended on it. He was rich, but if he failed this oral exam, should he default the money? Could he in good faith keep what his mother would have given his sister had he failed to continue his education?

"Billy?" came the cheerfully familiar voice.

He looked up quickly to see Dr. Lockhart smiling by her door.

"Ready?" she asked with a twinkle in her eye.

"I'd better be," he shrugged as he pulled himself up to the crutches.

"You're right about that," she said with a laugh. "Let me get your backpack. You just wobble on into the office."

"Thanks."

Billy moved inside to the brightly decorated room and took the seat opposite the large, crowded desk. Sunflowers covered the walls, as well as framed photographs of children, grandchildren and dogs. There was no empty space available anywhere except for two chairs and paths to them. Billy looked around to see if there was a place he could lay his crutches.

"Hand 'em here," she chimed as she followed him. He gave them to her, and she leaned them against a pile of books near the window. "That ought to hold them until we're finished."

She handed him his backpack and then made her way to her own seat behind the desk. She folded her hands together and placed them gently in front of her as she gave him another big smile. It was almost sincere enough to put him at ease.

"Nervous?" she asked as she gazed at him.

"Depends," he said as he cleared his throat.

"Depends on what?"

"On whether I'm being graded for masking vulnerability or being transparent."

Dr. Lockhart leaned back in her chair and bellowed out a laugh. "You're just too charming for your own good, Mr. Marcum. That'll be a real asset to you in the teaching world … should you pass this test."

"I appreciate the vote of … uh … confidence," he said shakily. "I guess."

The amusing smile now turned to one of curiosity. "I do have a question for you before we get started here." She leaned forward again on her desk. "Just how are you and Samantha related? I believe the words she used were *in a roundabout way*."

"If I tell you, does it improve my chances of passing?"

"Are you so unprepared for this moment that you need something more than your vast knowledge of education to pass?"

He looked at her doubtfully. "Sam's my ex-wife."

That information was obviously a total shock to the professor. Her eyes now widened as she put her hand up to her mouth. "You're putting me on."

"Is that worth a passing grade?" he asked hopefully giving his best puppy dog eyes.

"You were married to Samantha Marcum?" she asked still unconvinced. "Sam—with the ponytail and glasses? I've seen eighteen year-old girls literally drooling over you when you left a room and you're telling me that you were hooked up with Samantha Marcum in holy matrimony?"

He was a little irritated by her insinuation that Sam was something inferior compared to other girls. "We were married. It was several years ago. By the time she got into the Master's program, I was a bleak memory."

"Uh huh," she nodded as she shuffled a few papers. "She's a really sharp girl … kind of threw Dr. Hardin for a loop a few times."

"The math professor?"

"She came up with some stuff that nobody could figure out," Dr. Lockhart explained as she opened a folder. "Dr. Hardin said she should have taught in college … or even higher." She looked up at Billy. "She's a brilliant girl … but odd. Never had much of a social life at all. I always wondered how she would do as a teacher, but the school says she's incredible."

"She is," he defended immediately. "The kids love her too. She even helped me a few times make some chemical equations more understandable."

"Hmmm," she sighed as she pulled out a piece of paper. "So what was the attraction between you two?"

He was the one grinning this time. Dr. Lockhart's curiosity was obviously getting the best of her.

"Well, it was strong," he said teasingly, "but I'm afraid that all answers will have to wait until you've emptied my brain of all these things I'm supposed to regurgitate to you during this little session."

Dr. Lockhart peered over her glasses at him. "Uh huh," she said again. "I get your message. It would almost be worth it to just pass you anyway to hear the full story."

"I'm game," Billy smiled at her hopefully.

"Yes, I 'm sure you are. But I have a standard to keep. Here." She handed him a paper. "If you'll just sign this, we'll get started on this little examination."

☼☼☼

Hal looked harshly at Cindy and asked her to repeat what she had just said.

She took a deep breath and told him, "Kyle took Billy to Florence for his final. He can't drive because of his broken leg."

Hal shook his head as if trying to rid it of something horrible. "So, he didn't come in on Monday, and he's not coming in on Friday either? Does this go down as vacation time?"

"He had a funeral on Monday!" Cindy exclaimed. "The pastor's grandson!"

"I don't care who it was!" he yelled back at her. "I'm sick and tired of how this entire church staff runs around without any rules or any standards and does whatever they please and then shows up on Sundays and Wednesdays like they're God's gift to the congregation!"

Cindy was about to blow. "You are out of line."

"Am I? And you're the one to judge propriety?" Hal now gave a slightly wicked grin.

She stared at him. She had never wanted to slap anyone so badly in her life.

"Let's see," he said musingly as he put his finger to his head. "Cindy Marcum Sarkos. Wild child, slept with anybody until her mom got cancer, then got hired on by the sympathetic pastor. Then somehow managed to seduce the recently divorced minister of music, another story in itself, and bed him too."

"You have just stepped over the line," she said this time through gritted teeth.

"You know what gets me about all this?" he continued. "That no one seems to care about your past or Kyle's past … or the fact that Kylla isn't even your child."

"She is legally my child!" Her voice was beginning to rise.

"Sure … legally! But biologically? How old was she when you two met?"

"Who cares? When we married, I adopted her. She's my child, and that's all that matters."

"And it doesn't bother you that your sweet little darling minister boy used to spend his nights with one of the most elusive Hollywood debutantes of all time—or that your little girl is really hers?"

She tried to keep her composure. "We've all made mistakes in our pasts."

"Yeah, but yours seem to make everyone else's pale in comparison. Shoot, your reputation goes all the way back to high school!"

She couldn't believe this. "And my slate has been wiped clean. It seems like God's grace is sufficient enough in everyone's eyes but yours!"

"Oh, here we go again," he said smugly. "That seems to be the answer with everyone in this office. Anytime something a little questionable comes up, we all sweep it under the little religious rug and everyone is just supposed to smile and move on. Well, guess what, sister?" Hal smiled again. "Those days are over."

Cindy stood, grabbed her purse, and raced toward the door.

"Don't forget," Hal called after her. "You get paid by the hour! You can't just take off anytime you please and still draw a salary like the other two!"

She didn't dignify him with a response. She walked out the door and headed straight for the Jeep. She didn't do this job for the money; she did it for the ministry. In fact, she didn't even need the money anymore after her mother's inheritance check. And the more she thought about it, the more she began to think she might never step foot into that office again.

Sixty-Two

Stephen pushed away from the table and rubbed his tummy. "That was an awesome meal, Annie. I'm beginning to think your real talents may lie in the kitchen."

She laughed as she picked up her plate and his and took them to the sink. "I'm glad to know I at least picked up something from my mother."

"The cooking would definitely come under that," he said as he stood and came over to her, wrapping his arms around her. "But where did all the musical talent come from? I've never heard your mom or dad sing … or do anything musically."

"Who knows?" she said as she leaned up to kiss him. "But I do know that Stevie's at school and Ellie's with Cassie and Angie, and we're all alone in our big house."

He pulled her closer. "Let me guess, you want to bake a cake for me?"

She grinned seductively and pulled him down into another kiss. "Not exactly."

The moment was interrupted by a buzz on the intercom from the front gate.

"What on earth could they want?" he groaned as he leaned in for another kiss.

"Ignore them," she whispered. "Whatever it is, if we don't respond, we don't have to know."

No such luck. The guard spoke into the system. "Mr. Williams? There's a guest here for you saying you'll let him in if I call you."

Stephen furled his eyebrows. "That's a lame statement. Anybody could say that." He walked over to the intercom, pressed the button and said, "Anybody could say that. I'm not expecting any visitors. Send him away, whoever he is."

"But sir," the guard explained, "he's in a limo, and I recognize the name … and the face."

Stephen glanced back at Annie, then asked into the intercom, "Who is it then?"

"Benjamin Brenner, sir."

They both turned white.

"Ben Brenner?" she whispered faintly. "You invited Ben Brenner here?"

"No!" he said immediately, but his face was flushing at the thought.

"Then why is he here? I thought we had decided …" but she

stopped. She put her hands on her hips and turned back toward the sink.

"I swear, Annie," he pleaded as he walked over, "I never told him to come here. I never told him anything … concrete."

"Concrete?" she asked in anger as she spun back around. "But you've talked with him? Even after I asked you not to?"

"He called *me*."

"About what?" she said throwing her hands up in the air.

"About working with him on a new movie trilogy."

"What?" Her temper was going to get the best of her. "How convenient! One day you tell me you're thinking about working with him, and suddenly, hoo-hah! He asks you to do that very thing? You expect me to believe you never contacted him?"

"I didn't directly," he tried to reason with her. "I did call his company, but he wasn't there. When they asked if I wanted him to return my call, I said no. I thought that would end it."

"End it! I thought we weren't even beginning it!"

"*You* thought," he clarified.

Annie gave him a hard look. "Yes. *I* thought. I didn't realize you were out soliciting work. I assumed this would be something we would decide together."

"And it is," he said as sincerely as he could. "I hadn't decided anything. He just made the proposal. I intended to think about it, and then if it seemed interesting, I thought we'd talk about it. I never told him I'd do it."

"No," Annie's face fell, "but you talked to him. And you knew I wasn't in agreement with that."

They stared at each other in silence until the intercom broke through again.

"Mr. Williams?" the guard asked. "Are you still there? What about Mr. Brenner?"

Stephen walked back to the speaker and pressed the button. "Send him on."

"What?" Annie practically screamed. "You're gonna let him in?"

He looked at her astonished. "Of course I am. He came all the way from California. I'm certainly not gonna say, *My wife has something in her craw about you. You'll have to turn around and go home*!"

She glared. She knew he was right, and what else could she do? They couldn't very well turn Benjamin Brenner away simply because she knew a deep dark secret that involved both he and Stephen. She closed her eyes and folded her arms around her.

"Annie," he said softly, "I know you don't care for him for some strange reason, but this could be an opportunity …"

"Stop," she said in defeat. "You let him in, you talk to him, and I'll be cordial. But I thought we were retiring, for at least a little while. We haven't even been out of circulation for a year. And all these ridiculous things, like the whole ordeal with Angie and us being pounded again by the paparazzi, those things will start to fade, and we can begin to live like normal people again."

She said nothing more but began to rinse the dishes and place them into the dishwasher. As she put the leftover food away—the food from her wonderfully romantic lunch with Stephen—a knot began to grow in her stomach. There was something not at all right about this situation. Either Stephen wasn't being up front with her about his conversations with Ben, or Ben was being incredibly pushy to get Stephen on his team. Why? He definitely didn't *need* Stephen to write music with him. So why else would he come all the way to Dockrey, Alabama, to Nowheresville, to talk with him?

When Stephen answered the doorbell, Annie felt the knot lurch inside of her. She had a bad feeling about all of this. Why didn't she tell him at the very beginning about her trip to see his father in Chicago? Or for that matter, why hadn't she told him about it at any point in the past six years of their relationship? One thing was for sure, when Benjamin Brenner left today, she would come clean with Stephen about the identity of his real father. This was the last day she was going to live with this burden.

"Stephen!" Benjamin Brenner gleefully shouted as the door opened. The large, hefty man literally pulled Stephen into a bear hug. "Good to see you, boy! This is one nice country setup you've got going here. I was beginning to wonder if Dockrey actually existed!"

"Well, you found it," Stephen said as he awkwardly pulled away. "Congratulations … I guess." He motioned him on inside. "Come in and have a seat. We've got a fire going in the den."

Ben followed Stephen past the living room and the kitchen into the cozy family room that overlooked the back deck and pool. Annie was there warming herself by the fire.

"Annie, the wonder girl," Ben smiled. "How are you doing?"

"I've had better days," she said honestly, or bluntly. She had never been good about hiding her feelings.

"I'll bet," Ben said almost knowingly.

She gave him a strange look.

"So, what brings you to our humble dwelling?" Stephen asked as he stood next to Annie by the fire. "I don't imagine Dockrey was on your itinerary for the week."

"No, Birmingham was," Ben said as he ran his fingers through his thick, gray hair. He glanced out toward the pool and Annie realized just how large of a man he was as he turned sidewise. "Then I remembered you had moved down here … somewhere … called the office and had the girls do a little investigative work … and … well," he turned back toward them, "… here I am."

"Here you are," Annie repeated with a hint of sarcasm.

They actually sat and visited for about thirty minutes. Annie knew the point of his being here was to talk Stephen into working with him, but as they continued to share family histories, her nervousness began to escalate. And there was a particular look Ben continued to give her that didn't settle at all. As he talked about Indiana and teaching there at a college, she began to get antsy inside, wishing she could leave, but knowing she'd better stay.

Finally Ben got to the point. "Stephen, you have to know I'm here to convince you to come and work with me. I've thought of nothing else for the past while, and I'm here to do whatever I can to get you on board for this project. What can I do to make it worth your while?"

Stephen looked over at Annie before answering. "I'm still not really sure this is something I want to do. I just retired."

Ben laughed loudly and slapped his knee. "Boys like you don't retire! You go into anonymity for a bit, but you never retire. I'm offering you a chance to come out of retirement early!"

"What if he doesn't want to?" Annie asked with a controlled, stern stare. "Maybe he enjoys spending time alone with his family for the moment."

"The moment … the moment …," Ben repeated. "But you do know that moment will end, don't you, Annie? You won't keep someone like Stephen from continuing to make his mark on the world … no matter how incredible you yourself may be."

"I don't want to keep him from anything," she replied. "But I'd like him to be able to settle down for a few years and get a chance to live a normal life for a change."

Ben nodded and stroked his lush, gray beard. "I can understand that. Especially with the horrific childhood he grew up with."

Both Annie and Stephen stared at him in shock.

"How do you know about my childhood?" Stephen asked him. "Nobody knows about … my past … nobody."

"Not even your extremely talented, beautiful and intuitive wife there?" Ben asked as he raised an eyebrow.

"Sure, Annie knows. But that's it."

"And Edrew, of course," Ben said with that knowing look at Annie.

Her stomach now dropped.

"Edrew!" Stephen exclaimed. "You knew my father?"

"Well," Ben said slowly as he stood from the loveseat and moved toward the fire, "let's say I've had that dubious pleasure … more than once."

Annie leaned back on the couch and closed her eyes. Her world was about to capsize, and she had no one to blame but herself.

"How do you know my dad?" Stephen asked wide-eyed.

"He used to live in Indiana … where I taught."

Stephen shook his head. "I don't think so. He's from Chicago."

"Actually, no," Ben said assuredly. "He's from Indianapolis. He and Ellen relocated to Chicago when they married."

Ben looked directly at Annie, and she now realized he obviously knew she was aware of all of this.

"Are you sure?" Stephen asked him. "They never told me about this. Not at all. I think you might be a little bit confused."

Ben shook his head. "Nope, I'm pretty clear about a lot of things now … like what happened to your mother after the last time I spoke with her."

"You knew my mom?" Stephen stood from the couch beside Annie and walked over to him. "How? How did you know her?"

Ben leaned around and looked to Annie. "Should I tell him, Annie? Or would you like that privilege?"

She refused to look at him. She kept her head back on the couch and her eyes closed.

"Annie?" Stephen asked in utter confusion. "What's going on?"

Ben put his arm around Stephen's shoulder and led him over to the loveseat. "You'd better sit down for this, my boy. It's a doozey." Stephen sat and Ben began to pace around the room.

"Once upon a time," he began, "I used to teach at the University of Indiana … a music professor. There were several students there who were very promising, but one young lady in particular caught my eye. She had more than just talent; she had that special … oh, I don't know, charisma maybe? Probably the same thing you saw in the lovely Annie there that made you know she could be a star. And this girl had it all. She had spunk, drive, could sing like a bird, and was awesome on the piano—like no student I'd ever seen. She sang in this nightclub in the evenings and had invited me there several times to hear her, but I always had something or other going on.

"But then one Friday evening, I had nothing at all to do, and so I showed up. When she took the stage, I was mesmerized. This girl had a presence that was way beyond nightclub. She had *it* … know what I mean, Stephen? *It*?"

Stephen nodded.

"And she was gorgeous," Ben said as he closed his eyes in memory. "She had this flowing blond hair, slight wave to it, found out later it was major curly and that she *ironed* it. But she was incredible. After that first night, I knew I had to do something … anything to get her *out there*. Now you've got to realize, all I was at that time was a struggling college professor. I was making a minimal salary trying to teach college kids how to play together in an orchestra. I was a nobody, but I was gonna give my all to make sure I got this girl introduced to someone … important … you know?

"Well, one thing led to another, and before I knew what was happening, she had so captivated my life and imagination that I ended up having a … fling … I thought, with her. But it wasn't long before I realized I'd fallen head over heels in love."

Ben paused as he looked down at Stephen.

But Stephen shook his head as he asked, "Mom? Are you saying this woman was my mother? It couldn't have been. She had no, well, her hands were disabled. They were gnarled. She couldn't play the piano. It would have been impossible."

Ben knelt down beside Stephen. "She was incredible, Stephen. She was beautiful, bubbling, and could play the piano every bit as good as you."

Stephen squinted his eyes in confusion.

"Here's the sad part," Ben said ruefully. "I'd been offered my first real break … a gig writing some stuff for a television network. It was gonna pay well, but more than that, it would begin to introduce me to some people who could make things happen. We started dreaming about the possibilities, and they all centered on Ellen. She deserved it. I was gonna be her hero … until she came to me one night and told me she was pregnant."

Ben stood again and walked back to the fire. "I told her she had to be crazy to think we could have a kid right now. It would ruin everything. I should have known she'd never think otherwise, but like an idiot, I thought I could talk her into an abortion."

Ben now looked back at Stephen, and his eyes were definitely showing remorse. "I told her the best I could do at the moment was pay for the abortion. She slapped me." Ben looked out toward the pool. "I never saw her again after that. I even went to her parents' house, a huge mistake there. They were these devout Catholics, and when they found out she was seeing a Jewish boy, you would have thought the Apocalypse had come. All they said to me was that their fallen daughter deserved whatever she got. And I deserved whatever I got because I was the devil that led her into fornication."

Stephen was in shock as he tried to process all he was hearing. "But her hands …"

Ben shook his head. "Her father did that to her … with a hammer."

"What?" Stephen cried out. "He … what? How could anyone …?"

"Edrew was this sleaze bag that hung around the nightclub," Ben continued. "He had a major thing for Ellen, and she was always nice to him. She'd get on to me for talking bad about him, but he wasn't even in her class. She was this incredible, vivacious package of pure talent and beauty, and he was this greasy factory worker that would sit on the front row and gawk at her whenever she sang."

"Why did she marry him?" Stephen finally asked something coherent. "How could she? He was such a … lowlife."

Ben shook his head. "He found her with her fingers smashed, parents disowning her, and me, the idiot lover who tried to force her to kill her baby because it was too inconvenient for my plans—and Edrew became her hero instead. He took her away from all the things that had hurt her so bad that night, and he gave her a life of escape far away from Indianapolis."

Stephen stood up and tried to shake the thoughts from his head. "Why?" was all he could ask. "Why did you …?"

"There are many unanswered questions in all of this," Ben confessed, "and many that can be answered, but the answers are really pitiful." Ben walked up to Stephen and put his hand on his shoulder. "I regretted losing her back then more than I could ever tell you. But when I found out the truth … what her parents did to her, that she actually married Edrew, that *you*, Stephen Williams, are really my son, I couldn't sit back and just keep silent."

"I should think not!" Stephen said forcefully. "How long have you known?"

Ben looked over at Annie. "Not near as long as your loving wife."

"What?" He was even more confused now than before. "Annie didn't know about this. How could she have?"

Ben sighed and scratched his gray mass of hair again. "You want to answer that, Annie, or do you want me to just keep on going?"

She shook her head in complete disgust and said, "Have at it. You seem to really be enjoying it."

"Annie visited Edrew in Chicago several years back," Ben told him.

"You're kidding?" He looked at Annie. "You saw my dad in Chicago? When? How?"

Annie finally spoke, but she knew with every word she was nailing herself to a cross of her own making. "It was when I went up to Big Time Advertising to check about the whole music stealing incident. I looked up Edrew. I had some time on my hands so I drove out there and …" She stopped.

Stephen walked over to her slowly and shook his head. His face was pulsing with grief. "He told you? You knew all this?"

She turned away as she nodded.

"Why didn't you tell me? How could you *not* tell me? I told you everything about my life—my hurt, my anger, my deepest pain. Annie, how could you *not* tell me?"

She bit her lip as she tried to explain. "Because he had promised Ellen he would never tell you. She didn't want you to know. It was a big burden for me and a huge struggle. But who was I to challenge your mother's wishes? I didn't feel it was my place. I didn't know what to do, Stephen."

"You didn't know what to do?" he cried out. "You've been with me every year to see him at the holidays, and you've watched me abase myself before him again and again and again—begging, pleading, hoping for some kind of acceptance from him, and all the while you knew he wasn't even my father?"

She jumped to her feet. "I wanted to respect your mother!" she attempted to make him understand again. "Your memories of her were nothing but good and pure! I wanted you to keep that, Stephen!" She took a step toward him. "That's all you had of her. How could I tell you this? It would have tarnished her image … her memory. I couldn't bring myself to be the one responsible for that."

Stephen took a step away from her. "You could've told me the truth. And trust me; the truth would've been so much better than the lie … the miserable lie I've had to live with all these years."

Annie looked at Ben. "Congratulations. I think you've accomplished exactly what you came here to achieve today."

Ben replied by saying, "I came to tell my son that his past wasn't his past, and that he can choose whatever future he wants to choose … with or without the approval of his very beautiful, talented, though extremely deceptive wife."

Stephen walked to the French doors and stared out at the pool. There was no way he could process all of this right now. He needed time away, time alone, and time to evaluate his life. It seemed that nothing at all was ever as it appeared, and that everyone he held dear, including his mother and his wife, were liars. Only his father, his real father, the man who had wanted him murdered even before he was born, was willing to tell him the truth. Who could he trust? Who else did he have in this world?

He turned around and looked to Ben as he asked, "Does that offer still stand?"

"The trilogy?" Ben smiled. Stephen nodded. "You betcha."

He looked to Annie this time. "I think I've had enough of retirement for a while. I'll pack a few things and head back with Ben to California."

Annie, ever in control, nodded slowly. "I take it that you won't be spending Christmas with the children."

"I'll see a lawyer as soon as I get out there," he said coldly. "You'd better find a good one. We might as well let them start hashing this out."

That statement hit Annie with reality. He was leaving her, not for a little while, but for good.

"If that's what you really want," she forced herself to say. "I think we should talk to a counselor before we talk to a lawyer."

"Talk to whoever *you* want," he said without looking at her, "but I'm only talking to a lawyer."

He left the den and headed for the stairs. Part of Annie screamed for her to run after him and beg him to stay and work it out, but the proud part that stood there with Ben Brenner refused to budge. And as usual, that was the part that won.

Annie sat alone on the couch for nearly an hour. She needed to leave to get Stevie from Kindergarten, but her mind was completely wrecked. How did she explain this to her children? How did she tell them their father was gone and they would be spending time traveling from one end of America to the other to visit their parents from now on? How did she upset their perfect little life? How did she tell her family? How did she tell the world?

Before she could answer any of those questions, the bile had risen so high in her throat she could no longer stand it. She ran to the bathroom and threw up what was left of her wonderful lunch with Stephen. As she knelt on the floor, finishing the heaving and trying to regain control of the lurching in her stomach, her emotions began to explode. She sobbed in a way she never had before, and she felt so completely lost that she wondered if she could even move again. One thing was for sure: she was in no condition to get Stevie from school. She had to call somebody … fast.

Sixty-Three

"William James Marcum," the voice reverberated throughout the auditorium. Billy stood from his seat, thankful for the new boot that allowed him to at last get rid of the clumsy crutches. As he hobbled across the platform to receive his diploma, he looked to the area where he knew his twin sister was sitting. He pumped his fist high into the air and yelled, "Yeah! I did it!" The audience broke into applause even though most of the group had no idea who he was. He saw Cindy grin big as her eyes sparkled from tears, and she gave him a wave as he made his way to the president. He shook hands firmly and then received his folder containing the coveted document that would have made his mother proud. He looked toward the camera and flashed his best smile, and a few girls let out some whoops in response. When he sat back down in his seat, his heart was so full he felt he could burst. He had done it. He had accomplished something legitimate, something worthy, something right.

When the ceremony was finished, the graduates said their final goodbyes and began to look for their families and friends. As Billy headed for the van, someone yelled out his name amidst the scurrying. He turned around, not wanting to miss the chance to get another hug from a young, dazzling girl. He saw a hand waving above the heads and maneuvered his way to get a look. Sam. As soon as their eyes met, his heart began to melt, and every other girl he had held that night faded from his mind.

"Wow," he said loudly, trying to shout above the noise. "I didn't expect you to come … not at all."

"How could I not?" she shouted back. She then looked down at his leg. "When'd you get that? Where are the crutches?"

He smiled briefly but then began to look around trying to find a place they could go for a moment that was a little quieter. He spotted a door which led to an empty room down the end of the hall and motioned Sam to follow him. She shook her head in confusion, so he took her hand and led her. He walked inside, turned on the light, and then shut the door behind them.

"There," he said softly. "That's better." He turned toward her and smiled again. "Thanks for coming. I owe you a bunch for this."

"I know," she replied with pretend smugness. "That's why I had to come. I couldn't miss the chance to see my handiwork in action. It was sort of like watching some of those football players finally graduate from high school. I'd struggled through Algebra and Geometry with many of them."

"So, where's Crandall?" Billy wondered. "I figured he be shadowing your every move by now."

She blushed a bit. "He had to work … but he told me to come on anyway. He knew it was important to me."

"He seems like a really great guy."

She half-nodded. "I'm not here to talk about Jeremy. I just wanted to see you do this with my own eyes. I nearly jumped out of my shoes when I saw your name in the paper with the list of graduates this term."

"Me too," he grinned. There was so much he wanted to say to her, but he had come to terms with the fact that he needed to let her go so she could build a real life for herself.

"So, what's next?" she asked him as she picked a small piece of something from his tie.

"Subbing for the rest of the year. There's an English teacher in Dockrey that's about to go on maternity leave, and they've asked me if I'm interested in taking her place for the next couple of months."

"English?"

Billy shook his head. "Definitely not my forte', but it would be a consistent job for a little while."

"Will you be living with Cindy?"

He nodded. "Yeah … until I can figure out where I'm going. I'll be putting in applications all over Alabama and hopefully by the summer I'll have a more definite idea of where I'm headed."

"Sounds like a plan."

"Yeah, it does," he said proudly. "Can you believe all of this is really happening?"

Sam looked up at him with an unusual expression. "Actually, I can. I always knew you had it in you … that you could do anything you wanted. You just had to learn that things worth having can't be *charmed* out of life—you have to work for them instead."

He thought for a moment and then nodded in agreement. "It's been a hard lesson to learn."

They stared at each other silently then he asked, "What are you up to right now? We're heading over to the tower for a celebration supper. Wanna come?"

She shook her head. "No, but thank you. This is a time for you to be with your family."

"Well, you're *practically* family. You still have our last name."

Sam forced herself to smile. There was nothing she wanted more in life than to be a part of this family again. "Yeah, but I'm a teacher too, and I have some major Trigonometry homework to grade."

"Oh, come on. Let me twist your arm a little bit. Do something unpredictable."

"I'm a math person—everything is predictable and logical. It goes against my nature to be spur of the moment."

He raised his hands in surrender. "At least come and say *hello* to Cindy and Kyle. She'll be bummed to know she missed you."

"Then don't tell her you saw me."

He looked at her briefly and sighed. "Okay, you win. But only because I don't feel like arguing with you … not because I don't want you to come."

"Fair enough," she smiled back at him.

She offered her hand, and he took it and shook it, but he wouldn't let go. Instead, he pulled her to him and held her in a tight embrace. She reached her arms around his waist and let herself become enmeshed in the moment. It wouldn't matter where she went in life or whatever she did, this would always be the place she would long to be. She let herself linger way longer than she should have. When he finally pulled away, her eyes were close to watering.

"Sure you won't come?" he asked one more time.

She could only shake her head.

"All-righty then," he shrugged doubtfully. "I guess … uh … I'll see you around, huh?"

She nodded, but she knew they wouldn't make contact again. Each goodbye was getting harder.

When he left the room, she forced herself to breathe and stand tall even though she felt her entire world had just been crushed. She let the scent of his cologne weave around her head a few more moments before she turned out the light and left the room. When she walked outside, it was cold, dark, and pouring down rain. This had to be the wettest winter she could ever remember, and they had already had one good snow. She stepped out into the cold and let the biting rain sting her cheeks as she trotted toward her car. She wondered what had possessed her to wear high heels on a night like this. Well, that was easy—Billy.

The rain began to fall even harder, reminding her of the night she had brought him home from the ER after the wreck. It had been just as cold and just as wet, but at least he was there … with her. Now she was utterly alone … again.

She fumbled in her purse for the keys as the rain went another notch harder. She was now completely drenched, and she couldn't find them anywhere. If only she had a light or something. She shook her purse hoping to locate them by the jingle, but no jingle sounded. She reached into her coat pocket to see if perhaps she had placed them there. Nothing. Had she dropped them in the auditorium? Lost them in the room? Left them in her car? At this moment it really didn't matter anymore. The cold of the night was nothing compared to the cold in her heart at the finality of losing the love of her life a second time.

Slowly the sobs began to make their way to the surface, and before she could gain control, the first one escaped, then another, and another, and she slowly slid to the ground beside her locked car. As the rain poured down upon her body, her soul stormed inside. She dropped her face into her hands and cried like she did the night he left her years ago. Only this time it was worse because she knew if she had said the word, he would probably come back.

But then the thoughts of his second wife at Blue Bayou entered her mind, and the despair she was feeling began to dissolve into anger. She remembered clearly why she could never have him back—she would never be enough for Billy Marcum. No matter how hard she tried, how much she loved him, how far she might go for him, *she* would never be enough. There would always be women in his life like Angie and Kirstie, women who were larger than life that captured his imagination. She might have captured his heart, but again, that would never be enough … never … and she had to come to grips with that and find some way to move on … again.

☼☼☼

Annie didn't want to answer the phone. It had been two weeks since Stephen had left, and they hadn't spoken once. She stared at his name lighting up her screen. What would she say? What *should* she say? Was there any way to heal their marriage and start over again?

She braced herself and finally answered. "Hello?"

"Annie." It was unemotional … plain … uncaring.

"Yes," she replied in like manner. She could never let him know the depth of hurt he had caused her.

"We need to talk about Christmas," he said gruffly.

"Concerning what?"

"I'd like the kids to come out here and spend Christmas with me."

"What!" she exclaimed a little too loudly. "You've got to be kidding!"

"Believe me, I wouldn't dream of picking up this phone to call you if I weren't serious. I want to see the kids for Christmas. After the holidays we can began to work out some kind of custody schedule."

She could feel her insides begin to wrench. "Stephen, you may despise me, but don't do this to the kids."

"Excuse me?" he said sternly. "And what is it that you think I'm doing to the kids?"

"For heaven's sake, you've taken off and left them for two weeks without so much as a word, and now you want to rip them away from the only security they've known during that time. Can you imagine how hard it's been trying to answer all their questions about their Daddy? The only thing they've been looking forward to is the fact that they get to spend Christmas here with my family."

"Yeah, well these are issues you should have considered through all the years you lived a lie with me."

What a zing. She was guilty. There was no way she could fight against that accusation, yet everything within her told her that sending the kids away from what was familiar would be pure disaster in their little lives.

"Stephen," she would try reasoning with him one more time, "just take a moment and think about what you're asking. At least let them get through Christmas, and then we can discuss some kind of visitation plan. I have no intentions of trying to keep you from seeing them, but I don't think this is the time to upset their lives any further."

"Either we can work out something here … now … over the phone, or I can contact my lawyer and have something drawn up legally within the next 24 hours."

She couldn't believe he was going to play hardball with her over the kids. She couldn't bear to allow them to be a part of this battle.

"Don't do this," she pleaded with him. "I'm more than willing to be fair, but …"

"Either send the kids here for Christmas, or be prepared to receive some kind of legal demand tomorrow."

Anger began to rise and she knew it would erupt if she didn't get off the phone immediately. "Fine!" she yelled. "Be a jerk about this! It appears that we're both big liars now! Me about your father, and you about your genuine concern for your children!"

"You are out of line!"

"Am I? You don't speak with them for two weeks and then you call and demand they leave all their plans and dreams for the holidays to be with you? I don't think there's anything out of line with my thinking."

"No, I suppose you don't! You always think you're right, always entitled to your personal opinion! Well not anymore!"

She wanted to slam the phone to the floor, but forced herself to remain on the line. "Whatever," she finally gave in with exasperation. "If you insist on acting like a rear-end through all of this, I'm certainly not gonna play this game. Get your reservations and give me the details, but I'm not sending them on a plane alone. You'd better get a round ticket for my father too."

"Your father is *not* bringing my kids to California," he said firmly.

"Fine!" she bellowed this time. "Then call your overpaid lawyer and come up with a better plan! But I'm not sending my children on a plane alone … or with any stranger … all the way to California only to further upset their holidays! If you want to keep this clean, you'd better give just a little bit. I'll bend only so far, Stephen. I admit I brought all this on myself, but I won't see my children tortured in the midst of it all."

He was silent as he thought through the offer. "Okay," he said begrudgingly. "I'll make arrangements for your father to fly them out, but I have no intentions of speaking with him when they arrive."

"Don't worry," she shot back. "I don't imagine you're his most favorite person in the world at the moment either."

That comment actually stung Stephen because Jonathan had been more of a father to him than any other man ever in his life. As he hung up the phone, the bitterness within him concerning Annie's deceptiveness began to sweep over him again. It wasn't fair. Not only had he lost his wife and kids, he had lost a family that he never dreamed he could have. No, he didn't *have* to leave, but he couldn't bring himself to forgive her. She knew a powerful truth, something that could have relieved much misery from his past, but she never told him … for six years.

He threw the phone across the room and found himself aching for the life he had walked away from. For two weeks he had gone over movie plots and scripts with Ben. He had stayed out late at night doing the Hollywood scene and come into the office early mornings because sleep continued to elude him. He was absolutely miserable and he missed his family terribly. He wanted to believe it was just his kids, but the truth was he missed them all … even Annie, but he refused to let himself believe that. She had done the unthinkable, and no amount of love could ever cover such an incredulous mistake.

Sixty-Four

Doug walked through the hallway at the church toward Hal's office to take some measurements for shelves. He stopped by the water fountain for a quick drink and was startled by Hal's voice behind him.

"So, it's the illustrious Doug Mason to the rescue."

Doug spun around to face a smirking Hal.

"I suppose," he replied unsure. "I'm coming to measure the walls in your office."

Hal bit his lip and continued to smile condescendingly. "How does it feel to be the low boy on the totem pole in a family of superheroes?"

"What?" He had no idea to what Hal was referring.

"Sure," Hal balked mockingly as he headed toward the office with Doug following beside. "You've got the most righteous-reverend for a father-in-law, the musical genius for a wife, the world famous sister-in-law and her entertainer husband, then the missionary doctor with a dead son that the whole community thinks she's next to God." Hal paused as he looked over to Doug. "Then there's you—manual-labor man."

Doug sneered and shook his head. "Yeah, that's me, but it puts food on the table and a really fine roof over our heads."

"And so you're okay with that? Being the … well … the bottom of the family pile?"

Doug would have pelted the guy had they not been standing on church property, but he continued to act as if it all were a big joke. He chose to ignore the comment and walked on into the office.

"I don't believe you wiped your feet at the door," Hal remarked. "It's very muddy outside today."

Doug ignored him and began to measure the wall behind the desk.

"I don't want any shelves there," Hal said as he folded his arms and leaned against the open door.

He put down the tape measure, sighed deeply, and turned back to face him. "Then which walls would you like me to work on?"

"Hmmm," Hal muttered as he glanced around the office, "I'm not completely sure."

Doug clamped his jaws shut and folded his arms as he waited for a reply, but Hal just continued looking through the office.

"Look, Buddy," Doug said patiently, "I've got some *manual labor* to get back to, so if you could point out where you want the shelves, I'll take the measurements and be on my merry way."

Hal still didn't seem satisfied with whatever he was trying to accomplish. "I'll tell you what, why don't you just measure them all, except for the one behind the desk, the *wrong* one, and when I decide, I'll give you a call and let you know."

He slipped his tape and pencil back into his tool belt and shook his head. "I'll tell *you* what," he said calmly as he headed toward Hal and the door. "Decide where you want the shelves and then call me. When I can find another block of time some afternoon between all my *menial* jobs, I'll try to fit you in."

Hal put out his arm to keep Doug from leaving. "You seem a little disturbed, Mr. Mason."

"Not near as disturbed as you're gonna be if you don't move your arm from the front of the door."

"Are you threatening me?" Hal asked as he continued to condescend. "Are you suggesting you might do bodily harm to me if I don't comply with your every wish?"

"Not at all," Doug smiled at him. "I'm just *suggesting* that this is one of the few days I have time to come and measure a place where I'll do work for *free*. The possibility is growing strongly that your new set of shelves will not be custom built, but rather bought from Dollar General." Doug firmly gripped Hal's arm and moved it down as he walked past.

"Well, that may be better anyway," Hal scorned. "I wouldn't want any two-bit, cheap-rated shelves."

Doug smiled and shook his head. "Nope, I don't suppose you would. Your office won't look anything like Jonathan and Kyle's cheap offices. Instead of oak and mahogany, you can get the lovely pressed board shelves you put together yourself with an Allen wrench."

As Doug walked off, the smile on Hal's face faded into a scowl. The biggest thorn in his flesh at this church was the fact that Jonathan and Kyle had these magnificently plush, nice, and roomy offices, especially Kyle, and he had been consigned to a corner room with faded carpet and old paneling. His one hope had been to fix it up to such a point that it would be the envy of the other staff, but he now realized that his only chance to do that had just walked out of the building. Doug did all the carpentry at the church for free—the church just bought the materials. Hal had made big plans when he had heard that, and had even drawn out an incredibly furnished set of shelving complimented by a custom made mahogany desk. Without Doug, that wouldn't happen. He jammed his hand in his pocket and looked back inside the pathetic room. It really was ugly.

✪✪✪

"Of course I'll fly out there with them," Jonathan told a distraught Annie, "but I don't like the idea at all of them leaving here for the holidays. This is gonna break their little hearts."

Annie blew up at the hair dangling in her eyes. "I know, but I don't like the idea of starting this whole process by letting the courts decide what's best for my kids. And I don't like the idea of letting Stephen think he can make whatever demands he wants and I'll just roll over and comply."

Barbara wiped back the tears as she shook her head. "I still can't believe this is happening. Stephen was such a wonderful husband; he adored you. How could he just walk …"

"Because I was a royal jerk," Annie said as she cut off her mother's remark. "I knew some facts that could have relieved a lot of his suffering, stuff he suffered for many years."

Jonathan assured her, "You made what you thought was the right decision. You were trying to honor his mother's wishes."

"Yeah … well," she stood up from the table and moved toward the fire, "it was obviously the *wrong* decision. I'm really good at doing that, you know."

"Honey, don't beat yourself up over this," Barbara tried to console.

"You're kidding me, right?" Annie replied sarcastically. "I had this perfect life, the man of my dreams, two incredible children, my music known all over the world, and now a log home back here near my family, and it's all blown up into dust because of my stupid decision."

"No," Jonathan said firmly. "It's all blown up because Stephen refused to extend a little grace to you over this stupid decision."

"Thanks, Daddy," she murmured. "I feel so much better now that you've pointed that out."

"Glad to see that sharp wit of yours hasn't faded any," he said with slight disdain. "But you've got to understand something here, Annie—all the blame doesn't lie on you alone. Stephen took a vow. That vow promised to love you through the good and the bad … through …"

"Blah, blah, blah. You can go through the whole ceremony with me, but it doesn't change the fact that I knew something vitally important that he deserved to know, and I never said anything."

Barbara jumped in again. "But it wasn't a malicious holding back of the truth. You were only doing what you thought was most honorable. I'll be frank with you, Annie, I don't know if I'd have done anything differently. Stephen believed his mother was a saint. She died as a result of following *his* dreams—dreams she had to give up for herself because of her own indiscretions, and I can't say whether I would have kept that truth from him also. Why destroy his memories of her in the name of honesty? I don't think it's as simple as you and Stephen are want to make it."

"Or as simple as Benjamin Brenner tried to make it sound," Jonathan added.

Annie held back the tears as she turned to face the fireplace. "That all makes it appear so reasonable, but it doesn't eliminate the fact that what has happened, happened. I never believed I deserved him anyway. I was so pig-headed and stubborn, and he was so gentle and loving." She reached up to rub her watering eyes. "Who on earth was I to think I could ever be what he needed?"

"Hold on just a second there," Barbara said defensively as she walked over to her. "Stephen was a lonely hermit before you walked into his life. He was dark and brooding, simply finishing out a contract that had long ago lost its appeal. When you appeared on the scene, it was like sunshine rising again for the first time in years."

"Yeah," Annie nodded defiantly, "and I burned him badly, didn't I?"

"No!" Barbara persisted. "You brought him life, Annie … *real* life. He became a whole person when he married you. And his choice to throw all that away because of a mistake … a big one in his eyes … is utterly foolish."

"Annie," Jonathan now left the table and came over to the couch, "I appreciate the fact that you don't want to use the children as a weapon in all of this, but at the same time, you need to think about their needs very clearly. Don't let your personal guilt cause you to just lie down and roll over at Stephen's every demand."

"I don't want to fight this out in court," she said weakly. "I just want us to agree for the sake of the children and move on. I know Stephen adores them, loves them, cares for them. I can't believe he would do anything to deliberately hurt them."

Jonathan dropped wearily onto the couch, the couch that Stephen had bought him two Christmases ago. "I don't want to believe that either, but I would never have believed he could have hurt my little girl like this. I also am having a hard time understanding how he can selfishly demand that you send the kids to him for Christmas just out of the blue when this is their home—and this is what they've been anticipating for the past several weeks."

Annie had to wipe another tear. She hated feeling weak and defeated, but there was no other way to describe life at this point. And as much as she loved her children, they weren't her deepest love. Stephen had been her dream, her fulfillment, her deepest desire come true. The children were the result of that love, not the ends. The children were her gifts of life to him, one of the few ways she could give back to him all that he had given her. Without him, life was no longer complete, not even life with the children. And who was she to deny him any rights or time when it came to them? Nobody. That's who Annie Wright Williams really was—nobody. She had always known it, and now the truth had simply come to fruition. She didn't deserve Stephen, she never had, and the more she thought about it, the more she realized that had it not been the lie about his father, it would have eventually been something else.

The wrenching in her stomach was unbearable again. She grabbed her abdomen and practically ran to the bathroom.

"Annie!" he mother called out behind her. "Are you all right?"

She couldn't answer. She barely had enough time to slam the door and lift the seat before the bile came gushing up her throat.

☼☼☼

Sam sat sleepily in her last class before the holidays. The students worked nervously on their semester exams as she rubbed her eyes and took another swallow of coffee. She had been unable to sleep last night. Jeremy had dropped by on his way to the hospital to say he had Friday night off and wanted to take her somewhere special. She had agreed to his face, but inside she was reluctant. She knew she should be head over heels and overjoyed that such a man would give her this kind of attention, but the only image that came to her mind all night was Billy's smile. She wondered if there would ever come a time in her life when she wouldn't think about him, wouldn't continue to feel for him, and wouldn't long to be with him.

When she was with Jeremy, she enjoyed it. He was polite, witty, intelligent, and easy to talk with. He was a gentle spirit, and he literally treated her like royalty. But when he was gone, all she thought of was Billy—and Jeremy was most definitely not Billy. Jeremy was stable, hardworking, sincere, and logical. Billy was erratic, a drifter, a charmer, and a dreamer. Jeremy was a man she could easily trust, but probably never deeply love. Billy was someone whom she would always love, but could never trust again. But the reality was that Billy wasn't here and Jeremy was. Billy had walked out of her life … twice now … and Jeremy was begging to be in her life for as long as she would let him.

"Ms. Marcum?"

Sam opened her eyes to see Paulo standing at her desk. "I can't help you; it's an exam, Paulo."

"I know," he said slightly frustrated. "But I cannot remember the order of this one equation. It is one of two, and I always get them backwards."

"I'm sorry, but you know I can't help you." She honestly felt bad about it. Paulo deserved at least a hint of help. He had overcome so many adversities to rise to where he had. He was an honor student, a star athlete, and very well-liked by all the students. He was cheerful, helpful, and always gracious. His eyes pleaded for just an inkling of hope. She reached out her hand for the paper.

"Hmmm," she mumbled to herself as she looked at the problem where the pencil markings had stopped. She stood and cleared her throat at the front of the classroom. "Class," she said rather softly. They all looked up at her. "How many of you would use division to begin number fifteen, and how many of you would use multiplication … just for the first step. Division first … raise your hands if you'd start with division."

Two students raised their hands.

"Okay, what about multiplication as the first step?" The rest of the class raised their hands.

"Very good," she smiled. "I would say the majority rules in this situation."

She handed the paper back to an extremely grateful Paulo, and then smiled as the two boys who had raised their hands for division began frantically erasing their papers.

This is what I'm here for, she thought as she sat back down. *It's not about Billy, it's not about Jeremy— it's about Paulo … and those two idiots in the back of the class who were probably copying off of each other anyway.*

☼☼☼

"We don't wanna go, Mommy," Stevie whined again as Annie packed their bags. "We wanna be here for Christmas. Why can't Daddy be here for Christmas? He was gonna cut us down a big tree and then we was gonna put popcorns on it."

She struggled to keep her emotions in check in front of the kids.

"I wanna be *here*," Ellie joined in. "I wanna be with Cassie and Mimi and Gaga … and you." Ellie ran over to Annie and grabbed her leg. "Please, Mommy."

Annie didn't want to deride Stephen, but they were breaking her heart. How could she just pack them up and send them off like this simply because he had demanded it. She dropped down onto the bed and motioned for the children to join her. They both plopped down beside her, still sniffling and whining.

"Babies," she began gently, "I don't want you to go either. I wish we could all be together for Christmas like we had planned, but Daddy just isn't gonna be here this time. He hasn't seen you for a long while, and he needs to be with his babies … and you need to be with him."

"Then call him and tell him to come home," Stevie said simply. "Why can't we just be at Christmas together?"

How could she answer these questions? It would eventually come down to one of the parents taking the blame. It was so tempting to put it all on him, but that wouldn't be fair. In truth, it was her fault, but how could she tell that to her children? As she held them both, the knots in her stomach began to surge together again, and the bile was beginning to rise. She tried to gain control, but it wasn't long before she had to excuse herself and run to the bathroom.

Sixty-Five

The flight was only a couple of hours, but Jonathan's battle with his emotions felt like years as a grandchild sat on either side of him in first class. Neither was excited about the flight nor the visit to California with their father. They clung to Jonathan as though he was a lifeline back to their mother, and he wasn't at all pleased with the situation. He wanted to give Stephen a piece of his mind as soon as the plane landed, but he knew that would be the wrong approach. In fact, he knew Stephen was probably expecting that—and was ready for it. He was so full of bitterness and hurt toward Annie that even his judgment as a loving father was terribly clouded. Jonathan prayed desperately for God to help him extend grace to this man who had only learned how to protect himself over the years … and not think of others first. Stephen had never had an example of a loving father, and so he had no clue how to act when his deepest trust had been betrayed. And now he was working in the presence of a father whose first choice had been to terminate his life rather than sacrifice to bring him into the world. Jonathan shook his head in helplessness as little Ellie snuggled deeper into his safe and familiar arms.

When the jet finally landed, Jonathan and the children were escorted off first. As was typical, Stephen was surrounded by security. As soon as he saw his children, he broke through the guards and ran to them. But rather than respond with excitement, the kids held tighter to Jonathan's hands. Stephen looked at them in shock and hurt.

"Stevie … Ellie … it's Daddy," he said sadly.

Stevie nodded, but Ellie looked down to the floor.

Stephen looked up at Jonathan with disgust. "What kind of stuff have you been feeding my kids? They've never reacted to me like this before."

Jonathan looked as compassionately as he could. "They've never had their father walk out on them without saying *goodbye* before. They've never had to leave their mother behind at Christmas in order to be with their father. They've never been forced to go to a strange place without the security of a whole family before. Nobody's fed them anything, Stephen. They're just little children trying to deal with the reality that part of their world is suddenly falling apart."

"Right," he mumbled. "I should have known you all would rally around Annie and blame me for this. I bet she's had a heyday spilling out what a rotten person I am … to you … to the kids."

Jonathan shook his head. "Actually, all she keeps saying to us is that she never deserved you in the first place and your walking out on her is completely understandable."

"What?" He had been caught off guard. "I know Annie. She's probably badmouthed me constantly … especially to the children."

Jonathan continued to hold tightly to the nervous little hands. "Obviously you don't know Annie, because the person you just described has yet to show up in all of this."

Stephen knelt down to face his kids. "Look, no matter what your mom said about me, I still love you."

Ellie looked up at him. "Mommy loves you."

"Oh, that's good," Stephen chuckled, "very good."

"And it's true," Jonathan said gently. "Whatever you may think Annie's been doing or saying since you left, it has nothing to do with degrading you. If she had wanted to fight you over this, I wouldn't be standing here with these two trembling kids right now, ready to hand them over to you even though it's the absolute last thing I want to do. And no matter how much money you have, the only court in the land that would have forced these kids here at Christmas would have been a dishonest one … you and I both know that. The fact that they're here is simply because of Annie's guilt … and her desire to not hurt you any deeper … even at the cost of her children."

Stephen stood back up and stared out toward the landing area.

"There's a good way and a bad way to handle this, Stephen," Jonathan continued. "And you're not choosing the higher road."

Tears streamed down Jonathan's face as he flew back to Birmingham and to a house full of warmth, cheer, decorations and joy. He thought of his precious grandchildren that would miss it all, and of his gifted daughter whose life had been wonderfully changed by a man who was now choosing to destroy her for something done out of innocence, love, respect, and quite a bit of immaturity. Had he known, he would have guided her in a different way than the one she chose, but that wasn't possible now. And the only choice left was to extend grace to Stephen—the man who refused to extend any grace to his daughter … or his grandchildren. The root of bitterness had been planted within Stephen as a child, and now it had become full grown. Unfortunately for Stephen … and for Annie … he was unable to distinguish between deliberate hurt and ignorant hurt.

✿✿✿

Barbara finished putting away the food from supper and went in to join Annie and Angie on the couch. Her heart was heavier than she could ever remember. One daughter had just lost a child, and the other the love of her life. Everything had seemed so perfect just a few months ago, but now everything was falling apart. She desperately wanted to wave that imaginary magic motherly wand and bring happiness and joy back into all their lives, but there was no such thing. The best she could do was offer words of encouragement and always be available if they ever needed to talk, or needed a babysitter.

"Annie," Barbara tried to sound cheerfully, "why don't you and Angie go get a few of your things and you just stay with us for the rest of the holidays. You can have your old room."

Angie punched Annie and grinned as she said, "We can pretend we're teenagers again."

Annie shook her head. "Thanks, Moms, but I'd rather be at *my* home. Even though nobody's there, it's still my security … it's where I belong."

Angie remarked, "They say *home is where the heart is* you know."

"I know … and that's most definitely where my heart is right now. Even though Stephen and the kids are gone, it's my home. There's a comfort in being there. I don't necessarily understand it, but it's just where I want to be."

"But you've been so sick lately," Barbara reminded her. "I'd feel better knowing you were here so someone could take care of you."

"Sick?" Angie asked. "How so?"

Annie waved her off. "Just a nervous stomach or something. I'm having a hard time keeping food down at times."

Angie nodded. "You're probably right. With all you've been going through, it's bound to have some physiological effects." Angie shifted on the couch and then let out a sudden scream. Everyone turned their attention to her immediately.

"You all right?" Annie asked as she moved beside her.

"Hallelujah!" Angie yelled out this time.

"What is wrong with you?" Barbara said with great concern as she came running over.

"It's baby time!" Angie said excited. "It's finally coming!"

Annie's eyes grew wide. "You're in labor?"

Angie nodded enthusiastically.

"It's about time," Barbara said as she started wringing her hands. "Let me go get Michael. Annie, are you staying or going?"

"Definitely going … but not home," Annie grinned. "I'm headed to Tupelo to have a baby!"

"Should I stay with Cassie?" Barbara wondered.

Angie shook her head. "No way. Cassie's gonna be there when this one comes. After all she's been through with losing Carter, she deserves the chance to see this one come into the world."

"Are you crazy?" Annie was disgusted. "You're gonna let her watch?"

"She's watched everything else under the sun birthed," Angie explained. "Why not her little brother or sister? She knows the process well. I don't have a problem with it."

"She knows about how babies are born?"

"She's very inquisitive," Angie told her. "After a while the whole stork and baby business became completely illogical." Angie moaned out again as she grabbed her stomach. "Y'all had better hurry. I've been through this before, and when I start feeling like this, it's not long."

☼☼☼

Michael had passed out on the delivery room floor, but Cassie was as bright-eyed as ever. Two nurses had been called in to help get Michael back to consciousness, and the doctor actually gave Cassie a towel and braced her arm as he helped her deliver the second baby. When the first baby was delivered, Cassie squealed and Michael cut the cord. But as soon as the doctor said, "Hang on, there's another one," Michael turned green and fell flat to the floor. Cassie's eyes grew wide as she turned back to see, completely oblivious to her father's condition.

With Angie back in her room and Michael laid out on a cot beside her, Cassie kept complaining about not being able to see the babies.

"I need to have my brothers, Mimi," she kept telling Barbara. "I need to be with them. They need to know who I am and that everybody is all right. They might think Daddy is dead too."

Barbara knelt down to her level. "The nurses will bring them in as soon as they get them cleaned up."

"Mommy never does this," Cassie said sternly. "The babies and families are always together. This is not how you do it in Padawin. I don't like Alabama."

"We're in Mississippi right now," Barbara said calmly. Cassie couldn't comprehend the concept of 50 United States. To her, all of America was simply Alabama, and it was most definitely *nothing* like her beloved Padawin.

"But *we* should be with the babies," Cassie continued trying to explain the process of birth that took place in the clinic next to her house many times during the year. "They should be eating, and we should all be holding them. Those nurses are not their mommies or sisters."

"It's okay, sweetie," Barbara was struggling to explain. "They'll be with us any minute, and they don't ever have to leave again."

"Thank goodness," the exasperated four-year-old exclaimed as she walked over to the bed beside her mother and Aunt Annie. Annie instinctively reached for Cassie, and she gladly held out her arms. Annie pulled her up to her hip, longing desperately for her own little girl, and snuggled her head beneath her chin.

Angie reached out for Cassie's hand. "Everything will be fine in a little bit," she assured her daughter. "Twins require a little more attention than what I usually do back home."

Annie shook her head in unbelief. "How could you not possibly know you were carrying twins? How did the doctor miss it?"

Angie grinned as she dropped her tired head back on the pillow. "I knew I was big, but I had no idea why. And I've always been premature. Because twins are often premature, it never occurred to me that I could have two in there."

"But why didn't the doctor pick it up at your last visit?"

"You mean my *one* visit?" Angie reminded her. "All he did was listen for a heartbeat. Because we didn't know they were twins, we didn't listen for the other heartbeat. She did no sonogram; there was no need to."

"Are you ready for twins?" Annie almost whispered. "I think I would die if I was sent home with two babies at one time."

"If Cindy Marcum can raise twins, I know *I* can!" Angie insisted. "She was totally not the mothering type. Besides, and I know y'all get tired of hearing this, raising children in Padawin is totally different from the states."

Barbara gave a tired laugh. "So Cassie continues to tell us."

Angie looked down to Michael who was still very pale and very weak. "How you doing down there, sweetie?" She reached her hand to his.

"Embarrassed," he said shyly as he took her hand.

"Don't be," Barbara assured him. "I nearly passed out myself when Annie ran out to tell us Angie had twins. It was quite a shocker."

Annie sighed. "It seems like our lives are full of shockers lately." She rubbed her hand over Cassie's back. "I'm glad that at least one of them is joyous."

Michael tried to explain his reason for blacking out. "When the doctor said there was another one coming, my first thought was Carter … and what he said just before he left us."

Angie couldn't remember. "What did he say that made you think of him right then?"

"He loved them boys."

Immediately Angie's eyes pooled and her hand came to her mouth. "He knew," she whispered. "He knew we were having two boys."

☼☼☼

Stephen tried to get his children to enjoy the morning, but he was failing at even the simple task of getting them to eat breakfast.

"How about some Pop-Tarts?" he suggested. "I could make a call and have some here in fifteen minutes."

Stevie shook his head, and Ellie never even looked up.

"I want turtle pancakes," Stevie said softly as he reached up to rub his sleepy eyes.

"I can't make turtle pancakes," Stephen hated to admit.

Ellie spoke up for the first time. "Mommy can."

"Yes, I know," Stephen gritted his teeth. "But Mommy isn't here."

"Then call her," Stevie suggested hopefully. "She'd be here in fifteen minutes too."

Stephen shook his head and leaned back in his chair. "Mommy isn't gonna come here."

"Then let's go there," Ellie said quickly. "I want to see Mommy, and I want to have her turtle pancakes."

Stephen rubbed his hands across his knees. This was getting harder and harder. "Mommy isn't coming here, and we aren't going to see Mommy. You're gonna stay here for Christmas, and then you can go back to see Mommy for a little while again."

Stevie looked up at him with big blue eyes. "A *little* while? We have to stay for *Christmas*?"

"I don't want to be here!" Ellie now cried out. "I want to be at Mimi's for Christmas! We're having Christmas with Cassie!"

"Daddy, it's not fair!" Stevie began to cry also. "We helped decorate!"

"And we have our tree," Ellie protested as alligator tears began to stream down her face. "I wrapped a present for you and Mommy 'neath that tree."

"Mommy didn't say we couldn't come back for Christmas," Stevie whimpered. "She wouldn't have made us come see you if she knew we couldn't come back for Christmas. Mommy isn't that mean!"

Stephen was losing this battle fast, and he felt like a heel about it all. It only made his bitterness toward Annie even stronger. She could have made all this easier if she had wanted to. She probably planted all these thoughts in their minds anyway. They should be thrilled to see their father, the man who had been with them every single day of their lives. It had only been two weeks since he had gone. There was no reason for them to feel like he was a stranger and that Annie was their only parent.

"Look, kids," he had to try a more direct, honest approach. "We need to understand some things here. Well, *you* need to understand some things." He leaned back in his chair again. "I'm not going back to be with your mother. Some things have happened, and we aren't going to be … uh … that kind of family anymore."

"What?" Stevie asked with fear in his eyes. "But we're a family. You can't stop our family."

Stephen shook his head. "We *were* a family. We're not gonna be one anymore."

"So our family is dead … just like Carter?" Ellie asked.

"Not like Carter," Stephen said as the hurt in his children's eyes began to grow. "We will all still be alive. Nobody is going to die."

"But we won't be together," Stevie understood. Stephen nodded.

"We're gonna be divorced, aren't we?"

Stephen hated to hear the word, but that was exactly what was going to happen. "Not all of us will be divorced, just your mother and me."

"I don't want that to happen," Stevie was almost sobbing now. "I want us to always be together! You promised us we would be together! You aren't a liar, Daddy! You aren't a liar!"

Ellie disagreed. "You are a liar, Daddy!"

She jumped up from the kitchen chair and ran for the front door of the loft.

"Ellie!" Stephen called out as he ran after her, Stevie following right behind. "I didn't lie! Things have happened that you don't understand!"

"Daddy's a liar!" she screamed again as she tried to open the door. "I want to go home, and I want to be at Christmas at Mimi's, and I want my Mommy!"

Stephen grabbed Ellie just as she was about to open the door. "Ellie, you can't run away out here! It's dangerous!"

"You are a liar!" Stevie cried out from behind him. "You said we would always be together!"

"No!" Stephen screamed out in pure anger. His expression and demeanor scared them both, and they stood petrified and still. "Your mother is the liar," he said as the rage in his eyes grew stronger. "I had to go away … because … because … your mother told me a very, very big lie. Too big … it was just too big."

Stevie walked over to Ellie and took her hand. "Then you have to forgive her and come home, Daddy. That's what Jesus would say."

Stephen stood, walked to the door, and locked the chain which was too high for the children to reach. He tried to regain his composure before facing them again. He knew what he was doing made no sense to them right now. All the talk of love and forgiveness and God and grace were meaningless in a situation like this. Those words and ideas were for situations where people took their vows seriously and were open and honest. Deception destroyed trust, which in turn would eventually destroy love. His mother had deceived him and caused him unbearable pain. Had she told him the truth, the words of Edrew Williams wouldn't have stung so much, and the physical hits could have been borne much easier. Had his wife told him the truth, there could have been six years that he didn't continue to abase himself, continue to plead for Edrew to be proud of him, to buy him off with treasures and comforts. Instead, those he had loved the deepest and trusted the most had deceived him the greatest.

Sixty-Six

For the Wrights, holidays had always been times of great celebration. Even when the family couldn't be together, there was still comfort that all were happy and rejoicing in their own homes. As this year's winter season came and went, the only joy found was in the two new lives that had graced the family that December. At times they could almost forget that Carter was no longer with them. When things were going well and everyone was laughing and having a grand time, they could almost forget that Stephen wasn't there beside Annie or taking videos and snapshots of his children and newfound family. And as January followed, Andie could almost forget when things got so hectic with the other four still at home that Adam had gone to public school, joined the band, and demanded a cell phone to keep up with all his new friends. Billy could almost forget, as he taught a high school English class, that Sam was only an hour away basking in her new life with her new love and moving on without him. And Jonathan could almost forget as he gazed out the serene window of his office that his church was beginning to fall apart, attendance was dropping, business meetings were now debates, and everyone was fearful the new building program was going to bankrupt the church.

The phone buzzed Jonathan away from his thoughts. He pressed the intercom button. "Yes, Cindy, what is it?"

"Tom Richards on the phone. Line 2."

Jonathan frowned. If Tom was calling this early on a Monday morning, there must be more trouble somewhere. Tom was an ally in all of this—an encourager. He was on the *good* side.

"Thanks, Cindy," he replied tiredly. "I've got it." He pressed the button, picked up the receiver, and rubbed his already throbbing temples as he gave a weary, "Hello, Tom, what's up?"

"I thought I should let you in on this as soon as possible, Jonathan," came the answer. "The sooner we address it, the sooner we can nip it in the bud."

"I don't think there's any more nipping to be done, Tom. The nipping should have happened *before* we called Hal Bridges to this church."

Tom sighed before responding. "I really tried to get them to check him out. I said we needed to check references, finances, education—the works. They felt it would be an attack on his character to do such things."

"I remember. I'm just wondering why they think a person puts all that stuff on a résumé' to begin with. I suppose they believe that in church work it's just a matter of formalities."

"I guess. But the plot thickens. Yesterday morning in Sunday School, Nancy Beth Tate said she had a request she desperately needed to share ... in confidence ... but she had to get it off her chest."

"Oh, boy," Jonathan rolled his eyes. "*In confidence*? Sounds like the beginning of a gossip session."

"It probably would have been had I not been there. Be thankful I wasn't an offering counter yesterday."

"And so what was the request?"

"Nancy said there were some serious problems between staff relations here at the church."

Jonathan closed his eyes. "She wasn't wrong on that account, but I'm willing to bet her perspective was way off base."

"Way, way off, in fact. She claimed that Hal was excluded from all staff get-togethers during the holidays, and with his office being stuck way off down the hall away from the *inner circle*—and those were the words she used—he was never included in any decision making. She thought it was a horrible affront to our new, honorable, *doctorate* staff member who was only trying to do his job. She also commented that it showed the maturity level and spiritual level of our staff to be so exclusive to the new guy."

Jonathan shook his head in utter astonishment. "Do you want to know the real story, Tom?"

"Actually I would. How this guy manages to turn things around like he does proves he's extremely intelligent. But as far as his ministerial ability, I've yet to see anything worth paying him the weekly salary he demanded."

Jonathan switched the phone to the other ear as he swiveled his squeaky chair back toward the window. "Every year we have a staff Christmas outing. We did the gift exchange thing the first couple of years, but decided we'd rather spend the money going out to dinner somewhere nice. We planned the same this year and told Hal we'd all be going out to Huntsville on December fifteenth. Finding a date that's free for everyone is really hard because the staff is generally invited to everybody's Christmas party in the church. The fifteenth was open on the calendar, so we planned it. Hal checked his blackberry and said he and Lisa couldn't make it and that we should check with him before making any dates like that. Immediately we said it was no problem and we'd come up with another date. We asked what was open for him, he checked his little machine-thingy and said the eighteenth. We actually had conflicts, but agreed to change the date to accommodate *Dr. Bridges*. We'd rather blow someone else off than irritate our new staff member any more. So we changed it to the eighteenth. We agreed to meet at the office and take the church bus so we could all be together. At five o'clock we're all sitting on the bus—well, me and Barbara, Kyle and Cindy, but no Hal and Lisa. We waited for twenty minutes. Finally, after flipping coins and Cindy losing, she called him to find out where they were. He said that something had come up and they were on their way to Memphis. She reminded him about the staff outing, and he said they obviously wouldn't make it because they were headed to Memphis. The end."

Tom actually laughed. "That isn't even close to the story I heard … or the Sunday School class."

"And as far as the *inner circle* office situation goes, we meet with him every Monday, unless … say … I have a grandson dying in a hospital or a church member about to have surgery, or have to escort two little kids on a plane to California to see their Daddy who has left their mother, or am at another hospital as another daughter delivers twins. Other than that, we meet faithfully with him. He seldom comes down to where we are, and I'll be frank with you, Tom, I'm glad … really glad."

"And what do you discuss during these Monday meetings?"

"Everything that Kyle and I did wrong on Sunday."

"Seriously?"

"Dead serious. It's so bad at times that I've actually laughed out loud at him. It's almost as though he's trying to push us out and place himself in the role of savior here at our pathetic church."

"Man, Jonathan, our church hasn't been *pathetic* since you've been here … until now. What's this guy up to?"

"I have no idea, but I'm about ready to start going through some of those references the committee refused to check."

"That's not a bad idea. In fact, I still have my copy. If you want, I'll fax you one this morning and we can divvy up the sections."

"Don't fax it here," Jonathan said quickly. "One of his moles might spy it and begin to make accusations."

"Moles?"

"Well, you tell me where Nancy Beth gets her info."

"I'd say there's not a mole anywhere—it probably came straight from the horse's mouth."

"Probably. Look, just take your time. You can drop it off at my house when you leave work today."

"Will do … and Jonathan?"

"Yes?"

"There are a lot of people behind your here, and there are a lot of people who are totally confused. We just need to be patient and work through the right avenues."

"Thanks, Tom. I appreciate it … and appreciate you too."

☼☼☼

Annie tried to be patient as Stephen continued to list his demands concerning the children, but he was starting to cross too many illogical lines.

"Stephen, I don't want to be hard-headed about this, but I can't just pull Stevie out of school every few days and zip him out to California when it's convenient for you."

"*You* don't want to be hard-headed?" he mocked sarcastically. "Since when?"

"Since it comes to the stability of my children." She didn't want to raise her voice, but he was pushing buttons she never knew she had. "There are laws, not only in Alabama, but also in California. A child has to be in school a certain number of days."

"Okay then, we'll take him out of school and hire a private tutor."

"Oh, there's a great idea!" She yelled at last and winced at the sound of her voice. "His life has already been turned upside down because of this. The only thing that's remained untouched is Kindergarten. I refuse to pull him out just so he can fit into your schedule."

"If you don't comply with me, Annie, I'll hire a lawyer, a really good one, and I'll take the kids away from you … completely."

She bit her lip. "And you think this would be best for the children? Especially after the fiasco of a Christmas you gave them."

"Don't play games with me—you're poisoning them against me! You want to punish me even more! It's not as if you've already hurt me to the core. Now you want to take away my kids … the only real family I've got!"

"And don't you play games with me!" she spoke clearly into the phone. "Through all of this mess I've never said anything negative about you to the kids! However, they come back after two weeks with you to say you told them I was a liar!"

"And you are!" he was now screaming. "Look what you've done to us! Look what you've done to our family! Look what you're doing to our kids!"

"I didn't walk out on us! I made a mistake!"

"There's a huge understatement."

Annie knew there would be no reasoning with him. "Look, you'd better go ahead and hire that *really good* lawyer you keep threatening me with. I'd hoped we could settle this without the court system, but with you being so pigheaded about the whole thing, I can see we'll never come to an agreement."

"All I can say is that …"

But Annie cut him off by shutting down the phone. She wouldn't speak to him again. Every time they talked, he would inundate her with more and more guilt. She felt horrible about what she had done, but she had no idea it could have had this kind of result in her life. How could all of this be happening to her? It wasn't her desire to hurt Stephen or even be dishonest to him. Her ultimate motive was simply to protect him and to protect his image of his mother. But in the end she had done neither. And the last thing she wanted to do in this situation was withhold the children from him, but she couldn't take Stevie out of Kindergarten every couple of weeks to go spend time with his father. Something had to be worked out, and it appeared the only way that was going to happen would be for the legal system to decide what was best. She could only pray that Stephen's lawyer would simply be good and not crooked. And as for her own lawyer, where should she start? How do you hire someone with enough competence to go against the connections Stephen Williams had?

Again she felt her stomach begin to tighten. Every time she talked with him she ended the hang-up by either lying down or throwing up. She slowly moved toward her bedroom and eased herself down onto the lonely bed. Until he had left, she and Stephen had never spent a night apart. It killed her to sleep alone, and she was tempted every night to put one of the kids in there with her, but she knew if she didn't remain strong throughout this ordeal, she might not be able to recover. She had to get over him, and she had to move on. If she didn't, she would collapse completely. The emotional strain was almost more than she could bear, but she knew worse things could happen.

She took several deep breaths as she tried to ease the nausea, but they weren't helping. She tried to will herself not to get sick, but nothing seemed to work. She lay as still as possible on the bed with her legs pulled up to her stomach, the top one propped on a pillow. She tried to force her thoughts on something else, but wave after stronger wave kept bounding over her. At last she jumped from the bed and ran to the bathroom. This had to be the worst feeling in the world.

✪✪✪

Stephen could get nothing accomplished concerning music. The only thing on his mind was his family. In fact, the honest truth was he hated California, he hated writing music again with a deadline, and he didn't particularly care for Ben Brenner. The man was definitely a gifted genius when it came to composing, but he was completely despicable socially. Stephen wondered if he had always been that way, or if years of incredible success had bred it in him. No wonder the man had been married five times.

"What's your problem today?" Ben asked after Stephen exploded over not being able to come up with anything new or innovative.

He rubbed his throbbing head as he replied, "Just life." He didn't want to get into another discussion about Annie and the kids with Ben. Ben's answers were always self-centered, and they justified any action necessary to avoid discomfort. How could his mother have loved a man like this? She was so much his opposite.

"It's Annie and the kids again, isn't it?" Ben said knowingly.

"Yeah." Why lie? It was the truth. When Annie came into his life, it was as if Stephen began to really live for the first time. And as they added children, life only became sweeter.

"Look," Ben said as he laid down his pencil and walked over to the window where Stephen was standing, "you've got to give yourself some time. You've lived with this woman and those kids several years now. You can't just forget about them in a couple of months."

"Forget about them?" Stephen wondered at his suggestion. "I don't want to forget about them. They'll always be a part of me."

"Of course they will if you keep moping around like you've been doing. You've got to get out! Has it not occurred to you that you live in Hollywood? The best parties on the planet are happening every night all around you, but you're sulking in your loft over a woman who blatantly lied to you for many years. And the kids? Good heavens, man! What are you gonna do if you get custody of them? Hire some nanny to take care of them? That would be priceless. Then they could whine to mommy about how you're never with them but this other woman always is, and she can take you back to court … and it just goes on and on and on."

Physically exhausted and emotionally worn out, Stephen dropped into a chair. Ben's description pretty much summed it up. What if he did sue and make good on his threat to Annie to get the most manipulative lawyer money could buy to ensure his getting custody? Then what? The kids had hated their two weeks with him. They had cried every day, refused to eat almost anything, and made it clear they didn't want to be there. When Jonathan appeared at the airport to take them back, you would have thought he was the loving father. This isn't how Stephen wanted it all to turn out.

"Tell you what," Ben said soothingly as he put a hand on Stephen's shoulder. "Let's call it quits for the day. Go back to your loft, take a long, hot shower, and then be ready to go by six o'clock. I'm gonna show you the town tonight, buddy, and if you don't have the time of your life, then you flat out don't belong in L.A."

☼☼☼

Tom Richards looked down the list of names and numbers on Hal's resume' as he sat with Jonathan at the dining table. The list of credentials and accomplishments was intimidating. The only problem was they couldn't imagine how the man they had come to know could possibly be the same man described in this resume'.

"I almost hate to even think this," Tom said hesitantly, "but what if all this is a bunch of hooey?"

Jonathan sighed as he raised his eyebrows and nodded. "And what if all these numbers are just some padded phony list he concocted?"

"There's one way to find out. We start by calling the numbers first." Tom reached inside his briefcase and found a copy of Hal's resume' he had marked for Jonathan. "I noted the numbers I thought you might be able to handle better."

Jonathan sighed as he resigned himself to finally taking action. "I guess so. But exactly how do we go about this? I've never done anything like this in my entire life."

"The best thing I can come up with is to be as cunning as a fox, but as gentle as a dove."

Jonathan gave a nervous chuckle. "That'll do, I suppose." He took his copy of the resume' and looked down the list of check marks Tom had made. "When do we get back together?"

"How does same time next week sound?"

"Like a plan."

Sixty-Seven

Billy didn't care for English at all, but he enjoyed getting to know a lot of the students. Many of them had heard of him as a football star years ago in Dockrey. It did wonders for his ego to be somewhat of a celebrity. It was also fun living with Cindy and Kyle. He felt eerie about staying in his mother's apartment—the very place where she had died—but he spent very little time in there. Most of his afternoons and evenings were taken up with teasing the kids or getting into some intense discussions with Kyle. The more he was around Kyle, the more he liked him. It still blew him away on occasion to watch his sister live life with such a godly man. Cindy was definitely a different woman than the girl he grew up with, or the lady he saw occasionally during their adult years. If all the evidence had been gathered and shown, she had actually been wilder than him. Of course, that assumption was based on the fact that she was a girl and he was a boy. His sleeping around and partying was just looked on as being *one of the boys*. Hers, however, earned her the label of a *loose woman.* He remembered many times he was actually embarrassed for people to know she was his sister.

But here she was looking as pristine as possible in her white pantsuit and apron as she leaned over Kylla's shoulder to give some help with homework. The picture was completed by the wooden spoon in her hand with which she had been stirring some homemade meal on the stove. How could a person change so drastically? He knew what she would say. She would give all the glory to God and claim that He had changed her life completely. Billy couldn't argue with it because she had changed. Actually, she had transformed. Even her smile and her eyes seemed different. The only times he ever saw hints of the old Cindy were when he would talk about Sam. It was as if she were on a mission to protect Sam from ever being hurt by him again. He tried to assure her he had no intentions toward Sam and had let her go, even so much as pushing her into a relationship with Dr. Crandall, but she was always dubious about his sincerity.

He wondered why she was so doubtful about his ability to change as she had. Why couldn't he be transformed by God and then become the perfect man who could be the perfect complement to Sam, his only love? Well, that was obvious—he refused to give his life over to God. First, he was mad at God for taking his parents. But then again, he couldn't blame God for doing it. He had been the epitome of a rebellious son and caused nothing but agony for them. God had every right to take them away and stop the hurt he had made happen. Then that brought up another issue—Billy didn't deserve God's transformation. But did Cindy? He hadn't been any worse than she, and yet she ended up with a wonderful man, a beautiful family, and a changed reputation.

"You're in deep thought," she said as she waved her hand in front of him.

"Uh huh," he acknowledged as he turned his eyes up to meet hers. "It happens on occasion."

"So what are you thinking about?" She pulled up a chair and sat in front of him.

He sighed and looked over at Kylla who was grinning big. "Your family … how good your life is … wondering if I could ever have anything close to this."

Her smile was sympathetic. "It seems too good to be true, doesn't it?"

He nodded.

"It's just the grace of God," she told him again. "There's no other explanation for it."

"So what hope is there for me? I don't think I can do what you did … just put everything behind and pretend it never happened. A lot of the deeds … and the scars … are way too deep."

Looking intently at him she said, "Nothing … not a single thing … is too deep for God to reach … or to cleanse. I should know, Billy. And the thing about it is that when I think about my old life, it's almost as if it never really happened. That wasn't me back then—it was some other person struggling desperately to find meaning but looking for it the wrong way."

"But see, I have found meaning, only without God. I've stopped drinking, stopped doing all the stuff I did with women, and went back to school. I now have a Master's degree and am putting out résumé's for a real job."

"And you're happy with all that? I mean … is that really enough for you?"

He shrugged. "Sometimes it is. When I stay busy and don't have too much time to think about what I'm missing."

"So what are you missing?"

He looked around at the house, the kids, and then back at Cindy. "I don't really know. A family maybe? A wife to share it all with? But then, I had that once, or should I say twice, and it wasn't enough either. I want you to know that I really care for Sam. I love her, Cindy, but I agree with you that I don't need to hurt her ever again. So I've pulled away from her and tried to move on, but I can't stop thinking about her … missing her … wanting her."

He expected to see the familiar scowl on her face that appeared whenever he talked about his feelings for Sam, but instead her compassion seemed to grow deeper.

"I wish you could see that even Sam can't make you fully happy. She couldn't before, and you didn't love her any less back then. Yeah, you've matured some, and you've laid down some bad habits, but inside you're still the same person. What guarantee does she have … or do you have … that two people with the same problems, the same baggage, the same tendencies they had before could make it work a second time without a major change somewhere. You don't have to talk to her very long to realize she's still the same little girl, abused and frightened, that she was before. And you don't have to spend much time with you to realize that you still carry the guilt of all the things you've ever done wrong."

"I'm sorry, okay!" he blurted out, startling both Cindy and Kylla. He lowered his eyes and his voice as he explained, "I just can't let go of stuff like you did."

"I couldn't either. That's what I keep trying to tell you. It took something bigger than me. It took way more than just turning over a new leaf. I had to abandon everything, including my pride … and my anger … in order for God to do a transforming work in my life."

He shook his head. "I don't get it, I guess. I can't be religious like you."

"Neither could I—that's what I keep trying to tell you. If I had tried this on my own, I'd still be selling real estate, sleeping with the pick of the month, and then trying to numb it all with alcohol and parties when everything got quiet. When I abandoned my old life and asked Jesus to really take control, it's as if I gave Him the reins and just let Him lead. It was tough. I had to give up my incredible salary, my riverfront apartment, and my non-committal lifestyle. I had to risk my heart by caring for Mother, by being there with her through the pain and the struggle. Was it worth it?" Tears began to fill her eyes. "I learned what it really meant to *love* someone. I started by loving Mother, and then God brought Kyle into my life. I turned around, and there was Kylla. I was so full of love that it scared me to death. I wanted to run away from it all because I knew the kind of person I had always been. I knew that in my own strength I would let every one of them down."

"But you didn't," Billy assured her. "You were there with Mother right to the end."

She smiled shakily as she wiped her eyes. "Only because God changed me … totally … completely. I wouldn't dream of walking out on what I have now. But six years ago I would have cringed at the thought of living like I'm living. It would have cost too much for me to be here."

She reached out and took her twin's hand. "You've already sacrificed so much, Billy. Why do you hold back? Look what sheer willpower has done for you. Why don't you give God a real shot at putting your whole life back together instead of just a few pieces here and there?"

He turned away from her as he said, "Because God can't do that with me. I'm different than you, Cindy. I can't be all this domestic and committed stuff."

"Actually, you could if you'd ever admit it's what you really want. I know what you're afraid of. You're scared to death you're gonna lose yourself to something … or someone … and that you'll never recover. You're afraid you're gonna tie yourself to something you can't get out of. That's why it takes God, Billy. Our walls are too high to knock down in our own strength."

The beeper on the stove began to sound and Cindy gave a small laugh. "Duty calls." She stood to go back into the kitchen but added, "Don't try to reason all this out or you'll never go anywhere. Believe it or not, God even has a plan for you. The sooner you yield to that, the sooner you'll get your life together."

"There's a novel idea—me getting my life together."

"No more novel than mine."

☼☼☼

The following week Tom Richards and Jonathan sat again at the Wrights' table going over their notes from the week's contacts. Many things weren't adding up in their search.

"So this was a carpet business?" Jonathan asked as he circled the name of Rev. Bill Tidwell on his paper.

"Tidwell Carpets," Tom affirmed. "I called the number listed and got an answering machine referring me to another number. When I called that number, a lady answered *Tidwell Carpets*. I asked to speak to Bill and was told he was gone for the week. I asked if he was a minister, and she laughed almost uncontrollably."

"So what do you think?"

"I think it was a phony setup. I think Rev. Tidwell is just a guy Hal knows who's a bit shady and is willing to do a little lying for whatever reason."

Jonathan pointed to a number he had called. "And this was a cell number. The guy was at a ballgame of some type. When I said I was calling in reference to Hal Bridges and that his name was listed on a resume', the guy's whole tone changed. He gave a glowing reference for Hal, but whoever he was sitting with had some mighty flowery speech."

"What about the church in Arizona?" Tom asked as he moved his pen on down the page.

"Got it, but boy was it weird."

"How so?"

"First, the receptionist didn't answer by saying the name of the church. I wish I would have anticipated that and not asked, 'Is this Friendship Baptist?' Because as soon as I said that, she jumped in immediately with apologies and said she was new and just getting used to answering the phone."

"Do you think it was phony too?"

"Who knows? But the pastor wasn't there. When I asked if she knew Hal Bridges, I got a glorious report. It struck me funny that she was new, yet had a complete rundown of Hal's accomplishments at the church."

"Did you say that?"

"I asked her about it, and she said Hal was famous all over Arizona for his ministerial expertise."

Tom pulled off his glasses and folded his arms. "You know, I think we're going about this the wrong way."

"How so?"

"If Hal is the character that you and I believe him to be, he'd be too smart to not cover his tracks with this résumé'. Let's just pretend for argument's sake that all these references are phonies. He's told all these people to expect calls from a 256 area code and to lay it on thick. He's been here a couple of months, so we've been catching them off guard. But as soon as we mention his name, they remember and go into their praise of the great and mighty Hal."

"Ok, I'll pretend that with you. So what do we do then?"

"We start with the numbers he didn't give us." Tom gave a sneaky grin.

"I don't know what you mean."

"Well, I don't buy that the *Friendship Baptist Church* I talked to was a legitimate church, but I'd be willing to bet there's a Baptist church somewhere in Arizona that Hal worked at, and because he went to seminary in California, a couple of churches out there too he actually did serve. I'd say forget about calling *his* numbers. Let's start over again, but this time try to turn up some real stones instead of just what he's planted.

Jonathan shook his head at what they were imagining might be true. "What happens if he *is* a charlatan and we have all this proof? Who do we bring this to? The deacons? The committee? Do we face Hal with it? Frankly, Tom, at first I just wanted to do it for peace of mind, but after this week and realizing what might actually be going on here, I'm a little fearful. What kind of man would possibly deceive a church? And for what reason?"

Tom circled the names of the towns and churches Hal had served and connected them with a big question mark. "I don't know, but I think at this point there's no turning back. I'm like you—I didn't actually expect to find the things we're finding. But now that we are, we just have to believe that God is guiding us."

"And we just take one step at a time."

Sixty-Eight

Stephen had agreed to go out on the town again with Ben—it would be the third time in a week—but he didn't anticipate having women in the limo waiting for them this time. His first response was a flood of guilt washing over him. He may have left Annie and his kids in Alabama to come to California and think through things for a while, but the fact remained that he was still married. Even the thought of being with another woman sickened him. Annie had been his everything, and although she had betrayed him deeply, it didn't mean he could just cast aside his feelings.

"Ben," he whispered discreetly as he leaned over the seat. "I'm not comfortable with this at all. You said *we* were going out, not that we would have dates."

"What fun is going out on the town if there's not a woman at the end of it?" Ben laughed.

Stephen shook his head. "I don't want a woman right now."

"You don't know what you want," Ben bellowed as he handed Stephen a beer from the icebox. "Down a couple of these before we get there, and you won't care what's going on."

Stephen refused the beer. "This isn't who I am, Ben. I don't want to do this."

"Correction," Ben grinned at him, "this isn't who you *were*. It's time you made a change, my boy. Life is out there for the taking. You and I are privileged enough to have the kind of money, power, and fame that all other men would kill for. You need to learn how to appreciate who you really are."

"I told you, though, this isn't who I am."

"Oh, come on, Stephen. That pansy father-in-law minister you had has put some nutty ideas into your head about right and wrong. You might think that Annie was hot at one time, and I'll hand you this, on stage the girl flat out burned it up. But six years with her won't even touch one night with Sassy over there. She's highly paid because she's highly trained."

"What?" Stephen exclaimed. "These girls are hookers?"

"Call 'em whatever you want; they don't care. And by the end of the night, neither will you."

"I can't do this," Stephen insisted as he began to feel flushed. "I'm a married man."

"Since when? You walked out on her. You left her high and dry. You gave her your life and your love, and she betrayed you big time, my boy! This isn't infidelity … this is getting even—sweet revenge. This is saying that nobody messes with Stephen Williams, not even a hot woman."

If Ben used the word *hot* to describe Annie one more time, he was going to slug him.

"Look," Ben said calmly, "I'm not saying anything has to happen here tonight between you and Sassy, okay? Just relax, enjoy the evening, and let the town melt away your troubles. And a couple of beers would really help right now."

Stephen shook his head. "I don't drink … never have really. If it takes intoxication to enjoy the night, I might as well stay at my loft and sit on the couch."

"Suit yourself, buddy, but you're gonna have to relax and get Annie off your mind."

Stephen sat back and ran his finger beneath his collar hoping it would somehow relieve the tension penetrating his body. It might have worked, but when Sassy scooted over next to him and looped her arm through his, every muscle in his body contracted. He shouldn't be here, and he shouldn't be doing this.

☼☼☼

Lisa Bridges was livid. "Hal! How can you just sit there and act as if it doesn't matter that someone is checking into your background? You've got a lot of skeletons in your closet! *I've* got a lot of skeletons in my closet."

"I'm not worried about the skeletons," Hal assured her.

"Exactly what did Connie say?"

"She said someone called and asked if it was Friendship Baptist. It took her a second to put it all together, but then she remembered and made something up about being new. So what's the problem?"

"What's the problem?" Lisa threw her hands up in disgust. "The problem is the same as it always is! *You* can't cooperate! *You* can't just go with the program and do whatever it is you're supposed to do! *You* have to make waves and usurp everyone's authority to somehow make yourself feel like a big man!"

Hal stood up to slap her, but she stood defiantly where she was, refusing to cower before him.

"Go ahead, Hal! Put a nice, obvious bruise on my face! That'll really fix your problems!"

He held back his arm and breathed deeply to gain control. "I don't have any problems."

"Not yet … but they're coming … and you know it."

"It'll be different here—trust me."

"You've got to be kidding!" she said even louder. "How? People are digging up your skeletons already! How do you intend to fight that?"

He smiled a wicked smile and revealed, "This time I intend to fight skeletons with skeletons."

"What are you talking about?"

Suddenly a loud knock on the door startled them both.

"Who could that be at this time of night?" Lisa complained. "I sure hope they didn't hear us yelling in here."

Hal motioned for her to calm down as he went casually to the door. He could see Alice Vordeman's face looking sternly through the pane.

"Great," he mumbled, "I don't need this right now."

He opened the door and greeted the landlady with an endearing smile. "Hello, Miss Alice. You're out mighty late tonight."

She walked on in but never returned the smile. "Hal," she said cordially, then acknowledged Lisa. "How are you, Lisa?"

"Fine, Miss Alice," she replied nervously. "What brings you here at this time of the night?"

"The rent," Alice said plainly. "You've been here two months … at least … and you've yet to mow the field. I've tried not to bug you about it, tried to be pleasant and understanding, tried to give you time to settle in, but I think a couple of weeks should have done that. It's to the point of being downright defiant."

Alice looked to Hal waiting for a response.

"I'm afraid I've been very busy," he said with an unmoved expression. "You need to understand that I'm to be obedient to the Lord before anyone else."

"Poppycock and hogwash!" Alice said contemptuously. "A man's integrity and character are a part of obedience to the Lord. I know what backbone is, Mr. Bridges, and you haven't got an ounce of one. In good faith I assumed you were a man of God which meant you would be a man of your word. But all I've gotten from you is one excuse after another, and I'm tired of it. Either you mow the field tomorrow, or get out of the house by the end of the week."

Hal looked at her so condescendingly that Lisa shivered at his gall.

"Miss Alice," he said soothingly, "I'll do my best to mow that field tomorrow, but if something important comes up, I won't be able to get to it."

"If I were you," Alice was unmoved, "I would consider mowing the field an important something that just came up, because if it's not done, you will be served papers the following morning."

Alice didn't wait for another smoothly delivered lie. She opened and slammed the door, hopped on her General Lee, and fled the scene.

☼☼☼

"Why don't you stay the night?" Angie asked Annie as they each rocked one of the twin boys. "There's no school tomorrow so you don't have to get Stevie up. Cassie would love to have a sleepover with Ellie, and you could take a turn with the boys tonight when they wake up for one of those two a.m. feedings."

Annie looked down into the grayish eyes of tiny Christian Collins and marveled at the hope of new life this little one carried. "I don't think so, but I appreciate the offer."

"It wasn't an offer," Angie insisted. "It was more like a plea."

Annie glanced over to her sister. "Please. Between Michael and Moms and Daddy, I'd have to wrestle to get a hand on one."

"If you stay, I promise you can take one for a feeding."

Annie groaned as she shifted to a more comfortable position.

"Are you all right?" Angie asked with concern.

"My stomach muscles are a little sore, that's all."

"Are you still throwing up a lot?"

Annie nodded. "This is the worst case of nerves I've ever had in my entire life, but then I feel guilty whenever I start feeling upset about it all"

"Guilty?" Angie exclaimed. "You have very valid reasons to be upset! Your husband walked out on you."

"But he's still alive … out there … somewhere in California," Annie confessed. "And both of my kids are healthy and laughing and enjoying life in spite of it. I made a huge mistake, and I'm justified in paying for it. This is nothing compared to what you and Michael have been through."

"Lands sakes, Annie! No wonder you're a bundle of nerves! You're trying to hold all of this in on my account. You've got to stop. Carter is gone. I'm not thrilled about it, but I did everything I could to stop it. Now I have Caleb and Christian here, and still little Cassie, and I've got to move on through the pain."

"But you didn't deserve to lose Carter."

"And you certainly didn't deserve Stephen's walking out on you!"

"Yes, I did," Annie said adamantly. "You all keep trying to act as if Stephen is somehow the one in the wrong here, but he's not. I'm the one who lied to him."

"You did nothing malicious to Stephen. You thought you were protecting him. What you did was out of love. And I'll be honest with you, I believe that had you been the one to tell him and had the chance to explain why you kept it from him, it would have been a completely different story. But instead, old Ben comes waltzing in deciding to play Papa after thirty-eight years, and he twists the plot just enough to make you look like the villain."

"But the fact remains that I didn't tell him." Annie could feel the emotions beginning to rise again. "I should have told him from the very beginning."

"Yes. Given how he responded to the news, you should have told him. We'll all agree with that, but it's after the fact, Annie. He could have responded any number of ways had the setup been different. You really need to sit down with him face to face and talk through all of this. The guy was crazy in love with you. It was even sickening at times watching the two of you moon over each other. You don't get over all of that because of an honest mistake."

Annie shook her head vehemently. "I can't talk to him. In fact, the only talking I intend to do again will be through our lawyers."

"Don't even go there, Annie! You've got to jump in to this head first and begin to try to heal things between the two of you."

"It's not gonna happen," she insisted. "We can't decide civilly how to handle the children. I don't even want to think about trying to work through the mess of our relationship." Another wave of nausea began to roll. "No … not again," she moaned.

"Give me Christian," Angie said quickly.

Annie stood up, handed the baby back to his mother, and then moved quickly toward the bathroom.

That night as she lay in bed all alone, another wave flooded over her. She determined herself not to give in. This was getting ridiculous. She reached for a Saltine and began to nibble gently on one corner when the phone rang. She grabbed it from the side table and read the display—Stephen.

No. I can't talk to you again. All we do is argue and fight, and somewhere in the middle of all the ugliness about how to handle our children, you always manage to bring up the fact that I am your betrayer … your Judas. I know what I did, and I know what I am, and I refuse to hear you tell me that again.

Stephen waited through nine rings and then hung up. His night with Ben and Sassy and the other girl—what's her name—had been terrible. And to top it off, the paparazzi had been everywhere. Next week his face would fill the tabloids, and he would have no excuse before Annie about their marriage. Until now, he had been totally in the right. He should have left the limo as soon as he realized what Ben had up his sleeve and called Annie to talk things out. Instead, he endured the most loathsome night he could remember, and had to fight off a call girl at every turn. At one point she had told him she always gave her money's worth, and he might as well give in. It was then that he called a cab and left. All he wanted to do was get back to his loft and call Annie and apologize and forgive her, but now it might even be too late for that. He had to get to her before all of Dockrey saw the tabloids next week. If not, his life, the only life he ever wanted, would be over.

Sixty-Nine

Sandra Allen nervously tapped her fingers on the desk as she waited for the University to answer. She hadn't seen Samantha in many years and was nervous about telling her the news. It was quite possible that she hadn't even graduated from North Alabama. She knew that was where her scholarship had come from, but when Sam left Toombs County, her plan was to never return.

"University of North Alabama. How may I direct your call?"

"I need to speak with the alumni department." Sandra thought that would be the best starting point. If they had no record of her there, she would try another angle.

"UNA alumni. This is Kathi."

"Hi, Kathi. My name is Sandra Allen, and I'm trying to locate someone whom I believe should have graduated from UNA ten or so years ago."

"Sure. Could I have the name?"

"Her name was Samantha Conwill."

"Just a moment, please."

Kathi scrolled through her computer lists looking for a Conwill first. She found several, but none of them had *Samantha* in the name. "Could she have had another first name? I can't find a Samantha at all."

"No, it was just Samantha Conwill. She didn't even have a middle name or initial."

"Could she have married while here? If so, it's possible she could be listed under her married name because most alumni might remember her as that."

"Oh, goodness, I have no idea. I haven't seen her since she graduated from high school."

"Would you like me to pull up all the *Samanthas* we have listed?"

"I'm afraid that wouldn't help." Sandra was hitting a dead end, and she was running out of time. "I have an emergency situation that I need to inform her about. Her father has died, and her mother isn't capable of … well … handling anything … including herself."

"I'm so sorry," Kathi replied sincerely. "Can you give me any more information on her that might help us narrow the search?"

"The only thing I can think of is that she would probably have been a math major."

Kathi looked over to Denise who was idly glancing through a

magazine. "Do you remember a Samantha who went here several years ago who was a math major?"

Denise thought for a moment. "I think that one blond girl with the glasses might have been a Samantha. She was a math whiz."

"Do you remember her last name?" Kathi prodded.

"Wait!" The light bulb seemed to go off in her mind. "She was actually married to that cute guy who just graduated last month. You know … the blond who broke his leg."

"Billy Marcum?"

"That's him! Yes! Samantha Marcum!"

"Samantha Marcum was married to that guy? How did that happen?"

"Go figure," Denise yawned. "Opposites attract … or something like that."

"Ms. Allen," Kathi returned to the phone. "I think we might have a possibility. There was a Samantha Marcum who majored in math and is now a teacher in the Florence area. She married one of the students here. We don't have her listed as Conwill, but I could give you the number of the school and you could try and reach her there. We don't have any personal information on her—she's not big on updating her files with the alumni office … not the most social bird in the herd. But we get a lot of her students here. They say she's a super teacher."

Sandra's heart swelled just a little bit with pride. "I would appreciate the number so much. It's to the point of desperation that I get in touch with her."

☼☼☼

Sam was getting frustrated with her Trig class. She was ready to believe she had never had as much trouble in all her years of teaching as she had today. What was it about this particular operation that made it impossible for them to grasp? Turning back to the board to begin another attempt at explaining, a knock sounded.

"Great," she mumbled as she walked over to the door. "How many more interruptions could I possibly get within one hour's time?"

Paulo was standing there, and even though she had a soft spot for him, if he came to ask for help with his homework today, she might possibly give him detention for roaming the halls. She had had her limit.

"This had better be good, Paulo," she began, "and why are you out of class."

"I'm an office intern this period," he said timidly in response to her gruff demeanor. "I have a message for you. It has a phone number so they wanted me to deliver the note personally."

She felt guilty now. He was just doing as he had been told.

"Thanks," she said more humbly as she took the note. "Sorry for the attitude—Trigonometry is no fun for anybody today."

"Woo," he said softly with a grin, "I can hardly wait for my turn next year."

She smiled after him as he turned back toward the office, and then she stuffed the note into her pocket. There would be no phone calling until this class understood exactly how to complete an entire problem.

When class was finally over, she dropped into her chair and removed her glasses. Rubbing the top of her nose where the spectacles had sat she began to wonder if perhaps it was time to delve into contacts. Between the sweat of frustration and the building headache, glasses would be a nice thing to do without at the moment. However, when she reached into her pocket to retrieve the slip Paulo had given her, the glasses had to go back on in order to see the numbers.

She squinted at the scribbles and tried to make out the message:

Sandra Allen
Emergency
Please Call as Soon as Possible
Do not Wait

Following the note was a number. Sam sat in her chair stunned. Why would Ms. Allen be calling her and what could the emergency be? But even more than that, how did she ever find her? Sam hadn't contacted any one in Toombs County since she had left for college, and no one there would know her married name. How did Ms. Allen even know where she was?

She carefully punched in the number and then waited tensely for the voice from her past. Her palms were actually beginning to sweat.

"Hello?" It was the exact same voice, just as she had remembered it.

"Ms. Allen, this is Samantha Marcum … uh … you knew me as Conwill."

"Samantha! Thank goodness! Oh, I'm so glad I found you! I can't believe I found you."

"I can't believe it either."

"How in the world are you, dear? I've wondered about you so many times I couldn't even attempt to count them."

"I'm doing well," Sam replied carefully. She was very nervous about having her past find her. "My note said there was some kind of emergency. Is everything all right?"

"Oh, no, dear, not at all. Things are in a big mess. Your father passed away last night. He's had some severe heart problems for the last couple of years, and last night he just … well … he's passed on."

Sam was silent. This wasn't an emergency—this was a declaration of celebration in her mind. "I wouldn't put that into the *emergency* category."

"I'm sorry to be telling it all to you like this, but your mother has been left in a horrible situation. She's still very incompetent, but your father has been with her all these years. The law has stepped in and declared her unable to live on her own. They're giving her three days and then if no one steps up as a legal guardian to make some decisions, they plan to put her in an institution and sell the house, keeping the proceeds for the institutional expenses as well as all her social security and your father's assets."

Sam sat stunned. As far as she was concerned, they could bury her mother right along with her father. She wanted nothing to do with either of them ever again. Her mother had been the source of her greatest embarrassments in life, and her father, the most perverse abuses. "I don't care, Ms. Allen. I really don't want to deal with this. I'll appoint you to handle it or something."

"It doesn't work that way, dear," she explained sadly. "You're the only next of kin listed."

"Who on earth listed me?"

"Your father."

"You've got to be kidding! My father would rather see me dead than list me as an heir to that pile of junk!"

"It's more complicated than that. Your father has a significant amount of money invested, and his brother Farris would love nothing more than to see it all go to waste because he could never get his grubby hands on it."

The very mention of Farris' name sent chills through Sam's body. There wasn't a more repulsive, disgusting creature on the planet. Still, she had no desire to receive anything her father might have left.

"I don't care," she reiterated. "Send it all to the loony bin right along with my mother. I don't want to get involved with this."

"Samantha," Sandra continued, "there's so much more to the story. Look, I know you're probably very busy, but if you could just come here for a couple of days, you could meet with the lawyer, work something out for your mother, and then end up with a nice little inheritance of your own."

"I don't want his inheritance."

"Fine, then take it and give it to some charity. But don't give that louse of a man the chance to gloat over nobody having it if he can't."

Just the thought of Farris turned Sam's stomach. She could see him peeling off the oversized overalls from his sweaty, shirtless body, and then coming toward her with the look of insatiable desire blazing in his eyes. She literally had to come to her feet to get the image out of her mind. As much as she hated her father, and as little as she cared for her mother, the thought of Farris Conwill taking any pleasure at her expense was more than she could take.

"Do I have to come there?" Sam wanted to know. "Can't I just do a phone conference or something with this lawyer? I could give him all the details and …"

"You have to be here, Samantha. It's so much more than just collecting the money. You have to make funeral arrangements, and you have to decide what to do with your mother. If you want her committed, at least you can designate a place a little more dignified than the state institution."

Sam knew it wouldn't matter where her mother was. She wouldn't understand it anyway. She would still be crazy, still think things that weren't true, and still be clueless about life in general.

"How quick can we make this happen?" Sam couldn't believe she might actually make the trip. "I just want to get there, handle the business and get back."

"I'm not sure, but I would guess you could leave at least by Saturday. Since today is Wednesday, if you drove here tomorrow, you could set up a meeting on Friday with the lawyer, you could work through all the arrangements, and then you should be able to leave on Saturday."

She hesitated again. She didn't want to do this at all. The only thing pushing her in that direction was the thought of Farris feeling vindicated in some way. And what if she had to face him? Could she bear that? And then there was Farrell, the other uncle. Was he still there too? Was he clamoring also for what little money her putrid father had managed to stash away?

"Where's Farrell?" she asked almost fearfully.

"Oh, he died years ago," Ms. Allen told her. "He was hit by a train while he was drunk on the railroad tracks."

Sam chuckled, "You're kidding? Too bad Farris wasn't with him, or Frank for that matter." She couldn't bring herself to call her father any term of endearment. From fourteen on she had called him by his first name.

"So, you'll be coming? You want me to set up a meeting with the lawyer, or do you want to call him yourself?"

"I suppose I can call him when I get there. Where's he from?"

"He's all the way over in Hinesville."

"Well, at least Frank was smart enough to get something better than a smalltime local redneck to handle his business."

☼☼☼

Jeremy Crandall drove into Sam's driveway and pulled out the small jewelry box from beneath his seat again. He desperately wanted to propose, but he knew it wasn't time yet. However, he had actually run out of time. His residency was finished, and he was biding his days with erratic shifts at all three of the local hospitals hoping that at some point Sam would give him an inkling that she was ready to settle down … with him. He had thought Valentine's Day would have been ideal. He had made reservations and planned out a wonderfully romantic evening, but Sam's mood was definitely not into romance. She had remained distant and quiet the entire night. Now as February came to a close, he really needed to make some permanent plans, but he wanted her included in them. Surely she understood his intentions.

He placed the box back beneath his seat and headed for the front door. Sam was a one of a kind, the kind he had waited for his whole life, and he was willing to continue to wait and do whatever it took to have her with him. He inhaled deeply and tried to prepare himself for whatever atmosphere awaited him this afternoon. It might be good, or it might be cold, but whatever the situation, he would be patient and understanding through it all.

"Hey," Sam said morosely as she opened the door. "Come on in."

"What's wrong?" he asked with concern. This wasn't one of her typical moods.

"My life is once again a big mess, and I seem helpless to do anything about it."

"Your life has never been a mess," he said cheerfully. "Spill it all out to me and maybe I can help you work through it."

She shook her head. "You have no clue about my life." She grabbed her mug of coffee and walked toward the bedroom.

"I'm more than willing to learn," he said hopefully as he followed her. He was stunned to find a suitcase laid out over the bed. "Are you going somewhere?"

"Unfortunately, yes." That was all the information she would offer.

He knew he was treading on fragile ground, but if he planned to spend his life with this woman, she would have to open up to him at some point.

"What's going on, Sam? You can tell me. You know I care about you and would do anything in the world for you."

She only nodded.

"Can I go with you?" he suggested. "I'm just on call. I don't have to be anywhere at any time. I could help you through … whatever this is … and could spend some time with you in the process."

She shook her head as she went to the bathroom for her toiletries.

"Sam, come on," he pleaded. "Let me into your life. Tell me about this. What does it concern? I'm sure there's got to be some way I can help."

She grabbed a few things from the bathroom and then packed them in the suitcase.

"Sam, please," he begged again. "Let me help."

She stopped, closed her eyes and shook her head. "You can't, Jeremy. I'm sorry, but there are some things about my life that you'll never know. And this is one of them. I've got to go back home for a few days and try to clear up some stuff that has to do with my mother and … it's all complicated. I don't want to get into it."

He came over to her and took her hands in his. "Sam, you can tell me. You can trust me. All I want is to be a part of your life. I want to know everything about you … the good and the bad." He looked into her eyes, and he had never seen her so sad or fearful. What was she facing? "Tell me, Sam. Share this with me."

She pulled away from him and shook her head again. "I can't talk about it. I *won't* talk about it. It doesn't help when you spill stuff like this out. People say it does, but it doesn't. It only makes you vulnerable. It forces you to trust and to give yourself to people more deeply than you really should. And I can't go through it again with all of this." She looked up at him. "I'm sorry, but I just can't."

He was deeply hurt, but he tried his best not to show it. Whatever Sam's past held, it was bottomless and it was brutal. He wanted to believe they could move beyond it and that perhaps it wouldn't be a barrier, but he was too smart to live in that delusion. They would have to face it together at some point if they were ever going to be together.

"Wherever you're going, I don't think you should go alone," he tried a different approach. "I'd be glad to just be there, but not get involved. I could be moral support or something." He did a little dance to try and lighten the mood.

When she looked back up at him, he knew he was about to be hurt, but he wasn't prepared for what she said next.

"I'm gonna call Billy to come with me."

She might as well have stuck a sword through his heart. "Why?"

She turned back to her dresser and took out some socks. "Because he's the only one who knows. He's the only one who can understand."

"That's not fair, Sam," he purely ached. "I can know and understand too. Just give me a chance."

"I can't do this again!" she cried this time. "I told Billy; he was it. I don't want to tell you—I don't want to tell anybody! I don't even want to think about it! I don't want to live through it again!"

He was crushed.

"Please try and understand. I can't go through my life thinking that every time I start to get close to somebody, I have to spill my guts out again! I did it once, Jeremy … and it nearly killed me." She closed her eyes at the memory. "I can't go through it again."

He leaned against the wall and blew out a deep breath. "Then this will never work," he admitted, more to himself than to her. "I can't do this all by myself, Sam."

She barely whispered, "I never asked you to."

He nodded as he kept his eyes on the floor. Was it that she just didn't care for him at all, or was it that she was so afraid of baring her soul again and being hurt that she would rather be alone than take a chance and lose another love. But had she really lost Billy? That was another big mystery he could never pull out of her. What had broken them up, why were they still cordial, and why did Billy live with her during his recovery? They both insisted that the marriage, thus the relationship, was over, yet there were all these unanswered questions bouncing around. And of course, Sam was never willing to answer a single one of them.

Seventy

As Billy sat with Cindy and her family eating an after church snack she had baked, he began to wonder if he was putting on a little weight. He was tempted to reach down and undo his belt, but his vanity still ruled. He sat up straighter, and that seemed to alleviate the pressure for just a little bit. But when his cell phone went off, he had to stand to actually pull it out of his pants pocket, and even then it was a challenge. When he glanced at the screen, the name displayed nearly sent him for a loop—Sam.

"Hey," he said softly as he quickly left the room and made his way outside to the back deck. He didn't want Cindy listening in. "What's up, ponytail?"

"A big mess." She was down, and it was more than obvious in her voice. "I'm in a big mess, Billy, and I'm calling in a favor from you."

"Anything," he replied quickly. "You know I'll do anything for you."

"You owe me big," she reminded him.

"I certainly do. And I promise—whatever you need, I'm here."

She paused for what seemed like forever. "Frank died last night."

The words filled him with rage and delight at the same time.

"There's some kind of legal mess involving my mother and some assets that I need to address. I don't exactly understand it all, but if I don't go and lay claim as the heir, everything goes to the state, my mother goes to an institution, and somehow Farris gets vindicated by it all because he couldn't get his hands on Frank's stuff."

"Okay," he sighed as he sat down on a step in the freezing air. "That does sound like a mess. Do you have to go?"

"Apparently, yes. At first I just said *whatever*, but the thought of Farris getting any pleasure out of this literally eats at my soul."

"Believe me, I understand." He rubbed his arm trying to warm himself as he gathered information. "So when do you leave?"

"As early in the morning as *you* can get here. It's probably about a ten hour trip. I can't remember exactly."

"Me?" he choked. "You want me to come with you?" He hadn't anticipated the favor was for him to tag along.

"I know this isn't much notice … a teacher's nightmare … but I've only got three days to make claim, and one has already passed."

"Hey, it's no problem. Mrs. Miller left all the plans. Any sub could come in there and do what I'm doing. I'll call the principal tonight and be there for you bright and early in the morning."

There was more. "What if I see him? Farris? I don't know if I can handle it."

"That's why you called me, remember? I owe you big. Facing Farris and Toombs County will move me closer to being even again."

"If you get me through this, I'll owe you my life."

☼☼☼

Stephen punched in Annie's cell this time instead of the cabin's number. She was obviously not at home, because he had called five days in a row, and she had never answered—nor had the kids. What did he expect? For her to sit at their home all alone and pine away for him as she wallowed in guilt and despair? Actually, that is what he'd hoped she would do. He wanted to punish her for holding the truth from him for so long. He wanted her to feel what it was like to be abandoned and alone in this world. But Annie wasn't like him. She had her family, and that was one reason why she was so strong. No matter what she went through, they would always be there for her.

As the cell number began to ring, he tried to remember the last time they had talked. It had been over a month. They had argued about the kids, he had threatened to call a lawyer, and then she had hung up. Since then, she had managed to dodge his calls. The kids would answer a lot and talk for a while, but he couldn't get her to the phone. He needed to talk to her. He needed to know how she was doing. He needed to hear her voice. He had actually listened to their last CD just to remember all the things about her that he had treasured so much. And he had cried.

No answer. He had to arrange the details for the kids' visit, and he didn't want to do it through the stupid lawyers. Every time he had a suggestion, the only response he could get through Stevie or Ellie was that Mommy said to call her lawyer. He only had himself to blame. He was the one who had threatened it every single time they had spoken, and for Annie to actually avoid confrontation was something he didn't understand. She was a fighter. She demanded that everyone see her point of view whether they agreed or not. He had anticipated a long, fiery separation, and then possibly a try at marital counseling to see if there was any hope. But things weren't going at all according to his plans. In fact, his life was falling apart quickly.

Annie looked down at the phone, recognized the area code from California, and immediately pressed *ignore*.

"Who was it?" Angie asked as she nursed Caleb to sleep.

"I didn't recognize it," Annie shrugged. "Must have been a wrong number."

"Liar."

Annie rolled her eyes as she glanced over to her sister.

"You need to talk to him," Angie encouraged.

"I don't have anything to say to him anymore," she said with a tired stretch. "Daddy's taking the kids out there Friday and going back to get them next Friday. That's what he wants, so that's what he gets."

"And you're just gonna let him have whatever he wants?"

"For crying out loud, Angie! What am I supposed to do?" she cried in exasperation. "I couldn't reason with him, he threatened to try and get custody of the kids, and the only thing I knew to do to avoid any more hurt was to let the legal system settle all these stupid issues!"

"He wouldn't be calling you every day if he didn't want to talk with you."

"I think he's talking to plenty of women out in California. Every time I get online, his name is plastered in the Entertainment news."

"That was over a month ago. And it doesn't happen every time you get online either. I get online too, and I actually go out shopping where they sell those stupid magazines. For a couple of weeks there was all that stuff, but it hasn't happened since."

"Oh, I'm sorry," Annie bit out sardonically. "It's just a little hard having your husband's indiscretions standing next to the cash register in your home town for everyone to read and gawk at."

"Like it or not it just comes with the territory. You knew all of this when you agreed to be his wife. You knew what you were giving up and what you were gaining, and you felt like it was a fair trade."

"Yeah, but divorce was never in that little world I envisioned."

"Speaking of divorce," Angie continued, "what's the deal with that? It's like you both just keep dragging it all out. Are you divorcing or not?"

"I have no idea! I haven't spoken to him in over a month! I keep assuming his lawyer will present his case, give me some papers, and then I sign it and we're through!"

"Why don't you initiate it?" Angie asked more out of wanting to draw the truth from Annie than from curiosity.

Annie looked at her with pure defeat and confessed, "Because I don't want a divorce—he does." Her emotions began to roll and tears started to flow.

Angie put a sleeping Caleb down in the portable crib beside his brother and then walked over to Annie. She put her arms around her and pulled her close as Annie sobbed for a long time. The cell phone rang again, but Annie wouldn't even look to see who it was. As she began to pull herself together, Angie made a suggestion.

"I brought over a carton of Bryer's butter pecan ice cream. How 'bout I get two spoons, we turn on the TV, and we watch some corny old movie like in the old days?"

Annie smiled but shook her head. "I'm too nauseous, but thanks. It was a nice try."

"You're eating has been horrible lately."

"It'll pass. Just like everything else in life—it'll eventually pass."

"Well," Angie sighed as she rubbed Annie's arms, "if you don't mind, I think I'll take myself up on the ice cream. Are you up for the movie though?"

"Sure … and Ang, thanks for staying the night."

☼☼☼

"I think they know," Lisa said as the lines in her forehead grew deeper. "Why aren't they saying anything?"

"Because they don't know anything," Hal insisted. "I covered my tracks well this time."

"Why do you have to do this, Hal?" she asked in near rage. "Why can't we just go somewhere and live like normal people?"

"Because we're *not* normal people!" he matched her rage. "I will not belittle myself to be subjected to anybody ever again! Do you understand me?"

"Even if it means costing you a decent life, a decent reputation, a chance to just relax and live for a change instead of constantly having to stay two steps ahead of everybody else? Look at this pitiful apartment! We were in an awesome house, quaint and nice, but you had to be the big man and refuse to mow the old woman's field because *nobody tells Dr. Hal Bridges what to do*. Sometimes it's worth taking a humble bow now and then in order to get a little bit of that good life honestly. She's almost eighty, Hal! Could you not sit on a tractor for an hour a week for the luxury of a nice home?"

"That self-righteous pastor and precious music man didn't have to ride a tractor to get their luxurious homes, did they?" he yelled at her. "No! They just waltz through the church handing out their little ideas and singing their little songs, and everyone gives them whatever they want! Well, that's where I'm gonna be, and this is that place!"

"How?" she was completely dumbfounded at his unbeatable confidence. "The people love them here! This isn't like any other church you've ever been in before, and yet even in the torn apart churches you couldn't manage to pull anything off."

Hal had had enough. He pulled back his arm and flung it toward her face as hard as he could. But she had been expecting him to blow any moment and managed to duck just in time. Instead of hitting her, he hit a small column between the kitchen and living room breaking it in two and breaking his hand also. As he grabbed his hand, he looked over at her and said through gritted teeth, "You stupid girl. I told you before—this time I am fighting skeletons with skeletons." He winced as he cradled his hand. "Get the keys. You've got to drive me to the ER."

Seventy-One

Billy pulled into Sam's driveway shortly before six a.m. as he drained the last of his coffee from MacDonald's. He jumped from his car, anxious to get to the bathroom as the coffee had already run through his system. He rapped on the door anxiously because the extra-large caffeine was doing a number on him also. Of course there was always the possibility that he was nervous about seeing her again. He thought they had said their final goodbyes when he had left her house after finishing student teaching. Then there was graduation—and he had to do it all over again. Now he would be spending two days with her in the most horrible situation she could possibly face, all to end with yet another *final* goodbye. It was getting harder and harder to do this.

When Sam opened the door, Billy knew right away she had slept very little that night, but what caught his attention most was she wasn't wearing her glasses. Even when tired, her green eyes were penetrating and beautiful. If he could have one of many wishes for her, it would be to get rid of the thick, ugly glasses so that every time someone looked at her they could see her true beauty.

"Rough night?" he asked as he instinctively reached his arms out to her.

"Miserable," she responded as she immediately melted into his embrace. "I can't imagine that I'm about to do what I'm about to do."

"Hey." He pulled back, reached for her chin, and lifted it up so he could speak eye to eye. "You're not doing this alone. I'm gonna be there with you every step of the way. We're in this together, okay?"

Her expression changed from tired to something that had a slight hint of mischief. "Which reminds me," she said as she took his hand and pulled him inside the house. "As I did all that unstoppable thinking last night, I had an idea … I don't know if you're up for it, but it would sure ease a lot of questions I'm gonna get this weekend."

"I owe you big," he reminded her. "I'll do whatever you want." He then squirmed a bit and added, "But can I use the restroom first? I had a massive cup of coffee."

"You know where it is. I'll get my bags out to the car."

As he went to the restroom, Sam grabbed her suitcase and garment bag along with her keys and headed outside. She literally dropped her suitcase onto the sidewalk when she saw Billy's vehicle—a silver Ford Mustang. *Where in the world did he come up with that? He must have had some incredible insurance on that motorcycle.* Rather than take her things to her car, the ugly sedan, she left the suitcase on the sidewalk and draped the garment bag over it. If that was his car, that's what she wanted to show up driving in Toombs County. This trip was going to be more than just returning to take care of loose family ends, it was going to be the chance for everyone to size up Samantha Conwill and see what she turned out to be. Deception was the least of any guilt on her mind at the moment.

"Is that your car?" she asked as she walked back into the house.

"Yeah," he smiled as he rubbed his chilly hands together. "I got it last month."

"Where on earth did you get the money for something like that? Are they paying subs substantially more in Dockrey than the rest of the nation?"

He laughed. "It's a long story. I'll tell you about it on the way."

"Can we take it instead of my practical looking school-teachery car?"

"I was hoping you'd ask that," he grinned big. "I've been dying to take her on a good road trip."

He loaded her things into his car as she turned out the lights, got them both more coffee, and locked the door to the house. She then joined him in the Mustang. As they headed out on US72 toward I65 in Decatur, Sam finished her request.

"Would you be willing to pretend that we're still married when we get there?"

Billy swerved slightly from shock. "Seriously?"

"I'm Samantha Marcum, not Conwill. You're Billy Marcum, traveling with me. It would be so much easier just to tell everyone that you're my husband rather than try to explain why I'm divorced but still dragging my poor ex around."

"That's fine with me," he said calmly although inside the idea of pretending to be married again was a bigger thrill than he wanted to admit.

"We'll have to get a room together, but don't worry, they always have two beds … so … well … you know."

He cleared his throat. "Whatever … I'd sleep on the floor if I needed to. And you can use my credit card for the room … let me do all the arrangements so I will seem *husbandlike*."

Sam giggled. "You don't have to do that. This is my tragedy, remember? I just need you to play the doting husband the few times we're out in public."

"It's okay," he insisted. "I'll dote *and* pay."

"But you're practically broke, aren't you? You've barely been subbing, and $500 a month from your mom can't be all that substantial."

"Ah yes … I suppose its story time." He set the cruise control on the Mustang and began, "*Once upon a time* …" He went through the Monday when he thought his money had run out, only to discover that his mother had left him a sizeable inheritance instead. He reminded her of the night they went to Blue Bayou and how Kirstie had pretty much ruined everything before he had the chance to tell her. Then during the whole accident and student-teaching time, he never wanted to bring up the Blue Bayou night, so he never got around to telling her that he was financially set for the first time in many years.

"Wow," she whispered. "I had no idea. No wonder you were in such a good mood that night."

"Yeah, and I didn't think anything could ruin it." He reached for his mug of coffee. "Who would have imagined …?" He wouldn't finish that thought. "So, why didn't Dr. Crandall come with you?"

"Jeremy?" She leaned back in her seat and sighed. "He offered to, but I wasn't up to dealing with his questions about everything. This is a part of my life that I'd rather forget, and telling it to one more person would mean dragging it up yet again."

Billy looked at her with a frown. "You can't seriously think you can have any kind of relationship with him if you don't tell him about your past."

She shrugged. "I don't know. I think sometimes he's almost ready to propose, and I get all jittery and nervous. It manages to put him off."

"Why would you want to put him off? They don't make them any more perfect than that guy!"

She glared over at him and answered, "Because I don't know that I want to spend my life with him!"

"Why not?"

"Ever heard of love, Billy?"

He looked back toward the road. "Are you saying you don't love him?"

"I don't know what I'm saying, to be truthful. Sometimes I like being with him, and sometimes I wish he'd go away. He's very attentive and caring, but so many times I just want to sit and do nothing, not talk or go anywhere. I always feel slightly on edge when he's around, like I can't really relax and just be free to be … me."

Billy shook his head. "That's not good, Sam. If you're gonna marry the guy, you have to feel more than all that."

"I never said I was gonna marry him."

"No, but you said you thought he wanted to marry you. Look, you need to be honest with him. You need to tell him how uncomfortable he can make you … let him know that you're the kind of girl that needs her space. See, he probably thinks you're the kind that you have to prod everything out of them. You know, you ask what's wrong and they say nothing, but what they really mean is they want you to keep digging until they vent all the frustration."

"I am *not* that kind."

"And *I* know that, but Crandall probably doesn't. You need to tell him what kind of guy you need him to be."

She pulled a leg up beneath her and stared out the window. Why should she tell him what she wanted him to be? That would be completely unfair to him. Either they worked, or they didn't. And as day passed into day, it seemed more and more like they didn't.

"He's a good guy, Sam," Billy interjected.

"So you keep telling me. And why is that? I know he's a great catch, but if we don't mesh, what's the point? You and I mesh perfectly, but we can't seem to keep it together when it comes to a relationship. Why should I push so hard with someone that I can't even feel natural around?"

☼☼☼

Tom Richards shut the door to Jonathan's office and sat in the chair across from his desk. Jonathan was nervous about discussing anything concerning Hal at the church, but Tom only had a few minutes before leaving on a business trip and he really wanted to speak with him before he left.

"Just keep your voice down," Jonathan said as he made sure the door was shut tightly. "Sometimes I think this place is actually bugged."

Tom snickered as he opened his briefcase and pulled out a folder. "Here's the information I gathered the past couple of weeks. It falls right in line with everything else we've learned about the notorious Dr. Bridges. And to be frank with you, I wouldn't put it past him to bug someone's office after all the stories I've heard."

"So you found more churches?" Jonathan asked in genuine surprise.

"The man averages six to eight months at a church. And somehow he manages to have something else lined up about the time he leaves one … or is forced to leave."

"What exactly is he trying to do? I mean what's his purpose in all of this? Why can't he just go somewhere and do what he's supposed to do instead of stir up all this trouble?"

Tom opened the folder and gave Jonathan a list of addresses. "I did a little investigating on my own … outside of hunting down all the churches. Hal Bridges has managed to have twenty addresses in the last five years."

"You're kidding?" Jonathan exclaimed a little too loud. He immediately softened his voice as he looked down the page. "How did you find this out?"

"Let's just say I have a few strings I can pull on occasion, and I pulled them. Kind of bizarre, isn't it?"

Jonathan stared down the list. "It makes you begin to wonder about all kinds of things, doesn't it?"

"Things like does he really have a doctorate?"

Jonathan nodded and then added, "And the whole Navy Seal deal … is that for real? I couldn't say out right, but he sure doesn't seem to have the temperament to be in the Special Forces."

"I was in the military, Jonathan," Tom said firmly, "and I can't imagine the man making it very high in any field, much less one that required intense training and loyalty."

Jonathan took the information and went to his squeaky seat. He opened the folder and leaned over it as he read through some of the churches Tom had talked with. "Where do we go from here? Do we take what we've got, or do we try to find more?"

"This guy obviously thinks he has what it takes to pull the wool over everyone's eyes. Because of that, I feel like we need to make sure we have a loaded gun before we walk into anything or speak to anybody."

"Bad analogy, Tom," he winced. "The idea of having a gun anywhere near Hal Bridges makes my hair stand on end."

"Agreed. But I think we need to go one step further."

"Education check?"

"Yep … and military."

Jonathan ran his hand through his hair and frowned at the idea. What if all this got back to Hal somehow? He had already caused enough doubt and damage in this church to bring a split if pushed. If they weren't careful in their investigating, someone could let Hal know that people were checking up on him.

"Tom, we might need to slow down in all of this. I'm really uneasy about what we're learning."

"Me too, but at the same time, is this a guy you want directing spiritual issues in our church?"

"That's a definite no." He stood and went to his window. He was really edgy about it now. It was one thing to dislike Hal, it was quite another to discover that the man was an out and out liar in the name of God. "I just don't know what he might be capable of. I want to make sure we're doing the right thing in all of this."

"The truth shall set you free," Tom said with conviction. "I think it's time to find out the whole truth."

✪✪✪

Billy and Sam pulled up to the fairly new hotel and parked in front of the lobby. They both got out and made their way inside where a lady sat behind the counter watching *Jerry Springer*. When she saw them come in, she stood immediately but kept her eyes peeled toward the television. This was obviously a very good episode.

"Can I help y'all?" she asked with a brief glance.

"We have reservations," Sam told her. "I called last night."

"Yes, Ma'am," the lady replied as she grudgingly pulled herself from the screen and concentrated on Sam. "What's the name?"

"Marcum. Billy and Samantha Marcum."

The lady punched a few keys and found their names. "Got it right here." She printed out the reservation as she gave her attention back to the last of the program.

Billy leaned down to Sam and whispered, "Quality service they've got here."

She whispered back, "I told you what it was like. Now you can believe me from firsthand experience."

The form finished printing as the commercial break came, and the lady then gave them her full attention. "That'll be $62.95."

"Are you serious?" Billy asked not thinking. "The sign outside said $35.95."

"That's for a single. You add another person and the price goes up. That's extra towels and stuff you gotta pay for too."

"It's okay," Sam insisted as she gently took Billy's arm. "It's not worth driving back and forth from the city." She then looked back at the lady behind the counter. "We'll take it."

The lady smiled and then began to stare uncomfortably at Sam. "I think I know you from somewhere. Have we ever met before?"

Sam didn't recognize her and didn't want to be rude, but she also didn't want to be identified with her past. "I don't think we've met. I just have one of those faces."

"No, it's your eyes," the lady replied as she concentrated. "I've seen them before. I just know it. That green in them—very bright. Don't see that but once in a blue moon."

Billy handed the clerk his credit card and she swiped it across the machine. "Samantha Marcum. No, I don't know no Samantha Marcum. I don't know any Marcums from 'round here. I knew a Samantha once in high school."

Sam began to shift uneasily as the lady started reminiscing.

"She was a real brain," the lady went on. "Don't know much what happened to her. Think she got lots of money to go to college somewhere."

Sam was really antsy now. She knew who the girl was, Louise King, and she was hoping against hope that she wouldn't have to continue the trip down memory lane.

"Wait!" the lady stopped and stared back at Sam. "Her daddy done died the other night! Frank Conwill!" Louise now gave Sam a wide-eyed stare. "You're Samantha Conwill!"

Sam flushed from the recognition. This was like the beginning of her worst nightmare.

Billy stepped in immediately. “Actually, it would be Samantha Marcum now … has been for some time. And yes, she was awesome in math, got her Master's degree, and now is one of the finest higher mathematics teachers in the state of Alabama.” He put his arm around Sam's waist and pulled her close to him. “But right now she’s really tired and would like to get checked into her room so she can start dealing with all the arrangements surrounding her father's death. So if you'd be so kind as to hand me that paper and let me scribble my John Hancock on it, we can get busy with all that needs to be done.”

The lady now gave her attention to Billy. “Wow, they make 'em tall, blond and handsome in Alabama, I suppose. Where'd you find this treasure at, Samantha?”

“College,” Sam said shortly.

“Should’ave gone, then, I guess,” Louise laughed. “But I ain't never had the brains you did! We always wondered what happened to you. Now we know the rest of the story. He'd have kept me out of Toombs County too!”

Billy signed the form, got the card for the door, and then motioned Sam to head back to the car. When she was out of hearing range, Billy asked the clerk, “If we get any calls, would you mind just taking a message and a number?”

“Sure, hon,” she said with a flirty grin. “Anything you want.”

“I'd appreciate it.”

“And I mean that,” Louise said a little more seductively. “Anything … you … want.”

“Just a quiet, undisturbed couple of days with my wife is all I'm looking for.”

Louise pouted as he left for the car.

He keyed the door and opened it slowly as he juggled their luggage. She followed behind with her garment bag and purse. He eased his way in, dropped the suitcase on the floor, and then turned on the light. Uh oh … not the room Sam had reserved. He looked back at her.

“I think there's been a mistake,” he said as he glanced out the door.

“What kind of mistake?”

“One bed,” he pointed toward the sleeping quarters. “It's a very big bed, but only one bed.”

She walked on in and went for the closet to hang up her bag, making no comment concerning the bed.

“Do you want me to get a different room?” he asked as he draped his own bag over his shoulder.

“Oh, sure,” she said sarcastically. “Go tell Louise that Samantha and her hunky husband want separate beds to sleep in. That rumor will spread faster than a fuse on dynamite.”

He sighed. "So what do you want me to do?" He looked around and noticed a small couch and chair in the corner behind the door. "I suppose I can sleep on the couch."

"Whatever," she said as she moved toward the bathroom. "At this point in my life, at this place in my life, I don't really care where you sleep, Billy. Just as long as Louise thinks you're the doting husband, you can have the bed and I'll sleep on the floor."

"I wouldn't do that!" he defended immediately.

She grinned as she opened the bathroom door and walked in. "I didn't think you would."

Seventy-Two

It was another miserable night for Sam, just like the previous one. This time, however, not only did she have to deal with the constant dreams about her father and uncles, but she could hear poor Billy twisting and turning on the tiny couch in the corner. When she would awaken from a dream, she would practically will herself not to sleep, but because she was so exhausted from the night before, she would eventually drift off only to find herself back in another vivid nightmare.

As the sun arose, she decided to get on up. There was much to do today and she might as well get it started. A small coffee pot sat on the lavatory counter with some pre-measured coffee discs. Four measly cups should be enough to get her and Billy going, but she would definitely need more before calling Ms. Allen to find out how her day was to be ordered.

Sam went ahead and showered while the coffee brewed, and when she walked out from the bathroom, Billy had already started on his first cup.

"You'd better pour you some before I get the last of it," he yawned.

"There's another disc of that stuff in the little bag."

"Yeah, but its decaf." He held up the bag. "I checked. What's the point of drinking it?"

She nodded as she plugged in the tiny hair dryer which matched the tiny pot. She dried her hair thoroughly knowing it would be chilly and damp outside. The last thing she needed was a cold or sore throat to add to the already miserable situation. Billy emptied his cup and then went for his own shower.

After a decent breakfast at the local diner, Sam dialed Ms. Allen whom she assumed would most probably be in class. As they sat in the Mustang waiting for the phone to be answered, Billy reached over, patted her knee and gave her a thumb up. "You're gonna make it through this," he assured her with a wink.

She could almost believe it with him by her side. If for nothing but the brief weekend, it was nice having him back in her life. She tried to imagine if Jeremy had come with her instead, but the feelings were nowhere close. She wondered if she could ever feel for him the same way she did for Billy, and if she couldn't, would it be enough to stay with him the rest of her life.

"Sam?" Mrs. Allen answered cheerfully.

"Yes, ma'am. We've just finished with our breakfast and wanted to know what should be done first."

"Oh, my goodness! I wish you would come by here just so I can see you again! Could that be a possibility? I could tell the class that one can leave Toombs County if one is willing to use one's head a little."

"I suppose we could." She looked down at the clock on the car. "Is there any special time frame I'm looking at as far as having to meet with the lawyer and all?"

"I don't think so. But let me go ahead and give you his number so you can set up an appointment."

Sam took down the number and assured Ms. Allen that she and Billy would be on their way to the school in just a few moments. Once they said their goodbyes, she dialed the lawyer to set up a time to meet.

"Horowitz and Crumb law offices. This is Tammy."

"Yes, I need to speak with Daris Horowitz, please."

"I'm sorry, but he's not in right now."

"Okay, well, I need to meet with him as soon as possible concerning my father's assets."

"Mr. Horowitz will be out of town until Sunday evening. Could I make an appointment for you first thing on Monday morning?"

"Out of town?" Sam exclaimed. "I'm leaving here on Saturday! I can't wait until Monday!"

"I'm sorry, but he had a family emergency in New Jersey and had to fly out immediately."

"Well, I have a family emergency and came in by car from Alabama for the sole purpose of meeting with him sometime *today.* I can't wait around here until Monday! Besides, I was told I had three days to get this settled. If I wait until Monday it'll be too late and this whole trip will have been wasted! Can the other guy handle this case?"

"Is this Ms. Samantha Conwill?"

"Samantha Marcum." Sam winced at the truth she was about to stretch. "I'm married … now. I don't go by Conwill anymore."

"But your father was Frank Conwill?"

"Right."

"You have three business days, Ms. Marcum, to settle your father and mother's situation, so Monday will be fine."

"For him, maybe, but not for me. I need to be back at work on Monday."

"I'm so sorry, but this situation couldn't be helped. There's no possible way to meet with him until Monday."

"Okay, then what about the other guy—his partner?"

"Mr. Crown is on vacation in Europe."

"Great," she murmured under her breath. "What's the earliest I can meet with Mr. Horowitz?"

"He can be here at eight o'clock."

"Fine," but Sam was seething inside. "I'll be there at eight."

She practically punched the phone off and gave a quiet roar of frustration. "Did you get all that?" she asked Billy as she straightened her ponytail.

"You can't meet with him until Monday."

"He had to fly out to New Jersey for a sudden emergency!" she sulked. "Great! So I'm stuck here in earth's version of hell until Monday!"

He took her hand and flashed his most charming smile. "But hey, you get to be stuck here with me. This will give you the opportunity to show me all those places you yakked about back then. It'll sort of be like a dream come true."

"The only dreams that happen in this place are nightmares," she continued to gripe as she buckled her seatbelt.

☼☼☼

Annie stared at the white stick in her hand and knew the results were conclusive. Angie's suspicions and her own personal fears were now realized. This only added another deep burden to her life. How was she supposed to handle this on top of everything else that had happened? How did she tell the kids? How could she hide it?

She walked into the kitchen where Angie was cooing over baby Caleb as Cassie and Ellie ate their Captain Crunch. Annie must have looked awful because as soon as Angie saw her expression, she went to her immediately, balancing Caleb in one arm.

"What's wrong?" she asked Annie with alarm. "Are you all right?"

Annie merely handed her the stick. As soon as Angie read the little window, the lights came on.

"So it's true?"

"I guess so," Annie moaned as she rolled her eyes. "It's kind of sad, isn't it? Any other time we would be hugging and crying and talking about what an awesome gift of God I'm going to have. Instead, I'm just wishing like crazy that all of this was a big mistake and that … oh, man … Angie … I'm really pregnant … again. Un-stinkin'-believable… I'm not ready for this at all … not at all."

Angie took her hand and led her to the table. "Want something for breakfast?"

"You're kidding me," she retorted. "Like I could eat anything now."

"You've got to start eating, Annie, especially now."

"I was never nauseous with Stevie or Ellie. Why now? Why this one?"

"Oh, gee, let's see, then you were happily married, you were writing and recording your music, touring the country, basically making your dreams come true. This time around, life is considerably more stressful. Your body is struggling to handle it all."

"Tell me about it, but I certainly didn't need a pregnancy to let me know."

"How far along do you think you are?"

Annie shook her head. "I have no idea. You know me, I've never been regular."

"When did you start with the morning sickness?"

Annie thought back. "The day Stephen left."

"Hmm." Angie began to calculate. "That was about the first of December. That puts you somewhere around three months then."

Annie laid her head down on the table and groaned again. "I can't believe this!"

Ellie looked over at her with concern. "What's wrong, Mommy? Do you want some Captain Crunch?"

Annie lifted her head enough to glance at Ellie and said, "No, thank you, sweetie. I don't think I can eat anything this morning."

"You never eat anything anymore," Ellie noted. "I think you might be getting sick or something."

"Or something," she moaned as she put her head back down.

Angie came and sat down beside her and gently rubbed her back. "You need to tell Stephen."

"No!" Annie replied firmly. "That's the last thing he needs to know!"

"You can't keep this from him. He has a right to know, plus … it might make him feel … well …"

"Different?" Annie finished.

"Maybe."

Annie sat up and leaned back in the chair. "It would only make him madder."

"Why? He loves his kids."

"Because I had actually joked about having another baby when he mentioned working with Ben the first time."

Angie's jaw dropped. "Wo … I guess telling him might not be the best choice for the moment. But he's got to know at some point."

Annie stood and nervously twirled a strand of hair. "Just give me a few days to process all this, please. When I have it worked out in my head I'll be better able to decide what to do next."

"Are you gonna tell Daddy before they go?"

Annie wondered about that. Tomorrow her father was taking Stevie and Ellie to California to spend the week with Stephen. If she told her father, it was highly possible he would tell Stephen as soon as they arrived. But if she didn't tell him, it would seem deceptive … again … just like keeping the truth from Stephen.

"I don't know what I'm gonna do. Just give me a little while, okay? I'll have an answer by the time they leave."

☼☼☼

Stephen, Ben, and two movie executives sat outside at their table at an exclusive cafe' having breakfast as they discussed adding Stephen to the contract for the movie saga. Stephen tried hard to focus on the conversation, but the biggest thing on his mind was that his children were coming tomorrow to visit with him for a week. He had hoped to get Annie to come with them, but he couldn't get her to talk. He had called every number imaginable, but no matter what he did or said she refused to speak with him.

"What do you think, Stephen?" Ben asked him. "It sounds like a pretty fair deal to me."

He hadn't heard a word. He was imagining his two adorable kids getting off the jet accompanied by their incredibly beautiful mother whom he hadn't seen in nearly three months. The only thing he wished right now was that he could run to her, grab her, and hold her until he could make her forget all that had happened between them of late.

"Guys," Stephen said as he pushed himself away from the table, "I'm not ready to sign anything at the moment."

"But we want to get you on board," the shorter, bald man said with much excitement. "This is a big deal … Stephen Williams scoring his first movie. We're willing to do whatever it takes to make this happen."

"Yeah," Stephen said as he reached in his pocket for his phone, "but I'm not so sure I'm willing to do whatever it takes."

The three men looked at him in shock as though they couldn't imagine anyone refusing the deal he was just offered.

"Look," Stephen tried to negotiate, "why can't I just keep working with Ben for a little while longer until I know for sure if this is what I want to do or not? I've got a lot on my plate right now, and trying to sign my name onto a project for three mega movies isn't high on my priority list."

Ben looked at him in surprise. "You don't have anything on your plate right now! That's why we're offering this."

He closed his eyes as he fingered his phone. "My kids are coming for the week. That's what's on my plate—that's what's on my mind."

The bald man stood up. "Hey, it's all right. I know your whole family thing is a little disconcerted right now. Truth is—this probably wasn't the best time to meet. We understand," he motioned toward the other executive. "How about you get through the next week, enjoy your kids, and then we'll set up another time?"

Stephen nodded in relief. "I'd appreciate that. And I'm sorry about this morning. Ben didn't tell me we would be dining over contract negotiations. I just thought we were having a friendly breakfast."

"No problem," the shorter man insisted. "But don't just throw us out the window. Give us a chance to make you a good offer before you decide against this."

"Will do," Stephen nodded. "Now, if you'll excuse me, I need to make a call."

He left the table of men and made his way to a fountain located in the center of the outside dining area. He crossed his fingers, closed his eyes, and then dialed Annie's home phone. It was his best chance to speak with her and possibly talk her into coming with the kids for the visit.

Seventy-Three

"Samantha!" Ms. Allen yelled frantically when Sam and Billy appeared at the door of her class. She ran over to Sam and threw her arms around her. "I can't believe you're actually here!"

Ms. Allen looked her over and nodded in approval. Then she turned toward Billy and extended her hand. "I'm Sandra Allen, and I assume you're Samantha's husband."

"Yes, ma'am," he said politely as he took her hand. "My name's Billy ... Billy Marcum."

"Oh, my," the teacher giggled, "you almost sound like Bond ... James Bond when you do that."

A couple of the kids in the classroom snickered.

"Class," Ms. Allen said as she turned Sam's shoulders toward the students, "this is a student who graduated from here several years ago. Her name is Samantha ... Marcum. She is now a high school math teacher in Alabama."

The students weren't all that impressed, but Ms. Allen was beaming.

"Go ahead and get back to your work," Sandra told the class, "and I'll be just outside the door with Mr. and Mrs. Marcum. No foolishness, understand?"

Sandra motioned them outside, and then joined them as she shut the door. She hugged Sam again. "I can't believe you're actually here. I've thought about you so much these past few years and wondered what on earth you might be doing. Of course, after seeing the handsome Mr. Marcum, all my questions have been answered."

Billy grinned, but Sam blushed. She hated lying to all these people, especially Ms. Allen, but she didn't want to have to admit to any utter failures in her life. And as long as Billy was willing to play along, what harm could be done?

"I went to school for six years and then started teaching," Sam said shyly. "That pretty much sums it up."

"And when did you get married?" Sandra asked them.

"Just before my sophomore year."

"So you've been married a while," Sandra smiled. "And you are such a nice looking boy. Samantha used to complain about no one dating her around here. I told her to just wait until she got out of Toombs County and went to the big city. I knew she'd find someone wonderful. And it looks like I was right."

To Sam's total surprise, Billy reached his arm around her waist and gently pulled her close. "I think I'm the one who got the wonderful person. Sam's one of a kind."

Sam leaned in on him, trying to feel confident, but she knew she had to be blushing again. If only he still felt like that way about her. At this moment she was almost willing to sacrifice anything to have him back by her side … permanently.

After leaving the school, they went to the funeral home where Sam made all the arrangements. The viewing would be that evening with the service being conducted tomorrow afternoon at the chapel in the funeral home. She hoped her father actually had enough insurance to cover the costs of the funeral. She was still very curious about these *assets* he had that Farris wanted so badly. Perhaps there would be enough to cover the burial. She would just as soon have him cremated, but that was frowned upon in Toombs County. She imagined herself taking the urn of ashes and flushing them down the toilet.

They grabbed a bite to eat, and then Sam decided she had to face the unbearable—her mother. That thought both excited and horrified her. She couldn't believe her father had stayed with her all these years, but remembering the government help money settled that issue. Her father was always up for whatever was easiest to get, even selling his own daughter to his brothers for a little extra cash. She trembled at the thought.

She directed Billy down what used to be a dirt road, but now was nicely paved and manicured. They passed a couple of familiar aging houses before arriving at the driveway where Sam had spent many mornings completely mortified as her mother screamed after her while she tried to catch the bus. Sam could still remember the rude comments the kids made as she tried to find an untaken seat so she could be isolated from them all.

"It's a cute house," Billy stated as they drove past a large oak that had blocked their view from the drive.

Sam looked at it in shock. "Wow, they put up vinyl siding. It barely looks the same. And they screened in the porch and actually put on a new door."

"It's not bad," Billy told her as he put the Mustang in park and turned off the ignition. "And you're inheriting *this*?"

Sam shook her head. "I'm not really sure. From what Ms. Allen said, Mother isn't capable of living alone, so everything either goes to me or to the state."

"You could sell this easily, Sam."

She nodded, still dumbfounded at the surprisingly excellent condition of the little house. They left the car and walked up the steps to the screened-in porch. Sam didn't even bother knocking. If her mother was still in the same state as before, or worse, she wouldn't respond anyway. They walked to the door leading to the house and Sam paused.

"I don't know if I should just walk in or make some attempt at an announcement," she hesitated.

Billy only shrugged. He had no idea either.

She finally reached for the doorknob and slowly walked in. "Hello?" she called out softly. "Mama? Are you home? It's Samantha."

She heard a familiar voice reply from the living room, but she knew it wasn't her mother's. Suddenly, from around the corner of the kitchen where she and Billy were standing came her Aunt Millie, Farris' wife.

"Samantha?" Millie said as she put her hand to her mouth. "Is that really you?"

Sam nodded as she looked around at the kitchen. It had been completely refurbished. The appliances looked brand new, and custom built cabinets had replaced the ugly paneled ones that had always been there.

Sam looked back at Millie and asked, "Is Mama here?"

Millie nodded. "She shore is." Millie just stared. "I can't believe yore here. I hadn't seen you in so long."

Billy watched the odd exchange between the two women. They seemed to know each other, but they kept their distance as though complete strangers.

"Come on into the livin' room," Millie said as she now looked up at Billy. "Who's the man?"

"My husband," Sam said confidently. "His name is Billy Marcum."

"Oh, that's right. Sandra Allen had mentioned that you wuz married … said she had a hard time finding you." Millie smiled at Billy and said, "I'm Millie Conwill. I'm Samantha's aunt."

He nodded. "Nice to meet you."

The tension between Millie and Sam was thick, so when Millie turned back toward the living room and Sam followed at a distance, he fell in behind. He was nervous about Sam seeing her mother again. How would they react to each other? Beverly Conwill had been just about as big a blight on Sam's life as her father and uncles, only Beverly's problems weren't voluntary. There were times when Sam did express sympathy for her condition, but because it had caused so much humiliation for her, she mostly talked of her mother in terms of bitterness and despair.

"Look at this floor," Sam whispered to him as she hung back to wait for him. "It looks like genuine hardwood."

"It is," he acknowledged. "And it's beautiful."

"And the walls," Sam said as she ran her hand down the face of one. "This is sheetrock, isn't it?"

"Yep."

"We used to have this ugly old dark paneling. Mama must have gotten paid better as the years went by."

When they reached the living room, Beverly was leaned back in a recliner watching television. Millie kneeled down on the floor beside her and patted her knee.

"Beverly," Millie whispered, "Samantha's here." Millie pointed up toward Sam. "She came back to see you, Beverly."

Sam walked slowly to the front of the chair and stood in front of her mother. Beverly looked up at her, but showed no sign of recognition. Her dark curls had been perfectly kept, so she assumed someone must be dyeing her hair. Sam smiled slightly as she continued to stare at her mother. For the longest time, neither one said a word. Beverly continued to look into Sam's eyes as though she were trying to make sure it was her daughter, and Sam stood very still, unsure of what to do next.

"Mama," she finally said softly. "Do you remember me? I'm Samantha … your daughter."

Beverly stared a little bit and then began to shake her head. "Samantha's gone, and now Frank's gone too."

"No, Mama," she said calmly, but still keeping her distance. "*I'm* Samantha. I went away to go to college, and then I got married, and then I became a school teacher." Sam reached for Billy. "This is my husband, Billy."

He smiled and looked toward Beverly, but her eyes would only focus on Sam.

"Where's Samantha?" Beverly asked Sam. "Where's Frank?"

"Mama, I'm Samantha. Frank is gone. He's dead now. But I need to know what to do to take care of you. I need to know what you want me to do."

"Samantha, Samantha," Beverly shook her head. "You're too big to be Samantha. She's just a little girl. She's my little girl. I think they took her away."

"Mama, nobody took me away. I grew up and wanted to be a school teacher. I went to college. But now I'm back because Frank has died, and I need you to help me decide how to care for you."

Beverly took a deep breath and stared up at her, but she wouldn't respond with any recognition.

Millie finally spoke. "She thinks somebody kidnapped you. She's said that every day since you left. And every day Frank's told her that you done went away to school."

Sam took her attention from her mother and looked back around the living room. "What happened to this place? When I left it was a junk-heap … everything about it. Now it's actually a nice little house. Who fixed it up?"

"Frank did," Millie replied.

"Right," Sam said sarcastically. "Like Frank would do anything halfway decent."

"I swear, he did, Samantha." Millie sat down on the couch that was beside Beverly's recliner. "He took off for Las Vegas one week and came back with more money than any of us could believe. He changed his ways after that. He wasn't the same man anymore."

Sam looked back at Millie and almost laughed. "What? He gambled in Vegas and won? And then he did all this?"

Millie nodded. "I know it's hard to believe, but yore daddy had this big turnaround after all that happened. He started caring for yore mama, even hired me to come and keep her company during the daytime when he wuzn't here. He fixed this place up in all the ways that yore mama had talked about for so many years. He started going to church and …"

Sam's laugh cut off Millie's sentence. "You've got to be kidding me! Frank Conwill went to church?"

"He shore did," Millie continued. "When those doors wuz opened, Frank wuz there. And he gave money to the church and would cook Thanksgiving turkeys and such for 'em every year."

"Wait, wait, wait," Sam said as she put her hand up. "You're talking about Frank Conwill, my father, the drunk? You're saying that he had some kind of life-changing event in Vegas and came back here and started doing all these good deeds?"

"I swear it, Samantha. He really did." Millie's gray eyes looked totally convinced as she reached up to settle her bright red bouffant hair.

Suddenly the sound of a crashing door echoed throughout the house.

"Millie!" bellowed a loud voice from the kitchen. "Where in the tarnation did ya put my beer, woman?"

Millie stood tall in anticipation of his entering the room, and Sam felt chills go down her spine at the recognition of the voice. When he entered, it was a tossup as to who was most surprised—him or Sam. They both just stared in silence for a moment.

"Well, well, well," he finally purred, "ain't you quite the purty little thing?"

Sam stiffened as she backed against Billy. "Get out of this house," she said firmly.

"And howdy-do to you too, little missy," he replied. "I might not've recognized ya hadn't it been fer them four eyes and that blond ponytail still hanging on to ya. I'd thought by now you would've grown up a little bit and developed more into the woman you and I both know you can be."

'"I said to get out." Her body trembled as she leaned against Billy.

Millie looked to the man and said, "Farris, this ain't no time to be teasing Samantha. Why don't you go on home, and I'll be along shortly."

Billy suddenly realized that this was the uncle who had most abused Sam. He found himself clenching both fists as he gritted his jaw at the thought. The man was every bit as repulsive as Sam had described, and the thought of his forcing himself on her was almost more than Billy could take.

"And who is this pretty dude?" Farris asked as he inched toward Billy. "I'll be dad-blamed if he ain't purdier than you, Sammy. Tell me you didn't go out and find you one of them homo's, did you? Thought you might convert him, huh? I doubt it ... not with them four eyes of yores."

Billy moved Sam aside and stepped up to Farris. He towered him by a good six inches, but Farris probably weighed twice what he did.

"I believe she told you to get out," he said sternly as he looked down on the man.

"And I don't believe she has any right to come waltzin' back in here whenever she feels like it and start commandin' people to do anything."

Millie jumped in. "Farris, don't go causing no trouble. Just go on home, and I'll be there in a little while."

"Me?" Farris laughed obnoxiously. "I ain't causing no trouble. It's these two city slickers that's causing the trouble."

Sam stepped up beside Billy and threatened, "If you don't leave, I'll call the police."

Farris laughed again. "Go ahead, sweetheart! 'Cause that's what its gonna take to get me out of this house!"

Billy took another step closer to Farris. "We don't need the police. If he doesn't leave, I'll put him out."

"You and what army?" Farris laughed out again.

Very smoothly, Billy reached up and grabbed Farris' collar with one hand and began to move him backwards. Farris shrugged off the hand.

"Git yo hands offa me, boy!" Farris yelled in a different tone this time.

"Then get out of this house," he repeated.

Farris bumped back up to Billy. "I ain't leaving."

Sam spoke up. "Billy, don't mess with him. I'll call the police, and they can get him out."

"No!" he told her as the blood began to pulse through his body. "I'll get him out. In fact, I can say that I've been looking forward to this for a long time." He looked back at Farris with a degrading glare. "You've got one more chance, pal. Pack your butt out of here, or I'll move it for you."

Farris wouldn't budge, so Billy shoved his shoulders so hard that he fell back to the wall. Farris seemed undaunted and stood aright again, obstinate to be moved. What happened next seemed to go in slow motion. Billy clenched his right hand and drew it back behind him, but Farris only laughed. When Billy's fist met his face, the man fell to the ground with a warbling thud. Millie screamed at the sight, but Billy wasn't finished with the job. Rather than let Farris get back to his feet, he grabbed the shoulder strap on the front of the overalls and began to drag him across the slippery wood floor to the tile in the kitchen. Farris tried a couple of times to get up, but Billy would just shove him back down. When he got him to the door which led to the porch, he used every ounce of strength he could to pull Farris to his feet.

"Now," Billy said, "you can walk out the door on your own as Sam requested, or I can gladly finish the job."

Farris just stared at him, his face beginning to swell from the punch. Farris reared back his arm and attempted to hit Billy, but Billy ducked, spun around, and this time hit Farris smack in the nose. Blood splattered all over, but Billy wanted to get the man out. He grabbed him by the collar, drew open the door, and pulled him out onto the porch. Once he got the porch door open, he kicked him out into the yard. Farris swaggered a bit before finally falling over a rock. Billy wiped his hands on his jeans and felt a rush of adrenaline like he had never known before. For the first time in his life, he felt like he had really defended Sam. If only Frank had been here too.

Millie came running out of the house and threw herself down beside Farris. "Why couldn't you just leave? Yore so pigheaded! My stars, Farris! I think the boy broke yore nose."

Sam came up next to Billy on the porch and just stared at the sight. She wasn't sure whether to smile in delight or vomit at the image of Farris bleeding all over the sidewalk. She then noticed Billy was cradling his right hand.

"Are you hurt?" she asked immediately as she leaned over to check his hand.

He just smiled and said, "Who cares?"

"Samantha?" came a voice from the kitchen.

Sam leaned around Billy and was astonished to see her mother standing at the door. "Mama?" she replied.

"Samantha, where have you been?" her mother asked.

Sam walked into the kitchen and took her mother's hands in her own and said, "I went to college, Mama. I became a teacher."

Beverly smiled as if she understood at last. "You were always so smart. And you were very good at math."

Sam sighed as she took her mother's arm to lead her back to the living room. If she was having a lucid moment, maybe she could get some idea of what her mother wanted to do with the rest of her life.

Seventy-Four

"Daddy, you'd better not breathe a word of this to Stephen," Annie emphasized again. "I'm not ready to deal with this where he's concerned."

He breathed deeply and shook his head in disagreement. "I don't think you're going about this the right way."

"Advice heard," she said as she raised both eyebrows in seriousness. "I'm not ready. Just honor me on this … please."

He nodded reluctantly as he moved into the cozy den at her cabin. "No fire in the fireplace?"

"It's low on my list of priorities," she mumbled. "Besides, it's just too easy to flip on the heat."

"With rising gas prices, your bill is gonna be astronomical for heating this massive house."

She rolled her eyes. "Daddy, I've got more money than I'll ever know what to do with. In fact, if you'd agree to it, I'd gladly replace that antique heating unit you've got with something much more efficient."

He shook his head. "We're doing just fine. You, however, are another story. Annie, you've got to talk to Stephen about the baby. You can't sweep this under the rug. And eventually the kids are gonna figure it out, and you know they'll tell him."

"But right now, it's all just too new. I can't believe this actually happened!"

He let a small grin escape.

"And you think it's funny?" she said with a harsh glare.

"All of you are funny … at least you girls are. Andie's got five kids, Angie has three, would have had four, and here you are getting started on number three."

"But they both have husbands—they'll survive."

He stopped smiling and looked over at Annie without any hint of sympathy. "And you have a husband too, but if you don't start talking to him, he's gonna give up."

"Give up? He's already given up! He's in California … away from here, from the kids … as far away from me as he can get. And any discussion I've had with him since he left has been nothing but guilt-blaming, accusatory blah, blah, blah. I've had enough of that. Doesn't he understand I feel horrible enough already?"

Jonathan looked around the room at the photographs of happy memories and moments Annie and Stephen had wanted to capture and display. He agreed that Stephen had been harsh and impulsive in his response, but he was also convinced that Stephen was ready to talk beyond the emotions now. However, Annie wasn't someone you handled off the cuff. He should have known that. Granted, he was hurt, but if he hadn't intended his leaving to be permanent, he should have used a little more sensitivity with her.

"Annie," he tried to reason, "it's wrong for you to not at least speak with him. You have more than just a past with him. Look at all these pictures. They represent life that you shared. And these two children you have running around this house represent a love greater than most people ever know. You've got to give him some slack for his initial reaction about the news. And you've got to give him a chance to find his way back here again … if he wants to."

She stood slowly and went to the French doors overlooking the pool. "*If* he wants to come back." She sighed. "I don't want to think about *if's*, Daddy. I can't handle *if's*. The fact is that he is *not* here. That is the reality. It's also a reality that I never deserved him in the first place. I should've known from the beginning, all the trouble surrounding us ever getting together … I should've known it wouldn't work."

"But it *did* work!" he exclaimed. "You had six blissful years together! Now you're both ready to throw it away when you hit the first speed bump!"

"*I* didn't throw it away!" she screamed as she looked back at her father with huge tears. "He walked out. He left. And he still isn't here, is he? He arranges visits for his kids, but he is not *here*."

"And where are the divorce papers, then? Why hasn't he made any effort to make this separation permanent? For crying out loud, Annie, you still share the same bank account! Doesn't that say anything to you?"

She only shook her head as she turned back toward the pool. She reached up and wiped her eyes and then began to gently rub her tummy.

☼☼☼

Sam had Billy lie down on the bed as she filled up a bag with ice to put on his hand. His knuckles had begun to swell significantly, and she kept expressing fear that it might be broken.

"It's not that bad, Sam," he insisted as she examined it more closely. "It's just a little bruised."

"So you say. Are you gonna be up for the viewing tonight?"

"There's no way I'm letting you go there alone," he said quickly. "It's just my hand. Besides, I've suffered much worse than this."

She looked up from his hand and smiled. "Thank you. I don't know what I would've done today had you not been there. You do know that everything you think you ever owed me has been paid in full after all this."

He looked at her and desperately wanted to take her in his arms again. He looked past the thick rimmed glasses into her hurting green eyes, and then he glanced around her face to her hair … and the ponytail. She was so beautiful, but few could see it for the way she masked it with those two features specifically. Without thinking, he reached up and removed her glasses. She just continued to stare at him.

"You have the most incredible eyes," he whispered as he ran his fingers across her cheeks. "I dream of those eyes so many nights, that I wonder if they'll ever leave my head."

She smiled slightly. "Really? I had no idea."

"No," he said as he shook his head, "you don't. You have no idea how often I think of you, dream about you …"

He knew he should stop and turn away from her, but her eyes kept him entranced in a stare. He then reached up and caressed the hair around her face. "And why the ponytail, Sam? You're not sixteen anymore."

She shook her head slowly, but wouldn't break her gaze.

"Why?" he asked her again as he slid his hand back toward the base of her neck.

Instead of answering, she leaned into him and began to gently kiss his lips, first the bottom, then the top. He felt his head begin to swoon and he pulled her closer, kissing her back more eagerly than he meant. She didn't seem to care. She met his passion and then began to push him back on the bed as she carefully moved his hurt hand from beneath her. When she pulled back to look at him, he saw such a look of desire in her eyes that he could hardly breathe. He had to stop this, or it would be out of control before he knew it. But when she kissed him again, all thoughts of stopping fled. With his good hand still behind her neck, he moved it toward the ponytail and began to gradually pull the band from her hair. As the kiss deepened, his attempt to get the ponytail down became hastier. But just as he almost had it done, she cried out.

"No!" She pulled herself away from him and got up from the bed.

"Sam, I'm sorry," he began to apologize immediately. "I shouldn't have let that happen."

She held up her hand for him to stop talking. She reached back to where the ponytail holder was almost out, and she pulled it from her hair. She then looked at him as tears begin to slip down her face.

"Sam," he asked softly as he stood up in front of her. "What is it?"

She leaned down to the bed and picked up her glasses, but Billy kept her hand from putting them on.

"What's going on, Sam? This is more than the fact that we just shared a kiss, isn't it?"

She nodded slowly as she hung her head.

"Tell me, babe," he implored tenderly as he put his arms around her. "Sam, this is me, okay? This is the Billy that cares for you so deeply

I'd give my life for you. This isn't the one who walked out." He pulled her chin up to face him. "Whatever it is, you've got to tell me. You can't hold this inside anymore."

She collapsed into his chest and held him tighter than he could remember. He knew she was fighting sobs—he could literally feel them creeping into her throat.

"Sam, what is it? Is it the ponytail?"

She only nodded as her grip on him increased.

"I take it that its way more than just an easy fix for your hair each morning, huh?

She nodded again. Finally she managed to pull back and look up at him. Even though her eyes were red now, their beauty was still as prominent. Then another thought hit him.

"And the glasses?" he asked her. "You keep wearing the glasses because of something?"

She nodded again. Closing her eyes she breathed deeply, trying to regain control of her emotions.

"Oh, no," Billy whispered as the light dawned on him for the first time. He remembered Farris' statements about her glasses and her ponytail. "Farris," he moaned out in contempt. "It's because of Farris, isn't it?"

She nodded as her face began to contort into tears again. He was now putting it all together. Farris had made comments about her glasses, calling her four-eyes, and then talked about her ponytail and how she should have outgrown it by now. He had found them both despicable and said how much prettier she would have been without them. All these years she had deliberately tried to hide the two features that were her most attractive.

"Sam," he said firmly as he lifted her chin again. "I want you to listen to me … and listen to me good."

She looked at him and tried to keep from letting go into another cry.

"Farris has nothing to do with you anymore. You are an incredible woman, and you have this incredible beauty that you keep insisting on hiding because you are somehow afraid of … well … I don't know what. But you've got to come to a point, Sam, where he no longer rules your life. He's a pig, and he has no control over you."

He kissed her forehead and pulled her close. "It's time for you to move on, Sam. He's been in the back of your head far too long. But it's over now, okay?"

He leaned back so he could look at her. "I know the truth, Sam. I know everything now, so you don't need to hide anymore. You can let your beauty shine, babe, for everybody. It's time. It's your time, Sam; it's your time."

She buried her head into his neck as she threw her glasses back onto the bed. And no matter how good it felt to hear Billy pronounce her freedom, she couldn't help but cry. She had held this burden for so long, and had tried to hide for so long, that to hear Billy say it was almost too much. Could he really see into her soul like that?

When the moment finally calmed, he tried to lighten things up.

"Look," he told her, "you need to get in the shower. I'm gonna run down to that drugstore for a moment."

"For what?"

He just smiled his charming smile and shook his head. "You'll see. Put on your make-up, put on your best dress, but do *not* put your hair up in that ponytail tonight. Got it?"

She nodded and tried to smile as he left.

☼☼☼

Jonathan regretfully put the kids' bags in the back of the minivan. He would be staying the night with Alex and Megan, and then return the next morning. He dreaded seeing Stephen again because he had literally become like a son to him. What he wanted was to greet him with a strong embrace and then tell him to get his rear back to Alabama and take care of his family, but the walls were thick. He also knew that Stephen needed to be told about the baby, but he had to respect Annie's wishes … for the moment. She was fragile right now, more vulnerable than he had ever seen her in her entire life. But at some point he was going to have to insist that she meet with Stephen and they talk all this out.

Dear Father, he prayed as he looked toward heaven, *this is not what you want for either of them. Whatever it takes, Lord, whatever it takes to get them back on track again, do it. Please, do it. This is pure insanity.*

☼☼☼

When Billy returned from the drug store, Sam had just stepped out of the shower and begun to dry her hair. He dropped a couple of bags on the bed and then gave her a grin that was both charming and mischievous.

She turned off the dryer. "What are you up to? What have you got in there?"

He reached into one bag and pulled out a box of electric curlers and then into another to reveal a curling iron and a container of hairspray.

"What are those for?"

"You," he replied simply. "Growing up with a twin sister who knew how to bribe me to get me to help her with her hair has finally paid off."

Her eyebrows flew up in surprise. "What?" she laughed.

"Tonight, you're gonna look like the princess you really are. When I get through with you, the people in this pokey little town are gonna be bowing at your feet, babe."

Seventy-Five

As Billy pulled the Mustang into the parking lot of the funeral home, he wished he could infuse a jolt of confidence into Sam. She looked ravishing. Her blond hair flowed down her back in long, rich curls, and wispy strands framed her face as they fell from the barrette on top. He had also insisted she keep her glasses in her purse and rely on him for any necessary reading. If it got downright desperate, she could put them on for the moment.

"But I'll barely recognize people," she complained. "They'll have changed enough as it is anyway, but to not see clearly will make it even harder."

"Who cares?" he told her as he turned off the engine. "It doesn't matter who *they* are tonight. All that matters is that *you* are back for the weekend, and this is who you are."

"But it isn't really," she argued.

He took her hand immediately and forced her to look at him. "Yes … it is. And tonight, when people remind you of who they are, you just smile and let them know that you're Samantha Marcum, the girl who refused to bow to their perceptions back then—the girl who was determined to make something of herself even when every card dealt to her was a losing blow." He pulled her hand to his lips and gently kissed the back of it. "And tonight, I am very much your husband. You lean on me as though I'm your Gibraltar. Understood?"

She nodded as the lump in her throat nearly strangled her. Billy thrived on pretense like this, but it scared her to death. No matter what she might look like on the outside, she was still the same scared little girl on the inside, and it was unlikely that anyone passing that coffin tonight would ever believe she was anything more than transplanted white trash.

✪✪✪

Stephen looked around the huge room of his loft and wondered if it would ever be possible to make his children feel genuinely comfortable here. The colorful bunk beds in the corner, the trampoline with the protective netting in the middle of the large carpeted play area, and the huge collection of movies and games for the big-screened TV had yet to impress them. He understood though—they loved their mother. And as much as he knew they loved him too, he was here and not at home. And he was becoming more of a stranger to them with each day that he stayed away. He would give anything to just leave all this and return to the cozy log cabin nestled in the rolling hills of the lush north Alabama woods, but he was paying for his hasty decision … and his harsh words. When he had walked out, and when he had said all he had said, he had done it out of hurt.

He was Stephen Williams—he had earned the right to speak his mind and express his distaste for things. But when Annie had walked into his life, he had changed. Suddenly his fame and fortune paled in comparison to this spirited woman who had literally captured and imprisoned his heart. She had turned him down time and time again, but he knew that if she wouldn't be a part of his life, he would never enjoy anything again. He also knew she was hard-headed, but even that was a part of her attractiveness. She was someone whose affections couldn't be bought with all his impressiveness, and even when she had left him after declaring her love while in Paris, he refused to stop until she was back in his life again.

Yet here he was alone, miserable, and trying worthlessly to fill that hole in his life again with all those things that had become meaningless once she had entered. And even now, as he punched out a few notes on the keyboard beside a window that overlooked the Los Angeles skyline, it was all empty … again. If Annie was here, she would have heard his notes and then immediately hummed the next line to complete the phrase. That's who she had become to him—the completion of everything. In fact, it had been five years since he had written anything alone. He thought it was because he didn't want to, not because he couldn't. But as he worked with Ben the past three months, he had come to realize that Annie was not just a part of his life, but she had become a part of everything about him … including his music. Ben seemed thrilled with the puny melodies he pulled out of his brain, but to Stephen they all seemed trite, repetitious, and just a restating of something he had written before. They were stale and uncreative, and so was his life.

He reached into his pocket and pulled out his phone to try yet again for a conversation with her. He knew the chances were slim, but he was starting to get desperate. He knew Annie—if he didn't get to her soon, she would be so hardened against him that it would take a mighty act of God to ever turn her around. He clicked his menu and pressed the first name on the list. He then slowly placed the phone to his ear and breathed a prayer as he counted the rings. Two … then to voicemail. He knew that meant she had seen his number and chose to ignore the call … again.

He threw the phone across the massive room as hard as he could, and when it hit the wall it smashed to pieces. "Just like my heart, Annie," he moaned as he slammed the cover down on the keyboard. He paced the room, filled with anger and despair, wishing like crazy he could release the emotions by breaking something else, but it was pointless. "How can I apologize to you if you won't at least give me the chance?"

he screamed.

☼☼☼

When Sam saw her father lying in the open casket, she felt her knees almost give way. It was amazing how different he looked from the man she remembered. He was clean-shaven and dressed in a suit with a neat haircut. A large Bible was tucked beneath his hands, and a cross necklace made of small spikes emerged from one hand and draped over the Bible. She hadn't wanted to see him at all, but the receiving line would be right before the casket, so she didn't have much choice. Billy's hand constantly on her waist or shoulder was a huge comfort however, and whenever she would feel herself beginning to fail, his touch would cause her to raise her shoulders back and her head high.

"He looks dead," her mother said as she came up beside her at the coffin. It startled Sam for the moment and she let out a small squeak. "Did you know him?" Beverly asked her.

"Mama, I'm Samantha," she reminded her. "Of course, I knew him."

Beverly looked at Sam and shook her head. "Sam's gone … probably forever. They kidnapped her, you know."

She sighed and shook her head. "I went away to college, Mama. I'm teaching school in Alabama."

"They say Alabama is nice," Beverly continued conversing as though Sam was a total stranger. "It's a *sweet home* there, you know. Did you know Sam too?"

"I *am* Sam. I live in Alabama now."

Millie came up behind them and put her arm around Beverly. "He looks so nice, don't he?"

But Beverly shook her head. "He looks dead, Millie. He doesn't look right."

"He is dead, dear," Millie reminded her casually as though she were speaking of something as mundane as milk gone bad.

Beverly looked back at Millie and said, "Samantha should be here, you know."

"Samantha is here," Millie told her. "She's right beside you, Beverly … she and her husband. Remember when they came to visit you today at the house."

Beverly looked back at Sam and smiled politely, then turned to Millie again and whispered, "They've replaced her."

"Sam!" came a call from the door.

Sam looked around. She couldn't actually see Ms. Allen walking into the receiving room as everything was a complete blur, but she recognized the voice. She was a warm welcome in the midst of all the strangeness. The lady walked over to her and embraced her sweetly.

"How are you holding up?" she asked Sam.

"I'm fine," she said trying to sound more confident than she was.

"My," Ms. Allen smiled. "You look absolutely beautiful." She cupped her hands around Sam's face. "I always knew you were such a lovely girl. There'll be many a fellow come through here tonight wishing they had thought the same thing back then."

"I doubt that," Sam laughed slightly. "I don't envision too many people showing up to pay their respects to Frank Conwill."

Ms. Allen smiled and then took Sam by the hand. "Let's go to another room for a little while, why don't we?"

Sam shrugged as she went with her, and Billy followed immediately behind. They walked into the chapel which would be used tonight as a place of visiting and tomorrow for the service. Ms. Allen sat down on the front row and motioned for Billy and Sam to sit with her.

"Many things have changed since you left here, Sam," Ms. Allen began. "The biggest of those changes being your father."

Sam chuckled unconvinced as she leaned back against Billy's arm and shook her head.

"Honey, I know more than anyone else here tonight how bad things were for you. I know what a horrible father … shoot … what a horrible man Frank Conwill was to you. The truth is that he should've been locked away and punished severely for all he did. And if anyone knew, they'd agree. But you need to understand something before you start meeting all these people tonight—your father wasn't the same man that you grew up with. He changed in a big way, Samantha, and he became someone that all these people coming tonight admired."

Sam shook her head. "I can't believe that. He was a wretch of a man, and as far as I'm concerned, he deserves the biggest punishment God can offer."

"At one time, yes, I would agree with you. But he turned his life around in a way that you never saw."

Sam jumped up from the pew and nearly yelled, "I don't care! I don't care if he became the president or even the pope! He was an evil, evil man, and he ruined my life! He did things to me … let things be done to me … that he should have hanged for! And if another person tries to tell me how wonderful he was, I'm gonna puke!"

Ms. Allen stood and went to her. "Believe me, honey, I understand. I know all that happened, and if you would have let me, I would have had that man put away for many years … he and Farris and Farrell … all three of them. But you had lived through enough humiliation already. And when you begged me not to tell anyone, to just let you stay with me until you graduated, I was willing to do it." She put her arm around Sam's shoulder. "But sometimes God has other plans for people we can't understand, and your father was one of those people."

"Please don't call him my *father*," Sam gritted. "He was never a *father* to me. He was more like a pimp than a father."

"I know. So you've got to believe me when I tell you that for him to change like he did, it was more than just some surface game he was playing."

Sam walked back to where Billy was sitting and picked up her purse. "You know what? I really don't care. You and everybody else here can think he was some miracle from God if you want to, but all he ever was to me was the worst man … no, the second worse man … in my life."

"Samantha, you've got to come to grips with what happened to him or you'll never make it through the night," Ms. Allen said firmly.

"I *know* who he was—I lived with him," Sam said with a controlled anger. "I don't need anyone to tell me anything about Frank Conwill."

"Then ask your mother," Ms. Allen offered.

Sam laughed this time. "My mother is crazy and delusional."

"Sometimes," she agreed, "but not always. And Frank was very good to her these last few years. You need to know that, especially when you start making decisions about what happens to her now."

"She used to stand in the yard and scream in horror whenever I got on the bus in the mornings because she thought people from the TV were taking me away! She doesn't have a clue about my father! He could have cut her fingers off one by one and she wouldn't remember it!"

Ms. Allen walked up to her again. "You're wrong, Samantha. There are times when she is aware of her life. And Frank gave her a good life. You saw the house."

Sam didn't want to hear anymore. She didn't care what anyone had to say about Frank. She hated him, and that was a final and just decision on her part.

The night turned out to be much harder than Sam could have ever imagined. It was just as Ms. Allen had warned. Person after person would first comment on how awesome Sam had turned out, but then would immediately go into raving about how wonderful her father had been. Had Billy not been there, she would have walked out. But he continued to be her Gibraltar, just as he had promised, and she was able to listen to all the remarks and accolades and keep her composure. Something else Ms. Allen said also proved to be true—her mother had moments of what seemed like almost normal lucidity. Every now and then Beverly would reach over to hug Sam and tell her how glad she was that she was here, and then five minutes later would want to know who the pretty blond was standing next to her. She would realize that Frank was dead and that was why they were all there, and other times would wonder why on earth he was over there sleeping when all these people were coming to visit.

As the night wore on, so did Sam's nerves, but her composure somehow managed to remain sure. When the crowd had trickled down to just a handful of stragglers, however, that was when Farris decided to show—broken, bandaged nose and all. As soon as he walked into the room, his eyes lit up over Sam's appearance.

"Wow!" he exclaimed loudly as he whistled at her. "Now *that's* what I'm talking about!"

"Oh, shut up, Farris," Ms. Allen said with disgust as she moved toward Sam. "Couldn't you at least stay sober for your brother's viewing?"

"What fer?" he continued being obnoxiously loud. "He ain't given me a cent o' all that money, and after all my wife's done fer him all these years, he goes on and leaves everything to his runaway daughter!"

Millie stepped in to say, "And he's paid me well, Farris! Stop yore complaining. Besides, Samantha is his daughter and rightful heir."

He looked over at Sam with a spiteful stare. "Yeah … rightful heir. She don't show up for years and years, but when he dies, she comes in to put her mama away and claim all his money."

Ms. Allen quickly replied, "No one said Samantha was putting her away. And as far as the money goes, she wasn't even aware of it. She's here doing the right thing, Farris. Something you apparently aren't capable of."

Farris laughed as he swaggered past Sam toward the casket. When he neared her, he reeked of alcohol. It was a repulsively familiar smell, his body sweat and cheap liquor. She nearly gagged as the memory of it all began to flood her mind again. He leaned over the casket and gave the body a good once-over.

"Hey, big brother," he slurred. "You good-fer nothing. Can't believe you gave money to everybody under the sun but yer own flesh and blood. Dang … you even built a church. Ha! Who woulda' ever believed that? And now here you lay, dead as a derned doornail, and I'm still here havin' to scrape by for the rest of my life." He looked at the body one more time and then turned around to face everyone in the room. "Jerk."

Suddenly, without anyone expecting it, Beverly Conwill stepped up to him and slapped his face hard. He howled in pain as she had managed to hit his nose again.

"You hush your mouth, Farris Conwill!" Beverly said sounding as though she was in complete understanding. "You were never anything but pure trash, and Frank wasn't about to pour his money down the toilet … the place you apparently long to dwell! And I'll tell you this, if it weren't for the fact that Millie has been so good to me when I can't think clearly, he would have had you relocated long ago!"

Everyone stared at Beverly in astonishment. It seemed as though she knew exactly all that had happened.

"Relocated?" Farris bellowed. "What are you talking about you blasted crazy woman?"

"He wanted to get you as far away from his life as he could, and he almost hired some men to do it, but he knew Millie would eventually follow, and he knew I needed her!"

Farris laughed again even though blood was beginning to trickle from the bandage. "Hire some men? To do what, woman? You're as crazy as a derned bed bug!"

"To get you out of here!" Beverly continued. "He was gonna have some metal fabrication company in Kentucky hire you on. He had it all set up. They were gonna offer you more money than you were worth, and Frank was gonna pay the difference."

Everyone now was in complete shock. Was she telling the truth or was this another delusion? But the one in the most shock was Farris.

"What?" he asked as he took a step toward her. "He was gonna pay a part of my salary to get me outta here?"

"A *big* part," Beverly said with a sneer, "because you aren't worth much."

Farris dropped his head as he took in the thought. "He was gonna sell me out … my own brother."

Beverly sneered as she said, "You piece of dung. You worthless waste of human breath."

Seventy-Six

The rain was heavy as Billy drove silently back to the hotel. Once there, Sam wouldn't move. She just sat quietly in her seat and stared out the front windshield. The visitation had been harder than she could have imagined, and her emotions were confused and raw.

"I don't think it's gonna slack up any," Billy finally broke the silence. "Unless we plan on sleeping in the car, we're gonna get wet."

She turned and looked at him despondently. She obviously wasn't thinking about the rain. "Yeah … it's okay. Rain is the least of my worries right now."

He took her hand. "You don't have any worries right now," he assured her. "We're just taking this one step at a time. You got through tonight, and now it's over. Tomorrow we do the funeral. We'll handle that when we get there. Monday, we meet with the lawyer. Right now, Sam, you just need to sleep." He squeezed her hand. "Let's go inside where it's warm and dry. Okay?"

She squeezed his hand back and then opened the door. He ran up the stairs to their room, but Sam just kept a normal pace. He unlocked the door and turned on the lights, glancing back to see where she was. "Hurry up," he called to her. "You're gonna get drenched!"

When she finally reached the room, she walked inside but turned off the lights. He closed the door and sighed.

"Sam," he said softly, "I know what you're doing." He walked toward her, barely able to make out her figure from what little light shone through a crack in the drapes. "You don't have to hide your tears in the dark … you don't have to hide from me."

He put his hands on her shoulders, but she jerked herself away. "Just let me do this on my own, okay?"

He knew she was about to break because this was how she had always done it before. She preferred the lights off and to be alone in the dark.

"Don't do this alone, Sam," he whispered. "That's why I'm here … remember?"

She was silent as she sorted out her thoughts. "There were just so many of them tonight," she faintly said. "So many of them telling me how incredible he was … how good he'd been to them … all he'd done." A small sob escaped. "But all he ever did for me," she ground her teeth together, "was sell me out to that drunken sot of a brother of his." Another sob. "What am I supposed to do?" she asked weakly. "How do I reconcile the man they say he became with the man I knew he was?"

Billy honestly didn't know. If Frank Conwill had indeed changed into the image he had heard described tonight by person after person after person, he was as confused as Sam. He walked up to her, still trying to see in the darkness, and realized she had turned her back toward him. He wrapped his arms around her waist and rested his chin on her head.

"Sam, we'll get through this. I promise."

She pulled away from him again. "I don't need your pity, Billy! Okay? Just leave me alone!"

He reached out for her and grabbed her arm. "Yes, you do!" he countered. "Whether you like it or not, I'm all you've got right now. And yes, you need my pity. You need everything I can give you, because there isn't anyone in this place who really knows what happened to you. There isn't anyone in the whole world who really knows what happened to you." He pulled her to him again. "I'm it for you, Sam. Please … let me be here for you. Don't hide this from me … don't try to face it on your own."

She finally collapsed into his chest, but she still wouldn't cry. He knew her emotions were high, and there was probably as much anger as hurt, but her tears wouldn't come. As he stroked the back of her hair, now pasty wet from the hairspray and rain combined, he wished he could think of the right words to settle her heart, but he doubted they existed.

"We're gonna get through this," he told her again, but even that sounded shallow. "I mean it, Sam. This is the worst, okay? This is the worst that life can deal you. But in a year, this will be the distant past. Right now, just lean on me and know that we're gonna get through it."

He felt her head nod against his chest and took some satisfaction in hoping that maybe he had given her a sense of confidence instead of all the impending doom. She reached her arms around his waist and pulled him closer to her. He felt strong as he held her, and wished more than anything that all this was real, that he had never walked out on her, and that when they left this miserable place that they would simply go *home.*

She slowly lifted her head and he wished he could see her green eyes, no glasses, looking at him with thankfulness and surety, but the lack of light could only leave him guessing. But when she moved her hands to his neck and pulled his lips to hers, he forgot where he was or why he was here. He knew he should simplify the situation and gently pull away, but his emotions had been as frazzled as hers, and as they all began to dissolve into the passion of the kiss, it was too easy to continue. She seemed to melt into him as the kiss grew into another and then another, and he knew exactly where it was heading as she began to undo his tie.

He could hear Kyle's voice in the back of his head saying, *Don't give her the ball, Billy. Don't put that pressure on her. Stay in control and be the quarterback*. But as she pulled off his tie and began to unbutton his shirt, he was losing any control he might have had. With every ounce of strength he could muster, he pulled himself back.

"Sam," he whispered breathlessly. "If we're not careful …"

"Please don't reject me, Billy," she pleaded. "Not now … please …"

And with another kiss, he was gone, along with all his reasoning and rationale. He loved her, he really did, and he wasn't going to reject her on top of all she had been through that evening. This wasn't a situation Kyle could have foreseen, and as Sam began to remove his shirt, Billy lifted her from the floor and carried her to the bed.

✿✿✿

Jonathan sat thoughtfully on the last leg of the flight to L.A. as he held a whimpering Ellie in his arms. She didn't want to leave her mother again especially for an entire week at Stephen's, and her emotional protests when Jonathan had come to get her that morning had upset Annie horribly. He had watched his daughter grow from one shade of green to another as Ellie continued to scream about leaving. Stevie, however, remained quiet. Jonathan knew that his feelings were just as strong, but he had learned this was one area that was nonnegotiable. As much as he didn't want to stay with his father, he still had hope that maybe the family would get back together one day.

As the plane landed, the attendant advised Jonathan to be ready immediately to leave with the children because security was waiting for them. Obviously Stephen had come to the airport himself again. He tried to encourage Ellie to be happy about seeing her daddy, to which she replied she was happy about *seeing* him, just not *staying* with him. Of course, this broke his heart even more. He couldn't imagine what it was like to be a four-year-old who just months ago had the perfect family—yet now it was being torn apart month after month because of two stubborn parents. If he could, he would love to give both Stephen and Annie a good spanking.

As they left the plane, Ellie held tightly to his hand, but Stevie, carrying his own bag, almost acted like a grown-up as he let his sister be the one comforted. When Stephen's familiar face appeared through the sea of security, Ellie's hand tightened inside Jonathan's. How he hated being the go-between in all of this.

"Hey, buddy!" Stephen exclaimed with excitement as he approached Stevie. "Man, you're growing like a weed!" He stooped down and spread his arms out for Stevie, but Stevie moved closer to Jonathan instead. Stephen continued to smile, but he stood in disappointment.

"It's very hard on them," Jonathan explained. "They love their father, but it seems to come at the expense of their mother. They're too young to process all that's going on here, Stephen."

He nodded as he reached down to tousle Stevie's hair. "I know." He then looked at Jonathan. "It's hard on me too. I don't like how all this played out."

"Then why are you continuing to follow this course?"

"Because," Stephen said in exasperation, "I can't even get Annie to talk to me! I call and I call, but she refuses to …"

"Shhh!" Jonathan put his finger to his lips. "Let's get to your place, and then we can talk. Don't do this in front of the children."

Stephen nodded, a bit embarrassed at his outburst, and motioned for security to move them on through the airport.

Once they were at Stephen's loft, and the kids were occupied on the trampoline, Jonathan tried to reason with him. "She won't talk to you because all she got from you was anger and accusation and grief whenever you spoke on the phone."

"That was over two months ago! I was still shell-shocked over the whole incident."

"And you made no allowances for her judgment in any way, shape or form," Jonathan reminded him.

"I never said this was to be permanent. I told her I needed some time to get away and sort through it all."

"And since when has that been the best way to handle problems in a marriage? You don't walk away from a problem if you actually hope to work through it."

"Come on, Jonathan! It was a lot to process! It wasn't just the fact that Edrew wasn't my father, or that my mother did what she did. There was also the reality that Ben was my real father, and she had tried to … I don't know … keep me from even working with him."

"Yes," Jonathan nodded with a hint of sarcasm in his voice, "and he was conveniently there to suggest you take off with him when all the rockets started flying. Perhaps she had a little more insight into Mr. Brenner than you'd like to admit."

"I had to figure all this out," Stephen said weakly as he dropped into a chair. "I had to sort through it."

Jonathan ran his fingers through his hair as he felt a tightness growing in his chest. "And have you figured it out? Have you managed to sort through it all as you stay away from your wife and your children? Has it done you a lot of good? I certainly hope so, because in the meantime, Annie's heart is growing colder and harder towards you with each passing hour."

Stephen threw his hands up. "That's not what I wanted! I just needed some time … and space!"

"Baloney," Jonathan said unconvinced as he rubbed the tightness in his chest. "That's what you do, Stephen, when you're sixteen and you get mad at your girlfriend. You don't take a time out from your marriage to decide how best to put it together again!" He took a few deep breaths.

"Are you okay?" Stephen asked him.

He took another deep breath. "Could you get me a glass of water …?"

"Sure." Stephen jumped up right away and filled a glass with cold water from the door of the refrigerator. "Here you go."

He took several long swallows, put the glass down on the table, and then looked back at Stephen. "As I said, this isn't how a mature person handles a marriage."

"Mature? Do you call what Annie's doing mature? She won't even talk to me."

Jonathan folded his arms and looked with disbelief at Stephen. "You've got to be kidding me. You know Annie as well as I do—she's a person who thinks with her head, never her heart. In fact, if I hadn't threatened to throw her out of my house, she would have never spoken to you again after Paris … much less married you." The tightness was barely letting up.

"What do you mean she *thinks with her head*? Everybody thinks with their head."

"No. Most people think with their hearts, Stephen. Most people in Annie's position right now would jump for the phone every time it rang in hopes that it would be you. But no matter what her heart may want, it's her head that she listens to."

Stephen just looked at him in confusion.

"When you walked out on her, her head heard that it was over. You were leaving, she had betrayed you, and she didn't deserve any kind of courtesy as your wife of six years or the mother of your children. Then whenever you spoke to her, you continued to impound that fact, continued to insist on her deliberate guilt, and you just reinforced in her mind what she had already believed for many years—that she didn't deserve you in the first place."

"That she didn't deserve me? I never said that!"

"No, but she always felt it. Who was she, this small town girl from the sticks of Alabama, to think she could win the attentions and heart of her teen idol, the world famous most eligible bachelor, Stephen Williams?"

"I adored her …" He paused and put his head down. "I still adore her."

"But she was never really convinced that she deserved your adoration. And then the longer she held the secret about your past, the more guilt she felt about that. So when you left, and then verbally accused her of everything she already believed, all it did was reinforce in her mind what her heart kept telling her not to accept."

Stephen looked over at his kids. They had long since stopped jumping on the trampoline and now sat quietly, probably thinking about their mother and the fact that they would be away from her an entire week.

"So, what do I do?" Stephen asked hopelessly. "How do I get her to change her head … and follow her heart again?"

Jonathan shrugged. "Good question." He reached into his pocket for his phone so he could call Alex and Megan. "Cause right now, you're not reaching her heart—no one is. And if she keeps on like she's going, you aren't ever gonna talk to her again."

Stephen looked at him with wide eyes. "Then what do I do?"

Jonathan looked at him severely as he said, "Pray for a major divine intervention, boy. As I see it, that's the only hope at the moment."

Seventy-Seven

Sam knew it had to be late when she finally opened her eyes, but she didn't care. That was the best sleep she had had since this whole ordeal began. There had been no nightmares, no memories of her father or Farris, and no moans from Billy sleeping fitfully on the tiny couch in the hotel room. Instead, whenever she awakened, there was only his rhythmic breathing next to her, and his body … right beside hers. Several times when she had turned over, he would reach his arms around her, and she would gently fall asleep again. It was the sound of the shower starting that finally managed to rouse her completely.

As she lifted herself up in bed, she instinctively pulled the sheet over her chest. When she did, her hand touched a small strand of matted hair. It was a mess from the mixture of all the hairspray, then all the rain, and then the night in bed. She felt her face grow warm at the memory of all that had occurred.

She glanced toward the counter to check if Billy had perhaps made coffee and was delighted to see half of the tiny pot still there. She looked for her suitcase and spotted it across the room on a luggage rack. She laughed to herself at the hesitation she had about getting out of bed and walking across the room unclothed.

What exactly do you think happened last night? she asked herself as she finally got up and went for her luggage. *Besides, he's in the shower. Just throw on your robe, get some coffee, and wait your turn.*

When he emerged from the bathroom, it was definitely awkward between them. They tried their bests to carry on normal meaningless conversation, but it was clear things wouldn't be the same. Before, it had all been a mere rekindling of an old friendship. There had been an ease and a comfort in relating to each other, but now the line had been crossed. And no matter how much they both had wanted this to happen, it changed their situation.

Once Sam was ready, complete with the fancy hair style again, they left for the funeral home. Very little was said in the car, even though they both tried their hardest to carry on shallow banter, but when the funeral home actually came into view, all thoughts of the night before vanished. She had to face the reality again of her father, her mother, her uncle, and all those people who believed Frank to be a gift from God. Thoughts of what had happened between she and Billy last night faded as he turned off the engine and she watched the people file into the building.

The accolades about her father at the funeral would have been unbearable, but her mother seemed to be in her right mind during the entire service, and she kept turning to Sam saying how good it was to have her here through all of this. Sam wasn't exactly sure what to do with her mother anymore. After hearing her sail into Farris last night, and then getting glimpses of her—seeming to be almost in her right mind, but not quite—was disconcerting. Before she had actually seen her mother, she had pretty much decided to send her off to an institution, let insurance take care of her, and sell the house. She would invest the money from the sale in her own retirement, and never have to think about Toombs County or anyone there ever again. But as the complexities of this situation began to unravel, she doubted it would be as simple as that now. Not only did her mother seem to be aware of her situation at times, but whatever kind of money her father had, it was obviously a little more than a couple hundred dollars. She had heard over and over again last night that he was pretty much the one who had funded the building of a new church. And if the whole thing was true about his willingness to pay a portion of Farris' salary had he moved to Kentucky, there must have been a little more in the bank than what was needed to refurbish the house or pave the road.

But what was she thinking? This was her mother that had said that! Half the time Beverly had no idea who Sam was. However, the other half, she seemed to know exactly. This all now complicated the situation more than she had anticipated … or wanted.

After the service, the church had invited everyone to the Family Life Center for a pot luck dinner and fellowship. Sam really didn't want to go, but her curiosity about the church *her father had built* got the best of her. She had to see this place he had funded, however she didn't anticipate the grandeur that awaited her. The building was beautiful, made with chiseled stone and adorned with incredibly majestic stained-glass windows. The Family Life Center stood behind the main sanctuary, made with the same stone, and the entire area was lavishly landscaped. Neither Billy nor Sam said anything as he slowly pulled up to the stately edifice.

"Wow," he finally whispered as they watched the people pour into the door with pots and casseroles of food. "Somehow this wasn't quite what I expected."

Sam shook her head. "Me either." She glanced up at the height of the structure. "And they say Frank did all of this."

"Yeah."

She looked over at him and wondered out loud. "Just how much money did he win in Vegas? I mean, is it actually possible to go there with next to nothing and then walk away with enough money to totally change your life … completely? And then again, it's Frank Conwill we're talking about. For Pete's sake! Men like him gamble and win and then spend it all in some two-week drunken binge with all of their low-life buddies." She looked back at the church. "What happened here, Billy?"

"I have no idea, Sam, but if I were you, I think I would start listening to some of these people and what they've been trying to tell you." He reached for the door handle. "This isn't … average … you know?"

She nodded. "Tell me about it."

The people at the church were warm and kind to them. In fact, there were a few brief moments when Sam felt a twinge of homesickness for the place she had tried so hard to forget. There were many she remembered well, but she had a hard time believing they ever knew she had existed. There were even those her own age who had never spoken a word to her, never made eye contact with her all the years she had lived here, that came up and talked with her as though she were a dear old friend. They all expressed how proud they were of her and how they always knew she would do something wonderful with herself. Sam had no replies because all of it was completely unexpected. She had never considered any type of social interaction during her return to Toombs County, with the exception of Ms. Allen. This large get-together centered around the celebration of Frank Conwill's *homegoing* as they all called it, took her by surprise. She didn't know how to respond. She couldn't be rude; she wasn't that kind of person. But she also had no desire to open her heart up to these people. Yet here she sat … eating homemade pecan pie and talking about old times with Chere' Morris, head cheerleader during her years of high school, as though they had been the best of friends during the most miserable years of Sam's life.

On and off throughout the afternoon, Ms. Allen would come by and spend a few minutes with her, and her mother would drop by on occasion pleading with her to come over and visit with her Sunday after church. Sam's head was spinning in the emotional chaos of it all. When she first saw her mother yesterday the woman hadn't even recognized her, yet now she seemed clear-headed and in charge of her senses. It was all growing more confusing for Sam, and her need to make a decision about her mother's future was beginning to weigh on her heavily.

"Sam," Ms. Allen took her to the side as she was preparing to leave with Billy for the hotel. "I feel … well … there are some things that you need … oh my … this isn't easy for me, Sam … please know that. I understand what you went through. I know that accepting all of this has got to be one of the hardest things for you to do."

She nodded. "You're right. It's a hard pill for me to swallow."

Ms. Allen handed her a disc inside an envelope. "Please take this and listen to it. Do you have a DVD player in your room by any chance?"

"What's this?"

"Don't ask me. Just promise me you'll go back to your room and listen to it. Do you have a DVD player?"

"I have a laptop I can play it on."

Mrs. Allen shook her head. "That won't do. I know they have those nice big TV's in the hotel rooms. I'll be right back."

Billy came up behind her. "Are you ready to go?"

"Not yet. Ms. Allen gave me this," she said as she held up the envelope with the disc.

"What is it?"

"I have no idea." Sam looked through the plastic window to the writing on the disc. "All it has is a date from some time last year. It's a DVD of something."

"All right!" Billy teased. "We get to watch a movie tonight."

Ms. Allen came back carrying a small DVD player along with several cords. "Here, take this with you tonight and watch it for me. I think it'll help you to … well … understand some things more clearly."

"Ms. Allen, what is this? I'd really like to know before I sit down with it."

She shook her head. "No, Samantha. I need you to just trust me and promise me you'll listen to the whole thing."

Sam stared at her.

"Please," Ms. Allen said as tears filled her eyes. "You need to hear this as much as anyone ever did. Promise me."

If Sam's curiosity hadn't been peaked, she wouldn't have promised, but at the moment she was dying to see what was on the disc. "Okay. I promise. I'll watch it when I get back to the room."

"All of it," Ms. Allen emphasized. "From beginning to end … no fast forwarding … no stopping or turning it off … promise me."

Sam smiled and agreed. "I promise. All of it, beginning to end, skipping through nothing."

The older woman smiled with relief.

"But only because *you* asked me," Sam told her. "Had it been anyone else's suggestion here, I wouldn't have made that promise."

"Then I pray that your trust and respect for me pays off."

Seventy-Eight

As Billy hooked the DVD player into the television back at the hotel, Sam changed into a set of sweats. The comfort of being out of all the stuffy clothes felt better than she had imagined. The whole day had been filled with stress and pretense, and the confining outfit that Billy had insisted made her look *incredible* only added to how self-conscious she had felt. She wasn't *incredible*—she was just Sam. And all the hair and clothes and lack of glasses would never change the insecurities that lurked inside her. Not even a night with Billy Marcum again could change who she was inside.

"We're set to go," he said cheerfully as she walked out of the bathroom. "I don't suppose this is gonna be the most entertaining thing we've ever seen, huh?"

"I doubt it," she said as she climbed up into the bed and arranged the pillows so they could sit and watch comfortably.

"Maybe it's like an old classic movie or something, and she thought it would have some inspiring notions to get you through this period of death, doom and despair."

"We can hope," she smiled as she watched him crawl up beside her.

He took a moment to gaze at her, and then turned his attention back to the television. "Should I turn out the lights?"

"Yeah. It'll make it easier to see the screen."

"And to fall asleep if it's really boring," he mumbled as he reached for the lamp switch.

As soon as the credits started, they both realized they would be watching a church service from the elaborate complex where they had spent the afternoon. Not only that, but right up front it was made known that Frank Conwill was a huge contributor to the broadcasting ministry of the church. Sam shoved her glasses higher on her nose and sat back with folded arms as she now regretted making her promise. Obviously Ms. Allen wanted her to see all the things her father had made possible as a result of his generous financial gifts.

"Do we actually have to watch all of it?" Billy squirmed among the pillows uncomfortably.

She looked over at him and nodded. "I promised. But you're welcome to do whatever. You didn't make any promises."

"I'll be your moral support," he winked.

The song service was somewhat typical for a rural church, nothing like the type of stuff that Kyle did in Dockrey. In fact, Sam recognized the song leader as a local gas station owner, not a hired man full time in the church. Then a teenage girl went to the platform and sang a solo to the best of her ability—which wasn't all that great. Neither she nor Billy made any comments about the song, but it was hard not to snicker a time or two as she tried her best to hit some high notes, but never quite made them.

Then the pastor came to the pulpit. They both recognized him immediately as the one who had preached the funeral. He cleared his throat a few times and apologized for the laryngitis, but then asked them all to listen carefully to what he had to say. The look on his face was intense, as though something profound was about to be revealed. Both Sam and Billy leaned toward the television to make sure they didn't miss his comments.

"God has a way of working out things," he said through a strained voice. "I've tried for several years to get Frank Conwill to give his testimony, but he's always denied the invitation."

Sam gasped. Frank was going to speak in church, and Ms. Allen had made her promise she would listen.

"I can turn it off," Billy suggested.

"No," she replied resigned. "Ms. Allen wouldn't deliberately hurt me. If she believes this is something I should hear, then I'm willing to sit through it for her sake. I owe her that much."

The preacher continued. "I knew my voice was going during the morning service … as did most of you. And by the time dinner was done, so was my voice. God put it on my heart to call Frank and give him another try, and to my great surprise and pleasure, he agreed to share about the transformation that God made in his life. So, without torturing you any longer with my raspy utterances, please welcome a dear brother and faithful friend, Frank Conwill."

Just the sound of his name sent chills through her body, but when the camera caught the man who had raised her, who had destroyed her life, her jaw dropped in shock. He was in a suit and tie and his hair was as neat as it had been in the casket. There was no scraggly beard, and there was no beer belly pouching out from beneath the coat. He looked dignified, pleasant, and as much as she hated to admit it, handsome. The pastor helped him to turn on the lapel microphone, and then Frank Conwill did something Sam would never have imagined—he gripped the sides of the pulpit with both hands shaking and began to pray.

"God, I of all men don't deserve to be here tonight … standing in this holy place … saying anything about me or my life. I don't deserve any of the blessings You've given me. But I believe You need me to say something here tonight, so here I am. Make me a vessel, an instrument to be used by You, filled with Your words and Your power … and all for Your glory … amen."

Sam stared in awe. Had the man actually completed a sentence without using profanity? In fact, could he possibly be an imposter? There was no way this could be the same Frank Conwill she had known growing up.

"As most of you know, I was a worthless lowlife. In fact, the last day I saw my daughter, Samantha, those were the very words she used to describe me. And look, she hit the nail on the head. I don't think a day went by in her life that she didn't see me drunk or downright abusive because I couldn't afford enough liquor to get drunk. But I didn't think I had anything else to live for. I didn't think I had a reason to stay sober or live responsibly. I felt like I'd been dealt a harsh blow, and that I'd spend the rest of my life paying for a stupid mistake."

Frank slowly moved from behind the pulpit as if he felt the need to communicate more intimately with the congregation.

"I had life by the tail when I was a teenager," he said with a vacant grin. "Man, I was hot stuff … star football player, good-lookin' girlfriend and several scholarship offers for a promising future. I wasn't the brightest bulb in the box, but was downright mean on the football field, and coaches recognized the talent and couldn't wait to get their hands on me. Everyone believed I was bound for the pros—I believed I was bound for the pros. But in my cockiness, I got a little careless. And one afternoon after school, Beverly's dad and my dad met me at my truck with some serious faces. Beverly was expecting."

Frank stared down at the floor in a moment of silence as he shook his head. "I told them both I was sorry, but I had plans at the moment that didn't include Beverly or a baby. When my father shoved the barrel of his 12-gauge in my nose and told me the only plans I would be making would be to do the right thing by Beverly, I suddenly realized my plans had changed … and changed drastically.

"So, the very day after graduation, I married Bev, and a few months later, Samantha came along." His voice was getting a little shaky, and he went back behind the pulpit so he could hold on again. "I hated them both … Bev, Samantha, not to mention my father and her father, and every single person in Toombs County who knew I was a loser because I had to give up a life of football to sit here in this ratty town and rot away my life.

"And ya'll, I gave new meaning to the word *abusive.* The way I treated my wife and my daughter was downright criminal."

Sam stared in disbelief as his lip began to quiver and his hands began to shake even more.

"I should have been locked up and put away and had the key disintegrated with acid for the things I did to my girls." As the camera zoomed in, Sam could see tears clouding his eyes. "And then when Bev's mind began to go, it really got me, because now she wasn't even aware of how much I hated her. It didn't matter what I did—she just knew I was her husband and that I was taking care of her.

"When Sam left, when she got that scholarship and went on to fulfill her dreams, I was so jealous that I could have almost hunted her down and killed her." There were many gasps in the audience. "I told you I wasn't worthy to stand up here." He hung his head again. "I didn't think it was fair. My father had ruined my life by forcing me to marry Bev, and all I ever wanted to do was ruin Samantha's life just like she had mine. And when she left with a full ride to wherever it was she went, I seriously considered taking off after her and blowing her away. It just wasn't fair."

Sam found herself holding her breath at that revelation. He had hated her. So none of that had been her imagination. However, it was considerably chilling to know he had hated her so much that he had even considered killing her. That thought had never crossed her mind.

"But what was the point?" Frank asked the congregation. "So what? I knew I'd never see her again. If you knew the things I'd done to her, you'd know why she'd leave this place and never, ever even think about returning. I figured to just let her go. Why ruin two lives?

"Then one morning I was sitting on that wreck of a porch at our house, and I thought about what on earth I was doing. I had no job, living off my wife's subsidized government funds and whatever money I could manage to scrounge off of other people in a bet or by doing an odd job—and I hated my life. I figured I had nothing to lose if I didn't just take a chance … a big chance … a huge, stupid, unreasonable chance. I told myself that if I took the chance and won, I'd change my life, but if I took the chance and lost, I'd just kill myself. Either way, it seemed like the only choice I had left.

"And then it was like God just said something to me. I can't explain it to you … but it was like He suddenly let me see that all my mistakes and miseries in life weren't because of others, but they were because of my own choices. Bev didn't become pregnant because my father stuck a 12-gauge in my face. That was my fault—my choice. I was a cocky kid, just like a lot of you are sitting on those back pews right now. I thought I was invincible. I had a plan and the world begging at my feet, but a pregnancy which resulted from a bad choice I had made changed all that.

"So I told God I was a miserable wretch, a drunken sot, and a worthless excuse of a man. I told Him that if He thought I was still worth anything, He'd have to prove it, 'cause as far as I could see, I was the biggest mistake He'd ever made. I told Him I was taking Bev's next government check, was gonna ride non-stop to Las Vegas, and bet every cent of it on one bet. If He wanted to do something with my life, He'd let me win big, and I'd give it all to Him. But if He was through with me, and agreed that I was a sorry piece of flesh, then He'd let me lose it all, and I would end it all that same night."

Sam couldn't believe what she was hearing. If this was true, she knew how the story ended, and it was almost too incredible to even consider.

"So I lived off of coffee for three days straight and putted myself out to Nevada," he carried on. "And I think you all need to know, I wasn't really planning on holding God to this bargain. My plan was to end my life, but all this was an excuse to somehow ease my conscience. I could never take responsibility for my own actions, so by putting this burden on God, my suicide note would actually blame him for my death." Then Frank chuckled. "Leave it to God to throw a kink in all those plans … again.

"I walked into the first casino I came to," he said with a smile. "I took that money, exchanged it for some chips, and went straight to the biggest chance game around. The odds were huge—in fact, they were so big, that if I put all my money on one number and won, I would win twenty million dollars." He shook his head and then looked up toward heaven. "Everybody in the casino that night thought I was crazy, including me, but God knew exactly what He was doing. He must have laughed as he watched me slam those chips down on that one number, believing that I was sealing my doom, when all along He knew that whatever I picked would be the winning number for that round.

"People gathered 'round the table, and you could have a heard a pin drop in that big ol' room. And they all knew I had to be as poor as dirt. My hair was halfway down my back, my beard was scraggly and unkempt, my jeans had holes in 'em, and my boots should've been replaced years before. The only decent thing I had on was a silk shirt because I somehow wanted to die in style. It was like a last hurrah or something."

He began to climb down the stairs from the platform to the main floor of the church. "When that man called out my number, I don't know who was more shocked. The crowds were silent, the man's jaw nearly dropped to the floor, and I was suddenly very aware that my life was about to take a drastic change … a change I, in all honesty, didn't want to make. But it was right there staring me in the face. That man raked twenty million dollars worth of chips off the table and into a bag, and then had security escort me to a room to make the exchange. And I just followed blindly 'cause I knew what was coming next. I knew I had to go to God and apologize and make things right somehow.

"That night, I got a fancy room in that big hotel—compliments of the casino. And as I looked out that window onto the flashing lights of the city, only one thought came to my mind, and I looked up to heaven and said, *God, I can't believe that I really matter to You. I can't believe that I'm not about to jump out here onto the street below, or blow my brains out across the room. Instead, I'm standing here*, and then I fell to my knees and said, *No, I'm kneeling here, asking You to take my life and do with it whatever You want. As horrible and worthless and miserable as I've been, I want You to change me to the opposite.*"

Sam could almost envision her father kneeling in that Vegas room with his boots and long, dirty hair, pleading with God.

"I confessed every rotten thing, every sin, every evil thought and deed I'd ever even considered, and I just laid it all before God, reminding Him that He was taking the worst of sinners on there. I told him about how I hated my father, my wife, and even little Samantha, the most innocent victim in all of this, and that I didn't deserve His mercy or love or forgiveness because I'd never offered it to anyone else. But I couldn't get away from the fact that I'd bargained with Him, and He'd just won that bargain with twenty million dollars." Frank threw his hands into the air. "If He wanted me that bad, He could most certainly have me and do with me whatever He wanted, because nobody else ever would.

"I prayed all night that night, which is kind of unbelievable in itself because I'd been awake for three days already. But I was determined to make things right with God before I left there. I called the house the next morning, and bless her heart, Millie had been there the entire time with Bev. She gave me a piece of her mind, several pieces in fact, and I told her she was absolutely right and that I deserved everything she was threatening. It kind of took her off guard a bit, but when I told her that I was coming home, would be there that afternoon, and that I'd given my life to God, she just shut up. I mean … how do you respond to a man as low as I was when he tells you he's gotten right with God?

"So, I flew back to Georgia, bought a car, and walked into the house where Bev and Millie were waiting. And when I told them what had happened, Millie thought I was crazy, but Bev … sweet Bev … she just smiled and said how nice it was for me to finally believe in God."

Frank walked back up on the platform and opened wide his arms. "And so here I am. It took a long time for many of you to believe that God had worked a miracle in my life, but I didn't care. I'd spent a good twenty years proving to you all how bad I could be, so I was more than willing to believe it might take another twenty for you to see the opposite as well."

Sam found herself leaning toward the television as her father spoke his final words of the service.

"I just need you all to know something here tonight. If God loved me, as sorry and as filthy and as horrible as I was, and if He was willing to clean me up, forgive me, redeem me, and then use me, you've got to know that He loves you very much. It's kind of funny, had someone given me that twenty million just four days before, the day before I had bargained with God, I would've blown it in the most heinous and distasteful ways. But instead, I gave my wife the house she always wanted, I gave you all this church, and I gave many charities a desperately needed boost. And a lot of you know that I'd love to go on a mission trip to somewhere and tell people about how great the love of Jesus is, but my health is just too bad. That's why every summer and every Christmas I send many of you in my place to countries all over this globe.

"So tonight, I just want to ask you to think about your own life. Have you made some choices that have sent you down a path that's hardened your heart against God … and against others? In all probability, I'll never get the privilege of holding my only daughter in my arms and asking her forgiveness or declaring my love to her. I burned that bridge for 18 long, hard years. And every day I plead with God to not let her bitterness toward me burn out her ability to see Him and His love and care for her. But if Samantha ever steps foot back in Toombs County again, I plead with all of you to show her the love of her heavenly Father, and let her know that He's nothing like the miserable example she had to live with all those years.

"I asked Jim tonight if we could sing that simple chorus, *I Have Decided to Follow Jesus*, because no matter how far we've gone from God, or how deep in the pit of sin and pure evil we may be, His love and His grace are deeper still, and it's only a matter deciding to follow Him instead of drowning in the bad choices we made in the past."

As the song began, the DVD immediately went to a clip of the pastor in his study inviting all those who had heard the DVD to come and visit the church if they had the chance. Billy got up from the bed and turned off the TV before he got too much into his speech. The weight of Frank Conwill's words hung heavy on both of them, and neither knew what to say. Billy ejected the disc, placed it back in the envelope, and then looked at Sam.

"He didn't even look like the same man," she finally whispered as she pulled off her glasses and rubbed the bridge of her nose. "He almost reminds me of Cindy … you know? When you told me she had married a minister, I could have died laughing. Cindy? Our Cindy? But when I saw her again, she wasn't the same. And even now, when I've been with her, it's like she's a whole different person." She looked up at Billy as he continued to stand by the television. "I saw that in Frank just now too. That was his face, and that was his voice, but had I seen him on the street, I would've never recognized him. And had he ever tried to tell me all those things I just heard him say, I would probably have slapped him and walked away."

Billy went back to her on the bed and pulled her into his arms. "I wish I knew what to say about all this," he confessed. "But I'm as puzzled as you are. If all this is true, then I want to know why God chooses to save people like Frank … and even like Cindy … and yet he allows good people … like Mother, Dad … and Carter Collins to die. Why doesn't he take people like Farris, shoot, even people like *me* instead

… people who don't deserve another chance? Why do we live on?"

She tried to process her father's words, Billy's words, and all the things Cindy had told her during those visits to Dockrey, but at the moment, her physical and emotional exhaustion were at their limits. She didn't want to think about any of it right now. She just wanted to escape somewhere and forget her troubles and all the decisions that still awaited her.

She looked up at Billy and let her eyes plead for his attention again. It didn't take him long to get the message.

"Sam," he asked as he leaned down to kiss her, "are you sure?"

"No," she admitted, "but I'm less sure about everything else right now."

As he laid her back on the bed, she let herself get lost in his kiss and in his touch, and before long the passion drove away all thoughts of her father and the DVD. She had no idea where her life would be as a result of this weekend, but for the moment, she didn't care.

Seventy-Nine

Jonathan tried to focus on his sermon Sunday morning, but the weight of his world was bearing heavy on his shoulders, and at times he found himself just reading out phrases from his notes and moving on. Behind him sat Hal Bridges, continuously making notes in the bulletin, but not notes based on the preaching. Everything Hal wrote down was a criticism of the service, and it would be hounded to death the next morning in staff meeting. Then there was the obvious absence of Ellie and Stevie who would normally sit between Barbara and Angie along with Cassie. Every time he glanced that way, the image of Ellie pleading with him not to leave her in California with Stephen would replay in his head. And of course, the fact that Carter wasn't there, and never would be again, was just one more issue.

Annie hadn't been to church in months and it was because of the paparazzi again. Any step she or Stephen made was covered by photographers and info-seekers. When Stephen left for California, they went wild. In fact, they got downright rude and intrusive. After three months, the parasites had thinned down significantly, but not enough for Annie to comfortably leave for somewhere as public as church.

But just as distressing was the way he was watching the church divide. What had once been a happy and supportive congregation had now turned into a large group of people with varying opinions and views from everything to what color the carpet should be in the new sanctuary to how money was being spent in the church. Not that there was anything wrong with opinions on these issues, it was just that opinions had been given with attitudes, and these attitudes were developing into arguments which were quickly developing into sects and clicks—and the seating of the people this morning reflected the obvious grouping that had begun. Another tell-tale sign was that for the first time in three years the church had gone back to one morning worship service. It had literally been impossible to seat the entire Sunday morning crowd in the sanctuary … until the beginning of February. Now Jonathan was wondering if they had jumped the gun by starting a new building. If things continued as they were, there would be no need for extra space by the time it was completed.

Then, as much as he hated to admit it, there was the vulture-like presence of Vivian McCall in the church again. She had stopped coming over ten years ago. But shortly after Christmas, she suddenly popped back in. She never really fellowshipped with anyone or came to any other meetings, but she faithfully came on Sunday mornings, sitting in the very last pew on the back left, practically hugging the armrest throughout every service. She never sang a song, never opened her Bible, and never lingered to speak with anyone afterwards—but she was always there.

Suddenly the tightness that Jonathan had felt Friday at Stephen's began to grow in his chest again. Rather than fight it, he stopped immediately, breathed a few deep breaths, and then took a long drink from the bottled water on the pulpit. He would hear about this from Hal tomorrow morning. He tried not to indicate the extreme discomfort, but after about twenty seconds of silence, he forced a smile and said, "Sorry about that. It's been a long weekend."

☼☼☼

Sam and Billy sat with Beverly Conwill at the local buffet on Sunday afternoon after church. Sam had hoped her mother would have one of her lucid moments so she could talk with her about all the decisions that needed to be made. She also hoped that she could just *talk* with her mother. As far as Sam could remember, she had never really had a mother. She'd had this womanly figure that lived in her house, but as far as being a mother, she had never been that. Sam wondered why she couldn't remember times of Beverly being in her right mind while growing up, but then she had always tried to avoid her mother if at all possible. The only moments her mother would give her any attention was when she believed Sam was about to be abducted.

Billy drove them back to the little house, and Sam helped her mother into the plush recliner. She kept hoping she would give some indication that she understood again what was happening, but all she asked for was her remote and some time to take a nap because she was extremely exhausted. Sam stood in the living room and just stared down at her in deep disappointment. Nothing about this weekend had turned out right.

"Yoo-hoo," yelled Millie from the kitchen as she slammed the door behind her. "Ya'll in the living room?"

Billy walked back toward the kitchen to greet her. "Yes, ma'am. We're in here."

Millie walked in, still gussied up from church with her red hair shining from the bright sunlight through the windows. "I wanted to give ya'll some time together before I came over." She looked down at Beverly. "Hey, hon! Didja have a good time with Samantha here? I hear she took you to Buddy's Buffet."

Beverly looked distressed. "I haven't seen Samantha since they took her."

"Goodness sakes, Bev!" Millie laughed. "Sam's right here with you. She took you to lunch." Milled looked over at Sam and noticed the distressed look. "Honey, don't let her get you down. It's been a really tough week for her … losing Frank and all. She's not quite sure what all has happened to her, but she knows it's bad. It's gonna take her a while to sort through it … if she can."

Sam nodded, nudged her glasses up on her nose, and then let out a sigh of distress. "I'd hoped to get some information from Mama, but obviously that's not gonna happen. I suppose I could just talk with you. From what I understand, you've pretty much been her caregiver all these years."

"Just when Frank wasn't working." Millie motioned Sam toward the kitchen. "Why don't we go talk in there? Bev will probably be off to sleep in just a jiffy, and she generally needs a good long nap to keep her spirits up. If not, she starts getting all jumpy and suspicious about things."

They walked into the kitchen and took three seats around the table. Millie just smiled as Sam tried to decide exactly what needed to be discussed and what arrangements needed to be made.

"I'm in quite an unsettling situation," Sam began. "Having not been here for so long, I'm really not qualified to make any permanent decisions about my mother. I assumed she would be like she always was … out of touch, unable to reason at all. But that's not what I've found here this weekend. How is it, Millie, that there are actually times when it seems like she's aware of everything that's happening? Am I crazy, or was she like that when I was a kid, but I just never saw it."

"When Frank got the money, one of the first things he done was git her to a doctor … one of them *head docs* he used to call them. After several tests and such, they determined what was wrong with her and started giving her some medications. At first, it was kind of touch and go. Sometimes she would see things and get all upset, and then other times it was like the old Bev was back. Frank just cried and cried the first time she started making some sense."

"What was wrong with her … *is* wrong with her?" Sam wanted to know.

Millie shook her head. "It was a big jumbled mess of all sorts of things. They said some of it was psychological, and some of it was physiological in her brain … I've worked hard to learn them words too. It helps when people ask what's wrong with her. Anyway, they finally got all that medicine regulated … supposedly … and she began to settle down quite a bunch."

"So she's been normal all this time?"

Millie laughed and scratched the tip of her nose with her long, bright pink fingernail. "Goodness gracious no, child! But she stopped being so weird all the time. And when there was no stress in life, and nothing pressing or unusual, she would start having periods of normal. The longer time went by with nothing unusual, just a constant schedule, and everything being done the same, she'd stay normal for hours at a time." Then Millie shook her head. "But this mess with Frank's death has thrown her for a loop. I don't know if she'll ever recover from it."

Sam leaned back thoughtfully in her chair and crossed her arms as she analyzed the information. "And what was her life like? What was a normal day for her? What kept her feeling almost sane again?"

"Well, take Sundays. Frank would take her to Sunday School and church, then they would go eat at Buddy's. They'd come home, she'd sit in her chair and watch TV and nap, and they'd go back to church on Sunday night. After church, they'd go to the Dairy Delight with friends, come home and go to bed. Then on Mondays and such, Frank would go to work at eight o'clock and I'd come in. He'd come home for lunch, and we'd all eat together, then he'd be back a little after five. He had her from there. He used to try to take her different places on Saturdays just to see if maybe he could *broaden her horizons* he always said, but it just made her go cuckoo. It'd be days, sometimes weeks before she'd settle down again."

"Hmmm," Sam thought, "then I don't imagine taking her away from here would be good at all."

Millie shook her head. "Not for Bev," she said softly. "I know it'd be easiest on you, hon. And don't feel pressured to sacrifice everything for yore mama. She'll adjust to wherever she is eventually."

Sam sighed and put her face in her hands. "It's just so hard to figure this out." She took off her glasses and rubbed her tired eyes as she explained, "I wish I could just leave it all in your hands, Millie, but there's not a chance in hell I'd let Farris get his paws into any of this. In fact, I would prefer that he never step foot on this property again."

"Samantha, I understand," Millie said soberly as she placed her hand on top of Sam's. "Farris is a worthless sot. And yore Daddy would turn over in his grave if he ever thought Farris got anything other than a good butt-kicking. He'd have applauded yore husband there for knocking him out of the house the other day."

Billy gave an embarrassed smile.

"But who else do I leave in charge?" Sam continued. "And who would stay with her at night? She can't take care of herself all alone, and you can't be responsible for her twenty-four hours a day."

Millie shrugged. "Honey, I'll do anything I can, but I agree, it'll take more than just me."

Sam looked over at Billy and then back at Millie. "So what's the answer? What do I do?"

"Maybe the lawyer will have some suggestions," was all Billy could come up with.

✪✪✪

Angie rose from the Wright table and handed little Christian to Barbara. "I think I'm gonna go over and visit with Annie a little bit. She's got to be close to major depression at the moment."

"Good idea, hon," Barbara said as she took the baby and immediately began to kiss all over him. "If we don't give her a reason to live sometime soon, she's gonna become the Prozac poster child."

Michael, who was feeding Caleb a bottle, looked up at Angie in shock, but managed to control any laughing. It was seldom that Barbara ever came up with a real joke, and to do it at the expense of someone's calamity was unheard of.

"And I," Jonathan moaned as he stretched his hands over his head, "am so stuffed that I feel as though I should be rolled into the bedroom."

"A nap?" Angie asked in surprise. "Are you gonna take a nap on a Sunday afternoon?"

"Like I said this morning, it's been a tough weekend."

"Yeah," Angie remembered, "and what was that anyway? It was like you just zoned out for a bit."

"I did *zone out.* I can't handle this dropping the kids off with Stephen anymore. It's tearing me up inside."

Angie agreed. "I think that if Stephen wants to see his kids, he needs to come to Alabama to see them, not fly them across the country."

Jonathan went on to the bedroom, and Angie left for Annie's. It wasn't long before Barbara walked in quietly to check on him. She tiptoed around the bed, careful not to bump against anything that might awaken him.

"I'm not asleep, Barb," he mumbled as he opened one eye.

"I was hoping you might be," she confessed as she sat down beside him. "You seemed so distressed last night when you got back, and frankly, you've looked rather pale all day. At least you had a good visit with Alex and Megan and Ansley. I am a little jealous of that, you know?"

"You're more than welcome to come with me next time."

"No, thank you. I'll just wait for their next visit home. Besides, I've got two brand new boys to keep me company here for a while."

"Yeah, what happened to Christian? I thought you were taking care of him while Angie went to see Annie."

Barbara frowned. "He fell asleep on me again. Every time I get my hands on one of those babies, they just drop off to sleep. They won't let me have any fun with them."

"Why don't you let Angie or Michael bring them down tonight when they awaken at three o'clock? They'll give you some fun then."

"And I would do it gladly."

Jonathan rested his hands behind his head and closed his eyes in utter fatigue. "Who would have ever thought that Alex would one day be my *good* child?"

"Your *good* child? What on earth do you mean by that? Your girls aren't *bad* girls, sweetie."

"Andie's suffering major separation syndrome from putting Adam in public school. She's somehow forgotten that she's still got four at home who need her undivided attention. At least her ankle has healed up enough that she can get off those stupid pain pills now. And then Angie … good lands, she just lost a little boy, but immediately replaces him with a set of twins. How does she just keep going on and on? It's a good thing she married a low-maintenance, highly-attentive man. If it weren't for Michael, she'd be a basket case."

"And to think you didn't like him at all when you first met him."

Jonathan glared up at her. "That's ancient history, dear, and an uncalled for remark."

"My point is," she said as she gently took his hand, "is that things are always changing. This is a rough time, Jonathan—I'll agree with you one hundred percent on that. But one day it won't be like this, and we just need to rest in the grace and mercy of God as we face it all right now."

He took a deep breath and squeezed her hand. "I really believe Stephen wants to try and reconcile."

"What!" she nearly screamed. "Why didn't you tell me that last night?"

"Perhaps because I kept hearing my grandchildren pleading with me to take them back home."

"What makes you think he wants to reconcile?"

"Because he really believes he overreacted and wants to talk things out with Annie."

She closed her eyes and shook her head. "But Annie won't take his calls."

"Bingo. Thus, my third problem child. Strong-willed Annie has a heart so broken that she can barely manage to keep herself together, but she refuses to take any chances at healing herself. And now she's pregnant again. How do we convince her that she's got to see him and come to a mature understanding in all of this?"

"We can't," Barbara said rather nonchalantly. "You don't convince Annie of anything."

"So are you saying we just give up … let it all blow to pieces?"

"No, I'm saying that we pray God does something big here that forces her to see him and speak with him, and for heaven's sake, to tell him she's carrying another child of his."

Just then the phone rang, and Jonathan reached for it on the table next to the bed. "Hello?"

"Jonathan, this is Tom Richards. You got a minute?"

"Depends. Is this good news or bad news?"

Tom chuckled then replied, "Depends. It could be good, it could be bad."

"Hmmm, that sounds scary. Tell me what you've got."

"It's about our friend, Hal."

Jonathan winced, and Barbara immediately mouthed a *what is it* to him. He shook his head and motioned for her to leave the room. She grudgingly complied. "What's he done now?"

"It's more like what he's *not* done."

"Such as …?"

"Our boy was indeed in the military, but he was never a Navy Seal. In fact, he lasted eleven months and was given a dishonorable discharge."

"You're kidding me!" Jonathan was completely stunned. "How did you find out? No one would talk to me about him whenever I tried to make contact."

"I called in a couple of favors," Tom told him. "He was an a-number-one smart aleck, and his attitude and mouth are what got him kicked out."

"Wow, that confirms a few suspicions, doesn't it? And then it makes you kind of wonder what else he might be lying about."

"Uh-huh. Like perhaps the whole *doctorate* thing?"

"Man! Can all this really be happening? As I watch my church fall apart, all the evidence points to this charlatan, and yet I have no idea how to even bring it up! If I do, people will say I was out to destroy him and that's why I launched this attack on him to begin with."

"Patience, Jonathan. The time will come," Tom assured him. "Meanwhile, I think it's time you called the college and seminary in California to find out just how far *Dr. Bridges* actually did go in his education."

"I think you're right, although I'm not looking forward to it. Those people will think I'm a heel if he turns out to be for real."

"And what percentage of belief do you have that he was honest about his graduate studies?"

Jonathan sighed and replied, "Around two percent … maybe?"

"That high? Really?"

Eighty

Sam sat stunned on Monday morning as Daris Horowitz, her father's lawyer, quoted the figure of how much her father was worth. She had assumed most of the money would have been gobbled up by now.

"How does he have that much?" she asked dumbfounded. "For crying out loud, he built an entire church!"

Daris handed Sam a paper with a list of his investments. "He just made some lucky guesses, I suppose. He spent a minimal amount of it on a few things here and there, but all the rest he managed to place in some really smart markets. The thing is, all this now belongs to you. Because of your mother's situation, if you don't sign some papers of intent today, the state can take every bit of this … plus, they can basically put your mother away somewhere … anywhere."

She looked over the paper and tried to figure the math in her head. Frank had indeed made some really lucky choices. "Mr. Horowitz, I'll be honest with you. I want to help my mother—I want to do the right thing. I appreciate what Frank did for her, and what Millie has done for her, and I wish there was some way for all that to continue happening, but I just don't see how." She felt slightly guilty, but she admitted to him, "I'm not gonna leave Alabama. I have a home there, I have a good job there, and I'm settled there. That's where I belong, and that's where I'm gonna stay."

Daris added, "And it would also mean relocating your husband too. I understand all that."

She felt that twinge of guilt again about all the lying, but at this point it didn't matter. She had to get things settled today, sign some papers, and then get back to Florence. "And I can't move her there with me …" she looked over at Billy, "… with *us*, because according to Millie she can't handle change very well. Which also means that if I send her off to some assisted living place, she probably won't handle that very well either." Sam looked desperate. "And I don't want to just send her to an institution. If what Millie said is true, she knows who she is sometimes, and it would be horrible for her to think I just threw her away." She slung her hands up in sheer aggravation. "But there's no way I'm gonna put Millie in charge of all this money because Farris will force his perverted self into the middle of it somehow!"

"Mrs. Marcum," Daris said calmly, "may I make a suggestion?"

Sam looked fiercely at him. "You mean you have one? Please! Make a suggestion!"

Daris loosened his tie and reached into his file for a brochure. "Your father was very pleased with how Millie handled your mother. She was more than just kind to her. She joked with her, talked with her, acted like she was keenly aware of everything all the time. In fact, your father believed that was one of the reasons why your mother became more and more aware of things as the years passed. Because Millie treated her like that, your mother responded to that." Daris wrote a number on a post-it note and slid it over to Sam. "He paid Millie handsomely to do all that."

Sam looked at the figure and nearly fainted. "You've gotta be kidding! He paid her that much?"

"He felt she was worth it … and that she deserved it for all she'd put up with concerning his brother. I think some of it was just pure guilt, and he somehow wanted to make it up to her." He then put up his hand quickly and added, "But that's not my place at all to judge or even conjecture. The fact is, he had the money, and he thought it was a wise way to use some of it."

Sam turned the note around in her hand and eventually agreed. Millie had done wonders for her mother, and if Frank was willing to pay a high price to make sure Beverly's care was personal and genuine, then it was a very noble decision on his part.

"What I'm suggesting," Daris continued as he held up the brochure, "is that you consider keeping Millie on the payroll. You have the money, the assets, the investments—you control them. You could continue to pay Millie her salary, and she could continue to do what she's done for many years now. But," he opened the brochure, "you hire a professional service to come in during the nights and weekends. They're very expensive, and not many can afford it because in cases like your mother's, insurance just isn't gonna pay for something like this. But you … you can."

Sam glanced through the paper and began to feel the weight being lifted. "Will it be the same person all the time?"

He shook his head. "No, and that's a downfall with your mother's condition. Her care hours will be nights and weekends, the times that no one wants to work. I've talked with the service, and they understand the situation. They said they'd be more than glad to try and not rotate too many caregivers—try to be as consistent as possible. Also, since she takes sleeping medication, there'd be very little time actually spent with these people. Most of the time it would merely be a highly paid babysitting service."

Sam glimpsed at the prices. "Very highly paid."

"You can afford it, Mrs. Marcum," he reminded her. "And there's still plenty left to pay Millie, to build a mansion, to buy a yacht, to tour the world … whatever you want to do."

"Can I buy a jet?" Sam asked as she looked over the rim of her glasses.

The two men looked at her in surprise.

Daris nodded slowly and answered, "If you want, you can buy a whole fleet of jets."

"I don't really want to—I was just curious. It was the first extravagant thing that came to my mind." She finally breathed a sigh of relief and resolution. "How fast can we do this? I really need to get on the road."

"We can have all the preliminary stuff done in about two hours," Daris said. "For everything else, we'll just have to fax forms back and forth."

Sam blushed as she pushed her glasses back up her nose. "I don't have a fax machine."

Daris merely replied, "Then I suggest you get one unless you want to haul yourself back and forth to Georgia every few days. It's way cheaper than a jet."

The ride back to Alabama was mostly quiet and thoughtful as there were many things to consider. They had dropped by the little house to say goodbye to Beverly and Millie before leaving, and Sam had again desperately hoped her mother would recognize and say something for her to hang on to as proof that all those years growing up in this family were not worthless. But Beverly wasn't aware of anything other than the fact that Frank wasn't home.

Several times during the ride Sam's phone went off, and as she had done throughout the entire weekend, she would glance at the caller and then silence the call.

"Are you not taking anybody's calls anymore?" Billy finally asked after days of watching this, "or is it just one particular caller you keep choosing to ignore?"

She only smiled and leaned her tired head against the window. She didn't want to discuss this caller with Billy.

"That's what I thought," he mumbled "It's Crandall, isn't it?"

She sighed, closed her eyes, and nodded. "I just can't talk to him right now. I've got too much to sort through without having to bring him into the picture."

"And I haven't helped at all," he said with a tinge of disgust.

She reached over and gently rubbed his arm. "Please don't feel guilty about anything that happened this weekend. I needed you, and you were there."

"A bit too much *there* I'm afraid."

"Look," she turned in her seat so she could face him, "everything that went on back there was … well … needed, at least on my part. And no matter what happens down the road, I don't want to look back on that with regret."

"But I don't want it to be something that ruins your life yet again," he bemoaned. "I seem to be so good at that. You asked me to come with you because I understood the situation and could be moral support."

"And I asked you to pretend to be my husband so I …"

He interrupted, "… so you could avoid any unnecessary judgments about your life. All *that* was okay, Sam."

"Until I had to tell Daris Horowitz the truth. That was a little humiliating."

"He won't tell," Billy assured her. "He has to keep that lawyer/client relationship in confidence."

"But still, it's all kind of silly when you come down to it. Why couldn't I just be a big girl and face the music? Instead, I now have to come back home and … you know … say goodbye to you … to us … again. It's getting harder and harder each time we have to do this."

He nodded. "It would have helped if you had talked to Crandall a few times. It might have kept us grounded a little better."

Sam looked out the windshield into the pouring rain. Did she really want to be *grounded?* Jeremy was grounded, as grounded as they come. But Billy made her soar. "Is that what we really want out of life? To be grounded? Is that what it's come down to? It doesn't sound all that appealing to me to be honest with you."

He gave a light laugh and then reminded her, "Yes, we do indeed want to be grounded. Sam, if it could work between us, I'd run back to you in a moment, but we've tried this path, and all that seems to happen is heartbreak … again and again."

"I guess that phrase about love being all you need is just a myth, huh?"

"Yeah, I guess so." He drove silently a few moments then added, "Sam, Crandall's a good guy—the best. He'll love you, and take care of you, and give you everything you ever needed. And yes, as boring as it might sound, he'll keep you grounded … and predictable. There won't be any surprises, at least bad ones that you'll have to face. When he stays out all night, it'll be because he's at the hospital on call, or doing some kind of medical emergency thing. You won't have to wonder if he's gonna walk in one day and say it's all over … or treat you like mud." He cringed at his own description of how he had handled Sam during their marriage. "He'll treat you like a princess, Sam, and that's wonderful, because that's what you are."

She bit back the emotion and tried to remain light. "Awww, that's just a little too sweet and mushy for you, Billy."

He blushed a bit. "It is, isn't it?" He snickered. "Yuck."

☼☼☼

This was a call Jonathan had not wanted to make. He had put it off again and again, and even though Tom wanted every possible avenue concerning Hal Bridges investigated, Jonathan was uncomfortable with all the snooping. But after being belittled once again in Monday morning's staff meeting and then facing Hal with some common figures and percentages any seminary graduate should have known, only to see a blank look of ignorance on his face … it was all the nudging Jonathan needed to finish his part of the digging.

He was transferred to another person for the third time at the seminary. Everyone seemed to be passing the buck when it came to discussing alumni, but when he hit the actual alumni department he found a very cheerful and eager personality awaiting him.

"Yes, Mr. Wright," she said with a merry attitude. "I am very familiar with Dr. Harold Bridges. He's one of our most illustrious alumni. What would you like to know about him?"

Jonathan was taken back; he hadn't expected this. He really thought Hal had been lying about his education too. "Well, I guess I'd just like to confirm his degrees and all."

"Certainly. Give me a chance to pull up his information on the old computer here." She jabbed a few keys, but kept on talking. "In fact, Dr. Bridges is quite the speaker. He spoke at chapel here last month, and I made sure I attended. I'd go to his church if it were a few miles closer."

Jonathan scratched his head. Hal had spoken at the seminary in California last month? When would he have gone? He was here the whole month as far as he could remember. And knowing Hal, he would have made a big to-do about flying to California to speak.

"Here it is," the lady said. "He received his Master's in Theology in May of 1966, and His ThD in 1970."

"What?" Jonathan exclaimed as he shook his head. "That's impossible! He's only in his early thirties. He'd have to have been a child genius … in fact, I don't know if he was even born yet."

"Dr. Harold Bridges? Pastor at Sun Coast Baptist Assembly?"

A reality now began to settle on Jonathan. "No. Dr. Harold Bridges, Minister of Education at First Baptist Church in Dockrey, Alabama."

"Alabama?" the lady laughed. "We're most definitely not talking about the same man! Dr. Bridges has pastored at Sun Coast for nearly thirty years—still does."

Jonathan looked down at Hal's résumé'. He had been born in Sun Coast, California. "Can I ask you a question then? Does Dr. Bridges have a son who attended there also?"

"Well, he does have a son, but he never attended here."

"I see." Jonathan paused as he continued to peruse the résumé'. "Do you know if the son was also named Harold Bridges?"

The lady now became uncharacteristically quiet. "Sir, I don't really know if I should be giving you any more information than just the basic facts you asked about."

"I won't ask you anymore than what would probably be in that file. In fact, if you tell me *yes*, that will be the last question I ask at all."

There was a bit more silence, then she admitted, "Yes, sir. Dr. Bridges has one son, a junior … and quite a disappointment for such a great man."

Jonathan nodded as a few pieces of this miserable puzzle began to fit. "I thank you for the information, all of it." He was referring to the statement about the son being a *disappointment.* "You've been a big help."

"I hope you find what you're looking for, sir."

"I think I might have." He searched for a pen and asked, "What was the name of Dr. Bridges church again?"

"Sun Coast Baptist Assembly," she said slowly.

"Thank you, ma'am, and have a nice day."

Well, the doctorate was obviously pure make-believe, as well as being a Navy Seal. That in itself was enough to incriminate *Dr. Hal Bridges*, but Jonathan wasn't through yet. He knew not to call the number for Pepperdine University that Hal had listed on his résumé'. It would probably be a fake just like the number to the seminary which had sent him on an internet chase to determine the real one. Jonathan typed in the name on the computer, and then went to the official website for a real number. Sure enough, the actual number and Hal's listing didn't match.

After a little navigating, Jonathan was given the records department for the school. He decided to be a bit more professional this time. The jovial lady at the seminary had felt on the spot when she realized it wasn't personal information Jonathan had wanted, but rather incriminating information. This time he spoke bluntly.

"I'm checking credentials for a man employed here. His résumé' reads that he received his BA from Pepperdine, and I have reason to doubt that. I was wondering if you could confirm it for me."

"Absolutely," this lady said professionally. "May I have his name?"

"He has listed here that his full name is Harold Carroll Bridges."

"Well, I can tell you up front that Dr. Bridges did indeed graduate from Pepperdine University. He's one of our most notable alumni."

"I'm not talking about Harold Senior," Jonathan told her. "I'm talking about his son, Harold Junior. He doesn't have the *junior* listed on the résumé', so I wasn't sure if he would be listed like that in your records."

"Hang on a minute," she said as he heard the shuffling over the phone. "Do you have a social security number for him?"

"Yes, I do." Jonathan read off the sequence. "Although I can't guarantee that this number is actually valid."

"Oh, it is," the lady said slowly. "And yes, Harold Junior did attend here … but not for long."

"And his degree?"

"He didn't get one from here," the lady said with a bite of loathing in her tone. "In fact, he only managed to complete one year of schooling with us … and that was by the skin of his teeth."

"I see." He ran his hand through his hair and then shook out the few strands that had clung to it. "I don't suppose you have any more info on him other than that."

"Not really, but if its truth you're seeking, and he lied about a degree from here, according to what I'm looking at right now, this institution would be a poor character reference for Mr. Bridges. He managed to stay in disciplinary trouble most of the year … not for overtly bad behavior … just a smart mouth and a bad attitude."

He sighed. "I can believe it."

Now what did he do? What was the next step? Hal had lied about every credential he had, and yet the man had completely duped a huge group at the church. If He came forth with the information, there would be many who would leave out of pure spite. But then, many seemed to be leaving anyway. What was the wise thing to do? *How would Solomon handle something like this?* he thought. But then another idea crossed his mind—Dr. Bridges Senior. Jonathan wondered if it were at all possible to get in touch with the dad. Perhaps he could, if he were willing, shed a little light on the wayward son.

He typed in Sun Coast Baptist Assembly and hit the enter key. Wo—several impressive pieces of information jumped up immediately. He went to the main site of the church and began to scroll through all the lists. It was quite a church, and Dr. Bridges was quite a pastor. Jonathan clicked on the staff button and pulled up the info on the head pastor. The resemblance between him and Hal was uncanny. Jonathan had four children, and none of them came close to looking as much like him as Hal did his dad. He read through all the man's accomplishments and was astounded at the amount. He didn't know now whether to continue despising Hal or just feel sorry for him for trying to follow in the footsteps of someone who was almost untouchable.

Even though he doubted he could personally get in touch with Dr. Bridges Sr., it was worth a try. He had come this far, why not reach for the stars? He punched in the church number from the website and tried to gain his confidence in addressing the situation.

"Good afternoon! Sun Coast Baptist Assembly! This is Lucy."

"Lucy, my name is Reverend Jonathan Wright, and I'm calling from Alabama."

"Nice to speak with you Rev, Wright," she said very professionally. "How may I help you?"

"I'm not exactly sure how to go about this," he confessed feebly.

"Just tell me what you need, Rev. Wright, and I'll do my best to transfer you to the proper area."

This woman was quick and on the ball. He needed to stop dawdling for words. "The truth is, Dr. Bridges' son, Hal Jr., has been employed at my church for several months now, and he has wreaked havoc in the process. I did some checking today, and have discovered that anything on Hal's resume' that would be considered a credential is pure baloney, and I'm at my wits' end. I know that Dr. Bridges is a very busy man, but I'd appreciate it if at some time he could manage to give me a call back so we could discuss his son … and how I need to handle him."

The woman was actually speechless. "Wow," she said a bit breathless. "You have probably just hit the one situation I was never trained to handle."

"I can imagine," he smiled to himself. "Look, this guy has undone in just a few months what I've spent thirty years building. I don't have a mega-church like Sun Coast, but for a small town like Dockrey, we've done really well. But Hal has managed to do some pretty horrific damage here, and I really need some words of advice from someone who knows him well."

The receptionist took her time. "Rev. Wright, the only thing I know to do is to take your number and explain the situation to one of the associate pastors. Perhaps they can contact Dr. Bridges, and then he might call you some time, but I can't make any promises."

"I understand. If you could do that much, then the rest, we could say, is in the Lord's hands."

Eighty-One

Billy helped Sam unload her things hoping to get away as soon as he could. He knew exactly what she meant about having to say goodbye again, and he just wanted it over with so he could move on with his life … again … like he thought had already happened before the death of Frank Conwill. But now there was a whole new chapter written between them, and letting her go this time would be even harder than before.

"I suppose you're giving me these?" she asked as she held up the curlers and hair iron he had dropped onto her bed.

He grinned. "Something to remember me by. Besides, they won't do me any good. I've been thinking about getting a real haircut … you know, maybe start looking like a real man instead of just a *pretty boy*."

She shook her head. "Don't let Farris' comments about you being a *homo* sway your decision. The man is totally perverted."

"I won't say that he swayed me completely, but it probably is time for me to step into the 21st century."

She gave a really sad smile as she reached up to touch his soft, blond hair. "I'll miss it if you do."

They just stared at each other for a bit, knowing again this was their last and final goodbye. Billy so badly wanted to reach over and remove her glasses so he could clearly see those green eyes one more time, but he was afraid that if he moved any closer, the moment would become an embrace.

The sound of Jeremy Crandall announcing himself through the door put an end to that possibility immediately. They both took a step back from each other.

"There you are," Jeremy said with a welcoming smile. "I'm glad to see you made it back home." He glanced over to Billy. "Hello … Bill. Thanks for taking care of her … and all."

"Hello, Crandall," Billy managed to squeeze out. "It was … some weekend."

Jeremy looked back at Sam. "Did you make it through all right? Are you okay? Are you handling it fine? Is there anything I can do?"

She tried to smile, but all she could think about was Billy. Yes, Jeremy was wonderful. He was Mr. Right, Mr. Perfect, and any other positive adjective you could add to the end of *mister*, but Billy was … he was the love of her life.

"No, I'm fine," she forced herself to say as her heart ached to run to

Billy's side and boldly declare her true feelings. "Aren't you gonna be late for work?"

"Probably," Jeremy grinned sheepishly, "but when I saw that you were back, I had to stop. I wanted to … well … see you really bad. I missed you so much."

Billy cleared his throat. "And I need to get going."

"No!" Sam said quickly. "Not yet."

Jeremy and Billy both looked at her.

"I've still got some stuff in your car," she lied. "Just hang on a minute."

She looped her arm in Jeremy's to walk him to the door. "You need to get to work. We can talk tomorrow after school. Sound good?"

"You bet." Jeremy took her hand and pulled her with him. "I've missed you so much, Sam. It practically hurts to be away from you."

"That's very sweet," she replied. "Tomorrow we'll catch up, okay?"

"Absolutely."

She wouldn't kiss him goodbye even though she knew that was what he wanted, but she couldn't bring herself to do it with Billy in the other room. In fact, at this moment, if Jeremy Crandall were to disappear from the face of the earth, she wouldn't care. Once Billy was gone for good, she would sort through her feelings for Jeremy and then decide how to proceed. But for now, all she could handle was Billy.

Once she shut the door, Billy peered around the corner. "So what did you leave in my car?" he asked with a knowing look.

"My sanity," she replied as she turned toward him.

"Really? And how do you plan to get it back?"

She just looked at him for a moment. "I have no idea … don't know if I can." She then locked the door, pulled off her glasses, laid them on the table, and walked over to him. "Don't know if I want to."

He looked down at her and tried to keep his heart intact. The clarity in her unobstructed eyes was melting him again, and even though Jeremy had just oozed emotion all over her, Billy couldn't bring himself to look away.

"Sam," he whispered lowly, "I really need to … leave."

She continued to gaze through him. "I know," she whispered back. "But I really need you to stay."

He was confused. "Stay?"

She reached for his hands and moved them around her waist. "I can't be here alone … right now … not after everything I faced. Don't make me stay alone tonight … please … not tonight."

He knew he should leave, but he ached to be with her. How could he walk away when she felt the same? He only hesitated for a second, because when he looked back into her eyes, he immediately moved in for a kiss. There was no holding back this time. Pure passion began to sweep them away, and Billy threw any common sense to the wind. As if in a dream, he picked her up, still kissing her, and carried her to the bedroom—the one they had shared years ago when they had believed true love had found them and blessed them 'til death alone should part them.

☼☼☼

Jonathan reached into his pocket for his phone as soon as the catchy tune began to sound. He was locking up the gym at the church which was kept open during office hours for those who wanted to come and walk or play. He checked the display for a name, but only a number appeared.

"Great," he muttered, slightly out of breath from the brief jog he had taken to avoid getting too wet from the rain, "a stranger." He turned on the phone and placed it to his hear. "Hello?"

"Yes, I am trying to reach a Rev. Jonathan Wright."

"Then you have overwhelmingly succeeded. What can I do for you?"

"Rev. Wright," there was a pause, "this is Harold Bridges … from Sun Coast."

Jonathan literally stopped in his tracks. He hadn't expected the illustrious Dr. Bridges to actually call him back. "Dr. Bridges, yes, good afternoon."

"So, is it true?" the pastor asked him. "Hal has made it all the way to Alabama now?"

"Yes, he has." Jonathan felt the stress begin to build in his chest again. "I'm sorry about contacting you, but I'm in quite a mess here, and the more I find out about Hal, the less surprised I am with the trouble we're in."

"Rev. Wright, let me begin by saying you have no need to apologize. I'm the one who should be on my knees over this. Believe me when I say you're not the first pastor who's called me about my son."

"I wouldn't know," Jonathan responded solemnly, "because I've been unable to actually speak to a real pastor with whom he has served under. I've come to discover that every single reference he gave us was contrived."

"I would commend you for checking references before hiring him, but from what I heard concerning your conversation with our secretary, you've already hired him."

"November."

"Ah, then you've come to know Hal real well by now."

"Actually, I don't know him at all. I wish I did. I wish I knew what could make a man out and out lie to be in the ministry, and then walk into a church and literally tear it apart bit by bit."

"Well, I can help you there," Dr. Bridges said rather mournfully. "It's the result of being raised in an extremely successful ministry by a man who knew how to grow a church, but neglected his family in the process."

Jonathan didn't reply. That was quite a statement of admission from someone as flourishing as this man.

Harold continued, "I didn't really think that's what I was doing. I thought by putting my ministry as the priority, God would take care of everything else. I could go to high school football games because it was important that I be seen there, but I couldn't make it to little league to see my own son because it just wasn't important … not a single game, Rev. Wright … not a single one."

Jonathan couldn't relate at all. Between four kids in eight years, he had been to so many games and concerts that sometimes he wondered if he had any energy left with which to preach.

"So what Hal learned," Harold tried to explain, "was that you could sacrifice anything for the ministry … even integrity. He really did try to make a career of other things, but his bitterness and anger always flared up and managed to ruin the possibilities. I guess at some point he just decided he could fake the ministry since he knew it so well."

"I suppose," Jonathan sounded doubtful. "I'll be honest with you, I didn't trust him the moment I met him, yet most of the members of the committee thought he was the absolute answer to every prayer ever uttered. They were ready to follow him off a cliff if he suggested it, and I've about come to believe that's exactly what's happening here."

"He doesn't like pastors, or any real minister for that matter. He has a special detesting for music guys too."

"Well then why doesn't he preach? Why the whole education and administration route. It's like he wants to run the church, but he doesn't want to be the pastor. I don't get that. And I've definitely noticed the dislike for music guys. We have an incredible minister of music, but Hal has let him know that he is extremely displeased with his style. Every week we both get a lecture about all the mistakes made during the worship services the day before. If they weren't so obviously petty, I could have gotten my feelings hurt quite a bit."

"He has no gift," Harold said bluntly.

"Gift? What do you mean?"

"He can't speak, can't preach, can't sing. It used to irritate him that so many from our church went into the music ministry because they got such great training and exposure here. It nurtured and flamed some incredible talents, but Hal has no gifts for anything like that. He thought one time he could fake the preaching thing, and the church was eager to call him because he was my son. But when he went to preach in view of a call, it was a complete disaster. He thinks the only thing wrong with him is that he lacks a gift."

"You'd never know it. Ho obnoxiously oozes with confidence."

"See, that's his take. He assumes that if he belittles everyone else and boosts his own abilities … that somehow makes him way more impressive than the rest of us who can *charm* people."

"I've yet to see what his abilities actually are," Jonathan confessed.

"Well, believe me when I tell you that they don't lie in the area of ministerial expertise."

"I believe … I believe." He tried to process all the information and determine the best course of action to take. "So what do I do now? How do I manage to deal with Hal and not hurt those he's influenced all this time?"

"All I can tell you is to be careful. I hate to say that, but it's the truth. Hal is a bitter, ugly man, and if you're not cautious in dealing with him, he'll react like a cat caught in a corner—he'll come out scratching and gladly take anyone down with him."

"Thanks," Jonathan replied sarcastically. "That's just the advice I wanted to hear."

"He's left a trail of broken churches and pastors, Rev. Wright. I'd hate to see you join the list of casualties."

"Yeah, me too."

As he walked the hill back to his house, he decided for the moment the best course of action was to take no action at all. He and Tom both had enough evidence against Hal to embarrass him significantly, but until it was absolutely necessary, they might as well just sit on it. Maybe there was hope for Hal to come to his senses.

Meanwhile, Jonathan said to himself, *I watch my church fall to pieces.* He looked up to heaven as he approached the gate to his house and said, *God, I need more wisdom than ever before. This isn't just about me or my family—this is about Your body. Don't let one evil man destroy all the good you've done here for so many years.*

He reached for his chest and tried to rub out some of the tightness that seemed to be growing there lately.

"I obviously don't get enough exercise anymore," he mumbled as the pressure began to ease when the walk turned downhill.

Eighty-Two

It had been three, long, miserable months since Jonathan had talked with Dr. Harold Bridges Sr., and things had only gotten worse at First Baptist of Dockrey. Attendance was down, giving was down, and the whole attitude in general was down. If things didn't pick up soon, they would have to stop the building program in mid-progress. As far as the truth about Hal Bridges, only Tom and Jonathan knew—they had even chosen not to tell their wives the entire story, only bits and pieces. The fact that such deception was going on in the church was bad enough, but Hal had deliberately targeted Jonathan and Tom several times publicly in the church, and if the wives knew the truth, it was highly unlikely they would stand by and allow it to happen without revealing the whole unbelievable mess.

But Sunday had been disastrous, embarrassing, and as close to evil as Jonathan ever wanted to see in a church again, and as he walked up the hill toward the office at eight o'clock rather than nine-o-two, he had already determined that this was the time to face Hal with his past. He had never taken lightly what the senior Dr. Bridges had told him—*always be careful when dealing with Hal.* That was the biggest reason why nothing had been said … until today. As usual, Hal's car was already parked at the office, and Cindy and Kyle were pulling up as he came nearer. He cringed when he saw the twins jumping out from the back because he knew Hal would make his rude comments again about the church not being a daycare. He had to admire Kyle and Cindy, however, for not buckling beneath the criticism. As Kyle put it, if the church wanted to fire them over this fact, then they could do so, because at the moment working here was definitely no picnic. Jonathan actually smiled as he imagined Hal's words when school was out and Kylla joined the family at the church for the summer.

"Morning, Sarkoses," he waved as they all approached the door. "Did you folks have a good night's rest?"

Kyle gave him a bitter stare. "You're kidding, right? After yesterday's fiasco? What was that man thinking?" Kyle tried to release the anger with a big breath, but he pointed toward the office door and added, "Yesterday was the last straw, Jonathan. I'm afraid it's gonna have to be either him or me, and I intend to tell him that this morning in staff meeting."

Jonathan put his hand on Kyle's shoulder. "How about you let me handle staff meeting this morning? I've got some things I need to talk to

Hal about privately, and hopefully it'll settle this issue once and for all."

"I'd like to be there."

"Trust me with this, Kyle. Let me do it by myself. This could be potentially humiliating for Hal, and I think the fewer involved, the better the results might be."

Kyle shrugged. "If you say so, but if you need moral support … or a good right hook, just yell … loudly …down the hall … 'cause I'll be waiting with baited breath."

"I understand."

They all walked into the office together to face the indignant look they knew Hal would have on his face. Sure enough, he sat on the desk with his arms crossed and then glanced up at the clock as the twins began to squeal. He immediately gave them an icy stare, but it had no effect on them whatsoever. It didn't even bother Cindy anymore. She had admitted to hating Hal, so anytime she did anything that irked him, it gave her a secret sense of satisfaction.

Hal lifted his coat sleeve to reveal his watch as he said, "Early this morning, aren't you, pastor? Probably a good thing. Staff meeting, my office, now … let's go."

"Not all of us," Jonathan said immediately. "It's gonna just be you and me today."

"I don't think so," Hal countered. "This is a staff meeting, and all three of us are gonna be there."

"No," Jonathan stated firmly. "It is a staff meeting, but I'm the pastor, and still the head of this church … and the head of this staff. This meeting will include only the two of us."

"But there are things Kyle needs to adjust."

"No, there aren't, pal. Not today."

Hal was obviously peeved. Jonathan could tell he was trying not to bend to the power play that had just been pulled.

"Then I'll talk to *you* later," Hal said sternly as he pointed toward Kyle.

Jonathan shook his head. "No, you won't. From now on, any criticisms you have of Kyle will come through me, and then I'll determine if they're legitimate or not. I can choose to pass them on, or I can choose to leave them in the garbage."

"Excuse me?" Hal said in shock. "Since when did you become the boss?"

"About thirty years ago." Jonathan didn't give him a chance for another retort. "Let's go … now," he said firmly as he motioned Hal toward his office.

When they got inside, Hal was livid. This wasn't how Jonathan had wanted the meeting to start, but Hal had a way of disarming anything meant to be nice and neat.

"Who in the world do you think you are?" Hal started as the anger in his voice rose. "You have absolutely no right to come in here barking orders to me and saying who I can speak to and who I can't! You didn't hire me, pastor! This church did, and I fully intend to …"

"Sit down, Hal," Jonathan said patiently. "You can rant and rave when I'm finished."

"I will not be treated like this!"

"I said," Jonathan spoke considerably louder this time, "to sit … down!"

Hal crossed his arms and leaned against the wall instead, refusing to fully comply with any command of Jonathan's.

"After yesterday's debacle during the worship service, I can no longer just sit by and watch you do the things you do. I don't care how much you may dislike me or dislike Kyle, but to interrupt the song service to take a vote on the style of music we as a church would prefer is not only insulting and disgraceful, it's downright ungodly. You crossed a line, Hal, and this type of stuff is gonna stop. You have single-handedly ripped this church apart, and it's gonna stop today."

Hal's expression showed no sign of remorse, but rather a sinister grin. "Or you'll do what, pastor? Ground me?"

Jonathan could feel the pressure in his chest begin to rise. He wanted to drop himself into the chair and take several deep breaths, but he couldn't show weakness when dealing with this man. He also had hoped that somehow Hal would change his ways or move on without Jonathan having to ever confront him, but the time for any miracles in that department was over.

"I know about your past," Jonathan finally said. "I know that you lasted eleven months in the Navy, one year at Pepperdine, and never even entered seminary. I know who your father is, and I've also talked with several pastors you served under—the real ones by the way, not the contrived people you put on your résumé'. I know about Lisa's massive gambling debts, and I know that when it comes to really wanting to serve the Lord, that's the farthest thing from your heart. I'm not completely sure what your real motives are, but as of today, the seeds of dissension you've been sowing here are gonna stop."

Hal pulled a piece of lint from his jacket and flicked it away as though Jonathan had said nothing of particular importance.

"I'm serious, Hal. It stops now."

Hal looked over at him as though he didn't have a care in the world. "Exactly what stops, pastor? I just start being a good boy and let you go back to having your way, or are you attempting to fire me … which you actually don't have the power to do."

"You'd be surprised what kind of power I have here."

"What kind of power you *used* to have," Hal emphasized. "If you kick me out of this church, a third of the congregation will leave too. Then what happens to your flock?"

"Then we start over. Those who have followed your lies … hook, line and sinker … have done nothing positive here except to reveal who has a heart for God, and who doesn't."

"There you go again," he laughed. "Being the self-righteous one. You and Kyle just think you guys have got this whole religious thing in hand. You think you can wave your little Christian wands and everyone will just bow in awe at your …"

"Enough!" Jonathan slammed his hand on Hal's desk as the pressure in his chest kicked up another notch. "This is going to stop now! I'll give you two weeks to make a dignified resignation and get out of here. If you don't, then I'll make it publicly known that you're a complete charlatan and have caused unmerciful damage to this church."

"Why not go all the way and just call me an agent of Satan?" Hal smirked.

Jonathan gritted his teeth and replied, "Don't tempt me."

Hal arranged a few of the things on his desk as he mulled over the offer. "The one bad thing about threatening to reveal one's skeletons is that a few of your own might get revealed in the process." Hal grinned as he peered up at Jonathan. "Are you sure you're willing to take that chance?"

"I don't have any skeletons," Jonathan said firmly. "I've always been an open book before this church, admitting my mistakes and failures before anyone had a chance to dig them up."

Hal's grin became even more disturbing. "If I were you, pastor, I'd make sure of that before I went around making threats."

Jonathan turned toward the door, and without looking back he said, "Two weeks, Hal. Two weeks … then it's over … one way or another."

✪✪✪

Billy sat in his last class Friday afternoon as he read through the three applications for teaching positions in north Alabama. It had been two months since he had stopped the temporary position of English teacher for Mrs. Miller on maternity leave. From then on he merely filled in when necessary. Just a couple of more weeks and school would be out. As a substitute teacher, that would mean no income whatsoever. The sooner he got hired, the sooner he could begin to think about his future, a future that obviously wouldn't include Sam.

It had been three months since her father had died, and they hadn't spoken to each other since, not even over the phone. He had strongly encouraged her to give Jeremy Crandall the best benefit of the doubt and to believe that he could give her the finest life imaginable. He supposed she had taken his advice. He still wondered if he could have changed enough to really care for her in a way that would have benefited her, but with all the pain of her past, some of it his doing, it wasn't a chance he was willing to take, or a burden he was willing to bear anymore. For now, he would just have to believe that Sam had moved on and was doing great.

He also had been thinking seriously about God. He hated to admit it, but after hearing Frank Conwill's testimony, something inside of him had changed. Frank had been the worst of the worst, maybe even lower than Farris for allowing all that had happened to Sam, but God had obviously transformed his life in a miraculous way. Then there was the evidence in Cindy. He had known her better than anybody, and when she gave her life to God, the change was unbelievable. In fact, his first impression was that it was all an act in order to win over Kyle, but years of consistency had proven his impression dead wrong. Not only that, he had lived with her since December, and the mother and wife that she had become was even more convincing than what he had seen before.

The one thing holding him back was the bickering he had discovered at the church in Dockrey. He had never seen anything like it before. To him, that church had always been a haven, a safe place no matter what he was facing, but since he had moved back, he had seen things there that were the opposite of what he had always heard Christianity should be. And on Sunday morning when Hal had gone to the pulpit right in the middle of one of the songs to complain about the worship, it didn't sit well with Billy. He actually wanted to jump up from his pew and throw Hal Bridges out of the church as he had thrown Farris Conwill out of Sam's house in Georgia.

Sam. There she was again invading his thoughts. He never believed in the whole idea of consequences resulting from sex outside of marriage, but for the first time in his life he felt unbelievable guilt … still … over his weekend with Sam … three months ago. There wasn't a night when he laid down that he didn't think of her, and he couldn't help but believe it was because of the intimate connection they had shared that weekend. He could only hope that she had been able to move beyond it all and find contentment with Dr. Crandall that would give her the opportunity to live happily ever after.

"Have a great weekend, Mr. Marcum!" a sophomore girl said with her most alluring smile as the last bell rang.

"Most definitely," he replied. "You too."

"Oh, I will!"

Billy just shook his head at the very idea. Why was it that even a fifteen year-old would make an obvious pass at him, but his only thoughts were of a math teacher with thick glasses and a blond ponytail who was probably making wedding plans for the summer that didn't include him?

Eighty-Three

Jonathan hated this part of the plane trip. The kids knew they were descending, and in a few minutes they would be forced to stay with their father for another week of the most miserable fun Stephen could make up. He tried hard to be a good father and show them a great time, but it was impossible for them to get their thoughts off of home and Annie. Jonathan imagined it might have been different for them had Stephen and Annie fought all the time. They might have welcomed the separation and felt relief that the tension was gone, but Stephen and Annie had the perfect marriage. There had been much laughter and affection, and seldom had there been disagreements, especially in front of the children. They couldn't understand why their family was being torn apart, and to make matters worse, Annie was now six months pregnant. They were about to have a baby brother or sister, yet their mother cried more often than not, and they weren't allowed to tell anyone … not even their father.

When they disembarked the plane, as usual Ellie clung to Jonathan's hand. She had learned that whining and protesting did no good. She wasn't sure what a lawyer was, but she knew if she didn't go to her daddy's every few weeks, the lawyers would make big trouble for her mommy. Jonathan knew Stephen didn't want it to be like that, but Annie still refused to talk with him, and still believed their marriage was over. It also seemed the farther along she went in the pregnancy, the more determined she was to refuse any attempts by Stephen to have a face-to-face discussion.

When Stephen appeared amidst the massive security that had become larger with each visit, Jonathan took a deep breath as he prepared for the encounter. He anticipated Stephen's frantic questions about Annie—*is she all right, how is she coping, can you get her to just call me and talk a few minutes*? Jonathan always answered as truthfully as he could without giving away the fact that Annie was expecting their third child, seldom ate but threw up a lot, and absolutely never left their plush log cabin. And as far as getting her to talk with Stephen, Jonathan had pleaded, begged and threatened Annie as much as a father, and grandfather, could, but she refused with no exceptions. In her mind the marriage had ended—giving life to all her doubts and fears—the day Stephen left in December.

"How you doing, son?" Jonathan asked as he reached out his hand in greeting once they reached the entourage.

Stephen returned the handshake, but his expression was grave. "As good as can be expected," he said sedately. "I dread all this initial stuff," he confessed quietly. "It takes at least three days just to get them out of mourning at having to be here. Then I have to continually promise that when Saturday comes, they will indeed be heading back to Alabama … and Mommy." Stephen knelt down beside Ellie and gently touched her face. "Hello, little angel. Are you ready for a big week?"

Ellie shook her head vehemently.

He stood back up and looked Jonathan in the eyes. "I can't handle much more of this. I've decided to give Annie what she wants."

Jonathan furled his brows. "Which is what?"

"She refuses to communicate with me in any way except through the lawyers. She won't even send messages through the children. So the best I can assume is that she wants a divorce."

The word hit Jonathan harder than anything else he had faced the past few months. It was worse than the whole Hal situation, worse than finding out his oldest grandchild had been heard using profanity just a few weeks after beginning public school again, possibly even worse than watching his youngest grandchild die. He knew that neither Stephen nor Annie wanted the divorce, but the situation had so deteriorated that no other solution seemed possible. Yet at the same time, it wasn't a solution. The whole problem wasn't the marriage but the complicated reality that two people had responded to each other in ways that violated respect, honor and love, the very foundations of marriage. Stephen's initial reaction to Annie was done impulsively and without any thought concerning the consequences his actions might bring. Thus Annie's resulting action was in response to deep rejection which made her build a wall bigger than even she herself could scale. The whole thing was a big mess, and caught right in the middle of it were two adorable children whose worlds had been torn apart.

"Stephen," Jonathan tried to think of what he could possibly say to change his mind, "do you really believe this is the best answer? Is this what you want, to divorce her forever, to never have her in your life again?"

"It's not that I believe it's the best answer—it's the only answer. I've tried my best to talk with her, to just make contact …"

"No, you haven't," Jonathan contradicted him. "You've made efforts, but you haven't actually shown up in person to prove that you're willing to do anything to get her back."

"It's not as simple as that. I would have flown to Alabama in a minute if I thought I could get a few minutes of her time, but then that means fighting through the press and the paparazzi—the one thing in this world Annie hates more than me. We would've been plastered over every tabloid rag in the nation!"

"And that's not a worthy sacrifice for your marriage?"

"She would hate me even more," he insisted. "You know what she's like as well as I do."

Jonathan indeed knew. "Yes, I know … and you know … so why did you leave her like you did? You had to know you couldn't just walk out on her and then come back when it was convenient."

He sighed as he looked down at his two despondent children. "I was hurt, and I wanted to make her pay. At the moment, I just didn't care. I wanted her to feel my pain and understand that to me marriage meant total honesty and transparency."

"Well, congratulations. You did an excellent job of doing just that."

He shook his head at the thought. "I guess at *that* moment in time, I didn't realize that my love for her, my *need* for her was stronger than my hurt."

"The price of impulsiveness is often a hard lesson to learn."

"Believe me, I know that … now."

They stood a moment longer, hating the discussion, then Jonathan asked, "So what are your plans … concerning the divorce?"

"If you brought me no word from her, no consent for a meeting or anything, then my lawyers will contact hers tomorrow with the papers."

The pain hit Jonathan's chest again, this time harder than ever before. "Ahh!" he moaned as he looked for a seat.

"Are you okay?" Stephen asked quickly as he helped him down. "Can I get you anything?"

Jonathan whispered through the pain, "Some water … please?"

"Gaga?" Stevie asked cautiously. "Are you all right?"

Jonathan nodded as he rubbed the pain in his chest. "I'll be okay."

Stephen sent one of his men to get some water immediately and then knelt down beside Jonathan. "I'm sorry, Jonathan, I just don't know what else to do."

Jonathan stared at him with tears forming in his eyes. "Not only does Annie lose a husband and my grandchildren lose a full-time father," Jonathan closed his eyes, "I lose a son." He shook his head as a tear brimmed. "I lose a son, Stephen."

☼☼☼

The following morning, Sunday, was the lowest attendance Jonathan had seen in years. That, however, wasn't near as disturbing as Hal Bridges sitting in his same seat on the platform, with his same highlighter, continuing to make big marks in his bulletin that represented everything done wrong during the service. Then there was an almost smiling Vivian McCall perched in her back left corner, still not social, but always there. He tried to focus on the song service and put his mind and heart where it should be—ministering to the flock—but as of last week, one-third of the church had voted they didn't like the song service anymore and wanted to go back to just hymns and southern gospel, the way it had been before Kyle came. Of course, that wasn't true—that was only what they had been indoctrinated by Hal to believe. The guy before Kyle had actually been the opposite. He had tried to move the church toward a completely contemporary worship method, but when Kyle came, he gently blended every form of music imaginable, and it had worked miracles.

A miracle, Jonathan whispered quietly in his heart to the Lord as the special music was being sung right before his turn to preach. *I desperately need a miracle right now. My church is falling apart, being divided from the inside out, and tomorrow my daughter will be served divorce papers from the love of her life. I don't even know how I'm supposed to stand in that pulpit and preach anything because there'll be a third of the people out there only looking to criticize and destroy … regardless of You or Your Word.*

As the song finished, Jonathan stood slowly and made his way to the pulpit. Before Hal had come, a deacon in the church would have come up and placed a strong arm around Jonathan's shoulder and prayed for a mighty word from the Lord this morning, but Hal had convinced them all that it was a showy, tactless, and meaningless gesture. His reasoning had been that if Jonathan hadn't prepared properly, no amount of prayer would change that fact. It was the pastor's responsibility, and not a deacon's prayer, to deliver a message that would stir people to action. So Jonathan stood in the pulpit, weak, nearly hopeless, and most definitely helpless. He opened his Bible, pulled out his notes, and then looked out at the congregation. He couldn't even remember what he was preaching on, so he glanced down at the title to jar his memory.

"Ah, yes," he said softly as he looked back to the congregation. "If you will, take your Bibles this morning and turn with me to 1 Corinthians, chapter 12. We're going to look at the importance of unity in the Body of Christ, the importance of not only everyone being on the same page, but everyone taking up his own or her own responsibility in the Church and carrying out whatever it is that God has called us to do."

As the pages rustled and Jonathan waited patiently for everyone to get there, he noticed the back door of the sanctuary open and one of the ushers pointing a man with dark glasses toward an empty spot near the back. He couldn't place the man, but there was something assuredly familiar about him. As the pages continued, Jonathan watched as the stranger shook his head and pointed more toward the front of the church. The usher nodded, and the man began to walk toward the front, slowly, deliberately, as if he were there to be noticed, not to slip in quietly during the middle of church. As he came closer, the recognition began to dawn on Jonathan, but he refused to believe it could be so. The tightness in his chest returned, but this time it was hard and unbearable. Jonathan gripped the pulpit with both hands as he knew the pain threatened to throw him to the ground. And as it became more intolerable, the man just came closer. Slowly eyes began to turn toward the stranger, and as he reached the fourth row, he stopped, removed his glasses, stared at Jonathan and then took a seat.

Toby! he screamed in his mind, although nothing came out of his mouth. The pain in his chest was exploding, and Jonathan's left arm began to tingle and ache. As he stared down at Toby, all he could imagine was that this horrible relative—a man he had let into his house time and time again—had molested his girls, and severely abused his only son for several years. Jonathan grabbed his chest and could no longer keep his footing. He plunged forward toward the pulpit, hit his head and then fell to the floor. That was the last thing he remembered about Sunday.

☼☼☼

The entire Wright family, with the exception of Annie, sat stone silent in the waiting room of the Birmingham hospital's cardiac care unit. It was nearly two in the morning, and Jonathan had yet to regain consciousness after the massive heart attack in the pulpit yesterday. Of course, the waiting room had not always been silent. The anger from the sudden appearance of Uncle Toby had been discussed for hours, and no one had a clue as to why he had suddenly shown up when he did. Along with the Wright family were many others from the church as well. The doctors had been with Jonathan for a long time, and the discovery was that there was major blockage and that immediate surgery was needed. But Jonathan was still unresponsive. The doctors couldn't understand this particular problem, but they were going full blast to get him in a stable state so they could do the surgery before another attack incurred.

"Moms," Angie asked her mother gently, "can I get you anything at all?"

Barbara smiled gratefully and replied, "Another cup of coffee would be wonderful."

"I'd rather see you skip the coffee and try for a few hours of sleep."

"Coffee or no coffee, you know there's no way I could sleep right now."

Angie nodded. She understood. She went to the decanter and poured another cup for her mother and began to add sugar and cream. She felt so guilty. Angie knew her father had been under incredible pressure, and she had seen him rub his chest more than once the past few months, but it had never occurred to her that her father—her big, strong, invincible father—could be having problems. Had he shared with her what had been going on physically, she would have made him see a doctor right away, but instead, he put on a strong front, and everyone, including Angie, admired him for staying unshaken through all that was happening.

She carried the coffee to her mother and then went to join Michael on the vinyl couch. He had both of the boys laid up on either shoulder with Cassie's head in his lap. As she gently sat down beside him, he slowly opened his eyes and looked over at her.

"Any news?" he asked quietly.

"No," she regretted to answer. "I should've known, Michael, that something was wrong. I look back now and see all the signs."

"No, Angie, *he* should've known. He should've realized not all was right in his body, and he should've gone to see a doctor."

"But you can't always tell," Angie explained to him. "Many times there's no warning, and people suddenly have heart attacks and just die." She looked at Michael, and then Christian, Caleb and Cassie. "I don't know if I could handle losing Daddy so soon after losing Carter. I really believe that might be beyond what I could handle."

He only nodded because he agreed. Jonathan was as much a father to him as to Angie. It had been Jonathan's faith and unwavering support that had helped Michael get over Carter's death. There had been several times Michael had snuck away from Angie, times when he didn't think he could go on another minute, and spent an hour or two pouring out his heart, his hurts and his fears to Jonathan. Somehow Jonathan was able to go beyond the personal impact of the situation on himself and minister to Michael as a pastor, as a shepherd, as a man who knew God intimately and was willing to pass that on. Now Michael wished he had been the same to Jonathan. In Padawin that was Michael's role, but here in Dockrey he didn't think about ministering, especially not to Jonathan Wright, the very rock of Christian example.

Cindy Sarkos stared down at her empty cup as she made designs in the Styrofoam with her fingernail. If Jonathan died, this would be an unbearable pill to swallow. She had lost her father to a sudden heart attack five years ago, and her biggest regret was that he had died without ever seeing her come to truly know Christ. Jonathan had stepped in and become her surrogate father. He had given her away in marriage to Kyle and then performed the ceremony, but only after months of patient advice to bring her to the place where she could even consider being the wife of a minister. How could she go on without Pastor Jon always being there when she lost her grip? But the thing that weighed on her most was the fact that she hadn't seen how hard his life had become. She and Kyle had leaned heavily on him during the whole Hal situation, griping and complaining about everything Hal did, only to receive encouragement to remain patient through this trial and to trust God to see them all through.

Suddenly one of the doctors burst through the door with a beaming smile. Everyone ran to meet him except for Michael who was still the bed for three sleeping children.

"He's awake," the doctor said in exhaustion. "And he wants to see his wife … first … alone. The rest of the family can see him after that if his strength holds up."

Angie immediately began to ask the right questions concerning his medical condition. "Is he in pain?"

"A little," the doctor replied, "but we're working on that."

"Does he understand his condition?"

"Yes, and he also knows we're prepping for surgery as soon as possible."

"What are his chances of survival through this?" Everyone looked at Angie in shock as she asked the question. "I'm sorry, it's just that I need to hear a percentage … I need to get an idea of what we're looking at."

The cardiologist smiled in compassion knowing she was a doctor. "I'm not giving you any percentages right now," he said empathetically. "Besides, I think we could all agree that it's not the percentages we're depending on here."

They all nodded, knowing he was a strong Christian.

He continued, "He seems in good spirits, he's not very aware of all that happened, and he understands about the blockage and the absolute need for surgery. Other than that, let's give him a little bit of time to really wake up and gather his wits about him." The doctor then looked to Barbara. "Mrs. Wright, would you like to go in now?"

"Please," she smiled weakly. "I really would."

The doctor led Barbara back to the area where Jonathan had been since early that afternoon when they had flown him from Dockrey. He still looked pale, but at least he was awake. For the past several hours that had been her only prayer. *Please let me talk to him at least once more, Lord. Don't let this morning before church be my last words to him. Let me touch his heart once again.* Over and over she had prayed it, and when Jonathan finally glanced her way, the dam holding her emotions burst, and she literally ran to him and took him in her arms.

Eighty-Four

When the phone rang on Monday afternoon, Annie ran for it thinking it might more news about her father. She so wanted to be at the hospital with the rest of her family, but if she were to leave the house now, the big news on every network tonight would be her pregnancy. She had literally not left home since the beginning of March, and everyone in the world knew she and Stephen weren't together. This kind of news would take precedence over every other scummy idea, real or contrived, that any news organization, real or contrived, might find. Rather than risk having Stephen discover it this way, she chose to stay home alone and cry by herself as her father fought for his life several hours away.

She glanced at the display on the phone first—always careful to make sure she knew the number. It was her lawyer. Great. There was nothing legal she felt like discussing today. She would tell him the situation immediately and hopefully he could call back another time, preferably next week.

"Hello, this is Annie," she answered.

"Annie, its George."

"I know. This isn't a good time, George."

"I didn't figure it would be, because the news I have for you probably won't have you dancing in the aisles any time soon either."

She hadn't anticipated this. "Really? What's going on?"

"Stephen has filed for divorce," he said slowly. "I know this was what you were waiting for, but now that it's actually here, I don't imagine it's what you really wanted." He paused, "I'm sorry, Annie—I'd really hoped it would work out."

The hurt that hit her heart was unexplainable. "Wow," she barely breathed. "So this is really gonna happen?"

"Looks like it, but at least he's being very fair. He's pretty much giving you everything you guys have acquired together, including full rights and royalties to any songs, albums and productions you collaborated on."

"You're kidding?" Guilt began to spread.

"The only area you aren't going to like is where the children are concerned."

"Does he want joint custody?" she asked alarmed. She didn't want the children to become pawns at all.

"Actually, no, but he does want to see them more than once a month, and for at least a whole month during the summers when they're out of school."

She nodded. "Wow, this is quite a … I don't know what to say right now. My father is very sick … in the hospital in Birmingham. I'm not exactly ready at the moment to deal with looking through divorce papers. Can I have some time before I actually sign them?"

"You've got all the time you need," George told her. "The ball's in your court now. When you're ready to really end this, you sign your agreement, and then we go to work putting a permanent end to the marriage."

The whole lingo made it sound so stale and unattached, like having a wart removed at the doctor's office. She could feel the emotions rise in her throat, and in her stomach, as she imagined Stephen being totally out of her life.

"Just let me call you when I'm ready," she suggested.

"That'll do."

☼☼☼

Stephen felt like the most miserable man in the world as he leaned his head against the limo. Stevie and Ellie were both exhausted from spending the day at Disneyland, all with special treatment of course, yet they had had a miserable time. He couldn't imagine any child hating Disneyland, but Stevie and Ellie were so homesick that not even Mickey himself could draw them out of it. The only smile that came across Stevie's face the whole day was when one of the theme songs from a movie was heard playing in a restaurant—it was the one that Stephen and Annie had written and sang for one of the animated films. As Stevie heard his mother's voice play across the room, his smile grew bigger and bigger at the thought of her, but when the song was over, so was the smile.

He wondered how Annie had taken the news that he was filing for divorce. Was she thrilled that it would all be over now? He knew Jonathan had said her fear of being verbally ground down by Stephen was the real reason she wouldn't speak with him, but after six months of it, he believed it had to be more than that. He really believed she so enjoyed being out of the spotlight and scrutiny that came with fame, that she was more than happy to end a life with him. She wanted a quiet place to live with none of the trappings that came from being linked to him. He had enjoyed their serene life there in the cabin. Now he regretted, more than anything he had ever done, telling her he wanted to work again. And then when Ben Brenner came along and offered him the perfect opportunity, not to mention a very good excuse also, he had just run with it. And in the wake of his selfishness lay the love of the most incredible woman he had ever met, as well as the trust of his two young children.

With a little help, he managed to get the children up the elevator to his loft and into their bunk beds, clothes and all. As he tucked in each and gently gave a kiss to their angelic sleeping faces, all he could think of was how it used to be with Annie. He would kiss them goodnight, thinking life could barely get any better, except for the fact that his inconceivably beautiful wife was waiting for him in their own room down the hall. But now he would go brush his teeth, squeezing the tube any way he wanted with no comment of conflict about it, even though the comments were always given with a wink. Then he would climb into an empty bed with no arms to hold him, no thick, full lips to welcome him, and no secret words of passion and love to carry him off into the deepest sleeps he had ever known. That was not his life anymore, and he really hated the life with which he was now stuck.

☼☼☼

Jonathan looked soberly at his wife as they prepared to wheel him away to surgery. They had said much the past two days, and as ready as they were for this to happen and for all the questions to be put to rest, they still knew there was the possibility that this could really be goodbye. He held her hand tightly and marveled at the strength she was showing in the face of what was about to occur. Everyone else had literally broken down before him, but after her initial emotional outburst, Barbara had managed to care for him as though he merely had a cold and all would be better when he woke up in the morning.

"Life with you has been precious … and sweet," he said tenderly as he gazed into her weary eyes. "You have truly been a helpmate in every sense of the word."

"And you have truly been someone who needed my help," she replied.

He laughed. He was thankful she was making this easy.

"But seriously," she continued as her smile dulled, "you've been a wonderful man to help. When I married you, it was for the long haul. We have a lot to be proud of together—four wonderful children, 11 grandchildren … at least I think that's the last count, and many souls brought into the Kingdom as a result of our collaboration. I couldn't have asked for anything more in life."

"I did promise you I'd take you to Paris one day," he said sadly. "I could never afford it, Barbara."

"*We* could never afford it," she corrected him. "And as much as I would've liked to have gone, what part of our wonderful life should I have sacrificed for the sake of a trip? The ministry?" She shook her head. "I don't think so. That's who we are and what we were created to do, Jonathan. No regrets there." She placed a finger thoughtfully to her temple. "Perhaps not had any children? Or not had all of them? Which ones should we have refused for the sake of a trip over the ocean?"

Jonathan squeezed her hand. "You're good. I don't feel quite so bad about it now. But I promise you this—if I make it out of here, if I live through this, I will get you to Paris."

She smiled again. "I don't want to go to Paris anymore."

"Really? Why not?"

"Because it would mean sacrificing to put money away for a simple sightseeing tour, when there are greater needs right here and deeper wants right now … like spoiling my grandchildren, or cooking meals for the elderly, or sending a young couple away for a second honeymoon when they're struggling with a newborn or young children … the list could go on and on." She gently kissed the back of his hand. "My life is as full as it could ever want to be, and if you pull through this thing, we aren't gonna waste the next section chasing something as silly as all that. We're gonna make it count just as much as it did before. Agreed?"

He nodded. "Absolutely."

☼☼☼

"I can't do it!" Annie yelled to both of her sisters as they insisted she would be the one picking up the kids from Stephen's on Saturday. "Come on, he just filed for divorce! I can't fly out there, six months pregnant no less, and act like everything is fine here on my end and I'm just getting the kids as usual!"

Andie would hear of no other plan. "You've put this on Daddy for all this time, refusing to own up to the fact that you're in this situation because of your own lack of judgment …"

Angie put up her hands and stood between them, "Hang on," she said reasonably. "Let's not start dragging anything into this except for the fact that Annie needs to be the one to go."

"Great!" Annie yelled out again. "So you both think I'm responsible for Daddy's heart attack? Wonderful! I almost killed my father!"

Angie shook her head. "No, he has a physical condition. Stress or no stress, he still would've had a heart attack. It was inevitable."

Andie wouldn't give in so easily. "But you, Hal Bridges, and Uncle Toby did wonders to help bring it on."

"Thank you," Annie replied snidely. "I really appreciate the extra pounds of guilt as I prepare to sign papers that'll end my marriage, which I'm fully aware is all my fault."

Angie rolled her eyes. "It is *not* all your fault, and Daddy's bouncing back and forth across the United States isn't what caused his heart attack." She glared at Andie. "Could you not show a little bit of compassion here?"

"Actually … no," Andie said firmly. "I've watched this whole thing self-destruct for six months now. Trust me, Annie, Doug and I would've divorced many times if I would've treated our problems the way you've treated this?"

"Me?" Annie asked wide-eyed. "He left me! He told me …"

"And then he's tried to talk to you … again and again and again and again!" Andie reminded her. "But no, your pride had been wounded, and you weren't about to lick your wounds and make amends until you had destroyed every ounce of hope that was left. That's how you've always operated, Annie. You make rash judgments in life, and then when you have to face the consequences, you'd rather crawl in a corner and die than say, *Hey, everybody, I was wrong, but I'm willing to get over it!* Annie, for the sake of everything that is right and good, you are NOT perfect! You never have been, you never will be, and when you can finally realize that, you can begin to live life happily! Let yourself off the hook! Nobody will ever do everything right! Get … over … it!"

Annie just stared in shock. "I never said I was perfect."

"No," Andie agreed, "but you sure have tried awful hard. It's time to join the human race, Annie Wright Williams. It's time to get your head out of the sand. Swallow your dang pride, get on that plane tomorrow … yes, show the world that you're pregnant … and go to Stephen. And before you sign those stupid papers that will forever ruin the best thing that ever happened to you, at least look him in the eyes one last time and ask yourself which is more important to preserve—your pride … or your marriage?"

"He doesn't want to preserve our marriage," Annie replied regretfully.

"You have no idea," Andie said firmly. "You don't know what he wants because you've been too stubborn to bend your ear long enough." She put her hands on Annie's shoulders and forced her to face her. "This is your marriage, Annie. This is your future, the future of your kids, and even the future of Stephen Williams—all this lies on the line. If Daddy had been smart, he would've made you do this a long time ago, but he couldn't stand to see you hurting. Life is hard, sister. And for you, it's a bit harder right now than it is for the rest of us … but not by much. Angie lost a child, I have an adolescent who I feel I've just thrown to the wolves, our church is about to split in two, and our father just had a quadruple bypass. Welcome to the planet."

Annie closed her eyes and walked over to the French doors to look outside. She didn't believe she had the strength or the courage to face Stephen again. And if she walked into any public place as obviously pregnant as she was, it would only be a matter of minutes before the rumors began to fly. But in her heart she knew Andie was right. Half of her problem was her stubborn pride, her need to always be perfect, and that included a problem-free, perfect marriage that would be set on a pedestal for all to see. That's what Annie had wanted with everything in her life but had always fallen short. To face Stephen would be to face the biggest failure ever, bigger than challenging a music professor or greasing instrument valves or even being kicked out of college. To face Stephen would be to do it in front of the entire world, on every newsstand, and on every national television station. This would literally be the hardest thing she had ever done in her life, and what made it so difficult was that so many things always came easily to Annie. To do this would require more of herself than she had ever given before, and she honestly didn't know if she had it in her.

☼☼☼

Billy packed up his satchel for the last time this school year. It was Friday, and next week was final exams. He would be doing no subbing then. He had sent in the three applications, and then added another one that included the school here in Dockrey. The principal had notified him on Tuesday that the junior high science teacher would be retiring and the position would be open. Billy hadn't really wanted to teach junior high, but it almost seemed unbelievable that this position would open at this time. He had talked with Kyle and Cindy, and they all agreed the best plan would be to submit an application here also, and the school with the best offer would be the choice to consider. Then they had prayed with him, asking God to be very clear about His plans for Billy's life.

He smiled and shook his head in wonder at the very thought of considering God in any of this. His life had taken many turns the last few years, but the fact that he was seriously considering really giving everything over to God was the most shocking. Did God really love *him*? Could God really make something useful and decent out of his life after all the rebellion and misery he had caused others over the years? And could God use his testimony to encourage others not to take the same path he had—much like Frank Conwill's—and let Billy be someone people could look to as an example of God's grace? God had certainly done that with Cindy, and she often pleaded with Billy to just let go and let God take over.

When he got back to the house, he made a peanut butter and banana sandwich, poured a full glass of milk, and then sat in front of the television to watch a game show before everyone got home. He clicked on the remote to his favorite afternoon station, and then sat back in the recliner as he took a huge bite of his sandwich. But as if in perfect sync, a newsflash sprang out across the screen.

"… continue with this breaking news. Here's Carole on the scene at the high school to give you the latest details," the announcer said in a serious tone.

Immediately the shot was cut into a live scene somewhere in the viewing area. Since the anchorman had mentioned a high school, Billy gave it more attention than he normally would have.

"Thank you, Bob," the on-the-scene lady said. "There's a lot of commotion going on right now, so it's hard to actually make sense of what has happened. According to most reports, there was only one gunman, and apparently he was a student. Several shots were fired, and so far three ambulances have left the scene, so that's why we kept hearing speculation that maybe it was more than one person. I haven't spoken with the principal yet, but I did speak with one of the teachers who was actually in the building when the shots occurred."

The camera then panned from the reporter to the alleged building. Billy stopped chewing. It was Sam's school, and the building on the screen was the science/math wing.

"According to the teacher, there was one shot fired and then a lot of screaming. He said it sounded as if it were right next door. Because of the nicer weather, he had the classroom windows open, so everything sounded very clear. After approximately thirty seconds, another shot was fired along with more screaming and pleading. And then within just a few seconds, there was a third shot. The teacher said after the first shot, he had snuck out into the hall and was attempting to look through the door when he heard the second shot. He then looked inside and saw the student fire the third shot, which apparently did hit the teacher in that classroom."

Billy spit his food into his plate as a knot began to rise in his stomach. "Who was the teacher?" he asked the television as he felt the blood rush from his face.

"Of course, we're not allowed to give out any information on the alleged shooter because he is a minor, but I also cannot give the name of the teacher until family has been notified. I've been told, however, that she is one of the high school math teachers here. As soon as we have more information, we'll give you an update. Back to you, Bob."

Billy sat stunned. It couldn't be. He tried to think if there was another high school math teacher there who was a woman. The answer was no. There was no mistake. That was Sam's school, Sam's building, and Sam was the only female math teacher in the entire high school. His hands trembled as he reached for the remote and came to his feet. He left his sandwich and milk in the living room as he ran by the counter to grab his keys and head out the door. She had no family, so if the injury was serious, or even fatal, no one would be there for her, unless she happened to have already married Dr. Crandall. He paused for a moment; that could be a possibility. But what if it wasn't? He was the closest thing to family she had anywhere near here, and the only other option was to call her mother, and that wasn't an option at all.

On his way out, Cindy, Kyle and the kids were unloading from the van.

"Where are you going in such a rush?" Cindy asked him. Then she noticed the color gone from his face. "Billy, what's wrong?"

"I think Sam's been shot," he replied out of breath. "I've got to get there."

"Wo, hang on there a minute," she stopped him. "Take your time, and tell me what's happening?"

"I don't have any time!" he said in desperation. "I just saw a report on the television that a lady high school math teacher was just shot by a student at Sam's school! There were three shots, Cindy," he bit his lip. "Three. What if one of them killed her?"

If this were true, Cindy didn't believe she could take much more. Her father, her mother, Carter, Jonathan, and now Sam. At least Jonathan had lived. If Sam had just been killed, she didn't know how she could handle it—or if Billy could at all.

"Go!" she said emphatically as she rushed him on with her hands. "And call me! Please call me as soon as you find out anything!"

"I will!" he shouted as he pulled open the door to the Mustang and threw himself inside.

Eighty-Five

"When I asked God for a mighty work, this wasn't exactly what I had in mind," Jonathan told his wife as he tried to maneuver himself to a different position with the minimalist pain.

Barbara laughed slightly as she tried to help him adjust. "Nevertheless, it's still a miracle. Annie is flying to California to pick up the kids. Do you think we should call him to let him know she's coming? It would give him the opportunity to think about how to approach her and possibly get her to stay and talk with him."

"If God can strike me down in the pulpit with a massive heart attack in order to get her to go, I think we can trust God to do whatever else needs to be done in order to get them back together."

"I suppose you're right. If you weren't so sick, I might be tempted to fly out there on an earlier flight just to see Stephen's expression when he sees her walk off the plane … six months pregnant."

"Well, I, for one, am thrilled *not* to be flying to California to make this exchange," he winced as he made a sudden turn. "Ahh! I've got to stop doing that."

"Yes, sweetie, it would help if you would remember they sawed your chest open and repaired all those blockages around your sweet little heart in there." She helped him to relax and then sat back down in her chair beside his bed.

"You know this doesn't mean that all will be well in *Williamsville* if our Annie is involved," He reminded her cautiously. "She can cause the simplest of solutions to become calculus meltdowns."

"I know, but you and I, and the rest of the family, and anyone else we want to call in on this can pray from now until four o'clock tomorrow afternoon that God will soften her heart. Like you said, if He could do all this to just get her there—He can do the rest to get her to stay."

✪✪✪

As Billy entered the Shoals area, he tried to think clearly about where Sam might me. If the ambulance took her to the ER closest to the school, it would have to be Helen Keller Hospital. He decided to head there first. He took the quickest route possible, but traffic was busy, and no matter which lane he switched to, it would always be the one that piled up behind the red lights. When the hospital finally came into view, he heaved a restless sigh and pulled quickly into the parking lot. He assumed his best bet would be the emergency entrance.

When he ran into the ER, he approached the desk in a bit of a panic. His best bet to see Sam was to assume she was still a Marcum and that no one had been contacted. He would pass himself off as her husband and cross his fingers that the plan would work.

"Is this where Samantha Marcum is?" he asked with obvious alarm. He pulled out his driver's license and showed it to the receptionist. "My name is Billy Marcum, her husband. She was the teacher recently shot at the high school. I had to drive all the way from Dockrey … that's where I teach."

The lady's eyes widened and she picked up her phone immediately as she said, "Just a minute, sir. We've been hoping for family to show up." She punched in the extension and spoke almost frantically. "The school teacher's husband just walked in. He had to drive from Dockrey." She listened carefully for instructions and then put down the receiver. "She's in the Critical Care Unit right now. They asked for you to go on up."

"Thank you," he said as he stuffed his license back into his wallet while running toward the stairs. To wait for the elevator would be too slow.

God, let her be okay, please let her be okay. Don't let this be the end … not for Sam … please.

He took two, three and four steps at a time until he reached the CCU floor. He jerked opened the door and ran to the place where his mother had spent several weeks near the end of her life. He hated the sounds, the smells, and the sterile appearance of it all, but at this moment the only thing that mattered was getting to Sam and making sure she was all right … and alive.

As he rounded the last corner, he spotted Mr. C. sitting in the waiting area. "Mr. C!" he called out. "How is she? Is she okay? What happened? How did it happen?"

Mr. C. stood and an astonished expression flooded his face. "Billy," he said in near awe. "I can't believe you're actually here. Do you realize that you're an answer to prayer?"

Billy shook his head as he tried to catch his breath from the run up the stairs. "No … sir." Another breath. "How's Sam?"

"She's stable, but they need to do surgery," Mr. C. said as he pulled Billy aside. "They've been waiting for someone to come in who can speak for her."

"I'll do it," Billy said as he turned toward the station.

"Billy!" Mr. C. called him back. "Listen to me." He made Billy calm down as he tried to explain the situation. "You need to know a few things before you go barreling in there barking out orders."

Billy nodded as continued to breathe hard.

"First, Sam is pregnant."

Billy nearly fainted at the thought. Sam, his Sam, was carrying another man's child?

"Then where's Crandall?" he asked angrily. "If she's having his baby, he should be here! I know it's not his hospital, but he should still be here! Surely someone called him to let him know!"

Mr. C. shook his head. "Crandall is gone, Billy. He's out of the picture."

"What? He left her … even when she was pregnant? That doesn't sound like him!" He was enraged. How could he leave her like that?

"He went back home to take over a practice in his hometown."

"And he left Sam?" He was getting more furious as the conversation continued.

Mr. C. shook his head again and forced Billy to sit down. "Listen to me, okay, and don't interrupt. There's a lot going on here that you don't understand."

"But shouldn't I see Sam? Shouldn't she be in surgery?"

"Trust me—this is more important than even that. She's stable for the moment, but you won't be if you run in there like this without knowing everything. So stay put for a few minutes and let me get it all out." Mr. C. looked soberly at him and waited for a response.

Billy finally sat back and nodded—Mr. C. began the story. "A couple of months ago Sam started acting … looking … unusual. She seemed very tired, a little pale at times, yet at the same time very content and happy. I knew something was going on with her, but you know Sam, she doesn't open up easily. So I invited her to supper one evening … told her to bring her boyfriend with her. She said he wouldn't make it, but she'd love to see Mrs. C. again and would be delighted to come. She thought it was all innocent, but shortly after eating, I just flat out asked her what was going on in her life. I wondered if she was sick or if she was having a hard time … or what. And to our surprise, she opened right up to us and said she was relieved to actually be able to share all this with someone."

"Share what?" Billy was completely in the dark.

"She told us she was pregnant."

Billy flinched at the very sound of it again, especially knowing that Crandall had left her.

"Then she explained that Jeremy had gone home."

"Jerk!" Billy spat out.

"Hang on, son," Mr. C. said cautiously. "He's considerably more noble than what you're thinking right now. He wanted to marry her and raise the child … as his own … but Sam wouldn't hear of it."

"What do you mean raise it *as his own*? It wasn't his baby? Sam was *with* somebody else?" The thought actually made him insanely jealous. "Who else was she with?"

Mr. C. gave him the strangest look as he said, "You tell me! Think about it, Bill. Who else was she with three months ago … in Georgia … burying her father."

As the reality began to hit him, the ramifications of it all began to overwhelm him. He slowly stood to his feet and ran his hand over his shorn head of hair. Sam was carrying *his* child, and Crandall was decent enough and in love enough with her to be willing to still marry her. He shook his head at the thought. "Why didn't she marry him? He was so good."

"Because she's in love with you. She told us that night that when she realized she was pregnant, she knew it was over with Jeremy. She tried to love him, mainly because you had insisted he was the man she needed to be with, but she said she could never marry him and carry a part of you with her for the rest of her life … namely, the baby. So when she insisted to him it was over, and that her heart would always belong to you, he decided to just leave."

Billy walked toward one of the long windows and glanced down at the courtyard below. He was going to be a father … with Sam. The thought almost overwhelmed him until the reality of her situation hit him. "How's the baby?" he asked now feeling more helpless than ever. "Where was she shot? Is the baby harmed or …"

"I don't know," Mr. C. said shaking his head. "By law, they can't give me any information. But as her ex-husband, and the father of her baby, as well as someone carrying the same last name, you might be able to find out significantly more."

Billy reached into his pocket for his wallet again. "Do they know she has an ex-husband?"

Mr. C. grinned and shook his head. "I rode with her in the ambulance over here, and I prayed the whole time that God would somehow get a hold of you and get you here." His grin grew. "And here you are."

Billy nodded as he headed for the door to the nurse's station. Sam was carrying his child. It was almost more than he could contain. He burst through the door, held up his license and said, "I'm Samantha Marcum's husband. How's she doing … and how's my baby?" As soon as he said the words *my baby*, tears began to form in his eyes.

"Mr. Marcum," one nurse said as she came to him immediately, "are we ever glad you're here. Right now she's stable, and the baby seems to be fine, but we can't get her to respond to anything."

"Can I see her?" Billy asked as he looked into all the patient areas trying to locate which one held Sam.

"Absolutely. In fact, we'd really like to see her awake before we take her into surgery. Follow me."

The nurse led him to an area that had been enclosed with a large, encircling curtain. She pulled open a section and motioned him to follow her inside. There on the bed was Sam hooked up to a million machines with quite a bit of blood around what must have been the bullet wound.

"On her arm?" he asked. "Is that where she was shot? No one's told me anything."

"Actually it was more near her right shoulder," the nurse explained as she walked over to Sam and pointed out the area. "There was a lot of damage done. I doubt her right arm will ever be the same again. Was she right handed?"

Billy nodded. He didn't care about her arm right now. He only wanted to know that she was going to pull through this.

"Talk to her, Mr. Marcum," the nurse said kindheartedly. "Bring her back, okay?"

"I'll do my best," he said as emotion began to well up inside him again. "But the baby is okay?"

"For now. No damage to Ms. Marcum's lungs or any other major organ. A lot of blood loss, but we're pumping it in her right now. However, if things don't change soon, we can't say what will happen … to the baby, or even to her."

Billy very carefully sat down on the edge of her bed and looked into her face. How he wished she would open her eyes so he could see their beauty and know she was alright. If she pulled through this, he would never leave her again. He slowly looked down her body until he came to her stomach. He gently lifted his hand and placed it on top where he softly rubbed it back and forth.

"Sam," he whispered emotionally, "why didn't you tell me? Especially after Crandall left, why didn't you tell me?" He shook his head. He knew why she didn't tell him. "It was because I pushed you away. It was because I kept trying to convince you that I was wrong for you and the nice doctor was right." He sighed as he looked back up to her face. "I still believe it's true—he would've been the better choice, but he's not an option any more. It's you and me now, Sam. You've got to come out of this—you've got to wake up. We have a baby to raise." A tear fell from his face onto the sheet, and he could feel himself beginning to really lose control. "Come on, Sam, wake up. Tell me what happened. I'm here for you now, and I'll never leave you again, Sam … never—I promise."

He reached up to touch her face and caress her hair. He then looked for another wound, but saw nothing. Surely the nurse would have mentioned it. Then he remembered the reporter saying that three ambulances had left the school, and the teacher had seen Sam receive the third shot.

"Wake up, Sam," he said a little louder. "Tell me what happened today. Who else was shot in that classroom? Who did it, Sam? Why did they do it?" He leaned in closer to her. "Sam, please wake up and talk to me."

But she remained motionless. As the minutes dragged on, Billy began to get worried. He had been in there almost an hour trying to rouse her, but she hadn't moved a muscle. The nurse had returned several times to see if he had made any progress, but he would just shake his head.

"Keep trying," she would say. "They've got her scheduled for surgery in a little over an hour. It'd be really nice to have her cognizant before then."

"Come on, Sam," he said over and over. "It's Billy, and I'm here for good. We're gonna do it right this time. And we've got a baby, Sam. We've got a baby." Nothing. "You've got to wake up. You were shot in the shoulder, and they need to do some major repair work on it, but they want you awake and aware before they get started. The sooner you get going on this, the sooner we can begin to put our lives back together … all three of our lives."

He still couldn't believe she was pregnant. Until now he had been rather perturbed with Stephen Williams. Kyle and Cindy and Angie often discussed Annie's situation, and Billy had grown to think that Stephen deserved everything he got—including keeping the news about the baby from him. But now he felt very differently. What if Sam had never told him, which was highly likely if this bizarre event hadn't happened?

Billy looked up toward heaven and asked, *Is this what it took to get my attention, Lord? Was I so stubborn and wrong that You had to do this to Sam in order to bring me back to her … and to our baby?*

Suddenly she began to stir.

"Sam!" he said excitedly. "Sam, are you waking up? Come on, Sam, it's Billy. I'm here … please wake up!"

He touched her face again and she slowly began to roll her head from one side to the other.

"That's it, girl. Wake up! Sam, you need to wake up."

Her expression changed from that of peaceful sleep to one of deep pain as she began to rouse. As she tried to open her eyes, she began to moan.

"That's it, Sam!" he said as he reached for her unhurt hand. "Come on, babe! Wake up!"

"Noooooo," she began to whimper as she closed her eyes tight instead of opening them. "Oh, nooooo …"

"It's okay, Sam," he said more gently now as he leaned down over her. "Wake up, ponytail, and tell me what happened."

She shuddered at the pain in her shoulder as she finally began to open her eyes. A few more cries escaped before she became all the way conscious, but as she looked around, she was obviously disoriented. Billy knew she couldn't see well without her glasses, but they were nowhere to be found in the room.

"Hey, Sam," he said softly as he got right up to her face. "It's Billy. How do you feel?"

"What?" Then she smiled. "Billy? Why are you … I'm dreaming here, aren't I?"

"No, babe," he said as he gently kissed her forehead. "I'm here, Sam, and I'm never gonna leave again. I'm staying right here with you … and with the baby."

She furled her eyebrows and asked, "How did you know about the baby?"

"A little science teacher out in the waiting room told me."

"What waiting room? Why is he in the waiting room?" She looked around again and was baffled at her surroundings. "Where are we? What is this place?"

"You're in the hospital, Sam? You don't remember what happened?"

She suddenly grew alarmed. "Did something happen to the baby? Is the baby okay?"

He calmed her immediately. "The baby's fine. Everything's fine but you. The bullet hit your shoulder—it was nowhere near the baby."

She looked confused again. "What bullet? Why am I in the hospital?"

"You don't remember? You were shot at school today? Someone shot you in the shoulder. They say it was a student."

Sam began to roll back the memories of her mind, trying to recall what had happened before waking up here. She vaguely remembered the ambulance, and that Mr. C. had been in there with her. Why was she there? She thought back, but it was all unclear. She remembered falling to the floor and trying to catch herself so she didn't hit hard or hurt the baby. Then, as if in slow motion, she saw Patrick Page, a large and somewhat odd student shoving himself into … into …

"Oh … noooo," she began to whimper again.

"What is it, Sam?" Billy asked as he tried his best to hold her without hurting her. "Do you remember?"

She nodded as she opened her eyes again. "Paulo," she whispered in despair.

"Paulo got shot too?" Billy asked stunned. "Why would anyone shoot Paulo? Why would anyone shoot you?"

She shook her head. The images were returning now and they were very vivid.

"Who did this, Sam? Who brought the gun, and who pulled the trigger?"

She didn't want to say it again, but Billy didn't get it. "Paulo … he had the gun … he pulled the trigger."

Eighty-Six

"Michael and I will be glad to drive you to the airport," Angie told Annie on Friday evening as they sat in the living room at the log cabin avoiding the subject of Annie's trip to pick up the children on Saturday. Angie was tired of not talking about it.

Annie just shook her head.

"Really, we wouldn't mind."

"Then you'd have to wait around until I returned, and if you're actually willing to do all that, you might as well just make the trip for me." Annie gave her sister a helplessly hopeful look.

Angie giggled and reiterated, "I'm not picking up your children." She sighed and looked thoughtfully at Annie's ever-expanding belly. "He needs to know, Annie, and you need to at least see each other face to face before you actually sign those papers."

"Ah, yes," she moaned as she rubbed her tummy, "the ever present big *D* papers, the ones that prove Stephen has no desire to talk to me other than to negotiate visitation and custody rights concerning our children. And once he gets a good view of this," she patted her stomach, "it'll take the negotiations to a whole new level. It's kind of crazy, isn't it? He won't be here when this one's born, he won't be here to raise it, yet by law, he could demand the right to force visitation on it also."

"What's crazy is that you've been so utterly stubborn about all this that you have no clue what he will or won't do. You don't know what he thinks, what he feels, if he has regrets, or if indeed, as you seem so convinced, if he's moved on and made a whole new life for himself … without you."

Annie rolled her eyes. Yes, she believed that, but to hear someone else say it rather than the voice inside her own head made it sound horrifying. A few months ago she would've died to think that Stephen would leave her and she would have to live the rest of her life without him by her side—yet as it was all now a reality, she realized life could go on. She didn't want it to, but she had no choice. And even though she continued her protesting about having to make the trip by herself tomorrow, there was this very small part that held a flicker of hope that perhaps seeing her again would soften his heart just enough that he would miss all they had had before … just like she did. She knew things could never be the same, but just to be on cordial terms with him would be comforting. Before he had ever been her husband, he had been a musician that had touched her heart deeply, and she would hate to have all of that marred forever because of harsh feelings.

Cassie came trudging into the room full of her typical furrowed brow attitude as she carried a book to her mother. She plopped the book in her mother's lap and then pointed to a picture.

"Why are there no crabs in Alabama?" she demanded to know. "Look at all these. Why can't just one of them live in Alabama?"

"Actually," Angie tried to explain, "I think there are crabs in Alabama, but they live down on the coast … on the Alabama beach."

Cassie's eyes grew wide with excitement. "They have a beach in Alabama? Can we go, Mama? Can we go today?"

"It's a long way from here, sweetie. We're not traveling that far just to chase a few crabs for an afternoon."

"Hmph," Cassie pouted. "Then I'll ask Daddy. He likes the beach too, and Caleb and Christian would like it—I know they would."

"Caleb and Christian can't even walk yet, baby. They're a little too young to go to the beach."

"Carter never walked and he loved the beach!"

Just the mention of Carter's name at times could throw Angie into an emotional tizzy, and for some reason Cassie's timing was bad. Immediately Angie's eyes began to pool and her lip began to tremble. She turned away quickly not wanting Cassie to see any more tears over Carter.

"You know what?" Annie hopped up immediately and went over to Cassie. "I know a place where I bet you could get a good look at some crabs. I don't know if you can touch them or not, but when Ellie comes back tomorrow, perhaps your Daddy could take you and Ellie, and maybe even Lainey, on a little trip for the day."

The idea was appealing to Cassie. "And is there a beach there too?"

Annie shook her head. "Nope. It's a big aquarium though."

"Like the one at Mr. Kyle's?" Cassie had been fascinated at the idea of keeping fish inside the house. The rule in Padawin was that anything caught had to be released at nightfall. It turned out to be a better rule than either Angie or Michael could have imagined because Cassie brought in several potential pets daily.

"But this is a huge aquarium," Annie clarified. "It's as big as a building, in fact, there are several buildings, and they have fish and things from all over the world!"

"All over the world?" Cassie reached for the book in her mother's lap and handed it up to Annie. "Will all of these crabs be in there?"

Annie looked over the pages and had no idea if the Tennessee Aquarium in Chattanooga had crabs or not, but it had enough sea creatures to keep Cassie's inquisitive brain occupied for several hours. In fact, if Annie could swing it, perhaps they could get Cindy and Kyle to keep the twins for the day, and maybe Annie, Angie and Andie could all spend the day together just themselves. All three of them could use a good break from the struggles in their lives for the moment—the apex now being their father laid up in a hospital after quadruple bypass surgery. And the possibility was very high that Annie would sign her divorce papers after tomorrow's visit. A good distraction was definitely in order and would be appreciated by all.

☼☼☼

Sam's surgery was taking longer than any had anticipated. There had been significant nerve, muscle and bone damage, and the reconstruction was difficult. In fact, it looked like there would have to be more than one surgery if she was to have a chance of ever using the arm again normally.

"Look at it this way," Mr. C. tried to encourage Billy, "had Patrick Page not jumped on Paulo when he did, the gun would not have nudged to the left, and the shot would have probably … killed her."

Billy shut his eyes tightly. "I don't even want to imagine that." He sat in one of the many seats in the waiting area and rested his weary head in his hands. He then looked back up at Mr. C. and asked, "Why did Paulo do it? He wasn't a violent guy at all. And when you think about it, it's just not his nature to do something like this. He was a good kid, a hard worker, a guy with dreams and goals. Why would he throw all that away in a couple of minutes? And why Sam? She was always so patient and good to him. He was one of her favorites, always giving him extra time and attention, always making sure he had a clear grasp of how to do the problems. She wanted to see him rise above his circumstances and do something big with his life, and he was most definitely on his way. What happened?"

Mr. C. pulled off his glasses and rubbed the bridge of his nose. "I don't know, but something I've learned after years of teaching is that what you see with kids at school isn't always a clue to what life at home is really like. I do remember meeting Paulo's parents once at an awards' assembly. They could barely communicate in English at all, and they were embarrassed to be there because of that. It occurred to me then that he was fighting bigger odds than most. All those kids surrounding him at school, on the sports teams, they're all typically spoiled American kids. They drive expensive sports cars, have everything they could ever want, and pretty much get to do whatever they want. Paulo has none of that. Most kids like him end up running with a gang somewhere and getting into all kinds of trouble. Maybe all of it just got to him and he snapped—it happens, you know?"

Billy didn't agree. "Not Paulo. He knew that education was his ticket out of all that. That's one reason why Sam took such an interest in him. That's exactly what her situation was like. She knew if she wanted to get out of that life for good, she had to make the grades that would give her a ride to a college and to a new life."

Mr. C. stared down at Billy. "Sam's life was bad … really bad."

Billy rubbed his eyes and leaned back in the seat. "Oh, yeah. Take the worst you could imagine and double it, and then you'd have Sam's life."

"I'm glad she has you … at least someone in her life that she can be truly transparent with." Mr. C. paused, and then looked at Billy soberly as he asked, "She does have you now, doesn't she?"

"*If* she'll have me. I was never good for her, and I really treated her wrong as our marriage began to fall apart. And truth be known, our marriage didn't actually fall apart, I sort of pushed it in that direction."

"So you've said before. But it's been a long time since then. You've grown up quite a bit from what I've heard … and seen with my own eyes. And Sam's had to come to deal with reality herself. She's taught school, paid bills, lived on her own, and matured in a lot of ways too. I have the feeling the two of you will be entering this new time in your lives with your eyes opened a little more, and with a whole lot of wisdom and experience that you didn't have before."

Billy chuckled. "You'd think." He then looked up at Mr. C. and said with as much sincerity as possible, "I just don't want to hurt her again … never again."

Mr. C. smiled and said, "Then don't. If you really don't want to, but you love her and want to be with her, then you commit to always doing right by her."

"Yeah, like Jeremy Crandall would've done."

Mr. C. slapped his hands together. "See, there you go again!"

"What?"

"You keep wanting to pass the buck, Billy! You want Sam to be treated right, but you don't necessarily want to be the one who has to sacrifice to do it! You love her and want to see her happy, but not more than you love yourself and want to keep yourself happy!"

"That's not true," Billy defended. "I just have this past of being … well … self-centered … and …"

"Exactly what I just said isn't it?" He waited for Billy to acknowledge that truth. "Well?"

Billy thought for a bit and then half-nodded. "I reckon. But it's not a deliberate thing that I've tried to do. I just tend to do what comes naturally."

"Bingo!" Mr. C. yelled out. Several in the waiting area looked over at him, but he kept up the energy. He had an important point to make with Billy. "We're all selfish, Billy, every single one of us in the human race. True love is defined when you care about the needs of someone else more than you do your own. You claim to love Sam, but you're willing to let some nice guy like Jeremy Crandall come in and do the honors because your track record has been that when the going gets tough, you get out. But has that changed your love for Sam? All these years later, when you met her again, had your love for her faded? Were you glad that you had divorced, glad that she was out of your life, or did you sit and whine about all the regrets as a result?"

Billy mumbled in reply, "Regret. Definitely regret."

"Exactly. So here you sit again, professing your love for her, but scared that you can't pull it off. Yet you've already confessed that having your way—loving her but leaving her because you weren't willing to sacrifice to keep her—only gave you a life full of regret. So what's the better choice here? Love her and live with her, be willing to sacrifice your own needs and wants at times when things get tough, or let somebody else do it who's already learned that sacrifice is worth it when it comes to doing the right thing and thinking about others first?"

"You make it sound so … obvious," Billy protested.

"Because it is!" he exclaimed in frustration that Billy was still arguing this point. "Did you really want to see her living happily ever after with Jeremy? In the bottom of your heart, is that what you *really* wanted? Or were you hoping for some kind of guarantee that if you stayed with her this time, *you* would have the integrity to love her and stick with her no matter what?"

Billy had to really think about that question. He loved Sam—loved her with all his heart. He wanted to be with her and thought it would be a simple decision when he suddenly came into all the money his mother had left him. But when Kirstie had walked into Blue Bayou and he saw the degree to which he had hurt Sam again, he realized that even when he tried to do the right thing, she ended up hurt anyway. It seemed inevitable. And when Jeremy Crandall walked in at that point in time, it appeared like the noble thing to do was let Jeremy have her.

"Even when I don't want to hurt her, I somehow manage to," Billy confessed wearily. "I just have this knack for making mistakes. Jeremy Crandall never did anything to hurt Sam."

"Two things here, Billy—first, Jeremy had no past with her and had only known her a few short months. Somewhere, sometime, he would've failed. And that brings up the second point—she loves you, not him. When you fail her, you get back up on your feet because you love her and because she loves you, and you put your life together again. But what would have happened when Jeremy failed? Why should Sam hold on? Her heart's always been with you. Talk about being hurt, she would have resented you more than you could know because you had convinced her that Jeremy was perfect … and that even if she didn't love him, life could still be good. When all along, Billy, she never wanted to be with him anyway. All she's ever wanted is you."

Billy gave him a questioning gaze. "She told you that?"

"More or less. She certainly didn't want Jeremy Crandall raising your child. This child would always be a reminder of her love for you—it would never die. And no matter how wonderful Jeremy might have been, he would never be you."

An attendant came into the area and walked over to Billy and Mr. C. "Mr. Marcum?" she asked softly.

"Yes, that's me," Billy said as he stood quickly. "Is she all right? Is it over? How's the baby?"

She smiled, and it gave him a small sense of relief. "Everything's fine for the moment. The damage was way more severe than they initially thought, but I believe they already told you that."

He nodded.

"They do think that a total reconstruction is eventually possible, and they did enough repair this time to hopefully encourage a positive healing process. In a couple of months, they believe a second surgery will most probably take care of it, with the possibility of a third, depending on how this one heals."

"And the baby?" Billy asked again.

"It was monitored throughout the entire operation, and I'm pleased to report that all vital signs are very positive."

"Positive? Is that like *good* positive and everything's okay, or is that like *okay* positive and we need to keep a watch on it?"

The lady grinned. "No one used those terms exactly, but I would say that everything is fine, but they will keep a watch on it no matter what to ensure the safety of the baby."

He took a deep breath and rolled his head around to release some of the tension that had hung on him since that first revelation on television that afternoon.

"Would you like to see her?" she asked him.

"Really?" Billy was surprised, but he had forgotten the hospital staff believed him to be her official and present husband, not her ex. "I can see her?"

"In a few minutes. They're trying to bring her out right now, and she'll be in quite a bit of pain. But as soon as they've got everything stabilized, I'll come back in to get you."

He felt more tension leave. "Can I stay with her tonight … you know … in her room?"

"Absolutely."

It was longer than a few minutes before they came to get him, and for a while Billy began to get edgy again. When the attendant finally reappeared, her warm smile put him at ease.

"She didn't want to wake up," the lady explained this time. "But she's alert and very grumpy at the moment. This would be the perfect time for her husband to see her."

Billy followed her past the main door and through several hallways before coming to the recovery room. He took a deep breath as they walked inside and hoped to find a way to ensure her of his commitment to her without revealing to any medical staff around that he wasn't her *real* husband. The lady pointed him toward a bed where Sam lay still wearing the puffy hat with her hair stuffed inside. He walked over slowly and gently leaned over her when he reached the bed.

"Hey, ponytail," he said softly. "I hear you've been giving them a hard time."

She barely grinned, but then asked first thing, "Is the baby all right? That's all I've been thinking about. They keep saying *yes*, but I don't see how it can be when I hurt so badly."

"The baby's fine," he assured her. "And they're keeping a good eye on it."

"How?" she wondered. "They can't even see it."

He looked at all the wires and plugs attached to her. "I'm guessing that some of this stuff is somehow connected to the baby." He tried to follow the wires. "This one," he pulled on a piece of rubber tubing that seemed to lead further down than the others, "looks like it might be headed to your lower areas."

A nurse walked by and commented, "That's her catheter."

"Oh," he replied quickly. "I guess that doesn't have anything to do with the baby. Let's see," he looked again.

"It's okay," she mumbled as she reached for his hand. He took hers right away. "I can't go back, Billy. I can't do it." Tears began to fall down the edge of her face. "He took away my life there. How can I go back? How can I trust any of them ever again?" She swallowed hard. "It was Paulo," she sniffed. "I … I … loved him … like he was almost my own son. How could he try to kill me?"

Billy had no idea what to say. "You don't have to go back, Sam." He knew that she needed to go back, that teaching was what made her most whole, but there was no way he would tell her that now.

"And what about Randy and Kurt?" she asked weakly.

He had hoped she wouldn't ask that now. Mr. C. had filled him in with all the horrible details while Sam was in surgery, and Kurt's father had been down twice to check on her. The story went that Randy had been the first to try and disarm Paulo. He had stood between Paulo and Sam and told him to calm down so he wouldn't do anything crazy. When Paulo told him to move, Randy had said he would have to shoot him before shooting Ms. Marcum. So Paulo shot him … right in the heart. He had died before the ambulance even got to the school. When Kurt saw that Paulo was serious about using the gun, he had tried to come at him from an angle and disarm him, but Paulo saw him and turned the gun on him. Kurt took a bullet in the gut, and was in critical condition.

"How are Randy and Kurt?" Sam asked him again.

"They're tough guys," Billy decided to say. "They'll probably pull through this better than you will."

"I hope so," she whispered, tears still streaming down the sides of her face. "They saved my life, Billy. I don't know if I can handle knowing something had happened to either one of them."

He reached over and wiped the tears from each side as he tried to imagine how much information she could take. It was bad enough that it had happened at all, but if she found out that Randy had died as a result, it would devastate her. And what kind of effect would that have on the baby? Could this situation get any more complicated?

"Mr. Marcum?" asked one of the nurses as she tapped him on the shoulder. "We'll need you to go on back to her room now if you don't mind. We have a few last minute procedures to finish up with here, and then we'll be moving her there."

"Not critical care?"

"No sir. She's not what we would term *critical* any longer. Her vitals are fine, the baby appears to be safe for the moment, and everything seems very stable. But the staff in her area will keep a close watch on her the next 24 hours. If you were planning on catching up with your sleep while staying in her room for the night, that ain't gonna happen."

"No problem," he assured her.

Eighty-Seven

Annie felt the emptiness of the house again in a big way. It had been hard enough with Stephen being gone. Each night lying down in their big bed all alone, realizing that she had never spent a night without him since they had married, had been close to impossible. Had she been a weaker woman, she would have refused to even try. But Annie was determined to somehow get on with her life. Even so, the nights never got easier. What was worse was when she would dream about him and everything was back to normal, and then she would awaken and reach over to hold him only to find he wasn't there. Then she had to face the reality all over again.

Angie and Michael had gone back to the little apartment over her parents' garage so they could wash some clothes and straighten things up. Since Jonathan's heart attack, everything had been chaotic, and the house had fallen in from every side. So at Annie's there were no babies cooing or crying, no Cassie demanding answers for the existence of everything she saw, and no Michael crawling around on the floor playing with his daughter or telling his infant boys about the life they would find when they returned to Padawin.

She knew she needed to pray. She needed to pray for her father who was still not out of the danger zone. And even when he recovered, he had to walk back into a church that was falling apart. Then there was the whole issue with Uncle Toby. Why was he there? Why had he come? No one had seen or heard from him again since the heart attack, and it all just seemed downright fishy.

And poor Andie. Adam had pleaded with her to let him go back to public school, and as much as she didn't want to do it, it just seemed like the most logical choice. His subjects were getting harder, and as bright as Andie was, her gifts had always been in music, and that was pretty much it. Then there was the homeschooling with the three others, plus little Lainey tagging along behind her every second of the day who happened to be almost as inquisitive as Cassie, just not as demanding for complicated answers. Because of all that, spending large amounts of time with Adam trying to explain algebraic concepts that she had never quite gotten herself was becoming too much. Her broken ankle didn't help either. But when a teacher, who happened to also be a deacon's wife, took she and Doug aside at church to tell them that she had overheard Adam using some harsh profanity—not just the *average* type, but the *hard core* stuff—Andie was devastated. When she and Doug had faced Adam with the information, he just clammed up and wouldn't admit to anything. They told him that because he had no defense, they had to assume the teacher was telling the truth. When asked why he would fall into such a thing when he wasn't even allowed to hear profanity on television because of their foul-language-filter, he just shrugged and looked the other way.

Annie should also be praying for Samantha Marcum, Billy's ex-wife. She had met her once, and she seemed like a really nice girl. She wondered why Billy had left her, but then, he was Billy. What woman could possibly tame Billy Marcum and turn him into a faithful, one-woman-man? But he was now at her side at the hospital in Sheffield as she had been shot by a student and severely wounded. Maybe this would bring Billy back to reality and make him realize that love is worth the sacrifice.

Love is worth the sacrifice? she asked herself. *Is it really?* She thought about all that Andie had said to her, about her pride, about her need for perfection. Annie knew those to be true, but was she so stubborn that she was willing to sacrifice the love of her life to save her self-built reputation, to keep her image in tact? Here she was so ready to condemn Billy Marcum for not being willing to unselfishly give up everything for the sake of the woman he loves, and yet she was pretty much in the same boat. Her reason for not talking with Stephen did start out with the fact that she was tired of his demeaning her and reminding her of her mistake. But when he had brought up talking through the lawyers, she snapped. At that point it became very much a personal vendetta. No one would threaten Annie Wright Williams. No one made the rules but her. And rather than give their marriage a chance to heal, she chose to make him eat his words. It would have worked perfectly … had her father not had that heart attack on Sunday because of Toby, or Carter, or Hal Bridges.

It was then that a horrible thought hit her. *Surely, God, this isn't all my fault. This didn't happen to my daddy just to make me swallow my pride and be forced to speak with Stephen. You wouldn't do that to Daddy, would you? Or to Moms?* She shook the thoughts from her head and tried to close her eyes in the disconcerting silence of her huge house. As the hours passed, she realized it was highly unlikely that she would show up in California looking refreshed and beautiful when she saw Stephen again for the first time in six months. And it was impossible that she would show up not looking extremely pregnant.

✪✪✪

Stephen opened the door of his loft to see if Jeff, his personal bodyguard, was still on duty. There he sat—faithful and alert outside the door.

"Stephen?" Jeff spoke as he jumped up from the chair. "Is

everything alright?"

Stephen calmed him with his hand and assured him, "Everything's fine. I just needed an ear for a moment. Are you available?"

"Absolutely." Jeff grabbed a folded chair from the wall, opened it, and placed it beside him in the hallway. "I don't need to leave the door for another hour and a half." He then chuckled. "I can protect you, I suppose, just as well if you're sitting beside me as locked up in there."

"This is fine," Stephen said as he turned the chair around and straddled it, leaning his arms across the back. "The kids are asleep, and I'd rather not take the chance of waking them. I don't want them to have black circles under their eyes when they fly back to Annie's tomorrow."

Jeff nodded.

Then Stephen began with the big one. "I sent her divorce papers on Monday."

Jeff was taken aback. "Wo, I didn't realize it was all that serious … that final."

Stephen slumped over his arms. "I didn't know what else to do. She won't talk to me no matter what I do. I've tried everything possible, but she's shut me out big time. I assumed the only thing left to do was let her have what she apparently wants—a permanent and legal separation from me."

Jeff rubbed his hands on his knees and glanced down the hall as a matter of habit. "I can't believe that, Stephen … that she really wants to be divorced. You guys had a great thing, and I ought to know."

"You ought to know?" Stephen sniggered. "You've never been married."

"No, but I've been around enough married celebrities to know what works and what doesn't." He glanced down the hall again and then gave his full attention to Stephen. "Listen, I worked for two other people before taking on this job with you. Both of them were married, at least in name and on paper. But their marriages were jokes. As you know, they're both divorced now, but that was no surprise for me.

"But when Annie came on board, even before the two of you had a *thing* for each other, there was this dynamic about you guys that I'd never seen before."

"Dynamic?" Stephen teased him. "That's a pretty intellectual word for a bodyguard, isn't it?"

Jeff smiled. "Yeah, go on and make fun of me. But who's the guy you're spilling your guts to right now."

Stephen sobered. "Good point. So go on—Annie and I had this *dynamic* about us."

"Yeah … it was like you were on the same level. You were an awesome pianist, so was she. You wrote great music, so did she. You could work up an audience and have them eating out of your hand, and she just jumped in there right beside you, taking it to a whole other level."

Stephen smiled at the memories. "You're right about that, and yet she was so nervous about performing in front of that many people … especially *my* fans. She thought they'd hate her."

"Fat chance," Jeff laughed. "In fact, if you hadn't been so infatuated with her, you would have been jealous. And then when you guys fell in love, it was like WHAM!" and he slammed his palms on his bulky thighs. Stephen jumped. "Suddenly everything that you were became better. You played music together, and it was another level higher. You wrote songs together, and suddenly *Autumn Sunset* just became the warm up for *Winter Passion*. And you ate it up. It was like everything you did before was mediocre compared to life with Annie."

"Absolutely true, Jeff."

"Then came the kids," he said with a gigantic grin. "Man, I had never seen you so happy … never. And the two of you together as parents was just as *right* as the two of you on stage with your music." Jeff looked back down the hall and tried to think of the best words to describe them. "Man, Stephen, you just *worked*. Know what I mean?"

"Yes. Completely. Unmistakably."

"I guess that's why I'm so confused about all of this. You guys had this great communication thing going. I can't tell you how many times one of you said something that could've easily gotten the other all riled up, and believe me, I know about stuff like that. I literally pulled a guy off his wife one time when she set him off real good. But one of you would say something, and the other would just diffuse the whole thing with a laugh or a gentle remark or even an embrace. I was amazed. After a while I just stopped worrying. It was kind of a relief, you know? It wasn't like either of you was this major star, major talent, and the other should be pleased to grovel at your feet. Instead, you were these two really great people who appreciated each other's greatness."

Stephen was stunned. "Gee, Jeff, I never knew you were so sensitive … or so observant."

"Well, I am." Jeff cleared his throat. "Which leads me to a question I really have no business asking."

Stephen raised an eyebrow. "Go for it. I'm seeing a whole new side to you here, buddy. If we have many more discussions like this, I'm gonna call Oprah and see if we can get you your own show. We could call it *Dr. Jeff*, or something really catchy like that."

He gave a little laugh, but then pondered his question again. "What happened?" He shook his head. "I just can't imagine what happened."

Stephen began from the beginning. What did he have to lose? Jeff had been with him even longer than Annie had, and he had obviously seen the difference she had made in his life. He laid out the whole story and then waited for Jeff's analysis.

"Wow, Stephen," Jeff said as he shook his head. "That was really stupid of you."

He was startled by his honesty, but he did need to hear that truth. "Thanks for breaking it to me easily. I feel so much better about it all right now."

"Don't get me wrong," Jeff responded instantly. "It wasn't right of her to keep that from you, but that's where *you* broke the harmony."

"The harmony?"

"Right. Remember when I said that you two could diffuse each other? You didn't this time … and you wouldn't let her do it either. She tried, but you wouldn't listen. And then the stuff you insisted on about the kids, man, that's what the nut-head celebrities do. And Stephen, no offense against Annie, but you know how she is. She's a little hotheaded, a little stubborn, a little opinionated. You kind of have to take that into consideration when you're dealing with her." Jeff gave him a serious look. "I don't think you forgot about all that; I think you just didn't care for a while there. And I think you're paying the price for it."

"But what about her?" Stephen claimed his defense. "What about what she did to me?"

"Heavens, man! She apologized! She let you have the kids with very little protest! If you would've been in your right mind, you would've called on the way to the airport that day and said you'd overreacted and asked if you could come back and talk! Instead, you let Ben Brenner and his lack of moral excellence become your voice of conscience and you just kept on and on, nailing it in that what she did was unforgivable. Obviously it didn't take her long to believe that."

Stephen bit his lip. He didn't want this to be his fault, but if truth be known, it was his pride that had taken over, and it was his pride that had cost him the most wonderful gift he had ever received … faults and all.

"So what do I do, Jeff?" he finally asked. "She won't talk to me—she won't communicate in any way. She doesn't even send messages through her lawyer. If I ask something, her answer is always to do whatever I want, even with the kids. I mean look at the timing of this visit!" Stephen went quiet as his face turned red.

"What? What about it?"

Stephen hated to admit it, but his own guilt was eating away at him. "I demanded they visit me the week before the last week of Stevie's school year because I assumed it would rile her up and she would say something … anything … about it."

Jeff shook his head. "And here they are. Let me guess, with no protest from Annie."

"Nothing from her. Stevie has griped about it quite a bit —missing his field trip—but Annie just sent them on."

Jeff looked at him and sighed deeply. "If I were you, man, I'd start praying harder than I ever had before."

"I have been," Stephen said hopelessly as he stood from the chair and began to fold it. "Apparently God has chosen not to answer me either."

Eighty-Eight

The nurse wasn't kidding; if Billy had slept a total of two hours altogether that night, not just at one time, he would be surprised. His neck ached from the impossible positions he had maneuvered himself into on the makeshift chair-turned-into-bed, and he desperately needed to brush his teeth. As the next nurse came in to take Sam's temperature and blood pressure, as well as check all the machines to make sure everything was functioning as it should be, he decided to get on up.

He practically crawled from the contraption, sore and stiff, and slowly stood to his feet. After a good, long stretch and a trip to the bathroom, he quietly checked on Sam, careful not to wake her from the sleep he hoped she was enjoying. She had moaned off and on all night, and even screamed out at one time. When he jumped up to see if she was okay, she mumbled Paulo's name and then drifted again. He figured she had no idea he was even there with her, and he could've gone on back to her house to at least get a decent night's sleep, but that's not what he wanted. He wanted to be there for her every moment and to make sure she knew she could count on him from this time forward.

As he examined her closely, he took note of how much bandaging was on her shoulder. The doctors kept emphasizing the damage was significant and there was a chance that her arm may not be of much use if things didn't go well. He thought of Sam's declaration after the surgery that she didn't want to teach again. As a right-hander, that might end up being a good idea just out of practicality. But he couldn't imagine her not teaching. It was her life. It was as if that's what she was born to do. It had brought her the greatest fulfillment and had been her salvation for many reasons. If she didn't teach, what else would she do?

The baby. She would be a mother. The thought made him smile, and for a moment he let his mind drift to a place somewhere in the future where the three of them were altogether, happy, and at last complete. Then he thought of Cindy. When he had called her yesterday evening to let her know Sam's condition and that she had gone into surgery, he had conveniently left out the news of the pregnancy. She would freak. She had pounded into Billy the fact that he had better take things really slow, extremely slow, so slow that it wasn't even moving in any direction. He had listened well, but the weekend surrounding Frank's funeral had brought out … what? What had it actually revealed? What really had happened there that was any different from all the other times they had been together? He had lived with her for over a month after his accident, but nothing had happened then. Of course, the consistent presence of Jeremy Crandall had helped to put the brakes on during that time.

He thought of how confused and vulnerable and broken Sam had been during that weekend in Georgia. Then he remembered how he felt knowing that she had chosen him to be the one to go with her and not Crandall. As they pretended to be married again, he was determined to play the role publicly to the tee so that no one would doubt his and Sam's joy, as well as her ability to leave her lousy life and find happiness-ever-after. He knew she was showing a strong front around the community, but when she would go back to their room, she would melt to pieces. He couldn't handle that. He should have still been married to her, nothing should have been a show, and her whole life since their divorce should have never happened—he never should have left her … never.

So how did he tell Cindy? At some point she was bound to find out, and simple math could easily add up the months to determine when it all happened. But was he putting the cart before the horse? He had yet to explain his decision to Sam. What if he had rejected her so much by pushing her toward Crandall that she now had no desire to put her heart in a position to ever trust, or love, him again?

"I have so many questions, Sam," he whispered softly as he gently removed a strand of hair from her face and tucked it behind her ear. "I need you to get better so we can plan our life again … so we can decide what to do when we become a family." He leaned down and barely kissed her forehead. "But sleep for now."

✡✡✡

Because of the sudden change in plans, this time the plane was leaving out of Memphis, and Annie was glad she had decided to call a limo rather than let Angie drive her to the airport. This would also give her and the kids a chance to calm down after the flight home from California that evening. Annie despised flying with as much passion as she loved music. She had slowly grown accustomed to it during the years that she and Stephen had toured, but she had never liked it. She appreciated its speed and the fact that even though her children might be a thousand miles away, they were only a few short hours by air. But she still didn't like it. The last times she had flown, Stephen had always held her hand tightly and sang some silly song to get her mind off of the take-offs and landings, but he wouldn't be with her this time. She wondered if he would even show at the airport. So far, her father had said he was always there, both for the drop-off and the pick-up. She had so psyched herself up to face him that if he didn't show, it would be a miserable letdown.

The limo driver knew exactly where to take her so they could avoid the crowds as well as lose the seven cars that had followed from

Dockrey. No one had actually gotten a look at her through the dark windows, but with all the paparazzi still camped outside the gate of her property, several had jumped into vehicles just in case she was in the limo, and they were bound to have put it all together that it was the day the kids were to be picked up and Annie was actually doing the job herself this time. She knew that every flight from Memphis to L.A. would be covered by several reporters and photographers hoping to be the first to get a glimpse of Annie Williams after months of being a hermit. Phone calls would have been made, and preparations were no doubt in place to capture this big emergence for all to see. And what a sight it would be! Annie in all her six-month-pregnancy glory! She found herself laughing at the thought.

Sure enough, as soon as security escorted her into the building and moved her toward the gate, cameras began to flash frantically and questions began to be yelled out.

"How far along are you, Annie!'

"Is this why you've been hiding!"

"Are you and Stephen divorcing!"

She said nothing but continued to walk steadily toward the inspection area where she knew the staff would let her immediately come to the front and pass her measly bag through the machine. The entire time she was going through the scrutiny, cameras were flashing and questions were being fired out. When at last finished with the security check, she headed down to her gate. A few paparazzi had actually bought tickets and were waiting inside for her. As she prepared to walk through the long tunnel leading to her flight, she paused for a deep breath in hopes of fighting off the horrid sense of claustrophobia she always felt at this point. A few more cameras flashed, and a few more questions were yelled. She rolled her eyes, took another deep breath, and wished like crazy for a Valium to make all this ugliness just go away.

☼☼☼

Stephen took one final look around the loft to see if the kids had left anything. This was one of those situations that he had never really learned to appreciate Annie for. She always managed to pack for herself and both of the kids very efficiently, while he was lucky to leave with enough underwear for the allotted time. As he glanced through the apartment, he found several things that had not made it into any of the luggage. Usually the kids just had carry-on stuff to avoid the whole baggage claim business, but because of a trip to Disneyland and another to a famous costume shop, the souvenirs had gotten out of control. He ended up with a very large extra suitcase to carry all the memories in, and was hoping he could sweet talk the attendants into stashing it somewhere on the main deck of the jet.

He opened the extra case and tried to stuff five more things inside.

"Stevie!" he yelled as he couldn't quite get it to shut. "Stand on top of this thing so I can buckle it, will you?"

"Take out that stupid crown," Stevie suggested. "Ellie ain't a real princess anyway. She don't need it."

Ellie shot right back with, "And you ain't Spiderman! Take *it* out, Daddy."

Stephen buckled the case and then smiled. "We *ain't* taking anything out, but I doubt we're putting anything else in here." He grinned at his use of the word *ain't.* Annie despised it, and every time the kids had used it she would go ballistic. But it seemed to be a very acceptable word in Dockrey, so no matter how hard they tried, the kids had picked it up anyway and found it easier to use than *proper English.*

"Is Gaga gonna be there when we get there?" Ellie asked anxiously, always worried that this particular part of the whole visitation might fall through. She was never completely sure that she would be returned to her home.

"He always is," Stephen assured her.

"Good," she nearly fumed as she grabbed her stuffed Thumper and tossed her backpack onto her shoulders. "Let's go."

"Yes, ma'am," Stephen said with a salute.

The ride to the airport was typical. Stephen tried to point out some major landmarks to help familiarize them with *his* town now, but all they wanted to do was talk about seeing their mother, sleeping in their own beds, playing with their cousins, and eating *real* food again. Stephen tried not to be disappointed, but he was slowly losing his children, and it was killing him inside. He had lost Annie, and when it came right down to it, he knew it was his own fault. Like Jeff had said last night, he knew her temperament, and at some point he should have eased off and told her all he really wanted was space, not separation. But he hadn't done that, and now he stood on the verge of losing everything in his life that was really important.

And what about the children? Was it right for him to continue to demand they visit him like this? They hated the visits, and he had to confess that when they left it was a huge relief. He had to give himself a full day to merely recover, and then another week or two to get over the emotional letdown. He knew they loved him, but he wasn't a part of their family any longer. Somehow they understood that he was the one who had abandoned them, had left the family, and wanted to build a life away from them. They didn't want to lose him completely, but at four and five, they couldn't make sense of one home in Alabama and one in California, yet the family didn't live anywhere together. Daddy lived at one, and everyone else lived together at the *real home.* Daddy's was lonely and strange and cold, but the other one was warm and happy and familiar. One was filled with cool, yet unfamiliar items, while the other was filled with memories. How could he continue to do this to them? They were so young.

The limo followed the familiar path, and Stephen had expected the typical fare of reporters and photographers, but he wasn't prepared for the crew that had gathered there today. He pressed a button and slid open the window separating the back of the limo from the driver.

"Bill," he said as he leaned his head forward, "is there an alternate entrance into the airport? The paparazzi are like a plague out there today."

"Way ahead of you, sir," he said as he held up a phone. "They're going to let us go to the north entrance. They're notifying security to meet us there."

"Super," Stephen said with relief. "You're a fine man, Bill, a fine man."

"Very good, sir. That's what you pay me for."

The limo pulled in through a different entrance and threw those waiting outside for a loop, but Stephen knew there would be just as many on the inside. He wondered what on earth could have set them off this time. All it took was a little tip from someone somewhere that something even insignificantly newsworthy might take place, and they would come crawling from every cave in the area.

Sure enough, as soon as they were spotted inside the building, cameras and questions began to start. He tuned them out. All he wanted was to get to the gate and see Jonathan standing there with his sympathetic smile. Security was always good about letting Stephen go through inspection with the children and then stay with them until they boarded. Today was no different.

"Have a good day, Mr. Williams," one of the security said as they put their shoes back on.

"I appreciate it … Bobby," he replied as he glanced at the man's nametag.

Ellie's steps got a little bit faster the closer they got to the gate. Her anticipation of seeing her grandfather was directly related to her return to normalcy. Stephen's heart sank a little bit each time this happened. It was just another reminder of all he had lost.

Jeff stepped up next to Stephen with a worried look. "Something's up," was his simple statement. "Look at all the cameras and stares. It's almost like someone was tipped off about something, and they're here to catch the big moment."

Stephen opened his eyes wider and looked around. Jeff was right. Stephen held Ellie's hand a little tighter, but Jeff scooped her up in his arms.

"Get Stevie," Jeff commanded to an officer walking with them.

"No," Stephen said instantly as if some baser instinct took over. "I'll get him. You guys just keep a good watch. I don't like what I'm seeing here."

Stephen picked up Stevie and quickened the pace to the gate. He was relieved to see that the plane had landed and was in the process of getting hooked up. The crowd was very attentive to all that was happening, and Stephen watched Jeff pull Ellie a little closer. He did the same with Stevie. Whatever was happening here was obviously a mistake. It must be a slow news day and everyone was planning on making his and Annie's separation the main story this next week.

Then it hit him—the divorce. Someone had let out the news of their divorce! Someone in one of the lawyer's offices had jumped the gun and let the press know that Stephen had sent the papers. It could also be highly possible that Jonathan was bringing them with him and would hand deliver them to Stephen himself. He felt his stomach begin to grow nauseous. He didn't want this to be a public display. Someone, at least one person, maybe more, would lose their job over this leak. He was livid.

Jeff leaned into him and asked, "You okay?"

He ground his teeth together and tried to keep his cool. "I figured out what this is. Someone must have spilled the news that I sent Annie the papers. Her father is probably bringing them with him." He shook his head slowly in anger. "Someone will pay for this."

"That's all conjecture," Jeff said confidently. "Just stay cool. Don't give them anything to shoot."

The first of the attendants came through the doorway, and Stephen knew that meant Jonathan would be next, but when cameras started flashing from paparazzi who had actually bought tickets so they could enter this area, he began to wonder if this was even about him. There must be someone else on the jet. He peeled his eyes toward the exit and waited to see who would come through, but he wasn't prepared for what happened next.

As soon as Annie appeared, the kids screamed in delight. They wiggled relentlessly in both Jeff and Stephen's arms, but it took the men a few moments to catch up. They were preparing themselves for something slightly atrocious, and Annie wasn't at all what they had in mind. Jeff got it together first and realized that Stephen was standing there in a daze. Jeff let Ellie go to her mother, and then took Stevie from Stephen's arms so he could join the greeting. Stephen just stared. There she was, as beautiful as ever, though extremely pale, her face thin and gaunt … and her middle very pregnant. The sound of cameras whizzing and flashing and the shouts of strangers toward him and Annie didn't exist in his world at that moment. All he saw was her, and he couldn't believe she was here.

Jeff came up beside him and grabbed his arm. "What are you

waiting for, man? Get over there! You've just been offered the chance you were praying for!"

Stephen swallowed and began to slowly move toward her. It literally seemed like a dream to him, and he was almost afraid that, like in his dreams, if he reached her, she would disappear. So far, she had avoided his gaze, but when she saw him coming toward her, she stopped noticing the children and just stared at him. So much was written on her face that Stephen felt like falling to the ground and confessing his wrongs in all of this. The hurt and the despair were so evident in her eyes that he felt anger begin to rise in his belly … all directed toward himself.

He then looked down to her stomach. She was definitely pregnant. He slammed his eyes shut as another wave of guilt flushed over him. All this time she had not only been carrying the guilt of what she had done, but she had been carrying his child, a reminder of the passion and joy they had always shared throughout their marriage. When he finally reached her, no words could be said by either of them. The kids were jumping and giggling, thoroughly thrilled at this turn of events, but Annie and Stephen could only look at each other in frustration. They should embrace or smile or something, but then again this wasn't like before. They were divorcing, they were no longer together, and the hurt and rejection and betrayal that had passed between them were standing thick like a fortress. Neither could move, either forward or backward. They just continued to stand.

Jeff finally stepped in and suggested, "You guys need to go somewhere … private. You want me to arrange that?"

Annie shook her head, her long hair in a loose ponytail hanging way down her back. Stephen longed to reach his hand up and touch the silkiest hair he had ever felt.

"I've got to get going toward the return flight," she said weakly. "I've only got about forty-five minutes."

Jeff leaned toward her, "Forget the stupid flight, Annie. I'll personally pay for another one later."

She just shook her head and looked away as her eyes began to water. But Stephen immediately took her hand, causing her to look back at him.

"Please," he begged, his tired eyes giving away the desperation he was feeling. "Please don't go … yet. I'll do anything, Annie, if you'll just come back with me so we can talk … just a little while … please."

Her heart was pleading with her to go with him, but her head reminded her that it would avail nothing. There were divorce papers sitting on her computer desk back home in Alabama, and that was the reality.

She shook her head again. "There's a lot going on back home. I need to get back there … soon."

He squeezed her hand tighter. "Please," he pleaded. "I'd rather not get on my knees here in front of all these strangers trying to invade our life right now, but if that's what it'll take to get you to spend a couple of hours with me, I'll do it." He then leaned in close enough that she could see the flecks of gray in his blue eyes and added, "I have no pride when it comes to you, Annie. Nothing is more important than you. Please."

"Let's go, Mommy!" Ellie yelled in excitement. "Let's go home!"

"Hang on," Stephen said firmly, never taking his eyes off Annie. "Mommy's going to come to my house for a little bit."

Ellie didn't look thrilled about that idea, but Stevie's eyes lit up. "Really? Mommy's coming to your place?"

Annie looked down at their children and her heart could have broken at the anticipation in Stevie's face. She wanted to go with Stephen right now more than anything in the world, but her pride was holding her back. He had admitted to her that nothing was more important, not even his own pride. Could she not just take this one step and put her pride behind her also?

Without looking back up to Stephen, she nodded and said, "Yes, we're all going back to Daddy's, but only for a little bit. We need to get home tonight."

That was all Stephen needed to hear. If he could have just one hour with her, that would be enough to abase himself, declare his love, and confess his utter stupidity in all of this.

Jeff was on the go immediately. This time he grabbed both Stevie and Ellie and began to move the entourage quickly toward the exit. He yelled over at one of the other security men, "Let Bill know Stephen needs to be picked up immediately."

"Will do," the man replied as he pulled his phone from his pocket.

The crowd of photographers was almost impenetrable, and the cameras were capturing the moment with constant flashes. The group pushed through the crowd without too much trouble, and Bill was waiting at the door with several of the airport security surrounding the car. The kids were ushered in first, and then Stephen helped Annie inside. Normally he would have turned to the cameras and smiled, saying something witty or appreciative of the support, but at the moment all he wanted was to toss a grenade in each direction and blow them to pieces. They had no idea what was at stake here, and they were clueless as to how stressful they were making it.

As they rode back to Stephen's loft, the kids were in high gear. Stephen wished they could somehow be removed to somewhere else for just a little bit so he could talk to Annie alone, but he knew that wasn't going to happen. He was pleased to hear them talk about Disneyland as though it had been a great and glorious experience. Perhaps he hadn't lost his appeal to them as a father completely. If he could work things out with Annie this afternoon, perhaps they could all start over. Maybe they could be a real family again and live like they did before, as though the world were perfect.

Eighty-Nine

Sam's discomfort remained intense all day. The doctors were allowing a large amount of pain medication the first 24 hours to help take the edge off, but Billy was beginning to worry. That couldn't be good for the baby, and Sam was barely able to say anything intelligible. He had tried to talk her through some of the pain, but it was to no avail. She wasn't communicating anything to anybody except that she hurt horribly.

Cindy had called twice, and he had updated her on everything, everything except his concerns for the baby. Thankfully Mr. C. came by which allowed him the opportunity to vent his fears and frustrations. Mr. C. had tried to talk to Sam and then prayed for her before he left, and just that little sense of giving it all over to God, even the baby, was comforting to Billy. As he sat beside her and stared helplessly, realizing there wasn't a thing he could do to help her, he nearly broke. He felt overwhelming guilt because there had been many times in his life when he could've helped her but didn't. He hadn't wanted the responsibility of making her happy or caring for her when it was a little inconvenient. But now he was willing to do whatever it took to see her happy and healthy again.

He took his hand and gently ran it over her tummy. He had no idea how big a three month old baby might be, but in his mind he could imagine it curled up comfortably inside her, clueless of the turmoil going on with its mother.

"Hang on in there, little one," he said softly. "It's gonna be tough for a while, but I'm gonna do everything I can to make sure you show up in one piece … everything I can."

The emotions were overwhelming. He felt guilt, but he also felt relief at finally having made a real decision about Sam. He loved her, and as soon as she was ready, he wanted to marry her. But he felt scared because of the agony she was in right now. He knew it was possible for infections or complications to set in, and Sam wasn't out of the woods yet. And everything that happened to her also happened to the baby. He had only known he was a father-to-be for twenty-four hours, but it had changed his whole outlook on life. All the dreams, all the goals, all the things he had worked for were meaningless compared to Sam and this baby. But what if he lost them both? He had lost his father and mother. God's final just blow on his life might be to take Sam and the baby too. That would utterly destroy him.

Sweat began to bead up on his forehead—almost as if his fears were actually surfacing. He jumped up from the chair and went to the window. Glancing out over the lights of the city, he thought of how easy it was to turn one off or turn one on—just the flip of a single switch. Sam's life could be gone just like that. God could flip the switch and … blink … her light would be out. That's how it had been with his father. Billy hadn't even been able to say goodbye. He couldn't make any promises or tell him what a great dad he had been. He couldn't thank him for the sacrifices he had made or for the opportunities he had offered. But most of all, he didn't have the chance to tell him he was sorry for all the rebellion and humiliation that had swept through his life.

His mother went slowly. As Billy had watched her deteriorate, he realized he had the chance to make a real change before she died, and that she could go believing he was on a right path at last. It had worked and given him a small bit of relief from the guilt he had felt with his father.

But Sam was different. She had been persecuted and tortured her whole life, yet when she met Billy, he could have been everything she'd ever dreamed of. And he was … for a while.

He squinted back the tears as he looked up toward the rising moon.

Dear God, he whispered softly in prayer, *if You can hear me, and if what Cindy says is true, that You love me, that You really do love me and sent Jesus to die for my sins, then I only have one request for You. You don't have to save me; I'm not worth it. But if You love Sam half as much as I do, spare her life and the baby's too. I suppose that really counts for two requests, but I'm desperate here. I know You listened to Cindy and You turned her life around. You gave her a husband and a family, and she has a reason for living that's more than just about pleasing herself. Mr. C. was right when he said I was too selfish to really care about Sam, but if You'll give me another chance, I'll love her so deeply and so fully that she'll never doubt that love again.*

He had been such a fool. All those years running around like some cocky stud, thinking everyone was graced just to be in his presence, seemed like a pure waste now. What he would give to go back and start all over. He would begin by listening in church and trying to be obedient to God and his parents instead of being so obsessed over Angie Wright's body during the services. And he would treat her with the respect she deserved. Good lands! She had grown up to be a missionary, had a slew of kids, and even lost one, but considered the little time she had with him a gift from God. He would also have listened to his father and have respected his work. He would have taken the summer jobs his dad had always offered. And he would have applied himself in school and gone on to finish college just like his mother had pleaded with him to do until her dying day.

But I can't go back, God, can I? All those wasted years … gone. All the people I used and abused … the deeds are done, and I can't take them back. You changed

Cindy, and you changed Frank. You cleaned them up and gave them a reason to live again. Can You really do that for me? I know I was bad, but I wasn't as bad as Frank. Surely, God, You can change me too.

Billy had been in church from the time he was one week old until high school graduation. He knew the doctrine and the language, but it always seemed foreign to him. It wasn't that he doubted God—it was more like he just didn't want God. He had his life all wrapped up just as he liked it, and the thought of bringing God in to do a little rearranging wasn't promising at all. Yet here he stood at the most desperate time in his life, and the only One he could turn to was the very One he had always rejected.

He found himself falling to his knees as he began to silently weep over his life. He had nothing to show for it that was worth anything to God. God had blessed him abundantly, but every blessing God had given, he had taken and used for his own advantage. Even his diploma would be worthless if Sam were to die, or worse, reject him.

I'm sorry, Lord, he softly cried out. *I don't deserve anything from You, least of all Your mercy. But if You are the God that Cindy says You are, then I'm pleading for my life here. I'm so full of myself and sin, that I don't know where one starts and the other ends. And even when I think about my baby whose life lies in the balance at this moment, I'll always remember that it was even conceived in sin. I can't escape the wretchedness that I've always embraced, but if You could, if You would, let the blood shed by Your Son on the cross come and wash away all that's unholy and impure inside of me. Just make me new, Lord, like You did with Cindy and with Frank. My baby may have been conceived in sin, but it'll be brought up in a home that trusts God and hates evil.*

And Sam, Lord, let her give her life to You. Help me to be so changed that I can really love her like she needs to be loved. Don't let me keep on hurting her and rejecting her, because that's exactly what I've done. And dear God, don't let her believe that I can only love her if it's something physical … but that I'll love her always … and forever.

As he stayed on his knees, a peace began to wash over him, and the tears of anguish and regret that had been flowing from his soul began to change into tears of joy and delight as he realized for the first time in his life he was out from beneath the burden of impressing the world with who he was. From now on he would simply do one thing—seek to obey God.

Ninety

The ride in the limousine to Stephen's loft was mainly filled with talk and laughter from the children. Stephen and Annie said nothing except to answer a question or respond to a remark. She avoided his eyes as much as possible because she wasn't ready to be really honest with him yet. It would take more than a simple gesture for her to open up after all the hurt she had experienced. But when she did catch his eyes, the love that had always been between them rose inside her, at first she thought like a fountain, but the longer the drive lasted, the more it seemed like a volcano. Her heart was ready to scream out to him to please forgive her and to hold her and to never leave her side again. But then there was that other part, the part of Annie that always won. It was the part that was going to kill this marriage if she didn't find some way to shut it up between the airport and the apartment.

When Stephen opened the loft door, the kids ran inside and immediately began to climb on the trampoline.

"Look at this, Mommy!' Stevie called out. "Look what Daddy bought for us! We can jump inside!"

Annie glanced over at the trampoline in shock, but then she began to look around the loft. It was a massive room, and Stephen had filled it with things she knew he believed would attract the children. There was a whole area with a large screen television where they could sit on bean bags and watch TV or play video games. There was a small swing set in one corner, complete with a slide and teeter-totter. It was really a kids' dream home.

She then realized that the loft was it—it was the only room with the exception of one corner that held a bathroom. His king-sized bed was on one side of the room, and the kids' bunk beds were on the other. She almost laughed because she knew what a light sleeper he was, and that Ellie was known for talking, jerking, and yelling in her sleep. He had probably started out closer to them but moved the beds out of desperation.

"Can I get you something to eat?" he asked her as he looked with deep concern. She was way too thin to be this far along in her pregnancy, and her face was more pale than he had ever seen.

"No thanks," she said politely. "I'm not hungry at all."

Ellie burst out with, "She never eats anything anymore, Daddy!" Bounce, bounce, bounce. "And when she does, she just gets sick!"

"Does not!' Stevie yelled out after her. "She likes soup crackers! She eats them a lot!"

Stephen's look of concern grew more sober. "Really? That's why you're so thin? You're not eating?"

She shook her head as she took a tired breath. "I just need to sit down."

"Of course!" he said embarrassed. "I'm sorry, Annie. Here." He led her to a cozy couch, the most comfortable looking thing in the room with the exception of the huge bed covered in the thick, down comforter. "I should have offered you a seat before something to eat."

He watched as she maneuvered herself down slowly. The couch was low, and since her balance was off center because of the baby, an awkward move could lead to an awkward accident. Stephen instinctively wanted to help her, but he knew he wasn't truly welcomed. He could still feel the tension between them, and it wasn't going to leave any time soon.

"Food," he went back to his original thought.

She shook her head again. "I'm really not hungry, but if you'll tell me what all you've got in the kitchen, something might pop out as appealing."

He started to blush. "There's … uh … nothing in the kitchen."

She looked up at him in surprise. "Really? Nothing? You've gone back to your bachelor ways, I see."

"Old habits die hard," he confessed. "Besides, I wasn't gifted with your culinary upbringing. About all I can do is grill steaks. Other than that I'm a wash at it all. But hey, this isn't Dockrey. I can order just about anything you could want and have it here between fifteen and thirty minutes."

"Chinese!" yelled Stevie from the trampoline again.

"Yeah!" Ellie agreed. "Chinese!" She then followed with each syllable corresponding to a bounce. "Sweet … and … so-ur … chick-en!"

Stephen looked down at Annie. "Sound good to you? The kids have lived off of that stuff."

"I'm really not hungry. To be frank with you, I'm a little nauseous at the moment. Maybe a soft drink or something?"

"Tell you what, I'll order some wonton soup along with Pork Egg Foo Yung, Shrimp with Lobster Sauce, and a thing of fried rice. If you're still not hungry when all those aromas begin to swim around the room, I'll force you to eat a few bites of the soup and ease my conscience."

She smiled. He had just listed her favorites from a Chinese menu. She wanted to stay hard and protected, but his concern and insistence that she eat was a huge step in tearing down a little bit of that wall.

Supper came within twenty minutes, and Annie was shocked at how the kids gobbled down the battered chicken dunked in the red sauce. She had come to believe the only food they would eat from a restaurant had to be packaged in a little box with a toy. She started with the wonton soup, and it tasted so good that she took a few bites from some of the other boxes. But she could feel the nausea beginning to grow again, so she put down the chopsticks and pushed the food away.

"That's it?" Stephen asked in shock. One thing she had always done during her pregnancies was eat … a lot.

"That's it. If I eat any more, I may not make it through a conversation." She looked away. "It's been really, really hard to keep food down … at all."

He reached for her hand which obviously surprised her. When she looked back at him, he simply said, "I believe you."

He then jumped up from his seat and said, "All right, kiddos, your mom and I have a lot of talking to do, so I need you to find something quiet to do for a long time."

"Trampoline!" Ellie yelled out first thing.

"No way," Stephen said firmly. "The trampoline isn't quiet. You can watch a movie if you want, or play a game or something, but you need to leave Mommy and me alone for awhile."

Stevie took charge. "Let's watch that movie again we got at Disneyland."

"The one about the kitty cats?" she squeaked in delight.

"Yeah, and they play on that piano by walking on it," Stevie laughed as he herded her toward the television.

If Stephen didn't know better, it would appear that Stevie understood the importance of this conversation and was trying to get along with Ellie rather than irritate her.

"Thanks," Stephen told him. Stevie smiled.

Annie had gone to the bathroom, and when she came back out, she instinctively started to put away the food.

"No," Stephen said as he took her hand and led her back to the cushy couch. "Forget about cleaning anything. I don't know how much time I have with you, Annie, and I don't want to waste any of it. The kids should be into that movie a little over an hour, so that might be all we have … and I have so much to say."

Annie didn't want to take his hand, she still wanted to be guarded, but it seemed too natural to follow his lead. She sat down awkwardly again, thankful that he kept his distance as she did. She arranged a pillow to help support her back, and then gave him her full attention for the first time. She could have died when she saw he was looking directly at her belly.

"How long have you known?" he asked in an extremely dejected tone.

"A little over three months," she replied trying to sound stronger than she felt.

"And it's been a tough one … this time?"

"Very," she admitted. "It's been nothing like the other two. In fact, pregnancy never occurred to me. It was Angie that suggested that might be the problem."

He nodded in understanding then looked up at her face. "How did you manage to come today? Was it those stupid papers? I didn't really want to send them, but I thought you … I thought … I don't know, Annie. I don't know what I thought."

"All this has been really hard on Daddy."

He nodded. "I know. I always felt sorry for him whenever we had to do this."

"And then there's the whole crazy church thing with the new minister of education."

"*Dr.* Hal Bridges?"

Annie raised an eyebrow. "Yes. Then add to that Angie losing Carter in December."

"So you gave him a break?" Stephen surmised.

Annie looked at him squarely and explained, "When Uncle Toby walked down the aisle of the church Sunday morning just as Daddy was beginning his sermon, it was the straw that broke the camel's back. Daddy had a massive heart attack right there in the pulpit and then had quadruple bypass earlier this week."

Stephen jerked his hand to his heart. "Annie … no," he whispered. "Is he … okay?"

She nodded. "He seems to have pulled through it all."

Suddenly it dawned on him who Toby was. "Wait a minute … Uncle Toby? Is that the relative that tried to molest you and ended up … the one who … did all that to Alex?"

"The one and only."

"Why? How did that happen?"

She shrugged. "No one knows, or at least no one's talking. And nobody's seen him since."

Stephen fell back into his recliner and closed his eyes. He had thought she had come of her own accord, but that hadn't been the case at all. He had better act fast or he was going to lose what little chance he had here.

He flew from his chair and flung himself to his knees at her feet.

"What are you doing?" she asked in alarm.

"Begging for forgiveness," he said tensely. "I don't deserve it, Annie. I know that I treated you horribly, and that it was totally selfish of me to have walked out on you and the kids like I did. And I know it was wrong when I talked with you over the phone and made all these demands and insisted you were the lowest thing on earth for what you had done … but … no! There is no *but* in this—I was just plain wrong. I'll do whatever it takes to get you back in my life. If you want to see a counselor, I'll see a counselor. If you want to make any other demands at all, I'll do it." He lifted himself up so he could look her in the eyes. "I don't just hate my life without you—I hate everything without you in my life."

Annie was stunned. She had anticipated a long drawn out explanation with perhaps a hint of an apology mixed in, but he was taking the blame full force. "It's not just your fault, Stephen."

"Yes, it is! I know that what you did wasn't out of malice. I still wish you would've told me, but I can't imagine what kind of difference it would've really made."

"You would've known who your real father was."

He laughed. "Now there's a good joke. Ben Brenner is as big a jerk as Edrew, only on a different class level. I don't know which one would've been worse to have been raised by."

"But I thought that you really wanted to work with him."

He settled back down on his knees and gave a sarcastic chuckle as he shook his head. "You can't even begin to imagine what it's like working with him. I'd ask him about a particular scene and what he envisioned when he thought of the melody, and all he said was *money*."

"Money? Are you serious?"

"Yeah, and then I told him I needed something to go on in order to *feel* the melody line. I wanted to visualize the characters and try to display their emotions through the music." He looked back at her with a hint of devastation. "You know what he said? *Oh, you mean like that Autumn Sunset crap? Are you still trying to write music out of sentimentality? You've got to grow up, boy, and begin to move beyond that. Music is like math—there's a logical beginning and end to it all, and our job is to figure that out.*"

Annie stared in near horror. "That's not music!"

"I know," he said as he lifted himself up again and put his hand on the baby for the first time. "This is music," he whispered. "It's when you create something out of a passion so deep you can literally feel it sweeping through your body. Music is when you've made something tangible that before you could only feel. It's when a melody doesn't just catch your ear, but it captures your imagination and eventually your soul." He gently rubbed her tummy. "Each song is like a child. It comes from you, conceived in passion, and then reflects to the world a little bit of who you really are."

She felt his heart but couldn't help to smile. "Please tell me you didn't say that to Ben Brenner."

He smiled back. "Not in a million years. I just nodded and played a catchy little tune on the keyboard that he thought was downright amazing." He now was grinning. "And I was thinking about you the whole time."

"You're teasing me now."

"I promise," he said as he leaned in closer. "I imagined you being in there in the room with us and all the things you would have said, and that little melody just began to pop out. He thinks it's brilliant, but it really was a good tongue-lashing from you."

"You'll have to make sure you point it out to me when the movie comes out."

"Does that mean you plan on attending movies with me in the future?" he asked hopefully.

Annie's tired eyes were almost beyond the point of being expressive, but he could tell she was still afraid he could hurt her deeply again. Then he remembered what Jonathan had told him—talk to her heart, not her head.

"Annie," he said as tenderly as he knew how, "what happened between us, this whole mess, can never be erased. If I could somehow turn back time I'd do it in an instant, and I'd do everything differently." She dropped her head in despair, but he lifted her chin so she would look at him. "But I can't. I can't change a single thing about any of it, just like you can't change the fact that you never told me about your visit with Edrew. But we *can* learn from it."

She turned her head to the side and closed her eyes. "You can't just sweep it under the rug, Stephen, and pretend it never happened."

"That's not what I'm saying at all," he insisted. "I'm saying we learn from it. We learn about each other, and we learn about ourselves. We learn that honesty and openness are always the rule, but we also learn that when one of us makes a mistake, it's not out of spite or vindictiveness. We're just human, Annie."

She wanted to believe him, but his words had cut her to the core. How could she trust that he wouldn't get angry with her and leave again? What if this became a pattern that she had to live through with him over and over during their lives? She couldn't walk back into a marriage that always had that possibility hanging over her.

"Talk to me, Annie," he pleaded. "Tell me what's on your mind. What are you thinking? Don't leave me in the dark. This is our marriage, our life that we're discussing here."

She stared down at her hands as she said, "I can't hurt like this again, Stephen. I know that I deceived you, but when you left, I felt …"

"Betrayed?" he finished her sentence. "That's because you were betrayed. When I walked out, that's exactly what I did." He made her face him again. "I should have sent Ben on his way and talked it all out with you. You can't know how badly I've wanted to talk it through with you all these months."

She closed her eyes and said, "I'm sorry I wouldn't talk to you. I just couldn't handle another scolding about how horrid I was."

"I know." He sat back on his heels again and dropped his head. "Annie, for six years we got it right, as close to perfect as any couple could. I can't even sleep without you—it seems so wrong that you're not beside me. I can't write music without you—I've become accustomed to you as my inspiration." He looked back up at her. "You've become my life. Please forgive me and let me try again, and this time I'll get it right. I promise, Annie. I'll get it right."

The battle in her heart was unmerciful. Neither side would give in, and just when she thought she could either walk out or embrace him, the other argument would step up. She rubbed her head as if to help clear the thinking, but nothing was clear. She loved him and wanted him back in her life more than anything in the world, but she couldn't allow herself to be that vulnerable again to anyone, especially to the man to whom she had given her heart so deeply. But there could be no marriage if she couldn't give herself to him completely, holding nothing back, yet how could she ever truly do that again?

"Stop analyzing, Annie," he pleaded tenderly as he finally reached up and took her head in his hands. He had wanted to touch her hair since he'd seen her at the airport, and being this close to her was about to drive him mad. "This isn't like math," he whispered as he pulled her close. He then leaned into her ear and softly said, "This is like music. There's no logical beginning or end—it's just something you create as life goes on."

He felt her body tense as he pulled her closer, but he went on, refusing to give up. "Sometimes the music is soft and beautiful, while at other times it's passionate and fiery. And then some music is so powerful that it scares you as you hear it, as it seems to pulse through your body and unwind your emotions."

He pulled back and looked into her eyes again. "This has been scary, Annie, but it's only a part of the whole sonata. It was a movement that was tense and unsettling, but it's over." He reached down with one hand and tenderly touched the baby again. "We have so far to go, and this little one is only a tiny part of it. Take me back, Annie, please … please."

If he had moved away from her, she could have stayed strong. Or perhaps if he had left the baby out of it she could have resisted him better. But her body was tired, as well as her mind and her emotions, and she had fought so hard for so long to resist any thoughts of him, that when he only looked at her lips, her resolve collapsed. She practically lunged at him as she started the kiss, but he responded with no hesitancy. In fact, he nearly pulled her off the couch onto the floor.

"I love you, Stephen," she confessed as she caught her breath. "I'm so sorry."

"Please tell me it's all behind us," he pleaded one last time.

"All of it," she said as she pushed her lips again into his. "It's over. Please don't ever leave me again."

He reached for her waist and pulled her onto his lap. "Never. I wouldn't dare. I can't live without you … never again."

The passion was rising fast, and in another situation that wouldn't have been a problem. But over against the wall sat their two children engrossed in a movie that had only begun. And even if it had been over, the bunk beds and the big bed were all lumped into the same room.

"I hate your apartment," she mumbled as she began to kiss down the side of his neck. "It has no bedroom. What were you thinking?"

"I wasn't thinking this. In fact, I was just hoping for a good talk tonight."

Annie giggled as she ran her fingers through his curly locks. "I need to call my poor limo driver who's waiting for me at the Memphis airport."

He kissed her again. "And probably your family. They'll be wondering where you are."

Annie leaned in for one last kiss and then forced herself to pull back. "We've got to stop … now."

"I know." He helped her to slowly get to her feet and then gave her another kiss before she went for her purse and her phone.

☼☼☼

That night as Annie lay quietly in his arms, his hand gently rubbing her tummy, she felt secure again. Her head kept trying to raise suspicious thoughts about it all. But as the baby swirled inside her, and Stephen breathed gently on her neck from behind, and as Ellie flopped around on the bottom bunk across the room causing the bed to squeak, her heart was just too full to listen to her head anymore. The life she wanted was this one. It wasn't perfect, and she couldn't always be proud of it, but it was the life that fulfilled her more than anything else in this world. Her head would just have to learn how to deal with it.

Ninety-One

Billy spent another restless night on the makeshift bed, but this time instead of drowning in fear and dread, he simply prayed. He prayed a lot that night. There was much to say to God, not only about Sam, but about everything over the past thirty-five years. As he thought back, he could see many times when God had tried to get his attention, but he had only hardened his heart more with each attempt. As the sun began to creep through the cracks of the window blinds, he decided to stop the torture of trying to sleep on a sleepless apparatus. If Sam was still highly medicated today, he would go back to her house and take a hot shower to get the layer of grunge off his tired body.

He stood up and stretched his long legs, but every kink gained throughout the night was making itself known. He glanced over at Sam. She was sleeping peacefully. He quietly made his way to the bathroom so he could brush his teeth and get ready for another day. He was actually grateful for his short hair now. Before, it would have been a tangled, blond mess by this time, but it didn't look much different now whether it was clean and combed or oily and slept-on. He grinned at the change, not only with his hair that he had always taken so much pride in, but at the peace inside his heart for the first time ever in his life. If he had only known that giving up all those things he thought brought him pleasure could be this easy and fulfilling, he would have done it long ago.

He walked out of the bathroom and tried to decide if he should get some breakfast or wait to see if Sam would eat this morning. She hadn't actually been conscious since before the surgery. She had come to a few times, but nothing coherent had come out of her mouth. Even through Mr. C.'s visit she had remained unresponsive as she drifted in and out. He walked over to her and noticed that at some time during the night they had changed the IV drips. He couldn't remember that and wondered if it were actually possible that he had not awakened during that particular nurse's visit.

"Good morning, ponytail," he whispered, not really wanting to wake her. "Are you gonna show some signs of life today?"

He didn't expect a response, but when she moaned, he drew closer. "Sam? Are you awake?"

She began to slowly move her head as if she were genuinely trying to rouse herself.

"Sam?" he asked again with a little concern.

"What … is … this?" she asked very drawn out as she laboriously opened her eyes.

"Hey," he said with a warm smile as he moved his head over hers. "Welcome back." He reached up and moved a strand of hair from over her eyes.

"Billy?" she asked confused as she squinted to focus.

"Yeah, it's me," he replied. "I've tried to find your glasses for you, but they don't seem to be here anywhere."

"Glasses?" she asked groggily.

"Yeah. They must be at the school or something."

She continued to squint. "Is that really you?"

"Yeah. I've been hoping you'd wake up."

She looked up at him in confusion. "Your hair … what happened?"

He chuckled. "I decided to look more like a man than a teen idol. Did it work?"

She smiled slightly and then closed her eyes. "I don't know where I am, Billy." She opened them again and looked slowly around the room. "This is a hospital, isn't it?"

"Yeah," he said gently as he reached for her hand. "You don't remember?"

She shook her head slowly. "How long have I been here?"

He cringed at the thought of having to remind her again of all that had happened. "About a day and a half."

She only looked more confused as she turned her gaze back toward him. "How long have you been here?"

He grinned. "About a day and a half minus maybe one hour or so."

"The whole time?" she asked raising her eyebrows.

"Yeah. I didn't want you to wake up in the middle of all this and be alone. I kept thinking I should go take a shower or something at the house and see if I could find you an extra pair of glasses, but I was afraid that would be the time you would decide to come back to life."

She shook her head again. "I don't need glasses."

"I can imagine. I'm not too fond of hospitals myself. But it would be helpful if you could actually see the food they're trying to get you to eat here."

Again she shook her head. "No … you don't understand." She swallowed hard as she tried to lift herself up in the bed. She then cried out in pain.

"Take it easy!" he said immediately as he reached over to ease her back down. "Your shoulder is in really bad shape."

"Yow …" she whispered as she let him maneuver her back to a more comfortable position. "What happened to it? Was I in a wreck or something? The rest of me feels fine."

He dreaded this. She had no memory of the shooting for the moment. He wondered if she could have blocked it out completely. "You don't remember what happened in class on Friday?"

She closed her eyes to think. "I don't even know what day it is now," she confessed. "Did I pass out?"

Billy gently took her hand again and leaned down to kiss her forehead. "I don't want to do this, Sam," he told her earnestly. "If you can't remember, I don't want you to remember."

She looked at him with complete bewilderment as she began to squint again. "What are you talking about?"

He took a deep breath and then closed his eyes. How did he explain it casually? "You don't remember anything at all? You were in class and … and … someone brought a gun."

She tried to recall it but shook her head and asked, "Did someone try to shoot me?"

He nodded as he pulled her hand to his lips. "Yeah … and they succeeded." He motioned toward her wound. "He blew your shoulder to pieces. You were in surgery for several hours as they tried to put some of it back together."

"Well, that explains the pain," she sighed as she glanced down to her shoulder. "So, what happened?"

He didn't want to be the one to do this, but better him than anyone else, especially an unfamiliar nurse or physician. "It was Paulo, Sam." He paused as her expression began to change. "He, we don't know why yet, brought a gun to school … and then, for some reason, he tried to … well … I wasn't there … haven't talked to anyone in your room … but they say … he … uh …"

The memory began to turn her face pale, and her eyes immediately began to fill with tears.

"A lot of the details are still vague, Sam," he tried to sound reassuring, "so I can't really tell you much more."

She nodded slowly as the tears began to track down the sides of her cheeks. She looked back up at Billy and complete devastation filled her face. "Randy?" she asked first. "Kurt? He shot them both. They were so brave." She closed her eyes again as a tiny sob escaped. "I thought they hated me, you know? I was always so tough on them … the only teacher who wouldn't bow to their athletic prestige." She paused as she grimaced at the memory. "I don't think anyone believed he would pull the trigger. Randy just stood in front of him and … and … told him," she closed her eyes as she saw the whole scene vividly again. "Randy said he would have to shoot him before shooting me." Another tear fell. "So he did." She looked up at him as the emotional hurt began to wash through her again. "I can't believe it. What was he thinking?" Sam turned her head to the side and took a deep breath. "He didn't live, did he?"

What could he say? Did he lie again, or did he tell her the truth? *The truth will set you free, my son.* Billy looked at her with as much compassion as he had ever felt in his life and admitted, "No. He was gone before the ambulance even arrived."

Her face contorted as sobs began to flow. Billy took her head in his hand as gently as he could and moved his shoulder to her. She buried her face into him and wept as the memories and the reality became vivid again.

"Kurt's doing okay, though. They managed to put him back together pretty well."

She nodded in acknowledgment, but continued to cry. He moved so he could sit beside her on the bed while he gently held her head against him. He wanted to say that everything would be all right and that they would pull through this, but he knew right now Sam's world was crumbling … again. But this time he would be there to put it back together, not to be the cause, but the help and the healing.

☼☼☼

As Kyle gave the guest minister a rundown of how the morning service would happen, Hal Bridges walked in. He attempted to dismiss Kyle as if he was completely in charge and Kyle a blabbering idiot. Jonathan had explained prior to his surgery all the information they had discovered about *Dr. Bridges* and that Jonathan had suggested his resignation. Kyle just assumed Hal would pack up and leave without a word to anybody, but apparently he had a different plan.

When Kyle finally pointed the guest minister toward the sanctuary, he addressed Hal. "What do you think you're doing?"

Hal smirked as he replied, "Someone has to be in charge. The pastor is seriously ill and may not ever return to this pulpit. As I see it—that makes me the number one man at the moment."

"Then you'd better let me clear your vision, pal," Kyle said with controlled anger. "You're no longer on staff here. Your resignation has been demanded, and you have nothing more to contribute to this church."

Hal only smiled condescendingly. "Told you, did he? I thought he was the only one who knew … well, he and Richards."

Kyle shook his head in disbelief. "He said his being in the hospital might give you some crazy idea that you could do a little extra weaseling in all of this. I told him I didn't think even you were *that* evil. Apparently Jonathan knows the real you."

"So, what are you gonna do, Sarkos? You gonna stand before the congregation today and just reveal everything? Huh? Is that what a worship leader should do?"

"Don't put it past me," he replied through gritted teeth. "As I recall, you can't worship in the midst of deception. I believe it was Jesus who said, *True worshippers worship in spirit and truth.* Or are you familiar with Jesus, Hal? In fact, are you even familiar with what *Truth* really is?"

"Do what you want, Golden Boy, but I'm not out of here … yet. Unless you intend to actually stand up today and tell the whole church what you know, which would be quite a step for you … causing commotion and division instead of trying to put band-aids on everyone's wounds … I'd suggest you just shut up and sing." He glared at Kyle with what appeared to be pure hatred as he gave one final comment. "Frankly, I don't think you've got it in you. And I believe that so much that I'm willing to stake my whole reputation on it."

Ninety-Two

Stephen had been awake a long time, but he didn't want to move. He only wanted to continue watching Annie sleep beside him. They had laid in bed for a long time last night saying nothing, just holding each other and taking comfort in the closeness. There was so much he still needed to say, but he realized his first priority in all of this was to win her trust again. She loved him, she needed him, she longed for him to be in her life, but if she couldn't trust him again, it would be a pointless life.

As he continued to watch her, taking in all the familiar characteristics of her face and her hair, his heart literally ached. How could he have walked away from her so easily? He had been in L.A. for six months, and there was no beauty here to even compare. But more than her beauty was her fire in life. Everything about Annie was passionate. The people here were plastic and pretend, and even though they had their *passions* about many things, there was nothing engaging about them. It was as if they were always performing, on or off stage, in or out of the studio, in front of or far away from the cameras. They kept up appearances that always reminded everyone of how talented and exceptional and gifted they were, as if they ever let down the facades people might see that a normal person lay underneath. He had lived with that for eleven years before Annie, and it had been miserable. But when this enormously talented woman just accidentally showed up in his life, the misery turned into utter repulsion. She had more untapped ability than he had ever witnessed, more genuine passion about absolutely everything, and nothing about her was pretend or put-on. Every other person and pursuit in his life dimmed in comparison to this woman who had totally captivated every fiber of his being, and had she asked, he would have walked away from it all just to be near her.

But now he had walked away from her—and all that passion and fire and utter honesty had been squelched … because of him.

He slowly moved from the bed and began to think of how to start the day. With her father lying in a Birmingham hospital recovering from quadruple bypass surgery and her missionary sister on furlough with two newborn sons after the loss of a previous one, he knew she would want to return to Alabama soon. He had one more shot this morning to assure her he wanted a life with her more than anything else in this world, and convincing Annie of anything that wasn't already cemented inside her head would be immensely difficult. As he slipped from beneath the linens, she stirred slightly, but only rolled over. He held his breath—he wasn't ready for her to awaken yet. He had nothing for breakfast.

Stevie was the first one up, and he was easy to satisfy. A bowl of Lucky Charms did the trick, and then he settled onto a beanbag to fight Zurg as Buzz Lightyear on a secret intergalactic mission. Stephen had told the guard outside his door to just walk on in when the man from the bagel shop came so as not to awaken Annie or Ellie with the bell. He knew that Ellie would climb right up into the bed with her mother as soon as she got up, and Stephen was hoping to be the first face she saw that morning.

When all was ready, he put the items on a tray and gently eased himself onto the bed beside a still slumbering Annie. He softly began to sing:

So while I'm waiting for someone to love me
Someone who knows me through and through
I'll watch the Autumn Sunset from my single room apartment
And hope and pray that dreams can still come true
And long to hear the words, "I love you"

Annie smiled before her eyes ever opened. As she turned to face the music, she was startled by the sight beside her.

"What's this?" she asked as she clumsily dragged her body and belly to a sitting position.

"This," he said with a warm smile as he placed the tray beside her, "is commonly known as *breakfast in bed*, but for the sake of honesty and openness, we'll call it what it really is this morning—*sucking up*."

She laughed, something rare for her to do so soon after waking. "You don't have to *suck up* to me. We're on even ground here, you know?"

He shook his head. "No, I don't know. What I do know is that I walked away from all that ever gave my life any kind of meaning, and I'm scared to death you're gonna walk out of here not convinced of that."

She gave a gentle smile, something else rare for her to do this early. "I will graciously consider the whole sentiment of this breakfast thing, but I must decline. I haven't kept breakfast down in six months." She nudged the tray away.

He smoothly nudged it back toward her. "That's because you've never actually had breakfast in bed. It's way different than regular breakfast."

"You're right about that. In all the years that we've been married, I don't ever recall you *making* breakfast, much less *bringing* it to me in bed." She looked at the full mug. "And coffee? I thought you'd forgotten how to make coffee?"

He grinned sheepishly and shrugged his shoulders.

"But one thing I think you did forget," she said with a frown, "I don't drink coffee when I'm pregnant. I don't drink caffeine period when

I'm pregnant."

"Decaf," he said with a triumphant smile.

"Decaf? Since when did you start drinking decaf?"

"I don't," he explained as he settled his back against the headboard. "Ben does. It's the only health issue he actually pays attention to. He carries around an extra couple of hundred pounds and doesn't think that affects his heart at all, but he's worried that a jolt of caffeine might just be the thing that pushes him over the edge."

Annie gave him a quizzing look. "So Ben drinks a lot of coffee over here? You two doing some father-son bonding?"

He shook his head. "There's been very little bonding going on here. I hate to admit this, but I don't know which of the two men made the worst father. Edrew was harsh, uncaring, and resentful. Ben is completely full of himself—nothing in life matters other than getting whatever he wants." He looked over at Annie. "It makes me wonder how my mother ever fell for him."

"That's easy. She had stars in her eyes. Here's this literal musical genius, her professor, building her up and making her all these promises. I don't think she had to actually *know* him in order to ... well ... *know* him."

Stephen stared toward the area where Stevie was saving the universe and tried to imagine what life would have been like with Ben as a father rather than Edrew. Then he realized something. "Had Mom decided to go with Ben, I would've probably never known him as a father anyway. I would've been conveniently *eliminated* out of his life."

"Maybe not. Maybe your mom would've talked him out of it."

He shook his head. "You don't talk Ben *out of* anything. You know, I wondered for a while why she gave up so easily. Why didn't she go back to him and try to talk him into making things work." He glanced over at Annie and explained, "You don't talk Ben *into* anything either. He does exactly what he wants." He sighed. "She knew that. She had no choice but to tell her parents. If Ben had said the only way she could go on with him was to abort me, then that was that. She wasn't gonna kill her baby—that was so unlike her. And after talking with Ben, he apparently had derided poor Edrew over and over again. He considered him to be a worm among peacocks in Ben's world, and not worthy of a decent word. Yet there he was, Ben said, every night that Mom sang at that club, sitting on the front row taking in every lyric, gesture and expression.

"He adored her."

Stephen nodded. "Obviously. And then when he found her—all mangled and pregnant and broken and rejected—he became her savior. He took her away from everything that had destroyed her, and he gave her a new start."

Annie reached for the coffee and took a careful sip. "Mmmm," she said with a grateful smile. "This is my first morning coffee in four months. I never thought decaf could be so good." She then asked, "Do you think your mother ever loved Edrew?"

He had considered that many times the last months. "I believe she did. She was always tender with him, and their relationship was really almost normal. It was *me* who was out of place there, and now I know why."

"I should have told you," she said guiltily as she reached down to her belly and shook her head.

"No!" Stephen snapped immediately. He took the tray and placed it on the floor and then crawled up beside her. "I want us to get one thing clear here and now—there can be no more regrets between us about what did and didn't happen. And even if you had told me, Annie, what difference could it have made with my childhood? That's where the damage was done." He took the coffee from her hand and placed it on the tray also then took both of her hands in his.

"Annie, I wish I could tell you how many times I've replayed that day in December over and over in my mind. I would've done it so differently. I would've told Ben that he needed to leave so that I could have some time with you alone to sort through all of this. I should've told him had my mother listened to him, I wouldn't even be here, so why should I be listening to him now? I would then have talked through all of it with you … dealt with the emotions and the confusion. We would've cried together, probably yelled a little bit … only because you would have been involved in the conversation." He winked at her. "Then we would've come to a reasonable decision and gone to bed and lived happily ever after when we woke up the next morning."

Annie looked at him deeply, a way that no one ever in his life had been able to do. "Then, and I hate to ask this … but I have to, Stephen … why didn't you? Why the other choice … leave me … leave the children … leave our home?"

He leaned back on the headboard again, bringing his knees to his chest and placing his head in his hands. "Because I'm just a stupid man, Annie. I'm an imperfect, stupid and prideful man." He looked over at her. "I let a moment of pride grip me, and I somehow thought that … dang it … I don't know what I thought!"

Annie pulled him to her and smiled. "You thought that as you stood before this man that you had idolized, somehow standing up to me in his presence would make you look more like a man than telling him to leave. Everything happened so fast, Stephen, that all you could do was act on basic instinct. Had I told you years before, you wouldn't have been put in that position."

"No, but that doesn't excuse the fact …" he threw his hands into the air. "Annie, we can't keep doing this! We can't try to undo something that is and forever will be *done*! I blew it, Annie, and you blew it too. Can we just admit that we're both a little imperfect …"

"… and a little stupid?" she added.

He nodded. "If we can't put this behind us, we'll never be able to move forward. It'll always be hovering there in the background, right above our heads, buzzing and buzzing. And every time one of us makes a move that seems a little threatening, the buzz will just get louder." He furled his brows as he pleaded, "I'm totally releasing you from not telling me about this. It's all okay, and I understand why you did it. I also know that if we could turn back time it would happen the same way again unless we could somehow see the future … and that *never* happens. It just doesn't." His eyes searched her face for hope and agreement.

Annie felt her heart beat faster. If she actually did this, actually released him from the past six months of utter pain and heartache, it would be the first time ever in her life that she had absolved anyone from everything. She was a grudge holder, always had been; it was who she was. It had defined her in many ways just as much as her music, and to really let go of something this deep went against her very nature. Yet if she didn't, the one thing she loved more than her personal justice would be forever lost.

She reached for his hand again and held it to her chest. "You know me well, Stephen," she nearly whispered. "And you know how impossible this is for me."

He nodded sadly.

"But there's no way I can live with you and hold on to this at the same time." She smiled as she realized the thing she wanted most right now was the bagel sitting on the tray down on the floor with a dish of butter and two packets of jelly on the side. There was no nausea, but more importantly, there was no resentment. "I release you, Stephen—completely."

"Seriously?" His face held pure astonishment.

"You know me well. I'm serious or I wouldn't have said it. I don't play games like that."

He let out a deep breath and fell back on the bed. "I can't believe this just happened." He looked over at her and asked cautiously, "Does this mean I can come home?"

"If you don't, it'll make me question your sincerity."

"Today?"

"You want to leave L.A. today?"

He grinned and nodded. "I wanted to leave this place months ago, but I couldn't get you to talk to me, much less forgive me."

"I just thought you'd have to do some negotiating or something. You have this loft … and the work you're doing with Ben …"

"I'm not that stupid, Annie," he said soberly. "I never signed a contract."

"What? Are you kidding me? You've worked on this for six months and they've never given you a contract?" She was now in business mode and found this whole idea atrocious.

"They've offered, but I could never bring myself to accept one."

As she realized what that meant, that he sincerely had wanted to be with her more than writing scores for movies with Ben, her smile grew bigger. "So you've just been sitting here stewing all this time?"

"Stewing, suffering, suffocating … if you give me some time, I could write a really melancholy song with a lot more *S* words, all in rhyme of course, but I'd just as soon forget it … all of it."

Annie leaned in to kiss him, but the baby inside made it impossible to maneuver. He jumped up and smiled with deep relief as he met her more than half way. She giggled as his rough beard tickled her lips, but it didn't matter. They were back, and so was her hunger.

"So," she grinned as she reached up to rub his stubbly face. "Do you think all this apologizing has now given you permission to grow excessive facial hair?"

"I forgot," was all he could say. "It's a bad habit I've gotten into."

She kissed him again and giggled a second time at the sensation. "I don't want to get used to it, but if you'll let me have that bagel on the floor, I'd be willing to forgive it this time."

"Done!" he said right away. He sat up and retrieved the tray, careful not to spill coffee on the bed. He placed it beside her and handed her a knife and the dish of butter.

"Butter and jelly," she said with a grin. "Did the restaurant sneer at your request?"

"They did ask if I wanted cream cheese with it and informed me that they now have flavored cream cheeses."

Annie made a sour face. "Yuck."

"Exactly," he told her as he watched her bathe the top of her bagel in pure, yellow delight.

Ninety-Three

Sam said very little after being reminded about the shooting, but there wasn't much free time to talk. Nurses and specialists began to buzz in and out of the room, examining, questioning, poking and prodding. She lay there almost like a robot, answering questions and signing forms as she was told, but there was no emotion in her responses. It was as if she was numb to the whole process. Even when they changed the bandage on her shoulder, she looked down at the horrid wound but gave no reaction. Billy knew what she was thinking, and he would have felt the same—how could Paulo do this? This was completely unlike him. He was a peaceful boy, a *good* boy. He was responsible, punctual, thoughtful and respectful. In fact, Billy would have put Kurt and Randy in the *angry, young teenager* category long before Paulo.

When everyone had finished with their interrogations and examinations, she ate a little lunch, and then lay back in exhaustion and pain.

"Can I get you anything?" he asked eagerly, hoping to ease some of the turmoil he knew she was experiencing on every level.

She shook her head. "No … but thanks." She turned toward him and added, "You don't have to stay with me, Billy. You look about as tired as I feel."

"Maybe I'll head to the house in a little bit and freshen up," he told her. "I could get your glasses too. I'd turn the TV on for you, but I figure you can't see it well enough to be swept away in escape."

Sam smiled for the first time in ages. "I don't need them anymore."

He was shocked. "Why? Did you finally get contacts?"

She shook her head. "Surgery."

"You're kidding?" he said with excitement as he came over and sat on the edge of the bed. "When? Why?"

"In March. I thought about all you had said to me back in Georgia, about all the things that still bound me even though I was geographically far away from my past. When we went back there, it was almost like I'd never left. I was still just a helpless little girl trying desperately to survive the present day. All I had fought to escape still clung to me in certain, almost subconscious ways … I guess."

"I just thought you had really pretty eyes," he teased.

"Thanks, but …" she winced as pain shot through her shoulder.

"Are you all right?" he asked immediately, wishing he could somehow ease the pain.

She nodded as she caught her breath. "I've got to," she gasped again, "try to remember not to make sudden movements. That really hurt."

"They have significantly cut your pain medication," he explained.

"I know … I'm awake now. That makes a *significant* difference."

He chuckled. "Thank heaven for that dry sense of humor. I've missed it."

She eased herself back into the pillow and tried to relax.

"Mr. C. came by yesterday," he told her. "Do you remember?"

"I don't even remember how I got here."

"Yeah, I just wondered."

"Does he have any news? Anything new about Kurt … or Paulo?"

Billy didn't want to answer that question, but he knew if he was going to start things out right with her this time, honesty would always have to be his first choice. "Sort of … he said that Paulo wanted to talk to *me*."

"You?" Sam's eyes grew wide with wonder. "Why?"

Billy shrugged. "Mr. C. didn't say. He was able to go in and see him in the jail. He said he was in horrible shape, just muttering and mumbling, not making much sense at all. He would cry and shake a lot. Mr. C. told him that I was here with you and that we had been … well … married."

Sam's jaw dropped. "Mr. C. told him *that*. Nobody knows except Mr. C. It'll be all over the school by the end of the week."

"Apparently that gave him some kind of positive hope. He begged Mr. C. to tell *me* to come see him … said he had things he needed to tell me."

Sam relaxed her head. "Unbelievable." She closed her eyes and began to relive the whole scene again. "He just looked so resolute and so scared. I actually laughed at him when he pulled out the gun. I thought how totally ironic it was for Paulo to do a prank like that."

Billy scratched his oily head as he wondered out loud. "Do you think I should go see him?"

"Are you kidding?"

"I could walk in there and just punch him, Sam!" he exclaimed. "I could even strangle him if I'm not careful." He gazed into her face with a burning anger. "He tried to kill you, and would have … had some students not taken him seriously."

"But why? We both know he's not like that. What could possibly have driven him to do it? If he's willing to talk to you, Billy, that might mean I could have some answers."

He felt his body shaking in anger. "I … I … don't think I can … not yet."

"You keep asking what you can do to help me. I can't think of any better way. You say you've sat here in this room with me the whole time, but I can't even remember it." She then looked at him in confusion. "How did you get here anyway? How did you find out what happened?"

"I saw it on TV. I saw the school and then the math/science building. When they said it was a high school math teacher who was a lady, I knew immediately it had to be you."

She nodded. "Oh … I thought maybe Mr. C. had called you."

He shook his head as he rubbed his stubbly face. "No, but he was really excited to see me when I walked in."

"I'll bet." She tried to readjust without moving her shoulder as she explained. "I remember now being in the ambulance. He was there with me. He said to let him call you, and I told him not to."

"Why not, Sam? I should be here for you."

"Since when?" she asked with a sarcastic attitude.

The question cut him deeply. All she knew about him was that he had bailed on her time after time. Even after Georgia he had pushed her back to Jeremy Crandall—a man she didn't love—in order to avoid having to love and protect her on a regular basis. She knew he loved her, but not enough to really lay down his life to be with her.

"It's not gonna be like that anymore," he said softly and slowly. "I'm … different … now."

She smiled appreciatively at the sentiment, but he could tell she didn't believe him.

"Sam," he sat down beside her on the bed again, "there are things we need to talk about. I don't think right now is the best time."

"He told you about the baby, didn't he?" He nodded, but she closed her eyes in hurt. "I asked him not to."

Billy rubbed his tired eyes. She could remember no conversation they had had in the hospital before today. "I don't know that he actually intended to tell me the baby was mine. I started badmouthing Crandall about leaving you with a baby and then he … well …"

"He told you how wonderful Jeremy was," she moaned, "just like you always told me about him. And he was …" Sam paused to collect her thoughts. "He was the perfect man … I suppose. And if I had any sense, somehow I would've let him raise your child and tried to be happy."

"No!" Billy said with disgust as he heard the words actually come out of her mouth.

She stared at him in surprise.

"Never … again … will I let you be forced to do something … without … me." He hung his head at the statement.

"I won't let you love me out of pity, Billy, and I can't get any more pitiful or helpless than this."

"That's not even close to the truth." He stood up and rubbed his temples as he tried to clear his head from all the emotions that were running through him. "I'm good with words, Sam, especially when I'm trying to pull something over on someone. I seem to have a gift for deception and charm." He looked back at her. "But when it comes to just being honest and telling the naked truth, I run."

"What is the truth, then?" she asked in frustration. "Here you are! But I have no clue why!"

"Because I love you, Sam," he said as earnestly as he could.

"That means nothing to me! You should know that by now. You loved me before, but it was pointless, wasn't it? You loved me three months ago, but it was pointless too. Jeremy loved me … enough to raise your child as his own, but it was meaningless because I didn't love him back. As I see it, Billy, love has gotten me nowhere but in a big mess."

"Sam …"

"And let's talk about trust for a little bit," she continued. "I always thought the two sort of went hand in hand … love … trust … two sides of the same coin. I *loved* you, I trusted teaching, and here I am carrying a fatherless child in a hospital because a trusted and treasured student tried to blow me away in the classroom … in *my* only sanctuary!" The frustration turned into grief. "What do I have left?" she asked through tears. "Where do I go from here? Teaching was my only solace, my only goal. When I step out of this bed, where do I head?"

"You go with me," he said softly.

She laughed at the suggestion. "There's a great idea," she said scathingly. "I think we've tried that before. It didn't work, remember?"

"No," he insisted. "I never … all of that … it was different then. *I* was different then … or rather, I'm different *now*."

She shook her head. "I'll admit that you've changed, Billy. But a couple of degrees behind your name and a nice inheritance doesn't change who you are at the heart. And in your heart you'll always be someone …" she grimaced at the thought, "… someone who ends up hurting me … again … and if I don't stop it now, you'll end up destroying me altogether."

Billy wouldn't let her end with that thought. "I know that's what you believe, but when I talk about change, I'm not referring to the education or the money. I *am* referring to my heart, Sam. I did something," he began to try and put it into words. "I came to this point where I realized that if I really lost you again, everything I've accomplished would be … meaningless."

She only closed her eyes as though he was trying to merely charm her again.

"I don't even know how to tell you this," he said as one utterly lost. "How do I begin?"

She said nothing. He knew she had to be empty from the years of trying to pull the truth out of him.

"I did the God thing, Sam," he finally said with a huge release of his breath. "I gave myself up … to Him."

"You what? When?"

He walked over to the window where he had knelt and wept for hours last night. "I was really scared that I was gonna lose you for good. And not only you, but the baby." He glanced back at her with intense remorse. "And I knew that you'd never know how much I really did love you or how badly I wanted to hold that baby." He looked down at her stomach and then back up to her tired eyes. "I knew everything I'd ever tried to accomplish or be impressive about was nothing if I was never able to share it with someone … and the only one I really want, have ever wanted … is you … Sam."

She smiled, but he knew it wasn't sincere. "That's nice, Billy, and I do appreciate all the gushiness at the moment. I'm tired … I'm weak. I have no fight in me. You can tell me you're gonna change the world right now, and I'll willingly believe it. But when I leave, and I have to face all the realities of life again, you won't be here … you never are."

"That's what I'm trying to tell you," he said as he came over to her. "I know that's been my pattern, but I hate it … I hate that life. I told God I knew it was empty, and that I'd do whatever it took to be the man that you really need." He sat down beside her. "I gave it all up to Him, Sam. I know you may not believe it, and that you're gonna need proof … more than just my words, but I intend to spend the rest of my life proving to you that I can be a husband … and a father … a real one … a real man … not just some phony guy with a phony smile and phony words he throws around."

"Fine," she sighed unable to fight. "Whatever."

He took her hand. "I'm serious, Sam." He waited until she looked up at him. "I asked God to forgive me of everything."

That got her attention. Billy Marcum asked for forgiveness? "Forgiveness? For what?" She was curious now.

"For what?" It was really more of a rhetorical question. He stood and threw his arms into the air. "How about everything! What haven't I done that wasn't saturated with pure selfishness? Can you think of anything? Can you name one thing in my life that was ever done out of purity in heart?"

She just stared at him. She was in shock that he was taking responsibility for being the charming jerk that he really was.

"I looked back over my life and saw one selfish decision after another, and then I saw the wreckage I left behind. My father had tried his hardest to get me interested in something that wasn't controlled by my hormones, and I just pushed as I hard as I could to go in the other direction. I always knew of my mother's disappointment in me, but I'd smile and try to act charming and disarming and pretend that the disillusionment wasn't there. Then there was *you*," he said with great embarrassment. "I had the chance to sort of make up for all of my irresponsible shenanigans, but I just drug you through the mud too. And as if that wasn't enough, when I showed back up in your life this fall, I did it all over again! I'm a total and complete loser when it comes to doing the right thing, Sam. And what's worse, even when I actually *want* to do the right thing, I'm so scared I'll fail, that I just bail out before I get in too deep." He looked down at her. "What kind of man does that, Sam?"

She shook her head.

"I'll tell you," he said with disgust. "Men like Frank and Farris Conwill."

She gasped at the comparison. "You are *not* like them," she insisted.

"Yes, I am!" he contested. "I am *just* like them! I'm a user … someone who does everything for his own good and never considers what consequences others might have to face because of my selfishness." He came and sat down beside her again. "I couldn't get Frank's words out of my head. Every time I'd try to do something, I'd see him standing in that pulpit, gripping the sides with all his might, and hear him talk about how God was able to change him … *really* change him … from the inside out, and I knew that's what had to happen to me if my life was ever gonna make sense."

He reached for her tummy and gently ran his hand over the sheet. "This child was on its way to being just one more mistake to mark up in my book … one more failure … one more wreckage I'd leave in my path. And I don't blame you for not telling me. I certainly wouldn't have told me. But I gave it to God … I really gave it all to Him. Sam, in myself there's no way I can be what you need … or what this baby needs. I can't do it. But that doesn't matter anymore because my life isn't gonna be controlled by me. I told God He was free to do anything He wanted with me, and everything starts with you … and with our baby."

She couldn't believe she was hearing this from him. "I did it too, Billy," was all she could say in response.

He looked at her with uncertainty. "What do you mean?"

She shook her head and admitted, "I couldn't get my father's words out of my head either. In fact, for three weeks I would put that DVD on every night and just stare in amazement at him as I listened to his testimony over and over. He didn't just sound different, he looked different, he *was* different. I had hated everyone at the funeral for telling me how wonderful he had become, but when I saw the recording, I had to admit that there was way more than a surface change."

"So you became a Christian?" Billy asked with excitement for the first time as he began to see that perhaps the boat wasn't sinking altogether.

"Not at first. I still *wanted* to be bitter. Not only at Frank, but also at God for allowing it all to happen. Why didn't he save Frank when I was five instead of thirty? Why did I have to go through all those years of abuse when God was willing to save the man all along? If God was so sovereign and powerful, why didn't He step in and intercede back then? What good did it do me now?"

"Did you get an answer?"

Sam nodded. "It's almost impossible to believe."

"Try me," he grinned as his enthusiasm only grew.

"Mr. C. has invited me to church every week since the day I met him."

"Me too," Billy chuckled.

"So one Sunday afternoon after watching Frank's testimony again, I started asking God all the same questions. It was burning me up inside. I decided to go to church and find Mr. C., and then just explode on him with all my doubts and uncertainties.

"So, I showed up at church and sat in the very back hoping to avoid being noticed, but when the welcome time came, they started playing happy music and people were coming from all over the massive sanctuary to shake my hand. Several of my students came by, and I tried to act cool and collected about it all, but inside I was seething. I just wanted answers from God, not a barrage of smiling people jerking my arm off.

"Then the pastor started preaching about how Jesus told Peter he would die a martyr's death. Peter got a little riled and asked Jesus about another disciple, John. And Jesus simply said, *He has nothing to do with you.*" She shook her head at the memory. "And I heard myself asking God over and over again, *What about Frank? What about Farris?*, and it was like He was telling me they had nothing to do with me. What He did and how He worked—or didn't work—in their lives was none of my concern. The real issue was what I was gonna do about Him in my own life. I'd worked so hard to achieve so much, but I was completely empty. Frank had been the biggest loser imaginable, but God had given him real life. If He could do that for Frank, couldn't He certainly do it for me?"

Billy shook his head in amazement. "And so you did?"

"That night," she said as her voice trembled. "When the preacher talked about getting things right with God and to stop putting it off because we're so concerned with everyone else in our life and how unjust it all seemed, it was like he was talking directly to me." She paused. "So I went up. I took his hand and told him I had no idea what I was doing except that I needed God. He took me to the steps of the altar and we knelt down to pray." Her lips quivered as she recounted the prayer.

When the story was finished, Billy and Sam sat speechless. God had managed to put their lives back together after all they had been through, and it had to be more than coincidence that they were sitting together in this room at this moment in time.

Billy finally reached for her hand again and he looked intently into her eyes. "I can't promise you perfection, Sam, but I can promise that the mistakes I make in the future won't be the same as the mistakes of the past. And not only do I promise to take care of you, but I promise to be a father to this baby, and to be a man of God … if you'll just give God in me a chance."

Sam was afraid to let herself believe it could work with him. She had never stopped loving him and never stopped dreaming that there would be some way for them to be together again, but every time it looked like things were going good, something would come and crash them into pieces. She couldn't handle heartbreak from him again.

He continued with his plea. "I know it's hard to believe me right now, but if you could see inside me … really see inside me, you'd know that this is no game. I'm not trying to charm you, Sam—I'm trying to be as transparent as I can. And I'm not just committing myself to *you* this time. God's gonna have to be first if anything in my life is gonna work. And then there's the baby. I can't abandon our baby." He actually had tears in his eyes. "I don't want it to be this enigma of shame, and I don't want it to be another reminder of how many times I failed you. I simply want it to be the product of our love, a perfect little creation that God has given us." He squeezed her hand. "Please say *yes*, Sam. Please give me a chance to be everything you ever needed."

She tried to breathe, but everything seemed impossible at the moment. "I'm not sure what you're asking me. Yes, you can be a part of our lives? Is that what you want? I'm not completely …"

"No," he said cutting her off. "I'm asking you to marry me … again. But this time it'll be for real. I won't cross my fingers or look for a loophole. I want to be in it for good this time."

She sank back in the bed. She was too tired, too hurt, too weary and too emotional to try to give Billy any kind of answer. And just because he claimed to find God wasn't a good reason to commit her life to him again. And even the baby wasn't a good reason. It was tempting, but not enough. "I need time, Billy," she finally replied. "Let me get through this shoulder thing first. Let me see what's gonna be on the other side … where I'm headed … and then I'll see if …"

"… if I fit into your life?" he interjected. "It's not gonna work like that this time, Sam. If you tell me no, I'm still not leaving. I intend to be by your side every step of this recovery." He then gave one of his mischievous grins. "Besides, everyone here in the hospital believes I'm your husband. Why do you think they've let me stay in here all this time?"

She shook her head and smiled. "You told them we were married?"

"As far as I'm concerned, we are." He raised his eyebrows in question. "All we need is to make it legal again, and we're set."

She smiled, but wasn't ready to agree. "I just need time, Billy.

Ninety-Four

"You told Bro. Daniels not to come back and speak tonight?" Kyle was livid. "That wasn't your place to tell him anything! You shouldn't even be here as far as I'm concerned. Jonathan asked for your resignation."

Hal wouldn't budge. "The great and mighty Jonathan Wright didn't hire me, and he has no authority to fire me."

"You're absolutely crazy! I don't know who you think you are!"

"I am *formerly* second in command here."

"Well, at least you're getting closer to being correct," Kyle mumbled derisively. "There was a time when you believed you were first on the totem pole."

"A totem pole that is quickly crumbling," Hal said snidely.

"You'd better watch your mouth, Bridges."

"Or what? You're gonna take me to task? I'd actually like to see you try. That would be an interesting thing to watch."

"Well, I don't know what you had planned tonight, but you're definitely not in charge of the service."

"Oh, I believe I am. And I'll be preaching too."

Kyle was actually ready to punch him. He knew the whole Navy Seal thing was just a scam, yet Kyle was trained in Karate. If he wanted, he could give him a mighty blow right now that would disable him for several months.

Kyle pulled himself together and said, "The only way you'll ever preach in this church is over my dead body."

Hal laughed. "As I said, Golden Boy, bring it on. What are you gonna do to stop me? Stand up in front of the church and tell everybody the truth? I would stake my life on the fact that you don't have the backbone to even attempt it."

"You will not make a mockery of Jonathan Wright … nor my Lord."

"They're both pretty close together in your estimation, aren't they? But I have news for you, pal, it's all a big show. And as I see it, I'm the one giving the award winning performance."

"You're sick!"

"I've looked for a church like this a long time," Hal told him with great pride. "It took a lot of patience and a lot of moving around, but I knew I'd find one because they're spread out all over the place. Sure, I could have gone to some bumbling country church in the middle of nowhere with a handful of people, but that wasn't good enough. I wanted a big church, and here in Dockrey you could say I hit the jackpot."

"What are you talking about?"

"You and Jonathan Wright … what a humble pair. I'll say that Jonathan's got it over you when it comes to forthrightness, but he's still too sweet and meek for his own good. It was only a matter of time before I turned the majority of this church against you both so that I could step in and take over, helping them to *heal all the wounds* caused by your ineptness."

"You're out of your mind! There's no majority here in your favor!"

Hal put his hand up. "You can hush now. Your days are numbered. If you know what's best for you, you'll tack your tail between your legs and run for cover. I'm sure there are a few skeletons in your closet too."

"What are you talking about?"

"Ever wonder where *Uncle Toby* came from?"

The whole Toby story came out after Jonathan's heart attack. Even Kyle hadn't known about the molestations, but someone did, and Hal had obviously been tipped off. It was bad enough for the man to walk down the aisle, but when the rumors began to circulate as to *why* he had caused such trauma for Jonathan, they began to realize that someone else had to know also.

"You?" Kyle asked in unbelief. "You brought that man here?"

"Now … I know that you and your sweet little wife have such a reputation for being the perfect couple. But it wouldn't take much to get people riled up about the fact that Kylla is from your first marriage and that Cindy was pretty much the high class town whore in Florence for many years."

Kyle felt his hands beginning to ball into fists. Forget the Karate … he was going to punch him directly in the face.

"But see," Hal went on, "you men have been convinced that meekness is somehow a strength in God's eyes. I'm sick of it. So, unless you intend to change your colors, tonight I'll be preaching, and I guarantee you it'll be exactly what these itching ears have been dying to hear."

Hal left before Kyle could pull himself together enough to stop him. But Hal was right. Everything within Kyle told him not to let him in the pulpit tonight, but what could he do without causing a commotion? And if he caused a commotion, what kind of man would he be? Would he not be stooping to Hal's level? Wouldn't he be playing the same games?

Kyle practically ran to his office, slammed the door and fell to his knees. He needed a strength and wisdom that came from somewhere deeper than the supply within him at the moment.

☼☼☼

Billy walked into the jail uncertain if they would even let him in, but since Paulo had asked to speak with him, he figured he would try. He was only doing this for Sam. He wanted to string the boy up by his toes and beat him like a piñata, but Sam wanted to know the truth. If Billy was going to be the man she needed, he had to prove he was willing to do the job.

"Is there any way I can see Paulo?" he asked the lady at the front. "I was one of his teachers. And also, someone said he was asking for me."

"Could I have your name?"

"Billy Marcum."

The lady looked up at him in shock. "Marcum? Are you related to the lady he allegedly shot?"

Allegedly. Billy was ready to walk out right then. Yes, he knew in America everyone had rights, but there was a classroom of thirty students who saw Paulo pull the trigger three times, and one of those shots hit Sam. There was nothing alleged about it.

"I am related," was all Billy would say. He figured he should also stop lying about being married to her. "Look, I wouldn't be here if Paulo hadn't asked. If you don't want me to see him, that's fine with me. I'll walk out of here and tell the lady whom he *allegedly* blew apart at the shoulder that I wasn't able to make the visit."

"Hold on," she said quickly as she got up from the desk. "I'll be right back."

Billy folded his arms and leaned against a wall as he waited. He didn't want to be here. It was late, and he wanted to get back to Sam. He had left that afternoon to shower at her house, and ended up cleaning her kitchen while there. He also put on a load of clothes and waited through the wash and dry so they could be folded. Part of him knew it was procrastination—he had promised Sam he would try to see Paulo. But another part wanted frantically to help her in some tangible way. Cleaning up a little bit at her house gave him a small sense of accomplishment. He also assumed that if he got to the jail too late, maybe they wouldn't allow him to visit. He glimpsed at the clock on the opposite wall. It was five-fifty-eight. If visiting hours were over at six they probably wouldn't let him in.

The lady returned and motioned him to the door. "You may go in."

He was surprised. "Really? For how long?"

"As long as you need."

An officer met him at the door and took him to another room. "You'll need to empty your pockets and take off your shoes."

"Really? Why?"

The officer just looked at him.

"I'm not gonna pass him anything," Billy defended. "I'm a teacher, not a gang member."

"I don't want you killin' him either," the large man explained soberly.

"Oh," Billy muttered as he backed down and began to take off his shoes.

Once through security, the officer led him down a corridor and through another series of seriously locked doors. It was then that Billy saw Paulo. His whole demeanor was broken. He lay curled up on a small cot in the farthest corner imaginable, with his knees tucked up beneath his chest. This was the Paulo that Billy remembered—humble and gentle. He couldn't imagine what had possessed him to bring a gun to school and then turn it on Sam.

"Paulo!" the guard yelled out. "Against the bars!"

Paulo jumped at the voice, but his face lit up when he saw Billy.

"Mr. Marcum," he said softly.

"Against the bars, boy!" the guard yelled out again.

Paulo sat back on his cot and stuck his hands behind him through the bars of his cell. The guard then handcuffed him to a bar.

Billy asked sadly, "Do you really have to do that?"

"The boy's an alleged murderer … first degree. I might be doin' you a favor, sir." He placed a chair just outside the cell for Billy. "I'll be supervisin' the entire visit. Everything you say and do will be seen and heard by me … just so you know."

Billy eased himself into the chair. The lack of sleep and the stress of the past two and a half days had gotten to him more than he realized.

"Mr. Marcum."

Billy turned to face Paulo. He looked as tired as Billy.

"Paulo," he said restrained. "I heard you wanted to see me."

Paulo closed his eyes in humiliation as he nodded. Billy sat stiffly in the plain metal chair. When the boy finally looked back up, Billy saw tears in his eyes. How could he keep this angry exterior when something inside told him that Paulo could have never done anything like this out of pure maliciousness? There had to be more to the story.

"Why am I here, Paulo?" he asked him this time. "Why did you want to see me? Whatever you had to say could have been said to someone else."

Paulo shook his head. "Mr. C. told me that you and Ms. Marcum used to be married. He said you were at the hospital with her. He also told me you were going to have a baby with her."

Billy raised his eyebrows in surprise. "I guess Ms. Marcum and I have absolutely no secrets anymore then."

Paulo put his head back down as he tried to manage a comfortable position with his hands handcuffed behind his back. "I won't tell anyone … nobody. Mr. C. knew that."

Billy nodded as he bit the sides of his mouth. "Why do you want to talk to me, Paulo? I'll be frank with you—I don't want to be here right now. I want to be with Sam … Ms. Marcum. But she insisted that I come."

"I didn't want to do it!" Paulo cried out in what appeared to be pure agony. "I didn't want to hurt anybody, especially not Ms. Marcum! But I didn't have a choice!"

"Why? What possessed you to bring a gun to school in the first place? What were you thinking?"

The boy shook his head as huge tears fell from his eyes. "They made me! They threatened Marianna!"

A little bit was making sense, but it was still unclear. "Marianna? Your sister?"

"Yes," Paulo cried from the cot. "They hate me because I don't want to be like them."

"Who?" Billy wanted to know.

"Them," Paulo said again. "All of them from the neighborhood." Paulo tried to wipe his nose on the shoulder of his shirt. "They think life is about being tough and being strong. They tell me I'm a wuss for playing sports and studying so hard. At first I would just ignore them. That's what Ms. Marcum would tell me to do. All I wanted was to not make trouble for anybody, but then they started saying that I thought I was better than they were. They said I thought they were trash … Latino trash." Paulo's eye's pleaded for understanding. "I never called them that. I never did. I just studied and practiced and played."

Billy nodded. "How did they threaten Marianna? What did they say?"

"Last Thursday, they pulled me aside when I was coming home from practice. They threw me into this alley and pinned me against the wall." Paulo grimaced as he gave the details. "They said they were tired of me trying to be like the white Americans. They were gonna have to teach me how to be a real Latino … what it feels like to be a real man.

"They handed me the gun and told me they had a job for me to do. If I didn't, they would take Marianna … and … and …" he shook his head.

"I can imagine what they said," Billy said softly.

"No, you can't," Paulo insisted. "You may think of something as simple as rape, but what they described was way worse than that. It wasn't even human, Mr. Marcum." He sniffed again and reached down to wipe his nose on his shirt. "And then they said they would kill her when it was all over."

"And they told you to shoot Sam? They actually used her name."

"They didn't know her name," Paulo explained mournfully. "They just referred to her as the meddling math teacher who thought she could change the world."

Billy actually smiled at the description, because that indeed had been

Sam—at least it was before the shooting.

"Wasn't there anyone you could tell?" Billy asked. "They have protection for people under threats."

Paulo slowly raised his head to face Billy in the eye. "Not for illegal immigrants."

Billy nodded gradually as the impact of it all began to make sense. "Wow … what a position to be in."

"The last person on earth I would want to hurt is Ms. Marcum … or my sister." Paulo looked back to the floor. "I would have shot my own parents first, but they don't despise my parents. My parents are heroes to them. They came in and bled the US system. They get food and money and healthcare."

Billy actually felt sorry for Paulo. If he had been in his place, he probably would have done the same thing. It was as if he was backed into a corner with no way out.

"And I got an education," Paulo said sadly. "I worked so hard to be someone America would want, but my own people turned me into something America hates. Right now they don't even know what to do with me. My parents aren't citizens, and yet I'm in this American jail, promised a just trial, but no one knows where to start. If I was thirty, they could do something, but I'm only sixteen."

"Have they offered you any kind of deal … or help?"

"Are you kidding?" Paulo said in hopelessness. "They hate me here. They treat me like I really am a murderer."

"Do you even have a lawyer?"

Paulo shook his head. "I don't have anything … or anyone. My parents have left town because if they are caught, they are in trouble." Paulo seemed resigned to his situation. "I have no one—I have nothing, Mr. Marcum." He slid back toward the bars and explained, "Had this been any other situation, I would have called Ms. Marcum and asked her for help. She was always so willing to help me." He choked on his words. "But I can't … I don't have anyone."

Ninety-Five

Kyle was beyond distracted as he tried to lead the worship portion of the service. Inside he knew Hal was right. Here he was trying his best to put on a religious exterior, while inside he was dying to expose the real Hal and crucify him before the whole church. Maybe Hal was right. Christianity had been boiled down to leaders with no backbone in the name of Christ, and godly men like Jonathan Wright were hung on poles for trying to display the true character of Christ.

Kyle's stomach seethed as Hal went to the pulpit, Bible clutched in his hand. He could still hear Hal referring to Cindy as the *high class town whore*, and his anger went up another level. Normally he would leave the platform on a Sunday evening after the music to sit with Cindy, but tonight something made him stay put. Kyle looked down and found Cindy's confused gaze. She mouthed the words to him, *What's going on?*, but he just shook his head and rolled his eyes. Everything about this felt wrong, but what was the right response, the godly response? Would Jesus just sit here quietly and let this man mock everything the church was about?

"Change," Hal said with a very distinguished tone. "Sometimes it's all about change."

Several people nodded in the congregation, but most of them just stared in surprise. Hal had always made it clear he wasn't a preacher.

"This," he said as he signified himself in the pulpit, "is a big change. Sometimes we are thrust into roles that we would not have chosen for ourselves." He paused for effect. "That is where I humbly find myself at the moment."

Humbly? The man was not only a lunatic, he was an overt liar! Less than thirty minutes ago Hal had told him that the humble were weak and worthless for the most part, yet here he was claiming the characteristic as his own.

"What happened to Pastor Jon was indeed unfortunate," Hal continued. "He is a man with a heart of gold, but obviously not a heart strong enough for the moment to continue leading this church. So, until Pastor Jon is back on his feet, I feel it is my duty to take over the pastoral care of this flock until further notice."

Suddenly a vision popped into Kyle's mind. He saw Jesus carrying a whip he had carefully woven Himself and walking into the temple. As Jesus began to thrash the whip in righteous anger, He threw over tables and ran the charlatans off. Before Kyle knew what was happening, he had jumped to his feet and walked briskly to the pulpit.

"Thank you, Hal," he said as he stood directly in front of the microphone. "I believe I should take it from here."

Hal gave him a look of total disbelief.

"If you're gonna take over the pastoral duties of this church then it needs to be put to a vote." Kyle looked out in the dwindled crowd to find Tom Richards, the man who had chaired the committee last year to rewrite the church constitution and by-laws. "Isn't that right, Tom? Any ministerial position is to be voted on by the church."

Tom looked confused, but he gave a huge nod.

"Okay then," Kyle's hands were trembling as he stood firmly behind the pulpit, "let's get this done." He looked down at Cindy and she appeared utterly baffled at it all. Kyle whispered to himself, *Get some backbone, Sarkos. This isn't about you. It's about Jonathan and about the body of Christ that meets here. It's time somebody other than Hal Bridges did something overt.*

"Before we vote," Kyle said with a swallow, "I think it would be important to review the committee's findings and Hal's qualifications for the ministry."

Hal gently shoved Kyle to the side as he spoke into the mic. "I don't think my credentials need to be spread out before the church again. That's a bit overdoing it, Kyle, but I appreciate your willingness to remind everyone of my accomplishments and degrees."

But Kyle shoved back. "Not at all, Hal. In fact, would all the committee members that are responsible for bringing Hal to our church please come forward and join me up here?"

One by one the five committee members left their seats and came to the platform. Hal still seemed undaunted by it all. Kyle knew he was still figuring he could pull the wool over their eyes again. After all, this was the church he had waited for he had said.

"Let's begin with your most impressive credential, which really has nothing to do with church leadership, but it sure seemed to impact the committee." Kyle reached out his arm toward Floyd Benson and motioned him toward the pulpit. "Floyd, why don't you tell us what Hal's résumé' said concerning his military career."

Floyd walked confidently up to the microphone and explained in his raspy voice, "Yes, Dr. Bridges served our country in the military in the branch of the Navy, and he was given the honor of being a member of the Special Forces as a Navy Seal."

"Thank you, Floyd," Kyle said jovially as he helped Floyd back from the pulpit. "So, for whatever its worth, we know that Hal has incredible military training. Now, let's see, education. I believe your undergraduate degree was earned at a school in California known as Pepperdine. Is that right, Hal?"

Hal nodded, but his normally calm and controlled exterior was beginning to sweat.

"Nancy Beth, you want to tell the church something about that?"

Nancy Beth Tate looked totally confused as she walked up to the center next to Kyle. "Uh … well …" she stammered uncomfortably, "I guess all I need to report is that he received his Bachelor's from … uh … what was it? Peppermint … mine … mime?"

"Dine," Kyle corrected her. "Pepper-*dine* University."

"Oh … yeah," she blushed. "I'm not real familiar with the California area … schools … places. I know about USC and … uh … that other one …" she searched for the name and then exclaimed, "UCLA!"

"Thank you, Nancy Beth," Kyle smiled.

She sort of nodded and half-bowed as she returned to her place in the line of committee members.

"Okay," Kyle said as he tried to think what should come next. "I guess that leaves the issue of seminary. Tonya? Would you like to take that one?"

Tonya shrugged, obviously embarrassed at whatever Kyle was doing, but she was still very pleased with their find in Hal Bridges, so she would go along with whatever game he was playing. She stepped up to the pulpit and leaned into the mic as she announced, "Hal received both his Master's and Doctorate from Golden Gate Baptist Theological Seminary in, hmmm, I don't really know the name of the city."

"Mill Valley," Kyle reminded her, "also in California."

Tonya just shrugged and went back to her place in line. She looked as though the whole thing was ridiculous.

"Okay," Kyle said as he tried to remember everything he had seen on the résumé' personally as well as everything Jonathan had told him in the hospital. "Now, if I can remember right, there were several impressive churches in California and then Arizona where Hal served as Minister of Education." He looked back at the committee for agreement. They all nodded. "Of course, if I'm correct, I don't believe any of this was ever actually checked out."

Hal's face turned white, and the committee, with the exception of Tom, began to show signs of nervousness.

"No big deal, of course," Kyle said. He then looked toward the sound and video booth in the balcony and said with drop-dead seriousness, "You guys need to turn off the cameras."

The church went completely silent as they realized this must be more than what it appeared. Kyle had always been very predictable, and generally very much in the background. He led music and worship during the service, but that was about it. Whatever he had to say was never like this.

"However," Kyle said as he gripped the pulpit and looked soberly into the eyes of the congregation, "I'm afraid that even though our committee had the best intentions at heart, they made some grave mistakes in judgment. My father always told me that if something looked too good to be true, it probably was." Kyle looked back to Tom Richards. "Fortunately, we had a pastor who wasn't as impressed with that piece of paper as the committee was, and one member of the committee that felt this church deserved more than an impressive résumé', but a good solid background check … you know … just in case."

Kyle felt foolish in one sense. What he was doing was utterly ridiculous, but as he looked over at Hal Bridges and saw the sweat beading up around his face, and as he remembered Jonathan falling to the floor last Sunday morning as Toby walked down the aisle, he felt justified in his foolishness. They could fire him if they wanted, but he had enough of being the spineless nice guy, and he had most definitely had enough of Dr. Hal Bridges.

"Tom, if you don't mind," Kyle continued, "would you mind sharing with the congregation the revised version of Hal's credentials?"

Tom tried not to smile as he approached the pulpit, but his heart was right with Kyle's. He had watched this man systematically dupe the weak-minded and snub the ones who genuinely had the heart of the church and the will of the Lord in mind. He looked over at Hal as he began from memory to recite the realities.

"As most of you know, I have quite a few contacts with the military. In lieu of some long overdue favors, I was easily able to discover that our Dr. Bridges was indeed in the military … for a total of eleven months."

The congregation gasped, and the committee looked in shock toward Hal.

"I think most of you could do some simple math here and deduct that there was no way possible for Hal to have trained and served as a Navy Seal. Of course, the commanding officer I spoke with explained that Hal was in no way Seal material, had never been considered for the program, and was given a dishonorable discharge because of his uncooperative attitude and insubordination to officers.

"I also talked with the actual churches Hal claimed to have served at. Unfortunately, the numbers he gave me weren't numbers for church members. The area codes were all wrong for most of them. California has several different area codes, and Arizona is a whole different story. When I looked up the actual church numbers and talked with various secretaries and ministers, some had indeed worked with Hal, and they gave far from glowing reports. Others had never heard of him at all."

People began to stare at Hal as Tom continued the list of results, but Hal never moved a muscle. He stood there tall, arms crossed in front of him, no expression or evidence that anything out of the ordinary was happening. Only the sweat dripping down his face gave any indication of his true condition.

"Then Jonathan called the University, Pepperdine, and found out that Hal did attend there, but he only completed one year. He never received any kind of degree. As for seminary, he never attended … period … well, I take that back. He didn't attend Golden Gate, the one listed on his résumé Perhaps he made a mistake in citing that one and attended somewhere else … perhaps …"

Tom had given all the information, and the congregation was stunned. How were they to respond to this? How could such a thing have happened? People would look from Hal to the committee, and then back at Hal again. Who was to ultimately bear the blame in this fiasco?

"Thanks, Tom," Kyle said as he went back to the pulpit. He looked out over the church, some whom he knew would give their lives for him and Jonathan, and some who would gladly kick them out after the past few months of influence from Hal Bridges. He had no idea what to do next—all he knew was that he couldn't allow Hal to stand in the pulpit and desecrate Jonathan, the Lord, or this church ever again.

"I don't know what to do," he confessed. "I know we can't officially vote on Hal. In fact, I don't even know who takes over a business meeting when the pastor's not here." He hung his head. "Our pastor has never missed a meeting before. He's always faithful and busy and moving about in the Lord's business." He looked back up. "Pastor Jon's had a tough year. He lost a grandson among several other issues that have put undue stress on him. But when the family secret walked down the aisle last Sunday, the one that was meant to keep his *son* from humiliation and degradation, it was just too much." Kyle looked over at Hal who was still standing unmoved in his position. "You did that too, didn't you Hal? That's pretty much what you told me this afternoon. You somehow found out about the uncle, and that was your final payback when Pastor Jon asked you to quietly resign from the church so as not to cause all the ruckus that I'm causing right now. Even though you've torn this church apart, it wasn't enough. When Pastor Jon faced you with the truth, rather than just move on, you had to arrange one final dig."

Kyle turned back toward the people. "For the record, church, I feel sorry for a man who would go to such depths to destroy something … a fellowship … that at one time had been wonderful. But I suppose we asked for it. We got so big and so great that we began to lose sight of who God is and who we aren't. Rather than every one pitch in and begin to take up some duties instead of insisting that the same people do all the jobs, we decided to hire someone with a fancy résumé and just pay him to do it." Kyle sighed as he stuck a hand in his pocket. "I guess we deserved what we got.

"But I'll tell you the one person in this church who did *not* get what he deserved—that's your pastor. Pastor Jon tried to urge the committee to check Hal out. He told them to take their time. He pleaded with them to pray about it and to really seek the person God had for us, and Tom Richards was right there in agreement with him. But everyone else pushed for something fast as though a quick fix would solve all the problems we had developed."

Kyle couldn't help it as his body began to shake with grief. "I'm sorry," he said one last time as he began to cry from the pulpit.

Cindy jumped from her seat and practically ran to the stage area. She put her arms around him and held him close. Slowly people began to move from their seats. A few left the building in bewilderment and embarrassment, but most went to the altar or knelt somewhere in the aisles.

The committee members stared at Hal as movement began. They weren't sure how to react. They felt conned and slighted because they believed that a man of God was like Jonathan Wright—his word was truth and he could always be depended upon. But rather than trust the man God had given them to lead them and guide them, they had pushed Jonathan's warnings aside, going so far as to even accuse him of jealousy, and pursued a man who was only a pretender.

Hal finally left the stage, going through the choir loft and out the back. Lisa had left long before Kyle had finished, and Hal knew she would be fuming when he got to the car. Who cared anymore? His theory about churches must obviously be wrong. Maybe it was more than just a show, more than just a man with a strong personality manipulating the minds and pocketbooks of people. Whatever the key, he obviously didn't have it. Maybe it was time to try something different.

Ninety-Six

As Annie slowly opened her eyes on Monday morning and consciousness began to dawn, the first cohesive thought that hit her mind was that *normal* was so nice. She liked *normal.* She wasn't one for spontaneity or surprise, and the few years she had spent touring with Stephen had done a number on her *normal* preferences. There were no *normal* bedtimes or eating schedules as time zones could change from day to day, and the weather in each zone was just as different as the hour. Leaving one city at 101 in the shade and landing in another with subfreezing temperatures had happened more than once. When the cabin in Alabama was finally finished, and the last tour date was marked off the calendar, Annie imagined life becoming slow and … *normal* again.

As she looked over at Stephen and watched him dream, she felt a hole form in her stomach at the thought of almost losing him. Would she trade *normal* again just to be with him for the rest of her life? She had done it before. She had left the simple, predictable life of northern Alabama and followed him literally all over the world. In the process they had borne two children and built a life that was far from what anyone could call *normal.* But *normal* had lingered in her mind and tugged at her soul. When Stephen's contract had finally ended, he had said all he wanted was to settle down and live a *normal* life. They made their plans, bought their land, built their home, and then finally retired. To Annie it was perfect. She had her *normal* again, but she had Stephen and the children added to it all. It was almost too good to be true. And that's when the bottom fell out.

When Stephen began to talk about working with Ben Brenner, she should have recognized right away that her version of *normal* and Stephen's version were different. She should have come clean right away, told him everything she knew, and then suggested an alternative kind of work. Instead she had tried desperately to hang on to her *normal*, and in the process had almost lost everything.

She eased herself out of bed, trying clumsily not to awaken him, and made her third trip to the bathroom since hitting the sack after midnight. Stephen had chartered a jet from Los Angeles to Tupelo in order to avoid the press, but all the procedures involved in his leaving California took hours to pin down. As soon as they were inside the limo and on their way back to Dockrey, Annie had fallen asleep. She awoke long enough to make sure Ellie was tucked into bed, and then she collapsed for the night.

She carefully made her way down the stairs to the kitchen and went for the coffee pot. She wouldn't be drinking any, but she would make sure there was enough for Stephen to have at least two cups when he awoke. That was *normal.* She then pulled out a block of cheese from the refrigerator and began to make a tray full of cheese toast for everyone.

Normal. This was all wonderfully *normal.* The last six months had been so far from *normal* that Annie had seriously begun to wonder if she would survive. She had tried hard to go to bed on time, get up on time, set a schedule for the children, and make things as predictable as possible, but in the hidden corners of her mind a nagging voice constantly reminded her that this was all a big mess and there was nothing *normal* about it.

As she poured herself a glass of orange juice and sat at the table, she smiled at the smell of coffee brewing. The decaf Stephen had made for her yesterday had been wonderful. Perhaps she should consider giving it a try for the remainder of the pregnancy. One aspect of *normal* that she had missed was she and Stephen having coffee and a devotion each morning together. Then they would often meander off in conversation to every subject imaginable. Annie had thought it was heaven, but as she looked back, she realized Stephen would need more than all this in order to be really happy … really fulfilled. She had made a vow before God to stick with him through the good and the bad, and after having almost broken that vow, she realized for the first time what was meant by *marriage is hard work.* If she was to be the wife he needed, it was going to take willingness for her to sacrifice her ideal of *normal*, and a willingness to work *normal* in whenever it was possible.

As she heard his footsteps padding down the stairs, she felt a smile grow throughout her whole body. Yes, she was most definitely willing to sacrifice her ideals in order to live life with this man.

"Good morning, sleepyhead," she said sweetly as she rose from the table and went to greet him. His curly hair was disheveled, and his face was still unshaven, but she no longer cared. She wrapped her arms around his waist and placed a lingering kiss on his lips that left them both wanting for more.

"Do I smell coffee?" he asked as he buried his face in the hair flowing around her neck.

"Yes, sir," she replied as she leaned into his ear. "And if you'd like, I'd gladly make you a cup, lots of sugar, lots of cream."

Stephen pulled back and looked into her eyes with intense longing. "Anything you're offering right now, I'll gladly take it." He looked out toward the deck and the pool and thought of how close he had come to losing all of this—especially Annie.

She started to go, but her he pulled her back. "Annie, I know there are no guarantees in life, but I want to give you one."

She looked up at him, and his heart overflowed as he saw the depth of love in her expression.

"I'll never leave you again," he whispered as he cradled her face in his hands. "Nothing in this life is worth doing if you're not in it with me. I don't ever want to live like that again … never."

She smiled and pulled him closer. "I was just thinking the same thing." She gently kissed him. "And whatever it is you want to do," she kissed him again, "… wherever it is you want to go," and again, "I'll be there with you." She kissed him longer this time. "I promise."

Suddenly the baby kicked hard enough to cause her to jump and she began to laugh. "It's already coming between us and it's not even here yet."

"It?" Stephen questioned her. "Are you telling me you don't know if we're having a boy or a girl yet?"

She shook her head.

"Is that possible?" he asked as he pulled her back from him. "You're actually going to willingly give yourself to the element of surprise?"

Her expression turned soft and sad as she looked up into his blue eyes. "To be totally honest with you, I didn't *want* this baby enough to even care about discovering the sex." She closed her eyes. "Angie forced me to see a doctor. She thankfully put me on some prenatal vitamins to help counter all the … lack of food."

He pulled her close and gently touched her forehead with his. "Your face is so thin … gaunt … thinner than I ever remembered. It was the first thing I noticed when I saw you at the airport." He kissed her nose. "Then I saw the baby."

"I was so afraid for you to find out," she confessed in a whisper.

"Why?" He pulled back again to see her face.

"Because," she hesitated, "I had joked about having another baby whenever you mentioned trying to find some kind of work." She glanced briefly into his eyes again. "I was afraid you might have thought I did it on purpose … to try and trap you … or something."

Stephen let out a mild laugh as he said, "You've got to be kidding me? You swore to me you wouldn't go through pregnancy and labor again."

She buried her face in his chest and admitted, "And I was so scared of going through it alone … without you." She sighed deeply.

He caressed the back of her head and began to rock back and forth with her. "If I had known, Annie, that you were carrying our child, I would've been back here in a minute. I really would have. I would've thrown all my reasoning away and flown back here and …" he sighed. "Anyway, it doesn't matter. I'm here now … forever … okay?"

She pulled him down into another kiss. Nothing did matter

anymore. They were here together now, expecting their third child together, and planning their future … together.

☼☼☼

Cindy needed to balance the monthly accounts and get out an e-mail of all the updated prayer requests for the week, but there were too many other things on her mind and her heart to successfully accomplish anything. The result was that she spent most of the morning staring out the large window watching her children play gleefully on the playground beneath. There was great relief that Hal Bridges was gone, at least she assumed he was gone. He hadn't shown himself after church last night, and he hadn't made it in this morning either. That would be one stressor in her life gone, and hopefully gone for good. But the other stressor, the fact that Billy had apparently been at the hospital with Sam ever since the shooting, was gnawing at the back of her mind constantly. This wasn't a good sign.

"Hon, what's going on?" Kyle asked as he walked in for the third time to find her distracted. "Can't handle all the peace and quiet with *Dr. Bridges* out of pocket?"

She smiled at the question, but replied seriously, "I'm thrilled with peace and quiet—I just can't get Sam out of my mind. Billy talked about how serious everything was on Saturday, and I just feel this urgency to present Christ to her."

"Then go!" he said unexpectedly.

"What?" she nearly laughed. "Are you kidding me? That's all we need … for someone to show up and find me gone the day after we push Hal out of the church."

"And anyone willing to champion Hal Bridges after all that was revealed yesterday should be hung by their armpits over the pulpit Sunday morning!"

She smiled. "I hate to admit I like that idea." She then cocked her head to the side. "You've become rather assertive of late. What's going on with you?"

He shrugged as he came over to look out the window at the kids on the playground. "Pastor Jon's heart attack, I guess. If I'd been a little more *assertive*, as you put it, before the heart attack, you know, taking up some of the slack instead of letting him manage all the heat, it might have eased things up on him a little more. Perhaps he would've had some symptoms indicating there was a problem instead of wham—he drops in the pulpit."

Cindy shook her head. "And if Pastor Jon knew you were even considering the blame in any of this, he would probably have another heart attack."

He sighed and stuck his hands in his pockets. "Whatever … the fact is that Hal is gone, Jonathan is in the hospital and will be recovering for weeks, and that makes me in charge." He looked back toward Cindy. "So, following Jonathan's lead, I'll make the choice on the side of ministry and say that you should take off for Florence and go visit Sam. If there's a burden there, you should follow that prompting and go."

Cindy leaned back for a moment and considered it. Kyle was indeed right—Jonathan always sided with ministry over any other administrative duty. As far as he was concerned, they could close up office for a month if ministry needs were to mandate it. She pushed back her chair, stood to her feet and walked over to him with a huge hug.

"Associate pastor," she smiled as she kissed his cheek. "You're not a flunky here by any means. And after yesterday, I defy anyone to suggest that."

Kyle smiled nervously. "But with great power comes great responsibility."

She drew her eyebrows together and asked, "Is that from *Star Wars*?"

"You think everything comes from *Star Wars*. How many times did you actually watch the movies?"

She shook her shoulders and head. "Not many. But there were a few good lines … I think …"

"*Spiderman*," Kyle told her.

"What?"

"That line came from *Spiderman*."

"Oh," she nodded. The she looked at him confused. "I've never watched *Spiderman*. Jonathan must have used it in a sermon or something."

"You've never watched *Spiderman*?" he asked in shock. "Are you American?"

"And you've never sat through the entire movie of *The Sound of Music*," she countered. "I think that's more un-American than *Spiderman*."

"There's nothing American in that! It takes place in Austria!"

"Are you calling Julie Andrews un-American?"

Kyle rolled his eyes. "Yes—she's British!"

Cindy thought for a moment. "Oh … okay. You win then. I'm gonna visit Sam and convince Billy to go home."

Ninety-Seven

Cindy prayed during most of the trip to Sheffield. She prayed that Billy and Sam would find salvation. She prayed that he would be reasonable about leaving Sam alone. Her thoughts then moved toward the church and the devastation that would be left in the wake of Hal's destruction over the past six months. She prayed for Pastor Jon and what effect this heart attack would have on his leadership in the church, and then she prayed about the assertiveness that had suddenly come over Kyle in the absence of the pastor. Was God shaping him to become more in the ministry than he had ever been before?

When she pulled into Helen Keller Hospital, she saw Billy's silver Mustang right off. She should have known he would still be here. Where else would he go? His home was now in Dockrey. She had to do all within her power today to make him leave. Sam needed to face this without the crutch Billy managed to offer for some reason, and she needed to be able to get through this without his emotional interference.

After parking, she went to the back of the van to retrieve a small booklet which Kyle gave to those to whom he often shared Christ. It was a copy of the Gospel of John with a small Bible study for new Christians. She almost took a second one in case Billy was interested also, but decided against it. If all went as she planned, Billy would be leaving with her today. He could get one at home. She tossed the book inside her purse, closed the hatch, and then pressed the lock button on her key. As the van gave a slight *beep* signifying it was indeed locked, she squared her shoulders and moved with confidence toward the hospital.

Once outside of Sam's room, she paused at the cracked door to listen before entering. She wanted to make sure there was no examining or medical stuff happening. She wanted to enter with the sense of purpose clearly in her mind—she was here to share the Gospel clearly with Sam, and to enforce the priority of Billy leaving … for good. As she leaned in closer, she was totally shocked by what she heard.

Billy's voice read, "The thief cometh not, but for to steal, and to kill, and to destroy: I am come that they might have life, and that they might have it more abundantly. I am the good shepherd: the good shepherd giveth his life for the sheep." Billy paused and then began to explain, "I remember hearing Pastor Jon once talk about how stupid sheep were." He chuckled at the memory. "He got very animated about it all."

"I really like the way he preaches," Sam said. "It's like everything makes sense when he explains it."

"And to think I grew up with that but learned to just tune him out."

Cindy finally walked on in. "Hey guys."

"Cindy!" Sam exclaimed. "Wow! It's so good to see you!"

Cindy walked over and gently hugged her, careful to avoid her shoulder. "Hey, girl. How you doing?"

Sam grinned tiredly. "I've been better."

"I'll say," Cindy remarked as she stared at the major bandaging. "What's the prognosis? From this side it looks horrible."

"From this side it *feels* horrible," Sam moaned.

Billy jumped in to explain. "They began taking her off some of the major pain medication yesterday morning, so it's been quite a struggle adjusting to reality."

Cindy asked, "So the pain is really severe?"

"Usually. When I first get a dose, it takes about ten minutes to become tolerable again. Then as it starts to wear off …"

Billy interrupted, "… about four hours …"

"Yeah," Sam nodded, "it gets really unbearable again."

Cindy didn't want a rundown from Billy in any of this. She was here to see Sam, and here to get him out.

Sam asked her, "Are you not working today?"

"You were really on my heart so Kyle suggested I come on up here and see you."

"Well, I'm glad he did," Sam smiled as she relaxed back on the bed.

Cindy decided to jump right into it. "I noticed you guys were reading the Bible when I came up. That's sort of why I'm here. I wanted to just stop beating around the bush concerning the whole God issue. I wanted to make it really clear that God loves you and has a purpose for you that goes way beyond just existing in this life."

"I know," Sam smiled at her.

"And that there's more to making peace with God than just deciding to somehow live honorably and try to do your best not to be too evil."

"I know," Sam said again.

Cindy stopped talking and stared down at her. "You do?"

Sam nodded and smiled gently. "I accepted Christ as my Savior a couple of months ago."

Cindy leaned back against the wall. She was shocked. "I didn't expect to hear that. In fact, I came in here all revved up and determined to share the Gospel with you so clearly that your only choices would be to accept Him … or reject Him. I didn't anticipate this at all."

Sam explained, "You can take a lot of the credit for my decision. It was the change I saw in you that really impacted me the most. The way you were before—your total wildness—used to scare me at times. I'd never known anyone like you, so … well … immoral, who had changed so completely."

Cindy blushed in humiliation. "I wish I could have some excuse for all that."

"It doesn't matter," Sam told her. "God used all that to show me that He had to be real … that He had a power that could really change lives. Had I not seen it in you, I might have never believed."

Cindy was so overwhelmed that she couldn't speak.

Billy then added, "And that's why we're reading through the book of John. We started last night, just taking a chapter or two, and then we would stop and discuss something if it seemed important."

Sam jumped in, "Not that all of it isn't important."

Cindy smiled and looked to Billy. "That's nice of you to read it to her. If we could get her glasses to her, she could read it herself when you're gone."

"She doesn't need glasses anymore," he said proudly.

"I had eye surgery. I can read, drive and cook without having to shove those things up on my nose anymore."

"Then you don't need Billy here, do you?" Cindy suggested. "You can read all by yourself."

"Actually," Sam looked over at him and then back at Cindy, "he's been a huge help. I didn't even realize he was here all through Saturday, but he was a lifesaver yesterday. I don't know if I could've made it without him."

"Well, I'll tell you what," Cindy said energetically, "I could stay here with you for the rest of the day, and Billy could go on home."

They both just stared at her. Cindy had to get Billy out of Sam's life, and the fact that she was leaning on him right now at such a vulnerable time wasn't a good sign.

"I don't really want to go," he confessed as he stood a little closer to Sam.

"But you look horrible," Cindy told him. "You could definitely use a good night's sleep, and probably a shower or something."

"I showered at Sam's yesterday."

"Well," Cindy was grasping, "perhaps you smell all right, but those big bags under your eyes can't be washed away with soap and warm water."

Sam sighed as she reached for Billy's hand. "But I don't want him to leave." Her tired eyes cut through Cindy's defenses. "I know it's hard on him, but he's been such a huge help and a big comfort. Right now I'm so helpless that he's been like my right hand."

Billy quickly insisted, "It's not that hard on me, Sam. And it's not like there's anything else I need to do at the moment. The school's having final exams and averaging grades, so no one's gonna call me in."

Cindy decided to change the subject fast before she ran out of luck altogether. Her best bet was to just carry on with them for a while and then persuade Billy to walk her out to the van. She would corner him then and remind him that Sam didn't need another heartbreak to go along with all the physical problems this injury would entail. She didn't want to hurt Sam, but it was obvious the only chance to get Billy away from her would be to force the issue of all he had done to her in the past.

She stayed with them over an hour, and as the time neared for Sam's pain medication, her discomfort began to grow. Within 15 minutes of the medication being administered, she began to relax and then doze. Cindy took that as her opportunity to get Billy outside and alone. He walked her down to the van, and she then remembered the little book of John with the Bible study. She almost pulled it out for him to give to Sam, but then remembered that she hoped he wouldn't return.

"Billy," she began as she turned toward him and leaned against her van, "you need to leave."

He smiled and shook his head. "I'm not gonna leave her. She needs me."

"Oh, please," she practically snarled. "She *needed* you ten years ago."

"I agree. And I think it's about time I began to be what …"

"Don't even start in on all that baloney," Cindy cut him short. "You've hurt her so deeply that the only hope you can possibly give her at this point in time is to just leave. Don't do this to her again."

"Cindy, I've done everything you said I needed to do before I considered trying to patch things up with her. I finished school, started living responsibly, put away some money—a lot of money, thanks to mom—and have applied for teaching positions all over north Alabama." He looked down at his feet before adding the next line. "And I became a Christian yesterday."

"What? Are you serious?"

"Yesterday morning," he affirmed. "I realized how impossible it was to try and make sense of all this within myself."

"Wait a minute," she said as she put her hand up to stop him. "You can't think that just because you … man … Billy, this is Sam's life you're playing with here!"

"Don't you think I know that? I'm tired of hurting her. But shoot, Cindy, I'm tired of hurting everybody! That's been the story of my life! Sam, Mother, Dad … everyone that I ever really loved I've managed to hurt as deeply as possible."

"Thus, the need for you to leave … now … before it gets any deeper." She glared at him in disbelief.

He took a deep breath and said, "I intend to marry her as soon as possible."

"No way!" she nearly screamed. "You've got to be out of your mind!"

"I'm gonna do it right this time. I'm not leaning on my own power

… or my own needs. I'm gonna focus on Sam."

"Yeah, right," she said sarcastically as she looked away from him. "You get saved one day and then expect God to just take over the next."

"Actually, I do. I'm tired of holding on to my life. That's why I turned it over to Him."

"Well, how convenient for you, Billy. Now you're using God to get things done your way."

"It's not like that. And you're being really unfair to me." He waited until she looked back at him. "You've told me, and shown me, the difference God can make."

"And it's not a show! It's something that took place deep within me that required a daily commitment and understanding of what I'd done. It wasn't an instant answer but just a beginning. It took time and growth and … well … time!"

"I don't have time," he said soberly. "She's pregnant."

Cindy's jaw dropped as she stared at him in more shock than before. "Then why didn't the father marry her? Is that your fault too? Did you butt in so much that the wonderful Dr. Crandall finally left her … carrying his child?"

Billy shook his head. "It's not Crandall's baby … it's mine."

"You've got to be kidding me," she said with disgust as she closed her eyes. "No wonder he left her. I kept trying to figure out why *he* wasn't with her and *you* were."

"Actually, he offered to marry her and raise the baby as his own."

Cindy looked back up at him with repulsion. "When did you sleep with her? How did you manage all this?"

Billy hated to tell her because he knew another lecture would ensue. "That weekend that I went with her to Georgia to settle her father's estate."

She nodded in remembrance. "Wonderful. So you just *comforted* her above and beyond the call of duty."

"It was wrong. And for the record, I knew it was just as wrong then as I do now. But that doesn't change all the facts that we're talking about at this moment."

"Right … your decision to step back into her life again … full force."

"I love her, Cindy. And whether you can understand it or not, she still loves me. The reason she couldn't marry Crandall had nothing to do with the baby. It was the fact that she still … loved … me."

Cindy just continued to shake her head.

He continued. "I'm not asking your permission. I believe this is the right thing to do. I was hoping Kyle could come and do it as soon as possible. But if you aren't willing to give us your blessing, I'll get someone else."

Cindy was speechless for the moment. She had come here with the full intent of persuading him to leave Sam for good, and yet here he was asking her to sanction another marriage.

"I can't believe she's pregnant," Cindy seethed out. "What kind of an idiot are you?"

"The worse kind," he admitted freely. "I've made more stupid mistakes than I ever want to count. But God has wiped my slate clean, and I now have a chance to start over … to really start over. Not just quit a job and go to college, but really do something that's positive for other people … other people that I can have a profound effect on." Billy actually had tears as he said, "I have a baby with her, Cindy. Even if I walked away from her and never spoke to her again, we would be eternally connected. Besides, I really do love her … really. I can't make her face this recovery and this child all alone. That would be downright cruel." He sighed and finished by saying, "If you can't trust me anymore, then I'm asking you to trust God in me … the same one that you trusted to take you from what you were … to where you are now … to an incredible woman of God."

She couldn't speak. She just shook her head and got into the van. Yes, God had worked a miracle in her life, but she knew how hard and how long it had taken. For her brother to just change overnight was not possible.

With God all things are possible.

Perhaps, but in this case she was most definitely a doubting Thomas.

As Billy watched her screech away, as close to two wheels as a minivan could get, he shook his head in disappointment. He knew she thought he was just playing another game.

Dear God, he whispered in his utter exhaustion, *this life isn't mine anymore. Help her to understand that what I've done is for keeps. You changed Frank Conwill—You're now transforming me.*

Ninety-Eight

The following Saturday found the Wright house hopping. School was out, Jonathan had come home the evening before, and Stephen and Annie were back together. Jonathan was still in a lot of discomfort, but that was to be expected after the ordeal he had been through. Things almost seemed normal to him, but what had once been normal would never be that way again. Carter would never be a part of these celebrations. As the years passed and Angie would return with her family from the mission field, they would never comment about how big he had grown, or what a fine young man he was becoming. They would never make on over the special skills God had gifted him with, or talk with him about his plans for the future. There would always be an unmentioned sadness because the family would never be truly complete again on this side of heaven.

And even though Hal Bridges was long gone to somewhere, the innocence and accord that had once characterized First Baptist of Dockrey was gone too. It would take years for the hurt and anger and resentment he had sown to be forgotten. In fact, it would probably take another generation. The committee was humiliated. Three had even left the church—Nancy Beth Tate, Tanya Rogers, and Stan Preston. And then poor Kyle felt ambushed. A literal third of the church had openly voted to express their disapproval of how he led worship. When Hal left, six members of the choir quit. They now sat out in the congregation with folded arms and defiantly refused to sing any congregational song, hymn or chorus. Yet all of this had caused Kyle to rise to the occasion rather than shrink in defeat. He mourned the struggles, but would square his shoulders every time he faced the church … and stayed on his knees asking God to show him every move to make where this ministry was concerned. Even this had galled some of the members. They had enjoyed being able to brow-beat him over every little issue and watch him squirm—but Kyle no longer squirmed.

Then there was Adam, the oldest of the grandchildren. As he had hit 13, he no longer fit in with the fun and games of the rest of the kids. He sat off on in a corner of the couch and continued to text message on his phone with anybody he possibly could that was not a part of this family. He barely looked anyone in the eye and kept his arms folded when his hands weren't occupied with the phone. It irritated Andie, and she took no pains to hide it. Jonathan wanted to take her aside and tell her to give him some space, to let him work through all that was happening to him, but Andie had never been one for advice. Besides, how do you tell a parent first dealing with a child entering the teenage years that things will never be the same? As a parent you just want to hold and protect them for as long as you can. Jonathan smiled and thought, *and you still want to hold and protect them even when they're grown.*

Stephen. Yes, he was back. Little Stevie was ecstatic as his life had been put back together. Annie was glowing as an expectant mother should, thrilled to have the love of her life back at her side. Jonathan was proud of her for finally managing to swallow her pride, one of the very few times in her life. But there were some issues concerning Stephen that he just couldn't release. Several times their eyes had met, and Stephen would immediately divert his attention. Guilt. It was written all over his face. Things would need to be settled if they were all going to attempt to live here together in Dockrey, so he walked slowly over to Stephen with a decision to set it straight before dinner was served.

"You and I need to talk," he said sternly as he held Stephen's uncomfortable stare.

"I thought that was probably the case," Stephen nodded. "I'm all ears."

Jonathan looked around the room and said, "Not here. We need to be somewhere more private."

Stephen swallowed hard. "The back porch? Your bedroom? I don't think you need to attempt the climb upstairs."

Jonathan glanced around again and then asked him, "Have you ever split wood before?"

"No sir, but I don't think you need to be splitting wood in your condition."

"I have no intention of splitting wood," he told him soberly. "But I think it's time *you* learned."

Both Stephen and Jonathan knew there was no need to tell anyone. As soon as they would discover them at the woodshed, everyone would know a serious conversation was taking place.

Jonathan pointed toward a long tool and suggested Stephen grab it so they could get started.

As Stephen picked it up and looked it over, he remarked, "This is a funny looking axe. It's really dull. Will it cut well?"

"It's not an axe—it's called a maul, and its purpose is not to cut wood but to split it."

"Oh," was all Stephen said as he watched Jonathan look over a pile of wood.

Jonathan finally began to point out certain pieces. "Grab that one … and this one over here … and then we'll try this one."

Stephen gently leaned the maul next to a tree and began to move one log at a time. Inside he was wishing Jonathan would just spit out the conversation and forget all the wood-chopping business, but that wasn't how Jonathan handled things. Stephen knew that whatever was about to be said would be serious and probably life-changing, so he just complied.

"Take that medium-sized one first and set it upright on this concrete slab," Jonathan said as he slowly eased himself down into an old, metal chair.

Stephen did as he was told, standing the log in the middle of the square.

"Now, lift the maul as high as you comfortably can, and then slam it down with considerable force right into the center of the log."

Stephen gave him an incredulous look. "Are you kidding me? I'll probably miss all together and end up chopping off one of my legs right below the knee."

"Naw, the blade's too dull. It might seriously bruise your leg, or even break it at the most, but it won't leave a scratch or cut through those jeans."

Stephen's jaw dropped as he looked back to Jonathan, but as the older man's eyes began to twinkle, Stephen smiled slightly. He looked back down at the log. "You know that deep inside I'm still just a city slicker, don't you?"

"We'll see. Place the maul in the center of the log first so you can get a feel for where it should land."

"You mean where it supposedly should hit after I've held it above my head and then forced it down with all my might?"

"Exactly."

Stephen shook his head again and placed the edge of the maul in the center of the log. He lifted it up about a foot a couple of times and gently brought it back down, trying to get a *feel* for it as Jonathan had suggested. He then lifted the tool above his head, held his breath, and brought it down with all his might, very tempted to close his eyes but not stupid enough to actually do so. When the maul hit the log, smack in the center, the one piece of wood became three cascading down to the concrete slab.

"Wow," Stephen said in awe. "I never thought I would do that."

"And on the first try, too. Not bad." Jonathan then pointed to the split wood pieces lying flat on the slab. "Now you need to add them to the pile under the woodshed here. Put them on this side where the fresher, less seasoned wood is."

He complied, and then went for the second log. He raised the maul again and came down right in the middle, sending the log into several different pieces. It was then that Jonathan began to really talk.

"You know, Stephen, as I lay on that table waiting for them to wheel me into surgery, knowing I might not wake up again on this earth, there were a lot of regrets that ran through my mind. But the first one I thought of that I regretted most was that first time I took the kids to see you in California at Christmas, and that I didn't pull my fist back as far as I could and way-lay you in the face with all my might."

Stephen was stunned. He just stopped and stared at Jonathan for a second.

"Had I done that instead of trying to play the humble Mr. Nice Guy, perhaps it would have knocked you silly enough to have avoided all the pain you put my daughter and grandchildren through these past few months."

Stephen was now leaning on the handle of the maul as he continued to stare at his father-in-law.

"Surprised, huh?" Jonathan snickered. "You work—I talk."

Stephen grabbed the third log as Jonathan continued.

"Instead, though, I tiptoed around the whole thing for the sake of my broken-hearted, guilt-ridden daughter, who might possibly have disowned me had I followed *my* feelings rather than *hers*."

As Stephen set the log on the slab, he commented, "I deserved anything you felt like dishing out. I know I blew it, and in a big way too."

"You certainly did, and it was hard toting those kids back and forth with their broken little hearts trying to explain to them that we loved them and didn't want to hurt them, yet left them with you in tears and fear."

Splat! The third log split as easily as the first two.

Jonathan then said, "But you need to know that I forgive you."

Stephen stopped and looked over at him again. "I don't deserve your forgiveness, sir. I know that."

"Actually," Jonathan sighed as he motioned for Stephen to continue with his job by placing the wood in the shed, "you do deserve my forgiveness. If God in Christ could forgive me, I most certainly can forgive you. Forgiveness is a gift God gives us, son, but the hard part is the forgetting."

Stephen paused as he walked toward the shed and dropped his head.

"I don't know what you were thinking, Stephen, when you walked out on your family like that. And where was God in all of it? Did you just think you could do whatever you felt like doing and then somehow go to God at a later date and have it all made right?"

Stephen dropped the last of the wood on the pile and confessed, "I don't really know what I was thinking. Perhaps I wasn't thinking at all."

Jonathan disagreed, "Oh, you were thinking all right. You were thinking only about you. And here's the sad part about sin—yes, you're forgiven, but the only one who'll be able to forget this, to separate this deed as far from the east is from the west … is God. The rest of us will remember it as long as we draw breath and have a clear mind."

That thought was sobering to Stephen as he tossed a couple more of the logs over toward the slab.

"I can choose to forgive you and let you back into my home and back into my life, but I can't humanly forget what you did to people very precious to me. Every time something comes up, I'll be sitting here on pins and needles praying that it doesn't happen again, praying that you learned your lesson, praying that you're a bigger man because of all this."

Stephen stopped him right there. "I won't do it again. I assure you I've learned my lesson."

"I wouldn't have thought you could've done it before. But I've come to believe that the man who left my daughter wasn't the same man that I agreed to let my daughter marry. Before you asked to marry Annie you spent a lot of time in discipleship with me. We went through *Experiencing God*, *The Mind of Christ,* and *Disciple's Prayer Life*. We would talk at least once a week about how things were going spiritually, and you kept yourself accountable to me. You assured me that when you and Annie married you would keep each other accountable, and let's face it—she needed it as much as you."

"And we did, for a long time, until … I guess … until the kids came," he explained as he set up another log.

"So the children came and Annie was exhausted, as well as you and you just dropped the ball spiritually," Jonathan surmised. "And whose fault do you think that was?"

Stephen lifted the maul again and slammed it even harder onto the log as he felt the tension build within him. "I suppose it was mine," he confessed. "You'd told me how important it was to be a spiritual leader for Annie … that she struggled with her faith often." Stephen wiped some sweat from his forehead. "It was hard to focus on that with all the stuff we were doing—a new baby, a new album, a new tour."

"That's why you needed a church, Stephen. You need someone who can keep you on your toes and encourage you to keep the main thing the main thing."

Stephen piled the wood into an arm and toted it over to the wood shed. He now understood why work and talk went together so well. It genuinely was helping to relieve the tension that was thick from this conversation.

"It happens to all of us at some time or another," Jonathan went on to explain. "I've been there myself. The only difference was that the people I fell back on weren't the high and mighty elite in the entertainment business. They were men and women of God who prayed for me and supported me in the Body of Christ. I know that you and Annie have a hard time with the press, but there are other options for fellowship and discipleship if they are things you indeed consider important."

Stephen nodded as he placed another log in place. "Like what you and I did before we got married."

"That's right. And back then, Stephen, we did that because you had the same problem as you do now—accountability. You're used to calling your own shots, handling your own matters, and it's something you've pretty much had to do your entire life. But God designed the church to need each other, each member relying on the gifts of all. When we pull away from the Body, it's hard to find that source of life."

He whacked away at the log, split it into pieces, and then carried them over to the pile. He knew what Jonathan was saying was absolute truth. Even though it did seem impossible for him and Annie to attend church most of the time, he could find a way to do something. When he had first fallen for Annie and realized her father wasn't going to accept just any average man spiritually for his strong-willed daughter, Stephen had dedicated himself to becoming a man that Annie could lean on spiritually as well as every other way.

"The reason you could walk out on Annie and your children," Jonathan finally detailed to him, "was because your vows and your family were no longer seen as pledges to and gifts from God. They became something much cheaper in your eyes at that moment, and there was no one there to tell you that your focus was way off. All you thought of was your own selfishness, and then you acted on it rather than call it into check."

"What about Annie in all of this?" Stephen asked a little perturbed that he was getting all the blame. "She did deceive me … for six years. That was a little hard to swallow."

"Was it now?" Jonathan raised his eyebrows. "The use of that word *deceive* gives the idea that she did something with evil intent—that she deliberately held that information from you out of malice and with the purpose of hoping to hurt you horribly. Is that what you really believe she did to you? Is that where you think her mind was?"

He shook his head. "No sir. I guess that's a bad word for what she did."

"Yet you and Annie have both used that same word time and again to describe what she did. And so it justified everything you did, and then it served as a tool to drive her deeper and deeper into a guilt that really wasn't fair."

Stephen stopped working, looked over at Jonathan and asked, "So what do I do now? I've lost your respect, I've lost my walk with the Lord, and I almost lost my family. I'd ask you to disciple me again, but I don't imagine you'd do it."

"You imagine correctly," Jonathan replied. "I'm not the one to do it anymore. Like I said, Stephen, I forgive you, and I really do mean that, but I don't see myself ever forgetting that it happened."

"What do I do, then? I don't want to fall back into this old life ever again. I've been more miserable these past six months than every other day of my life added together."

Jonathan thought for a while before he answered. "There are men in our church who could mentor you, but that isn't enough anymore. You need to lead your wife and your family back to church."

"But the paparazzi will hound us like crazy! It'll be more of a distraction to the church than a blessing!"

"Or," Jonathan said thoughtfully, "it could be a testimony to the world of your faithfulness to the true and living God … and an example to other men with issues and justifications about skipping church—they can look to your example and find encouragement to do the right thing also."

Ninety-Nine

"He's not letting up on Stephen," Annie said as she watched out the back window. "I don't like the idea of Daddy taking my husband to the woodshed. That was always just a family sort of thing … Stephen shouldn't have to do that. It's a bit humiliating."

"Or," Angie put her arm around her sister, "it could be an honoring thing. This lets Stephen and everyone else know that no matter what he did, he's still very much considered a part of this family. The fact that Daddy's taking him to task is a good thing. If he didn't, I know I would …"

"… or me," Andie said as she joined them at the window. "I'm glad to see it. Daddy's not an idiot. Whatever he's saying right now has been well thought out and carries some life-changing possibilities."

Annie sighed. "I suppose so. I hope he doesn't leave me again over all this."

"He won't," Angie assured her. "Believe me—he knows what he almost lost when he left you, and I don't imagine he'll ever try that again."

Cindy walked up and looked out the window with them. "What are they doing out there and why is Stephen having to chop wood? It's the end of May. Pastor Jon has enough wood stacked up to heat two winters already."

"This has nothing to do with wood," Angie told her. "Daddy always does this when he has to have a heart-to-heart with someone."

"I wish I could send Billy out there with him then," Cindy pouted. "He could use a big dose of heart-to-heart with someone other than me."

"What's he done now?" Angie asked.

Cindy made them all go out and sit down on the back porch as she explained the whole, long, drawn out story. And as she finished, she mournfully said, "And now he wants to marry her … again."

"Bravo!" Angie clapped. "I can't believe it! Billy Marcum got saved!"

Cindy stared at her in unbelief. "Supposedly … how do we know it's not just another trick? Billy is famous for saying and doing whatever is necessary to get whatever he wants."

Angie stared at her and sternly said, "And so were you."

The remark took Cindy off her guard. "I know, but I didn't make my peace with God one day and then up and marry Kyle the next. There was a lot of growth and time that took place."

Then Angie reminded her, "But you weren't pregnant with his child either."

"Are you saying that pregnancy is a good reason in itself to get married? Now not only does Billy have the opportunity to screw up Sam's life, he can mess up the little baby's too."

"What a minute," Andie broke in. "In Billy's defense, even before he professed salvation, I saw some major changes in him."

"Me too," Angie agreed. "When I first came back from Padawin, married to a missionary no less, he was still trying to hit on me. It was humiliating! But after your mother's death, it's like God began to finally peel back the layers. And from what you've told us, perhaps this shooting incident with Samantha was the final layer to go. Maybe, at last, God really did get his attention."

"But we don't know that!" Cindy defended her point. "It would be just like him to pull something like this so he could come off being the hero … but only for a little while."

"Or," Annie said with an authority that shocked everyone, "it could be the hand of God directly touching his life and putting it back together again."

Cindy sighed as she slouched back in her seat. "Seeing is believing is all I can say."

"No," Angie countered. "Praying is believing … then believing becomes seeing. Right now he needs your prayers and your confidence that God can work in *him* just like He did in *you.* It almost sounds like you don't believe God's powerful enough to change your brother."

Cindy hated to admit it, but, "You're probably right. It was easier for me to believe that God would somehow remove Hal Bridges in what appeared to be an impossible situation than it is for me to believe that Billy could really turn his life over to the Lord. I'm sorry, guys, but I've never seen Billy do anything other than whatever ultimately pleased Billy."

Barbara walked out on the back porch drying her hands on a dishtowel. "Angie," she said with a strange expression, "security has just alerted us that Levi Taylor is here to see you." Barbara held up her hands. "I told them to send him through. I hope that's alright."

Angie jumped from her seat. "Levi? You're kidding me!" She turned back to Cindy, "Go find Michael right away. Whatever this is about, he needs to be with me."

Angie followed her mother back into the main house and then ran to the kitchen window to look out. Sure enough, there was Levi's Mercedes SUV pulling up to the house. She knew better than to greet him outside the door—the paparazzi would have a field day with that whole scene again. Instead, she walked to the door and waited patiently for the knock.

"What's up?" Michael asked as he came trotting down the stairs.

"Levi's here," Angie said as the knock sounded. "I wanted you beside me so we could face whatever this is together."

He smiled reassuringly as he took her hand. "I'm here … for always."

Angie gently kissed his cheek and then opened the door. "Levi," she said softly. "It's really good to see you. Come on in."

Levi walked in and shook Michael's hand first … then he hugged Angie. "I really need to talk with you both."

"Sure," Angie told him. "Come on in and have a seat."

"I hope I'm not interrupting anything," he said warily. "I noticed a lot of cars out there."

"It doesn't matter," Angie said with a warm smile. "Even if it were some major important event, whatever you're here for has now become more important."

Levi laughed gently. "Good ole' Angie. You always knew how to put people at ease." He looked over at Michael. "You're an incredibly lucky guy, you know?"

Michael only nodded. He knew.

"So what brings you to the sticks of Dockrey?" Angie asked curiously. "I didn't think you went to places this out of the way anymore."

He smiled, folded his hands together, and then leaned back against the recliner. "A lot has happened in my life since Carter's death … starting with the fact that I almost lost it when he died." He shook his head as he remembered. "I couldn't believe that it all took place right there under my own roof. I was so determined to save him … to prove to you both that I had the power you were claiming your God had."

Angie and Michael both looked at him in surprise.

"All that talk," Levi continued, "about God and how real and awesome He was to you just grated on me. I told Gail that very night right before you discovered him sick that I was gonna be the one who healed that boy, and I was gonna make sure you both knew it. When you came running down to tell me how fevered and sick he was, a knot began to rise in the pit of my stomach that told me I'd made a huge mistake … I'd taken on your God.

"Cassie almost had me convinced … that little four-year-old … when she started talking about the reason I didn't see God was because I didn't like His *stuff* … I only liked my *stuff*. For all your years of explanations, Angie, none of them came close to hitting me as hard as Cassie's."

Angie wasn't offended. Instead, she squeezed Michael's hand and smiled proudly.

"I was determined to fight the infections and give him his life back, but everything I did was pointless, worthless. I was absolutely helpless. When he died, it was as though God was telling me I had no power … only whatever He was willing to grant me. I couldn't accept that. If that were true, what was the point of all the education and training? God was gonna do whatever He was gonna do anyway. I was simply a stupid puppet in His hands.

"When Gail went to the funeral, she was really convicted by your words, Angie. She was so moved that while she was heading back to Memphis, she saw this little Baptist church by the side of the road and noticed a couple of cars there. She was crying and upset and messed up about her whole life. She felt worthless and meaningless and believed our marriage was over. She went inside the church and found the pastor there. She began to pour out her confusion to him, and by the time she left, she had accepted Christ."

Angie practically jumped from the couch. "No way! Are you for real?"

He nodded. "Very for real. In fact, when she returned from the funeral, that was the first time I'd come back to the house. She saw me and grabbed me and told me that God was indeed for real, and that all we needed to do was put our lives in His hands. Well, you can imagine how that went over with me."

Michael suggested, "Like a ton of bricks?"

"Two tons," Levi added. "I told her I didn't want to hear anything about this God anymore. I was sick of Him and would spend every last ounce of energy proving that He wasn't real." He smiled and shook his head. "She asked why I was trying to fight someone I claimed didn't even exist. If I didn't believe in Him, why did it matter if I proved or disproved Him?" He paused. "I couldn't answer. I was just so mad at God—I felt if I could hurt Him it would somehow vindicate me.

"I would have left, but she actually begged me to stay. She said not to give up on our marriage. I told her I'd try it, but she was never to mention God to me … never. She asked if she could go to church, and I told her she could go every day if she wanted but to never ask me to step foot there. So she didn't. But man, the difference in her life was unbelievable. And what's so funny was that all the things that had once attracted me to you, Angie, began to come out in her life. I found her turning into this caring, considerate and nurturing being. She took care of me and loved me like I'd never been loved before. Finally, one day, I couldn't stand it and I asked her what had happened … what had made the difference. She just smiled and told me she couldn't tell me. I asked her why, and she said because I told her to never mention God again."

Levi smiled at Angie and then at Michael. "I released her. I said tell it all to me, from beginning to end. As she did, I knew in my heart it was all the truth. I realized too that it wasn't actually you, Angie, that my heart had longed for all those years. It was God in you. Having grown up in an agnostic family, I craved the reality of God but refused to accept it. But when I saw His power work in Gail's life day after day, week after week, month after month, never failing, never falling, I could no longer deny the truth."

Angie's jaw dropped. "You became a Christian?"

"Three weeks ago," he grinned.

Angie jumped from the couch with a scream and pulled him up from the recliner. "Why didn't you call me then?" She pulled back to look him in the eyes. "We've prayed for you and Gail every single day since … well … since we moved into your house."

"I didn't know," he shrugged. "I thought for sure you'd gone back to your island with Cassie and the new baby. I didn't imagine the States held anything more for you here."

"Babies," Michael corrected him.

"What?" he asked.

"We had twin boys," Michael said humbly. "God blessed us with two this time."

Levi only shook his head again. "Unbelievable. At least I know now why you were so dog-gone big."

"We had no idea until they were born," Angie explained.

"Can I see them?" Levi asked hesitantly. "If they're asleep, it's okay."

Angie smiled her typical smile and motioned him toward the stairs. "These boys could sleep through a tornado."

One Hundred

The following Friday Billy found himself frantic over the rings as he searched every nook and cranny in the Mustang.

"Would you hurry up?" Cindy said impatiently and she and Kyle stood outside waiting for him to get it all together.

"I can't find them!" he moaned as he hit his head popping up from the car.

"Can't find what?" she asked.

"The rings! The wedding rings!" he exclaimed as he bent back down into the car. "I thought for sure I had put them here between the seats."

Kyle smiled as he tapped Billy's back. "You gave them to me, pal … back at the house before we left."

Billy popped back up and hit his head again.

Cindy reached up to rub his head. "You need to settle down. Everything's just fine. We're here, Sam called this morning to say she was ready and waiting, and you're about to become a married man … for the last time, I hope."

He gave a crooked smile. "Absolutely the last time. I can't believe I'm this nervous. I wish it could be at the church in Dockrey with a pretty ceremony and all our friends around, but I don't want to put it off. I want Sam to be my wife, and I want our baby to carry my name."

"Well then," Cindy said impatiently again, "why on earth are we standing outside this hospital talking?"

Billy closed the door, locked the car, and led the trio hurriedly toward the door of the building. He had wanted to wear a suit and tie, but considering Sam would be in a hospital gown, he figured a Polo shirt and khakis would suffice. At least he had remembered a bouquet of roses for her. He glanced down at the pink flowers and then lifted them to his nose for one more sniff. It brought a smile to his face. Sam loved roses. He wondered if Jeremy Crandall had ever figured that out.

They found themselves rushing from the elevator toward the room when Kyle caught the twins by the arms and pulled them to an abrupt stop.

"Guys," Kyle said softly. "Can you both just settle down here a little bit … for Sam's sake? We don't need to go barreling in there like a herd of buffalo. Let's just stop, take a deep breath, and slow down. She's probably nervous too, and I don't imagine this is exactly her dream wedding."

Cindy rolled her eyes. "They had the dream wedding once. That should suffice. But we need to get moving so they can take her down to run those next tests. I don't want them waiting on us."

"Yeah, right," Kyle said sarcastically. "Like the medical staff is actually waiting on us to do anything. They're always running behind."

A large nurse walked by and snidely remarked, "I heard that, boy. I'd like to see you waltz in here and do any better."

"Sorry," Kyle called out after her. "I was really just making a point, not a criticism."

She turned back without stopping and said, "Uh huh."

They slowly opened the door to Sam's room and found her reading the Bible quietly as she sat up in the bed. The sight warmed Billy more than he could have imagined. The new life that he and Sam had found in the Lord was bonding them in ways they had never understood before.

"Hey, ponytail," he said softly as he went to her and presented her the roses. "Your bouquet."

She put her hand to her mouth and tears begin to wash her eyes immediately. "You didn't have to do that."

"Well, it's just the kind of guy I am," he replied with his most charming grin.

Kyle grabbed her toes and wiggled them beneath the covers. "Are you ready to do this? Ready to become a part of this family again?"

Sam nodded confidently. "Truth be known, I don't think my heart ever really left this family."

"It didn't," Cindy confirmed as her tears were beginning to form also.

Billy sighed and closed his eyes. "How can you two be crying? We haven't even started the ceremony yet?"

Suddenly the large nurse came in. "So we're making the deception real at last? I can't believe you had us believing you were her husband."

"In name I still was," Billy tried to reason.

"And we could've been sued over all of this," the nurse replied curtly with no apparent sense of humor at all. "We'll know better next time someone saunters in claiming to be a husband, flashing around a driver's license."

"Stop complaining," Sam insisted to the nurse. "Had he not been here, it's very possible I wouldn't be here too." She reached for his hand. "I think he's the only reason I was able to hang on for a while there."

"Well," the nurse sighed, "let's just chalk it up to a miracle and leave it at that. Are you ready? I don't have a whole lot of time here to serve as a witness. The medical staff is already too slow for the likings of some." She raised an eyebrow towards Kyle.

☼☼☼

Stephen and Annie showed up for church on Sunday morning followed by a pack of paparazzi. The famous couple refused to speak, look, smile or even nod in the direction of the cameras. A few managed to follow them on into the church, but it wasn't near the problem it would have been had the entire church actually been there. Jonathan did make it clear during the pre-service announcements that this was private property and picture taking of any kind was prohibited because it interfered with the worship. All were welcome, but anyone choosing to disrupt the service for any reason would be escorted out and on to jail if necessary.

After the singing Jonathan slowly moved toward the pulpit. He reached back to turn on the lapel mic and then looked out over the congregation. It was just as he had anticipated—one-third of what had already dwindled had left also. A part of him hurt over that fact, but another part actually rejoiced. It hurt because that meant those who were gone had been something else at this church other than the fullness of God. It hurt because they had fallen prey to an ungodly leader instead of trusting leaders who had sacrificed their lives for the sake of the ministry—would have laid down their lives for any member in need. It hurt because it gave evidence that what Jonathan had thought was a thriving part of the Body of Christ was really only a faithful remnant with a large group of thrill seekers simply catching the ride for what it could offer them. No wonder it had been so hard to get workers to fill up the spots needed to carry out all the ministries that were growing as a result of the numbers.

But he found joy at the faces of the faithful. Those who were here now were those who desired to do the work of the Father and to walk with the Father. These were the ones who filled the positions, who sought to obey God and follow their pastor, and who had probably questioned Hal Bridges from the beginning as the sixty-forty vote had indicated. These were the ones who wouldn't question what to do now, but would simply pray and volunteer to be a part of whatever plan was offered next.

"Good morning, flock," he said warmly. "It's a bigger blessing than you know to see these particular faces here this morning."

Slowly the church began to applaud and come to their feet. He was moved at the response, but he quickly quieted them with his hands and motioned for them to be seated.

"There is much to be said from this pulpit today, and though I know many of you believe we should leave the cameras on for all those absent to see this service, I'll be frank with you—I don't want anyone back here out of guilt. Guilt won't compel ministry, and that's the point of this church. I've never been in this for the reputation, and I won't start now by complaining that our numbers are significantly down.

"When I began pastoring here over thirty years ago, I promised you I'd be up front with you and never pretend to be more than I was." He paused to catch his breath. He was still quite weak. "However, I now need to confess to you for pretending to be less than I was. The griping and complaining about the fact that I sit in on every committee meeting, even though it's plainly stated I'm to do so in the constitution, it was beginning to grate on me. My goal has never been to control this church but to lead it. As the undershepherd of this flock, I'm held accountable to God for what goes on here. When I see evidence that we're heading in a direction that doesn't line up with the purposes of God for this church, I'm bound by my call to make it known. But folks, I'm as human as the rest of you. Being accused of trying to be a big shot, trying to force my personal ideas and goals over what the rest of you want is hard to swallow. So as I sat and listened to the search committee mull over Hal Bridges, I knew there was something about it that wasn't right. Call it a hunch, call it being led by the Spirit, call it just a good dose of trying to be careful … I don't know … but I do know that had I said anything, had I rightly discussed my misgivings, I would have been accused of things that weren't true, and my leadership concerning this church would have been questioned … again."

Jonathan looked toward Tom Richards and then down at Floyd Benson. "I find it interesting that only two members of that committee have chosen to remain here. And Floyd, I think the fact that you didn't leave with the rest of them says a whole lot about your character."

Floyd nodded in appreciation, but Tom Richards suddenly raised his hand and stood.

"Pastor Jon," Tom said with authority, "if you don't mind, I'd like to say something here."

"Why not?" Jonathan replied. "This is gonna be a very unconventional service anyway."

Tom stood where he was as he explained to the church, "You all need to know that Pastor and I knew the truth about Hal a couple of months ago, but he didn't want to divide the church, nor did he want to hurt the committee or cause any kind of embarrassment. Because of that, he said the best we could do at this point was to sit on the information and just pray for God's timing. His real hope was that Hal would stop playing games and just come clean. Pastor was more than willing to give him a second chance to do the job for real if Hal would just … I guess … repent. But when he took the vote that Sunday morning about what kind of songs Kyle should be leading, your pastor realized that Hal was now openly defying a minister in the church, and it wouldn't be long before this church became more about loyalties to men than loyalty to God.

"I know many of you are concerned about the new building and whether we can afford to carry on with the project," Tom continued. "Frankly, I don't care anymore. As far as I'm concerned, it can be a stigma of humiliation reminding us what happens when we begin to think we're bigger than we really are—and when we begin to look for newer, flashier things and newer people over what we've seen and known to be truly trustworthy."

Tom sat down, but then Stephen raised his hand and stood. "May I say something?"

Jonathan nodded again.

"First, I want to thank all of you for your prayers and your concern for our whole family these past few months. You've been as much of a blessing to me as I would allow you to be. And I want you to know that the new building outside will never become a trophy of disgrace for this church—some half-built structure that reminds you of a tough time we all went through. Annie and I will gladly add to whatever is needed to see the building not only completed, but up and running and fully functional on all levels as it was originally planned."

There were many verbal responses to Stephen's statement, and Jonathan could begin to feel healing take place already. More people stood to talk, all reaffirming that it wasn't the size of the church that concerned them, but rather the hearts of those who attended. Others confessed had they been more willing to disciple some of the newer members, perhaps all of this would have been handled with much more maturity. Still others began to express the need for more consistent and pointed prayer in the church. As the service began to draw toward a close, Jonathan felt encouraged for the first time in months.

"Now," he said, leaning against the pulpit as he was beginning to tire significantly, "I need to say one more thing." He was getting emotional, something he hoped wouldn't happen, but he couldn't help it. "I personally have no desire to stop pastoring."

"Neither do we!" yelled a man from the congregation.

Jonathan smiled. "But my doctor has a different opinion."

The reality of what he had said slowly dawned throughout the church.

"I never intend to stop ministering," he told them soberly. "When someone finds me dead, it'll be with a Bible in one hand and a Gospel tract in the other. But Dr. Norman says the old ticker can't handle this kind of stress anymore."

There began to be gasps around the room.

"I don't plan to just walk out and leave you high and dry," he reassured them. "Kyle is here with me, and he'll make an excellent associate pastor working by my side while you search for a new over-pastor. And when you find the right man, I'll then get the opportunity to do something I've never been able to do—mission work. We've sent teams from this church all the way from South America to Montana, but I've never been able to go because my job was to pastor here. So I'll get to move on for a change … perhaps even visit some missionaries I'm very close to down in the South Pacific." He winked toward Angie.

"But I want to close this morning with a thought that I hope will inspire you as our church faces this new era." He glanced around the room trying to look into each face as much as possible. "Very soon summer will be upon us. The days will be predictably warm again and we'll enjoy time with family and time with friends that just doesn't seem to happen the rest of the year. But just as in the summer, even now, each morning we awake with a sunrise. Sometimes its cloudy or rainy—which it has been an awful lot this winter—but nevertheless the sun is always there and always faithful. Even though we may not see direct sunlight for days, it's still there. But in the summer … ahhh … it just seems so much brighter and definitely so much warmer."

He stepped from behind the pulpit and went to the edge of the platform. "This church has seen a tough, bitter and rainy winter, but there's a summer sunrise just on the horizon. I challenge all of us to forget the cold, forget the old, and begin to see what new things God has in store for us. Anticipate with me the sunrise, the warmth, the return of the summer, and let's just begin again. As Paul said so clearly, *Forgetting what lies behind and pressing on* …" He nodded as he held out his right hand to the church. "Who will look with me … look for the next summer sunrise?"

Stephen leaned into Annie's ear and whispered, "Do you think there's a song in there somewhere?"

"Summer Sunrise," she said thoughtfully. "Do you want to take the words or the music?"

"I don't know yet," he replied. "When we get home, we'll just see what comes out."

One Hundred One
(Christmas Eve—Seven Months Later)

As the Mustang rolled into Dockrey, Sam continued to lean her head against the window. This wasn't what she had wanted to hear, especially on Christmas Eve. She had assumed the doctor's desire to meet with her on the doorstep to Christmas was to impart some wonderful news to brighten up the holidays. Instead it had been to give her the final blow. She had managed not to cry the whole way home from Florence, but as they drove into town, the emotions were ready to overflow.

Billy reached over and took her hand as he said, "Sam, this is all gonna be okay. It could've been worse. At least you do have partial movement, and you can lift it almost to your head now."

She squeezed back, but her thoughts weren't near as positive. "I can't even pick up my own baby by myself," she choked out. "I'll never be able to reach down into Will's crib and pick him up on my own." A tear finally fell.

"You don't know that yet, however, there are so many other things you have that you can be thankful for. Sam, I'm just thrilled to have you in my life, to have the Lord in my life, and to have Will in my life. I wouldn't trade anything for those … not even a good arm for you."

She leaned her head back against the seat and sighed. "I know you're right, and I should snap out of all this before we get home. It's not fair for me to rain on everybody else's Christmas just because I'm depressed."

"Then don't be depressed anymore," he said as he flashed her his charming smile.

"Just like that?" she asked as she glanced over at him.

"Yes," he said resolutely. "And you can start by being thankful for all that you do have." He held up his five fingers and added, "Give me the top five things you're most thankful for."

"Just five?"

"See there," he chided her, "you have so much … you're already complaining because I'm making you limit them to five. So start—give me your top five."

She looked out the window as she tried to think of her list. He was right—she had much to be thankful for. "First would be that God finally got a hold of my life and saved me through and through. Nothing can outshine that."

"Agreed," he said enthusiastically. "That's number one. What's next?"

"Hmmm, that's a tossup. I don't know who to list first, you or Will?"

"Start with Will," he insisted. "I'm a big boy. I can hold my own with third if I must."

She started to grin a little now. "I have a very healthy little two-month-old baby boy. And I'm thankful that he was *not* a twin."

"Then we'd better not plan on having any more. With me being a twin, we could end up like Kyle and Cindy."

She shook her head. "One at a time is all I want. I can't believe they're expecting again in the spring."

"Well, keep in mind, twins could happen to us just as easily," he reminded her. "So what's number three? I believe it had something to do with me, didn't it?"

She gently punched his arm. "Of course—number three is that you have most definitely become the man of my dreams. Not only do I have my Billy back, but I have a wonderful Godly husband who caters to my every whim. I didn't think you actually had it in you."

"And we're just starting out. Have I got some great surprises for you during our first Christmas together as a real family."

She raised her eyebrows. "Really? What kind of surprises?"

"That's so like you—trying to make me tell you what I've got up my sleeve." He shook his head in mock disgust. "I said they were surprises, and that's what they'll continue to be. Now, what's number four on your list?"

She took a deep breath as she pondered. "I guess the fact that we're building our own house on the property right next door to Cindy. That has to rank in the top five somewhere."

"Agreed again," Billy nodded. "It's been great living with them since I got that Jr. High teaching position here in Dockrey, but I do miss our privacy, especially since Will's come."

"But they're good about letting us have time alone," she reminded him. "And Cindy's been wonderful about helping me with Will since I can't … you know … pick him up … alone."

"Don't start on that again," Billy said immediately. "We're talking about being thankful, remember? Which brings us to number five. What's last on your list?"

"Last makes it sound so final … like that's the end of it."

"But it's not—it's just your top five. So what is it?"

She had to think long and hard about this one. If it rounded out her list of most thankful things, it had to be worthy. "I guess that we're building a special room on the house for Mama to come and live in." She smiled, still surprised by her decision.

"I agree with that one too. The last two times we saw her she remembered you. I know it'll be hard for her to leave Georgia and come to a strange place, but at least you'll be here for her."

"And she can help me with Will."

Billy reached for her hand and gently kissed the back of it. "So, are you happy to be alive, with or without the full use of your right arm?"

She nodded with another smile as she answered, "I believe I'm even more than happy. I would say I'm close to ecstatic." She rubbed his hand. "Thanks for reminding me what matters most."

"I'm good, ain't I? How did you ever live without me?"

☼☼☼

Cindy continued to jostle little Will in her arms as Kyle stirred the pot while talking on the phone to Stephen. Will had never been separated from Sam this long before, and he was hungry and tired. Cindy had offered him a bottle, but he would have none of it. He wanted his mother and that was that.

When Kyle was finally finished with Stephen, he came over to Cindy and held out his arms for the baby. "Let's trade for a bit. You finish supper, and I'll try and calm the baby."

"I'm fine … really," she insisted as she pulled back with the baby. "I seldom get my hands on him, and I'm loving every minute of this … even if *he* isn't."

Kyle smiled as he watched Cindy's attentiveness toward the child. "I bet it's a whole different story just having to handle one baby at a time."

Cindy gave him a big grin and a nod. "I'm just getting in some practice ahead of time. At least when this one is born," she motioned toward her expanding tummy, "Sam and Billy will be right next door. I'll have built-in extra help."

Kyle came up and wrapped his arms around her. "Life is good, Cindy. Even though we've had some tough times through it all—it's still good."

She smiled back, but tears began to fill her eyes.

"What's wrong, hon?" Kyle asked concerned.

She just shook her head; she couldn't talk about it at the moment. "Tell me," she choked slightly, "about Stephen and Annie."

Kyle understood. Cindy had become very emotional around the holidays. Having Billy and his family with them had been wonderful, but it made her miss her parents all the more. She wished desperately that they could have seen this legacy … in their home—their children finally walking with the Lord and raising their families to do the same.

He would talk about something neutral for a moment. He had been meeting with Stephen once a week since July to disciple and mentor him in his faith. Also, Kyle had let go of the youth and become the associate pastor along with the music to help take up some of the slack needed as Jonathan began to slow down. A new youth minister had been hired fresh out of seminary, and Kyle felt comfortable and relieved to place the reins of that ministry into his hands. Jody was a whole different man than Hal had been, and he fit into the staff and church perfectly. He had become a part of the family, and Kyle felt as though he was a little brother in many ways. Jody had even talked Billy and Sam into helping with the youth. They had chaperoned youth camp last summer, and the teenagers fell in love with them as a result.

"Needless to say, Stephen and Annie are loving their holidays," Kyle told her as he went back into the kitchen to stir the pots again. "He says Annie's tan is so awesome that she could give Angie a run for her money."

"Really?" Cindy replied with surprise as she began to gain control of her emotions. "She never was one for sunbathing."

"The kids are having a ball," he continued. "They actually think this whole little Christmas getaway was designed specifically with them in mind."

"I can imagine, although I'd be scared to death to let my kids run around on something like that."

"They've got a fulltime nanny with them specifically for this trip … not to mention a huge staff."

"I know, but still, how do you trust strangers like that with your children?"

"I guess they're used to it by now."

Cindy shifted Will to her other arm and was thankful he had finally begun to settle. His sleepy eyes were heavy, and he seemed content enough for the moment to just chew on her finger. "And what about the baby? How is little Emily handling being away from home? I can't imagine taking a trip like that with a four month-old."

"Me either," Kyle admitted.

Suddenly Devin came bustling around the corner of the room. "They're back!" he exclaimed, but in a soft voice. He had been very worried about Will because of all the fussing and decided to make himself sentinel concerning Billy and Sam's return.

Cindy quickly put her finger up to her lips. "Remember—we don't mention that Will wasn't happy about their being gone. Aunt Sam will never leave him with anyone again if she thinks he's unhappy all the time."

"But he was unhappy … the whole time," Devin replied.

"But until he realizes that sometimes his mama can't be here … and that she always comes back eventually … he'll fuss like this every time she leaves. Let Aunt Sam go a few more times, and we'll have him happy as can be before long."

"If you say so," Devin moaned doubtfully turning back toward the door.

One Hundred Two

Doug placed the last of the put-together gifts beneath the tree and then joined Andie on the couch. He stared at all the money represented by all the gifts and smiled. "As an only child," he told her, "to have seen something like this would have blown me away." He reached for her hand and said, "I think having five kids is downright cool."

"Or crazy," Andie said mournfully.

"Well, babe, we've been doing pretty good," he teased. "We haven't had a kid in four years. Do you think we're through, or should we try for one more?"

Andie said nothing, but only glared at him.

"What has got you so bah-humbugged tonight?" he asked a bit irritated. "All day long we've been doing all this last minute, festive, Christmas Eve-y stuff, and you're acting like it's the end of the world."

She sighed. "Sorry. I didn't realize it was so obvious."

"Is it the turkey thing?" he wondered.

"What?" she looked at him with slight disdain. "What turkey thing?"

"Well, I know you've been real nervous about cooking a turkey for the first time ever in your life. But don't worry about it. I told all the kids to just pretend it's the greatest thing they've ever tasted … no matter how it turns out."

Andie's glare now became more severe. "Tell me you really didn't do that."

"Actually," he looked horribly guilty, "I really did."

He watched as Andie balled her fist.

"Why do you do that?" he asked in an attempt to change the subject. "You always threaten to whack me whenever I do something that grates on you, but the truth is—you've only actually hit me once. Wasn't it over that comment I made about Delilah Motes in the high school beauty pageant? We were juniors, I think."

"For crying out loud, Doug!" Andie exclaimed. "Her name wasn't Delilah! It was Delia! And the reason I slugged you was because you said you would love to play *Samson* to her *Delilah*."

Doug thought for a moment. "Really? I don't remember it like that at all. I thought all I said was something about wishing they had a swimsuit competition. No wonder you never hit me again. All this time I had it wrong. The thing that makes you mad enough to pound me is Biblical comparisons?"

Andie just shook her head.

"So, what are you all bummed about this Christmas Eve?" he asked her again. "It's been unnaturally relaxed today compared to what we're used to … hauling everyone over to your parents and all the typical Wright clan chaos."

Andie sighed again. "I suppose that's what I'm missing … all the chaos."

Doug's eyebrows flew up. "Are you serious? You don't think it's great just being here with our family alone for a change?"

She shrugged. "It's not so much the *our family* thing as much as it is that *my family* is out of the picture for the first time ever in my life. Do you realize I've never spent a Christmas season without my parents?"

"Really?" He considered it for a moment. "I guess you're right." He then grinned at her and said, "I guess it's about time. The first official Christmas holidays at the Mason house."

"I know we've spent Christmas *Day* here the last few years, and it's been wonderful, but the rest of it, the holidays leading up to Christmas, and of course, always Christmas Eve—has been spent at my parents'. It's like … I don't know … tradition or something. I'm having a hard time feeling Christmas-y without all of that."

"With five kids, babe, we'd better start our own Christmas traditions. I mean … we don't need to be hauling Adam and Arly and their wives and kids all over to your parents' place every year. *Our* place is the one where they need to be going. And we need to have some traditional things of our own too … things that didn't happen at your parents."

"I suppose." There was no pulling her out of the glum mood.

"We could start with you cooking a really bad turkey," he quipped. "Every year we could anticipate it and …"

"My turkey will be great, Doug," she said firmly. "Moms told me exactly how to prepare it and cook it. You're gonna have to come up with something better for tradition than that."

"She really told you how to do it? I guess I'd better tell the kids to lay off all the turkey compliments tomorrow then … and put the M&M's back into hiding."

"What do you mean by that?"

"When Adam and Arly and Ashley were Christmas shopping with me that last time, we bought a big bag of M&M's to munch on throughout Christmas day in case we couldn't fill up on your … well, your turkey."

Andie stared at him and shook her head. "Why do you do bizarre things like that? Our kids are gonna be so warped by the time they leave home."

"Warped? I was just thinking about keeping your feelings intact."

Andie snickered for the first time. "You're not right, Doug. I guess it's inevitable that our kids will be warped in some way."

He pulled a piece of paper from the coffee table containing some assembly instructions, wadded it up, and then tossed it into the fire. He hit it perfectly. "Ah … three pointer! Warped, but very impressive when it counts."

Andie pulled his arm around her and leaned into him on the couch as she stared at all the presents in the living room. "Did we go into debt this year over Christmas?"

"Absolutely!" he said with mock excitement. "We'll be finished paying it off hopefully before next Christmas."

"Why did we do that?" she wondered. "Nobody really needed a new bike … or a Barbie house … or a video game system."

"Nope, but then Adam didn't really need a new expensive electric guitar with a 125 watt amp either, did he?"

"Actually, I think he did," she disagreed. "After all we went through with him last spring, I was beginning to think we'd lost him … and he was barely even a teenager. Then when he found out Jody was coming to replace Kyle, you would've thought he had reached his darkest moment. Without Kyle leading the youth, church had officially lost what little luster it had left for him."

Doug smiled as he rubbed her shoulder and added, "But he hadn't planned on Jody being so … what was the word Adam used?"

"Awesomazing."

"There you go. And then youth camp with him this summer totally changed his life."

"So, I'm thinking," Andie concluded, "that an expensive guitar and a twenty-five watt amp was a worthy investment."

"It's a 125," Doug corrected her.

"What is?"

"The amp … 125 watts … not twenty-five. A twenty-five watt amp would be rather puny and pathetic … pretty embarrassing to plunk down on a stage."

"One twenty-five … one twenty-six … whatever … the point is, if he wants to lead worship in the youth group rather than learn new choice words of profanity with his school buddies, the amp and guitar are good gifts."

"Agreed." He grabbed another set of used instructions, balled them up, and tossed them toward the fire. "Yes! Douglas Mason scores again. It must be awesomazing being married to a guy like me. So much so, that I bet I could get your mind off of the fact that your mama and daddy are gone for Christmas, your two sisters are gone for Christmas, and even your itty bitty baby brother won't be home for Christmas."

Andie gave a skeptical glimpse. "And how do you propose to do that?"

He grinned and pulled her closer. "We could try for number six?"

Andie actually punched him as she jumped up from the couch. "Doug, if I end up pregnant again, you might as well just commit me somewhere."

"Okay … okay," he backed down. "I was really just kidding anyway, but I thought it might be a good line … you know … to sort of … well …"

"Get me in the mood?" she said contemptuously.

"Well … yeah … but I'm realizing now that it probably was more like a bad joke … huh."

She wouldn't respond. She merely tapped her foot impatiently.

"A really bad joke," he said meekly as he came to his feet. "How about I change directions and try a more eclectic approach?"

"Eclectic?" she nearly laughed. "Do you even know what that word means?"

"Absolutely! Instead of boxing the whole thing in to just baby-making, let's move toward the *one hot mama* arena. That leaves the possibilities wide open."

Andie just smiled and shook her head. From fifteen to thirty-eight, Doug had changed very little, but that was probably why she still loved him. As other men grew old and boring, Doug still pretty much acted like an adolescent always on the verge of a great practical joke. If he had ever become too serious, they would have probably drowned in melancholy together.

"Well," she yawned, "your *one hot mama* is ready for bed."

Doug gave a loud whoop and pulled her into a firm embrace. "That's what I'm talking about!"

One Hundred Three

Annie couldn't remember the last time she had read through an entire novel. As she set on the front deck of the yacht overlooking the Mediterranean Sea and the Greek Isles, she felt not only warmed by the sun and her surroundings, but also warmed at the calm in her life at last. The year had started out horribly and had gone downhill from there. Even after Stephen came back, there was still a lot of unspoken tension concerning him with the rest of her family. It hadn't been until Emily's birth that they began to see how important family was to Stephen, and that he truly regretted the actions he had taken. Her birth had broken him.

The delivery was much harder than the first two, and when complications began to develop, there was a possibility they might even lose the baby. Stephen fell apart, blaming himself for any problem that his stress toward Annie might have caused. He had grabbed Jonathan and Doug and pleaded with them to pray with him in the chapel. During that time he confessed more than he imagined he could ever confess before those men, but it brought about a healing that *he* needed … as well as them. Both men had struggled with harboring resentment and distrust toward him, and he had felt it. When the doctor decided to do an emergency C-section, Andie had run down to the chapel to inform them all. That's when Stephen really broke.

"Miss Annie," came Rodney's English accent out on the deck. "Do you know where I might possibly find Mr. Stephen?"

Annie put down her book and gave him her attention. Rodney kept the boat and the staff running smoothly. The only thing he didn't do was drive it, and she was thankful for the effort he had made to ensure that this truly was a vacation for relaxing and remembering.

"I honestly don't know where he is," Annie replied. "What time is it?"

"Precisely three-o-two," he said as he glanced down at his watch.

Precisely. Annie smiled. Every answer Rodney gave was always *precise*. "You might check the exercise room. He's been taking the mid afternoons trying to get back in shape."

"Very good. He has a phone call … appears to be rather urgent."

Annie's interest peaked. "Really? From whom?"

"She said she was his agent … a Miss Artie."

"Artie's calling him while he's on vacation? It must be urgent."

Rodney headed back for the door. "I'll see if perhaps he is working out as you suggested. Thank you, Miss Annie." And with that he gave a slight bow and left, almost running into Constance and the baby who were heading for Annie on the deck.

"Oh my!" Rodney exclaimed as he backed away quickly. "Please excuse me. I had no idea you were there, and I was in the midst of trying to find Mr. Stephen for an important phone call."

Constance's sweet expression put him at ease at once. "It's no problem, Rodney. Continue your quest."

"Very good, mum," he said hurriedly with a bow as he headed down the stairs.

Annie reached out her hands as Constance approached with a fussy Emily. "Is someone ready for her mama?"

"Very much so," Constance said with all the grace and poise of a beauty contestant. It was hard to believe that someone so accomplished and intelligent would hire herself out as a nanny. "She has finally decided that my bag of tricks will no longer suffice."

"Glad to hear it," Annie remarked truthfully. It had scared her to think Constance would be spending this two week vacation watching the three children right under Annie's nose, but Stephen had insisted that Annie have a true vacation. Constance had come highly recommended, and highly priced, but Annie could understand why—she was perfect. And Annie had enjoyed the time to herself. She had done a lot of reading, a lot of praying, and a lot of nothing … just sitting in the warm sun on the deck of the yacht drinking in the beauty of the sea and the islands.

"I'm beginning to think that she got more of your genes other than just the dark hair and dark eyes," Constance said with a playful grin.

"And what exactly do you mean by that?" Annie asked as she took little Emily into her arms and nuzzled her head beneath her chin.

"Oh, you know that reputation you have," Constance teased, "always striving for perfection."

Annie laughed. "And you're saying that this four-month old is a perfectionist already?"

"Unmistakably!" Constance dropped down into a chair beside her. "This child knows exactly what she wants and will not be placated with anything less. She'll tolerate me as long as she's not exhausted, but when she reaches that point, I'm learning that only mama will do."

"That's my girl," Annie smiled as she looked deeply into the baby's big, dark eyes.

Constance took in the sight and added, "I find that very admirable … and very rare."

"Really?" Annie was surprised. "Why do you say that?"

Constance leaned back and closed her eyes against the sun as the wind off the sea blew about her willowing blond hair. "In my line of work I seldom find a truly doting mother. I'm basically hired to become the surrogate mother." Constance reached over and ran her finger gently down Emily's fat little arm. "And you're the first mother I've worked for that actually nurses a child. All of this is almost turned around for me. Generally I'm the one the children are crying for."

"I can't imagine that," Annie shook her head. "I'm not wired that way at all."

"It's kind of sad for me really," Constance explained. "I have worked in three different homes, and each time I was handed extremely confused and maladjusted children. But within a few short weeks, we developed a wonderful bond."

"Three? That seems like an awful lot for someone so young," Annie noted. "I would imagine that you would stay with them throughout the years."

"That would be my plan too, but the rich and famous often have egos the size of Godzilla," Constance said sadly. "The first family, and you would know them if I told you, was very pleased with me at the beginning. But when the children no longer found them interesting and would rather be with me than displayed somewhere at an event or outing, the mother became indignant, accusing me of poisoning her children against her."

"You're kidding me!"

"Not at all. Yet they were so young. They felt secure and loved with me, and it was so hard to leave them." Constance shook her head as she recalled the scene. "Then the second family … well … the wife thought the husband had a thing for me. She even insisted I wear these drab, ugly uniforms and keep my hair pulled up in a bun."

"Why do you put up with all that?" Annie wondered. "You're too good to be treated so unfairly."

"When you've been trained as extensively as I have, and are paid as highly as I am, you come to grips pretty quickly with the fact that women carry a lot of guilt when they see someone doing an excellent job at something that's really their job in the first place."

Annie glanced at Constance over the rim of her sunglasses. "I can see how intimidating you could be."

"It's not intentional. I just love children, and I take my job seriously."

"And what about the third family?"

"Yes, that was rather sad. They're not as *rich* and *famous* or as busy as they used to be. They could no longer pay me."

Annie nodded. "Well, I'm very glad that you were between jobs long enough to take this little cruise with us. The kids have had a ball."

"And they're so adorable. I'm never with children who get normal family attention. I usually have to work through quite a bit of emotional baggage before the children and I can begin to get along—but Stevie and Ellie just welcomed me into the family." Constance poked Emily's chubby tummy and added, "But this one has made it clear that her mommy and daddy are the loves of her life, and the nanny is a force to be tolerated for a while."

Annie grinned at her sleepy little girl. Emily had settled down significantly since finding Annie's arms, and would probably drift off to sleep even without being nursed. But she was tired and needed a good, long nap, so a full tummy would encourage that better than just letting her give in at the moment.

"Well," Annie said as she carefully stood with the baby. "I'd better head inside and nurse her before she snoozes. I don't mind my picture plastered in the tabloids as I enjoy my vacation, but I'd rather not take the chance of someone *exposing* me to the whole world."

Constance laughed as she stood also and held her hands out in confusion. "So what do I do now? You're getting the baby to sleep and Stephen is exercising with the big kids. That kind of leaves me in limbo."

Annie pointed to a canvas bag beside her chair. "Look in there. You might find some wonderful fiction to take you away for a few hours until dinner."

"You're not paying me to read books," Constance reminded her guiltily.

"Stop complaining. Find a book and enjoy a little time to yourself for a change."

Annie took Emily down the stairs from the deck into the luxurious parlor connected to the bedrooms. She plopped onto the couch and smiled into the sleepy eyes of her daughter as she prepared to nurse her to sleep. Maneuvering the baby into a comfortable position, she noticed the light on her cell phone blinking.

"Hang on, little one," she said softly as she reached for the phone on the table next to the couch.

As Emily settled in Annie popped open the phone to see if perhaps a family member had called to wish her a merry Christmas. A voice message had been left, so she punched the button and waited for the connection.

"Annie, this is Artie. I've been trying like crazy to get in touch with Stephen, but he's not answering his cell. I've left messages but haven't heard from him yet. I'm trying you now. Please, if you get this before he does, have him call me immediately. There's some news he needs to know. Thanks … and hurry."

Annie closed the phone and wondered what could be so important on Christmas Eve to warrant a call from Artie. Apparently the lady had found the number for the yacht's phone and managed to contact Stephen that way. As she placed the phone back on the table, Stephen came walking into the parlor. His face was red from working out, but his expression was disturbed.

"What is it?" she asked him immediately. "Did Artie have bad news?"

Stephen sighed and nodded as he wiped his face down with a towel and walked over to the couch. "Ben Brenner died last night. He had a massive heart attack followed by several stokes." He looked over at Annie and painfully said. "He died Annie, and I spent six months with him and never mentioned salvation. I was so caught up in my own struggles, and I knew how anti-religious he was that I just reasoned it away … thinking a day would come when it would be more convenient."

Annie reached out and took his hand. "I'm so sorry. You only found out last year that he was your father, and now … well … I'm really sorry."

Stephen shook his head. "It's not the father thing." He leaned back against the couch and ran his hand over the top of his bushy hair. "Even if I had spent years with him he would've never been a father. As much as I hate to admit it, Edrew was probably a better father than Ben would've been. Had Mom gone on with him and had me, I would've been a huge inconvenience in his lifestyle."

Emily was out. Annie gently moved her toward her shoulder, but Stephen reached out his hands to take her instead. Annie handed her to him and he carefully placed her on his shoulder as he tenderly patted her back.

"There's more," he said without looking at her. "The movie execs have contacted Artie about finishing the score for the movie."

That didn't surprise Annie. They had called him several times over the past months pleading with him to come back and work with Ben. They wanted Stephen's name in the credits and the acclaim for being the company that nabbed him first after his recording career.

"They've made quite an unbelievable offer," Stephen continued. "I didn't give Artie an answer; I told her I needed to discuss it at length … with you."

Annie tried not to appear disappointed. Stephen hadn't mentioned work again since returning from California, but it never left the back of her mind. She knew he was who he was, and to force him to choose between his family and what he was created to do in this world was unfair. She had come to grips with that inside her own heart but had never discussed it with him. She didn't want to leave their home in Dockrey for California, but she wasn't going to force him to ignore the passion for writing music that had driven him for so long.

"So, tell me about the offer," she tried to sound positive. "What hoops are these guys willing to jump through to get you on their team?"

Stephen stood from the couch and gently rocked Emily, still on his shoulder, as he paced the carpet.

"First," he began, "they said I could stay in Alabama."

She was shocked, but thrilled. She nearly came off the couch at that announcement.

"They also said that when it came to actually recording the score, we could go to Muscle Shoals. They've contacted a studio there that would be willing to accommodate an orchestra and set aside the time needed to get it done."

"You're kidding?" Annie was stunned. Hollywood was going to bow to Stephen Williams?

"… and … they want you to work with me."

Annie did stand up this time. "Me?"

"Yep. And they would really, really like for us to sign on for the two sequels. They're offering the two of us together more than they were paying Ben."

"That's unheard of," Annie said as she shook her head and tried to imagine if this would work. She and Stephen would be making music again, in the comfort of their own home, only venturing an hour away when it came time for actual recording. "What do you think?" she asked him.

He looked over at her and shrugged. "What do *you* think?"

She took a deep breath and considered the ramifications. It wouldn't be near as much of a spotlight career as their life had been before, yet they could continue to do what they did best … and on their own terms. "I think there must be a catch somewhere," she said suspiciously.

"There sort of is," he admitted.

"Okay … what is it?"

"We have to attend the premiere in Hollywood … the whole red carpet bit," he explained, "and also any award ceremonies if the music is ever nominated."

Annie raised her eyebrows. "That's it? Just the premiere and the awards?"

"That's it." He carefully moved Emily from his shoulder and cradled her into his arms. "I don't think anyone could offer us a better deal … anywhere. I mean if we ever want to continue in this business, this is a good way to go."

Annie grinned as she walked over to them. "You're not kidding." She caressed Emily's little sleeping face and thought how wonderful life was at the moment. Would this be a good choice … or a bad one? "How much time do we have to decide?"

"Two weeks."

She nodded again and then looked up at Stephen. "So we can just put it out of our minds until we get back home … right?" She grinned big. They both knew that would be absolutely impossible.

One Hundred Four

Angie nervously scurried around the concrete block house trying to make sure everything looked as close to perfect as possible. If only she could somehow keep her house as spotless as she kept the clinic. The fact that the twins were both walking, thus climbing, had added another layer to the normal chaos. Out of sheer frustration, Michael had finally suggested he take all three of the kids down to the beach to swim and play for an hour or two so she could manage to undo messes without having another set added while she cleaned. When the bunch returned from the water, Cassie walked into the house from the back deck with eyes wide open in surprise.

"Wow, Mommy," she whispered in awe. "Our home has never looked like this."

Michael admitted to himself, though never out loud, that indeed the house in Padawin had never appeared this nice before. The six years he had been married to Angie he had never seen her put this much effort into cleaning. Even when their missionary friends, Chet and Vicki, and their kids would come to visit from the capital city of Taveren, she would merely straighten things up moderately and act as though they lived in a palace. But today was different … very different. The most special guests ever were arriving, and it meant more to Angie than she could say to realize they were finally going to be in her home.

"The house looks great, hon," Michael told her as he swept his arm across hers. "Stop worrying. They're gonna love it."

She smiled doubtfully. "I can't believe I'm so anxious about this. I have wished and prayed for a long time that this would happen, and now that it's here, all I can wonder is if I'll meet their approval."

He shook his head and marveled at this particular insecurity, one of the few this vivacious woman held. "How could they not approve? You have given your life to missions. You live on an island in the South Pacific in a concrete block house with a former hermit and three incredible kids. Explain what part of this they would find unacceptable."

She leaned in to kiss him. "Thank you," she said sweetly. "Somehow you always manage to put my feet back on the planet. I guess when it comes to the whole housekeeping thing, my sisters have me most definitely beat. They have these gorgeous designer houses, and their kids' rooms look like magazine pictures. Here … I don't know … those things just didn't matter … until now."

"And the truth is," he assured her, "it really doesn't matter now.

Once they're here and settled in, they'll fall in love with this place just like we have … and like our kids."

She closed her eyes and took a deep breath. The smell of the lush forest mixed with the sound of the rushing river and the view of the nearby ocean could almost remove any thoughts of fear or anxiety, but today was different. She looked down at her growing tummy … again. She had told her parents she had a big surprise for them when they came, and she was very relieved that she could tell them she knew for certain that only one child was on its way this time.

Cassie yawned as she emerged from her bedroom with her wet swimsuit to hang on the deck. At least she had managed to impart a few necessary household skills to the family over the years. She knew there was probably more she could do, but after non-stop cleaning and straightening and organizing for three days, she was spent. Surely Jonathan and Barbara Wright would just be glad to be here … at last.

"Mommy," Cassie said tiredly as she came in from the deck, "I'm hungry. Can I just have one piece of chicken before they get here?"

Angie reached for her tanned little five-year-old with the bleached out hair. Cassie wearily collapsed into her arms.

"How about a banana?" Angie suggested. "The chicken is still baking in the oven and isn't quite done yet."

Cassie shook her head. "How can I eat a banana and be happy when I smell that chicken all through the house?"

Angie chuckled and hugged her tightly. "I didn't realize it was a matter of happiness—I just thought you were hungry."

Cassie sighed as she trudged toward the couch to lie down. "That doesn't make sense, Mommy. You say the weirdest things some times."

"Copta!" yelled Christian as he hobbled toward the door totally naked, having gladly stripped himself from the swimsuit before anyone had a chance to dress him.

"What?" Angie asked surprised as she followed him to the door. "You hear the helicopter?"

"Copta!" Christian yelled out again.

Angie scooped him up as she hurried toward the door. She could hear it now too.

"Michael!" she yelled before she stepped outside. "They're here!" As she started toward the landing area, she realized that Christian was still nude and this might not be the best first impression for her parents to have when she welcomed them to Padawin. "Christian …" she moaned as she turned back toward the house. "Can you not stay with your father long enough to even get a diaper on?"

Michael was on his way out as Angie approached the door. "Aha!" he laughed as he looked at Christian. "There you are!" He held Caleb, fully clothed, and then suggested to Angie, "You wanna trade?"

She grinned and held a wiggly Christian out to Michael. "Good luck. Once he's run around naked, it's hard to make him go back to the restrictive clothes again."

"Dr. Angie! You must hurry! Your parents are here on the helicopter now as it is landing!" yelled a villager as he ran toward the chopper.

"Yes, I know!" Angie yelled back at him. ***"But my baby is naked!"***

"This one's not," Michael handed Caleb to Angie as Christian wiggled incessantly in his other arm. "I'll get him dressed and join you as soon as I can." He turned around and walked back into the house. "Cassie," he called out, "Mimi and Gaga are here."

Angie hurried toward the helicopter bouncing Caleb the entire way. He giggled and cackled as though this were one of Michael's games he often played with them.

"This isn't for your benefit," she smiled. "In fact, you're wearing me out. Running with you on my hip and the other one inside is just about to take me down." She panted as she slowed herself down. "I've got to walk the rest of the way."

When the chopper landed, they were a bit overwhelmed at the sight. They knew the native Padawin people were very dark-skinned, but it seemed even darker next to their bright clothes and shining, white smiles. They waved at the Wrights as though they were long, lost friends, and it warmed their hearts right away. Then Barbara spotted Angie in the distance. She was hobbling awkwardly with a baby in tow … and another one on the way.

"Oh … my … goodness!" Barbara exclaimed as she grabbed Jonathan's arm. "I have just discovered Angie's big surprise."

"What is it?" he asked as he followed the direction of her point.

"She's expecting … again," she replied in unbelief.

Jonathan squinted until he finally found Angie and one of the twins moving toward the landing area. "Well I'll be," he chuckled as he shook his head. "What is it with our girls and all these babies?"

"I'm not sure, but whatever the cause, it must be your fault."

He looked at her in shock. "Why would you say that?"

"Because everything irrational comes from your side of the gene pool," she reminded him as though this were common knowledge.

"What?"

She smiled and patted his arm. "Just kidding, sweetie. What can I say? Our girls like the idea of family … *lots* of family … I suppose."

One of the pilots turned around and explained in very choppy English, "You take off belt now and you see Dr. Angie. We get things and take to doctor place for you."

"Thank you," Jonathan nodded politely. "Thank you very much."

A kind-eyed man reached out to help Barbara. She took the dark hand and let him guide her down to the ground.

"Thank you," she said with a smile, knowing he probably had no idea what that meant.

"Sojay," the man said as he pointed to himself.

Barbara recognized the name right away. Without thinking, she reached out and embraced him as though he were a friend from years ago. Sojay's faith and perseverance had been told to the Wrights since before Angie even went to Padawin.

Jonathan eased himself down from the helicopter and Sojay extended his hand.

"Jonathan," Sojay said choppily, and then he pointed to his chest as he introduced himself. **"Sojay."**

Jonathan nodded in understanding and shook his hand. There was no sense in trying to speak. He was clueless when it came to any words from the Padawin language.

Suddenly the brightly colored crowd began to part, and Angie made her way through with Caleb smiling on her hip. As soon as her eyes met with her mother's, tears began to well. Angie couldn't believe her parents were here in Padawin for the holidays.

"Merry Christmas," Barbara said as she reached first for Caleb. He willingly went into her arms. They had been back in Padawin for nearly six months, but Caleb still seemed to remember Barbara and Jonathan. "How's my big boy?" She then embraced her daughter and glared down at her obvious baby bulge. "Do you want to explain this to me?" she asked her.

"Are you kidding?" Angie teased. "Daddy hasn't told you what causes babies yet?"

Barbara playfully slapped her arm and blushed. "Don't even go there."

Angie then reached for her father and gave him a full two-armed embrace while Barbara held Caleb. Jonathan held her tightly as he realized this was the result of many years of tearful praying. She had been their only overtly rebellious child, and as a teenager they wondered if she would ever return to the Lord. But when Angie had decided to cast her lot with Christianity, she had gone in head first, committing herself to medical missions. Years of education and training had finally culminated in all that he was seeing right now, and as much as he wished she could be near him every day, letting her go in obedience to the Lord was a peaceful experience.

"So," he grinned down at her, "show me this village of yours that I've heard so much about."

"Gladly," Angie beamed as she took his arm and began to walk leisurely down the well-worn path.

Some men from the tribe grabbed their things and carried them toward the house as Angie excitedly explained all the aspects of the Podakind village. She pointed out the many fields where Michael had taught the men how to grow their own food, and then showed them the water system where he had introduced water purification. She motioned toward a fence that kept livestock and then to the pavilion and building where church and school took place. She explained how the huts were built and told them every family's name as they passed a hut or a group of family huts. But her greatest pleasure was watching the awe in her parents' eyes as she told of the blessings this life had brought her.

When they came to the door of her own house, she paused as an unsettling emotion swept over her.

"What is it?" Barbara asked as she immediately noticed the change.

Angie frowned and then looked intensely at both of her parents. "In all of my preparations, you know … house cleaning and preparing your room … it never occurred to me how … uh … meager my home will seem compared to Annie's and Andie's."

"Sweetie, you know that won't matter a bit to us!" Barbara replied right away.

"It's just that I've always been known as … well … a slob. I know that," she grimaced. "And I've never been one who catered to the finer things in life. I guess living here seems to fit me perfectly, but it's very different from what y'all are used to."

Barbara reached for Angie's hand and assured her, "Don't you think we know that? And don't you think we also know that God placed within you a desire for missions that supersedes every other desire in this world? If you lived next door to us in a mansion with twenty-four hour maid service, I know you would be miserable and out of God's plan for your life. So stop thinking that we're gonna consider your home as anything other than what it truly is—your home."

Angie tried to smile confidently, but after the months in Dockrey, shuffling between Andie and Annie and their plush dwellings, it was hard not to feel a little inferior. She bit her lip, squared her shoulders, and finally opened the door to the house. The greatest sight ever was waiting inside. Michael was sitting on the couch with a clothed Christian asleep on his shoulder and Cassie fast asleep with her feet in his lap.

"Welcome," Michael smiled warmly as he waved toward the door. "It's nice to finally have you in our home."

Jonathan walked over to the couch and shook his hand firmly. "The feeling is indeed mutual. I can't believe I'm actually here, in Padawin, in your home, smelling something incredible that's cooking."

"Those would be our tiny chickens," Angie told him as she made her way to the kitchen.

"I don't care what size they are," Jonathan said as he followed behind her. "Anything is better than whatever that was we had on the plane."

Before he could make it into the kitchen, however, the deck and the river caught his eye. "Good heavens," he whispered in awe as he walked out and caught sight of Mt. Podakind. "It can't seem possible that this is what you wake up to every morning."

Angie came out beside him. "And go to sleep to each night. There's nothing quite so calming as the moon reflecting on the river, the mountain," and then she pointed down to the right, "and the ocean."

Jonathan could feel his stomach turning flips at the magnificence of it all. "I'll say this for you," he grinned as he put his arm around her and pulled her to him, "you've got Andie and Annie beat by a mile when it comes to location."

When Barbara joined them, she put her hand to her mouth stunned at the view. She looked up at the mountain, then down to the river, and then over to the ocean. "I understand now," she had to choke out. "I understand."

Angie looked at her in confusion. "Understand what, Moms?"

She looked at her daughter and smiled with tears as she said, "Cassie. I just thought perhaps she was a bit too free of a spirit for the States." She shook her head. "How do grow up in this and then leave it all behind?"

Angie sighed as she put her arms around both parents. "That's what I've been trying to tell you guys for years."

One Hundred Five

Hal hesitated outside the door of the massive house. The decorations looked like something from a grand old movie, and the brilliantly adorned tree glowed through the window of the great room. On one hand it seemed familiar and warm, but on the other it was cold and indifferent. It was Christmas Eve and he had nowhere else to go. Lisa had left him right after the fiasco in Dockrey, and he had decided to just do menial work for awhile. He was considering actually going to Alaska to find some miserable, hard-working job that paid well but wore the body out. He was just ready for change … and here was the best place to start.

He took a deep breath and closed his eyes tightly as he tried to conjure up some of that confidence he used to portray so easily. It was gone now, and pretense was getting harder and harder to muster. He forced his finger to the small lighted button and heard the faint ringing of *Amazing Grace* echo inside. He took a step back and glanced around at the swaying palm trees in the warm California breeze. Had he listened to Lisa and just stopped the power playing he could still be in Dockrey, sipping hot cider next to a blazing fire, having one arm wrapped around his beautiful wife as they spent a second Christmas in Alice Vordeman's cozy old house. Instead he had lost everything … everything … absolutely everything.

When the door opened, Hal was shocked to see the senior Dr. Harold Bridges at the threshold. He had assumed one of the help would have answered the ring. He wasn't yet prepared to meet his father face to face again.

"Hal?" Harold asked unsure of the bearded, bushy haired man standing on the front steps. "Is that you, Hal?"

Hal took an awkward step forward and half nodded. "Yes … sir. It's me."

Harold slowly smiled and shook his head in dismay. "I would've never thought in a million years you would turn up here on Christmas Eve."

Hal shrugged. He was now feeling uncomfortable and wished he hadn't come. "I was near the neighborhood and thought I would stop by and wish you and … Mother … a merry Christmas."

Harold, still stunned, just stared at his son. "Wow, I'm speechless." He then looked around behind Hal. "Is your wife here too? I'd love to meet her."

He shook his head. The disappointing consequences of his stupid choices were already being illuminated and he hadn't even been here more than a minute. "I'm not married any longer."

Harold nodded in understanding. "Then I suppose you're all alone this Christmas."

He didn't want to admit that, but what was the point in lying. He had ruined his life, driven every one away, and was miserable.

Harold at last walked out onto the concrete and reached out his hand. "Your mother's making some kind of wonderful snack for us to eat before we go to bed. I know she'd be thrilled if you'd join us."

Hal shook his head. "I need to get back to … uh … my … well, I just need to get back. I only wanted to drop by, you know, and say what I said."

Harold nodded but continued to offer his hand. "I wish you'd stay." He reached up and put his arm on Hal's shoulder. "It would mean a lot to me … if you would."

Hal glanced up into his father's eyes and saw regret, kindness, and perhaps even a love he had never seen before. He nearly buckled beneath the hand on his shoulder as he had wished so many years prior for that hand to reach out to him in love and support. He almost shrugged it off, but he was too broken to disregard any tender gesture,

"Maybe," Hal said shakily, "but only for a little while. I don't want to ruin your plans for Christmas."

Harold slowly and carefully pulled Hal into a gentle embrace. "There are no plans I could ever have that would be too important to keep me from my son." He pulled him in tighter. "And if you'll give me a chance, Hal, I'll prove that to you from this day forward."

☼☼☼

Stephen rolled over in the bed on the yacht and instinctively reached for Annie, but rather than finding her waist, he discovered she was sitting up in the bed staring out the large window behind them.

"Are you okay?" he asked as he tried to focus from his sleep.

She smiled and gently rubbed his arm. "You know how sometimes you just can't get something off of your mind?"

"I can most definitely relate. What's on yours?"

She stared back out the window and the moonlight on her face was breathtaking. For a moment he even forgot what they were discussing or why they were awake.

"Summer Sunrise," she whispered as she sighed into the night. "I've had these words all jumbled up inside my head for months now but could never make sense of them because there was no meter … or melody."

Stephen slowly sat up beside her and ran his fingers down her shoulder and the side of her arm. "And so they're causing you a lack of rest in the middle of the Mediterranean on Christmas?"

She grinned. "Sort of … but mainly because they're all starting to come together now. I'm having to fight the urge to run to the keyboard and start putting it all on paper. Then I remember—we have no keyboard anywhere on this boat. So I'm trying to run it all over and over in my mind until it sticks, then in the morning I can at least write out the words and perhaps a few chords I think might work."

Stephen pulled her back down into the bed and softly kissed her forehead. "If you're feeling this creative, why don't you just sing it to me now? Then maybe the two of us together can remember enough of it to last until we get back home so we can focus on more *fun* things while vacationing." He now ran his hand down the side of her body. "We're not supposed to be working at all while on this trip. It's an *escape* if you'll remember, and right now I would love to escape with you somewhere other than songwriting."

She pulled up close to him and gazed into his face reflecting the silver light of the moon. "It's not a very fast song," she teased. "It might take longer than you would like."

He slowly kissed her full, warm lips as his hand slipped around her back. "Sing it," he whispered. "We've got all night."

She lay back on the pillow and hummed until she found the most comfortable key. "Ready?"

"… and willing," he grinned as he took her hand beneath the covers and squeezed it tenderly.

Just this once I'd like to have an answer
Just this once I'd like to feel assured
Just this once why can't I be the dancer
Who felt the music and still endured
But silence screams within this darkness
Every fire is smothered by this cold
The music's faded and I am helpless
The dance is heartless, dry and old

But just as sure as the moon that's shining
Just as sure as the dove's soft song
The Heavenly Father's ever watching
Loving, guiding me along
Nothing He has planned is wasted
So as I look through weary eyes
I recall the joys I've tasted
And know the summer sun will rise
I need the summer sunrise

Annie looked over at him. "What do you think? Ben Brenner would probably refer to it as *sentimental crap*."

Stephen reached his arm around her and pulled her close. "Then be very glad you're married to me, the *Autumn Sunset* boy." He kissed her softly and smiled as he said, "Because I love sentimental … absolutely love it."

"Good answer, city boy," she whispered as she kissed him back and reached up to touch his face.

He pulled back for a moment and asked, "Will I ever not be a city boy?"

She grinned. "Let's hope not, because the only man I ever wanted is a full-fledged, Chicago raised, New York transplanted city boy. Anything else just wouldn't do."

"I can live with that," he kissed her again. "Most definitely—I can live with that.

So Close to Paradise

Meg MacAllister's life is anything but simple, but when an old friend shows up, suddenly things become even more complicated. Phillip Barton is tired, burned out from ministry, and ready to make big changes, but Meg knows that God placed a call on his life, and she desperately wants to see him return to what he is most gifted to do. As she tries to help him regain his confidence, she finds old emotions and attachments beginning to resurface...and all the baggage that comes with them. As hard as it may be for Phillip to overcome his present, it is just as hard for Meg to overcome her past. Will she learn that forgiveness is full before she makes a serious mistake in judgment? And will Phillip ever understand that sometimes our trials drive us to exactly where we need to be?

www.ingramcontent.com/pod-product-compliance
Lightning Source LLC
Chambersburg PA
CBHW021831010726
47493CB00005B/1351

* 9 7 8 0 6 1 5 9 5 8 2 8 6 *